ALPENA COUNTY LIBRARY
8604 9100 035 765 0

W9-CLR-932

FIRES OF FORTUNE

Also by Patricia Shaw

Valley of Lagoons
River of the Sun
The Feather and the Stone
Where the Willows Weep
Cry of the Rain Bird

Pioneers of a Trackless Land
Brother Digger

FIRES OF FORTUNE

Patricia Shaw

St. Martin's Press New York

 For information, address St. Martin's Press,
175 Fifth Avenue, New York, N.Y. 10010.

ISBN 0-312-14336-2

First published in Great Britain by
Headline Book Publishing

First U.S. Edition: May 1996

10 9 8 7 6 5 4 3 2 1

To
Evangeline Holly Shaw,
Lynne and Garry,
and Desirée Shaw

Drought

Judith Bandidt

Day upon day with no relief
as the pastures bake in the searing heat,
when the water-tanks and bores give out
we know we're facing drought.

As the dams dry up to stinking bogs
the cattle stand in hopeless mobs,
for the dingoes stalk them as they graze
and watch through the shimmering haze.

The crops die off, just a waste of time,
bullocks are sold before their prime,
and we graze the roads 'mid dust and flies
while fodder prices rise.

Our family's future lies in this land
but it can't work out now as we planned,
the man from the bank's been 'round again –
and still it hasn't rained.

1994

Chapter One

In his mind's eye Ben was a seafarer, a proud and fearless mariner who would take his ship down the river to Moreton Bay and then swing out with the winds, his sails riding high, to the ocean blue. In fair weather and foul he would be at the wheel, a brave captain greatly admired by his loyal crew.

He would be wearing a peaked cap and a fine jacket with brass buttons, just like Grandfather Beckman in the portrait over the mantelpiece. Poor Captain Beckman! He went down with his ship on a dark and stormy night on the Great Barrier Reef. Ben could imagine him standing there – upright and true, the storm raging about him – shouting to his men to save themselves, but refusing to surrender his honour by abandoning ship. That, to Ben, was the best part of the story, as told to him many times by Oma Beckman. It was a fine thing to have a hero in the family.

Ben scrambled to the edge of the dusty orange cliff and dropped down to a ledge, his favourite vantage spot. From here at Kangaroo Point he could look across to the town of Brisbane and, in the foreground, the long, busy wharves. This was the most exciting lookout in the whole world. No ships could pass without his scrutiny. Well . . . a few might slip by. It annoyed him to find he'd missed one, caught up in house and yard chores and Oma's interminable lessons. Those lessons! She never let up. When he complained, his mother threatened to send him to school so that he'd never have time to watch his ships.

He smiled at that, as he noted an old paddle steamer thumping upriver. She was the *Louisa Jane*, not very interesting. She carried stores and passengers up and down from the settlements on the south coast: a dreary life for a captain. Ben always let her pass. Sometimes he lined up strange ships with a piece of clay piping that was his cannon and blasted them out of the water for daring to pass his fort without permission, because he was the Queensland navy, the harbour master and the suspicious customs officer all rolled into one.

Send him to school! That was a good one. Ben knew as well as his mother did that he couldn't go to school, not here, not anywhere. The kids who hung about the wharves told him that. But he always pretended to be scared of that punishment to please her. He loved his mum. She was a good-looking lady and very tall, but he was catching up. She and Oma often measured him with a ruler flat on his head, cutting notches in the timber wall to mark his progress. Grandma, Oma Beckman that is, said Mum spoiled him, but it was Oma who came to his rescue when Mum really put her foot down, threatening the strap. She'd make excuses for him, so the old razor strop still hung in the laundry, unused since the days when it had travelled far and wide with the Captain.

Some days, when the ferryman was in a good mood, Ben would cadge a ride on the ferry and wander about the wharves, especially when the big ships were in port, caught up in all the excitement of the loading and unloading and the strange voices of passengers milling about on the decks, eager to disembark or calling tearfully to families and friends as the gap between ship and shore widened. Although what they had to weep about, he couldn't imagine. Ben had decided that one day, when he had his own ship, he would take his two ladies, Mum and Oma, all around the world. Even across the Pacific to the Spanish Main, where great treasures were to be found. He had dreamed once that he'd found a fabulous treasure chest in an old cave, and it was such a wonderful dream he made an effort to keep remembering it, although it was slipping away these days.

Below him fishing boats were returning, accompanied by screeching seagulls, and he waved to the crews, who were sorting their catches with swift hands, ready for the markets. They waved back to him in their good-natured way, so they were safe from his cannon. He would protect them when he was a buccaneer captain with his own ship, which he'd already decided to call the *Black Swan*, after the swans that sailed his river like tiny dignified galleons.

Whenever he stayed too long on the wharves, he ran into trouble, because the ferries were crowded and that meant a long walk in the opposite direction to the Victoria Bridge. Once across the bridge he'd have to run for miles through the dank and scary streets of South Brisbane and then on up to the Point. Many a time drunken men had grabbed him as he'd sprinted past the taverns and brothels:

'Where you goin' in such a rush, sonny?'

'You're a pretty boy. Hold here a while.'

'Come on, I'll buy you a rum.'

Frightening as they were, they were nothing to Diamond's anger when he was late home. Diamond, his mum, worried so much she'd be in a real panic by the time he came sprinting down the street, and what an ear-wigging he'd get! She didn't like him to go to the wharves, she said it was no place for kids. And it had been a mistake to tell her that he never stole like the other kids or slipped aboard the ships; that only made her worse.

Diamond yelled at him. 'You keep away from those wharves, I tell you! Stay on your own side of the river. They're bad, those people.'

Defiantly he'd turned to Oma. 'The Captain was a seafarer! Why should I be afraid of seafarers?'

But on this point Oma agreed with Diamond. 'The Captain was a good God-fearing man. You don't know who those people are.'

'But I want to know. It's boring over here. There's nothing to do.'

Another mistake. Diamond soon found him more chores. But every so often he still managed a ferry ride, churning across the river to see his friends, the skinny lads and the wild-eyed girls he'd met over there. Most of them had no real homes at all, finding refuge in the big woolsheds or under the warehouses or over the road in sheds behind shops. They hung about the wharves for a purpose: to survive on pennies earned or whatever pickings they could find. Ben found them exciting company. They wore ragged clothes and they grinned at Ben's neat shirts and knee-breeches and long socks, but they accepted him. He wasn't a squealer. He saw what they did: the pilfering; the sly, shifty encounters with men behind the sheds; the swift shuffling of grog cases to baffle customs men; and the pickpocketing, moving silently among the excited new arrivals from passenger ships.

He saw it all, astonished by their boldness but deeply aware from the pinched faces that necessity drove them on. Oma's larder was well stocked and she expected their 'growing boy' to help himself whenever he felt the pangs of hunger between meals, so he was able to stuff his pockets with food filched from the shelves to give to his friends.

His best friend was Willy Sloane. He was the same age as Ben, and the leader of a gang. Willy had a hideout somewhere on a rooftop which, he boasted, was free from rats. He knew that Ben lived on the other side of the river but, like the others, never asked where. They were all too busy.

Many a time Willy had dragged Ben out of the way when the police were on the rampage, marching him down to the gardens to sit awhile.

'But I haven't done anything wrong,' Ben would complain.

'A lot they care, mate. Just make yourself scarce or you'll cop it like the rest.'

Ben often thought that when he had his own ship, Willy could be his first mate. He'd never met a smarter person than Willy. He'd have liked to have invited him home but nobody much ever came to their house, and a restless, fidgety boy like Willy would probably find it deadly dull.

Over the fence, the neighbours had plenty of visitors. But theirs was a big house, 'A mansion,' Oma called it. There was no envy in Ben's heart, though. He looked from the cliffs back to his own home. It was a lovely white weatherboard cottage set well back towards the street, and it had a big garden. Inside there were three bedrooms, one for each of them, and that was all they needed. From the windows of his room he could gaze out at night at the gaslit fairyland of Brisbane and conjure up more dreams of the world out there.

The next-door house was two-storeyed; he figured there'd be a great view from the balcony up there. The couple who lived there – Dr and Mrs Thurlwell – were very important people, so naturally they didn't talk to the Beckmans. They stayed on their side of the high fence and, according to the newspapers, entertained all the society people – even the Governor, though Ben had never spotted him.

The Thurlwells called the mansion Somerset House, and Ben was familiar with every inch of the grounds. For years he'd been sneaking along the cliffs and wriggling through their hedge to gain entry to the colourful gardens shaded by stately pines and rustling palm trees. The lawns and bushes were carefully trimmed and flowerbeds bordered paths that wound down from the side of the house. The front garden was even more spectacular, especially when the big flame trees were in bloom. Under cover of the lush greenery he was able to watch carriages and gigs crunch down the long drive to the front door, and observe servants in fancy dress opening doors and bowing to their betters. Ben marvelled at the show and at the beautiful people who lived in this house. On the cliff side, at the rear of the building, was an elegant veranda where ladies in dazzling white dresses and fine gentlemen took the air, resting languidly on easy chairs and sofas.

Occasionally the gardeners would catch him and chase him off, but they knew he was from next door and never made a fuss.

Ben sighed, tossing stones down the cliff. After the wharves, Somerset was his favourite place. He'd miss it when he went to sea. He'd miss her too, that girl, Phoebe Thurlwell. Not that he ever spoke to her or let her know he was hiding in her garden.

It seemed she'd always been there, graduating from dolls and tea sets to reading books and playing games with girls who came to visit. None of them were as pretty as she was, though. She looked like a doll herself in her soft summery dresses and long blonde plaits, always neatly tied with bright ribbons that matched the sashes at her waist. Ben had met plenty of girls on the wharves, cheeky girls with sharp eyes and whiny voices, and had found their company no different from that of the boys. They could filch and fight and run like the wind when they had to. No, the 'girl' thing didn't bother him – after all, he lived with two women – but that Miss Phoebe had him beat. It irritated him that a silly girl could turn his legs to jelly, make him too shy to even attempt to speak to her.

Sometimes she'd be naughty and venture past the hedge to the cliffs, and maids would swoop, pulling her back, threatening to tell her mother. On such occasions Ben imagined himself her protector. If she were in danger at the cliff edge he would save her. He would fling himself forward with the ground crumbling under him and throw her back to safety so that, gratefully, she would ask his name and he could tell her he was Ben Beckman from next door. And she would tell her mother, Mrs Doctor Thurlwell, who would be so pleased with him she would invite him up to the white house for a fizzy drink, but Ben, being respectful, would not accept. He knew his place. It was enough that he had been recognized as a hero . . .

Diamond was calling him, so he turned to climb back up from his ledge, but as he reached for a tuft of grass at the top, a snake was waiting. He wondered how long it had been sitting there, just above his head, coiled on the warm rock, contemplating the back of a boy's head. And he wondered if this snake were an honourable fellow who did not strike from the rear but waited to face the enemy before it killed him, for as sure as eggs this yellow-belly meant business now!

For that matter, he pondered, as he remained motionless, his right hand still clutching the grass, his feet firmly planted on the ledge, was there ever a taipan that didn't mean business? This one was unmistakable, with its metallic yellow and black skin and its big head poised, tongue spitting, only a few feet from Ben's face.

As if to distract him, force him to make the first move, the snake brazenly uncoiled some of its polished length but its head remained still, beady eyes fixed on its prey.

Ben's arm was becoming stiff; he'd have to let go of the grass soon, but those powerful eyes seemed to forbid him to do anything but pay attention. Maybe the snake was trying to hypnotize him, Ben thought fearfully, to prevent him from considering an escape route. Because there was one. He could fling himself backwards and take his chances over the cliff. And break his neck and his legs and his arms as well, and that would hurt a damn sight more than a snake bite.

Where was his mother? She had called him, so why didn't she come looking for him? She had a gun, she could shoot this brute whose head was now shifting slowly from side to side as if it were listening to his thoughts, taking its time, still challenging him with its flicking tongue to have a go.

A little honeybird flipped out of a tree by the wall and fled. Without altering his gaze Ben could see that tree behind the snake. It was a big old thing, with spreading branches, growing in Somerset grounds but overhanging his garden. He'd often used it as a short cut home. Painfully still, he wondered what had spooked the bird, and then he saw among the branches, the girl next door in her white frilly dress, staring at him. He wanted to call out to her but he didn't dare, and as he hung on, he was vaguely annoyed to see her in his tree, although he allowed that the gnarled old thing was an easy climb for a girl.

Desperately, he forced his mind back to the snake, which he knew now was trying to wear him down, as cats did with little birds, frightening them so much they lost the nerve to fly free. If he didn't make a move soon, try to bat that head out of the way, he'd be too stiff to move fast enough. But there in the background the silly girl was climbing the tree even further, and stepping out to the overhanging branches, hanging on to the ones above her. She was coming over the wall!

If she came over here he'd kill her. If he lived that long, after she'd stirred the snake and got him bit. Petrified, he watched her drop down on to a branch and hang over the high wall, her britches showing with the frills of her dress caught on a twig, ready to let go and drop to the grass below.

Ben wanted to groan, hoping she'd get stuck there. Old man taipan was still flicking at him, not in any hurry. His eyes glazed over, shutting out the background scenario; he wished he could close them, but he figured that could be a signal for the snake to strike so he snapped them wide open again, deciding to sit out this menace. Maybe he could. Maybe not. Then he saw Diamond standing over them. His mum seemed to have come out of nowhere. He hadn't seen or heard her approach, she was just there, his lovely mum, in a long black skirt that brushed over her bare feet.

Ha! he thought. Mr Snake, you're in trouble now. My mum will shoot you dead!

Ben braced himself, but then realized that Diamond hadn't brought her gun. He had been hoping that the girl Phoebe had seen his predicament and run for help, but obviously not. No doubt she'd just galloped off home to play with her stupid toys, leaving him to his fate.

But instead of going back for the gun, Diamond lowered herself to sit cross-legged behind the snake. Terrified, Ben wanted to scream out to her to get away, that she was placing herself in danger now because the snake could strike her at that distance. She put her fingers to her lips, compelling him to remain still and silent, and tears sprang to his eyes as he realized she was trying to draw the taipan's attention from him.

And then she began to sing, in a very low voice, a strange song with muttering repetitive words, the palms of her hands flat on the ground, as if proving to this horrible snake that she carried no weapons. Ben was angry with her for her foolishness; he didn't want her to die, he loved her. Diamond and Oma were his whole life. Diamond's song took on the rhythm of a lullaby now, and the damn snake reached out, widening its sway, the vicious forked tongue still flicking as it leaned from one to the other of the humans, deciding which, Ben thought frantically, it could hit with one fast jab.

His mother's eyes, dark liquid, began to draw the snake away from him. There was an expression of such sweetness on her face that Ben was shocked. She should have taken a big stick and belted the thing, but instead she was exposing herself to the taipan. He released his grip on the tuft of grass and allowed his hand to slip down ever so slowly, as the snake reared away from him, listening to her. The coils unravelled and began to retreat, the strong head facing Diamond. She continued her chant, watching as the tongue disappeared and the snake swayed seductively in front of her, almost as if it were trying to please her.

She smiled, an audience now, watching it dance for her until it slowly drew back and, after what seemed an eternity to Ben, was gone.

He scrambled up the cliff. 'Quick, Mum! Kill it before it gets away!'

'No,' she said. 'He lives here. I've seen him many times. This is his home. You frightened him.'

'But he would have bitten me and I'd be killed dead!'

'Maybe. Next time you be more careful. I've told you before to keep off the cliffs, stay on clear ground at the top. Many little animals and birds live in burrows over the edge. You frighten them.'

Oma came running, her skirts billowing in the breeze, to throw her arms about him: 'The little girl, she was so frightened! She saw the snake. She came to us crying. Are you all right, you poor boy? Ah, Diamond, the poor boy, bring him in, bring him in!'

'Where is she?' Ben asked. 'The girl.'

'Gone home,' Oma said. 'She was too shy with her dress all torn. I tell her I sew it up so no one ever know, but she wouldn't stay, she ran off out the front gate. I think Miss Phoebe, she like our little Ben.'

'Oh pooh!' he said. 'I'm not your little Ben and she don't like anyone, that girl.' Although he was surprised that Oma knew her name.

But what an embarrassment to have her save him! To have her get help for him, after all his daydreams about being her protector. What a dope she must think he was.

As the weeks passed, however, his attitude changed. She had been smart enough to run for help without disturbing the snake, and so now he owed her. Probably his very life. And one day he would be there when she needed him and he would come to her rescue, a pirate captain rescuing the Lady Phoebe from a doomed ship . . .

The ladies were charmed. Lalla Thurlwell's 'long' room was a delight. As she explained, since Somerset House already had a parlour and a drawing room she'd been quite at a loss to know what to do with this room when she first saw it.

'One could hardly use it as a sitting room, it's too large, running the full width of the house. And since it is sheltered by the wide veranda, it's not a sun room. With the glass doors opening out all along the river side it reminded me of a greenhouse, so I decided to be brave and decorate in that manner.'

'And it's perfect,' Mrs Sutcliffe, wife of the Speaker of the House, enthused. 'With all this superb white cane furniture amid these glorious potted plants, especially the tall palms, it's a study in green and white. And it is *so* cool, I really must congratulate you, Mrs Thurlwell.'

'Thank you.' Lalla beamed. 'I could hardly ask you to take tea with me in the "greenhouse", hence the "long" room.'

Mrs Buchanan was equally enthusiastic. 'The wonderful rugs and those beautiful little white statues really set it off, Mrs Thurlwell, but would I be out of order if I asked from where you obtained all this furniture? It's so solid for cane, and so roomy.'

Her mother, the formidable Belle Foster, a leading Brisbane socialite, glared at her. 'Clara! Don't be so crass. You are, most certainly, out of order.'

'I just thought,' Clara said, shrinking, 'that before we go back upcountry I could speak to my husband. We do need new furniture and it's difficult to know what to buy. It can get so hot.'

'Of course it does,' Lalla said kindly. 'I'll send you the catalogue, Clara. We imported all of this furniture, the chairs, tables and stands, from Hong Kong.' She dropped her voice to a whisper. 'But I must say that when it arrived William got a shock.'

'What? At the bill?' Mrs Foster boomed.

Lalla giggled. 'Oh no! He didn't mind the cost. He was most impressed with the whole consignment, especially those big winged armchairs, but when I announced I intended to have them all painted white . . . well, you can imagine! He really bridled. But I just told him to trust me and went ahead. He's resigned to it now.'

'Just as well,' Mrs Foster said, looking about her. 'It wouldn't have the same impact in the dull old bamboo cane.'

All the women turned as Dr Thurlwell came to the door. Lalla glided over to meet him, the embroidered silk train of her dress making a slight shushing sound on the polished floor.

'My dear,' he said, kissing her on the cheek. 'You do look beautiful.'

The guests sighed their appreciation of this well-trained husband, for Lalla did look lovely. Her thick blonde hair was swept up into wide rolls framing her face, with pert little strands allowed to fall loose, softening her fine features, and her white tea dress, showing off her curvaceous figure, was a dream. A very expensive dream, they all noted, set off by an emerald brooch at the high lacy collar. They had heard that this woman dressed to match the colour schemes of her reception rooms, and here was proof to take away with them.

'The ladies are just leaving,' she told her husband and he turned, disappointed. 'Just my luck to be deprived of the company of three lovely ladies, but duty called. I hope you enjoyed your afternoon.'

'Oh, indeed we did, Doctor. The tea was quite superb,' Mrs Sutcliffe gushed.

Mrs Foster, a tall, bosomy woman, took the opportunity to snipe at her, in order to let the others know that she was not impressed by the office of the Speaker. Politicians, to Mrs Foster, were servants of the people and should be treated as such. She gathered herself up and looked down on little Mrs Sutcliffe: 'One would hardly expect less of Mrs Thurlwell!'

As the maid led the visitors to the front door, William nudged Lalla and whispered, 'Did they go along with it?'

'Of course.' She smiled confidently. 'Biddy,' she called to another maid, 'where is Phoebe? I want her to say goodbye to the ladies.'

'I can't find her, ma'am,' Biddy wailed. 'We've been looking everywhere.'

'Then look again!' Lalla hissed as she sailed forth into the white-tiled lobby.

Two light carriages had presented themselves at the front door to carry off the visitors. Lalla, making small talk, fumed. Where was that brat? She had told her daughter to make herself scarce during tea but to be there when the ladies were ready to leave. It was typical of Phoebe to disappear when she was needed. God alone knew why she'd been stuck with a daughter who not only had a lisp and was as plain as pudding, but was also a defiant child, never easy to deal with, always arguing, contradicting her mother . . .

'Good heavens!' Mrs Foster exclaimed, staring as Phoebe came towards them, cutting across the circular lawn, the centrepiece of the driveway.

Lalla was mortified. Neatness was almost an obsession with her. Everything in her house had a place and everything in it had to be in place, right to the inch. Family attire must be kept immaculate, perfectly laundered with not a loose thread or button.

And now look at her daughter! Phoebe had lost one of her ribbons, so one plait was unravelled, and worse, her dress was torn, the sleeve ripped and a hem frill hanging loose, dragging on the ground like a grubby streamer.

'Hello!' she said cheerfully, gravitating like a magnet towards Mrs Foster, the most powerful pole. 'Did you have a nice day?'

'Yes, thank you,' the woman replied. 'What happened to you, child? Did you fall out of a tree?'

Phoebe treated her to a toothy grin. 'Yeth I did! How did you know?'

'These things happen.' Mrs Foster shrugged as she stepped into the first carriage, and then laughed. 'Test the branches in future, child. Test the branches.'

Standing beside the wretched girl, a forced smile on her face, Lalla bade her guests farewell and then turned on Phoebe. 'What happened to you?'

'I fell out of a tree.'

'Haven't I told you, ladies do not climb trees!'

'Yes, but—'

Lalla shook her. 'I don't want to hear your buts. And what were you doing out the gate looking like that?'

'I was in next door. I saw the boy next door and he was—'

'What? You went next door?' Ever since they'd moved into Somerset House, the Thurlwells had refused to acknowledge their neighbours. In fact, many a time William had tried to buy that property, on the end of the Point, but the German woman living there had constantly refused to sell, and so it had remained, a rustic cottage out of place beside the Thurlwell mansion.

'I had to,' Phoebe argued and, infuriated, Lalla slapped her across her face.

'Get inside, you little wretch. Biddy! Give her a good bath and clean her up. I'll attend to her later.' She saw the frown on her husband's face and rounded on him. 'What are you looking at me like that for? Do you want her associating with them? Well, do you?'

'No, of course not,' he admitted lamely. William could never stand up to his wife's head-on confrontations. She was a slight woman, with an air of grace and refinement accentuated by the pale colours and expensive materials she chose to wear, and though he loved and admired her, he was always startled by her aggression when there was any hint that he might disagree with her. Over the years he'd learned it was easier to allow Lalla to have her own way rather than experience the discomfort of her wordy belligerence.

Right now, though, there were more important matters at stake. William was a dedicated anti-federalist whose family had pioneered the great cattle runs in north-west Queensland. Now a band of reformers wanted to amalgamate all the Australian states into a commonwealth, and to the Thurlwell family, and many of their friends, this would mean a loss of power and, of course, an increase in taxes. A federal government couldn't operate on thin air, so where else would the money come from but out of the pockets of men who were already supporting state governments? To William it was preposterous, and he was delighted that Lalla had taken up the cause with her usual energy.

'What did Mrs Foster say?' he asked her.

'She was a pushover. She can't stand politicians at the best of times and the thought of electing another batch has just about given her the vapours. She's happy to join our movement and will donate rather substantially, I believe.'

'Excellent.' He nodded. 'And what about Mrs Sutcliffe?'

'She's a fool of a woman. She let it slip that Harold Sutcliffe is in favour of federation.'

'Did she now? That's interesting. He's been giving the impression that he's against, and by God, he's on the committee chosen to produce a report on the subject.'

'He might change his mind.' Lalla smiled. 'Mrs Foster gave his wife a good talking-to. I didn't have to bother at all. By the time Belle Foster was finished with her she was all our way, and she promised to speak to her husband.'

'If he'll listen to her.'

'He might if she remembers to tell him that the Fosters hold a swag of votes in his electorate. But there's another problem. When the other two went for a walk in the garden, Clara Buchanan said not to tell her mother, but that her husband fancies the idea of a union of states. She didn't want to give me the wrong impression by not mentioning his attitude in front of Belle.'

'And did you tell Mrs Foster?'

'Of course not. Ben Buchanan has always had political ambitions. He could be useful.'

'Bloody idiot. Why doesn't he stay in the bush and look after his own affairs?'

'Because he's not doing so well these days. He sold his cattle station up north and bought another one outside Charleville. About five hundred miles due west, Clara says. All was well for a start but now they're facing a drought. Besides, he likes being in town.'

'But he's against us,' William said.

'Not necessarily. I suggest we find a way to get Ben Buchanan into the State Parliament. On condition he joins us in opposing federalism. He'd jump at the chance.'

William laughed. 'My dear, you should have been a politician yourself.'

'No. Even if ladies were admitted, I haven't the patience for it. Buchanan's easily swayed. We have to encourage him, so let's invite Clara and Ben to stay with us for a while before they go home. That should do it.'

'Now listen to me, darlin',' Biddy said as she brushed the girl's hair. 'Don't be answering back yer ma. Just be quiet.'

'She hit me again!' Phoebe snapped.

'Never mind that. She got a fright to see your dress all torn. She thought you must have been attacked or somethin'.'

'And thay I had been? Is that a reason to thlap my fathe? She'th a beast. I hate her.'

'Oh, dear Lord, you mustn't say things like that. And don't be getting upset, you're messing up your s's again. Say the practice words after me: Bess, mess, Tess, less.'

Phoebe repeated the words without a trace of a lisp, and Biddy smiled. 'There you are, you're perfectly good at them, you just forget when you get all het up.'

'Mother doesn't think . . . so,' Phoebe replied, making a special effort with 'so'. 'She . . . says . . . I'm a booby.'

'Oh never!' Biddy replied, but it was true. She worried as she tied an apron over Phoebe's clean dress. All very well to say children should be seen and not heard, but this poor little love was never allowed to speak in company, which was why she'd been shunted out of the way this afternoon, to be produced like a kewpie doll when the visitors were leaving. It was the missus herself who brought on the child's lisp, with her bullying ways; Phoebe was never as bad with the servants or with her father. Trouble was, the more madam bullied her, the more the kid fought back. She was a feisty little miss with a grand sense of her rights. Biddy sighed. Hadn't she herself learned the hard way to keep her mouth shut? But it was difficult to explain to a girl living in the lap of luxury. Biddy was nearly thirty but she felt as old as Methuselah listening to Phoebe.

When she'd been Phoebe's age, Biddy Donovan, the daughter of Irish immigrants, had been living in the shanty town on the south side. Jim Donovan had scrimped and saved to bring his family out here to find a better life, and an easier clime for his wife, who was suffering from consumption. But the long voyage had been too much for her and she'd died just as the ship was entering Moreton Bay.

Endeavouring to keep his promise to the dying woman to look after the girls, Jim had soon found a job on a road gang and rented a two-roomed cottage for his family. He slept on the tiny veranda, Biddy remembered sadly, with his three girls – Maureen, who was sixteen, Tess, thirteen, and Biddy, twelve – in the bedroom behind him, well guarded by their brave Dadda.

Maureen became the housekeeper, and Jim managed to place Tess and Biddy in a school just up the road. Schooling was expensive, a luxury for families like the Donovans, so Maureen had to be careful with her pennies in this land of bountiful food. In return for her success with his meagre budget, Jim insisted that the two younger girls share their lessons of an evening with their sister, so that she would be educated too. He always sat in, listening, and 'for fun' would ask the girls if he could have a try. Solemnly they included him in their lessons, knowing that Dadda had never learned to read or write, knowing that he was more eager than any of them to have an 'edjication'. Poor Dadda.

Then there was the time they came home from school to find the stove not lit, no dinner prepared, and Maureen, battered and bleeding, curled up on the bed they shared.

Jim's rage was terrifying. Neighbours came in to calm him, to no avail. It was the first time, but not the last, that Biddy was to hear the word 'rape'. Alone in the house all day, Maureen had been a prime target for their landlord, who'd made his way inside to inspect the house, and then attacked the girl.

Biddy could still hear her father weeping, blaming himself for not protecting his daughter. She could still hear women whispering that Maureen should not have fought back, that it would have gone better for her had she not, that she wouldn't have taken such a beating. And it had taken a long time for Biddy's rage to subside, for her to learn to stop fighting back, to bow her head and accept the hardships of factory work. When she found a better job in service, her battling days were over. Biddy could bob and say 'Yes, sir, no sir' with the best of them, no matter what she thought privately. That was what she was trying to teach Phoebe.

She could still see Maureen in the hospital, her head bandaged, her face like a purple balloon, her poor bloodshot eyes wild and frightened. She never recovered, dying in the loony bin six years later. As the neighbours said, the landlord, Tom Cranston, a beefy old butcher, had bashed the brains out of her.

When Jim had confronted him, he'd denied it all, denied the scratches on his face too, until Jim had torn the clothes from him, revealing the long weals on his chest and back, where Maureen had tried to defend herself. He'd knocked him down, as everyone expected he would, and that had seemed the end of it, until he'd returned to the hospital, with the doctors shaking their heads and Maureen not knowing anyone. Nor ever would again.

Jim Donovan took a gun and shot Cranston dead right in front of his butcher's shop. Biddy's father was still serving life in the Brisbane jail.

Neighbours had shunted the two Donovan girls from house to house, their schooldays over, until they'd ended up in a workhouse and then faring for themselves in a cellar in the shanty town. It always seemed strange to Biddy that Tess had taken to the streets, earning a living from the sex that had killed Maureen.

By the time Biddy had learned to make her way in service, she didn't want to know about men or sex; she just wanted to do her job, have a clean room and get paid . . . live a safe life. If others taunted her that she'd end up an old maid, Biddy didn't care. Better safe than sorry, she always said. She had visited her father in prison until he'd told her to keep away, that having a jailbird for a father wouldn't go down well on her history. He'd blessed her and told her to be a good girl and remember him in her prayers. He no longer made any mention of Tess, and by then Biddy had lost touch with her sister.

But as Cook once said: 'Misery isn't choosy. Rich or poor, youse can be miserable. And to my mind Miss Phoebe is just as bloody miserable as we was when we was kids. Pity that father of hers don't speak up. Weak as piss he is.'

The door opened, interrupting Biddy's reminiscences, and, well-trained, she came up with a bright response: 'Here she is, madam, none the worse for wear.'

She was ignored. Her mistress confronted the child. 'How dare you climb trees!'

'I had to get my ball.'

'We have gardeners. Why didn't you call them?'

'I forgot.'

She grabbed Phoebe by the ear and ran her to the window. 'You're lying. You deliberately climbed the tree to go next door. Get out of those clothes!'

Knowing what was coming, Biddy gathered her courage and spoke up: 'Excuse me, ma'am, she fell out of the tree, 'twas lucky she didn't hurt herself.'

'Did I ask you to speak?' Lalla flared, She stood tapping her foot as Phoebe removed her apron and dress to stand defiantly in her vest and bloomers.

'Now,' she said, her voice quiet and menacing, 'you didn't have the ball when you eventually came home. Where is it?'

'Thtill in the tree I thuppothe,' Phoebe lisped.

'Stop that baby talk immediately! You didn't fall out of the tree, you haven't got a mark on you. You took yourself over there to defy me. Isn't that the truth?'

'No!' Phoebe shouted. 'I saw the boy and the snake and he was frightened and he couldn't move, so I ran to find his mother and tell her, and she came out and the German lady came too—'

'Ha! Did you hear that?' Lalla turned to Biddy. 'She didn't fall out of the tree.' She shook Phoebe. 'Did you?'

'No. I jumped. I had to jump. I had to get his mother.'

'There you are, we have half of the truth, you little wretch! All of a sudden she's the heroine. A snake! If there were one, you didn't think those people could deal with it without your help?'

'I had to tell them.'

'I see.' Lalla's voice was silky. 'So you saw a snake in their garden, and completely unafraid, you leapt down into danger instead of staying safely in the tree. Then what?'

As Biddy watched, Phoebe mistook her mother's quieter tone for real interest, and launched into a breathless explanation, her lisp forgotten in her excitement. 'You should have seen what happened! The boy couldn't move, that big snake was right in front of him and it was waving its head all about, ready to bite him, so I ran to the house and the two ladies came out—'

'Ladies!' Lalla looked to the heavens in disgust.

Phoebe rushed on. 'I told them about the snake, and the boy's mother went down there and she sat on the grass on the other side of the snake and started to sing to it, a little song we could hardly hear.'

'Who are we?' Lalla demanded.

'The German lady. You know.'

'I do not know any such thing!'

Biddy stifled a sigh. The Thurlwells had been living next door to Mrs Beckman for more than twelve years.

'Anyway,' Phoebe continued, 'his mother sat right close to the snake and sang to it, and it gave up frightening the boy and turned to her, and it listened to her for a real long time and then it stopped poking its tongue at her and nothing happened. It just slid away like she'd told it to go home and be good.'

'I see. She told the snake to go home?'

'Yes.'

Quick as a flash, Lalla slapped her daughter's face again and Phoebe fell back, banging her head on the windowsill.

Biddy jumped, feeling the sting of the slap herself, but she dared not intervene.

'Pack of lies!' Lalla snapped. 'You expect me to believe that rot? You were in there playing with that boy. Did he touch you?' She was shaking her daughter. 'Where did he touch you?'

'Nowhere!' Phoebe screamed.

'So you were playing with him?'

'No.'

Lalla went to the cupboard and brought out the switch. She pushed her daughter over a chair and beat her until her own rage was assuaged, and then wearily turned to Biddy. 'I should have the doctor examine her by rights.'

'Oh no, ma'am,' Biddy pleaded.

Not one sound had Phoebe made during the beating, but now she turned on her mother. 'I hate you!'

Lalla sighed, delicately fingering her hair before the mirror: 'No you don't. I've never met a child who could invent such outrageous tales as you do. Now that you're getting older I have to be even more watchful of you. She thinks she's hard done by, Biddy, but a mother has to care. I know what girls can get up to.'

'Takes one to know one,' Biddy mumbled.

'What did you say?'

'I said, "It's hard to know, ma'am",' Biddy hastily improvised.

'Yes. Put her to bed. No supper.'

'But she didn't have any tea.'

'Give her bread and water then.'

Biddy nudged the child as she slipped the nightdress over her head, and Phoebe knew that though Biddy would bring her bread and water on a tray, in the pockets of her skirt there'd be some goodies wrapped in one of her mother's damask table napkins. She loved Biddy, and understood why none of the servants could talk back to her mother, no matter how mean she was to them. But she could. Her mother would have to kill her to shut her up.

When the adults had left the room, Phoebe lay on her stomach, allowing herself to groan. Her ear hurt and her bottom stung like fire. One of these days, she vowed, when she was certain she could speak without the baby lisp, she'd really tell her mother off in front of all her important friends. She'd so love to make a scene . . . one of these days.

Her mind drifted back to the neighbours. She couldn't understand why her mother hated them. The boy's mother was very dignified and had the most beautiful dark eyes. She hadn't panicked when Phoebe had run to her to tell her about the snake; her smile had been a caress in itself, as if she'd known Phoebe all her life. And she'd handed her on to the German lady, who had edged forward fearfully, clinging to Phoebe to watch the drama. It had been so comforting, so unfamiliar to be gathered into the skirts of this plump lady who smelled so fresh, like newly ironed linen, without the overpowering perfume her mother used, that Phoebe was astonished.

'Such a good girl you are,' the German lady had said when the snake had gone. 'You come in and I sew up your dress like new.'

'No, no! Thank you, but I have to go,' Phoebe had said, and fled. She hadn't worried that her dress was torn as she ran out of their gate and along the grassy patch to her own front garden, until she saw the women gaping and her mother's cold stare.

'Biddy,' she asked, when the maid came back with her miserable tray and a surreptitious supply of chicken sandwiches and crunchy butternut biscuits, 'why doesn't my mother like the neighbours?'

'I don't know,' Biddy replied, rather than try to explain.

'It was true what I told Mama,' Phoebe said. 'About the snake.'

'And I'd be believin' you, but leave well alone, my love. Leave well alone.'

The snake episode was long forgotten. As the years passed, Diamond became increasingly concerned about her son's future.

'He's fourteen, Oma,' Diamond said. 'We have to find him a job. He can't go on living here as if he's our gardener and handyman; he needs a *real* job.'

'I know, dear, I know,' Gussie Beckman worried. 'I've made enquiries but when I tell them he's a coloured boy, they say no. I tell them he's educated, his English is good but they don't want to listen.'

Diamond smiled. 'Something will turn up. You found me a job at that age.'

'As a housemaid,' Gussie sniffed. 'You deserved better.'

'It was the best you could do for a black girl, and I coped. Now, you're tired, and it's a chilly night. You go to bed and I'll bring you in some hot cocoa.'

Gussie packed away her embroidery and heaved herself out of the chair. 'Oh my, getting old I am, darling, but I can still make my own cocoa.'

'No you won't. Off to bed, I've turned it down for you.'

The old woman tucked her shawl about her shoulders. 'You're too good to me, you spoil me.'

'Good to you?' Diamond echoed. 'After all you've done for me? Get along with you.' She went through to the kitchen and stoked up the stove to boil some milk, then stared out of the window at the twinkling lights of Brisbane across the river, remembering the twelve-year-old Aborigine waif that these good people, Captain and Gussie Beckman, had adopted.

She'd been frightened out of her wits when they took her home, and on the first night had hidden in their woodshed, refusing to come out. But they'd been patient with her and had gradually gained her confidence. As Gussie often said, Diamond's arrival had turned her life about, taken away the loneliness of a sea widow in a strange land. They'd called her Diamond after the Countess Diamantina, wife of the Governor of Queensland. The Countess was European, and since Gussie was German, struggling with a new country and a new language, Diamantina was her heroine. Gussie's husband had been captain of a merchant ship that plied the route between Melbourne and Java, with Brisbane as home port. He was away for months on end, so her first years in Brisbane had been miserable until Diamond was put into her hands. With the energy of a woman long deprived of someone to care for, Gussie took charge of the girl. She taught her English, which to this day Diamond spoke with a slight German accent; she taught her to cook, to sew, and as their relationship grew, Gussie took on the education of the girl she now regarded as her daughter. There was always great excitement in the house when their beloved Captain came home, for then Diamond would read to him and show him her workbooks, where Gussie had taught her to write and to do sums. After the slap-up dinner, of course, which they had cooked for him.

Diamond sighed, remembering the welcome-home dinners. They'd been a happy little family, until tragedy struck. A happy trio, just as she and Gussie and Ben were now. But this wouldn't last either, she knew that. So many things she knew, that she couldn't explain to other people. They were earth stories, tribal thoughts, inherited from another plane of knowledge which she'd learned never to doubt. She couldn't pass them on to Ben because bereft of her heritage of inter-family traditions he could not hope to understand. His father was a white man. In her learned language Diamond called these thoughts intuition and left it at that, but already she could see a storm shadow over their happiness. Sometimes, of a night, she sat for hours out there on the cliff edge, searching for guidance, for a star plan in that brilliant ordered sky, a plan that would provide a life path for Ben.

She jumped as the milk sizzled, boiling over, then rescued the remains, cleaned the black stove and set Gussie's tray,

Oma, as Ben had been taught to call her – German for Grandmother – was kneeling by the bed in her nightdress, saying her prayers. As always, Diamond joined in the final refrain: 'God bless our dear Captain and from heaven have him watch over us. Amen.'

When Gussie was settled, Diamond handed her the tray. 'Ben seems determined to go to sea like the Captain,' she said, but the older woman shook her head.

'You mustn't allow this. It's not because the Captain's ship went down; that was the will of God. But a coloured boy on a ship would lead a terrible life, he'd be worth nothing. The best he could ever become would be a deckhand and he'd be lucky to survive that. Diamond, he's a handsome young boy.'

Diamond laughed. 'I know. I'm proud of Ben, he's beautiful. He has lovely olive skin and his father's straight brown hair, not frizzy like mine. When he grows up he'll be a handsome man. Why would anyone complain?'

As she spoke she saw the fear in Gussie's eyes. 'Oma, what's wrong?'

'Give me my rosary beads,' Oma said, and as Diamond handed them to her, she clutched them and whispered: 'The Captain never spoke of these things but I voyaged with him, as you know. When there are no women about, men do strange things. While I was aboard he flogged a man for attacking one of the deckhands, and when I visited the boy in sickbay I was shocked. I still didn't quite understand, so I searched the logbooks for similar floggings and found them. They were flogged for buggery. So . . . you listen to me, girl. Aboard ship Ben would be in danger, and a coloured boy might not have the protection of the officers.'

'If anyone touched my son like that I'd put a curse on him that would rot his innards,' Diamond said stoutly.

'A bit late,' Gussie retorted. 'I blame myself, filling his head with all my stories of the Captain. He only knows about the sea from the wheelhouse.'

'No, no! The presence of the Captain has kept us a family. If Ben persists I will just have to explain things to him. When he's a grown man he can make his own decisions.'

On the way back to the kitchen Diamond looked in on Ben, who was sleeping soundly under the soft down cover with its buttoned broderie sheet. One arm was flung wide and he looked so vulnerable she despaired.

Could she have taught him more? Taught him there were ways of protection? But what were they? They had only come to her over the years from the mists of time, like something that was already in place. Ben was half white. Would any of that knowledge ever filter through to him, the mystic other sense? He hadn't been able to cope with old man snake that time. If she hadn't come down to quieten it, he could have been bitten.

She remembered the incident of the cruel housekeeper. She'd never told Gussie about that.

When the Captain was reported drowned at sea, their world had fallen apart. Left with no means of support, Gussie was forced to return to her family in Germany, but she couldn't take Diamond with her.

'She did the best she could for me,' Diamond murmured.

Gussie had found her a live-in job as a housemaid and left her what money she could spare.

'Underneath it all, I was still a wild one in those days,' she recalled now, remembering the abuse and beatings she'd taken at the hands of the housekeeper. She still had a sense of guilt at her reaction. The woman had died of snake bite, and it wasn't by accident that the snake had found its way into her room . . .

No, Gussie would not appreciate that story. But she'd told her most of the rest. How she'd travelled north and learned to fend for herself against both black and white men, until she met and fell in love with Ben Buchanan, the owner of Caravale cattle station. That had been a wonderful, romantic time. With Ben as her lover she'd hoped she'd found a home at last, but it was not to be. Ben had decided to marry a white woman and had coldly ordered Diamond to leave.

For some years she'd struggled to earn a living any way she could.

Eventually she'd joined friends who were heading north for the Palmer goldfields, her only aim being to make contact with members of her own tribe, the Irukandji people. But it was the tribal people who'd shown her where to find gold, enough to last her for the rest of her life!

Then she'd heard that Ben Buchanan was also on the goldfields, and like so many others was dangerously ill, having succumbed to fever. Diamond nursed him gladly and brought him out to the coast, waiting to tell him her good news, that she had buried a cache of gold nuggets in the scrub. But as soon as he recovered he reverted to his old self, the arrogant pastoralist, treating her with contempt as his 'nigger woman' and eventually leaving her, as he thought, destitute in a little northern port.

Broken-hearted once again, and now carrying his child, Diamond had made her way back to Brisbane, believing that no amount of money could compensate for the loss of the man she loved so deeply.

She closed her son's door and retreated to the kitchen.

Time had healed the wounds; she wasn't bitter about that man any more, and the birth of their son was her greatest joy. And of course the gold had helped. She'd bought this house, not without difficulty since no one wanted to sell to a 'nigger', but she'd overcome that problem by writing to her adoptive mother, inviting her to return to Australia to live with her. Gussie Beckman had been thrilled to hear from her. For years she'd been living on the charity of relatives who resented her, so she was only too happy to board the next available ship to Brisbane.

An Aborigine with a hoard of gold would have created too much suspicion, so their solicitor, Joseph Mantrell, sold the gold for her, nugget by nugget, over the years. He opened a bank account in the name of Mrs Augusta Beckman and the house was also bought in that name. When Diamond told him it would be a long time before the Northern gold fields were mined out, he invested in gold shares for her and, incidentally, for himself. A very profitable venture for both of them. Only Mantrell knew that these two quiet, reserved clients of his were wealthy women.

Thunder rolled across the hills and Diamond closed the windows along the front of the house. The coming storm made her feel even more nervous. A storm was imminent in their lives too, and she felt helpless to prevent it.

'We must find something for Ben to do,' she whispered. 'I must be able to find a steady path for him where he'll be safe from the humiliations I had to endure.'

When Gussie came home with the good news that she had found a place for Ben, his mother was thrilled. 'Where, Oma? Tell me quickly.'

'It isn't much,' Gussie said, taking off her hat. 'But I saw a sign that said “Lad Wanted” and I marched right in. There I met a nice man, Mr O’Neill, who owns big stables and a saddle-making factory in New Farm.’

‘What would he want Ben to do?’

‘He said he could start off as a stableboy to learn to look after the horses, and if he proved to be a good boy—’

‘You did say he was a good boy?’ Diamond interrupted eagerly.

‘Would I not? I said he was a good lad, from a good family, and knew his lessons. Mr O’Neill was surprised to hear that he could read and write, even though—’

‘He is coloured?’ Diamond said.

‘Yes. No need to hang your head, missy. Mr O’Neill said he has a son of his own, a bit older than Ben, and it had been the devil of a job to make him learn his lessons. I saw the lad, his name is Cash, or that’s what it sounded like. He works in the saddlery now, and that’s why the gentleman needs a stableboy. He’ll be good company for Ben.’

‘If he accepts him,’ Diamond said.

‘Oh poof! He will, boys are all the same. I’m to take Ben there in the morning. Where is he?’

‘I don’t know. He wandered off after lunch. He’s probably gone over to the wharves again.’ She saw Gussie’s disapproval. ‘I can’t keep him locked up here, he’s not a baby!’

‘Yes, I know. But soon he’ll be working and kept too busy to be hanging about those places.’ She took out her purse and put several sovereigns on the table. Every month it was Gussie’s duty to draw cash and check their accounts. Sometimes Diamond went with her, waiting outside, and then they enjoyed an afternoon outing, strolling through the Botanical Gardens, which Diamond loved. When he was younger Ben looked forward to these days, but eventually he lost interest, although he still liked to accompany them to the busy markets, listening to the shouts of the spruikers, eating toffee apples and talking with his friends.

It was at the Saturday markets that Diamond had first met the ragged beggars who were Ben’s friends from the wharves, and although her heart went out to them, she recognized their sly, calculating eyes, old beyond their years, and she feared for her son in their company. Time and again she’d tried to tell Ben there was no need for him to mix with them, but her arguments fell on deaf ears. None of the white children in the street were permitted to play with him, nor did he seem interested in them. All the fun and excitement he required could be found down on the wharves, and in that world he’d made friends his own age. Or so he thought.

‘I brought home the bank statement,’ Gussie said.

Both women studied the careful handwriting. This was their lifeline and they guarded it minutely, watching for any discrepancies, convinced that bankers might attempt to cheat them. They never spoke of Diamond's gold these days, only of their shared nest egg which still stood at more than ten thousand pounds, thanks to their cautious lifestyle and their continuing success in the share market.

Having perused the statement, Diamond grinned. 'We're still not broke.' It was a standing joke between two women who desperately feared poverty. 'I'm glad you found Ben a job, Gussie. I was beginning to think we'd have to leave here and buy him a farm.'

'Good God! He's too young to own a farm, I'm too old to run one and you don't know anything about them.'

Diamond shrugged. 'It was just an idea. If he was a bit older I'd buy him a country property. That would be perfect for him.'

'Good money after bad,' Gussie sniffed. 'Let him learn something first.'

Diamond kept glancing at the back door, waiting for Ben as the afternoon sun began yellowing in the sky. 'If anything happens to me,' she said, 'will you give him an allowance, Gussie? But don't hand over the bank money.'

'Nothing will happen to you,' Gussie retorted. 'I'm the one making old bones. I've written my will and Mr Mantrell has it. It turns everything back to you. It frightens me, Diamond. You're settled now, no one will bother you any more. Let me transfer everything back to your name.'

'No. Ben is not a good judge of character yet, we've seen that.' She laughed. 'Probably because he hasn't had to learn the hard way like I did. You'll know when is the right time to hand on to him. When he is responsible enough to look after both of you.'

Gussie shook her head. 'Enough of this morbid talk. I think you've just got the willies because Ben is late home. You mustn't worry so much. He's a good lad, he'll be in soon.'

Ben was having a grand day. A big ship had come upriver, the *Southern Star* from Plymouth, and the passengers were being ferried ashore. Further down, a steamer was loading for the South Coast, and a picnic party of swells was waiting to board the lighter to take them to one of the islands.

He climbed on top of some wool bales to watch the busy scene. The immigrants in their heavy northern clothes – dark cloaks, shawls and bonnets – clutched bundles and stared open-mouthed at the laughing group of picnickers, the men in white suits and the women looking pretty in summery dresses and toying with gay parasols.

As the crowds grew, so did the noise and excitement, with sweaty porters trying to push their way through, shouting: 'Make way! Make way!' Ben realized there was an opportunity here to earn a few pennies, so he jumped down and ducked through to a portly gentleman who was standing, frustrated, with his family and their baggage, unable to catch a porter.

'Carry your bags, sir?' he called, but his friend Willy Sloane was there first.

'This is my job,' he grinned, 'but you can give me a hand.' He tipped his cap to the gentleman. 'Me mate and me, we'll carry the big trunk for you, sir, penny each.'

The man ignored this grubby urchin, and his wife and daughter huddled nervously beside him, but Willy was persistent. He jerked his head at the soft fluffy clouds gathering in the distance. 'Best you get movin', sir, them clouds can blow up in a second here, blow you off'n yer feet if they don't drench youse first.'

Ben stared at the clouds. They were harmless, they drifted over at this time every day and passed on without a drop of moisture to spend, but the immigrant had taken the bait.

'Very well,' he said. 'You can take these bags as well.' He dumped a bedroll and carpetbag on top of the trunk. 'We'll carry the rest ourselves,' he told the women.

'Customs and immigration shed down this way,' Willy said, the deal done. 'You take the other end, Ben.'

The trunk felt like a ton weight, but the two boys struggled manfully with both hands on the leather straps, trying not to spill the extra load, banging their ankles on the trunk.

'I shoulda said tuppence for this lot,' Willy puffed. 'Tuppence each. I bet it's full of bloody stones.'

The family had moved ahead of them, carrying their own pieces with ease, but when Willy and Ben stopped to rest and resettle the bags on top, their employer shouted at them to get a move on, obviously not impressed by their efforts. 'And don't scratch that trunk,' he shouted. 'A pretty penny it cost.'

'Chuck it in the river if he don't shut up,' Willy gritted.

'We're nearly there,' Ben said. 'And you can keep the tuppence. I'll find another job.'

'You're a good sport,' Willy said as they stumbled into the shed, where people were sorting themselves into queues. 'This'll do.' They dumped the heavy trunk and the man handed Ben, who was the closest, two pennies, without another word.

'Stay here,' he instructed the women, 'while I see what's doing.'

'See you later then,' Ben said, passing the pennies to Willy.

As he left the shed he turned back for a moment and noticed that the women were anxiously watching their man instead of keeping an eye on the luggage. And then it happened so fast he wasn't sure if it had happened at all. The carpetbag that had been resting on the trunk was gone, and so was Willy. Ben was confused. Had Willy pinched it? No, he wouldn't do such a stupid thing. Probably one of the women had lifted it down and it was in among the jumble of their other goods. He shrugged. He could hardly go back to make sure.

Outside there was a commotion. An old woman had collapsed and people were pushing and shoving, calling out that she should be given air as she lay on salt-worn timbers.

Ben managed to get to the front of the crush, curious as always. 'Is she dying?' he asked.

'No, it's just the heat,' a woman said, kneeling to help her. 'Can you get her some water, lad?'

Water? There were taps but no cups. Then he remembered that all the lorries that brought wool and produce from the warehouses carried water bags, so he darted through the sheds, unhooked one of the canvas bags from the back of the nearest lorry and ran back with it.

The woman was sitting up, though looking very dizzy, with other women supporting her, and she meekly accepted the water as they lifted the bag to her mouth.

'Thank you,' she said to Ben. 'I don't know what came over me.'

The drama was over and people moved away, but Ben waited: he had to return the water bag. With all chances of finding another portering job gone, he made his way back through the sheds and carefully replaced it. She hadn't drunk much, so it didn't need refilling. Haulers never minded kids taking a swig from their bags but they could be nasty if they were left empty.

Standing away from the wharves, which were quieter now, he decided he might as well go home, be early for dinner for a change. Besides, he'd promised Mum he'd clean out that damn chicken coop. They only kept a dozen or so chooks, down at the end of the side garden, and from his point of view they were more trouble than they were worth.

'There he is!' a man shouted, and Ben turned to see what this latest racket was about. He was stunned to find a group of men racing towards him, led by the gentleman from the ship, his coat-tails flying.

'That's the one!' he yelled. 'Grab him! He stole my luggage.'

'I did not!' Ben retorted, but two customs clerks grabbed him anyway and shoved him forward so roughly his head almost crashed into his accuser's stomach.

The man was in such a rage he belted Ben across the ear with a hand of iron, and Ben reeled back, his head ringing with the pain of it. 'You damned thief!' roared the new arrival. 'Where is it? You stole my carpetbag, and by the Lord you'll give it back!'

With a sinking heart Ben realized what had happened, but that knowledge wouldn't help him now. 'I never touched your bag, sir,' he said. 'I swear to God I never did.'

'Don't add blasphemy to your sins!' He made another swipe at Ben, who was able to sidestep since the interested clerks had loosened their hold on him.

This was the time, Ben decided, to make a run for it, but he'd left it too late; a policeman was bearing down on them. 'What's all this?'

'I've been robbed, Constable,' the gentleman said. 'I am the Reverend Craddock from Plymouth. No sooner stepped ashore than I have been robbed of a carpetbag of valuables. A disgrace I call it and I will certainly report this to the Bishop, but here's the culprit. I want him charged and my property returned.'

'I didn't steal anything!' Ben insisted, but the constable grabbed him by the ear.

'Where is it? And don't lie to me. I've had a gutful of you young hoodlums pinching every bloody thing you can lay your hands on round here. Tell me where it is and it'll go easier for you.'

'I didn't touch it!' Ben repeated, worried what his mother would say if she heard about this.

'He lies!' the Reverend shouted. 'He carried my luggage with another young scoundrel. I paid him tuppence and the minute I turned my back he was gone, taking my property with him, the ungrateful wretch.'

'Did you see him take it?' the constable asked.

'Of course I did.'

'You just said your back was turned,' Ben challenged him. 'So how could you have seen me? I only walked out the door to where the old lady—'

'Shut your mouth!' the policeman said. 'Don't get smart with me. Who was your mate? The one working with you?'

'I don't know,' Ben said. 'Just one of the lads. I don't know his name.'

'The hell you don't!' The constable turned to Ben's accuser. 'I'd say your bag's gone, Reverend. They work in pairs. This one's the decoy to draw you off. But they won't get away with it. I'll take him in and he'll soon put us on to his mate. They're not too smart once they see the inside of a cell. Now, where can I find you once I've got this sorted out?'

'St John's Church in Fortitude Valley,' the cleric replied, 'and I don't accept that my bag is simply "gone", as you put it. I want it found, do you hear me? I demand that my property be returned to me and these scoundrels punished. I expect you to see to it!'

He stormed away while the constable, cursing both the robbed and the robbers, clamped handcuffs on Ben and shoved him out into the street.

'Why won't you listen to me?' Ben complained. 'I never touched his bag. You wait till my mother hears about this,' he added, hoping the introduction of an adult on to his side might even the odds. 'She'll be really angry and you'll get the blame for arresting an innocent person.'

The constable stared at him. 'Jesus! For a kid you've got a mouth on you,' and then he laughed. 'Your ma's coming down, is she? Well, she'd better look out I don't lock her up too.' He gave Ben a hefty kick in the backside. 'Get along with you!'

After he'd slung the kid in the pen with the day's collection of thieves, drunks and rowdies, Constable Ray Dolan gave the details to the duty officer. 'His name is Ben Beckman. Looks like his daddy was a German. And I'll bet *he's* nowhere to be seen. Charge: theft of a carpetbag containing valuables from Reverend Craddock, who's a cranky piece of work, I might add. Bellowing at me to return his property. The half-caste kid had a partner on the job, could have been any one of them little bastards that hang about the docks.'

'And the Reverend's stuff would have been flogged off by this,' the duty officer said with a sigh.

'To be sure, them kids have got thievin' down to a fine art. But listen, the Beckman kid had the cheek to threaten me that his ma would be comin' down here on the warpath.' Constable Dolan smirked. 'So we'd better watch out for a black gin to come bowlin' in.'

'Scary stuff that,' the other policeman laughed. 'Do you reckon she's in on the thievin' too?'

'Nothin' surer. By the sound of things the contents of that bag would keep her and her mates in booze for a month. If she turns up we'll hold her too.'

Diamond was angry with Ben for being late, but she was also restless. She had a feeling that something was very wrong. She watched the last ferry cross the river but there was still no sign of him.

'Don't be worrying,' Oma said. 'He's a sensible boy, he won't be far away, and it's not dark yet, this fine evening. We'll wait dinner for a while.'

Impatiently Diamond went to the front of the house and then on to the front gate, standing awhile before she walked down the road a little, hoping to see him in the distance. The girl from next door, Phoebe, was strolling idly in the driveway of Somerset House.

'Have you seen Ben anywhere?' Diamond asked her.

Phoebe looked up in surprise. 'No, ma'am.'

'I thought he might have been wandering about here somewhere. He's late for dinner.'

'Will he get into trouble?'

Diamond smiled. 'Do you think he ought to?'

'Not if he has a good excuse,' Phoebe said stoutly.

'He always has that. He's a good talker.'

'I'm not. I get nervous and my tongue gets tangled up and I lisp.'

'You're not lisping now.'

'You don't make me nervous. I remember that you can charm snakes.'

'Well, there you are,' Ben's mother said. She broke a dead stick from a tree and drew a snake in the sand. 'I think if a snake could talk it might lisp but it wouldn't worry him.'

Phoebe laughed. 'I don't suppose it would.'

'You see. Who cares?' Diamond slid a soft dark finger down Phoebe's cheek. 'Forget about the lisp, it will go away.'

'When?'

Diamond pondered this. 'When you forget about it.'

Biddy came looking for Phoebe. 'There you are! Dinner's ready,' she called. 'Oh, it's sorry I am, ma'am, I didn't see you there.'

'Mrs Beckman is looking for her son, he's late,' Phoebe said.

'Isn't that just like boys!' Biddy grinned.

'I'm learning,' the neighbour said and flashed a smile at Phoebe before she went on her way.

Biddy was impressed. 'She's a gorgeous-looking woman that one,' she said to Phoebe. 'No matter the skin colour, she'd stand out against the best of them, I say.'

But Phoebe wasn't listening. 'I have to forget I've got a lisp,' she told Biddy.

'You do, do you?' Biddy said drily. 'Now get along. Your parents are waiting.'

Oma Beckman watched nervously as the sun dropped far too quickly from the sky. She used to tell Ben that it was in a hurry to light up the northern hemisphere, but now she wished it had taken its time, spared a little twilight for them, because Ben still had not come home.

'I'll walk down the road and see if I can find him,' she said, 'he might be playing down there somewhere.'

'No,' Diamond said. 'I'll go. It's dark out there now, I'll just keep walking until I find him.'

'Ah, you mustn't. You're not well, dear.'

'Nonsense. I've only got a cold. A walk will do me good.'

'Maybe you should wait a little longer. You shouldn't go down there at night.'

'Oma! You fuss too much. I can look after myself, I'm not your little black girl any more.' She disappeared into her bedroom and slipped a loose jacket over her blouse and long skirt, then unwound the colourful bandanna from round her head and replaced it with a grey scarf that she tied at the nape of her neck. Oma was right, of course, the dark streets of Brisbane could be dangerous for a lone Aborigine woman, but Diamond had lived in rougher towns than this and had long ago learned to fend for herself. She knew to wear drab clothes, so as not to draw attention to herself, and to move swiftly, with a determined air. And – she stepped behind the door so that Oma couldn't see her – to take precautions. While she moved freely about the town during the day, she rarely went out at night, but now if she had to go down to the docks it was best to be careful.

She opened a wooden box that she kept under her bed and searched the contents until she found the bundle she'd been looking for. Then she put her foot on the side of the bed and strapped the knife to her ankle. 'Just in case,' she smiled grimly, remembering the bad old days when a fast slash with that knife had saved her from serious assaults.

'But then you were young and beautiful,' she sighed, 'not just a dull woman out looking for her kid.'

She ran easily down the road, watching for Ben at every turn. When she entered the red-light district of Vulture Street she slowed, moving among dark groups of loiterers and peering into murky lanes and doorways. She approached several of the prostitutes to ask if they'd seen a young boy pass this way, and when they couldn't help her she began to search the dim taverns. Ben had often come home pleased with himself that he'd earned a few pennies doing odd jobs on the wharves, even though he knew she disapproved. Maybe he'd found some chore in one of these places. After all, he was growing up and, like any boy, beginning to seek independence.

With no luck there she headed for the bridge, loping along beside carriages as they clattered towards the town.

'Where is he?' she kept asking herself, frightened now that he might be hurt and lying in some dark alleyway. Maybe he'd been run down by one of the vehicles that hurtled through the streets. She avoided the gardens, guessing that he wouldn't be likely to be wandering through there at this hour, and kept to the busier streets that bordered the river. In no time she was back into the darker districts finding herself eventually on the deserted wharves.

Hours had passed. She was feeling hot and flushed, from the worry and all this exertion, she supposed, and was beginning to give up hope of finding him. What if she'd missed him and the little wretch was already safe at home with Oma? She thought of asking the police for help but she doubted they'd be interested in locating a coloured kid, and besides, she had an innate fear of the police. She'd never had any dealings with them, fortunately, and didn't want to start now.

Before retracing her steps she thought of enquiring at the hospital, but just in time, she realized that this would be a waste of time: they didn't treat coloureds. She sighed. She'd been living contentedly in the white world for so long now it was hard to remember that she wasn't really part of it. Oma Beckman was her buffer against them.

Sadly she remembered Ben Buchanan, whom she'd last seen up there on the goldfields. She'd loved him so much and had been so happy to be with him. And just when she was preparing to surprise him, to tell him that she'd struck gold, he had dumped her: 'You forget you're just another nigger, Diamond. I couldn't marry you!' He'd left her, gone back to his cattle station. Sometimes she wondered what would have happened if she'd run after him to tell him about the gold. At the time her pride wouldn't allow her to.

'Wonder all you like,' she told herself as she strode on. 'He would still have despised you. You were only his bed-mate.'

Lost in concentration she blundered into two men who barred her way. One took her arm. 'Looking for a man, love?'

'Get away from me,' she said, shaking him off, but the other man lurched at her, his foul breath sickening her.

'Don't you want to earn a few bob?'

He grabbed her belt and jerked her towards him, and instinctively Diamond's right hand shot out, palm flattened as she delivered a sharp blow to his throat with the side of her hand.

As he fell back, choking, clutching his throat, the other bruiser threw a punch at Diamond. She easily sidestepped and moved away from them, only to be halted by a policeman swinging his truncheon. 'What's going on here?'

'Nothing,' Diamond said. 'They're just a bit merry.'

'Like hell we are!' the first assailant yelled. 'That bloody black bitch attacked my mate here.'

The policeman grasped Diamond firmly and poked her in the back with the truncheon, preventing her from leaving. 'Not so fast, Topsy. What happened to him?' He indicated the other man who was still stumbling about, gasping for breath.

'I told you,' his friend said. 'She attacked him. She'd have rolled him if I hadn't been here to stop her.'

'That's not true,' Diamond cried. 'I was only walking down here looking for my son . . .'

'Pull the other leg,' the lawman snapped. 'Did you do that to him?'

'She's a whore, a street-fighter, this one,' her first assailant cried. 'Damn near killed him!'

'I did not!' Diamond argued. 'He'll be all right. Please, sir,' she said to the policeman, 'I have to go.'

He slammed his truncheon across her back. 'Shut your trap! You bloody boongs are a menace on the streets. What's your name?'

When he struck her Diamond stumbled under the blow, almost to her knees, but as she went down she knew she had no hope of winning this argument so she kept going. As she dived forward almost at their knee level, the startled policeman lost his grip on her. Before he could regain control she was off, running down the dark street.

In her day she had been able to run for miles across the dangerous territory adjoining the Palmer goldfields, but now she was hindered by her long skirt and by a shortness of breath caused by the cold that had lingered for weeks. She turned the next corner with the policeman chasing angrily after her, frantically trying to think where she could find refuge. And then she had it! She raced towards a road and down the other side, past staring pedestrians, hearing the shouts of the policeman demanding that someone stop her.

The cry went up of 'Stop thief!' as she fled down an alleyway that led to busy Queen Street but instead of continuing through, she dived into a gap between two brick walls, wedging herself firmly in the dark crevice.

Diamond hardly dared breathe as her pursuer raced by. As soon as he'd passed she moved swiftly to the back door ot one of the buildings, thumping on it with her fist, her heart thudding as she did so.

'Who is it?' a woman's voice called.

'Let me in!' Diamond cried, and the urgency of her tone spurred the person on the other side into action. She heard the heavy bolts slide back and as the door opened a few inches, she pushed her way in, slamming it behind her.

'Lock it,.quick!' she said. 'The police are after me.'

Her rescuer shot the bolts and turned to stare at Diamond in the dim light. 'Who are you?'

'Is Goldie home?' Diamond asked.

'Yes.'

'I must see her. I'm a friend.'

The woman was plump, fair-haired, her lips scarlet in a pallid white face. She clutched at her loose kimono and stared at this black woman: 'I never seen you before.'

'Hurry!' Diamond ordered.

The woman shrugged. 'Orright. Hold your horses. You wait here.'

Leaning against the door, Diamond was grateful for the respite. She'd met Goldie many years ago when they were both working in the Chinese brothel in Charters Towers. Goldie had remained in the business and was now the owner of this establishment, well known in Brisbane as The Blue Heaven.

Diamond would rather have forgotten those hard times in the mining town, but Goldie had befriended the bewildered black girl and extended many a kindness to her. In time Diamond was able to repay her.

Five years ago, when she'd been walking to the ferry with Oma Beckman, she'd met up with Goldie again.

'How're you doin', Diamond?' Goldie had said cheerily. Goldie had always been sharp. She caught Diamond's glance of warning and knew not to make any mention of their past in front of the white lady, who, Goldie assumed, was Diamond's employer.

'I'm fine, thanks,' Diamond replied, but she was shocked at Goldie's appearance. The other woman looked thin and tired. 'But are you all right, Goldie? You don't look well.'

'I'm gettin' along,' Goldie sighed. Then she whispered, 'Do you think the lady there could lend me ten bob?'

'I'm sure she would,' Diamond said gently. She asked Oma for a pound and handed the note to her old friend. 'Where do you live?'

'Right there,' Goldie said, pointing to a rickety boarding house. 'It's a flea-trap but it does me for now.' She turned to Mrs Beckman. 'Thank you, lady, you're very kind. I'll pay you back.'

'No, no,' Oma said quickly. 'No need. You keep it.'

'Gee, thanks. You're a good lady. I'd better go now. Nice to see you again, Diamond.'

As they boarded the ferry Oma looked back. 'Such a sad woman there, Diamond. She must have been nice-looking in her day, with that pretty red hair.'

'Yes.'

'Also she looks to me like she might be a prostitute. Yes?'

Diamond nodded. 'She helped me when I was down on my luck, Oma.'

Nothing more was said about the meeting with Goldie, but the next day Diamond boarded the ferry again, in search of her friend.

'I want you to have this,' she said when she found her.

'What?' Goldie opened the envelope. 'It's money!' she cried, leafing through the notes. 'It must be fifty pounds, Diamond! Where did you get it? Did you steal it?'

'No,' Diamond laughed.

'Is it from the German lady?'

'No, Goldie, it's from me. I was worried about you, I want you to have it. You will take it, won't you?'

'Will I what? I always said you were a good sort, Diamond, in more ways than one. And Jeez, I could do with a loan right now.'

'It's not a loan, it's for keeps. Now I have to go. You look after yourself.'

'But how can you afford this?'

Only the lawyer and Oma Beckman knew that an Aborigine girl had been one of the many returning triumphant from the golden gullies of the Palmer River, and she wanted to keep it that way. 'Ask no questions,' she laughed, knowing that Goldie would understand.

From there, realizing that life was too hard on the streets of Brisbane, Goldie had opened her own small brothel, and with the profits had invested in this blank-faced and very private two-storeyed house.

In a small town like Brisbane it was inevitable that the two women would meet again, and when Goldie was well established, she'd proudly shown Diamond through her plush and profitable house. But they never met socially, relying on chance encounters, and Goldie never asked her old friend any questions about how she'd become a respectable lady.

'Diamond!' she cried now, rushing down the passageway, her taffeta skirts swishing against the narrow walls. 'Is that you? What are you doing here? What's wrong?'

On their way upstairs to Goldie's sitting room, Diamond explained what had happened. 'It's all so stupid. I was just trying to find my son,' she said at last. 'And I got mixed up with bruisers and then the police. A black woman on the streets, fair game,' she added bitterly.

'They'll backtrack if they don't see you in Queen Street,' Goldie said. 'And like as not they'll come bashing on my back door, thinking you're one of mine.'

'A compliment at my age,' Diamond laughed. 'I see you've got some pretty girls here.'

'You're still a good sort, love, but I'll have to get you out of here. And you can't go walking about again at this hour.'

'Yes I can. Let me out the front way and I'll cut across to the bridge.'

'No. Leave it to me.' Goldie hurried out of the door, calling to one of her girls, then came back and bustled through to her bedroom. 'Put this hat on.'

It was wide and very fashionable, with a heavy veil. Diamond removed her scarf and pinned on the hat, which disguised her dark skin to a certain extent. 'I look mad in this. But never mind. What now?'

'There'll be a hansom cab downstairs for you. Come on.'

At the door, she stopped Diamond. 'What's your son's name. I'll ask about.'

'Ben. Ben Beckman. He's fourteen, tall for his age.'

Goldie opened the front door, and there was the cab. They could hear banging on the alleyway door. 'Go,' she said. 'Quick! Hop in the cab.'

Within minutes the horse was clopping over the bridge, with Diamond sitting safely inside the cab, hoping that Ben was home by this time. Her head ached even more, her chest felt empty, like bellows with a hole in them, unable to hold enough air for her to breathe properly, and her throat was sore. She promised herself that if Ben was home, she wouldn't chastise him, she'd listen to his reasons because he was a good boy, a dear boy . . .

As she climbed down from the cab and paid the driver, she felt dizzy but steadied herself. 'Could you wait a minute? I might need you again.'

'No fear. Can't do it. Me horse is dead tired now. We're goin' home.'

'Oh. I'm sorry.' Intimidated, Diamond let him go, took off the hat that seemed like a lead weight by this time, and made for the open front door.

'Is he home yet?' she asked Oma, who came hurrying out to meet her.

'No, dear. You've been out so long I was beginning to worry about *you*. Are you all right? You look flushed.'

'I'm fine. I walked so far I had to get a cab home,' she lied, so as not to worry the old woman. 'I looked everywhere but I couldn't find him.' She flung the hat with her jacket into her bedroom, relieved that Oma was so worried she hadn't noticed Goldie's chapeau. 'Oh dear,' she cried, 'where can he be, Oma? I know something terrible has happened to him.'

'He'll be all right,' Oma said. 'Come and have some coffee. Boys, they don't worry, he's probably fallen asleep at one of his friend's homes . . .'

'What friends?' Diamond said bleakly, glad to find refuge in their warm, snug kitchen. She was so depressed she was almost in tears. She wanted to believe Oma, that Ben had fallen asleep somewhere and that he'd be on the doorstep first thing in the morning. Maybe he'd stayed too long on the wharves and had been too frightened – a coloured boy, alone – to make the roundabout trek home in the dark.

But then Ben didn't see himself as coloured. Even though he was aware why, as a half-caste, he couldn't attend a school, she guessed that the enormity of the problem had not affected him. Not yet anyway, she thought ominously.

Her own experiences this very night had proved to Diamond that she'd taken the best course in keeping her little family to herself; not mixing with any of the Aborigine clans in Brisbane for fear of appearing patronizing. They'd want no part of her anyway, for she lived in the alien white world. She always had, from the time Gussie and the Captain had adopted her. And she had no relatives here. Her own tribe, the Irukandji, in the far north, had been scattered by the onslaught of whites.

Ten years ago she'd gone back, by ship to Cooktown, to see her mother and her dear blind brother again, ignoring Oma's advice:

'It'll be a journey of heartbreak, darling, don't go. They said their farewells to you when you left the Palmer district. They didn't expect you to come back. They love you but to them you're a white lady.'

'But it has been five years!' Diamond had argued.

Oma Beckman could be very direct at times. 'You're not going for more gold?' she accused. 'It's too dangerous.'

'No. I just want to see them. My father died long ago but my mother and brother are still there.'

But they were not. Timid tribal people who'd come down to the outskirts of Cooktown in capitulation had told her that her mother had died in a white raid and her brother, unable to fight, had thrown himself over a cliff.

She looked out from the kitchen window at the pinprick lights of Brisbane, where she hoped her son was sleeping peacefully. Diamond had been saved from the whirlwind that had engulfed her people. To the surviving tribal women she was a wonder of the times, a woman who had crossed over into a new age to live a happy and legendary life with many babies.

If only they knew, Diamond thought. I haven't crossed over anywhere. I am tolerated because I can pay my way, and I keep out of sight. And I haven't warned my son about any of this because I didn't want to frighten him. I wanted him to grow up confident of our love and sure of himself before I talked to him about these things. But what to say? And would he listen? Several times she'd tried to tell him about her people but he'd been more interested in 'his' people, white people. Ben, in his mind, was white, not black.

And that question in itself had been a problem. Ben Buchanan, the love of Diamond's life, and an arrogant cattleman, was his father. It always intrigued her that the English name, Buchanan, was so close to Oma's name, Beckman. But Oma said there was no connection and the names had no translation as Aborigine names did. They just were. But superstitious, Diamond saw a connection: they were as nature had ordered. Over the years she'd forgotten Buchanan, and the only living name to her now was Beckman. And so Ben became the grandson of the late Captain Beckman, and his widow loved and cared for him. He seemed to take it for granted that his father had also been a seafarer, son of the famous Captain, and the women had left it at that.

'Why don't you go to bed?' Oma said, interrupting Diamond's depressing reminiscences. 'I'll wait up.'

'No. I can't.' She took the old woman's hand. 'Oh God, Oma,' she cried. 'What is to become of Ben? I'm so frightened for him.'

Gussie Beckman smoothed a wiry strand of hair from Diamond's forehead. 'Dear girl. When the Captain died and I had no money I had to go back to Germany and leave you here. It nearly broke my heart. I cried every night on that long voyage. You were only a couple of years older than Ben is now.'

'But I had a job as a housemaid.'

'Diamond, think about it. Young people are resilient. You only had a few pounds to your name. You were alone, a black girl in a white town. Ben has us. We've built a fortress for him. He has a home and he'll never be as poor as you were. You survived.'

'I was lucky,' Diamond growled.

'You still had to struggle,' Gussie said curtly. 'I'm trying to say that your son has advantages you never had, so he'll be all right.' She stroked the tip of her slipper along Diamond's ankle. 'I pray that our Ben won't ever have to leave his home with a knife strapped to his leg.'

Diamond was surprised. 'You know about that?'

'So many years we have been together and I don't know these things?'

'You never said anything.'

'I tell myself you have good reason. You have always been a clever girl. Quick to learn. And I see you in Ben. If he is not home, he too has a good reason. At his age you never put me through worry and neither will he. Now you have a bad cold, you go to bed and I will keep the lamps lit for him.'

Diamond didn't sleep. Her sheets were wet with perspiration and wild images crowded her mind. She was up with the birds, sluicing herself down in the bathroom to cool the fever that assailed her.

'Worry,' she told herself. 'Just plain damn worry! As soon as I find Ben I'll be better.'

She was waiting at the Kangaroo Point landing when the first ferry berthed, but before she could board, a skinny lad accosted her. 'Hey, lady. Aren't you Ben's mum?'

'Yes,' she said eagerly. 'Where is he?'

The boy took her aside, walking ahead up the cliff path. 'He's been arrested. You better get down and bail him out.'

'What are you saying? Ben arrested? What for?' Diamond was frantic, her fears made worse by her innate suspicion of the police. 'Who are you?'

'Willy's the name. I'm a mate of Ben's. I met you once and I often seen you around. I was comin' up here to find you. I knew Ben lived up here someplace.'

'Where is he?'

'In the Valley lockup, I reckon.'

'How do you know this? When did it happen?'

'Someone told me he got nabbed yesterday.'

She glanced over at the ferry. 'Come with me. I have to find him.'

But the boy edged away. 'Nah. I got things to do.' He seemed to have the same fear of the police as she did. She gave him a shilling. 'Thank you for letting me know.'

'Ta,' he said and scuttled away up the hill before she could question him any further.

Rain scudded against the little ferry as it ploughed across the wide river, but Diamond hardly noticed. Why had Ben been arrested? What on earth had he done? Surely he wouldn't commit a crime. There must be some mistake.

She tried to think what to do for the best but the worry was making her nauseous, and when she stepped ashore she stood uncertainly in the drizzling rain, trying to make a decision. Under normal circumstances she would brace herself and go right into that police station, demanding to see her son. But what if that policeman from last night was there? She wouldn't be much help to Ben if she became entangled in an argument with the law. Maybe she ought to see her solicitor, Mr Mantrell, straight away. Have him make enquiries for her and act on Ben's behalf. No. He would make enquiries and then she would act.

Young Barnaby Glasson saw the tall Aborigine woman standing nearby when he opened the office, but he didn't take much notice. This was an important day for him. Mr Mantrell wouldn't be in the office today – he'd gone to Ipswich to plead a case for one of his wealthy clients – and Barnaby, his clerk, would have the place to himself. He jangled the keys importantly as he slid open his desk, then placed them carefully in a cubbyhole. Mr Mantrell would give him hell if he lost them. Then, in a carefree mood, he took out his pipe and lit it.

Normally, he wouldn't dare light a pipe in the office, even though Mantrell puffed away all day. If he were to become a fully fledged lawyer he'd have to learn to dress well and to pose like his boss. And that included a pipe. As yet, he had to confess, he hadn't mastered the art. He sat sucking the stem furiously to keep it alight and tapping two fingers on the bowl in the accepted manner. Although he wasn't sure why.

As the door opened he shoved the pipe aside in a guilty reaction, but it was only the black woman.

Barnaby stood: 'Good morning, madam, what can I do for you?' Precious little, he thought. She's probably in the wrong office, but manners were manners, as his boss insisted.

'Good morning,' she said, surprising him. The voice of an educated woman. 'When can I see Mr Mantrell?'

'He won't be in until next week,' Barnaby replied, avoiding offering an appointment in case Mantrell didn't wish to see her. As far as Barnaby knew, the lawyer didn't have any black clients; he'd been here six months and he'd seen Chinese clients but no Aborigines.

She looked so distressed, Barnaby felt sorry for her. 'Can I help you?'

She hesitated. 'I don't know. My son's in jail and so I need to talk to Mr Mantrell. I thought he'd know what to do. Do you mind if I sit down? I'm not feeling very well.'

'By all means.' Barnaby placed a chair by his desk for her. He was confused. The jails were full of blacks, but he doubted if any of them would call on the services of lawyers, or if lawyers would represent them. This was a new field for him.

'What did he do?' he asked.

'I don't know. He's only fourteen and he's been missing since yesterday. I only found out a few hours ago that he'd been arrested. He's in the Valley lockup.'

'Ah. I see, Well, the best thing to do is to go down there and enquire of the duty officer. He'll be able to tell you all about it.'

'No, I don't want to do that. Could you make the enquiries for me? I'm sure Mr Mantrell would but since he's not here . . .' Her voice trailed to an entreaty.

'I'm sorry. I wouldn't be able to do that.' Surely she didn't expect to walk in off the street and have lawyers run errands for her?

'Don't you go to police stations?'

'Oh yes.' He smiled ruefully. 'Quite often. For clients. When Mr Mantrell instructs me. For clients,' he repeated.

'My name is Diamond Beckman,' she said sharply. 'I *am* a client. I have been a client of Mr Mantrell's for many years. Although I haven't seen him for a long time.' Her dark eyes were steady now as she gazed at him, and Barnaby felt weak, as if their roles were reversed and she was in control. 'You must go down to that police station for me and enquire after Ben Beckman. I am willing to pay for your time.'

'It would be expensive,' he said gently, as if to explain to her the machinations of business.

'I haven't much money with me,' she began, and Barnaby nodded, expecting that. 'But I can give you an IOU for fifty pounds for a start. Will that be enough?'

Barnaby sighed. 'Mrs Beckman. I'd like to help you. Really. But I only work here. I can't take on a case with a promise of fees. Not without Mr Mantrell's say-so.'

'From a stranger, you mean?'

'Yes.'

She seemed to consider this for a while, then she shook off her damp gloves and placed them on the desk. She opened her handbag and then a small purse, and from a fold in the back removed a slip of paper. 'I always carry this in case of emergency,' she commented. 'It's a signed cheque form.'

'So I see,' Barnaby said curiously.

'A pen, please.'

She filled in the form carefully and handed it to him. 'The bank is two doors down the street. Would you cash it for me, please?'

He stared. 'It's for a hundred pounds!'

'Yes. And I'm in a hurry. If I go in there, a black woman, they'll stare at me and waste my time just like you're doing.'

He stalled. 'You don't need that much. You don't even need fifty. If we take the case.'

'Go!' she commanded, standing to allow him to pass.

As he hurried into the bank he inspected the cheque. It had been signed by one Augusta Beckman. The signature was in a different hand from the rest of the writing on it. He fully expected to be thrown out on his ear, but the notes were counted and handed to him without comment.

'There,' she said when he returned. 'Now that the fee is no longer a promise, do your duty, Mr . . . ?'

'Glasson,' he stuttered. 'If I go I'll have to lock up the office.'

'I'll wait outside,' she said calmly. 'But please hurry.'

She was standing there in the same place under the awning when he returned an hour later.

'Did you see my son?'

'Yes,' he said, searching for the keys.

'Is he all right?'

'He's scared and he's taken a few knocks I'd say, but he's well.' Barnaby didn't add that the company of the mean-looking felons in the overcrowded cell would be enough to frighten any kid. 'Come in, Mrs Beckman, I've got the details.'

At his desk Barnaby read from his notebook. 'Ben Beckman was arrested yesterday for stealing a carpetbag of valuables from the Reverend Craddock at the wharves.'

'Ben wouldn't do that!' she exploded.

'Arresting officer Constable Ray Dolan,' he continued. 'I spoke to the boy, who claims he is innocent.'

'Of course he's innocent!'

'I couldn't apply for bail because he hasn't been before the magistrate yet. That might take some days.'

'Good!' she said. 'By the way, a gentleman came to the door while you were out. I told him Mr Mantrell was away and you were out on an errand of mercy.'

Barnaby groaned. God knows who that was, he thought.

'So that's the best I can do for now,' he told her. 'And the fees so far are only four guineas. I'll find out when he comes up before the court and apply for bail.'

'No you won't,' she said firmly. 'I want you to write him a reference. He's a minor, he shouldn't be in there.'

'I'm afraid that doesn't carry much weight.'

'I know,' she said harshly, 'but money does. That's one lesson I've learned well. Write a reference to say he has never been in trouble before, he comes from a good, respectable family—'

'Excuse me,' he said. 'I hope you don't mind my saying, but obviously his father is white. I couldn't help noticing—'

'That he's a half-caste,' she said calmly. 'And it would be better if his father went to collect him. That's true, but his father is dead. And obviously, if I go in there, a black gin, no one will listen to me. So it's up to you, and I'll make it worth your while, Mr Glasson.'

'That's not necessary,' he mumbled.

'I think you'll find it is,' she smiled with a flash of humour that made him nervous. 'Ben isn't a street waif. We live in River Road, Kangaroo Point. A good address, you will note in your letter. So please write the reference. You can also say he is well educated. Mr Mantrell will approve.'

As Barnaby wrote, he forgot that she was black. He felt instead as if his old schoolmistress was standing over him, threatening punishment if he so much as raised an eyebrow.

'Good,' she said as he blotted and folded it. Then she peeled off five ten-pound notes and slipped them into the folds of the letter.

'What are you doing?' he cried. 'Do you want me to bribe them?'

'Yes.'

'Good God! I can't do that!'

'Mr Glasson, my son is innocent. He doesn't need to steal some preacher's dirty old carpetbag. You are simply arranging justice, shall we say? You know and I know that the police don't give a damn about coloured kids. But fifty pounds will buy my son a friend in the police station. You know them, you find that friend and get Ben out of there. I'll double it if necessary.'

'Fifty pounds is outrageous!'

'Exactly. I won't leave my son in a filthy lockup and I won't have him hauled into court at his age. His defence, with all due regard to you and Mr Mantrell, might lose if he comes before a bigoted magistrate.'

'You seem to know a lot about the system,' he said, not unkindly, appreciating her spunk, 'but I can't do what you ask.'

'You never know what you can do until you try,' she told him. 'And I doubt if there's a policeman in that guardhouse who has ever seen fifty pounds in his life. All I ask is that the charges be dropped. Try to find that Constable Dolan.'

He shook his head. 'I can see your point, but I don't know about this.'

She put the other fifty pounds on the desk. 'You get Ben out, pay Mr Mantrell's' fees and the rest is for you.'

'Now you're bribing *me*!' His voice sounded like a yelp.

'I'm begging for your help,' she said simply. 'There's no other way. I'll wait here. You bring me my son.'

'I'll try,' he said at last. 'But *I* shouldn't take your money.'

'You haven't earned it yet. But whatever you do, don't let Ben know that his release has been bought. It would be bad for his character.'

Barnaby started to laugh. 'You don't care about mine?'

'Consider it part of your education.'

It was so easy Barnaby was astonished. He found Dolan and handed him the reference and the cash, preparing his defence that it was a mistake in case the constable took offence. After all, that much money *was* outrageous. No one offered a bribe of that size to lowly policemen, he was sure. But when Dolan saw the money, his eyes lit up.

'What's this?' the constable asked, still holding the notes inside the letter.

'A reference. The boy comes from a good family. He's very young. They want the charges dropped.' Barnaby didn't mention the money.

'A reference, is it now?' Dolan grinned. 'For this lot, lad, I'd drop a score of charges. I'll get the little varmint for ye.'

When the lad was brought out, Dolan nudged Mantrell's clerk. 'Barnaby, me boy! You'll go far in the law. If it's ever a favour you want, you can rely on me.'

Barnaby wrote out a receipt for four guineas to the firm and pocketed the rest of the cash, wondering if he'd set out on a life of crime instead of being an upholder of the law. He called a hansom cab for the strange black woman and her son, and watched them leave.

He'd listened to the boy's story as they walked back to his office, and he believed him. Except for the part where Ben claimed he didn't know who had stolen the carpetbag. The kid knew all right, he just wasn't letting on. Fair enough.

'Keep away from the wharves in future,' he told the lad from the heights of his nineteen-year-old wisdom. 'I mightn't be able to get you out next time.'

'You sound like my mother,' Ben grumbled.

The woman intrigued Barnaby. When they were well away, he took out the keys and opened a locked cabinet in Joseph Mantrell's office, searching through private files until he came to one marked 'Beckman'.

'Well, I'll be damned!' he said, turning over pages that were more than a decade old. 'She's not Mrs Beckman, her name is just Diamond!' She'd initially come to Mantrell with four gold nuggets.

Mantrell's ledgers were neat and efficient. 'Gold sales,' he read, line after line. 'She must have fed gold to the old man over the years. I wonder where it came from?'

He whistled in amazement. The transactions went on and on, with Mantrell selling gold, and depositing the monies in the nearby bank in the name of Augusta Beckman. He found the deeds of the house at Kangaroo Point in the same name, but always the receipts for the gold, the source, were made out to Diamond. He studied entries of purchase and sale of gold shares, later, parcels in the prosperous Newcastle Coal Company, and found two sealed wills: those of Augusta Beckman and Diamond.

Who the hell is this Diamond? he asked himself. But he had work to do and a lot of money burning a hole in his pocket. He decided to ferret it away rather than spend it. Mantrell or his landlady might smell a rat. He had confidence in the woman that the transaction between them had been strictly private.

When Joseph Mantrell returned and noted that Barnaby had assisted Mrs Diamond Beckman by requiring that the charges against her young son be dropped, and had earned the firm four guineas for his efforts, the lawyer simply nodded his appreciation. He gave no hint of Diamond's background, and Barnaby admired him for that. The ladies had fared well at the hands of this honest broker.

Chastened, Ben was glad to escape to the job Oma had found for him. His mother had been so pleased to see him she'd almost hugged him to death in the cab on the way home, without a word of criticism, although he was faced with the inevitable 'I told you so'.

Oma, too, had whispered: 'You must listen to your mother. She knows what's best for you. You see you keep away from those wharves in future. Only trouble there.'

No need to tell him that, he mused. He'd never go near them again. He was still shocked by the unfairness of his arrest and more so by the treatment he'd received: punched, pushed, thrown into a cell with slobbering maudlin drunks and a wild blackfellow who'd screamed most of the night, terrifying Ben. They were not fed, and when a bucket of water was handed to the thirsty inmates it was soon knocked over. Ben didn't get a drop. It had been the longest night of his life, cringing in a corner of that stinking place.

He'd refused to allow Oma to escort him to O'Neill's stables: 'I'm not a baby, Oma! I know where the stables are.'

'But you're a day late. You must apologize.'

Diamond came into the kitchen. 'I hope they'll still take him.'

'If they won't, they won't,' his grandmother said. 'We'll just have to find something else. And I told *you* to stay in bed, you're not well.'

'I'm much better today. It was just the worry. And I wouldn't miss seeing Ben off on his first day at work.' She kissed him on the cheek. 'Isn't it exciting?'

He pulled away. 'Oh, Mum! It's just a job!'

'It's not just a job. You must do everything you're told and learn—'

He didn't wait for the rest of the lecture. Grabbing the lunchbox that Oma had stuffed with enough food to feed him for a week, he went on his way, running down the hill to catch the first ferry.

At the stables he soon located Mr O'Neill, a big man with a black beard flecked with grey, and a voice like a foghorn.

'So you're Benny?'

'Yes, sir. I'm sorry I couldn't get here yesterday, but—'

The boss cut him short. 'Better late than never, mate.' He called to a youth who was opening up the tall double doors. 'Hey, Cash! Get over here. This is Benny, the new stableboy.' He turned back to Ben with a grin. 'He's me son and heir. He'll show you what to do.'

Ben studied the youth. He guessed Cash would be a couple of years older than himself. He was taller too, with black curly hair, fine features and a flashing smile. And he had bright blue eyes that glittered with merriment. Ben thought he saw villainy in them too, a sort of mayhem. As if anything could happen with him around. He reminded Ben of Willy in one of his happy moods, but then Willy would never be as handsome as this, or as self-assured.

But the son and heir was kind, and Ben liked him. By the end of the week he idolized Cash O'Neill.

'This is where you start,' Cash had said. 'First up I'll introduce you to the horses. Do you know anything about horses?'

'No. We haven't got any.'

'Righto. Then let me tell you, they're not just horses, they're people, and a lot smarter. You treat them good and they'll treat you likewise. Me too. Never let me hear you hurt a horse or I'll give you a hiding.'

As they moved along the row of stalls, with Cash taking his time, talking to the animals, patting them, checking them, Ben was fascinated, not only by Cash's obvious affection for them but by the horses themselves. They seemed to know he was new, watching him curiously, assessing him.

'You shovel the manure into the wheelbarrow and take it to the tip out the back,' Cash was saying. 'Clean out the stables, and all this flagged area has to be hosed down. Fresh hay. Fresh water in the trough. Keep that clean too, no slime. Then you find Dennis and help him with the horses.'

'Who's Dennis?'

'He's your boss. What he doesn't know about horses doesn't exist.

Some of these are racehorses, others are for riding. Their owners are mostly a pain in the neck but you just keep out of their way.'

'You don't own them?'

'Of course not. Dad and me, we've got our own horses out in the paddock. These darlins are for minding. For town people who don't have their own stables.'

It didn't seem like work, just cleaning up and trotting about with Dennis, who was a wizened old bloke but as kind to his charges as Cash was. And it was a busy place with people coming and going all day, and always something to do – polishing saddles and things, and leading the animals back and forth from the blacksmith's next door, Ben's favourite spot. He loved to watch the blacksmith at work, fascinated by the molten-red horseshoes emerging from the furnace, and the double ring of the hammer on the anvil, and the understanding patience of the animals.

Oma and his mother were waiting for him at the ferry when he came home at seven o'clock, dying to hear his news.

'What are you doing here?' he complained, embarrassed again. They were treating him like a child when now he was a man, earning his living, three shillings a week.

On the Friday afternoon, Dennis showed him again how to put a bridle and saddle on one of the horses, and then shoved him on board. 'Time you learned to ride proper, Benny my lad,' he said, 'and we're gonna keep at it until you get it right.'

That night Ben came home triumphant, his wages in his hand. 'I can ride,' he told Oma. 'And old Dennis says I'm a natural.'

'Ah, that's lovely,' she said. 'But I want you to be quiet. Your mother's not well. Her cold's flared up again. It's this hot weather, it's very trying. You never know whether you've got a fever or you're just too hot. Now eat your supper, there's a good boy.'

Saturday was a busy day. Ben went through to the saddlery on an errand for Dennis and heard Cash arguing with his father.

'You'll not be gettin' the afternoon off!' Mr O'Neill shouted. 'You'll stay here and get on with your work.'

'But Ransom and Lady Lou are both running today.'

'I don't care if they're all runnin'! There's a load of work to be done here.'

'If you think I'm going to spend my life stitching up saddles you've got another think coming!' Cash retorted angrily. 'I want to be a trainer.'

O'Neill laughed. 'A lot of good that'll do you. You'd lose every quid you earned to the bookmakers. You're not going to the races and that's that. Get back to work!'

And yet, when the boss went home for lunch, Ben saw Cash stroll out into the street, all dressed up.

Dennis shook his head. 'The bugger's off to the races again! There'll be hell to pay when his old man gets back.'

'What'll happen?' Ben asked nervously.

'A lot of noise, with everyone gettin' the hurry-up, but he can't sack his son. Best we start again and check every bloody thing, or we'll get a bawling-out too.'

Chapter Two

On this occasion Lalla spared no expense to impress her dinner guests. Already the secret was out that her dress had cost more than two hundred pounds.

'Enough to buy four houses and then some,' Biddy complained to Cook. 'It's a fair crime for her to be spending that much on her back.'

'You be careful,' Cook warned. 'I heard the missus telling that dressmaker she didn't want no one knowing what it cost.'

'The hell she don't! She knows as well as we do that her fine Madame Grace is the biggest flap-mouth in town. Besides, when she comes down the stairs in that dress, everyone will know it's never a bargain. Any fool can see it's worth a fortune.'

Despite her disapproval of Lalla Thurlwell's extravagance, a note of admiration had crept into Biddy's voice. Cook was impressed. 'I'd love to see it.'

'I can't show it to you. It's up there on the stand covered by sheets in case it gets a speck of dust on it. If I shifted one of them sheets, she'd notice, you know what she's like. But I tell you, that dress is fit for a queen. It's made of heavy ivory satin and it's covered from tip to toe in seed pearls and little silver beads. I swear she'll outshine the chandeliers!'

'Dear God!' Cook breathed, eyes wide with awe.

'But pearls are tears,' Biddy sniffed.

'I didn't know that.'

'Bet she don't neither. Nor does Mr Edgar, the boss's brother. He gave her diamond earrings with pearl drops for her birthday. I bet she wears them tonight.'

'Why would he give her such an expensive present? She don't need them. She's got heaps of jewels.'

'Because she's throwing this shindig for him. He's the guest of honour.'

Indeed he was, and Lalla intended to make sure her dinner party was a success, because the Thurlwell fortunes were at stake.

She sat at the small desk in her boudoir, studying the list of last-minute details she had yet to check, with an occasional glance over her shoulder at the dress, shrouded in sheets. She couldn't wait to wear it, to step out on to the landing in one of the finest dinner gowns ever seen in the Colony of Queensland.

Apart from the fact that she would look stunning, that she would outshine the other women in the room, it was important to impress her guests with the Thurlwell wealth. Investors followed money, they ran it down like hounds, yapping and barking to be in at the kill, while any scent of danger could have them scattering in all directions, chasing false trails, retreating from the prize that Edgar held for them. He would make them all millionaires if they'd have the sense to listen to him.

Lalla sighed. Edgar was a big man with big ideas, an exciting man, strong, generous and decisive. The exact opposite of William, who was content to plod along in his older brother's shadow, busy with his medical practice, allowing Edgar to handle all their investments through their various companies.

It was Edgar who had taken himself off to America, talked with the fabulously rich railroad tycoons, visited their steel mills, ridden in their private rail carriages and come home with all the information he needed to construct his own railroads. Lalla had been spellbound at his account of his travels and his association with those American railroad 'barons', as they were known, and she was absolutely bowled over by his description of the splendour of their magnificent houses.

'It's all too simple,' Edgar told William, 'so we have to move quickly before someone else gets on to it. I have the papers ready; all you have to do is sign and the Western Railroad Company will be in business.'

'Doesn't sound simple to me,' William muttered. 'It sounds like a lot of work and rather too good to be true.'

'How can you say such a thing?' Lalla cried. 'Hasn't Edgar brought home living proof of the viability of private railroads?'

As if he had anticipated William's reticence, Edgar passed some papers over to Lalla. 'I'm touched by your enthusiasm, Lalla dear, because I took the liberty of including you as a shareholder. One thousand shares are set aside for you if you wish to take them up.'

'They are?' She was thrilled, but not unaware of the subtlety of Edgar's manoeuvre. If she were in favour of the project, William would not, could not, refuse to co-operate. 'You're so thoughtful, Edgar. It would be wonderful to have an interest, however small, in such an enterprise.'

'How does it work again?' William asked, weakening.

'I told you,' Edgar said. 'First we choose our routes. I have in mind Rockhampton west to Longreach, for a start. A vital link. Then we begin the first leg of the coastal route, Brisbane north to Bundaberg. It took twenty years for the government to complete the railroad from Brisbane to Charleville. We'll show 'em that private enterprise can be up and running in a couple of years! As in America, I expect the state government to come to the party, co-operate by transferring to us free grants of land all along the routes so that we have a clear run and no time wasted.'

William was still worried. 'Wait a minute. I can see that by not having to pay for the land the company would already have made a huge saving in capital expense, but why would the government donate the land?'

Lalla was exasperated. 'William! The Western Railroad Company would be doing them a huge service opening up the west for the pastoralists and for settlers. How marvellous for them to have a railroad for passengers and freight instead of having to rely on coaches and bullock teams on those dreadful roads. They couldn't refuse.'

'Keep in mind,' Edgar said, 'that towns will grow at our railroad stations. Knowing where they are to be located, we could buy up the land surrounding them and make an interesting set of profits for our real-estate company. We would practically own the towns as well, as do some of our American friends. This is the chance of a lifetime, William. We'll keep the bulk of the shares but we do need to bring in other investors for a project of this magnitude. I have already arranged to purchase the steel from British mills, so we are almost ready to go. All we need is more finance and then we can put the project to the government. They can't refuse!'

They can't refuse. Edgar's words echoed as Lalla unwound her hair to prepare for her bath. Ever since Edgar had begun outlining his project to banks and businessmen, the Jeremiahs had come out of the woodwork. They complained that Queensland didn't have the population for such a grand scheme, not realizing that the railroad would bring settlers. They jibbed at handing over so much land to private enterprise, wallowing in their mean and socialistic bogs. Some even called Edgar's American friends and advisers 'robber barons', which infuriated Lalla. They were so ignorant, not knowing what was good for them. And now this bugbear of federation had marched on to the scene!

Edgar had quite a few state politicians onside, but if the states federated then he'd have another set to convince – and, she smiled to herself, bribe if necessary. But there was already talk that if the states voted to unite into one nation, rail transport should be a federal responsibility, left to the federal politicians if and when they were elected.

'It's all too much,' she said, pressing the button to call the maid. What had begun as an exciting and financially brilliant plan was now delayed by this talk of federation. A wait-and-see attitude would have investors stalling. Edgar was now pouring all his energies into rallying support and relying on Lalla to assist where she could. As he explained, all she had to concentrate on was giving the heave-ho to ideas of a united Australia, which really meant government of the less populated states like Queensland and Western Australia from Melbourne or Sydney.

Even William was pulling his weight now. Convinced at last that Edgar was right, he was angry that politicians were placing obstacles in their way by listening to the lower classes in their mad rush for unity, instead of heeding men of substance who had the interests of their state at heart. 'Charity begins at home,' he'd often said. 'We'll look after Queensland and let the others look after themselves.'

Tonight she would have fourteen at table. More men than women, but that couldn't be helped. Lalla had always refused to bow to convention and dot her tables with token women, especially on occasions like this, when Edgar needed time to introduce the twin subjects of the railroads and anti-federalism. He agreed with her that trying to talk business with gentlemen after dinner, when the ladies had retired, was a waste of time. By then the men were usually half potty with too much wine and unable to assimilate or even recall the conversation.

Since the Buchanans were house guests, Lalla had no choice but to place Clara. And then, of course, Clara's widowed mother had to be invited.

Lalla giggled. Her brother-in-law, a bachelor, was wary of Mrs Foster, who seemed to view Edgar as a potential third husband, but he'd have to put up with her this time. Lalla hoped to subdue the talkative woman by placing her next to Edgar. His presence might stop her from monopolizing the conversation.

Lalla knew she had shocked local society by hostessing dinner parties with no other women present. Her 'smoke nights', they called them, but she didn't care. She catered so superbly that the men had no complaints, and she always retired from the room eventually, leaving the gentlemen to their brandy and cigars, having steered the conversation in the right direction without the inane interruptions of silly women.

Like Clara Buchanan. How a man like Ben could have married that frump was beyond Lalla. Maybe it was the Foster money. Although it was said that old Belle was a tight-fist. Not that money would help the Buchanans if their cattle station really was entering a drought situation. Money couldn't buy rain. Lalla shuddered – talk of drought and dying stock horrified her. Poor Ben, he was so handsome. Big and blond, a typical countryman – and unlike his wife, he was always cheerful, and excellent company.

She had often noticed Ben watching her. No, be honest, admiring her, as many men did, but there was more to it with Ben. He had an intensity about him that excited her. And Lalla loved it because William was dreary these days. When she'd first met him he'd been lively, full of fun, but now he was dull and pompous, full of his own importance as Brisbane's leading surgeon. She sighed. 'Oh well, as long as it keeps him busy and he leaves me alone.'

Tonight, she'd seat Ben Buchanan beside her, at the centre of the table, and let William and Edgar take the ends. Clara could go down by William, and the rest of the company of politicians and functionaries would be gathered about their hostess. An excellent arrangement.

Ben Buchanan was delighted, when all the guests filed in from the drawing room, to find himself placed next to Lalla, well aware that it was her choice. She fascinated him. She had to be one of the most beautiful women he'd ever met, so elegant and serene, but underneath, he knew, a strong, decisive woman with a sexy disposition.

The dining room looked brilliant, chandeliers and silver glittering in the candlelight; red roses with silver leaves trailed along the table that had no centrepiece so that the hostess would not be blocked out. The setting was perfect for Lalla, he mused, in that marvellous ivory gown contrasted by all the gentlemen in their dark suits. Not so good for Belle Foster's choice, a heavy checked taffeta. And Clara . . . well, she faded out of the picture in beige lace. Ben shrugged as they took their places. What Clara wore was her own business. He had more important matters to deal with. A new career was unfolding for him and he wasn't going to miss this chance.

Years back, the Governor himself had suggested to Ben that he ought to enter the political arena, and he would have done so, except that fate had stepped in. The death of his elder brother had forced him to take full responsibility for their cattle station since their father had also passed on. Still, sometimes things worked out for the best. He'd made a name for himself as a top-notch cattleman, married money and still moved in the élite circles of Sydney and Brisbane. Now, at thirty-eight, he was much better equipped to handle the political scene than he would have been at twenty-one. These Brisbane wheeler-dealers would be going some to pull the wool over his eyes now. The same went for the fast-talking Edgar Thurlwell, who had hinted that he and his cronies could make it well worth Ben's while to take up the vacant state seat of Padlow. And he might just do that if the carrots they dangled were worthwhile.

Parliamentarians were only paid expenses. As a young bloke that hadn't bothered him – a small price to pay for glory – but experience had taught him that many poor politicians had mysteriously become owners of newspapers and substantial shareholders in large concerns. Although Ben was by no means poor, Fairmont, his new cattle station near Charleville, was not the investment he'd hoped. The homestead had caught his eye in the first place, very large and cool and beautifully appointed, ideal for entertaining; and then of course the proximity to the Brisbane markets had been important. After years spent in the far north, a cattle station only about five hundred miles west of Brisbane was a Godsend and he'd snapped it up on the first inspection. How was he to know a drought was looming?

He shook off his doubts. Droughts could happen anywhere in Australia. He hadn't made a mistake. Besides, it could have rained out there by this for all he knew.

Ben stood, watching, as his hostess glided towards him with her alarming green eyes and that pink curve of a smile, so distant and yet so inviting. He felt the warmth of her as she took the seat beside him, her hand brushing his as if by accident, though Ben knew it was not.

'I'm so glad Mrs Foster could join us this evening,' she said sweetly to him.

Ben nodded. I'll bet you are, he thought. And don't tease me, lady. He said: 'Mrs Foster is delighted you thought of her.'

She sat demurely, allowing her husband to make the running in the small talk as everyone settled at the table, and Ben glanced down at the swelling breasts, the deep cleavage that met a band of satin. His hostess had a lot to offer.

Best view in the house, he mused as the chatter rose. Not only was this woman ripe for the picking, but she could be mighty useful to him.

With an effort he turned his attention away from her and struck up a conversation with his neighbour on the other side, Royce Davies, the Member for Ipswich.

The rows of crystal glasses came to life as waiters poured the wines, and the first course, magnificent salmon with a light lemon sauce, was served. His mother-in-law's voice boomed from down the table. Clara was silent. William reminded them all that Buck Henry, President of the Turf Club, to his right, was an excellent fisherman. The hostess, with studied aplomb, addressed those within earshot, her voice lilting with gaiety, setting the pace. At the same time Ben felt a stockinged foot rub along his leg.

Deliberately he ignored it, although it sent a flame through him. You want me, lady, you work for it. This will be your idea.

From an alcove three violinists began to play soft romantic airs, so quietly they were hardly noticed; plates were whisked away, a tasty clear soup was served, more wine flowed and they rose for The Queen.

Ben wasn't surprised when the conversation turned to the subject of railroads. He wished he could spare the cash to buy in: Edgar had come up with the best idea he'd heard in years. Maybe he could raise a loan.

But Royce Davies didn't seem too impressed. He drained his wine glass and interrupted the President of the Turf Club, who was sitting opposite him. 'Can't see the point. Let the government build the railroads.'

Lalla leaned forward. 'Mr Davies. You're fortunate that you already have a railroad to Ipswich. Spare a thought for other country folk. It will take a century for the government to get around to them. Surely you wouldn't be so cruel as to deny them.'

Davies, Ben noted, was a man who should settle for a beard. He had a permanent five o'clock shadow which gave him a shady, unsavoury appearance. Ben stroked his own thick fair moustache, watching Davies wilt – more as a result of his hostess's sweet smile than in a care for other country folk.

'You do have a point there, Mrs Thurlwell,' Davies admitted. 'I'll have to give it more thought.'

'Give it your support, more like it,' Belle Foster thundered from down the table. 'A vote for Queensland before we get squeezed dry by this mob of federalists!'

'They're just hot air,' Davies replied, snapping his fingers for a refill of his wine glass.

'Don't be so sure,' Belle said. 'A little bird told me that our Premier is at this minute preparing to travel to Hobart to take part in the conference of states. And not only that, according to southern newspapers he's leading the chase.'

'He can't be!' All eyes were on Henry Templeman, a wealthy grazier and Member of the State House representing the northern district of Gladstone. 'I'll get shot at dawn if I go back with that news. They'll blame me for selling out.'

'Then you'd better have a quick word with him,' Davies grinned. 'It's your party on the line.' He looked to Edgar. 'Federation will kill your railroad plan stone dead, Mr Thurlwell.'

Ben decided it was time to step in on behalf of his hosts, the people who had shown themselves anxious to support him. 'Royce,' he said easily, 'they can talk federation until they're blue in the face. My uncle is Premier of Western Australia and he says they won't have a bar of it. If push comes to shove they're likely to go it alone. After all,' he expounded, now that he had their attention, 'Western Australia is probably the biggest state in the world and they've got untold wealth in gold and other minerals. Why should they jump for a clutch of easterners?'

William, down at the end of the table, seemed confused. 'Would that matter? There could be a federation of the other states without them.'

Although he wasn't looking at her, Ben could feel Lalla's irritation with her husband throwing a spanner into the works as if he believed that federation was inevitable. The works in question being Edgar's Western Railroad Company.

To counter his host's lack of political tact, Ben spoke up. 'Hardly a federation, old chap, with half the continent missing. I doubt our gracious lady, the Queen, would countenance such an arrangement.'

'Hear, hear!' voices echoed and the conversation shifted to the ever-present interest in Victoria, the beloved Queen.

Lalla pressed Ben's arm. 'I can't understand why you haven't entered politics before this, Ben. You have such a grasp of these important matters.'

'Haven't had the time,' he said, giving her his full attention, his eyes meeting hers and drifting down to that inviting *décolletage*. 'Would it be correct of me to inform my hostess that she is looking adorable this evening?'

'Thank you,' she murmured, 'you're very kind.'

Lalla was an accomplished flirt. Her gaiety seemed directed at the company, but as waiters entered from the kitchen pushing dinner wagons, and enthusiastic voices were raised with: 'What have we here?' she leaned closer to Ben as she responded, and the warmth and excitement was there again. He wanted this woman, he had to have more of her than this circumspect visit, and sooner or later, he knew . . .

'It's a speciality dish I promised Mr Davies,' Lalla was telling the company. 'Previous guests speak of it. We have roast duck stuffed with pâté in cognac, or roast duck stuffed with lobster. You have a choice.' She laughed. 'Dear oh dear, I'm not sure which ducks are which but the servants will know.'

'Can we have both?' Davies asked, wiping red wine from his lips and surreptitiously dabbing sweat from his face.

'You take whatever you please, Mr Davies. We're delighted to have your company. You're so rarely available.'

The waiters toured the table with the steaming silver platters, and everyone was almost drooling in anticipation, laughing and talking, with sidelong glances at the crisp brown poultry and enticing side dishes. It was truly a jolly evening. Another success for Lalla Thurlwell.

And then disaster struck!

The butler lurched into the room, stumbling forward.

At first, facing the door, Ben thought the man must be chasing a cat or a dog as he dived low. But a boy ran into the room, shouting for the Doctor, dodging the butler's grasping hands. A waiter was knocked aside, his large platter wobbling. He almost managed to contain it but Templeman jumped up from his seat, reacting to the commotion behind him. Belle boomed at him from afar to be careful but it was too late. His shoulder upended the platter and it slid forward, slopping two roast ducks in their delicious-smelling juices across the pristine white tablecloth and sending glasses flying, wine spreading.

The boy tore past Ben, who imagined he sniffed the sour smell of horseboxes, colliding with other waiters. Someone grabbed at him and missed. Silver clattered and another dish crashed to the floor. Guests gaped and the fragile crystals of the chandelier shivered in shock.

William blundered to his feet. The boy was screaming something about his mother, at the same time as the Doctor was ordering him out. Edgar bristled with indignation, pop-eyed at this chaos, and Lalla gripped the table, eyes blazing, appalled.

At the stables all was quiet again, with Cash back at work as usual, but with a grin on his face. Ransom had won his race and Cash had won twenty pounds. Ben smiled. He thought he understood. He'd dearly love to go to the races himself to watch Ransom win. What a thrill that would be! He took an apple down to Ransom and palmed it to him quietly. 'What a grand horse you are,' he said, picking up the Irish expression. 'I'll be coming to cheer you on one of these days.'

Ben was happy. It was the best job out and he was making new friends all the time, not only among the men who worked in the saddlery but with the jockeys, those marvellous riders who were around every morning. He decided to ask his mother for a cap. Ben had never worn headgear of any sort but his friends at work, his grown-up friends, all wore caps, so he should too.

But Diamond's cold was worse. She looked terrible, gaunt and grey-faced, and she had an awful cough, propped up there on all those pillows.

'Will she be all right?' he asked Oma anxiously.

'Yes, dear, I'm sure she will,' his grandmother said as she poured boiling water into basins, steaming the room with the pungent smell of eucalypt, but Ben could see she was worried.

'Is there anything I can do?'

'Yes. Take some money out of my purse. Run down and wake up the storekeeper. I need some more of that cough mixture. Hurry, Ben!'

Gussie Beckman was very worried. Over the years she'd nursed many an influenza patient back to health, and Diamond had seemed to be recovering slowly, but this evening her temperature had flared and she was suddenly very weak. The sickness in her was developing into pneumonia, Gussie was sure.

She put a poultice on Diamond's chest to help her breathing, and Diamond took her hand.

'Look after Ben,' she whispered.

Gussie hushed her. 'Don't be silly now. You'll be well soon. Don't tire yourself.'

'I saw my mother,' her dear girl said, and Gussie nodded.

'That's right, you've been dreaming a lot, so you just rest.'

When Ben came back with the mixture, Oma was waiting for him with a note. 'I'm sorry, darling, you'll have to go out again. Take this down to the doctor in Vulture Street, you know the one?'

'Dr McNab? Yes, I know his house. Do you want him to come to Mum?'

'Yes, as quickly as possible. And be careful, Ben, don't talk to anyone.'

'I'll be all right,' he said stoutly, grateful to be able to help, afraid for his mother now. A doctor meant danger; they'd never called a doctor for Diamond before, only a couple of times to see Oma.

He ran and ran, down to Vulture Street, turning away from the busy centre, on two more blocks to rows of cottages. If he passed anyone he didn't notice, he was too intent on his mission. At last he came to the doctor's house and hammered on the door.

When a woman opened it, he was out of breath, so he pushed the note at her without a word.

She took it back into the light, read it, and smiled at Ben. 'The Doctor is out, he is very busy tonight, but I'll send him to Mrs Beckman as soon as he gets back.'

'When will that be?' Ben persisted.

'It will be late,' she said gently, 'but I promise you he'll be there. Tell her mother to try to keep her temperature down.' She patted him on the head. 'You're a good boy running a message for Mrs Beckman at this hour.'

Once he knew that the doctor would come, Ben was relieved. His mother would be all right now. He trotted home with the news.

'Late?' Oma cried. 'How late? She needs a doctor now. She can hardly breathe!'

He sat silently, petrified, listening to his mother drawing hard, rattling breaths, fighting for air, while Oma frantically tried to help her.

'Oh my God!' Oma said suddenly. 'I am so stupid, so stupid! There's a doctor next door. And he's a surgeon. He can make her breathe. Go there! Quick, Ben. Tell Dr Thurlwell your mother is dying!'

He stared. What was she saying? His mum? Diamond? She wouldn't die. Her eyes were on him and he could see a loving smile in them. Oma was wrong.

She wrenched him from his chair by the bed. 'Do you hear me? Go next door, Ben. Tell Dr Thurlwell it's urgent. I need him!'

Once again he was out of the door, through the gate, racing down their driveway, up the steps to the big, well-lit house. He could hear voices inside, a lot of cheerful voices. At least this doctor was home, and right next door. He should have come in here in the first place. He pounded on a large brass knocker, pounded and pounded.

The door opened to a great cave of white light that stunned him momentarily. Behind his own front door was a dim passageway, with rooms on either side, that led to the kitchen. Behind this front door, he now discovered, was a white-tiled entrance hall, blazing with candle-light from a massive crystal jewel that hung from the domed ceiling high above. Beyond that was a golden staircase that curled round the far wall . . .

'What do you want?' A man in fancy satins, white stockings and buckled shoes confronted him.

'The Doctor!' Intimidated, Ben's voice was a whisper.

'Get out of it!'

Ben roused himself. 'No! I have to see the Doctor. It's urgent!'

'Dr Thurlwell is entertaining,' the man intoned, moving to close the door, but Ben shoved against it.

'Don't shut me out,' he pleaded. 'My mother's sick, I have to get the Doctor!'

'*Your* mother?' The man grinned, clamping a firm hand on Ben's shoulder. 'Nick off! You're bloody mad!'

Ben kicked at him, twisting under his grip, but he was being forced out until a voice called: 'Let him in!'

He thought it was Mrs Thurlwell at first, that imperious voice he'd heard giving orders to the gardeners, but as he straightened up he saw it was the girl, Phoebe, standing on the staircase in a long white dressing gown, looking like an angel.

Instantly, to his astonishment, the doorman released him and stood back. 'My mother's real sick,' he called to her. 'Where's the Doctor?'

'In there,' she replied, pointing, and Ben dived across the hall, bursting open the double doors, knowing the doorman would come after him.

There were people sitting at a long table. Rows of people with blurred white faces. Startled faces. He could smell delicious food aromas, see the glitter, hear the shocked cries as he flung himself among them, but none of this really registered as he searched wildly for the Doctor. All the men looked alike in their dark clothes with flashes of starched white.

The Doctor identified himself. He stood angrily at the far end of the table. 'What's the meaning of this?'

With a rush of relief, Ben ran to him, grabbing his arm. 'Doctor, sir. Oma says to come quick! Next door. My mum is real bad!'

'Good God!' a voice cried.

'Bert!' the Doctor shouted to the footman. 'Get him out of here or by Jove you'll be out the door too.'

'No!' Ben screamed, clinging to the doctor as that gentleman struggled to disentangle himself. 'You don't understand. My mother is dying!'

'Then take her to the hospital!' Thurlwell was shouting angrily. It burst upon Ben then why Oma couldn't take Diamond to a hospital, so he fought harder as another man leapt up to help the doorman to remove the nuisance. He heard the word 'nigger' and someone snort his disgust. And he heard her, Mrs Thurlwell, answering a question: 'Of course he doesn't treat them. Good Lord, no!'

One voice, a woman's voice was raised for him. 'Perhaps you ought to see what it's about, William?'

'Shut up, Clara!' came a man's angry response, and through his tears young Ben looked over at a sweet-faced lady, about his mother's age, who seemed to be helpless to assist. He would never forget her voice. Nor would he forget Dr Thurlwell, who sent his guest back to the dining room as he marched beside the doorman who was carting Ben out by the scruff of his neck.

'Damned outrage!' he muttered to Ben, his face bright pink against his fair whiskers. 'You little brat! If you ever set foot on my property again I'll have you arrested.'

Over his shoulder he saw Mrs Thurlwell hustling Phoebe up the stairs, so there was no more help from that quarter. He stifled his tears as his feet hit the hard tiles and the doorman began to frogmarch him out, but he managed to twist his head to face the Doctor with one last plea: 'Please, sir, I beg you. Just for a minute. It won't take long.' His voice echoed in the high hall as he screamed: 'Oma says she's dying!'

'Take him to the gate, throw him out and then lock the gate!' Thurlwell snapped. 'It's outrageous that I should have to put up with something like this with guests in my house!'

'You bloody little bastard,' the footman shouted at Ben as he threw him down, adding a kick to send him on his way.

Ben limped home, straightening his clothes as best he could.

Oma was waiting eagerly for him. 'Where's the doctor?'

'Later,' Ben muttered. His pride wouldn't allow him to tell her that he'd been thrown out, or the reason why. That their neighbour, the high and mighty Dr William Thurlwell, didn't treat niggers.

It was after twelve that night when a weary Dr McNab reined in his horse and climbed from his gig in front of the Beckman house. The door was open and no one answered his knock, so he walked in quietly and found his way to a bedroom where an elderly woman was sitting on a bed, cradling a black woman in her arms. On the other side of the bed a young coloured lad sat motionless, staring at them.

Gently he lifted the woman away to examine the figure on the bed. 'I'm so sorry,' he whispered. 'I've been out all night, there's an epidemic of this influenza. I only just got your message.' He looked at Diamond. 'God rest her soul.'

* * *

They buried his mum in a rough, weedy patch behind the hundreds of tombstones in the cemetery, and Oma hugged Ben: 'Don't you worry, darling, we'll get her a beautiful tombstone, even if it is out here.'

Ben didn't understand what she meant by that, he had supposed everyone got one of those marble shapes, but then he wasn't understanding much at all. He felt dead himself, still unable to grasp that his mum had been made dead: Diamond, who to him had been invincible. She'd often told him of her adventures in the far north. She'd been to great cattle stations and to the goldfields and to many a wild bush town, but she'd stopped her roaming to settle down here and look after her son.

'That's a mother's job,' she'd told him, and of course she was right. So what had gone wrong? She should have been safe here. Ben worried about that, he couldn't think of anything else. Had he failed her?

A few people came to watch her being buried. Mr and Mrs Watkins from the store, an old white-haired preacher, a pretty lady called Goldie, whom Ben had never seen before, and Mr O'Neill, from the stables, riding up late on his old bay horse. Ben thought it was really nice that Mr O'Neill had come along but he couldn't talk to him, he was afraid he would cry – again – and make a fool of himself.

Another stranger had appeared too. Mr Mantrell. He seemed to be in charge. 'A lawyer,' Oma had told Ben, 'very important.' He was Barnaby Glasson's boss. He had called for them in his gig and escorted them home again when the others dispersed, and he was in the parlour now talking to Oma. He had never seen Oma cry before but now she didn't seem to be able to stop. Poor Oma, she'd be lonely now without Mum. That thought brought on another deep sob. So would he.

'I have to write a new will,' Oma said through her tears, but the lawyer hushed her.

'Time enough for that.'

'No, there's not!' Oma cried. 'My poor girl has been taken at the prime of her life. Why didn't God take me?'

Ben slid out of his chair to wander forlornly through the house.

'It's important,' Oma persisted, hardly noticing that Ben had gone. 'The money was all Diamond's. You know that. You must draw up a will for me right away, leaving everything to Ben. I won't sleep a wink until it's done.'

'Very well, Mrs Beckman. Is there anything else I can do for you?'

'No thank you.' She smiled wanly. 'You're a good man. Diamond always appreciated that you kept her financial affairs private. It's a difficult world for a black girl.'

'She was a very sensible person, though,' he said. 'She knew the pitfalls and I only carried out her instructions. The lad is fortunate that she was so far-sighted.'

'Oh, God bless him,' Oma wept. 'He's a dear boy. He's my life now, I'll take care of him.'

Ben dropped down the cliff and sat and sat among the dry crumbling rocks, not knowing what to do with himself now, despairing that his mother had gone and somehow it was his fault. The sun blazed on the ochre rocks, making them hot to touch, but he didn't notice. He plucked at yellowing grass that was fighting through the crevices. And then he saw the snake. It was sunning itself only a couple of yards from his feet, from his Sunday-best shoes.

'Bite me!' he muttered despondently. 'Go on, bite me. What do I care? She's not here any more. She can't sing you away and I don't know how to do it. She was a real Aborigine, she knew things. I'm only half a one.'

But the snake ignored him. It raised its head and seemed to stare past him, and then it slithered across the dusty ground to disappear behind a shrub that clung precariously to the cliff face.

He felt bereft again. As if the snake were his only company, the only one to understand how terrible he felt. How guilty. But something lingered, something he had said. Something he was sure the snake had understood.

And why not? he shrugged. Diamond was black. That's what it was. Blacks knew about nature things. Better than white people.

A nigger!

The word leapt out at him, and he recalled that terrible night when she was dying and that bastard of a doctor next door wouldn't come to her aid. He didn't treat niggers! The enormity of it hit him. Dr Thurlwell could have saved his mother. It wasn't Ben's fault at all! Hadn't Dr McNab apologized, sorry that he hadn't been able to come earlier? Which meant that if he had, Diamond would still be alive. Ben wept. He should have *made* Dr Thurlwell attend his mother! But he'd tried his hardest. He remembered being bundled out of the glittering room, out of the house like a mangy dog . . .

Wearily he made his way back to the house. Mr Mantrell had gone. Ben had wanted to tell him what had happened, but he'd gone. Oma was alone in the kitchen. Ben's anger rose. He couldn't tell Oma, she was miserable enough without that. He decided to tell Thurlwell himself. That his mother had died. That the Doctor had let his mother die.

Determined now, he marched out of the gate, along the street and back up that circular drive. But before he came to the front steps he picked up a stone, a good heavy stone, and hurled it point-blank at a front window. The sudden smashing noise it made was satisfying, so as he began to shout at the Doctor within, he found another stone, and another window.

He was feeling better now, fetching more stones, screaming abuse, but aiming well. He wrecked the leadlight windows bordering the front door and ran back to hurl stones through the other windows, smashing, smashing, doing a very good job. Paying back that bastard of a doctor.

The door burst open. Maids bundled out, staring. Gardeners ran at him, grabbing him, forcing the last stones from his hands.

'What are you doing? Have you gone mad?'

'Someone call the police!'

'He killed my mother!' Ben screamed over and over as they dragged him round the back and locked him in a shed until the police came. He didn't see the doctor, or any of the family for that matter. He was tied up and shoved into a police van, and taken away.

William Thurlwell was appalled at the damage. His wife was livid.

By the time they came home the servants had swept up the glass, but with every one of the tall front windows cracked or smashed, even the lovely leadlights she had designed herself, the house looked frightful: decayed, slovenly, as if this deterioration had taken place over years of neglect. She jumped down from the gig with an unusual display of vigour to scream at Bert: 'Who did this?'

'The kid next door, madam,' he replied, surveying the damage.

'You idiot!' she shouted. 'You incompetent idiot! Why didn't you stop him?'

He cringed. 'I'm sorry, madam, I wasn't here. I was off this afternoon.'

'Where were the rest of the staff? Can't I turn my back on my own house for one minute without having the place vandalized?'

'The women were out the back. They didn't know what was happening. Where the noise was coming from, like. 'Twas the gardeners caught him and locked him up.'

'Where is he now? I'll skin him alive!'

'The police came and arrested him. I always said he was no good, that kid.'

Phoebe, who'd returned home with her parents, walked along the tiled veranda, examining Ben's handiwork. 'Boy oh boy!' she breathed in admiration, pushing a loose piece of glass with the toe of her patent-leather shoe to assist his cause. It clattered to the ground and her mother screamed at her: 'Stop that this minute!'

Lalla turned on her husband. 'Don't just stand there. Do something!'

'What can I do now? Obviously the police have the matter in hand.'

'Really? And are the police ready to pay for all this damage? I told you years ago you should have got rid of that riffraff next door, and now look what's happened. Well, they'll pay for it, every damn penny . . .'

'It'll cost a pretty penny,' the doctor observed. 'Those big windows don't come cheap. Like as not those women won't be able to afford it and I'll get stuck with the bill anyway.'

'There's only one woman now,' Phoebe told them. 'The black lady died. There's only the old lady, Mrs Beckman, her mother.'

'Don't talk rot,' Lalla snapped. 'That German woman's not her mother, she couldn't possibly be. The gin was her maid.' She turned to William. 'You demand payment from the German woman, and if she can't pay, all the better. Put a lien on the house. You can buy the house, then she'll have the money to pay. She's responsible for that boy. She *has* to pay.' Lalla looked in the direction of the Beckman house. 'That woman has two blocks of land there. If we owned them we could have beautiful grounds that would really show off our house.'

William had no wish to be forced into conversation with their neighbour, so he sent Bert with his instructions.

Gussie Beckman was sitting in her room, fondly examining a box of mementoes of her dear girl. A photograph of Diamond with her baby, trinkets, crushed flowers, a band concert programme, her favourite headscarf . . . She reached over to the dressing table and picked up a newspaper clipping. She'd had it for weeks, meaning to show it to Diamond when she felt better. To ask her if she should keep it. The article spoke in glowing terms of Mr Ben Buchanan and his wife Clara, who were visiting Brisbane from their magnificent property out west. It noted that they were the guests of well-known Brisbane socialites Dr and Mrs William Thurlwell at their lovely home in Kangaroo Point.

She'd been startled to read about the Buchanans, and immensely curious, knowing that here was young Ben's father, right next door. Gussie had never met him but they'd read pieces about him in the social pages, many a time. 'One day,' she'd told Diamond, 'you ought to tell the boy who his father is. He has the right to know.'

'Yes,' Diamond had admitted. 'But not yet. When he gets older.'

Gussie sighed, placing the clipping in the box. One of these days she'd have to tell Ben herself. But later, when he was old enough to understand how these things happen.

'And what if, God forbid, you are taken suddenly with the bad heart, like your own darling Mutter?' she asked herself. 'The boy will never know his true parentage, and that would be a shame.'

There were more tears as Gussie took the clipping out again, staring at it. She found a stub of a pencil and circled the name of Ben Buchanan. After some consideration she wrote in the margin: 'Father of Ben Beckman.' She felt more should be added but she couldn't think what else to write, so, with guilty concern, she hid the clipping even deeper in the box and shut it away.

Someone was banging on the front door, even though she'd placed black ribbons on the brass knocker. Gussie marched up the passage, offended by this lack of decorum.

Bert was standing there, a manservant from next door. When Gussie heard what he had to report she didn't believe a word of it. She ran, stumbling, ahead of him to see for herself, and stood, just as the owners had, horrified by the destruction confronting her.

'My Ben wouldn't have done this!'

'He done it all right,' Bert said. 'Make no mistake about that, missus. Everyone seen him. I reckon he'd have set fire to the house next if the gardeners hadn't grabbed him. In a real rage he was, off his head. Them niggers, no tellin' what they'll do next. The master says you can't civilize them—'

'Stop that talk!' Gussie snapped. 'I wish to see your master.'

'He don't want to see you. He says he'll be sending you the bill for the damage and you have to pay.'

'Where's the boy?'

'The police have got him – you won't have to worry about him any more – but the master says you're responsible. You have to pay.'

Gussie was devastated. She stood there, wringing her hands, not knowing what to do next. It was hard to believe that Ben could have done this or why he would have committed such a senseless act. Maybe he was so upset at his mother's death, he just had to strike out at someone, something. In her long life, Gussie had seen many outpourings of grief, many violent physical reactions, but this time it seemed senseless, so unlike Ben. Unless, she pondered, Ben had expected Dr Thurlwell to come sooner to his mother's side. What had he said about that? She was so confused she couldn't recall.

'Get that woman off my premises!'

Mrs Thurlwell was standing at her front door, pointing arrogantly to her gate. Gussie ran over to her.

'Please, madam, if my boy did this, I'll pay for it whatever it costs. But please, tell the police to bring him back. He's a good boy.'

'Is this the work of a good boy?' Mrs Thurlwell threw out her hands in dramatic despair. 'First he wrecks a dinner party, and now this. I won't have him in the neighbourhood, do you hear me? He'll be banned from this district, and if you don't like it you can go too.'

'He was just upset,' Gussie pleaded. 'His mother was buried today. I beg you as a Christian woman not to be so hard on the lad.'

'What's the problem here?'

A gentleman strolled out to assist Mrs Thurlwell, who turned to him: 'Oh Ben, I really can't cope with all this. I feel quite faint.'

Gussie's eyes narrowed as she saw the woman switch from her mean and dominant attitude to what she had always called the 'clinging vine' type, and her dislike of Mrs Thurlwell intensified. But she'd also picked up the name, Ben, and guessed that here was Mr Buchanan in the flesh. She too changed her attitude.

'Perhaps I could speak to the gentleman?' she said softly.

'By all means,' Mrs Thurlwell replied, fluttering a lace handkerchief. 'Would you see to it, Ben? Neither the Doctor nor I could bear any more unpleasantness.' With that she wafted inside.

As usual Phoebe was eavesdropping. Biddy was always pulling her ear about that when she caught her. 'Only nasty little girls listen in on grown-ups like you do, miss!' she'd said. 'It's not nice to be sneaking about like this.'

Nice or not, Phoebe didn't care. The only really interesting things in this house happened when she was sent out of the room. Like the gossip in the kitchen. Biddy's daddy was in jail. The cook's daughter was in the family way with no husband. And Daddy and Uncle Edgar were plotting to make people give them lots of money for something. Then upstairs Mr Buchanan and his wife had rows. She wanted him to go back to the property where she, Clara, said he was needed, but he wouldn't go. He'd said he had business in town and she ought to go and stop nagging him.

If I were her, Phoebe thought stoutly, I'd just go! A cattle station would be far more interesting than town houses. But Clara was hanging on. Maybe she knew that Phoebe's mother was flirting with her husband. She'd have to be blind not to see Lalla going all girlish and stupid when Mr Buchanan was around. And Lalla was so old! As if a handsome countryman like Mr Buchanan would take any notice of her! Phoebe wanted, above all else, to visit his cattle station. After all, he had invited them. In the meantime she'd taken more interest in her riding lessons to prepare for country life, and Daddy had promised her she could have a horse of her own one day.

She frowned as she watched Mrs Beckman, the old lady from next door, take a seat on the veranda, and slid quietly into the parlour to try to listen in beside a tall broken window.

'Excuse me, sir,' the old woman said, 'while I get a breath. It's very hot and I came in such a rush without a hat.'

'The footman will escort you home,' Mr Buchanan replied, still standing. He didn't seem too pleased at being stuck with her, and Phoebe supposed that was fair enough. After all, it wasn't his problem.

'No, no,' Mrs Beckman said. 'You will please to give the Doctor my apologies and tell him I will pay for the damages.'

'Very well. Consider it done. Now if you will pardon me I must go.'

'Wait! What about my boy? You must not leave him with the police. I want you to get him back. I'll bring him in here to apologize to Dr Thurlwell. You see, his mother—'

'I'm afraid there's nothing the Doctor can do about that. He was caught in the act. Vandalism like this is a serious crime. The boy deserves a good whipping: he's obviously quite uncontrollable. A spell in jail is what he needs.'

'Oh, dear God, no!'

'Madam . . .' Mr Buchanan was becoming impatient with her. 'You might as well go home and rest. It's up to the courts now.'

'But sir, you are an important man. If you were to plead for him, they'd listen to you.'

Buchanan stared at her. 'Good Lord! Why should I do that? It's out of the question.'

She seemed to gather herself up, squaring her shoulders and thrusting out her chest like a little bantam hen. 'Aren't you Mr Buchanan from Caravale Station?'

'Yes. I did own Caravale.'

'And you went gold-seeking to the Palmer River. You were very sick there with the fevers?'

He was startled. 'How do you know that?'

'Diamond told me. You remember Diamond?'

He flushed and stepped back as if he'd been struck. 'I don't know what you're talking about! It's time you left, madam.'

But she persisted. 'Diamond nursed you, she cared for you.'

'I don't know anyone by that name,' he said angrily, but his voice was low, furtive.

'Sir, I am not here to cause you any trouble. But the boy, Ben, needs you. He is Diamond's son. Your son.'

'How dare you come here with your lies!' he snapped. 'You'd better leave before I have the law on you as well.'

'Oh no, you won't do that,' she said quietly. 'I'll never ask anything of you again, if only you'll go to the police and speak for the boy. You don't have to tell them why.'

'You're trying to blackmail me!' He seemed to be shouting at her but it was a whisper. 'You get out of here this minute, do you hear me? I don't want to hear any more of this from you or from the woman you call Diamond.'

Mrs Beckman stood up. 'We buried Diamond this morning, sir. She was a very fine woman, she deserved better than you.'

He stalked away and Phoebe could hear him calling Bert. She was confused. What was that all about? And what was blackmail? It sounded very dramatic. The poor old woman had been too distraught to make sense. Mr Buchanan couldn't be Ben's father, he lived in another house way out in the country. But it was rude of him to treat her like that. Phoebe's liking for their guest was fast diminishing. She was shocked that he didn't care about Ben going to jail or that Ben's mother had died. That was awful!

Ben Buchanan did call at the police station as soon as he could. He spoke to the senior sergeant on behalf of Dr and Mrs Thurlwell, informing them that Ben Beckman – and here he almost choked on the name – the boy they'd taken in charge, was uncontrollable. A fair young devil in the neighbourhood. That this was not the first time he'd caused trouble, even before his mother's death, so that excuse wouldn't hold water. The rascal should be made to feel the full force of the law.

Despite the fact that Mrs Beckman paid for all damages in full, and that the boy was represented in court by Mr Joseph Mantrell, Ben Beckman was given a harsh sentence of eighteen months' hard labour.

'But they can't do this!' Gussie wept. 'He's under age.'

'Not any more,' Joseph explained to her. 'He's fifteen now. They asked him his age and he told the truth. He turned fifteen several days after his mother's death.'

'In jail? Oh my God!' Gussie cried. 'Can I go to see him again? He's been so brave.'

'I'm sorry, Mrs Beckman, that won't be possible. He's been taken to a labour camp. They don't allow visitors. But you can write to him, and I'm sure a parcel or two would be permitted.'

Ben never saw her letters, or the parcels she so lovingly wrapped and sent to him. He was working in a white-hot stone quarry while she remained behind, a lonely old woman, steadfastly refusing to sell the house to her persistent neighbours. This was Ben's home and she meant to hold it for him.

'It's so kind of Clara to take Phoebe riding,' Lalla said to Ben Buchanan. 'I really do appreciate it. And Phoebe says she's an excellent rider.'

'She is that,' Ben agreed. 'My wife will make a good teacher for Phoebe.'

'Wonderful. Personally I've never gone much for riding, it seems so . . . well, unfeminine, although I do believe gentlemen admire ladies with a good "seat", as they say.' She smiled mischievously at him and spun about, deliberately swishing the bustle of her grey silk dress.

Ben laughed, picking up the *double entendre*. 'They certainly do, but I prefer the real thing. The trouble is, since those bustles came into fashion we never see them any more.'

'You don't care for the bustle?'

'Yes, they're very attractive and they accentuate pretty little waists like yours, but in my mother's day the outline was softer. She often complained, or pretended to complain, that gentlemen would surreptitiously pat her bottom. That's not possible now, is it?'

'Maybe the bustle was invented for protection. I'm sure I wouldn't appreciate having my bottom patted by all and sundry.'

'Then you'd better pray the bustle stays in fashion.'

'Why? Do you think I'd be a target?'

'I'm sure of it. Now, if you'll excuse me, Lalla, I have to go into town. I've taken a lease of rooms at Romany Court in George Street so that I'll have permanent accommodation when I'm in town, and I want to take a good look at them today. I think they'll need a bit of fixing up.'

'Are they furnished?'

'Yes. But not greatly to my taste. I want to make some changes.'

'Surely Clara could do that for you?'

'She won't be there very much. Someone has to stay on the property and she's happier out there. She's a country girl at heart.'

'But she's such a shy little person. Isn't she nervous on the property without you?'

He grinned. 'Clara's only shy in company. On the station, even though we have a manager, she will be very much in control. She grew up on Tarraburra Station, don't forget, a huge property: they ran sixty thousand head of cattle in her father's time.'

'Is that why you married her?'

Ben refused to be thrown by Lalla's direct question. 'I'm a cattle man too. I wouldn't take a city girl out to the bush.'

'Of course not. Very sensible of you.' She took a jube from a dish and popped it in her mouth. 'Have one, they're delicious.'

'Not just now, thanks.' He picked up his hat. 'I must be off. I'll take the ferry.'

'Don't be so independent. I'll have Bert send for the gig. But do you know what you're doing? I've never heard of a gentleman attending to decorating chores.'

He knew where her questions were leading but pretended to be unaware. It was important to him that she make the moves: he needed Lalla to be dependent on him, not the other way around, even though, God knew, he wanted her help. This conversation was crucial. If he invited her to come with him, alone, then she'd find him easy prey and lose interest.

'I'll work it out,' he said. 'It's just a matter of throwing up new curtains or drapes, or whatever you call them, and buying a bit of carpet. All that stuff.'

'But what about lamps and lighting? And a million other things? They have to match the décor.'

'Good God, Lalla! It's only four rooms. I don't need décor. I just have to buy enough to make myself comfortable.'

'You do not! As a Member of Parliament, which you will be within a year, you must have appropriate quarters, Ben. You will have to entertain, and you simply can't drag important people into dreary rooms.'

'They won't be dreary! I'm sure I'll be quite good at it.'

'Utter nonsense! Wait just a minute. I'm coming with you.'

He appeared worried. 'Are you sure? Would William mind?'

'Oh William! Of course not. He knows I simply adore decorating.'

'But do I?' he argued. 'I'm not sure that I want my rooms all prettied up.'

'Don't be silly! Leave it to me. You have to have rooms that are both elegant and comfortable.'

While he waited for her Ben smiled. Elegant and comfortable. And private. He'd seen to that last requirement. The four rooms also had a back entrance into a mews. Very private for a lady who might wish to visit him without drawing attention to herself.

'Why! They're quite charming!' Lalla said as she strolled through the entrance hall to the parlour, dismissing the concierge. 'Good high ceilings and the walls are in excellent condition.'

'Yes. The building is only a couple of years old.'

'And this is the dining room? Quite small, Ben, it will only seat eight. Where is the kitchen?'

'I don't want a kitchen. That involves staff. I'll take my meals out mainly, but the concierge tells me he can have meals sent up if I need them. There's a service staircase from this other room which I will use as my study.'

'Quite the bachelor quarters,' she smiled. 'But there's still plenty of room for improvement. You're right, those dull brown drapes have to go, and the carpet looks so tired! And Ben, my dear! Get rid of every stick of this horrible parlour furniture. It's too prissy for men.' She insisted he take notes as she progressed through the rooms, offering to lend him paintings for the walls and bring her own ladies to measure and make new curtains. Until eventually they moved on to the bedroom.

It contained a suite: the usual mahogany double bed, wardrobe and dresser.

'Oh dear. I'm quite exhausted,' she said at last, sitting on the edge of the bed. 'No one will see this poor room, so we can leave it for the time being. We have to get the public rooms right first. You've been so nice, Ben. You don't mind me making all these changes, do you?'

'Not at all. I'm grateful to you.'

'Then you might show it. You've been walking about looking bored for the last half-hour.'

'I'm not bored. I'm just sorry that the cupboard is bare and I can't offer you any refreshments. Next time I'll be prepared.'

'Next time I'll have servants with me.'

'Then the time after that,' he offered.

Lalla took off her hat and smoothed her hair before she stood up and moved closer to him. 'Will there be other times, Ben?' Her mouth was a fingertip away from his.

'I wouldn't dare hope,' he whispered, but her lips were on his, denying any false protest he might have invented.

They made love in his firm new bed, and he marvelled at her eagerness, which made up in some measure for her inexperience. She might be bold, he mused, as he held her in his arms, more interesting than Clara, but as a lover she had a lot to learn. And he would teach her. That would be exciting and it would bond her to him more than she could possibly imagine.

She moaned as he kissed her small breasts and moved her about the bed, taking her gently, lovingly, giving her the romance that he knew was lacking in her life with William, murmuring to her that she was beautiful, her slim body so white and so smooth, shocked that he should be thinking of Diamond.

Diamond, with her vibrant black body, had been the best of them all. Ever since those last days in the far north he'd never found a woman who could make love like Diamond, who had really loved him and knew how to please him.

But she was dead. Gone. He didn't care about that. She was history. But that old German woman had thrown her at him after all this time. He recalled Diamond talking about the German couple who had adopted her as a kid, but he hadn't taken much notice, hadn't cared. And now there was the son. Another Ben! Even though he'd called the woman a liar he knew that Diamond wouldn't lie. Diamond, even though she was black, was straight. She wouldn't know how to lie. Jesus! A kid, and a dark kid at that. The one who had come rampaging into Thurlwell's dining room demanding aid for his mother. What would he have done had he known this was his son?

Nothing. Absolutely nothing. Plenty of blokes out west had piccaninnies, but you didn't claim them. Yet he had to admit the kid was a chip off the old block. Diamond's son! She'd been afraid of no one. It was a wonder the boy hadn't carried a knife like she used to.

'You're smiling, darling,' Lalla said, nestling into him. 'Are you happy?'

'Yes,' he muttered, lifting her to him. 'You're incredible.'

'We don't have to go yet,' she whispered, lying limply beneath him.

'Good.' This time he forgot to be gentle, plunging on her, trying to resurrect real passion, not caring that her little moans had turned to gusts of shock.

They had no children, he and Clara. She never complained, she just hoped. He had felt humiliated, wondering if it were his fault. Now he knew it was not. He had fathered a child. More, maybe, but neither the blacks nor the prostitutes would dare accuse him. Only that German woman. Well, she could go to hell, and the kid too. And if this woman got pregnant it was her problem. At least he now knew that he wasn't sterile. He could prove it was Clara's fault. Not that he ever would, but good to know.

'I'm sorry,' he said, apologizing for his rough treatment, remembering Lalla's social status.

'Darling, never mind! Don't tell me you're having second thoughts at this stage?'

'No, of course not.'

'Then run along. Leave me while I dress.'

Her tone irritated Ben but didn't surprise him. She was accustomed to having her own way, and as long as it suited him she was welcome to the illusion.

On the return journey she was businesslike again: 'Edgar is willing to support you, Ben, for the seat of Padlow.'

'I appreciate that, but I was rather thinking of the Legislative Council. It would be much easier to accept nomination to a place in the Upper House rather than face an election for the Legislative Assembly.'

'That won't do at all. You'd have to wait for someone to die to get into the Upper House; they hang on like glue. And they're only rubber stamps. The real power is the Lower House.'

'Where the Premier is a dedicated federalist. I can't see much power for me in opposition.'

'She laughed. 'Don't be so pessimistic! You under-estimate yourself, and your friends. Premier Griffiths might be making the running now but it's early days, people are only just beginning to wake up to what federalism means.'

'I don't know why you're so dead against it, Lalla. When it comes to the railroads, something could be worked out.'

'Do you think so? Where are they proposing to locate the federal capital? Sydney, of course. Doesn't that give you a hint? And you know quite well that at the last convention the federalists made it plain they intend to take over railroads, immigration, defence, tariffs, all sorts of things. I'm amazed that you would consider selling out Queensland.'

Ben couldn't admit that he really hadn't given the matter a lot of thought except that it had sounded like a good idea at first. Until he'd heard the big money was against it.

'I'm being the Devil's Advocate,' he said calmly. 'One should look at all sides of the question.'

'Then you should listen to the New Zealand pastoralists. They won't have a bar of it. They won't even attend the conventions.' She touched his hand. 'You mustn't miss this opportunity, my dear. Edgar can be very generous.'

'In what way?' There was a tinge of boredom in his voice.

'He's prepared to sign over to you five thousand shares in the railroad company.'

'That's very gracious of him and in years to come, no doubt I'll reap the rewards but I'll have to look about for a business interest right now to offset spending so much time away from my property.'

'He's aware of that and I'm led to believe he can arrange for you to be offered a place on the board of the Southern Coal Mining Corporation. Would that interest you?'

Would it what? Ben was stunned. A director of one of the most prestigious corporations available. Money for jam. He hid his excitement by enquiring if Edgar was on that board.

'No, but his friends are. Interested?'

'It would be an honour. I'd very much appreciate such an appointment. It would also give me a more solid base when I stand for the seat of Padlow. I'll be representing both the pastoralist and the mining interests.'

'That did occur to Edgar,' she said smugly. 'Shall I tell him you're prepared to stand for the Legislative Assembly?'

'By all means,' he smiled. 'And with you as my campaign director, how can I lose?'

On Christmas Day Phoebe was awake by five in the morning, with the hot sun elbowing at her curtains. Although they were only slightly open she could feel the heat on her face, and rather than shut out this exciting day she jumped up to examine her treasures.

Santa hadn't come to her for years – that was for babies, her mother said – so Phoebe had appointed herself Father Christmas and had presents for everyone.

Yesterday, after some persuasion, Daddy had given her a purse of money and allowed her to catch the ferry into town on her own, so that she could shop for gifts. She'd had a marvellous time. The streets were busy with cheerful people, calling to each other, wishing Happy Christmas to all. Carol-singers dressed as angels stood at the corner of Queen Street, chorusing the familiar songs, their paper wings drooping in the heat, and generous passers-by dropped pennies in the basket at their feet. Phoebe did too, it made her feel part of all the celebrations.

She walked the length of Queen Street, so as not to miss any of the shops with their jolly decorations, and then took herself back to a café where she polished off two strawberry ices. Then, with the assistance of shop girls in various stores, she began her shopping in earnest, choosing her gifts with care, and not forgetting to buy coloured cellophane and ribbons to do the wrapping at home.

Anxiously, now, she tapped each parcel, reciting the names of the recipients to make certain she hadn't forgotten anyone. There were socks for her father, perfume for Mother – she'd taken a long time to make a decision there, because Mother seemed to have everything, but the lady in the shop had assured her that ladies always appreciated perfume, and this one, called Deep Violets, was a great favourite. It ought to be, Phoebe thought, it had cost her two shillings and tuppence, the dearest of all her purchases. Then there were chocolates for Biddy – she adored chocolates – and hankies for Cook, white stockings for the little scullery maid, tobacco for the gardeners, and a big man's hankie for Bert. She hated the footman but supposed it would be unfair to leave him out. She was grateful that Mother hadn't hired extra waitresses for Christmas dinner: her spending money wouldn't have extended to them.

Bert had placed a big Christmas tree in the lobby and Biddy had decorated it, with Phoebe's help. Now mysterious presents were sitting under it to be handed out at dinner time. Phoebe could hardly wait. She decided that her own presents were to be distributed right now, so everyone would get a surprise first thing.

Since the servants came in early, Phoebe ran downstairs and put the kitchen gifts on the plain scrubbed table, Bert's too, then hurried outside to place more coloured parcels at the door of the garden shed where they couldn't be missed. There were no cards on any of Phoebe's gifts; she would tease everyone if they tried to guess and tell them they came from Santa.

She left her father's gift outside his room and was just settling the small parcel at her mother's door when it opened.

'What are you doing up at this hour?'

'Oh, nothing,' Phoebe grinned.

'Then go back to bed and get some rest. It's going to be a very hot day.'

'Santa left you a present, I think.' Phoebe pointed to the gaily wrapped parcel.

'Good heavens! So he did,' Lalla said, picking it up as she made for the bathroom.

'Happy Christmas, Mother!' Phoebe called after her.

'Yes. And to you,' Lalla said absently, unwrapping the parcel. 'Oh! Perfume!'

Phoebe followed her into the bathroom and watched as Lalla unscrewed the bottle and sniffed it.

'Dear oh dear,' she said, recoiling. 'Did you buy this?'

Phoebe nodded. 'Be careful, you only use a little drop at a time. The lady said it's very strong.'

'You can say that again.' Lalla put the small gold top back on the bottle and handed it to Phoebe. 'I wish you wouldn't waste your money on cheap stuff like this. Give it to the servants. Go and smell my French perfume so that you'll learn the difference. It's important to know.'

'I'm sorry,' Phoebe mumbled, and ran back to her room. Back to bed, with tears of disappointment streaking her face. She clutched the bottle of Deep Violets and the perfume wafted faintly about her. It was lovely, a beautiful perfume. Her mother was just being mean. Phoebe was sorry now that she'd bought her anything at all. It had been a waste of money. She wouldn't give it to the servants, though. She'd keep it and give it to someone else. But who?

That took some thought, but eventually she came to a decision. The lady next door, old Mrs Beckman. She'd seen her about but hadn't spoken to her. She must be lonely with Ben still in prison. It had been more than a year since he'd broken the windows. Yes, she'd take it in to her this afternoon, after Christmas dinner.

Daddy gave her a pearl brooch for Christmas, and Uncle Edgar had sent over a tennis racquet and a pair of gold and silver bangles. Phoebe was thrilled. She left her mother's gift until last, after the lace gloves from the staff and the small gold watch sent to her by Mrs Foster, who seemed to have taken a liking to her.

Carefully she opened the box and read the card: 'Happy Christmas from Mother.'

Inside was the most beautiful hat. It was boater-shaped but made of coppery burnt straw with tiny lemon rosebuds resting on the rim, interspersed with lily of the valley. She loved it, but she steeled herself and placed it back in its nest of tissue.

'My dear, it's lovely!' her father enthused. 'Try it on, Phoebe.'

'No.'

'Come on. Let's see it on you,' he persisted.

She looked at her mother, her grey eyes cold. 'No. I don't like it.'

'I'll have you know,' Lalla said, 'that's a very expensive hat. It came from the Chic Boutique.'

Phoebe's face was impassive. 'Never mind, it won't be wasted. If I don't wear it I shall give it to one of the servants.'

They were entertaining guests in the long room when Phoebe slipped away that afternoon.

'Why! It's Miss Phoebe!' the old woman said. 'What a pleasant surprise. Come in, dear.'

'Oh no.' Phoebe fumbled with the bottle of perfume, which she had rewrapped. 'I just came to wish you a Happy Christmas.' She thrust the gift at Mrs Beckman, worrying now that she was making a fool of herself.

'Is this for me? How kind of you.'

'I just thought,' Phoebe stammered, 'that with the boy away . . .' She blushed, too embarrassed to use the word. Everyone knew he was in jail. 'I thought you might be lonely.'

'What a dear girl. Come through. You must have some Christmas cake.'

Before she could protest Phoebe was ushered into the small parlour, where she came face to face with a young gentleman, who leapt to his feet, spilling his tea.

She was glad of the few minutes of confusion, to cover her own surprise. It hadn't occurred to her that Mrs Beckman might have a visitor, especially a nice-looking young man with sandy hair and a merry smile. His name, she learned, was Barnaby Glasson.

'Two such thoughtful young people!' Mrs Beckman smiled as she opened Phoebe's present. 'First chocolates from Barnaby and now . . . oh, my! Beautiful perfume!'

To Phoebe's relief her appreciation of the perfume was genuine. Or she hoped it was, because she was feeling a little uncomfortable that the gift was only an afterthought. And worse, a slap at her mother.

'Deep Violets!' Mrs Beckman enthused. 'That's all the fashion now. I'll put it away for best.'

When they were finally settled with tea and cake, Mrs Beckman explained Barnaby's presence. 'He's training to be a solicitor,' she told Phoebe. 'And he'll be a very good one too. He's trying to help Ben. You know he's still in jail?'

'Yes. I'm sorry.'

'I can't do much,' Barnaby shrugged.

'But you have seen him, and you took him the Christmas basket.'

'Yes.'

'Then that's something. But I won't worry Miss Phoebe with my troubles.' She did her best, talking about her late husband, the sea captain, and of Christmas in Europe but Phoebe could see she was a very sad woman who really was delighted to have visitors.

Barnaby walked Phoebe home.

'How long will he have to stay in jail?' she asked the fledgling lawyer.

'A long time, I'm afraid. He has made two attempts to escape, but they caught him both times.'

'Really?' Phoebe was fascinated. 'Is jail as terrible as they say?'

'Worse. He's doing hard labour. Very tough on him. Fortunately he's healthy and is standing up to it, but I'm afraid that mentally, it's a different matter.'

This young man was talking to her as an equal, not patronizing her as most people did, and Phoebe appreciated that. When they reached her gate she made no effort to go in. 'What do you mean by that?'

'How well do you know him?'

'Not at all. He was just the boy next door.'

'Yes. Well, he's been well brought up by those two women. He's not accustomed to roughing it.'

'Of course. How awful.'

Barnaby nodded. 'My employer, Mr Mantrell, did his best to represent Ben but there was no defence.' He stopped, startled. 'It was your windows he smashed?'

'Yes.' Phoebe felt guilty for a second but then she grinned at Barnaby. 'He did a good job of it! He was really angry.'

'Maybe. But that's the attitude that is getting him into more trouble. Did you know his mother?'

'Not really.'

'I met her. She was a very strong woman. I had the impression that she wasn't a person to cross. This lad is a bit like her; instead of settling down and seeing out his time, he's fighting every inch of the way.'

'Good on him,' Phoebe said stoutly.

'All very well, but if he doesn't smarten up he may not survive.'

'You didn't tell Mrs Beckman that?'

'No.'

'What if you spoke to my father? Got him to say it was all a mistake?'

'It's too late for that. Besides, would he do it?'

'I shouldn't think so.' She turned away abruptly. 'If you see Ben again, remember me to him. I'm glad he broke their windows!'

Barnaby watched as she ran down the drive. A disconcerting miss if ever he'd met one, but he was touched by her kindness to Mrs Beckman. Phoebe Thurlwell! Pretty as a picture and brimming with intelligence. Very sure of herself too, the confidence that money bought, but different from most girls of her age. Nothing silly or simpering about Miss Thurlwell. He would have liked to talk to her a bit longer. She seemed older than her years, older than the fussy 'little girl' dress she was decked out in, anyway.

Mantrell had done his best. The case was closed. But Barnaby had a conscience. Diamond had demonstrated to him the power of money, and so, when Ben went to jail, Barnaby had used bribes to get to see him. He'd spent a pound here and a pound there until he'd finally come face to face with the lad. He felt he owed it to Diamond, spending the money she'd given him.

Meeting the kid again had been a shock. Gone was the coddled boy and in his place a wiry, brown-skinned prisoner with defiant eyes and a deep, resonant voice.

'What do you want?'

'Your grandmother asked me to come and see you. She's worried about you.'

'Tell her I'm all right.'

'Did you get the parcels she sent you?'

He shrugged. 'What do you think? Tell her I did.' He relented. 'Tell her not to worry, I'll be home soon.'

'Ben, you won't be home soon if you don't behave. You've already got a bad reputation.'

'But I'm still alive. Three of the niggers that came in with me are dead, and a couple of others have had their brains bashed in.'

'Then don't let it happen to you.'

'You don't know what you're talking about, Mr Glasson. If you're so interested, why don't you help me to escape?'

'I can't do that.'

'Then sit here until I eat as much of this food as I can stuff down my neck, because the minute you go, the warders will grab every crumb. Have some cake.'

Mrs Beckman, he knew, wasn't poor. Maybe heavy bribes would get Ben out, but to suggest something like that would put his own career at risk. That was too much to ask of him, thought Barnaby, too much.

Chapter Three

Warden 'Bull' Baker could not have known that this was the last day of his tenure on earth.

Had he known, maybe he would have fallen from his bunk in the stone hut to kneel and beg, with frantic devotion, that the grossly defaced slate of his life and times be miraculously cleansed while there was still time. Or perhaps, seeing no hazard in the recitation of his years, he might have been moved to pray that this was a terrible mistake, that another miserable dawn would see him swagger forth as usual, bullwhip in hand, ready to lash his foremen and prisoners into action.

Certainly, being a superstitious man, he would not have chosen this day to indulge in one of his more vicious pleasures once he had the quarrymen working full tilt. Even Warden Baker knew, although he never gave it much thought, that this was one sin guaranteed to incur the wrath of the Lord.

But then he wasn't to know that his hours were numbered when he dropped to his knees at the base of that low bunk to assault a bound and spread-eagled prisoner.

Bull Baker had been watching the pretty coloured boy for months, savouring this pleasure, there being no hurry. The convict, Benny Beckman, was only halfway through his extended sentence. To Bull, this one was a beauty: tall and slim with a body of bronze and smooth muscles that rippled as he worked on the rocky shelves.

Some of them came easy, afraid to resist or hoping to earn favours, but not this one. After three years on the work gangs, the pretty boy had become a tough customer, fighting all the way, defying the bosses, demanding his rights – they said he could talk underwater – a real bush lawyer! Watching him mature into a man worth his personal attention – Bull couldn't be bothered with kids – he'd been amused just listening to the bold bastard giving the foremen a hard time and earning himself plenty of pain. The silly bugger was playing right into the warden's hands.

After yet another altercation involving Benny and some of his mates against truncheon-wielding foremen, Bull strode down to intervene.

'I've had enough of this bastard!' he shouted, pointing at Benny. 'Bring him out! Bloody troublemaker. I'll show him who's boss here.'

As he was thrown forward, Bull's whip sliced across Benny's back. 'Another dose of solitary'll cool him down.'

He whistled to a couple of his pet trusties to hustle the prisoner up the hill, ignoring the sudden nervous glances of the other labourers. The introduction of these two hefty bruisers was a warning not missed by a long-term jailbird like Beckman. He began to fight, but was hampered by leg-irons and was no match for the hard fists of his captors.

At the edge of the scrub, Bull gave his trusties the nod. Once they were out of sight of the workforce, they by-passed the windowless stone cell used for solitary confinement. Benny began to fight again and, trailing behind them, Bull laughed: 'Don't worry, mate, we'll get to that! All in good time.'

He was in a good mood as he chortled to the knowing trusties, 'Never seen a prisoner so keen to get put in the pit!'

It was like trying to force a wild animal through the narrow doorway into Bull's hut, and that excited the warden even more. He waited outside, casually smoking his pipe as the gag muffled Benny's shouts and he heard the leg-irons clank to the ground. He shivered in anticipation, knowing that the long, firm body would be stripped bare by this. He could hardly wait to get a good look at it.

The trusties lumbered out and went on their way without a word, but still Bull waited. He wanted to give the pretty boy time to settle down.

Eventually he ducked through the low doorway.

Emerging an hour later, well pleasured, Bull strolled away. He cut through the bush to emerge at a rock plateau from where he could oversee his domain, and all those worker ants, as he called them, toiling in the sun. Standing there gave him a sense of power. His authority over these prisoners and their keepers was never questioned, except by a few mugs like Benny in there, and they didn't count for nothing.

He shuddered momentarily, thinking of Benny. The bastard, gagged, had turned his head and glared at him with such fury, such hatred, that for a second or so Bull had been startled. The brown eyes were round and flat and venomous, like a snake's eyes. Bull was scared stiff of snakes, and there was no shortage of them around the quarry.

He shrugged. The prisoner could glare until his eyes fell out as far as Bull was concerned. A week in solitary would take the shine off them. He'd come out half blind, and then he could go down to the floor of the quarry in the white heat reflecting from the sandstone. 'I'll give him glare!' Bull muttered, grinning at his pun.

If he'd had a notion to do so, another prisoner, Jim Donovan, might have warned Bull Baker to tread carefully round Benny Beckman. His daughter, Biddy, had written to him, asking him to seek out and offer kindness to the lad, the son of a neighbour.

It had taken a long time for Jim to make contact with the lad. The older men usually worked on the roads, but as a lifer he'd managed to wangle a job as a lorry-driver, taking sandstone blocks from the quarry to the river barges.

Right from the first, Jim had picked this coloured boy as an odd man out. Benny was another of those wet-behind-the-ears kids who deluded themselves into believing that they were entitled to just treatment in prison, and were noisy in their defiance of brutal guards until they started to wake up to themselves. In a typical reaction he'd twice tried to escape, so he was already branded as a recalcitrant, and the guards were ready for him. His behaviour fitted a pattern they had come to recognize very easily.

Jim had talked to him, warning him to settle down and stop drawing attention to himself, and although Benny admitted that the attempted escapes had been stupid, lengthening his sentence, he was still his own worst enemy, stubborn, cranky and argumentative. Every time Jim heard that Beckman had won himself another flogging or another spell in the pit, he despaired. How could he help a lad who wouldn't help himself?

He spoke to Benny's mates, the men who worked with him, the white men, but they only laughed. Benny, 'the mouth', was a source of entertainment. They egged him on, pleased to witness someone standing up to the guards, easing their own miseries and frustrations. Jim turned then to the black prisoners, but found they were in awe of the 'white' boy whose skin was so much lighter than theirs and who talked 'white' too. Finally he met a grizzled Aborigine called Moorak, an old lag who'd spent half his life in prison, protected from the noose by the general belief that he was crazy, a witless loony.

Moorak called to Jim one day as he passed by: 'No need you cry for him white boy,' the Aborigine commented, squatting in the dust, tapping a monotonous rhythm endlessly with two carved sticks, his treasures.

'You mean Beckman?' Jim said.

The old man nodded, and curious to hear more, Jim dropped to the ground, facing him. 'Why do you say this?'

He was rewarded with the twist of a grin exposing cracked and broken teeth. 'Him boy got the evil eye.' The black man nodded, as if to himself. 'Him carry big payback.'

'I dunno about that,' Jim said. 'He's gettin' plenty payback himself. He gets more whip than feeds.'

The old man went on nodding and tapping as if there were no need for any more words, so Jim shrugged and climbed to his feet. But as he walked away, the old man called to him. 'What happen to Mister

Crotty?' His voice sounded different, an ugly sound, deep and rasping.

'Crotty?' Jim asked. 'I dunno. Who's he?' Then he remembered that Crotty had been one of the foremen, a real mean bastard. 'Oh yeah, I know,' he recalled. 'But he's not here any more. He had an accident, fell from a ledge, broke his leg.'

'Plenty assidents,' the voice cackled.

'Some,' Jim admitted, remembering that a guard had recently been badly hurt in a landslide.

A gnarled finger wagged at him as if the blackfellow had read his thoughts. 'That one, he bash up your white boy, then whaap! Stones bash him!'

'Listen,' Jim snapped, 'that had nothing to do with Beckman. He's in enough trouble. Don't go blaming him. He was nowhere near that landslide.'

The nodding and the tapping commenced again and the old man lowered his head, muttering: 'Pow'ful spirits in this place. Blackfeller know.'

'Yeah,' Jim said, deciding to humour the old bloke. 'That'd be right,' and went on his way, dismissing the matter as an old man's ramblings.

Months later he managed a visit to the filthy barracks where the black labourers were housed, segregated from the white prisoners. Being coloured, Benny had been assigned to this overcrowded rat-hole. Jim had pleaded with the foremen in vain to move him to the white quarters, strangely, Benny himself didn't seem to care.

'What difference does it make?' he'd said. 'It's still a bloody prison.'

'For your health, son. I'll keep asking. Our quarters are flea-holes but they have to be kept cleaner than this. Nobody cares about these huts. I'm trying to keep you alive.'

'Don't worry about me, Jim. I'll stay alive, I've got things to do when I get out of here.'

'If you don't learn to shut that trap of yours you'll never get out of here.'

Benny looked at him curiously. 'You've got more chances than me. You're not even chained. Why don't you make a run for it?'

'My life's in God's hands,' the Irishman said. 'I killed a man and I expected to be hung for it. They said there were mitigating circumstances and so I was spared, but I have no repentance so I must accept His punishment.'

'Then you ought to repent,' the brash young man grinned. 'And get the hell out of here while you can.'

What was missing in this lad? Jim wondered. Taken on his own, away from the harsh world about them, he was a likeable kid, growing into what could be a decent man. A lot of his problems had emanated from standing up for others, often for blackfellows, who really got the rough end of the stick in jail. He had this mania about injustice – with good reason, Jim conceded, since his sentence for vandalism and destruction of property was harsh. But it was not unusual. There were men and women in Queensland prisons for far less, for stealing a little food or even a few spoons from their employers. Prisons were supposed to be the great reformers. What a joke that was.

And there was the dark side of this lad. He never spoke about his home life, refused to discuss the outside, and yet he was well educated, an oddity among half-castes let alone the throngs of illiterate whites. But there was no doubt he carried the age-old Aborigine rule of payback strong within him. Bad enough in whites, but as Jim had observed, practically law to the blacks.

In an effort to reform his protégé, Jim had tried to instruct him in the Christian value of turning the other cheek, but was startled when Benny had thrown back at him:

'Is that what you did, Jim? Turn the other cheek? Don't preach at me.'

One time, a nervous blackfellow took him to find Benny, who was lying on his mat – there were no bunks or hammocks in the black sector – battered and bruised, with blood caked on his face and ears.

'What happened to him?' Jim demanded to know.

The Aborigine prisoner rolled his eyes in fear. 'Taffy Welk, him foreman our mob, he bash up this feller good for givin' cheek.'

'What sort of cheek?'

'One of our blokes carryin' too heavy a load. Him fall down an' Taffy he start screamin' and beltin' him with a stick. Benny here, he start yellin'! "You cut that out, mister!" So Taffy givin' him the hidin' instead.'

'Oh Jesus!' Jim said. 'Get me some water and I'll clean him up.

'Will ye never learn?' Jim despaired as he slopped water from an iron bucket on to Benny's face.

'I'll be all right!' The patient was pushing him away.

'Like hell you will! You're bloody mad, Beckman! You'll end up a lifer like me, if you survive.'

Benny grabbed the cloth from him. 'I'll get out of here,' he grated, 'and then we'll see who'll survive. They'll be sorry.'

'Who's they? For Christ's sake! What's eating you, lad?'

But Benny had nothing more to say.

'Oh well, nothing broken,' Jim said as he swabbed Ben's face, noting that even with the poor diet the lad's teeth were intact, firm and strong. Sure sign of a well-fed youth in these times. His own teeth had decayed early.

'I'll get you something to eat,' he said and strode out to the line-up where the blacks were waiting patiently for their grub, pannikers in hand.

Moorak sidled up to him. 'White boy hurt?'

'Yes,' Jim said, handing over the metal dish. 'You get his grub for him.'

'More assident now,' Moorak grinned. 'Mister Taffy, he get the evil eye. Pow'ful spirits wakem up. You see!' He wagged a finger under Jim's nose, and came back untroubled with two dishes of mutton slop, busily devouring his own on the hoof.

That night, Jim heard a few days later, Taffy Welk had come down with the fever. By the next morning he was raving and by sunset he was rushed away to the infirmary back at the Brisbane prison.

Although he knew it was only a coincidence, Jim Donovan was shaken. He began to make a few enquiries. What were the circumstances of Crotty's accident? What about the other fellow, the one in the landslide? They'd all been overseeing gangs that included Benny Beckman. He didn't ask any more. He didn't want to know. Jim believed in good, so therefore he believed in evil. If there were angels there had to be devils. But this was all too close to home. He made the sign of the cross every time he saw Moorak, and kept well away from him. Not that he really believed this heathen stuff, but reason told him that the arm of coincidence could only stretch so far. He began to observe Beckman's tormentors more closely.

And had he had the confidence, and a notion to do so, he might have warned Bull Baker of the thing the blacks called the evil eye.

He was hitching his horses to the lorry for the return journey from the river when a guard rode down to taunt him with the news that Bull Baker had another 'customer' up in his shed.

'Oh holy God, no! Who is it this time?'

'Your mate,' the guard laughed. 'Benny the half-caste!'

'You bastards!' Jim shouted at him. 'Why don't you put a stop to that filth?'

'Nothin' to do with us. He's the boss.'

'Then the wrath of God be on ye!' the Irishman yelled at the departing rider.

All the way home he worried about Benny. 'Enough to send the lad mental,' he muttered to himself, urging on the big draught horses, hoping against hope that the information was wrong or that Benny had somehow managed to escape the devil's clutches. And if Benny was yet another victim, this time he couldn't let his conscience allow such a crime to go unheeded. Benny could write. Jim would have him write a letter to His Excellency the Governor, lodging a formal complaint, and he, James Donovan, would sign the letter. It would be an easy matter to smuggle it out on one of the barges. Writing materials he could get from the rivermen too.

While Jim Donovan was furiously concocting this plan, Bull Baker took his last look at the quarry, then turned away and tramped back over the exposed rocks, feeling right pleased with himself.

Suddenly he stopped, smothering a scream.

A tiger snake reared up in front of him, preparing to strike, its fangs bared, its coppery body gleaming in the sun. Petrified, he watched the brown eyes that were ringed with flaring orange, spiteful, cruel eyes.

Matching his own cunning against that of the snake, he knew he did not dare run. Instead he concentrated on the handle of his rawhide whip, surreptitiously moving his fingers along for a baton grip and carefully measuring the distance between himself and the rearing, gently weaving snake.

Without warning, Bull moved, confident that a hefty strike with his steel-lined whip handle would belt that leering head out of his way. But the snake was faster. Bull reeled back in shock as it hit him on the chest, fangs sinking viciously through his flannel shirt, locking on to his skin.

Screaming in terror, he tried to bat it away with the whip but was forced to grab the scaly body, trying to tear it from him, amazed at its strength. It fought back, head shafting at his neck like a spear, sending a searing pain through him.

Using both hands, he hurled the monster away from him and ran shouting down the hill, unknowingly assisting the poison to course freely on its deadly journey, until he collapsed at the feet of the returning trusties.

There was nothing they could do. There was no place for tourniquets nor did they know how to bleed the wounds. They were shouting now, shouting for help as they held the boss down to try to ease the spasms, watching as his eyes rolled in agony and foam spluttered from his mouth. Watching Bull Baker die.

From the hut Benny heard the commotion, but it was of no interest to him. He was still lying naked, bound to the bunk, waiting for the final humiliation of release, ashamed of the tears that still blotted his face.

Hours later, he was still there, forgotten. He tried to recall the distant screams and shouting he'd heard earlier, and concluded that there must have been some sort of a fight going on out there, not unusual in this warring pit of slaves and slave-drivers. He struggled against the rawhide thongs that bound him until his wrists were raw and bleeding, and by the time Jim Donovan found him, he had managed to work his legs loose, wrenching them free by sheer force.

Jim found a knife and cut Benny free from the sturdy timber bunk, then handed him his clothes. 'Come on, lad, let's get out of here.'

Avoiding Jim's eyes, Benny pulled on his trousers and shirt, ashamed again to be seen like this by the older man.

'The boss is dead,' Jim told him. 'Got bit by a snake. Now you just cut down to your barracks like nothin' happened. They're all runnin' about like headless chooks right now, they'll have forgotten about you.'

When Benny hesitated at the door of the hut, Jim cautioned him. 'You're not going to bolt, now are you, son?'

'No,' Benny whispered, his shoulders drooping miserably.

'Are you all right?'

Benny shuddered and Jim tried to spare him. 'No one knows,' he said quietly. 'For all they know, the snake killed him before he got to you.'

'Yes,' Benny said, his voice a sob.

He seemed blind to his whereabouts, disoriented, so Jim went with him, escorting him down to the barracks where prisoners were dancing about with glee that the hated warden was good and dead. Such a monumental event far outweighed Beckman's minor problem, so the pair wandered by unnoticed.

But Benny Beckman was changed. Scarred, Jim feared. The noisy, outspoken prisoner became sullen and withdrawn, no longer listed as a troublemaker, just another defeated blackfellow. Jim found some books for him to read on Sundays, some battered penny dreadfuls and another which he was told was poetry, and the lad seemed pleased, but his insolent demeanour had disappeared. To the others, Beckman had finally got the message and was simply accepting his sentence, but Jim knew that he was nursing a rage, and he feared for what would become of this young man when he was finally released.

The prisoners were mustered for a church service to pray for the soul of the departed warden, but no tears were shed for Bull Baker. When they were dismissed Jim was confronted again by the evil-looking old Aborigine, Moorak.

'Another assident, eh?' he wheezed.

Reminded afresh of Moorak's claims, Jim nodded. 'Maybe. Maybe not. But either way the bastard got his just deserts.'

'Pow'ful spirits mind white boy,' Moorak insisted.

'Well he needs them even more now,' Jim growled.

'He be al-ri',' Moorak grinned. 'That one comen up big-feller boss hisself.'

Donovan shook his head. 'I don't think so, mate. He's taken too much of a thrashing.'

Ever since that Christmas Day three years ago when he'd first met Miss Phoebe Thurlwell at her neighbour's house, Barnaby had been in love with her. It had been a gradual process, though, because it had taken a while for him to recognize what had happened to him.

At first the girl had simply dwelled in his thoughts. Little sunlit passages of pleasure in which he saw her smile again and heard the girlish voice, direct and cheerful, enough to brighten his busy day. And then he'd met her at a tennis party the following summer, and, amazingly, hadn't recognized her, his picture of her blurred by his mental thumbings.

'Barnaby Glasson!' she'd said, poking him with her racquet. 'I'm shattered! You've forgotten me.'

Never mind that inside him, his heart gave a whoop of joy. The picture he presented must have been pitiful. He whisked off his green-lined tennis hat, dropped his own racquet, which she picked up for him, and muttered that he hadn't forgotten her at all. Stumbled. Bumbled. Asked her how she was.

'How do I look?' she responded, as if they were lifelong friends. 'My hair's longer now and I'm allowed to wear it up at night. And I get to choose my own clothes. Do you think this tennis dress is too short? I'm getting peculiar looks from the old ducks in the pavilion.' She struck a pose for him. 'So what if my ankles are showing. Better than tripping over my skirts, don't you think?'

'Yes. Yes, of course,' he mumbled, not daring to examine those fine ankles too closely. How could a fifteen-year-old girl make him feel like a country bumpkin? After all, he had a legal career ahead of him, and several eligible young ladies welcomed his company. In fact Lucy Morrow was waving to him now, beckoning him over to tea.

'I'm dying of thirst,' Phoebe said. 'Have you finished your games?'

'Yes,' he told her, wondering why he sounded apologetic. 'I didn't do too well.'

'Neither did I. We ought to have a game one day without a net. The jolly thing's a nuisance. It slows up my game.'

He was laughing. As they walked towards the pavilion she gave him a running commentary on her disappointed tennis partners, most of whom Barnaby knew, and he listened to her outlandish views with delight. Her gaiety was so infectious he pretended not to see Lucy when Phoebe asked him: 'Where shall we sit?'

'Down here, I think,' he told her, finding a rickety table at the far end.

He often met her after that, with mutual friends, delighted that she always found time to chat with him.

The invitation to her eighteenth birthday party at the Thurlwell mansion was hand-delivered to the office, and Barnaby agonized over what to wear and what present he should buy until Mrs Mantrell came to his rescue. She was impressed that their law clerk should find his way so easily into society, and was determined that Barnaby should make a good showing.

Barnaby arrived looking very smart, he thought, in his first dinner suit, black tie and all, and handed over his gift with all the confidence in the world. It had been chosen with an eye to propriety, and Barnaby was grateful to Mrs Mantrell for her choice, although it had set him back five shillings and sixpence. It was a beautifully bound copy of Shelley's poems, which Barnaby had leafed through at home – with gloves on so as not to mark the pages – in case anyone asked him about them. He'd never had much time for books outside his required reading of law volumes and he found the poems difficult but accepted that they were fashionable and popular.

The party was a huge success: a superbly organized evening for several hundred guests, with a magnificent buffet, champagne flowing, and wandering minstrels in the lovely garden overlooking the river, strung with Chinese lanterns. But Barnaby hardly saw Phoebe, and he was only able to wish her a happy birthday in passing before she was whisked away by excited swarms of her friends. He felt like a common old bumblebee in this hive of elegance, with the queen bee far out of reach.

He did get to talk to her uncle, Edgar Thurlwell, but not by choice. Edgar collared him and sat him in a quiet corner of the parlour to expound on the virtues of his company, the Western Railroad, pleased to meet a young man who was *au fait* with the share system.

'We're going public now,' Edgar told him, puffing on his cigar. 'This dashed federalism talk has scared off a lot of investors, delayed my plans, but I'm working for the good of the country and when we get going, they'll be sorry. Damned sorry! A man must have vision to achieve anything in this world. But we're on our way now. Two of the most modern steam engines are already being shipped to Brisbane.'

'Shipping steam engines!' Barnaby was impressed. 'You'd think a ship would sink under their weight.'

'Maritime people know what they're doing. You want to mention to Mantrell that if he has any clients with spare cash about, they won't go wrong investing with the Western Railroad, but they'll have to get in early.'

'I'll mention it to him, sir.' Barnaby was happy to oblige.

They were interrupted by the Member of Parliament for Padlow, Ben Buchanan. Barnaby knew him by sight but had never met him before. Buchanan was a big blond man, well dressed, but as Mrs Mantrell often said: 'You can take the man out of the bush, but you can't take the bush out of the man.' And Buchanan was definitely a bushie, with a tanned face and big strong hands.

'A word with you, Edgar,' Buchanan said. Barnaby took the hint, but as he retreated he heard a sharp exchange between the two men and wondered what that was about.

He was home by midnight, feeling depressed. No, not depressed, he told himself as he peeled off his glad rags, more like distressed. For weeks he'd been looking forward to enjoying Phoebe's company at her party, but she'd hardly noticed him. It was then that Barnaby began to understand the depth of his feelings for Phoebe, and the next morning, instead of dwelling on his disappointment, he began to make plans to court this girl in earnest. He was known in his own field as an ambitious young man. He'd make the time to include Phoebe Thurlwell in his plans, another ambition, equally important. One of these days he'd marry her, and he'd love her madly and make her the happiest wife in the world.

To a certain extent his plan worked. Phoebe was too young to begin with to be permitted to walk out with any gentleman, without a chaperone, but nevertheless there was no shortage of beaux eager for her company.

Barnaby remained in the background, but he was never far away at parties and outings, and sooner or later, on most occasions, Phoebe would drift over to him, ostensibly for a chat, but more often to deliver her caustic comments on various members of the company. She had a wicked wit and she knew she could make Barnaby laugh, so he became her audience. And in time her confidant.

'Mother says I should encourage Richard Masefield because his people are very rich, but really, Barnaby, he always looks so pop-eyed!'

Unperturbed he smiled. 'I'm not surprised. He's not accustomed to young ladies with strong opinions.'

'So you think I'm opinionated?'

'No. But you are inclined to be rather dogmatic at times.'

'I am not! Anyway, I'm allowed to go to the Governor's Ball now that I'm eighteen, and Richard has asked to escort me. I told him I have already accepted another gentleman.'

'Who's taking you?'

'That's the trouble. No one. I lied. You have to help me out. You have to take me.'

He shook his head. 'I'm sorry, Phoebe, I can't. I haven't been invited.'

'I'll see that you are and then you have to promise to take me.'

'Very well,' he said lightly, his heart pounding. 'You do get yourself into some fixes, Phoebe.'

She threw her arms about him and kissed him on the cheek. 'Oh Barnaby, you're a darling! I hope you can dance.'

Although there was never any suggestion of them 'going together', Barnaby escorted her to various functions, usually when she was dodging a suitor, and her parents didn't seem to mind. They began to take him for granted since, to his dismay, Phoebe insisted that Barnaby was her best friend. That wasn't what he had in mind, but he dared not touch her or flirt with her, for fear of spoiling their relationship. Instead he was forced to listen to the stories of her juvenile love life, her crushes on this young man or that. Fortunately they never lasted long, but he feared the day when someone would come along and sweep Phoebe away from him.

The time was approaching when he'd have to speak up, to tell her how much he loved her, but it would have to be planned with care. She was never serious with him. They always had such fun, mixing easily with all their friends, that it would be difficult to introduce a romantic atmosphere. And what if she laughed at him? Barnaby shuddered at the thought and remained by her side. Her best friend. Dammit!

For her part Phoebe knew that Barnaby was fond of her, that he cared very much for her. When she was with him she could be herself, not the social butterfly everyone expected her to be. That became boring after a while which, she knew, was the reason she was often too outspoken or over-fond of pranks. Her mother, exasperated by her behaviour, said she was an exhibitionist and warned that she would get a name for herself.

She can talk! Phoebe thought meanly. She guessed that her mother was having an affair with Ben Buchanan, though she couldn't prove it, nor did she wish to. In fact she deliberately turned a blind eye to them, wondering if her father did the same. Nobody, except Barnaby, seemed to notice that there was a serious side to Phoebe Thurlwell, and not even to him could she confide her distress that her father was being hoodwinked by Buchanan. Her attitude to Ben Buchanan hardened and she was cool to him but never blatantly rude, worried that a wrong move on her part might alert the Doctor to the cause. Confused, she was desperately loyal to her father, who allowed his life to be ruled by his wife. He was weak, and no match for Lalla's tantrums.

Sometimes, in a fit of pique, Phoebe considered shouting at him to wake up to himself. To take note of what was happening between those two fakers, but she knew she'd come off second-best. That the Doctor would refuse to listen, would be angry with her, and that Lalla would win, pushing Phoebe further away from her father's affections.

Wasn't he already echoing her mother's words? That it was time she found a nice young man and settled down to married life.

Phoebe accosted her mother on the subject. 'You'd like that, wouldn't you? You'd like me to be married off, out of the way.'

'I don't know what you're talking about. Every parent has a responsibility to see their daughters well placed and happily married.'

'And in my case, out of this house, where I see too much for my own good. Or for your good, should I say?'

Lalla twisted about from her dressing table. 'What an imagination you have, Phoebe. Really, you're quite impossible. I'm very proud of you, even though your behaviour is far from ladylike at times. You've blossomed into a beautiful young woman.' Phoebe noticed that Lalla glanced in the mirror as she spoke, admiring her own features as if satisfied her daughter had managed to maintain the standard.

'Several young men, eligible young men,' Lalla continued, 'have already made it plain that they'd like to court you, *and* their mothers approve.'

'Like who?'

'Like the Masefield boy, and John Sherrington and Gavin Fortescue. *His* mother has hinted as much to me, letting me know that Gavin will inherit their big sheep property in New South Wales. He's their only son.'

'Richard Masefield is a dope, John is a drunkard, and Gavin is frightfully conceited.'

'Well then, we might take a holiday in Sydney . . .'

'I won't be touted around Sydney!'

'Oh, suit yourself!' Lalla smiled. 'Perhaps you'd prefer to remain a spinster.'

'I could marry Barnaby Glasson,' Phoebe threatened.

Her mother looked over at her serenely. 'Oh no you won't. You use him. You hide behind him like a hedge and he puts up with it. The Barnabys of this world are content with crumbs from the table. Why do you think I've allowed the fellow to visit so often? He won't compromise you. You're safe with him until the right man comes along.'

Phoebe ran and hid in her room in tears. Her mother's incisive remarks cut deeply. She was ashamed that Lalla had seen through her and hurt that Barnaby had been so demeaned, knowing that she was the cause.

'Who else is coming?' Barnaby asked her the following week as they boarded the *River Queen* for a twilight cruise.

'No one,' she said. 'I just thought it would be nice to go somewhere on our own for a change, and I've always wanted to take one of these cruises ever since they started.'

'Good-oh, we'll try it out. And Phoebe Thurlwell can announce to all and sundry whether it's a good idea or a bad idea.'

Phoebe had dressed with special care. After trying several outfits she had decided on a soft silk of blush pink with a lace bodice to accentuate her small waist and well-defined figure. Her fair hair was dressed into a fluffy fringe and swept into long curls at the back. To protect it from the wind, she added a gossamer scarf dotted with tiny beads to pick up the night lights. She was looking her very best, and Barnaby didn't fail to notice.

'Phoebe! You're looking absolutely beautiful tonight. Everyone is staring at you.'

'They are not,' she lied modestly, and sat with him on the outer deck in the warm night air as the boat slid away from the wharf. 'They're serving champagne,' she whispered to him. 'Why don't we have some too?'

'It's expensive,' he warned. 'It's not included in the ticket.'

'Oh Barnaby, I really want some. Let me pay.'

'No. I shouldn't be so mean. I'm celebrating tonight, so it's my treat.'

'What are you celebrating?'

'I passed my tests and I'm a fully fledged solicitor.'

'That's wonderful!' She kissed him on the cheek. 'I'm so thrilled for you.'

'And what's more, I'm shortly to take up a position on the staff of the Attorney-General. As a legal adviser.'

'That's fantastic. But what does Mr Mantrell think about this?'

'He's given me his blessing. He's delighted that one of his protégés should achieve such a prestigious post.'

As the cruise progressed they drank champagne; they laughed and talked and demolished two plates of delicious savouries that were set before them; and they listened to the sweet music of a gypsy violinist.

Barnaby, excited about his new post, was still talking about it when the boat began its return journey. The office was next door to that of the Premier, Sir Samuel Griffiths, so he'd be moving in exalted circles. Apparently his brief would be to concentrate on constitutional law, with the state moving closer to the federal union. 'We have to be very careful that we maintain our state's individual rights while moving to federation,' Barnaby told her, and Phoebe tried to pay attention while preparing her own, very important speech.

But in the end she didn't make a speech. Maybe it was the champagne, or her own nervousness, but finally she simply blurted it out. She hardly heard him telling her that he intended to visit his parents before he took up the new appointment. They had a small farm on the coast, only about eighty miles north of Brisbane. He wanted to tell them himself, they'd be thrilled. Much better than giving them the news in a letter.

'Barnaby,' she said, 'why don't we get married?'

He stopped mid-sentence and stared at her. 'What did you say?'

'You heard me,' she whispered, fumbling nervously with her scarf.

He thought she was teasing him so he managed a grin. 'I didn't realize you'd be so impressed by my new status. What will you say if I end up Attorney-General?'

'I'm serious. Don't joke with me.'

Barnaby looked at her intently. He should have been overjoyed that his dream of marrying this lovely girl was coming true at last, but instead, logic told him that this wasn't real. Icy beads of sweat pierced his forehead as he fought against a powerful urge to take her in his arms and say: 'Yes. Yes, of course we will.'

Instead he took the hands that were still fluttering with that scarf and held them still. 'What brought this on?' he asked her gently.

She was defensive. 'I thought you loved me.'

'Phoebe, I do love you. God knows, I've been wanting to tell you that for a long time. And I'll hate myself for saying this, but do you love me? Tell me the truth.'

'I've offended you now. I shouldn't have been so forward. You'll think I'm an absolute ass.'

'No I won't, and you haven't answered my question.'

She pulled away from him in a huff. 'How do I know? I think I do. Of course I do, or I wouldn't have asked such a stupid question and made a fool of myself.'

'Phoebe, love. You couldn't make a fool of yourself with me. I just have a feeling that this is one of your spur-of-the-moment ideas that you're likely to regret tomorrow.'

'Oh, marvellous! You're refusing me!'

'No I'm not. I'd marry you tomorrow but I think you need more time to think about this.' He didn't add that he was afraid it was the wine talking: she'd been nervy all evening, tossing down the champagne as if it were cordial.

She shrugged. 'All right. If you say so, I'll think on it.'

'And you don't have to look so miserable. Give me a smile.'

They walked to the aft rails of the ship to watch the white wake disturbing the velvety waters. Both were immersed in their own thoughts, Barnaby depressed that he'd passed up the opportunity of his life and Phoebe upset that she'd made an awful mess of things. She hadn't expected him to ask her point-blank if she loved him, and she wasn't sure that she did. She liked Barnaby. Wasn't that good enough?

A woman in a group behind them laughed, and Phoebe jumped. It sounded so much like her mother.

When they stepped ashore, Barnaby took her arm. 'How about we have another talk when I come back from my holiday?' he asked her, his voice reassuring.

'Yes, Barnaby. Yes, thank you,' she said, but her voice was distant. More of a sigh.

Another guest who never forgot Phoebe Thurlwell's party was Benjamin Buchanan MLA, and he wasn't likely to forgive Edgar Thurlwell for humiliating him.

Until then he'd been at peace with the world. His financial situation had greatly improved, even though the drought was still menacing his cattle station and causing, according to Clara, drastic stock losses.

'Sooner or later, the rains will come,' he'd told her, refusing to allow her to sell the herds at bedrock prices. Born and bred in the north, where the wet season was a matter of course, he stubbornly refused to accept that droughts could last for years.

In a few short years Ben Buchanan had become a power to be reckoned with in Parliament, even though he was still in the ranks of opposition to the Premier's party. He was a confident speaker, popular among his colleagues as well as with the mining and grazing interests whom he supported with a tenacity that brought him accolades from both sides of the House.

Even the Premier had called him in for a chat.

'We've got a lot in common, Buchanan. You ought to join our team.'

Ben was flattered by the invitation, but wary. 'If you'll forgive me, sir, your determination to tie Queensland into federation with the other states is too big a risk for me. Surely you know how unpopular such a move is. The arguments have been going on so long now everyone is sick of it. You're flogging a dead horse.'

'I know your people oppose the concept, but I wish you could see the wider picture. Instead of separate states, we could become one single country. A nation! Australia could take its place on the world stage and all of our people would be known as Australians. I shudder when I hear our gentlemen overseas referring to themselves as Anglo-Australians.'

'Why not? That's what we are. My parents are of British stock.'

'But you were born here, son. This is your country. Why won't you stand up for it?'

Ben had heard all this before. He sat through the lecture and then politely excused himself. Griffiths was becoming so obsessed with this wild dream that he was prepared to sell out Queensland to the more powerful southern states. To join his team, Ben was now convinced, would be electoral suicide.

It amused him, at Phoebe's party, to find himself much in demand with the ladies. And there were some real beauties among them. He went out of his way to be entertaining and to dance with several of them, not unaware of Lalla's angry glances.

Finally she managed to get close enough to him to complain. 'You're making a fool of yourself, flirting with those silly women.'

'My dear,' he murmured, 'I can hardly be seen to be spending time with you. We have to be careful.'

But his mistress would not be placated. 'You could spend more time with the gentlemen in the smoking room and consolidate your position.'

'I don't need to,' he smiled. 'I'm entitled to a break. By next week I'll be Leader of the Opposition. I've got the numbers.'

'In that motley lot? Don't bank on it.'

He bowed to a lady passing by. 'You're out of touch, my darling,' he murmured to Lalla.

'Am I?' she snapped. 'Then why is Edgar backing Royce Davies?'

Edgar was sitting talking to one of Phoebe's young friends, Barnaby Glasson, when Ben challenged him, causing Glasson to depart very smartly.

'How dare you support Royce Davies as Leader of the Opposition?' Ben demanded. 'The man's a socialist.'

Edgar looked at him coolly. 'The man doesn't know what he is. He wouldn't know a socialist if he sat on one.'

'Then let me tell you. A socialist will let you build your railroads and then take them over in the name of the people without so much as a by-your-leave.'

'Dear me, Ben,' Edgar sighed, puffing on his cigar. 'How you do go on. We'd have to have a socialist government for that to happen, and it's simply not possible here. I don't know why you're so upset.'

'Upset!' Ben lowered his voice as he dropped into the chair beside Edgar. 'You knew I've been lobbying for leader. You're deliberately undermining me.'

'And have you got the numbers?'

'Yes. But your interference will split the vote. I could lose.'

'That's a chance we'll have to take. I have it on good authority that Davies is leaning towards the government party. Now we can't let that happen, can we? You never know who Royce might take with him.'

Ben was furious. 'This is the business of Members of Parliament. It's nothing to do with you. I won't have you interfering like this.'

Edgar ground out his cigar grimly. 'You watch your step, Buchanan. And don't talk to me about interference. It wasn't interference when I bought your seat for you. It wasn't interference when I put you on the board of Southern Coal Mining, from which I hear you're doing very well indeed.'

'I appreciate that, but—'

'Let me finish,' Edgar grated. 'Don't you ever talk interference to me, you bloody pipsqueak! You're holding a swag of my railroad stocks, thanks to my generosity, and since we're about to go public, you're in on the ground floor. I should expect some gratitude.'

'And you're welcome to it,' Ben snapped. 'But if I'm Leader of the Opposition, Edgar, you'd have a much safer run than taking a chance on Royce Davies.'

'True. But Ben, you're already on my team. I need Davies roped and tied. Out of harm's way. He's so excited he's already buying his first decent suit.'

'And you consider making him Leader of the Opposition will tie him down?'

'Naturally. The man's practically grovelling. For all his fine talk he's as much a self-seeker as the rest of you.'

The insult was so blatant, Ben was taken aback. He was glad to cover the moment by accepting a drink from a tray proffered by a passing waiter.

'Don't take it so hard, Ben,' Edgar grinned. 'You can be his deputy.'

'The hell I will,' Ben exploded.

Edgar shrugged. 'Please yourself. It's all or nothing. I put you on that board and I can just as easily have you removed.' He leaned forward. 'You wouldn't want the identity of your mistress worded around, would you? I mean, the secret's safe with me but my dear brother is very popular in Brisbane and I hate to think what that mother-in-law of yours would have to say. That old harridan might come after you with a shotgun.' He waved to a couple who'd just entered the parlour to come and join him. 'Now you run along, Ben, and enjoy yourself.'

Now he was deputy leader of an opposition composed of independents with little in common, and less cohesion, thanks to a total lack of direction emanating, or not emanating, from Royce Davies, who was too busy basking in this undeserved limelight.

Ben knew he was trapped in Edgar's web, and it became of paramount importance for him to escape, to find ways to shake off the man's influence. His first move was to disassociate himself from Lalla. Their affair was over, he told her, without giving her a reason, and he steadfastly ignored her notes and pleading letters, though keeping them on file for a rainy day. He gave up the lease of his apartment, brought Clara back to town for a while, and, to her mother's delight, purchased a house only a few doors from Belle Foster's mansion in the sedate suburb of Hamilton, on the town side of the river. During the winter recess he retired to his cattle station and worked harder than he'd ever done, sinking wells in a frantic search for water, shocked by the poverty of the land. He sent drovers with great herds of cattle along what they called the long paddock, roadside feeding, hoping to fatten the animals up. All of which impressed Belle Foster, as he had intended, because his only hope of regaining control of his own career was to rearrange his finances.

He considered confiding in Belle. Telling her that he'd been threatened by Edgar, that if he didn't jump to attention for Thurlwell on political matters then he'd be removed from the board of Southern Coal Mining. But she was such a bombastic woman she'd probably go charging over there to tear a strip off Edgar. And that would be disastrous. He shuddered to think of Belle's reaction if she heard of his affair with Lalla.

Finally it was Belle herself who gave him the chance to make a move.

'Why don't you give up this politics business, Ben,' she said, 'and concentrate on your property?'

'I can't do that. I don't think you realize, Belle, how bad this drought is. Clara keeps up a brave face because she loves Fairmont Station, but it's draining me financially. And you can't sell land that's hardly showing a blade of grass. It's important for me to remain in Parliament: that gives me the status to be appointed to a board like Southern Coal Mining.'

'Yes, I suppose so,' she admitted. 'I hope that as a director you're properly remunerated.'

'That's another problem,' he said, and began to relate the lie he'd been rehearsing for some time. 'I have a very uncomfortable feeling that there are some peculiar dealings within the membership of that board.'

'What do you mean, Peculiar? Use plain language. Are you saying dishonest?'

'It could easily be,' he confided. 'I'm not privy to enough information to speak up without being sued, so it's a real worry for me.'

'Good God! Then you must disassociate yourself from them immediately.'

'With the cattle industry in such straits I can hardly do that. Southern pays its directors well. Maybe too well,' he added darkly.

'Stars above!' she grumbled. 'I don't know how you young people get yourselves into these situations! You are to resign immediately from that board. Call it pressure of business. I'll have to see what can be done.'

Within weeks of departing SCM, he was appointed a director of the Queensland Pastoral Syndicate and then gained an equally impressive position in the successful Brisbane Brewing Company.

He was living comfortably these days. Belle had appointed herself his hostess in the absence of his wife, relieving Ben of the expense of entertaining. He found her dinner parties, soirées and conversaziones, though lavish, deadly dull – she did not have the flair of Lalla Thurlwell – but since she was enjoying herself he was resigned to his new role of dutiful son-in-law. In public, at least.

With extra finance available, Ben quietly bought more and more shares in the Western Railroad Company, from the day Edgar listed it on the stock exchange. In a stroke of luck he had met an American visitor at the House who had confirmed all that Edgar had told them about those railroads.

'You can't go wrong investin' in railroads, sir,' he'd said. 'Got a hefty slice myself. They ain't just transport, they're money-making machines. Gold on wheels.'

His renewed interest pleased Edgar, who didn't even comment on Ben's resignation from the board of Southern Coal Mining, so he was able to remain on good terms with the Thurlwell family, having managed at last to persuade Lalla that they were both now too well known to continue their affair, even though he missed her dreadfully. And that was another lie: he was secretly glad to be free of her possessive attitude. His life had taken a turn for the better, and it was much more exciting to enjoy the pleasures of the ladies at The Blue Heaven, knowing that the proprietor, a woman called Goldie, was the soul of discretion.

Goldie had a large stable of attractive girls, including, for variety, two luscious Aborigines, two tiny Chinese girls, and a Japanese contortionist.

Buchanan was only one of the many politicians who visited The Blue Heaven but his preference for the Aborigine girls caught Goldie's attention and stirred her memory. Where had she seen him before? It wasn't important, it just irritated her that she couldn't remember. One day it would come to her, though. Goldie prided herself on her memory.

Chapter Four

Benny was out! He couldn't believe it. He'd been removed to the Brisbane jail with no explanation and shoved into an overcrowded cell, waiting, as he thought, for assignment to another bloody back-breaking job. But he was glad of the rest and slept as much as possible on his blanket in a corner, reacting angrily to any disturbance.

The other prisoners soon learned it was unwise to bother this morose half-caste. Big Tom Jenkins found out the hard way when he began to harass the new arrival, who was taking advantage of the hour in the yard to doze in the sun.

'Is this bloke a deaf-mute?' he asked the others, since Benny was ignoring his teasing attempts at conversation. 'He never talks! Say something, nigger!'

When he was still ignored he shoved at Benny with his boot, sending him sprawling.

Ben's reaction was so fast, prisoners and warders alike collected to watch the fun, as in one swift movement the burly Jenkins was hurled to the ground by the new inmate.

Shocked, Jenkins came up fighting, but the half-caste was ready for him. He grabbed his tormentor's arm, twisting it behind his back until Jenkins screamed in pain.

'Now get away from me!' he shouted, pushing Jenkins into the crowd.

Afraid of losing face as one of the toughest prisoners in the yard, Jenkins tried again, swinging punches at Beckman who retaliated with a hammer-like blow to the big man's stomach, sending him crashing, winded, to the ground.

'Get him!' the other prisoners shouted gleefully, expecting that the half-caste would finish off the bully with a few well-placed kicks. But surprisingly Beckman gave Tom his hand and helped him up as the crowd dispersed, disappointed.

'I'm sorry,' he said to Jenkins. 'I've taken too many beltings myself to want to hand out the same to anyone else.'

'Jesus! You *can* talk!' Jenkins puffed as he struggled to his feet. 'But you don't bloody fight fair.'

'What's fair?' Beckman said grimly.
'Nought, lad, nought!' Jenkins laughed.

The message had come from Jim Donovan in a letter that he'd toiled over for days with a scrap of paper and a stub of a pencil. This time he couldn't ask anyone to write for him because the matter was very private. While he guessed most of his fellow prisoners knew what had happened to Benny, he didn't want to resurrect the story. Nor could he tell anyone outside about it without embarrassing the lad, who was still taking it hard. Too hard. He wouldn't even talk to Jim these days. He never seemed to talk to anyone.

So Jim wrote to Biddy as best he could. He said she should see the people next door and tell them the boy was sick. That seemed the best excuse. And that they should try to get his sentence ended. Terminated was the right word, he knew, but it was too troublesome for his pencil.

It was only a few lines but it worried Biddy. She didn't really know Mrs Beckman. Phoebe did – she called in there occasionally – but Biddy couldn't show the note to her employer's daughter and admit that her own father was in jail for murder. Even though she liked Phoebe she was still very wary of the upper classes; you just never knew how far you could trust them.

For a few days, she did nothing. Then her conscience got the better of her and she slipped away one night to do as her father had requested.

Poor Biddy was nervous. 'You won't tell anyone me dad's in there too, will you?' she begged the old woman.

'No, dear, of course not. Your father must be a very kind man, no matter what he's done.'

'Is there anything you can do?' Biddy asked.

'If our Ben is sick I have to,' Mrs Beckman said. 'But what? I've spent years trying to get him released.'

'What about Mr Glasson? Miss Phoebe's friend. She says he knows your grandson.'

'Yes. First thing in the morning I'll go to see him.'

'You won't let him tell anyone about this note? It could get me, and me dad, into trouble.'

'Don't worry. That won't happen.' Mrs Beckman burst into tears. 'I feel so useless. I feel I've let Diamond down. Ever since she died and that terrible thing happened to our Ben, I haven't spent much of her money. It's all for him. I've earned money making these silk flowers for ladies' hats.' She showed Biddy a table covered in the silken evidence of her work. 'And I make baby clothes.'

Biddy picked up an exquisite baby's christening dress and examined the embroidery. 'Oh, Mrs Beckman! It's beautiful.'

She was so busy admiring Mrs Beckman's handiwork and wishing she could sew as well – why, she'd open a shop! – that she didn't register the old woman's reference to Diamond's money until she was on her way home, sneaking around the back to the servants' quarters. What was it she'd said? Diamond's money? That didn't make sense. Diamond had been black. None of them had any money. Maybe, Biddy reasoned, she'd been so beset with her own fears that she'd misunderstood. But she'd done her duty and that was that.

Barnaby was busy – this was his last week with Joseph Mantrell's office – but Mrs Beckman was so upset he agreed to see her.

'Whatever the problem is,' he told her, 'I'm sure Mr Mantrell can handle it for you.'

'No, no, no,' she whispered. 'I have a message and it's secret, and I want *you* to investigate. You must do this for me. I have been told that Ben is sick so we have to have him released to a hospital.'

'All right,' he said. 'I'll see what I can find out.'

Several days later he called on Mrs Beckman after he left the office. 'I don't know whether this is good news or bad. Ben is not sick, in fact, I'm told he's in extremely good health.'

'That's not true!' she cried. 'They're lying! I will show you a note, but you must promise not to say where it came from.'

Barnaby read the scrawl. 'Who wrote this?'

'His name is Jim Donovan.'

'And who is Biddy? It's written to someone called Biddy.'

'Never you mind. I trust this man better than the jailers. I can pay you, Mr Glasson, you must find out more.'

By the time Barnaby located Jim Donovan, he had taken his leave of Mantrell's office and should have left to visit his parents. He decided a few extra days in Brisbane wouldn't matter. He hitched a ride on a barge travelling downstream to Pitts Landing, where a disinterested foreman told him that if he hung about, the prisoner, Donovan, should be along with a load of sandstone.

Barnaby felt uncomfortable standing leisurely in the shade while haggard prisoners in leg-irons shambled back and forth, loading the barge with sandstone blocks. He hoped young Beckman wasn't among them. He walked up the track and hailed the next lorry driver. 'Do you know Jim Donovan?'

'That'd be meself,' the man replied and Barnaby took stock of him. He was a slight man with bristly grey hair and a weather-lined face, but for a felon, a murderer he'd been warned, he had a gentle smile. 'What can I be doing for ye?'

'I wanted to talk to you about Ben Beckman.'

'Ah, you do now? Then you'd better go on back to the landing. I can't stop here or the narks'll come chargin' up like I might be trying to steal their golden rocks.'

He slapped the reins and the two big draught horses strained on their way again.

Donovan had little time to spare. He hurried over to Barnaby as other prisoners began unloading his lorry. 'Who might you be?'

'I'm Beckman's lawyer.'

Donovan raised a shaggy eyebrow. 'The devil you are?' he said, startled. 'I wouldn't have thought the lad could call up someone like you. But more's the better. You'd better do your job, sir, and get him released. He's real sick.'

'Mr Donovan, I've made enquiries and I am informed that Beckman is in good health. Now what's all this about?'

The prisoner looked about him warily. 'If anyone asks, you tell them you bin talking to me about my case. Right?'

'Very well. But I want the truth.'

'Then you shall have it, but Benny won't thank you for the knowing. It's not somethin' any man wants spread about. Benny is sick, sir. He's sick in the head from despairin'. I been in here a good while and I seen the signs. He ain't gonna last, and that's a cryin' shame an' all.'

'Is he going mad?' To Barnaby it seemed that prison life could send a young boy like Ben quite crazy.

'Not that you'd notice. But he's had trouble, more than the usual. He's strong enough to stand up to the flogging and that hellhole of solitary . . .'

'Oh, dear God!' Barnaby groaned, remembering the fresh-faced boy he'd last seen years back.

'Ah, but it's the other business,' Donovan said.

Barnaby was shocked and disgusted when Jim told him in detail what had happened to Ben in the warder's hut. He shook his head in disbelief.

''Tis true now,' Donovan insisted. 'And I have to leave it up to you to get that boy free. He's worth savin'. But you keep in mind that's not somethin' he'd thank me for telling you. Now I've got to get going.'

Barnaby took some tins of tobacco from his pocket. 'These are for you, Mr Donovan. And thank you. I'll do my best.'

All the way home Barnaby worried at the problem, and he seemed to hear the woman, Diamond, insisting that there was a way. Her words were ringing in his ears: 'Fifty pounds will buy my son a friend in the police station.' And: 'You are simply arranging justice.'

While he'd been working for Mantrell he couldn't interfere, he wouldn't have dared. But for a few weeks now, he was his own man. The very thought of what he might do made him nervous. He tried to tell himself that perhaps he should wait until he was working in the Attorney-

General's department and go through the proper channels, but that would take time. And if he failed, his name would be tied to the case and it would be too damaging to his career to even consider bribes. Even the word made him shiver. But so did the thought of that dead woman, as if she were at his side, a powerful image, far from benign. Haunting him.

Feeling like a criminal himself, he spoke to Mrs Beckman about the possibility of obtaining Ben's release. 'It's a faint hope but I could try,' he said.

'Then do so,' she replied. 'Straight away. If my boy is sick then he should be here with me.'

Barnaby coughed, cleared his throat and finally came out with it. 'What I have in mind is not legal, ma'am.'

'So it was legal to jail a good boy all these years?'

He sighed. 'Mrs Beckman, it will take money. A lot of money, I think. And please, be sure it isn't for me. I don't want a penny. We'll have to be cautious and you must think on this very carefully.'

'How much?' she asked, her voice as determined as he'd ever heard.

'I know a policeman who might help for fifty pounds, but I'm led to believe these amounts go down the line. It could be more.'

'Make it five hundred,' she said grimly. 'And if you need more you shall have it.'

Dolan had been promoted to sergeant by this, and when Barnaby invited him for a quiet drink at the Valley pub, the lawyer also realized that the man was a Catholic. He would have to break his word to Donovan, for if Dolan was a family man, telling him the whole story might be the most effective way.

'How's your family?' he asked, fishing for information.

'They're all fine, thank you.'

'Do you have any sons?'

'Four strapping boys,' Dolan said proudly.

'Good. Then I've got a story for you.'

As Barnaby had hoped, Dolan was outraged.

'By Jasus! The bastard! I never knew that about Bull Baker, may he rot in hell.'

'Yes. We can forget about him, but the boy he raped is distraught.'

'And wouldn't you be yourself? By God, if any of them buggers touched one of my kids . . .'

'Then you of all people must understand that we have to get him out.'

'Aha! I wondered what this would be about. Who's the kid?'

'The same one. Ben Beckman.'

'Do you know what you're asking? I've been hearing of him. He's a bolter.'

'Not any more, Ray. Baker's broken his spirit. I mean, the kid only went in for smashing windows in the first damn place. He doesn't deserve this. No man's son does,' Barnaby added for emphasis. 'And his people are prepared to pay to rescue him from this happening again. But they want that story kept quiet.'

'For sure,' Dolan agreed. 'It might be done but it'll be costly.'

'Fifty for you for starters. And whatever you need from then on.'

'They must be made of money.'

'Wouldn't you do the same for a son of yours if you could?'

'Indeed I would. A magistrate will have to be oiled and given a reason.'

'That's easy enough. Parole for good behaviour. Another fifty for someone at the jail to send up a good report on him. Leave nothing to chance. Just keep my name out of it, for God's sake.'

'What's in it for you?'

'Nothing. I knew his late mother. And I get the feeling from up there that she'll strike me dead if I don't rescue her kid now that I know what happened to him.'

Dolan laughed. 'I reckon she's got you spooked. How much have you got on you?'

'Two hundred pounds.'

'That ought to do it.' Dolan drained his ale and got up to leave. 'Another drink for my mate here,' he told the barman, dropping some coins on the counter. He turned back and tapped Barnaby on the shoulder. 'You've got a lot to learn, mate. This one I would have done for nothin', but I can't speak for the rest.'

She didn't recognize him, this dusty, barefoot tramp who knocked and stood humbly at her door.

She was just about to ask him his business when the tears came flooding. 'Mother of God, it's my Ben!' she wept. 'And to think you had to knock at your own door! But you're so big now . . .' Oma was blubbering in a confusion of pain and joy. 'Why! You must be more than six foot tall, but then your mother . . .'

Without a word he put his arms about her and hugged her to him, comforting her, savouring the almost forgotten aroma of lightly scented soap and the magical clean scent of this house.

As they sat at the kitchen table, Oma did most of the talking. Ben was content to sit and listen while he munched on blessed cold chicken and thick slices of fresh bread. In truth, he couldn't think of much to say. What could he say to this sweet woman about those years that he'd now put behind him, except, dully: 'It was all right.'

But Oma was all for action. 'First I run you a good hot bath and you wash off all that dust. And then you have a good sleep while I make you a decent dinner. You're too thin, I'll have to fatten you up. And Ben, you'll need clothes. I'll have a tailor here to fit you out.'

'I can go to a shop, Oma.'

'No, no, no. You will have the best, just to please me. Now you go inside. I've kept your room just as you left it.'

A bed, he thought. A real bed. At last.

After soaking in the bath he slept the night through, but she didn't disturb him, and he woke at dawn, anxious and disoriented. It would be a long time before Ben could shake off the demons that invaded his dreams, resurrecting the worst of his prison days and leaving him shaking and unnerved.

Even with a wardrobe that any man would be proud of – new boots and suits, and jackets with dark velvet lapels, and silk shirts, some with ruffles – Ben had no inclination to leave the house until Oma insisted he go out and enjoy himself.

'I'm so proud of you. With a bit of condition on you, Ben, you're looking very handsome. You must start to live properly again.' After some persuasion he agreed, not wanting to distress her by reminding her that he didn't have any friends. He didn't know anyone any more.

'I was wondering if you could lend me some money, Oma. I'd like to buy a horse.'

'Lend?' she cried. 'What is this? All the money is yours. This is your house too. It was all Diamond's money we lived on. From the gold she found, remember? She only left it in trust for me, to mind it for you. You're not poor, Ben.'

He was so numbed the first week, with the tailor and his apprentice hovering about, he hadn't given a thought to payment, and now he recalled a cryptic comment from one of the warders in the jail that he'd been 'bought' out.

'Did you give bribes to get me out?' he asked.

'I certainly did, and I'd do it again,' she smiled.

'Thank you, Oma. I'm grateful to you. But the lawyers must have cost plenty too. And you had to live all these years. How much is left?'

'With the shares, good solid investments, Mr Mantrell said, you've got about eleven thousand pounds. It's in my name but it's all yours, Ben.'

He nodded, stunned. It was a fortune. Hard to comprehend. He wondered what the Thurlwells were worth. A lot more, he guessed.

Oma misunderstood his failure to respond, and her face fell. 'I did the best I could. I'll turn it all over to you right away.'

He kissed her. 'No, Oma, forgive me. I was thinking of something else. Leave it all in your name. I just meant I have to earn my own living.' Earn more, he meant, a lot more. Somehow.

'Then we'll call it our money, my dear. And if you need any or all of it, just tell me. You can't walk about with no money in your pockets.'

Oma had turned Diamond's room into a sewing room. For her hobbies, she said. To Ben the room was sad and depressing. When he was feeling strong enough to remind himself of his mother he went out to the cliffs, in a deliberate act of farewell. The Aborigines he'd known in prison had spoken of this ritual. It was time for him to finish his 'crying'.

Winds came storming in from the sea, carrying scuds of rain, but he stood his ground, revelling in his freedom. Flocks of birds screeched overhead, racing for shelter, and below him the big river still trundled on its way. The magic had gone. It no longer interested him.

With a sense of relief he realized he could think of Diamond now with pride, without that deadening misery, and conceded that the Aborigines were probably right. But there was another side to Ben Beckman. He turned to stare at the imposing mansion over the fence. 'I promise you, Diamond, they'll pay. Oh, by Christ, they'll pay!'

O'Neill's saddlery had gone but the stables were still there, much bigger now, surrounded by horse paddocks with white-painted fences.

Ben walked under the stone archway to the cobbled yard, where a young stablehand stopped him. 'You lookin' for someone, mister?'

'No. I was wondering if I could buy a horse here.'

'Hey, Cash,' the lad yelled, 'there's a bloke here wants to buy a horse.'

Cash O'Neill emerged from the office. He hadn't changed; he was still that curly-haired Irishman with the villainous twinkle in his eyes.

'A horse is it, sir. You've come to the right place. What was it you're wanting to pay?'

'I haven't decided yet.'

'And that's the best way to go. Now come down here with me.'

Ben followed, and then stood back while the stablehand led out a magnificent black stallion that pranced and reared, probably irritated at being disturbed from his rest after an early-morning run. And probably, he grinned to himself, the most expensive horse in the place.

'Have you ever seen a better mount?' Cash was saying. 'A man's horse, this lad, full of fire he is. A three-year-old, take you anywhere.'

'No. He's too flashy.' The last thing Ben needed was to draw attention to himself. 'I just want a mount.'

'Never fear. I've never let a customer down. Lenny, bring up Major.' He turned to Ben. 'A big feller like you, you don't need a pony. Major's a four-year-old but he's got plenty of stamina.' He stopped and stared. 'Do I know you?'

'You did. I used to work for you.'

Cash stood back to scrutinize this customer. 'By all that's holy! You're Benny. Benny Beckman! Where have you been all these years?'

Ben hesitated, but it was no use lying. Brisbane was a small town. 'In jail,' he admitted quietly.

'So you were! My old man, God rest his soul, was bloody upset about that. He reckoned you didn't get a fair deal.'

'He's dead?'

'Yes. A heart attack. Two years ago next month. I'm the boss now. I got rid of that bloody saddlery and expanded the stables. What do you think of my place?'

'Very impressive. Are you training racehorses now?'

'Sure I am. The brutes keep me poor but I love 'em.'

Lenny brought up a chestnut horse.

'This is Major. He's a good horse, Benny, I wouldn't sell you a dud. But he's got a bit of brumby in him so don't fall for his smilin' eyes. If you're not watching he's likely to take a bite out of you. His price is thirty.'

'You mean he's not properly broke?' Ben paused. 'Make it twenty-five.'

'For a mate, done.'

In the office they settled the deal, and Ben also bought a rug, saddle and bridle for the horse. 'I'll have to keep him here for a while,' he said. 'There aren't any stables where I live.'

Cash nodded. 'That'll be fine. Five bob a week bed and board. You know the drill. Nothing but the best here.' He produced a whisky bottle. 'Have a drink.'

'I don't drink,' Ben said.

Cash laughed. 'I don't suppose they've got a bar in jail. But you can have one now. Ease up, Benny, you're too tense.'

'No. I saw enough in the prisons of what grog can do to my people.'

'Your people! That's a laugh. You're more white than black. I wouldn't be wanting to offend you, there's no doubt you've got the touch of the tar-brush but you're too light-coloured to be calling yourself a blackfeller.'

Ben was grateful to Cash for his honesty, but he couldn't agree. 'My mother was black and proud of it, so I wouldn't let her down.'

'And your father was white.' Cash was curious. 'Don't you feel a loyalty to him too?'

Ben sat back, surprised. 'I don't know. I never thought about him. He died when I was very young.'

By the time Cash had downed his third whisky he was in an expansive mood and Ben was in no hurry to leave. He had a friend, at least for this short time, and he was loath to terminate such a pleasure.

'So what are you doing now?' Cash asked. 'You look as if jail didn't hurt you none, and them clothes don't come cheap.'

'My grandmother paid for them. But Cash, can I ask you something? How do I make money?'

'Not as a stablehand, if that's what you're thinkin'.'

'No, real money. I've been walking about the town, finding my way again, and there's a lot of rich people out there. How do they do it?'

'Buggered if I know,' Cash said. 'I'm up to my ears in debt. I'd never admit it to anyone else, but the old man was right. Backing horses is like dropping money in a deep hole. How come a man can have so much fun losing money?'

'I don't know,' Ben said, bewildered. He didn't understand how a man could own fine stables like this and still be poor.

'I've got a few ideas,' Cash said at last, 'and I could do with a partner. Let's go out and have a good time and we'll talk about it.'

That was how they ended up at The Blue Heaven, with Ben blushing as he was introduced to all those girls, and Cash laughing his head off at his friend's embarrassment. It was more like a party, with people singing at the piano or lounging about enjoying the exciting company in the crowded parlours. Ben did take some wine to boost his courage to go with a girl called Lily, and she was marvellous! He paid for triple time for her to stay with him, because in the luxury of her arms he was able to obliterate a bad memory. Though not the circumstances that had placed him in that trap.

'What a man!' Lily boasted when he came downstairs with her. 'You will come again, won't you, Benny darling? And you'll ask for me?'

Cash didn't mind the wait, he was enjoying the company too. He introduced Ben to the madam, Goldie.

That was another surprise. Ben found a quiet moment to speak to Goldie. 'I never had a chance to thank you, ma'am. I remember you came to my mother's funeral.'

'Who was your mother?'

'Her name was Diamond.'

Goldie wilted. 'Ah, you dear love. Your mother was my best friend. We had some hard times and some good times but she was a fine woman and as straight as they come. You ever need anything, Benny, you come to me.'

Goldie studied him, and when Buchanan arrived, demanding one of the black girls as usual and making straight for the stairs, she placed the politician at last. Her memory hadn't let her down at all. Buchanan, a cattleman from the north. The white man who'd been with Diamond in Cooktown. The love of her life.

As she watched the young man with Cash O'Neill she saw the resemblance, and she began to tot up the years. She was certain that this was the son of Ben Buchanan. It had to be. Diamond had given the child the same name as the father. But the two men had passed without a sign of recognition.

That wasn't unusual; maybe Diamond had never told the kid. Or the father. That'd be a waste of time. And no one would know that better than Diamond.

It was all very interesting but Goldie was, as ever, discreet. She kept her suppositions to herself. But if push ever came to shove she'd be on the side of Diamond's son. She didn't like Buchanan, he was rough – at times brutal – with the girls. Last time that had happened she'd warned him off and made him pay for the girl's medical treatment.

Diamond's lover and son were both worth watching.

The two men rode west, leading a packhorse, full of eager enthusiasm for this great adventure.

It had been Ben's idea in the first place. He simply wanted to get away, to ride out there into the wide open spaces, to nowhere in particular, just to wash away forever the rattle of chains and a lingering claustrophobia.

And Cash decided to join him. Word had it that there were herds of brumbies running wild outside the town of Dalby, and Cash was determined to round some of them up. 'It's only about a hundred miles to Dalby. We could set up camp in the bush, build a few fences and trap them. Water's short out there, they say. If we can find a waterhole we can't miss.'

'But how do we bring in wild horses?'

'We only need to break them into halters and keep them hobbled at night. Besides, a good horse-breaker only needs three weeks to get them used to humans. We can spare the time.'

'But what about your stables here?'

'The foreman, Callaghan – you met him – he can run the show as well as me. There's money in brumbies; you catch 'em free and sell 'em high. They've all got a bit of class in them somewhere, so I just tell folks they've got a dash of brumby.'

'Like you told me?' Ben grinned.

They rode up the range to the village of Toowoomba, the commercial centre for the graziers on the Downs, and camped right at the edge of the sheer cliffs, admiring the spectacular view of the coastal plains.

'I'd like a house up here,' Cash said, but Ben had other ideas. 'No fear. My grandmother has a cottage at Kangaroo Point. When I make money I'll build a really grand house there. It will overshadow all the rest!'

'You'll have to catch a lot of brumbies to do that.'

'I'll find a way.'

They rode on further west through increasingly dry country. It was all new to Ben, who loved to see the mobs of kangaroos and emus in the wild and was fascinated by the sheer numbers of bird life. Thousands of cockatoos and little corellas and magpie geese became common sights, and scrub turkeys were easy catches to roast over their campfire when they were too far from waterholes or rivers to fish.

In Dalby, a rough little country town, they put up at a shanty inn, mixing with the locals to learn more about the district. They heard that there were plenty of brumbies in the surrounding bush, but more importantly, there'd been a big gold strike further out at Sailor's Drift, on from Charleville.

'Gold!' Cash was thrilled. 'Let's go too. We could make our fortunes! I've always wanted to have a go at this.'

'But the goldfields are a long way from here, Cash. How would we find them?'

'We only have to follow the mob. And with a bit of luck we've got as much chance as any of them of striking gold.'

Ben wasn't so keen. He didn't believe in luck. 'What about the brumbies?'

'Later. We can get them some other time.'

Within days they'd joined the rush of frantic gold-seekers on the now busy track out to Sailor's Drift, riding through the hamlets of Miles, Roma and Mitchell until the bands of weary travellers were in sight of the goldfields.

At first they found the whole place chaotic, a maze of tents and lean-tos scattered among the dry, stringy trees. Food was in short supply, liquor in abundance, and clouds of flies tormented the diggers, but they managed to stake two claims and worked hard, inspired by the shouts of triumph when someone struck it lucky.

At night they sat about campfires, listening to stories of massive gold finds in other districts as well, and the prevailing fear of bushrangers. The miners clamoured for troops to escort the gold back to civilization, but so far none had appeared and travellers on the roads were at the mercy of the thieves. The worst of the bushrangers, known as Captain Jack, terrorized the district with just one offsider, unknown to anyone, unlike a lot of the other bushrangers, who worked in gangs.

Captain Jack had a price on his head for several murders as well as for his bushranging activities, but the police had been unable to apprehend him because he ranged through districts as far north as Charters Towers, wherever goldfields were proclaimed. And in the contrary attitudes of the mining populations, he had achieved quite a reputation of being brave and bold, thumbing his nose at the authorities.

A month of back-breaking work had only returned Ben and Cash a few ounces of alluvial gold, so they decided that brumbies were a better proposition. While Cash kept digging, searching for one last chance, Ben rode out to talk with some tribal Aborigines who were camped in sullen resentment a mile or so from the diggings, at the bend of a sluggish river.

Sharing quarters with so many black prisoners for years, Ben had picked up some of their dialects and was eventually able to make himself understood, but when he placed a pouch of tobacco at the feet of the headman it was ignored.

He asked what tribe they were, but they would not give him that information. Instead the headman enquired of his tribe.

'My mother was Irukandji,' he replied, but that made no impression on them. He noticed that the women were backing away and were replaced by stony-faced naked men who ranged about him, their spears held firmly in a threatening attitude; and that he still hadn't been invited to sit.

'Irukandji people,' he explained quickly. 'They live far, far up there in the hot countries. It takes many moons to walk there.' He couldn't think what else to tell them. All he knew was that he'd made a terrible mistake. They obviously didn't like miners. And probably with good reason.

'What do you want?' the headman asked him.

'Only greetings. A visit,' Ben said, trying to grasp some protocol. He guessed it was too soon to be asking favours. And too late to back off.

One man broke ranks. 'You touch our women, we kill you.'

'No, no. Women safe,' Ben told the painted face. None of the Aborigines he'd known wore these slashes of white paint, certainly not in prison, and he found the stark images even more disconcerting. He took off his gun belt and revolver and dropped them on the ground. 'I am a peaceful man. Why can't we talk?'

The headman was still unsure. 'You speak some parts of our language. Where did you learn this?'

He searched for the right word, and then realized that there was no such word in any of their languages. Aborigines did not have prisons. He stared about him in desperation and then came out with the English words. 'Prison. Jail.'

The headman understood. He stared at Ben and then translated for the others, who all registered fear.

'This place "lockup"?' the other speaker asked him.

'Yes. Lockup.'

'You lie. Blackfellers get lockup, not whitefellers,' the man retorted. 'You're too much of a whitefeller.'

Whenever he could, Ben had kept his socks on. He was ashamed of the telltale scars of the ankle chains that had worn his skin, in those early prison days, almost to the bone. On the goldfields it hadn't mattered so much – he'd noticed the same scars on many a digger sluicing in the shallows – but anywhere else, he knew, they'd always be a permanent embarrassment. Except for this situation.

Angrily he took off his boots and socks and revealed the scars.

'Aaaah!' The sound that rustled through the crowd was a wind of compassion. The most terrible thing that could happen to a tribal man who had the sky for a roof was to be locked up. Shut in. Obviously they all knew of the dreadful punishment white men could inflict on their people.

'You sit.' The headman put aside his spear and waved to the others to join him.

Ben returned to their camp with good news. 'I've made contact with a tribe out there and they tell me there are scores of brumbies south of here. They are willing to help us round them up. They even know the waterholes they use.'

'Why would they help us?'

'For fun. Something to do. Besides, most of this country out here has been taken up by cattlemen, and they don't like them any more than gold-miners.'

'Jesus! Who'd want land out here? They ought to give it back to the blacks; it's as dry as chips.'

'Ah. But this is a bad season. The blacks can cope, they know where the underground springs are, they think it's funny that the white bosses don't know.'

'And they're not about to tell them?' Cash grinned.

'Exactly.'

'I still wouldn't want a station out here. I've never seen so many rotting cattle carcasses in my life.'

'Well, when you meet them don't tell them it's crook country. They love it. They think it's beautiful. And they say the rains will come back again next year because the kangaroos are breeding again.'

'What's that got to do with it?'

'Kangaroos don't breed in bad seasons.'

'Ah, get out with you?'

'That's what they told me.'

'Jesus, you've been away two days. I thought they'd had you for dinner. You're not gonna go bush on me?'

Ben laughed. 'I'm about the most ignorant blackfeller they ever met. I think I'm a bit of a joke among them. They didn't want any part of me when I first turned up, but my scars saved the day.'

'What scars?'

Once again Ben took his socks off.

'Oh Christ, mate,' Cash said. 'I never noticed.'

'Then you might as well know, Cash, that I wasn't treated as a white prisoner. Because I'm a half-caste, I was always locked in with the blacks.'

'Jesus! And you were only a kid!'

'I was safer with them,' Ben growled. 'And they share everything.'

'Is that where you learned their language?'

'Not language,' Ben said wearily. 'Languages. Dialects. As different as French and German. It's a bigger country and more ancient than Europe so why wouldn't there be?'

'Are you trying to school me?'

'No, I'm only just waking up to the fact that my prison education might come in handy after all.'

'I could do without it,' Cash shuddered.

The massive landscape, hopelessly barren, was a pall of dusty brown as far as the eye could see. Squat bushes, their frail leaves a sickly yellow, clung to the diminishing topsoil, and stubborn trees seemed to lean towards them for succour as they passed, for there was none forthcoming from the pitiless blue sky. And as if to taunt them, the horizon was an insidious mirage of shimmering silver.

Ancient rust-coloured rocks were scattered about the vast plain in dishevelled heaps, as if some madman had gone berserk attempting to smash the mighty monuments into extinction.

Cash tied a handkerchief round his face, protection from the stifling dust, and cursed when a hot wind blew up, releasing more untethered soil into a stinging haze as they rode relentlessly on. Beckman didn't seem to be troubled, he mused angrily, nor were the two near-naked blackfellers who loped easily alongside them carrying long spears, boomerangs stuck in their cord belts. Their only attempts at dress were the fur sweatbands they wore around their heads and lap-laps of scraped hide to cover or protect their genitals – Cash didn't know which, and he didn't care. He didn't trust these granite-faced natives with their scarred coal-black bodies. They were beginning to get on his nerves, along with the torture of travelling through this awful drought-blasted country.

This was their second day out and there was still no sign of the wild horses that their guides had promised to find. By sunset Cash was ready to turn back.

The enormous sweep of sky had turned into blazing ridges of red and yellow like a fiery lava flow, and Ben was overwhelmed:

'The colours are amazing, aren't they?' he said to Cash, admiring the display.

'Hell more like it,' Cash growled. 'It's going to be another bloody boiling day tomorrow. These blokes are leading us nowhere. We'll turn back in the morning.'

'We've come this far,' Ben insisted. 'We can't turn back now.'

'Have a bit of sense! Horses aren't camels. We're a day's trek from the last waterhole. If there's no water further on, we're in real trouble. We have to go back while we still can.'

As they dismounted to make camp, Ben pointed to the two Aborigines, who were trotting down to a dried-up riverbed. 'They say there's water here.'

'Ah, sure there is! Forgive me if I'm the only one who can't see it.' He strode away to pour water from his canvas waterbag into a pannikin for his horse, and then took out a bottle of rum, angrily swigging on it while he watched the natives removing hardened slabs of caked mud from the wide, dry riverbed.

Ben went down to join them.

The grey-beard, Mandjala, seemed a surly fellow, rarely speaking, but his dark eyes were intelligent and alert and Ben felt reassured by his presence. The younger one, Djumbati, whom Cash called Jumbo, was more sociable, thoroughly enjoying the trek.

He stood up grinning as Ben approached, but his elder growled at him to keep digging.

The deeper they went, scooping out sand with their bare hands, the more Ben began to worry. Maybe Cash was right. Even if there had been brumbies out this way, what if they'd moved on? Wild horses could travel great distances. Blacks really knew nothing about horses, they had no need of them.

He had also told Ben that his clan was of the Kalkadoon nation, whose warriors had fought a great battle with the white soldiers about ten years ago. Djumbati had managed to explain to Ben that more than six hundred Kalkadoon warriors had massed to drive off the white men once and for all, but the guns had beaten them and only a few warriors had escaped. 'I was too young for that battle,' he said sorrowfully. 'But Mandjala, he was one of those warriors. He doesn't like white men much.'

'Then why is he here with us?'

'The headman is your friend,' Djumbati said simply. 'He tell him he must guide you.'

'Don't you know where the horses are?'

'No!' Djumbati seemed surprised that Ben hadn't known that. 'Mandjala told to show me this country, so I learn more. My family lost their country so we came south to join this family.'

Ben didn't bother to pass on this information to Cash. It was better for him not to know that their guide had no time for white men; he was already cranky enough about the whole expedition.

The hole in the ground was becoming wider and deeper but it was still dry. Ben was about to suggest to them that they try another spot when Djumbati gave a shout, hurling up damp sand. Before long, blessed water was welling up into a small pond and the crisis was over.

Later that night, when Cash had drunk half a bottle of rum, he became despondent and irritable again. 'I don't trust these bastards. They're just taking us on a bloody walkabout. I wouldn't be surprised if we're riding round in circles. If these blokes decide to disappear we could be lost out here.'

'No we won't. They say we're travelling straight, and when we get to the horses, a town is closer than the goldfields.'

'What town?'

'Charleville, I'd say. The end of the railroad.'

'And you believe them?'

'Yes, because Mandjala says we're only a half-day from the horses.'

'I see. And they're just standing there waiting for us.'

'Jesus, Cash! Will you stop your whingeing! They say the only decent waterhole for miles around is ahead of us. They know it and the horses know it. That's where the brumbies come to drink.'

'All right. I'll give it until midday tomorrow, and if we haven't found the horses we're getting out of here,'

Ben agreed. He had to. He didn't know enough about horses to cope on his own. 'One thing worries me, though,' he said to Cash. 'It'll be a long trek back to Brisbane with horses. How will we manage?'

For the first time in days, Cash laughed, a great roar. 'By God, you can be a dope at times. *If* they appear, and *if* we can catch them, we can't take them that far. We'll drive them into Charleville and sell them there. Then we'll see if we can locate any between Charleville and the next town. With more luck than we've got now, we could cash in all the way back.'

And that was his friend. Sometimes mean and moody, at other times bursting with humour and enthusiasm. His temperament was capricious, while Ben remained unassuming and anxious to please.

In the company of this man who had no trouble making friends with people from all walks of life, whether on the long trek west or in the goldfields, Ben was regaining his confidence. And for that he was grateful to Cash O'Neill. He would always stand by him, as he already had done back at Sailor's Drift, rescuing his friend from several drunken fights, which Cash didn't even recall the next day. But that was unimportant. This was the man who had accepted him just as he was, a half-caste and an ex-jailbird.

As Ben and his company travelled steadily on, they were hailed by two riders, who looked suspiciously at their native guides.

'Where are you lot off to?' the first man demanded.

Smiling, Cash returned the question with a question. 'Good morning to you, sirs. And who might you be?'

'We're boundary riders. You're on private property. This is Fairmont Station, owned by Mr Buchanan.'

'Is it now?' Cash replied. He looked about him. ''Tis a hard job you fellers have got in this terrible drought. I take me hat off to you.'

Mollified, the lead rider lowered his rifle. 'You can say that again, mate. Cattle are dying all over the bloody place. And we don't take kindly to strangers who kill our beasts for tucker.'

'I should think not, but don't look at us. We're city folk, we carry our food in tins.'

'What about them?' He pointed at the blacks, who kept well back from this confrontation.

'They find their own grub, but for the love of God don't scare them off or we might get lost.'

'Where are you from?'

Without batting an eye, Cash lied to them. 'We're from the Sailor's Drift goldfields, where we did no good at all. But we hear there's been a strike on from here, so we're off to try our luck.'

The two boundary riders stared at each other. 'I never heard of a strike out this way,' the second man said.

'Then you'd be doin' us and yourselves a favour if you keep it quiet. Us prospectors don't want a mob landing on us. First in, best dressed.'

'How far's this gold strike?'

'About another fifty miles as the crow flies,' Cash told them, as Ben listened fascinated. 'At a place called Spencer Gully.'

'Never heard of it,' the boundary rider shrugged.

'The blacks know where it is, they'll get us there,' Cash said, and the boundary rider laughed.

'You hope. Bloody mad, you diggers. But you keep going now and you'll be off our property in a couple of miles, and then you're on your own.'

'How far is it to the next waterhole?' Cash asked artlessly.

'There ain't no bloody waterholes left out here, mate. You take my advice and give it up.' He pointed: 'Head thataway, towards Charleville, or you'll end up joining the cattle carcasses.'

'By Jesus, no,' Cash said. 'We have to give it a go.'

'Ah, please yourself.' The boundary rider wheeled his horse about. 'Just get off this property!'

'We'll do that. And we'll be praying for rain for you lads,' Cash called as they cantered away.

'What was that all about?' Ben asked. 'What goldfields?'

'I was hoping you'd keep your mouth shut,' Cash laughed. 'If we'd told them we're after brumbies they'd have herded us back to Sailor's Drift with those rifles in our backs.'

'Are we poaching?'

'No fear. Brumbies are fair game, but don't you think they'd rather have them than us? Anyway, that's not the problem now. You heard what they said . . . no bloody waterholes out here. So much for your smart-alec blacks.'

Ben rode back to Mandjala with this news, and their guide nodded as if in agreement and set off at a trot.

'I don't think he understood me,' Ben told Cash.

'I think that bastard understands a lot more than he pretends,' his friend retorted.

Nevertheless, since Cash hadn't made a decision, they followed Mandjala. Ben watched miserably as the sun stretched across the sky, heat hammering at the parched intruders who had to pick their way across a rocky incline.

Ahead loomed a jagged cliff, starkly orange in this hard light, another remnant of some long-defeated mountain range, with sharp boulders perched atop at dangerous angles, as if the slightest nudge would send them crashing hundreds of feet below.

Keeping well clear, since it offered no shade at this time of day, they pushed on, on a parallel course to that impenetrable wall. Ben was intrigued. He was still unaccustomed to these sudden rock formations that jutted sheerly from the plains, and he found them mysterious and exciting. Unlike Cash, who rode stolidly by, Ben felt a yearning to investigate those ancient monuments, as if they held secrets of his mother's people, lost to him now.

Instead of heading on into the plains, Mandjala began to traverse the outskirts of this massive mound, beckoning them to follow.

'Now what?' Cash complained as they followed the uneven line of cliff for at least a half a mile until they began to enter a field of crumbled rock on the other side.

Rather than risk their horses stumbling, they dismounted and caught up with Mandjala, who managed a rare grin. 'Horses,' he said, pointing to tracks. 'Horses go down.'

'Where?' Cash cried eagerly, seeing no such evidence.

Ben noted that Mandjala had spoken in English.

They left their horses with a disappointed Djumbati and followed Mandjala through a gap in the rocks to a path that dropped ever so slightly into the cooler bowels of the cliffs.

They ran down a worn track bordered by thick undergrowth into a steamy stretch of rainforest, dropping sharply all the time. Their path turned and twisted under a canopy of greenery strung with creepers and robust loya vines, leading, inevitably, Ben guessed, to springs of some sort.

He was thrilled by this hidden oasis, an awesome relief from the desolation outside.

'What is this place called?' he asked Mandjala. In English.

'Winnaroo,' Mandjala replied with a knowing smile. 'This good place Winnaroo.'

Ben stopped to look about him. It was all so alive, a haven for birds of all descriptions and, he had no doubt, other wildlife beside the brumbies.

Cash broke the spell, shouting to him, 'Water! Down here!'

But Mandjala had been watching Ben's reaction to this hidden world. He put out his hand to delay him. 'What name you?'

'Ben. Ben Beckman.'

Mandjala nodded thoughtfully. 'This good place,' he said again. 'Important.'

'Yes, I'm sure it is,' Ben replied respectfully.

'You be good feller to Winnaroo.'

'We'll take care,' Ben replied. 'We only need water for the horses.'

Dark eyes searched his face. 'We talk longa time. Plenty spirits here. Allasame Dreamtime people.'

'I can believe it.'

Still Mandjala made no move to release him, and for the first time Ben took stock of the dark smudged face behind the thatch of grey hair and the wiry beard. Mandjala's features were firm, and strong teeth showed from the tight curve of his mouth. He held his head high on a leathery neck and stood tall as if unaccustomed to bowing to anyone. Here indeed, Ben realized, was the warrior, the survivor of those wars. Not a man to cross.

Cash was still calling to him. 'Hurry up! Come and see!'

'That feller no good,' Mandjala said suddenly. 'You look out.'

'Who? Cash?' Ben said. 'He's all right. His bark's worse than his bite.'

Mandjala made no further comment. He stepped aside to allow Ben to run on down the track and finally emerge at a pebble beach beside a deep lagoon. Cash had already thrown off his clothes and was splashing about in triumph.

'It's freezing!' he called. 'But bloody marvellous!'

Within minutes Ben too had plunged into the crystal-clear water, the heat and dust of the outside world forgotten.

He glanced back to see Mandjala standing watching them, and all about, the high cliffs protecting this place seemed also to be on guard. Inexplicably Ben felt anxious, his stomach churning as if there were something here that should bother him. But there was nothing. How could there be in such a serene hideaway?

Now there was business at hand. They had found the brumbies' secret watering hole. Next came the hard part. With the help of the blacks they worked for days building fences at the entrance to the cavernous springs, toiling, as Ben said, 'like prisoners in a quarry' to remove rocks in order to dig postholes. Further away from the trap, on more level ground, a holding paddock was constructed, and all the time they could see a couple of high-stepping brumbies circling the area, watching this activity with suspicion.

'They're the leaders of their mobs,' Cash explained. 'The boss men. They know this is a trap so they're keeping well away.'

'Then why are we wasting our time?'

'Because they need water. You heard those boundary riders. They said there aren't any waterholes out this way. Either they weren't telling or they don't know about this spot, but the horses do. Sooner or later thirst will get the better of those nags; they'll have to take a chance and come through our gate. Just pray they don't smash down our fences.'

'What?' Ben was appalled. 'After all our work!'

Cash laughed. He was enjoying this challenge. They spent the next few days strengthening the fence rails with lengths of tough, supple vines until Cash shouted: 'Look out! Stand clear! Here they come!'

An advance mob of nine horses came thundering towards them at a mad gallop, charging up the rocky slope with sure-footed ease, swerving through the open gate to dash on down to their waterhole.

Swiftly Cash shut the gate, on which he'd hung pieces of rag to spook the horses away from that outlet. He was jumping about with glee. 'This is all we can handle now, Ben. If you see another mob heading this way, fire your rifle into the air and keep them away.'

Their thirsts quenched, the horses came cautiously back. As soon as they realized that they were penned in, they reacted furiously, screaming, rearing, lashing out at the fences. One horse, unable in that small space to get a run at the fence, tried to climb over, but the Aborigines thrust it back with their spears.

'Don't get too close,' Ben was shouting at them. 'They bite. They'll kill you if they get half a chance.'

Finally, some of the horses began to quieten but their leader, a grey stallion, turned on them, lashing out at them with his hind legs to keep them fighting.

'They're his mob,' Cash explained. 'He doesn't care if he kills them as long as he can keep throwing them at the fences. If he doesn't settle down I'll have to shoot him.'

'No!' Ben screamed. 'You can't do that. He's a beautiful horse.'

'He's a killer,' Cash said, watching them. 'We can't sell horses that he's beaten up.'

'Then let's try to get him out first.'

They took ropes from their packhorse, and after about an hour of trial and error, managed to get lassos on the kicking, snapping beast and, with the help of their own horses, drag him down to the holding paddock.

For a man who would have shot the stallion, Cash was surprisingly gentle in the breaking process, using only a rope to circle the stallion, talking to him, occasionally allowing him to let off steam in a wild canter about the compound, then returning patiently to what he called 'the lessons'.

While he worked with each horse, another corral had to be built to hold the quieter animals, some of whom were almost content as long as they were in sight of the grey.

But feed was the problem. The horses in the trap could graze inside the springs, but there was little for their own horses. Besides which, the other brumbies, cut off from their water supply, were a pitiful sight, coming closer, almost begging to be allowed in. It was a relief for both Ben and Cash to be able to remove all their captured horses and allow the rest through.

'It's a damn shame,' Cash groaned, 'to have to leave them, but it's too hard to keep our own mob fed. I didn't think of that.'

Resistance faded as the horse-breaker took each of his captives down to the lagoon himself, gaining their trust, and as Ben watched he realized that on the next expedition they'd need better equipment. Cash was a good horse-breaker but too disorganized to handle a successful operation. Ben thought they were lucky to have caught nine horses, considering all the setbacks in this dry country, and he hoped Cash appreciated that they wouldn't have rounded up a foal without the tenacity and strength of their native workers. Who were still happy to trail along with them.

As they neared the town, Ben asked how much they could expect to get for the horses.

'About ten quid a head,' Cash said. 'They're a frisky lot and less than half broke. Maybe twenty for the grey.'

Charleville was a busy place, with the gold rush well under way. The one main street was packed with drays and wagons, and crowds of hopeful gold-seekers milling about, leading horses and donkeys. Some even carried swags, having just stepped from the crowded train.

Mandjala and Djumbati wouldn't come near the town, preferring to camp a few miles out by the river, so leaving them there, Ben promised to return in a few days with presents for them, and then he and Cash took their horses on to the saleyards.

Soon they'd joined the press of customers overflowing into the yard of one of the many pubs. They sank three large tankards of ale each, and then, their great thirst slaked, sat on a bench outside, eager for all the news. They weren't comforted to hear that another gold-bearing reef had been discovered near Sailor's Drift.

As always, the main topics of conversation were gold, the weather and horses.

Cash nudged Ben. 'Did you hear that now? Horses are in short supply in this here town. We've just upped the price.'

Later, though, he had an even better idea.

At noon the next day they brought the horses into town, and standing on a keg, Cash shouted the town to attention, announcing the auction of 'the freshest and finest horseflesh this side of the Curragh!'

He soon drew the crowds from the pubs and the stores, bantering with the wits, charming the women with his flattery and singing the praises of his horses as Ben led them forward one by one. For a shilling each, Ben had engaged the services of some lads to keep the rest of the horses hobbled and out of sight until he came for them.

Some experienced horsemen in the audience were inclined to make sarcastic remarks about Cash's fine horses, but instead of arguing with them, Cash gave them the wink and included them in his sales pitch.

'Now there's a gentleman who knows horses! What am I offered for this fine mount? Did I hear thirty? Thirty-two over there. Going too cheap. Sailor's Drift's got more gold than horses, mates! You'll never buy a horse out there, let alone a beauty like this.'

In the end his detractors were laughing with him, cheering as the prices soared. But when the last horse, the grey stallion, was brought out, a cattleman stepped up and handed Cash forty pounds. 'Don't put him to auction, lad, I'll take him. He's no more broke than a dingo and you know it, but he's too good to be dragging a wagon.'

With the sale over, Cash gleefully counted up more than three hundred pounds. 'Come on, mate, let's celebrate.'

'We can celebrate on the trail,' Ben told him. 'Half of those horses have never seen a bridle, let alone a saddle. There'll be hell to pay when they start acting up. And you'll be on the paying end.'

'Ah, you worry too much. For a price I'll offer my services as a horse-breaker.'

Just then there were screams and shouts as a riderless horse galloped down the street. 'That's one of ours,' Cash grinned. 'The colt I called Strike. Now he is a beauty, isn't he?'

But his grin turned to a frown as men tried to round up the wild horse, infuriating it even more. Strike reared and bucked, and, no respecter of traffic rules, bolted along the footpath, shouldering posts aside and causing awnings to collapse. He stopped short when men with ropes began to advance on him, then in another fit of fury began snapping at them with bared teeth and lashing out with his hind legs, smashing shop windows.

Watching the horse's destructive progress, a man standing beside Ben remarked casually: 'He'd make a great buckjumper, that one. You could take bets on who'd stay on him the longest.'

But Cash had seen enough. He nudged Ben. 'I think it's time to go.' He dashed into the pub to buy his supply of rum, while Ben brought their horses round from the back. Soon they were on their way, riding fast, laughing at the financial success of that adventure.

The two Aborigines were pleased to see them and eager to continue on this interesting walkabout, especially when Ben presented them with their pay, a saddlebag of assorted purchases: tobacco, tins of beans, peaches and boiled sweets, and two sheathed hunting knives.

'What did you give 'em them for?' Cash growled. 'They'll probably stick them in us if we cross 'em.'

'Spears would have been easier,' Ben laughed. 'It might be a good idea to keep off the main track to the next town. We don't need irate customers catching up with us.'

With a late start, dusk was upon them within three hours, so they made camp in the bush, relaxed now.

In the morning, they were in high spirits. They'd slept well without the constant need to keep watch over the wild horses. They kept Djumbati with them as a guide, and sent Mandjala off to scout for brumbies.

'This time,' Ben told Cash, 'if Mandjala spots horses, we can buy all the equipment and supplies we need and come back for them. I'm learning the ropes now. We can break them properly and when they're ready you can take them into town and sell them a few at a time.'

'Yeah. All right,' Cash agreed grudgingly. Ben knew that his friend was now losing interest in the hunt. The money was burning a hole in his pocket. With a sinking heart he realized that Cash was no different from so many they'd met on the goldfields. Men who'd strike gold, spend it in the next town on gambling, booze and women, and return, broke, to start again. But for Ben, his share of the three hundred pounds was only the beginning. A small beginning, but he would make more and more, and like his mother either invest or buy property just so long as that bankroll kept on increasing. He could never have enough to satisfy his ambitions.

As the trio struck east, with Ben leading the packhorse and Djumbati trotting along beside him, the native became increasingly nervous.

Sometimes he dropped back and then caught up with them again, until finally he came abreast of Ben's horse.

'Men following,' he whispered, as if in this great empty land someone might hear him.

Ben reined in his horse. 'What men?'

Djumbati shrugged. 'Two men, two horses.'

When they told Cash he wasn't concerned. 'So what? We don't own the place.'

'It might be a couple of our good customers,' Ben teased, 'come to get their money back.'

'They'd have to be keen for a few quid,' Cash laughed. 'If they give me any trouble I'll stick a bullet in them.'

They continued on their leisurely way, not needing to push their horses now, and by late afternoon called a halt near a creek.

'Where's that old blackfeller?' Cash complained. 'We haven't set eyes on him for days. What if he can't find us?'

'He'll find us,' Ben said. 'Don't ask me how, but he'll turn up.'

As usual Cash slumped under a tree to enjoy his rum and Ben set about the chores. There wasn't much to do so he didn't mind Cash taking a rest. He unsaddled and hobbled the horses to allow them to graze, while Djumbati lit a campfire. He slung a supply bag on the ground and was unpacking it when a voice behind him called: 'Stand and deliver!'

Thinking it was Cash playing a joke, Ben turned and rose, a smile on his face.

But Cash was already standing, his hands in the air. Djumbati was cringing by the fire and a stranger was confronting them with an ugly double-barrelled shotgun. This, he knew, was no irate horse-buyer; the mean eyes above the black cloth that covered the lower part of his face were those of a real live bushranger. He had a dark hat pulled down to his eyebrows so all that could be seen of his face were those eyes, and Ben knew there'd be no arguing with this one.

Not Cash, though. 'What can we do for you, sir?' he asked blithely, still keeping his hands raised.

Now Ben saw another man, a back-up man, standing at the edge of the clearing, his rifle trained on them, and he was angry with himself. Both he and Cash had guns, no one in their right minds traversed this country without weapons. He had a revolver which he'd dropped with its belt over where he'd unloaded the packhorse, and Cash's rifle, probably not loaded, was propped against a tree, also out of reach.

'I'll have your money for a start,' the bushranger said.

'Then you're out of luck here,' Cash said. 'We're only poor prospectors on our way home. We did no good out there.'

'You're a liar, you Irish bog-trotter,' the man grated.

But still Cash stalled. 'You're soundin' Irish yourself,' he said, exaggerating his brogue. 'You wouldn't rob a fellow-countryman. Now put away the gun and have a drink with us.'

'Shut your trap and hand over the money before I blast you.'

'I told you, there isn't any money.'

'You sold a mob of brumbies in town and sailed away with the takings. Now I'll have it.'

'Ah, dear God. Is that what it is now?' Cash said. 'If you bought one and you're not happy then I'll be pleased to refund the purchase money, but by rights you should give me back the horse.'

The bushranger turned to Ben. 'Your mate there, is he mad or something? I'll shoot him in a minute to shut his mouth.'

'If you know we sold the horses, then you'd know I lost the lot in a card game,' Cash said, but the bushranger had had enough.

He turned the gun on poor terrified Djumbati. 'You've got three seconds to turn over the money, or the nigger's dead.'

'Give it to him!' Ben shouted at Cash.

'Give what to him?' Cash replied coolly. 'I lost it in that card game.'

'You get it then,' the bushranger ordered Ben, 'or you're next.'

Ben had no idea where Cash kept the roll of notes. He didn't wear a money-belt so it could be anywhere – in a pack or in his saddle, anywhere.

'Where is it?' he shouted at Cash, in a panic now.

'Time's up,' the bushranger said, but those words gave Ben the seconds he needed before the gunman could carry out his threat. As the bushranger aimed the gun squarely at Djumbati, Ben leapt at him, punching the masked man with all the force he could muster.

The bushranger's gun went off with a thunderous blast as Ben fought him for it. Djumbati bolted into the scrub, and so did Cash as the other man fired wildly at him.

But he only fired one shot, and then stumbled forward to land on his face in the clearing with a long spear trembling in his back.

As Cash rushed back to grab the shotgun, the two men on the ground fell apart, and Ben yanked their attacker to his feet.

'Well done, Benny me lad,' Cash cried, and then turned to the bushranger, whose bearded face had lost its cover. 'You're not so smart now,' he taunted their captive, 'and I'm bettin' you're Captain Jack himself, you Irish clodhopper! Wouldn't that be right?'

The bushranger spat blood. 'Let me go and I'll make it worth your while.'

'What about his mate over there?' Cash asked, but there was no need for Ben to reply. Mandjala stepped from the bush and without a word retrieved his spear from the man's body.

'Is he dead?' Ben asked nervously, and Mandjala nodded.

'Good. One less to worry about,' Cash said, keeping well back from the prisoner. 'If we take you in, Captain Jacko, we could collect a hundred-pound reward, and that's a fair sum. So how could you make it worth my while to let you go?'

'I'll double it.'

'You've got two hundred have you? Then show me.'

'It's not here.'

'Ah, Benny, did you hear the poor chap? He didn't believe me and now he expects me to believe him.'

'Because I'm telling the truth and you were lying, you bastard!'

Ben interrupted the argument. 'We have to bury this other fellow. What was his name?'

'John Smith will do,' the bushranger said. 'He was of no account, the bloody fool. If he'd been doing his job I wouldn't be standing here listening to this bigmouth.'

'There's an old mine-shaft a way back,' Cash said to Ben. 'Search him, wrap him in his horse-rug and drop him down there. It's as deep a grave as ever you'd find. Get Jumbo to help you.'

It seemed the best thing to do, so Ben carried out the task. He didn't relish riding into one of these towns with the body of an unidentified white man who'd obviously been speared in the back. It could cause more trouble than the robber was worth.

By the time he returned, Cash and the bushranger had come to an agreement. Jack was prepared to buy his freedom.

'But he would have killed us,' Ben protested.

'I was only bluffing,' Jack said.

'The hell you were. Don't believe him, Cash, he could be leading us into a trap.'

'Not with both of our guns on him and your two mates there minding our backs.'

'But when we let him go, what's to stop him coming after us?'

'And how will he do that with no weapons and no horses?'

'Fair go,' Jack said. 'You can have the guns but leave me a horse.'

'Count yourself lucky we're not deliverin' you to the hangman, mister!' Cash growled. 'Now where's your hideout? And no tricks.'

While they saddled up, Mandjala edged over for a few words with Ben. He already knew where the bushranger's hideout was, having become suspicious of him the day before and tracked him into some nearby foothills.

Ben kept this information to himself in case Captain Jack did try any tricks but occasionally glanced back to receive a nod from Mandjala that they were on course.

Tracks around the area had been brushed clean and the low entrance to a cave was heavily disguised by bushes and fresh branches.

'I'll get you the money. Two hundred we agreed on,' Captain Jack said, as he dismounted. 'And we call it square?'

'You have my word as a gentleman,' Cash said loftily.

'Wait here and I'll get it for you,' Jack said.

Cash laughed. 'What is this? A bank you've got, with a back entrance and a few more guns? Not on your life! Jumbo, you get in there and have a look around.'

When Djumbati returned to report that it was a single large cave with no other outlets, Cash left the bushranger with Ben and explored for himself, carrying a lantern.

He came out grinning with delight. 'You sure have been busy, my friend,' he said to Jack. 'You've got supplies and guns and ammo, even a crate of whisky. But where's the money?'

'I'll get it for you,' Jack said.

'Ah no. Grab that spade, Jumbo, and come with me.'

This time Cash returned with two steel bank boxes that had been buried deep in the rear of the cave, their locks smashed. 'Signs of a misspent youth,' Cash chortled as he brushed the dust from them and opened them up. The first contained bundles of notes wrapped in oilcloth.

'I told you,' Jack said as Ben allowed him to dismount. 'Now take your share and get out of here.'

'There's no rush. What's in this tin?' Cash opened the other and stared in astonishment. Gently, almost reverently, he lifted out two leather pouches. One bulged with alluvial gold, the other contained a dozen small nuggets.

'Jesus, man!' he exclaimed. 'What were you going to do with all this?'

'Make my way to America,' Jack leered, 'when it gets too hot here. They've got plenty of goldfields there and I've had plenty of practice in lifting it.'

'You surely have,' Ben said, trying to keep a wary eye on their prisoner while darting fascinated glances at the gold.

'I can't see myself leaving a villain like you with all this loot,' Cash said eventually. 'I'm afraid we're going to have to take the lot.'

'I thought you would,' Jack said. 'You haven't got a gentleman's bone in your body.'

Ben, too, was looking greedily at this haul. It would take years to earn this sort of money. Captain Jack had no real claim on it, and if they took it back to the authorities they'd have to hand it over and come away with just the reward. It was bad luck on Jack's part to have tried to rob the wrong men. He would have to go on his way now and begin his career all over again.

Jack appealed to Ben. 'Take the money and leave me the gold. Fair go!'

Ben kept the gun on him: 'You stand over there while Cash finishes searching the cave. You never know what else he'll find. You're still in front, Jack. You'd never make prison, they'd hang you first.'

'You'd know about that, wouldn't you?' Jack snarled.

'About what?' Ben said, surprised.

'About jail. I can smell a jailbird a mile off. You're still "yessir, nossir" to that mate of yours. It takes a long time for them chains to stop rattlin'.'

Cash had taken Djumbati back into the cave, and Mandjala was standing back idly, one bare foot resting on his knee, his spear planted firmly on the ground. None of this seemed to interest him.

Jack looked over at him. 'He's a better man than you are,' he commented, trying to bait Ben. 'He's real. He won't do no portering for your white mate like the kid. Like you do.'

'Shut up!' Ben said to him. 'We'll leave you food. And the rest of your stuff. That's the best we can do.'

'And you'd better watch your own back. One of these days your mate will turn on you too!'

Ben ignored that. 'I'd be lying if I said I'm sorry. And you know as well as I do that we'd be mad to take your offer of money when we can take the lot. You've robbed other people, so stop whining because you're being robbed. And keep back.'

'You still don't get it, do you?' Jack said. He looked older now, and weary. He was fifty if he was a day, and an old scar cut a white slice through his dark beard.

'You listen to me, son. I've been working these roads from the goldfields of Gympie and Charters Towers. There's more where that lot in there came from. Down the hill we passed a mangled old fig tree with an eagle's nest in the top. The rest of my haul is in there. Come with me and I'll get it for you.'

Djumbati came out carrying an old travelling trunk, which reminded Ben of the time he was arrested for stealing on the wharves, when his friend Willy had left him to face the music. This oily old bastard was deliberately unnerving him. He wished Cash would hurry.

'We haven't got much time left,' Jack urged him. 'Shoot the Irish son-of-a-bitch as he comes out.'

'You're a madman,' Ben snapped. 'You didn't give a damn when your own mate was killed back there.'

Without warning, Jack called out to Mandjala in a guttural language that was too fast for Ben to understand. When he looked round, Mandjala was gone. What had Jack said? That the white men would kill him? Not that it mattered. Ben was certain he could trust Mandjala, he'd be back. This Captain Jack had more tricks than a bag of monkeys, he was the one to watch.

Clothing from the trunk was pulled out and scattered about, but Cash couldn't find any more loot.

'I'll watch his lordship here,' Cash said, levelling his rifle at Captain Jack. 'Pack what we can carry, Ben, and don't forget the whisky.' He slung over two empty saddlebags. 'Put the loot in here and strap it on to your saddle.'

That made Ben feel better after Jack's unnerving remarks. 'Where did you put our earnings from the brumbies anyway?' he asked Cash.

'In my boot,' Cash laughed.

'He would have shot Djumbati!'

'No he wouldn't. You heard him. He was only bluffing.' Cash hadn't even noticed that Mandjala had left the scene, but that wasn't surprising. As Ben had said, Mandjala had no interest in chores. He considered himself above them except when his expertise had been required to turn vines into twine or to chop trees for fence rails. He'd enjoyed the experience of working with Ben's sharp new axe.

Finally they were ready to leave. 'We've got two spare horses,' Cash called gleefully. 'You want to ride, Jumbo?'

Smiling, Jumbo shook his head. He still hadn't come to terms with these strange animals, sometimes tame as pets, other times fighting mad, although he was hugely impressed by them.

'Did you leave food for Jack?' Ben asked. 'We've taken everything he's got. We can't let him starve.'

'Sure,' Cash said. 'I've searched that cave the best I could but he might still have a gun hidden somewhere. Best we march him down the hill so we'll be long gone before he has time to get back for it. He's a wily old character, that's probably why he's lasted this long.'

So it was over. Ben breathed a sigh of relief as he rode down the hill with a fortune in his saddlebag, travelling slowly, leading the now heavily laden packhorse while Cash had charge of the other horses. They couldn't afford to allow the bushranger to make a bolt for it, so he was on foot, striding out as if he'd made this trek many a time, which he probably had. Looking back, Ben couldn't help admiring the choice of hideout. There was no sign of any cave on that otherwise stark hillside, not even the telltale signs of bats, which usually coveted such dark hollows.

'This'll do,' Cash said from the rear of the troop. He lifted his rifle. 'On your way, Captain Jack, and God be with you.'

Instead of turning on them with a last round of abuse for stealing his fortune, Jack began to run, crouching and zigzagging. Cash got him with his second shot. He crashed over a boulder and tumbled, dead, face up to the sun.

'You shot him!' Ben screamed. 'Why the hell did you do that?'

'Because he would have come after us. We'd have been looking over our shoulders for the rest of our lives, you fool!'

Ben felt sick. 'It was wrong, Cash. You shouldn't have done that.'

'I know it's hard to take. But we have to look after ourselves. We're heading straight to Brisbane now. We don't need brumbies any more. We're rich.'

He threw the bridle of a spare horse to Djumbati, who caught it warily. 'A present,' Cash called to him, 'for your work. He's yours!'

Jumbo looked to Ben, who was still in a state of shock. 'This horse mine?'

'Yes,' Ben said numbly. 'You go home now and take him with you.'

The Aborigine, in sentimental mood, came over to shake Ben's hand, and that gave Ben the chance to feel the comfort of the revolver in his belt. Captain Jack's warnings were beginning to make sense.

They watched Djumbati run with the horse, still not attempting to ride, and Cash laughed. 'What the hell will he do with it?' And then, as an afterthought, 'I'm losing my touch, Ben. I got carried away with the good fortune of all this. We should have kept him to dig a grave for his lordship there. Now you'll have to do it.'

'You shot him, you bury him,' Ben growled.

'Fair enough,' Cash said, 'but I can't claim to make too good a job of it. Needin' to dig it deep enough for two.' His voice hardened. 'Get down off your horse.' He now had the shotgun levelled at Ben, but having grasped the experienced bushranger's warning, Ben didn't waste a second. He pulled out his revolver and fired, only to hear a lonely click.

'I took the precaution of removing your ammo,' Cash said calmly. 'You must understand this is nothing personal. I like you. You're a bloody good mate.'

The malignant steel of the shotgun held fast on Ben, as, despairing, he stepped down. So this was his life. The love and nurturing of Oma and his lovely mother, Diamond, had come to nothing. The prison years of hope had come to nothing. The criminal neglect of that doctor who'd let his mother die would go unpunished. But most of all he thought of Diamond: how she'd loved him, and what dreams she'd had for him. She'd even talked, embarrassing him as a boy, of her grandchildren growing up in that home on the Point. A fury rose in him as he glared at Cash O'Neill, his so-called friend.

Cash was wise, standing too far back from him to make the mistake that Jack had made. 'Don't look at me like that,' he was saying. 'You're casting the evil eye on me as if you wished me dead. I can see it in your Abo face, but it don't work with me.'

Ben remembered the snake. The one that had killed Bull Baker. He tried to conjure it up. Diamond had loved snakes, she'd told him. They were her totem. Ben kept his eyes hard on Cash O'Neill, willing a snake to steal up and strike his enemy. Maybe to drop on him from the branches above.

But nothing happened, so he tried arguing. 'Think about this, Cash. Keep the money, I don't care. I don't need it. I didn't tell you before but I'm quite well off. I've already got money. There's no need to kill me, for God's sake!'

'If I believed you,' Cash said, 'that's even worse. You've got money and I've got creditors hard on my heels. Even if I sold the stables I wouldn't have enough to dodge them. But now, with this haul, I can sell the bloody place, pay them off and still have plenty to spare.'

'Do that then. I won't stop you. I told you, keep the lot.'

He realized that he sounded like Captain Jack now, trying to negotiate with a man who was beyond the pale.

'Captain Jack knew you would kill him,' he said. 'And he warned me that you'd kill me too.'

'Well, he was a smart man. He had a good run. He knew there was no such thing as sharing when it comes to a haul like this. That other mug, the one we dropped in the well, he wouldn't have seen a shilling of it. Jack would have disposed of him in time.'

'Like you're about to dispose of me?'

'Ha! Listen to him! Didn't I just see you fire at me? With an empty gun but no less a try!'

'That was self-defence!'

'So is this, me lad. I can't let you go now. Move away from the horse.'

Ben obeyed but at the same time Cash caught him glancing about the hillside. It was open country and Cash was standing in front of a lone tree that had survived the ravages of the drought.

'Don't be looking for your nigger mate,' he said to Ben. 'He won't get me in the back. And I'm out of range of a spear. He'll have to come out into the open to hit me at this distance, and if he tries I'll get him first.'

'If you kill me he'll come after you.'

'Don't kid yourself. He's probably bolted by this. But he won't want to try, I'll be watching for him. Then I'll be off. He can't outrun a horse. Now get a shovel and start digging. I'm staying right here.'

Ben considered refusing, but that would only hasten his death. He had to stall for time, hoping for some chance of life. He walked over to the packhorse, steeling his back in anticipation of a bullet. Cash was so het-up and trigger-happy, he could fire any minute. Ben could almost feel the impact as he reached for the shovel. Maybe Djumbati and Mandjala would come back, take on Cash from two different directions. But Djumbati was a trusting soul, he'd gone running off with the horse. Why would he think to turn back and check on the two white men?

And besides, Ben thought, an attack like that, in the open against a shotgun, would fail. They'd be hurt or killed. And Cash still had a handgun slung on his hip as well. No point in counting on that not being loaded.

He moved sideways under Cash's shouted directions to begin the dig, sickened to find himself staring downhill at Jack's corpse splayed out under the sun, broken, beaten, as if it had never lived. And he saw himself flung aside in the same way, a useless spent thing, as he jammed the shovel into the ground.

Stalling again, he called over to Cash, 'It's like rock! I can't make a dent in it.'

Out of the sun, a shadow flicked, hardly even the glimpse of a shadow as something passed by.

He heard Cash scream, a terrible scream of pain.

With an effort Ben turned full on towards that menacing shotgun. In a mad way he'd kept his back to it as much as possible, thinking that the blast might not hurt so much if it struck his back. Stunned, he saw that Cash had slid to his knees.

Every part of his being had been focused on that shotgun, the dual-eyed blue steel monster that threatened his existence, and now it was difficult to disassociate from it. Cash was still grasping it across his chest as he slumped back on his haunches, refusing to let go. Blood was pouring down his face. Ben snapped his brain from the gun, and forgetting everything that had happened, ran towards Cash in a kneejerk reaction. He saw Cash release the gun and fall forward on top of it. Then, as if he were standing apart listening, Ben heard himself scream.

Cash's mouth gaped open but nothing of his face was recognizable above it, only a bloody gaping wound where his head had been sliced open.

Ben reeled away, sick to his stomach.

Mandjala walked past him to retrieve his war weapon, his boomerang. Taking a handful of leaves he cleaned blood from the razor-sharp hardwood edge that had sliced Cash's skull as if it had been an apple.

The following night, sitting disconsolately by their campfire, Ben remembered to ask Mandjala what Captain Jack had said when he'd shouted at him.

'He warned me that the boss would kill us all.'

'And you believed him?'

'More better than that one, your friend.'

Ben nodded. He was still shocked that Cash had turned on him, and distressed at the miserable turn of events. But they had buried both men and now he had to report to the police, so he decided to keep going on to Mitchell, the next town.

Remembering Captain Jack's remarks, that he still had the air of a convict, he walked into the police station with his head up and looked the sergeant in the eye. Gone forever was his prison stance, eyes lowered in the presence of his betters.

Confidently he gave his version of the ambush, in which brave Cash O'Neill had caught Captain Jack off-guard and shot him, only to be slain by the second outlaw, who had escaped. To prove his point, he showed them Jack's horse, his hat and face mask, and his black jacket, a garment with a high, stiff collar that had seen better days. He made no mention of finding Jack's loot. Or of the Aborigines involved.

Not that it mattered. The police were too excited about the demise of the outlaw to bother about the details. The evidence that Ben provided was enough to convince them that Captain Jack's reign of terror was over. They showed Ben a sketch of Jack's bearded face on a reward notice. 'Is this the feller?'

'Yes,' Ben said. 'Except he had a scar down his face across the beard there, where the hair couldn't grow.'

'By God, he's right!' the sergeant cried jubilantly. 'The bugger was slashed with a sword in a fight with a trooper a year or so back.'

Ben offered to show them the graves, but no one was keen on disinterring the bodies out in that country.

'I'm sorry about your mate,' the sergeant said, 'but you'll be set for the reward.'

'I don't want it,' Ben told him. 'Mr O'Neill's parents are dead but he owned O'Neill's stables in Brisbane. I'd rather you sent the money there. It was Cash who shot Captain Jack, not me. The money should go to his next of kin.'

'That's right decent of you now,' the policeman said. 'Do you come from these parts, Ben?'

'No, this was my first trip out this way. We were looking for brumbies for his stables.'

'I see. But there's something familiar about you. I never forget a face, trained meself to remember. If you don't mind my asking, was your father a white man?'

'Yes, but I live with my grandmother in Brisbane.'

'Maybe your father comes from out this way?'

'Not that I know of. He died a long time ago.'

The sergeant nodded. 'Beckman,' he mused. 'Can't say as I know of any Beckmans in the district. You must just resemble someone. So where are you off to now?'

'Home,' he said. 'I own a house at Kangaroo Point in Brisbane if you need to get in touch with me,' he added, to establish his credentials as a man of means. 'Do you need me any more?'

'No. You've done all that could be done. We'll find the graves and put permanent markers on them. Leave that to us.'

Mandjala was waiting for him well out of town. Ben had already dumped all but necessities for the journey home, and had left the two horses that had belonged to the Captain and Cash with the police. He thanked Mandjala again and prepared to leave. 'Goodbye, my friend.' But Mandjala waved that aside. 'We meet again,' he announced.

Ben thought this unlikely but accepted that it could be polite form as well as an assertion of fortitude, despite the troubles that beset the tribes.

Well armed, with a fortune in his saddlebags, still shocked and dejected when he thought of Cash, Ben headed off on the long, lonely ride back to Brisbane. The police had already telegraphed the news of the death of Cash O'Neill and his bravery in defeating Captain Jack, so he knew he'd be spared having to face the O'Neill staff, and quite probably relatives, for a while.

The sergeant's questions about his father gave him something else to think about. At home they'd never spoken of him, only of dear Captain Beckman, the hero, who must have outshone his son, and now Ben began to wonder why. A man should know more about his own father. He'd ask Oma.

Chapter Five

Gussie Beckman was the only person he could talk to, and he told her the truth. All of it.

Her first reaction was sheer fright that Ben had nearly lost his life at the hands of a man he'd trusted. To her, the outback had always been a wild and dangerous place, and here was proof of it.

When he showed her the wads of notes and the gold, she almost fainted. 'There was only a loaded gun in that other tree,' he told her, 'another trick. Not unexpected by then. I had enough of poor old Jack's haul anyway.'

'But it is not your money, Ben,' Oma whispered. 'You must hand it in.'

'To whom? He was a tricky customer. The bags are all unmarked. He robbed so many people, who could prove a claim to any of it now?'

'You should give it to the authorities.'

Ben laughed. 'I might as well throw it in the river. Who knows where it would end up? If not in government coffers then in government officials' pockets. No, it's mine, my good fortune. I'd be crazy to hand it in.'

Oma wasn't happy about it but she admitted she wasn't sure about these things and supposed that Ben knew what was best. And he was right about officials; hadn't it taken bribes to have him released from jail? Instead she turned her mind to her greatest delight, the chance to cook for her dear boy again.

'There's something I wanted to ask you, Oma. About my father.' He saw her stiffen but kept on. 'Did he die at sea too?'

'I don't like to talk about the past, Ben,' she said quietly, her back to him as she peeled vegetables.

'You don't like to talk about your son? Was your husband so much more important than your son?'

She sighed and turned to him. 'My only son died in Germany years back. He never came to Australia. He wasn't your father.'

'I was just waking up to that,' Ben replied. 'Then who was my father?'

'A man Diamond knew in the north. He was not a good man, Ben, and your mother knew she was well rid of him. That's why she would not say his name. She wanted you to have our name, Beckman.' Gussie consoled herself that the lie was only a twist of words. Ben needed normality in his life now, more than ever. The last thing he needed to know was the proximity of that terrible man whose name she wouldn't even think of, in case it came tumbling out.

'When did she last see him?'

'Ach! So long ago it was, before you were born. One day, she said, she'd tell you about him, when you were older, but she never got the chance. It's better this way, Ben.'

'I suppose so,' he agreed. Oma was right. The white man had probably abandoned his mother, not an unusual happening, so why worry about him now? Or even think of him? He wasn't disappointed. Besides, he had other matters to discuss with her.

'Tomorrow I'll have to go to the stables to talk to them. I don't know who the owner will be since Cash has gone. But I do know that whoever it is will only inherit debts, thanks to his gambling.'

'What a shame,' she said, relieved to be over the other subject.

There was a constancy about his view of the river from the clifftop that always drew Ben back. He still never tired of watching it, as some enjoyed the ocean and others the pleasure of the splendid hiss of rain. It was this same river that had delivered him to the quarries, but it had also brought him back, and looking at the past, the monotonous misery of that time seemed to fade compared with the shock of his final encounter with Cash O'Neill.

He should hate Cash, but strangely he mourned him, mourned a friendship that might have been, because he had liked the man. But that, he supposed, was the way with confidence tricksters like Cash; they were amiable, likeable characters, that was their stock-in-trade. Hadn't he himself used the gift of the gab in Mitchell to rearrange, for his own purposes, the circumstances of the deaths of the two men? He was older now, he felt years older. Where the quarries had given him physical strength, Cash had given him something more valuable. Confidence. And by his treachery a bonus, a steely resolve to succeed.

Oma was sitting in her big cane chair on the veranda, a picture of contentment. Her eyesight had dimmed to such an extent that she could no longer sew under the lamps at night, so relaxing out here was a peaceful end to her day.

Ben pulled up a chair to join her. 'When I rebuild the house,' he said, 'we'll have a wide veranda upstairs for a much better view.'

'Why would you rebuild the house?' she asked. 'There's nothing wrong with it.'

'It's too small. I want you to have a really beautiful house with a proper dining room and big parlours, and your own big bedroom with your own veranda, not the poky little room you have now.'

'And what will happen to this house?'

'We'll pull it down.'

'Oh, Ben. Such a waste of money. What would I do with a big house? I'd be cleaning all day.'

'No you wouldn't, you'd have maids. Even a cook. You deserve to be looked after now.'

'A cook!' She was horrified. 'I won't have silly girls interfering in my kitchen!'

Ben decided to let the subject drop for the time being. 'Like I said, I'll go into the stables tomorrow to see everyone. They'll think it peculiar if I don't put in an appearance.'

'Yes, you should. And I'd like to come with you to pay my respects. Don't forget that Mr O'Neill, rest his soul, was kind enough to come to your mother's funeral.'

'Good. It will be better if we go together. But Oma, please don't forget that I told them Cash died a hero. You won't forget, will you?'

'No. I think that's for the best. No need to add to their sadness.'

The stables were still open but very quiet, and Rod Callaghan was worried. 'I didn't realize until Cash left that the firm was broke. There's no money in the bank; stabling fees have been keeping the animals fed but not the staff. There's only old Dennis and me left, I had to let the rest go.'

'What about the sale of horses?' Ben asked.

'Oh, sure. I sold the three I had left, but there's no money to buy any more.' He looked at him. 'The place is going to rack and ruin. It was a sorry day, I tell you, when Cash shut down the saddlery. That was the money-maker, it brought more people here, gave us more of a chance to show off the horses we wanted to sell, and let them see that horses stabled here were in good care.'

Rod turned apologetically to Mrs Beckman. 'I'm sorry, ma'am. I shouldn't be keeping you out in the sun like this with my goings-on. Come into the office and I'll make you a cup of tea.'

He found a cup and saucer for Gussie, who sat primly in her black hat and gloves until Rod returned with a billy of tea, apologizing, this time, that he didn't have any milk.

'Not to worry,' she said as Rod poured tea into enamel mugs for himself and Ben. 'I find black tea far more thirst-quenching in this climate.'

'Indeed it is, ma'am,' he said. 'It was very good of you to come, you and Ben, I've sent Dennis to tell Kathleen that you're here.'

'Who's Kathleen?'

'Why . . . she's Cash's sister. The last of the family now. It was her door the police came to with the news that Cash had been killed, and her home on her own, the poor girl, so it was a terrible shock. But she's bearing up. We had a memorial service for him at St Joseph's Church, and so many people came it was remarkable. Of course, Cash being the hero made a difference; he's famous now, poor lad. And wouldn't he have loved it in his lifetime!'

While they waited, Rod wanted to know more about Cash's brave actions, and Ben obliged, telling exactly the story he'd related to the police. All the while Gussie didn't interrupt, seeming more interested in the untidy office with its photographs and sketches of fine horses on the walls, and papers scattered on the grimy desk.

Kathleen O'Neill appeared at last. A petite woman, but so much like Cash that Ben was taken aback. The black clothes seemed to suit her, accentuating beautiful dark eyes swept with long lashes that lacked only her brother's merry gleam. She had creamy skin, black curls bobbed from under the severe bonnet, and red lips, so solemn now, had the same curve that Cash could turn into a cheerful grin or a sneer of derision.

Gussie stood up to take her hands. 'My dear, I am so sorry. Please accept my condolences. I am Mrs Beckman and this is my grandson Ben, who was with your brother.'

Ben followed with the same sentiments, which she accepted graciously, but when she was settled in a chair there was an awkward silence.

Unlike Callaghan, she didn't seem to want or need to hear more of the now-famous story from Ben. She simply repeated Rod's words. 'It is very good of you to come. It's nice to know he had such good friends.'

'The reward is coming to you, the reward for that outlaw Captain Jack,' Rod told her. 'Ben wouldn't accept it.'

'Thank you,' she replied dully.

'I hope this isn't a bad time,' Ben said. 'But Cash and I sold the brumbies we caught out west. We made three hundred pounds . . .'

'Is that what the outlaws wanted?' she asked.

'Yes,' Ben said. 'I think they heard about it in town and followed us.'

'And he got himself killed just for the money,' she retorted. 'Why didn't he give it to them?'

'I wish he had, miss, and that's the truth. If I'd know where it was hidden, I'd have handed it over myself.'

She stood up, extending a hand to Gussie. 'I must go now. I've got a lot to do. Thank you again for coming, Mrs Beckman. It's very kind of you.'

'Ben brought back the money,' Rod said in an effort to cheer her up, 'the money for the brumbies. There's three hundred in the drawer, Kathleen.'

She stared coldly at Ben. 'I was under the impression that you both caught the horses.'

'Yes,' Ben replied. 'And a hard job it was too, out there in that dry country.'

She went to the drawer and counted the notes, handing half of them to Ben. 'This is your share, Mr Beckman. I don't take charity.'

'I didn't even know Cash had a sister,' Ben said on the way home. 'He never mentioned her.'

'Some men are like that,' Oma sighed. 'They never like to let the right hand know what the left hand's doing. But she seems a very nice young girl. And very sensible. I wonder what will become of her now?'

'I wouldn't worry,' Ben said. 'I'm sure she has plenty of friends.'

'But no money.'

He grinned. 'She's good-looking. She's probably got a husband in mind.'

'You men! You all seem to think that husbands are the answer to a maiden's prayer.'

'Aren't they?' Ben laughed.

'Rarely,' Oma sniffed. 'And to a girl in her circumstances sometimes a tragedy.'

He was surprised. 'Why?'

'Because her choices are limited.'

When they arrived home, Gussie took off her hat and called to Ben. 'Come into the kitchen, I want to talk to you.'

'What about?' he asked, following her.

'Those stables. I think you ought to buy them.'

'Why? Because you're feeling sorry for that girl? I'm not that keen to throw money away. The place is a dead loss.'

'It's nothing to do with Miss O'Neill. You know that her brother ruined the business, he sent it broke. But you said yourself it was a good business in her father's time. And so did Mr Callaghan. I think you should buy it, run it properly and reopen the saddlery. Find his old workmen and bring them back.'

'I don't know, Oma,' Ben said. 'I think it's past saving.'

'Then what do you intend to do with yourself? You can't sit about here all day. Just give it some thought, Ben. The land itself will be worth a lot of money as the town expands. You'd be surprised how fast cities grow.'

To please her he did think about it, and by morning he was beginning to believe that it wasn't such a bad idea after all.

'There's only one problem,' he told her. 'I can't suddenly turn up made of money. I can't use that haul I brought home yet; people might ask questions about how I'm suddenly rich.'

'I've thought of that, and it's a blessing now that your mother left her money in my name. I will buy it for you through Mr Joseph Mantrell, our solicitor.'

'I'll reimburse you,' he said, but Oma laughed. It was the first time he'd seen her so excited, so happy, since all their troubles began.

'Don't be silly, you can't reimburse me for money that's already yours. I feel like a conspirator, Ben. If you need extra capital to put that business back on its feet then you can quietly make use of your own bank, the money you've got hidden in your room. We won't ever mention it again, it's just your own private bank.'

He smiled. 'Oma, I do believe you're becoming as devious as the rest of the world.'

Gussie looked at him seriously. 'The world has struck you some terrible blows, Ben, and it's time you had some luck. I don't know whether the money you brought home is tainted or untainted, I can't decide, but one thing I expect of you. I want you to put aside all that has happened to you and work truly and honestly. And one more thing. I never want to hear the name of that Cash O'Neill again. If you do buy the business, take down the name of O'Neill and replace it with Beckman.'

'He wants to buy the stables?' Kathleen asked Rod. 'Where would he get the money from? He was just a stablehand and you say he's been in prison.'

'Mrs Beckman has made an offer,' Rod explained. 'She lives up on Kangaroo Point and apparently she's quite well off.'

'But he wouldn't know anything about our business,' she objected.

'What does it matter? Once he buys the stables it won't be your problem.'

'No. The place is mine now. I'll run it the way Father did. There won't be any more expensive racehorses. I can pull it back into shape. We'll make money again.'

He shook his head. 'Kathleen, if you don't sell you'll lose your house too. Cash mortgaged it with the rest of the property.'

She was shocked. 'How could he do that? Father left it to the both of us.'

'I don't know. How Cash did things we'll never discover except through the growing list of creditors. He owed money everywhere. You'll have to sell quickly, and this is the only offer.'

'How that Ben Beckman must be laughing at us. From stablehand to owner in only a few years.'

'I don't think he's laughing, love. He's quite a nice feller.'

'Then if he's such a nice feller, tell him he can buy a partnership in the business. That will give us money to pay the most pressing debts and begin to set things to rights here.'

'No go. I suggested that, but he says he's not interested in a partner.'

'In a female partner, I suppose?'

'I don't know about that. He's seen the registered plan of the stables and adjoining land, and that's what he wants to buy.'

'And what do I do? Sit in state in my house, watching everything my father worked for handed over to a stranger.'

'I keep telling you,' he said angrily, 'at least you keep your house, and you'll have a little money left over. If it bothers you that much, you could sell your house in a separate deal and move somewhere else.'

'Never!' she exploded. 'This is my home. I was born here.'

'I give up, Kathleen. I'll leave these papers with you. You can sign them or not. It's up to you.'

'And I suppose you're going to work for him. And Dennis too?'

'Take care, Kathleen. Don't treat us like traitors. We did the best we could and now we need jobs. With pay.'

A few weeks later, she was furious to see a new sign that proclaimed: 'Beckman Livery Stables'.

'Lose the name, you'll lose even more business,' she muttered to herself.

But that didn't happen. More horses were bought, more staff employed to work in the elegant stables that Cash, profligate as he was, had built.

And then on the vacant land where the training track for Cash's racehorses had been, she saw a building under construction. Angrily, she stormed into Ben Beckman's office.

'What are you building there? Right next to my house?'

'A saddlery,' he responded coolly. 'Your father was on the right track, good saddlers are still needed.'

'I won't have a factory next to my house. Put it somewhere else.'

'That's not possible, Miss O'Neill. But if you wish to sell your house I could do with more space.'

'You're deliberately doing this to annoy me,' she snapped. 'I don't understand what Cash saw in you!'

The insult cut deeply. 'Nor I in Cash!' he retorted angrily as she flounced out through the door.

Ben was at his stables by five o'clock every morning. He had a staff of seven, which he needed now since business had picked up. The stables were immaculate, the horses well fed and groomed and even though he'd raised the charges for stabling horses none of his customers complained. On studying the books he'd discovered that charges had remained the same since Mr O'Neill's days, while costs had risen, so he'd soon lifted them to a level that would return him a good profit.

His saddlery was almost complete, and he'd scoured Brisbane for the best workers in that trade. Kathleen O'Neill was still miffed at having a factory next door, so he'd built a high fence to separate their properties, which had mollified her to a certain extent. A least she didn't ignore him when he raised his hat to her as he passed, allowing him a nod, so that was something. Ben was all for keeping the peace.

On Oma's insistence – to give a good impression, she'd said – the small office had been cleaned out, painted and neatly furnished, but Ben didn't spend much time in there. He preferred to be outside working with his staff or exercising the horses in the remaining paddock. And he had other plans too. Nothing as foolish as going after brumbies again. Once the saddlery was under way he could find additional premises and begin manufacturing other leather goods. One thing led to another, he'd discovered, in this business of making money, and he was determined to make a great deal of money. He grinned to himself. Diamond had given him a good start, bless her. And Captain Jack and sent him bolting out in front. But now he needed to prove to himself that he could be a success, that he could double and treble his capital.

His only disappointment was that Oma had steadfastly refused to allow him to rebuild the cottage, to pull it down and replace it with a more modern house that would overshadow the one next door. Preferably a three-storeyed building that would grant them spectacular views and look down on the private gardens of the Thurlwells.

It was only seven thirty but he heard a lady outside talking with one of the grooms. Her voice sounded vaguely familiar.

He put on his hat and went out to greet her. She was a small woman with the unmistakable light tan of the bush, and she was wearing a wool jerkin over a check shirt, baggy moleskins and neat riding boots. Most ladies who rode astride wore modest long divided skirts, but this one was dressed more for comfort than style.

She smiled at him. 'You must be the new owner. Mr Beckman, is it?'

'Yes,' he said, charmed. 'What can I do for you?'

'I'm Mrs Buchanan. My husband keeps his horses here. Your groom has just gone off to saddle up Talleyman for me.'

Ben winced. Her husband, a politician he was told, was an arrogant fellow but, as Ben had to admit, he knew horses. Not as much of a townie as he pretended. On the other hand, Talleyman was a strong stallion who liked his own way. Ben considered suggesting that this lady choose another mount but thought better of it. She looked as if she knew what she was about.

'I'll need the filly Gracie, too,' she was saying. 'A friend is coming to ride with me.'

'That's good,' he said. 'Gracie hasn't been out for a while but I keep her in trim.'

'I'm glad to hear it, Mr Beckman.' She walked across the cobbled courtyard still damp from the morning hosing and peered into a full, glistening horse-trough.

'What wouldn't I give to be able to waste water like this,' she said wistfully.

Ben was alarmed. 'Do you think this is a waste?'

'Good heavens, no, it's just such a luxury. I come from out west and the drought is a nightmare.'

Phoebe arrived in a gig, as indeed had Clara, though they'd come from different directions.

She stepped down, told the driver she'd only be an hour or so, and in her usual manner set her riding cap straight, adjusted her blue velvet jacket and shook out her heavy riding skirt.

She hurried through the gate and saw Clara across the courtyard talking to a tall, heavily suntanned man. In that instant she took in and appreciated this 'fine figure of a feller', as she liked to describe good-looking men. He had broad shoulders, strong arms, with his sleeves rolled up, a well-belted waist and dark breeches that met high tan boots.

Before she crossed the courtyard to meet this interesting stranger, she automatically loosened her long blonde hair at the back with one hand to make it look more attractive, and tipped her chin a little higher.

On closer inspection she saw that the suntan was colour, which was a disappointment, but he was still an attractive man.

'There you are,' Clara called. 'We're having Gracie saddled for you now.' Her own horse was being led out and Clara rushed to it eagerly. 'Ah, Talleyman. Isn't he beautiful?' Over her shoulder she said, almost as an afterthought: 'Miss Thurlwell, meet Mr Beckman. He's the new owner.'

His eyes were brown and beautiful and they seemed to be concentrating on hers as he smiled and said softly, 'How do you do, Miss Thurlwell?'

Phoebe knew who he was! It had to be that boy, now grown-up, but the smile? Was it recognition, or simple politeness? He gave no indication so Phoebe was confused. She could be wrong. But he had looked at her with such fondness – she was sure it was fondness, like a genial relation looking on a little girl he hadn't seen for a long time. But, oh my God! He was a jailbird! What could she have been thinking of to even consider flirting with him!

She dashed away and he made no attempt to follow her, allowing a groom to assist her into the saddle. Clara was already mounted on Talleyman, holding him steady, patting him and talking to him like an old friend until Phoebe was ready. When they rode out together, Phoebe didn't look back.

Ben hadn't recognized her at first but he was genuinely pleased to see her. The spindly girl had grown into a fine lady. He had nothing against her, only her people. And that he could never forgive. It worried him though that he'd seen disappointment in her face; the shine had been rubbed off as if with a cloth when his name was mentioned. She had been embarrassed and he supposed she had every right. As a neighbour she'd know his background down to the last detail, especially the prison terms. Something he never bothered to hide.

As Oma had explained to him: 'Hold your head up, boy. Be forthright. Whatever people try to hide, others scurry to find.'

He smiled, wondering when she'd stop calling him her boy. But what news he'd have to tell Oma tonight. Phoebe Thurlwell was a customer!

Oma had said that the girl had been kind to her, calling in occasionally with little presents, but she hadn't seen her for quite a while. 'Young ladies, their social life becomes important.'

Rather than embarrass the girl, he kept out of sight when she returned later in the morning with Mrs Buchanan. But he wondered if Phoebe had mentioned their acquaintance to her friend. Or worse, his story. Maybe it would cause the Buchanans to remove their horses from the Beckman Livery Stables. Not that it would matter, he shrugged. He had a list of customers waiting for space.

Phoebe didn't mention him to Clara. They rode well out into the country instead of along the fashionable track by the river, and had a good time talking about every little thing.

But that night Phoebe sat alone out on her balcony, knowing that he was home, right there, in that cottage. Probably sleeping soundly while she sat here, disturbed, completely thrown off balance. It was very annoying. No matter who he was, good manners required that she should have at least acknowledged him, saying: 'Oh yes, we've met,' or something inconsequential like that. But she hadn't. She'd run for cover. And he must have known that she was embarrassed. How awful! She'd never go near those stables again.

She wondered if he'd found her silence hurtful. But then, he could have acknowledged her, or asked if she were his neighbour.

No he couldn't, she argued with herself. It wouldn't have been his place to speak up. Not at all. Maybe he thought she was one of those hoity-toity women who would have cut him dead.

Clara had remarked that the new owner had seemed a very nice person. She hadn't mentioned his colour. But then Clara wouldn't. Out west she was accustomed to dealing with blacks so she'd probably hardly notice a half-caste.

Phoebe sat up in shock. Was that what the boy Ben was? A half-caste? As a kid she'd never thought about it. No wonder her mother threw fits at having them next door. Phoebe grinned. Wouldn't Lalla have another one of her fits if she knew the kid from next door had grown into a handsome man, *and* the owner of the best stables in town. And that was interesting. Where had poor people like the Beckmans got the money to buy a business like that? Not that it mattered one whit to her. None of it mattered. She decided to find a good book and go to bed and forget about Ben Beckman. For heaven's sake!

'Up early again, miss?' Biddy was surprised to see Phoebe coming down the stairs at this hour.

'Yes. Tell someone to bring round the gig. Mrs Buchanan has got me riding again, and I have to say she's right. This is the best time of the day, before it gets too hot.'

'Very sensible, miss. Would you like some breakfast before you go?'

'I'll get myself some tea and toast in the kitchen. You order the gig.'

She hadn't lied, she told herself, she'd just given the impression that she was riding with Clara this morning, in case her mother asked. She wasn't doing anything wrong. She had enjoyed the ride yesterday and she was entitled to do the same again today. No matter whose stables they were. Besides, as Clara had said, the horse did need the exercise, even if she did have to ride alone.

This time the groom recognized her and hurried away to bring out the filly. There was no sign of the owner of the stables, nor did Phoebe see him when she returned more than an hour later. But she had enjoyed the ride, this time along the river bank. She really had.

And on the following day she had Clara for company again, collecting the horses in her matter-of-fact way and returning them to the grooms without any need to see the proprietor.

'You've got me back into the habit,' Phoebe told her. 'I shall ride much more often now.'

'I'm glad. With Christmas coming on I won't have too much time, and then we're going home.'

'So soon? I shall miss you. Most country people stay a lot longer.'

'Normally we would,' Clara explained. 'But the drought's so bad it's important to be there to shift stock all the time, to find water for them. And some sort of feed.'

After that Phoebe rode every weekday on her own.

Ben saw her. Occasionally he nodded to her, smiled as she trotted the horse out of the gate, because she seemed a lonely person. He was reminded of the little girl who had played in that big garden next door, so often alone. Then he remembered her father. He wished he would come in! A few burrs under a saddle would give him a nasty ride.

Then, one morning, she came limping in, leading the horse, and he went out to meet her.

'Miss Thurlwell! What happened?'

'I fell off,' she said crankily. 'A man came riding a damn bicycle out of nowhere. Right in front of Gracie. She took fright and jumped out of the way and I was thrown. People like that ought to be locked up.'

'You're not hurt?'

'No. I grazed my hands and got a bump on my elbow, but I'll be all right.'

'Perhaps I should send one of the grooms to ride with you in future.'

'There's no need,' she snapped.

'Good-oh. Your gig's waiting out there. I'll take Gracie and settle her down. She looks forward to seeing you in the mornings now, sticks her head out of the stall, peering about, getting very impatient. And she seems to know the days you're not coming.'

'Does she?' Phoebe said, pleased. She patted the horse. 'What a good girl you are! I'm glad you weren't hurt by that horrible man.' Then she remembered the gig. 'It's late. Excuse me, I'd better go.'

She felt foolish on the way home. She had actually run to the gig! Why had she done that? Would he think she was running away from him? She really ought to stop visiting those stables. It was becoming boring riding on her own. But now he'd made her feel responsible for the horse. As if her absence would cause it to go into a decline. Gracie wasn't her horse. She belonged to the Buchanans, who had always allowed Phoebe to ride their horses because there were no stables at Somerset House. The horses used for the Thurlwell vehicles were kept at the coach house down the road.

It was a damn nuisance! She ought to take the horse out less and less, wean her off, so to speak.

But as usual, Phoebe was there again the next morning.

As she was leaving for her ride, Beckman himself emerged on a big chestnut horse. 'I thought I'd better come with you today in case Gracie is still jumpy.'

'There's no need,' Phoebe said. 'I'm sure she'll be fine.'

'If you'd rather I kept my distance, I don't mind.'

'I didn't mean that.' She didn't know what she meant. He looked so attractive, sitting there waiting for her to make a decision, she hardly knew what to say.

In the end she shrugged. 'Come on then. Can we go down towards Breakfast Creek?'

'By all means, anywhere you like.'

They rode in silence until Phoebe couldn't stand it. 'Do you mind if I ask you something?'

'No. Fire away.'

'Are you Ben Beckman from next door?'

'Right first go!' he laughed.

'Why didn't you say so before?'

'Why didn't you ask before?'

'I didn't like to.'

'Well, there you are.'

Phoebe was astonished that with his background he was so self-assured. It seemed to place her at a disadvantage, so she retaliated. 'You broke our windows!'

'And I paid for that, in spades,' he said evenly.

'Yes. I'm sorry.'

'Don't be. It's not your problem.'

More silence until he volunteered: 'Remember the snake?'

'The one that had you bailed up when we were kids? How could I forget? I was scared stiff!'

'Not half as scared as I was. If you hadn't called my mother he'd have got me.'

Mention of his mother made her nervous. Phoebe recalled the night he'd come screaming into their house begging her father for help. The night his mother died.

'I got into trouble for tearing my dress,' she said vaguely.

Their conversations were sporadic. Piecemeal. Taboo subjects evident. They dismounted at the creek and allowed the horses to drink, and then led them along the track that bordered the grounds of a former governor's residence.

'It's beautiful,' he said. 'I didn't know this track was here.'

'We're probably trespassing. Do you care?'

'Not unless someone takes a potshot at us.'

On the way home Phoebe found safer ground. The stables. He was proud of them and told her he was reopening the saddlery shortly, enthusiastic about his new business.

Ben found her pleasant company after all. She'd grown into a very nice girl, he thought, with an honest approach. Too honest. He'd noticed her efforts to avoid embarrassing subjects, just as he'd shied away from any thought of her family and that bastard of a father of hers. He really had gone out with her to keep an eye on the horse – and her, of course. She wasn't the best of riders since, though unhurt, she'd been unable to remount Gracie on her own after her tumble.

But it had been a good break for him, riding out with a pretty girl, and that she was, by God.

Two men from Cobb and Company were waiting for him, to discuss his plans to buy and train horses for them. But they were worried. Plans were afoot, they told him, to build more railroads throughout the state, railroads that would ruin their company. Listening to them he forgot about Miss Thurlwell.

But Phoebe didn't forget him. She knew it was wrong. She knew it was madness. But there was something about Ben, the Ben she now knew. He was the most thrilling man she'd ever met. Riding beside him had given her a rush of excitement, a feeling she'd never experienced before. She wanted to talk to him. To talk to him properly, like a person, not just the boy next door. To have him tell her what had happened to him during those years in jail so that she could show him she cared about his suffering. He must have suffered, she was sure. She wished she could make it up to him. But he was so damned offhand about everything.

It was a week before she found a chance to speak with him again, and even then she had to think of something to say: 'I was wondering, are you closing down over Christmas.'

'No, miss, only Christmas Day.'

'That's good. I think I'll go out to Breakfast Creek again today. Why don't you take a break and come too? You're always working.'

'I'd like to but I can't. I bought a colt at the yearling sales yesterday and he's a bit wild. I have to take him out to the back paddock and give him some lessons in behaving himself.'

'You wouldn't hurt him?'

Ben smiled. 'Of course not.'

'I've never seen horse-breaking. It sounds interesting. Can I watch?'

'If you want to. I'll probably still be there when you get back, but it's pretty boring.'

She cut short the ride and was back in time to leave Gracie with a groom and hurry out to the paddock, where he was teaching the young horse not to jib at a bridle. The animal didn't like it at all but Ben was patient and soon he called for a light saddle, holding the colt still as a groom strapped it on. The horse kicked and bucked, trying to dislodge it without success as Ben led it round and round, pretending not to notice the tantrum. Some of the staff were watching too, enjoying the action and calling out advice to Ben.

After a while it did become boring. No one seemed to be in any hurry to try to mount the horse, and Ben just kept on walking the animal and talking to it, so Phoebe slipped away. She had an appointment with her dressmaker and the woman would be waiting.

There were so many parties and social occasions this Christmas, she practically needed a whole new wardrobe, but it was hard to raise any interest. It was always the same people, the same crowd, only the venues differing. That was why she'd accepted Barnaby's invitation to the staff Christmas party at Parliament House. It was only a get-together of all the clerical staff, but she thought she might as well go. And she had to overcome that stupid proposal. Neither of them had spoken of it since.

When he called for her that evening, he was impressed: 'Phoebe! You're looking radiant. I mean, you always look good but tonight . . . well! You'll outshine all the other ladies.'

'It's a new dress,' she said shortly.

'Is that what it is? Then it certainly does the trick.'

'Can we go?' she said, on edge now, irritated by his compliments. 'Mother's not all that pleased I'm going out with you. Let's get away before she starts lecturing us.'

'Your carriage awaits,' he grinned, still dazzled by her appearance. The dress was lovely, Barnaby mused, as he helped her into the hired cab. It was the palest green in a very soft material, and so close-fitting it showed off her figure to perfection. The skirt swelled out to a fullness at the hem and was balanced by a light cape of the same material that gave only a glimpse of a low-cut bodice. Ideal for summer evening. And enough to send a man crazy, he added to himself. He longed to take her in his arms. Instead he made polite conversation.

'How are your parents?'

'They're fine. Except they're really cross with you now. When you went to work for the Attorney-General I thought you'd be doing law, and instead everyone says you're working on this federation business.'

'It is law. We can't have federation without a constitution.'

'I really don't know why you bother, Barnaby. No one wants it.'

'Your uncle is anti-federation because it might jam up his plans for the railroad.'

'It's not just that. We're independent here. Why should we want a parliament from a southern capital interfering?'

'They won't be interfering. Only in certain matters.'

'There you are, that's interfering! It shouldn't be allowed.'

'Don't you want to see us as a nation, one big country?'

'That's airy-fairy talk! I don't want to see this state ending up a backwater to the bigger states.'

'We are the biggest state on this side of the country, and we are already a backwater,' he said crossly. 'If we join up with them we'll really forge ahead.'

Since most of the talk at the party, among Barnaby's colleagues, centred on federation, and what a great job he was doing for their minister, Phoebe wasn't impressed. Although she didn't argue with anyone, for which he was grateful, neither did she make any attempt to be sociable.

Fortunately the small function, which was held on the front colonnade of the House, lasted only a couple of hours, and Barnaby was glad when it ended. His friends had all remarked on his beautiful girlfriend, which made him all the more miserable. She was not enjoying herself and it was his fault. He shouldn't have argued with her.

To make it up to her, he suggested she might like to dine at the new Victoria Hotel. 'It's very respectable and they have an excellent chef.'

'No thank you. I'm tired. I should prefer to go home.'

'Aren't we speaking, Phoebe?' he asked her.

'Of course we are. It's just that you're so adamant about this. Other people have different views.'

At her door, he tried to make light of the argument. 'Religion and politics! They shouldn't be discussed on social occasions, people say. That's what we get for breaking the rules.'

'I expect so,' she said vaguely, and with murmured thanks, she was gone.

As he travelled home he worried. It seemed as if they'd said goodbye forever. He knew Phoebe. The argument wasn't only about politics, there was something else. Maybe some*one* else. At times this evening he'd noticed her gazing out over the grounds, which looked soft and misty in the moonlight, with a faraway expression on her face. As if she were thinking of someone else. And that was quite possibly true. He supposed it had to happen sooner or later, though he hadn't heard of Phoebe being seen about with anyone in particular.

He bought some fish and chips and ate them in his room. A fitting end to a disastrous evening.

The name of Barnaby Glasson was becoming well known in the halls of power. He had applied himself diligently to the complicated subject of federation, studying the proposed constitution and the bewildering array of amendments put forward by those in favour of the merger of the states, and he was inundated with opinions from all sides.

'If the constitution has become such a battleground among the pro-federationists,' he groaned, 'what sort of a débâcle will it be when we go to the people and the anti-federationists join the fray?'

'Stay with it, Barnaby,' the Attorney-General, Thomas Creighton, told him. 'I'm convinced that sooner or later Queensland will join and we have to watch our state's rights, see that we don't get left at the post. Read every line of the speeches and debates coming up from the southern states, and let me have the reports as soon as possible.'

'All very well for him,' Barnaby muttered to himself as he worked late into the nights. The premiers of the four southern states were eager for the Queensland government to pass an Enabling Act to send delegates to the conventions working on this new Australian constitution, so they made sure that the Queensland premier was kept informed. Most of the paperwork found its way to Barnaby's desk and he did his best trying to unscramble all the legal aspects, often depressed that this seemed much too big a job for him. So far the Queensland politicians, with all their vested interests, couldn't even agree to send delegates to discuss the constitution, so the Bill was gathering dust on the table.

Adding to his despondency was the realization that interest in federalism was dwindling because of the long shearers' strike that was causing hardship for both the shearers and the squatters. The Ministerial Party was busy preparing legislation to outlaw the strike, which had continued for months in an atmosphere of violent confrontation.

Barnaby had seen the proposed legislation and had avoided any involvement with it by good luck rather than good management. He'd commented to the Attorney-General that he thought the Bill was too harsh and hardly democratic, at which his minister had told him crustily to mind his own business! That had resulted in a decision by Creighton to send Barnaby to Sydney for a few weeks to observe debates in the New South Wales parliament and meet, in person, the gentlemen who were drawing up the constitution.

He was thrilled, and it gave him an excuse to call on Phoebe Thurlwell, to tell her the good news. Their relationship had been strained since that evening on the boat, and the staff party hadn't helped, but Barnaby was determined not to lose her. She meant too much to him.

With more confidence, encouraged by the growing importance of his duties, he sent her a note asking if he could call on Saturday afternoon, and received one of Phoebe's typical replies, which simply said, 'Of course.'

Once again, though, there were young people everywhere at the Thurlwell mansion, where Phoebe had organized round-robin table tennis events for doubles and singles.

'Barnaby dear,' she greeted him, 'I'm so glad you could come. You're a good player and Beth Noakes needs a partner, so I've paired you with her.'

'You sound like your mother,' he said, knowing that would annoy her and distract her from burying him in the table tennis teams.

'I don't sound at all like my mother,' she snapped.

'Well then, what happened to: "Hello, Barnaby, What have you been doing? I haven't seen you for weeks"?'

'I know exactly what you've been doing,' she countered. 'I hear nothing else from my beloved family. You're working on a constitution that will send us all to the poorhouse. Actually, that's why I didn't send you an invitation to come today. You're out of favour with the parents.'

'And what about you?'

'You're always in favour with me, you know that.'

A young gentleman came dashing towards them. 'Phoebe! The referee is hopeless. Come and adjudicate!'

Barnaby turned on him. 'Excuse me, I was having a private conversation with Miss Thurlwell.'

'I beg your pardon.' The youth retreated in confusion.

'That wasn't necessary,' Phoebe said.

'Yes it was.' He took her into the quiet of the parlour. 'I want to talk to you.'

'Oh no. Are you never going to let me forget I made a fool of myself?'

'Never,' he grinned. 'Talking marriage with you was the most important event of my life, and it was I who made the mistake. I didn't handle it very well.'

'You turned me down. So we'll forget it.'

'That's only an excuse to dodge the issue, Phoebe, and you know it. You've had more time to think about it now. I do love you, very very much. I hate all these people being here, I want you to myself. The question is, Phoebe, do you love me?'

She twisted away. 'Barnaby, I do and I don't. Can't you understand that I'm not sure.'

'Do you love me enough to marry me? This isn't the best time to be asking you, but I'm going to Sydney for a few weeks and if you're happy about this I'll do it properly when I come back.' He heard himself pleading but was pleased that at least he was presenting his case with some coherence. 'I'll make you a good husband, Phoebe. I understand you and I'll always take care of you.'

'That's the trouble,' she said sadly. 'I know you would, my dear Barnaby. That's why I rushed at the idea so foolishly, and I don't know how to apologize for doing such a cruel thing. And you having the good sense and the courtesy to tell me to think on it has only made me feel worse.'

'You're saying you don't want to marry me?' he asked her gently.

'I think so. You're too good a friend. Does that sound stupid?'

'No. That's what I was afraid of all along.'

'Love?' she asked. 'What is it? I want to be madly in love. I want to be jealous. I don't know what it is to be jealous, not of anyone. Maybe I never will like or love someone that much. Perhaps it's just not in me.'

'I think it is. And I'm already jealous.' He took her to him and kissed her on the lips. 'That's to say I still love you, even if you are the most maddening person I ever met.'

She threw her arms about him. 'You forgive me then? I wouldn't hurt you for the world.'

The strange part of it, he mused as he made his way home, declining her invitation to stay for the games, was that he didn't feel hurt. Her answer had not been unexpected and it was some solace for him to know that there was no competition on the horizon. Nor was there for Phoebe for that matter. He'd met more young ladies in the last six months than he had in the years of seclusion in Joseph's office, but none of them could hold a candle to his lovely, wilful Phoebe.

Not so far, anyway, and there was no rush for him to find a wife. He had work to do, and mixing with politicians of all persuasions, he was beginning to get the bug himself. If federation ever came to pass with the inclusion of Queensland, a man's name would go down in history as one of the founding fathers if he were to be among the first members of an Australian parliament.

Sydney was a surprise and a delight to Barnaby. He'd enjoyed the adventure of sailing down the Brisbane River and across restless Moreton Bay out into the ocean beyond. He'd fared well on his first sea voyage, overcoming the dreaded seasickness within hours to appreciate the hearty company of his shipmates. When they finally sailed into Sydney Harbour, he was more disappointed at the end of too short a voyage than impressed with the grandeur of the great harbour.

But when he stepped ashore at Circular Quay and walked up the street, he was astounded by the solid sophistication of this city. Barnaby had always regarded Brisbane as a very important place, being the capital of the great state of Queensland; a fine town, unmatched in beauty, with its lovely botanic gardens, wide streets and busy commercial area. But Sydney was immense! Tall buildings, people a-bustle everywhere, no sign of rough carts or rumbling wagons in this mecca of elegance. Beside this city, Brisbane was ramshackle, still mainly one-storeyed except for a few public buildings while this place spread high and wide. His Brisbane, he had to admit, was still only a rustic town, so no wonder the politicians and king-makers of the south had never taken it seriously.

Until now, he thought grimly. Until now, when they needed the Queenslanders to come to heel or upset the whole applecart of federation.

Being a dedicated civil servant, he made straight for the Houses of

Parliament, pleased to note, in a surge of parochialism, that his own Parliament House, back home, was much more modern, having been completed only about twenty years ago.

He was referred to the office of the Clerk of the Parliament and then on to the office of the Chairman of Committees, where a genial clerk with a fluff of white side-whiskers accepted his credentials and offered him tea.

'In fact,' he said, 'the invitation was extended to your Attorney-General but I gather your government up there in the bush is troubled by strikes.'

Barnaby would not have referred to Brisbane as 'up there in the bush' but he let that go. 'I hope this doesn't mean that I am to be excluded from the meetings. I am after all my minister's representative.'

'Only a few top-level shows with the Premier and so on,' the clerk murmured. 'We'll find enough for you to do.'

'Thank you,' Barnaby said. 'And could you suggest where I might stay?'

'We had booked a room for Mr Creighton at the George Hotel, a very pleasant room indeed. You might as well stay there.'

'Is it very expensive? My expense account is rather meagre.'

'That seems to be the lot of gentlemen like us.' The clerk smiled mildly. 'But since the invitation was issued from here, this office would of course settle the bill, so you need have no worries on that score. I'll give you a note to the manager and you trot along to the George and make yourself comfortable.' He winked. 'We shouldn't want to let the hotel down, should we? They don't take kindly to last-minute cancellations.'

'It's very good of you,' Barnaby said.

'Not at all, Mr Glasson. You report here at eight sharp in the morning and we'll set you to work. You do have very important duties. Personally I find all the arguments a monumental headache, and if you can take home reports that will entice your parliament to get on with it, we shall be most grateful.'

His room at the George Hotel was splendid but Barnaby didn't see much of it. He was kept busy listening to debates, attending meetings – some in the committee rooms and some in public halls – and working on his notes at a small desk provided for him in a corner office. He was never asked for his opinion but as he grew more confident and the occasion permitted, be began to speak up. To suggest mildly that such measures as removal of border customs would see a loss of revenue to poorer state governments like Queensland, and that some forms of recompense might be in order.

'This is one of the main objections of our parliamentarians,' he said, 'even though our sugar and beef growers would welcome more open markets.'

'Then I don't see what the problem is,' one man replied testily.

'The problem is that the primary industries don't have a say yet. We have to get the Enabling Act past Parliament first. Past the Treasury benches.'

There were nods of understanding about the table.

'A sweetening might be in order,' the Chairman said. 'We'll have our taxation people look into it, Mr Glasson. There must be other ways for the states to raise revenue.'

Only on Sundays was Barnaby able to walk the quiet streets, to fully acquaint himself with this city. To sit in an inn on the harbourfront to have lunch and a quiet drink, and in the afternoon to ride the ferry to Manly and back. On the last Sunday he boarded a ship to return home, a changed man.

At all these gatherings he'd heard some sensible speeches, and some that were nothing short of ridiculous. He was no longer awed by big-city folk, he knew he could match, almost, the best of them. And he would fight even harder for federation, for this young lawyer was determined now, not just playing with the idea, to be among the first to enter a federal parliament, wherever it was located. That was just another problem to overcome. Where a Commonwealth Parliament House should be built.

His return to Brisbane was hardly noticed, there was so much gloom and exhilaration, depending on one's point of view, that the shearers' strike was over.

'Defeated they were by the sheer might of the squatters,' a Labor politician growled to Barnaby. 'What hope has the working man got?'

'Maybe you'd have a stronger voice with an Australian government,' Barnaby murmured.

'Like hell! I'd like to get rid of our Upper House, with all those pompous layabouts nominated to wear out seats for life. We don't want another one.'

'Wait a minute!' Barnaby scrambled through his papers. 'Look at this. An Australian government will be different. Much more democratic. The Upper House will be called the Senate, the members will have to be voted in by the people of Queensland, not nominated, and there will be no life members.'

'You don't say!' The politician studied the typed pages that Barnaby presented to him. 'Well, that's a bloody improvement.'

When the man had left, Barnaby found himself studying the same amendments, not to learn more, but to further his own career. Why hadn't he thought of it before? Every man and his dog would be rushing for the Lower House, which they understood better. The Senate wouldn't be a sinecure for swells; anyone could stand for it. Each state could elect an equal number of representatives, to protect the smaller states from being overwhelmed by the others. 'And by Jove,' he muttered to himself, 'what an opportunity! Senator Barnaby Glasson! That has a nice ring to it.'

His daydreams were interrupted by a summons to the inner sanctum of the Attorney-General, who accepted all of Barnaby's carefully prepared reports with grumbling approval. 'Good work. Don't know when I'll get time to read them. But I can see you've been busy.'

Barnaby sighed. Creighton was a bureaucrat of the first order seemingly convinced that the heavier the paper-storm, the better the work. And he'd noticed that several of the Attorney-General's staff played that game to the hilt, sending him reams of inconsequential letters, memos, summaries and long-winded arguments, knowing full well that the boss never bothered with half of them.

'This damn drought,' Creighton grunted. 'Costing us all a bloody fortune. Banks foreclosing. Graziers and squatters, some of our best supporters, shouting at us to do something. I keep telling them that federation will open the borders for them, give them bigger markets, but it doesn't help the men who've hardly got a decent steer still standing. It's hard to keep the federation ball rolling up here, with that Royce Davies, a Labor man, and Ben Buchanan, a cattleman, in cahoots, damning federation as the work of the devil.'

'I have a suggestion, sir. While I was in Sydney I met Mr Theodore Prosser. He's one of the best speakers I've ever heard, especially on the subject of federation. He's also on the executive of the Australian Natives Association.'

'What the hell's that? An Aborigine Club, for God's sake?'

'No, sir, not at all. They're a very powerful group of leading citizens who are backing federation. They are loyal to the Queen and want to remain in the Commonwealth, but feel strongly that we should be united as a nation, not a set of colonies.'

'Oh! Well, good on them. But what about this feller Prosser?'

'He's willing to come up, if he's invited, to speak in Brisbane and in as many country towns as might receive him.'

Creighton chewed his pen. Tapped his foot. 'Would he expect to be paid?'

'Certainly not, he considers himself a patriot.'

'He does? Then we'd better have him. I'll speak to the Premier about him. Maybe he can talk some sense into the drones in this place while he's about it.'

The suggestion to have Prosser visit country towns had been an idea of Barnaby's, a sudden inspiration, and he was sure that the enthusiastic Prosser would go along with it. And with luck he would be accompanied on his tour by one Barnaby Glasson, who would avail himself of the opportunity to become known in these far-flung centres. A senator had to be elected by the vote of all electors of the state, not just in one electorate. A tour like this would give him a flying start, without letting any other possible runners know that the race had begun.

Prosser accepted the invitation, noting that he should be proud to take the word throughout Queensland, but that owing to pressing engagements he would not be available until early in the New Year.

The Attorney-General confirmed the tour and promptly forgot about Prosser, having recently acquired a new headache: South Australia was in the process of granting women the right to sit in Parliament, a move that appalled him and was stirring Queensland women to demand the same right.

But Barnaby didn't forget Theodore Prosser. Every spare minute he could find he worked on the tour, studying maps and transport requirements and writing letters, under the official government seal, to town mayors and leaders, enquiring as to the availability of venues for public meetings. He did not give the name of the speakers or the subject matter, simply lodging enquiries at this stage. It became for him a recreational activity as exciting as preparing a Grand Tour of Europe.

Coastal towns could be reached by ship, and from those ports they could make their way to inland centres. He pored over a large Lands Department map with its few and far-flung black dots representing townships. From Townsville, for instance, they could travel west to the famous gold town of Charters Towers, a journey of about a hundred miles.

Then, returning to the coast, they could sail south to the port of Rockhampton and visit the massive Mount Morgan gold mines, and from there head inland again, this time to the pastoral centre of Longreach, made famous by the shearers' strike.

Barnaby gulped, taking out his ruler to check. That place was five hundred miles or thereabouts from the coast! Until now he'd had no idea of the size of this colony. He wondered if Mr Prosser would even consider such arduous journeys to the outback townships Barnaby had on his list. By now he was wishing that Edgar Thurlwell's great dream of inland railroads was a reality, not just plans in progress. He'd heard that to raise the required capital for such a huge enterprise, Edgar had gone public with his company and that the shares had soon been snapped up. He wished now that he had bought some of those shares, since the proposers of the federal constitution were, as he understood it, fast losing interest in nationalizing the railroads.

Distance would be a real challenge to anyone wishing to have his voice heard throughout this state, and Barnaby prayed, as he continued with his itinerary, that Prosser was as good as his word in boasting that he would go anywhere in the service of the nation.

* * *

For his part, Edgar Thurlwell wasn't so sure that a federal government wouldn't interfere with his plans. Hadn't the Premier and his cohorts already started backing off from granting him the necessary stretches of land so that he could begin laying the lines? If he couldn't trust his own state government, what hope would he have with politicians planted a thousand miles away?

'Typical of their usual lack of foresight!' he complained to William and Lalla.

'Then you should look at the problem from another direction,' Lalla said. 'Since you propose a railroad to Longreach, go there. Have the people of Longreach, and the towns along the route, demand that the government support your railroad.'

'Better to call it their railroad,' William advised. 'It makes people more involved.'

'Why should I have to go?' Edgar said. 'Haven't I got enough to do, battling with English steel mills to get on with my shipments, and a million other matters? As it is, I have to get down to Sydney to supervise the building of my rail coaches. They're coming along well but it's folly to turn one's back on factories like that. I'm paying for the best and I want the best.' He snorted angrily. 'The Americans never had to put up with dunderheads like we've got in government. They're go-ahead people, with entrepreneurs like myself encouraged all the way.'

'Get Buchanan on the job then,' William said. 'Send him to Longreach. He's been slacking off lately.'

'Only because, as an independent, you tied him in with Royce Davies, a Labor man, Edgar,' his sister-in-law said. 'I still think you made a mistake there.'

'No I didn't. Buchanan has his uses but he's not all that popular, he'd never have made Leader of the Opposition. You have a talk with him, Lalla. The man is only sulking but he still has shares in the railroad company. Get Belle Foster on to him.'

'I might be able to,' she said vaguely. 'Clara is in town. She'll expect me to call on her.'

'Good idea,' William said. 'Most of the squatters come to the coast for the festive season, that's a chance to bring 'em all into line.'

Edgar nodded. 'It's a comfort to know my family can be relied on. Now I must be on my way.'

As he left he smiled to himself. He'd noticed that since his remark to Buchanan, the man had been keeping as clear of Lalla as he could, but she was a determined woman. Throwing them together again could have interesting consequences.

Although he gave no inkling to any of them, he was a worried man.

Expenses were mounting; grants of land were the linchpin of the whole enterprise – without them the capital required would skyrocket – and he had already invested far more of the Thurlwell funds than he had originally intended. His application for grants of land was not a matter for the full Parliament, it could be done with a sweep of the pen by the Minister for Lands, the Honourable Jed Sweepstone. It was time Jed got on with it, or something would have to be done.

The problem here, though, was that Jed, a wealthy man and a member of the best clubs, was truly a gentleman of integrity. Whilst he was in favour of transferring the required land, and enthusiastic about a railroad to Longreach, for a start, he was prevaricating.

'It's only a slight delay,' he kept telling Edgar. 'I should prefer the Premier's signature over mine. I'm sure he'll see the wisdom of our endeavours when he has more time. I keep telling him that private enterprises like this will be the salvation of our great state.'

Sweepstone also graciously declined to accept the gift of shares in Western Railroad proffered by Edgar. 'Couldn't accept them, old chap. I have great confidence in the project, but conflict of interests, you know . . . can't be done.'

He had also made a 'slight change', as he called it, to the proposed transfer of land. Instead of grants, Edgar's company would now be given ninety-nine-year leases.

The switch infuriated Edgar. There was a big difference between owning those corridors of land and holding the leases, a loss of assets that he had already included in his prospectus. But the mild-mannered Sweepstone was not a man to be bullied. He had to be treated with kid gloves until Edgar could find another way to pressure him. He would have to take a harder look at the Sweepstone family.

The formal afternoon tea held in the grounds of Parliament House that December was one that would be long remembered. Not in the pages of Hansard, for it was never mentioned in either House, but in everyday households the gossip sputtered and spread like endless rows of tiny firecrackers. An event to be recalled again and again.

For this township of Brisbane, the capital of a state though it might be, sheltered an isolated community, intimidated by the southern cities and by the sheer size of their own state. As a result, local news, trivial, true or untrue, was seized upon with gusto to be munched over and masticated, replacing the all-pervading subject of the climate.

Invitations to the afternoon tea were issued by the Speaker of the House to the lists of family and friends submitted by the Members, and as numbers were limited the gilt-edged cards were greatly prized by those privileged to attend.

As the *Courier-Mail* reported, it was a fine, sunny day . . . if the temperature of ninety degrees and a humidity equal to a Turkish bath could be described as such.

Nevertheless, the stoic traditionalists arrived properly attired, the gentlemen in their Sunday best with stiff shirts and cutaway coats, damp handkerchiefs at the ready to mop flushed faces and the inside bands of toppers. Ladies were more to be envied, strolling the lawns in their summery, mostly white gowns and splendid hats, and carrying pretty parasols.

From a tall window upstairs in the House, Barnaby and other staffers who, naturally, were not invited, were impressed. It was a lovely sight, like a very elegant picnic, colourful canvas umbrellas hovering over tables set in starched white. Prim little maids in black and white were threading carefully with their trays through the assembly, and from the colonnade on the east wing a gorgeous military band was playing stirring marches.

He wasn't upset at not being invited; staffers knew their place, they were happy to have such a view and to be able to point out notables, friends and foes. Barnaby, though, was watching for a certain person, and when he saw her arrive with her family, his heart missed a beat. Several in fact. Phoebe looked lovely, as usual, trailing behind her mother as they made slow progress, chatting to all and sundry. He found some consolation that she was only partnered by her Uncle Edgar and not by any of the young gentlemen bounding about who would have been pleased to escort Miss Thurlwell.

Barnaby grinned to himself. That was typical of Phoebe. She had to be different! Most young ladies would be mortified at having to attend such an occasion without a partner from among their peers. It signalled that they couldn't catch a man and were bound for the dreaded shelf. But other people's opinions never bothered Phoebe. She made her own rules.

He saw the Thurlwells make for Ben Buchanan's table and turned away. No point in standing here gawking any longer, he still had work to do.

Phoebe turned to Clara Buchanan. 'It was very kind of you and Ben to invite us. Mother adores these shows.'

'So does mine,' Clara whispered. 'Personally I prefer to have my afternoon tea at home in comfort.'

When she had greeted all their guests she insisted Phoebe sit next to her. 'Stay with me, these formal affairs make me nervous. I'm never sure what we should be talking about. Politics confuse me.'

'They confuse everyone. Just do what I do.'

'What's that?'

'Try not to look too bored and stay awake during the speeches.'

Clara began to laugh and Ben frowned at his wife. 'My dear, control yourself. You're not in the bush now.'

'No, she's in the jungle now,' Phoebe snapped at him, annoyed that he'd caused Clara to blush and sink back into her chair.

'Don't talk such rot!' Lalla glowered at her daughter, but Phoebe pretended not to hear.

Clara was her friend, despite the difference in their ages. On her own, away from formalities, Clara was not really a shy person. It was just that her husband and his friends intimidated her, as did her mother, old Belle Foster, who had placed herself the other side of Ben as if she were the hostess. Since they'd started riding together some years back, Phoebe had found in Clara a woman she could trust, and she'd become very fond of her. She hated to see her cringe before her husband, but it was more than that. As Clara had said to her, ages ago: 'I really love the bush. I feel like a fish out of water in town.'

The band stopped, the speeches began and Phoebe sat praying for rain. Eventually, though, they were able to stop swatting at the flies that descended on the tables, get on with the cakes and scones, and chat without being frowned upon.

As soon as tea had been served and the jugs of fruit cordials replenished for the thirsty guests, some of the men began to move off to mingle, opportunities not to be wasted in this auspicious gathering.

Ben Buchanan wandered away. Edgar stepped over to take up an empty seat across from Royce Davies at the next table, and as other gentlemen excused themselves, only Dr Thurlwell remained happily with the women.

A young man stopped by to speak to Phoebe, with a bow to Mrs Buchanan, but since Phoebe didn't invite him to join them he soon moved on.

'Who was that?' Clara asked. 'He seemed to know me but I'm terrible with names.'

'Fontana Sweepstone.'

'Oh, of course! His father's the Minister for Lands. Very nice people, the Sweepstones.'

'Yes, they are,' Phoebe replied. 'Pity about him. I've known him since I was a kid and I never could stand him.'

'Fontana. That's a strange name. A family name, I suppose?'

'Oh yes, someone who was someone, Fontana has told me often enough but I keep forgetting.' She watched as Fontana strolled over to the Davies' table and drew up a chair beside Edgar, and then she lost interest. She'd slipped her tight shoes off under the table to cool her stockinged feet in the grass, and now she couldn't get them back on again.

'Good afternoon, Mr Thurlwell,' Fontana said. Edgar replied cheerfully, but Royce Davies was not so pleased. He nodded curtly at the intruder.

'I was thinking of investing in the railroad company,' Fontana said grandly. 'Tell me, Mr Thurlwell, what size parcel of shares would you suggest?'

'Whatever you can afford,' Edgar smiled.

'I'd suggest you pay your bills first,' Royce snapped from across the table.

'Are you addressing me, sir?'

'That I am, and it's just your damn cheek to park yourself at my table.'

'Shush, Royce!' his wife said, tugging at his sleeve. 'Don't make a scene. People will hear you.'

'I don't care who hears me!' Royce growled.

Fontana stood up, jerking his brocade waistcoat into place. 'If you'll excuse me, Mr Thurlwell,' he said, 'I shall leave. I am not accustomed to this rudeness.'

'You'll get used to it,' Royce sneered. 'All cheats do.'

Fontana spun about. 'Did you call me a cheat, sir?'

'What else? You don't pay your gambling debts, and in a game with my brother you were seen to cheat.'

'How dare you!' Fontana gasped. He picked up a jug of raspberry cordial and hurled the contents at Davies.

Unfortunately, since he was using his left hand, his aim wasn't too good. Some of the cordial splashed on to Royce but most of it sloshed over Mrs Davies, who was still trying to quieten her husband.

She leapt up, screeching, to survey her white organza dress, now soaked in red from the bodice to a large dripping splotch on the full skirt.

Even Fontana was stunned. 'Oh my God! I'm sorry, I didn't mean . . .' he stuttered, while women rushed, clucking, to the victim's aid, to attempt to minimize the damage with a flurry of handkerchiefs and table napkins.

Royce Davies went in the other direction. He sprinted around the end of the table to hurl himself at Fontana, grabbing him by the lapels and shaking him with such force that one lapel gave way. Edgar, being a much bulkier man than either of them, intervened, holding Royce back, and at the same time ordering Fontana to make himself scarce.

Young Sweepstone didn't need a second telling. He dashed away between the tables, brushing servants aside as heads turned from every corner of the lawns to follow this astonishing and outrageous event. The chatter had ceased and the only sounds to be heard were the sobs of Mrs Royce Davies and the consoling mews of her friends. Then a rustling whispering began and seemed to follow the Honourable Jed Sweepstone and Mrs Sweepstone as they rose from their chairs to walk stiffly over to the scene of the disaster.

It was obvious to all that they were offering their apologies on behalf of their son, because as guests craned for a better view, Mrs Sweepstone escorted the weeping Mrs Davies to the shelter of Parliament House.

When the women had retired from the scene, Jed, always a stickler for protocol, made his way over to the head table to proffer further apologies to the Governor and the Premier and their ladies. And with that, he too left.

Edgar remained with Royce Davies, ostensibly to keep him calm, but in reality curious about what had happened. 'What was that all about anyway?'

'The little bastard's a welsher and a cheat,' Royce said. 'It's common knowledge.'

'Is it?' Edgar replied. 'Oh well, I daresay his father will pay his debts and keep the lad away from the card tables in future.'

'Fat chance,' Royce said, still furious. 'And that's not the half of it. Those Sweepstones, always so high and mighty! I might not be in their social league but at least my son's a man!'

'I'm sure he is,' Edgar replied blandly, sensing something interesting here. 'I'm glad I don't have any sons to worry about.'

'If you had a son like him you'd have real problems,' Royce growled. 'Prancing about with his pansy friends. If I'd bred something like him I'd have strangled him at birth.'

'Good God! You're not suggesting . . .?'

'I'm not suggestin', I'm tellin' you.'

'Surely Jed doesn't know about this?'

'Of course not. People like that never see what's right under their noses,' Royce said bitterly. 'And that dress my wife's got on, it was brand bloody new! And cost a packet! I'll bet it's ruined. It's not easy for me to support a family with my wife having to keep up appearances like this. It's time politicians were paid for all the work they do.'

'I couldn't agree more,' Edgar said. 'Mrs Davies must be terribly distressed. Let me cheer her up. I'll get Lalla to find her a new one, just as nice.'

'Thank you, that's a good idea. And we'll send the bill to the Honourable Minister.'

'No, no. I'll pay for it. Let it be my surprise.'

'That's decent of you, Edgar.'

'Not at all. My pleasure.'

Edgar Thurlwell did not believe in employing the services of sordid private investigators, but he would certainly like to know more about young Fontana. This could be the lever he needed to make his old man toe the line. Gambling debts were one thing, but this other business . . .

'By cripes,' he muttered to himself when he arrived home, 'a word of this could have Jed Sweepstone grabbing for the pen.' Of course it would have to be handled delicately, but it could be done.

He sat in his parlour, nursing a brandy, and thinking things over.

He could suggest to the Minister that his son be bunged off to England in the same way that aristocratic English gentlemen sent their disorderly sons out here. Fontana could be a remittance man in reverse. That amused Edgar.

And there would be a price for his fatherly interest, for appraising Jed of the situation in time to prevent a scandal, and for his silence, of course. The least the grateful father could do was to sign that land over to the Western Railroad Company. It wasn't blackmail by any means; this action should have been taken months ago for the good of the state. 'Think of the jobs it will create,' Edgar would remind him. 'Prosperity stagnating simply because of your procrastination, Jed,' he would say.

'And,' Edgar added meanly in his rehearsal of the scene, 'he can forget those leases. I want freehold land all the way.'

If it were true of course. If Royce Davies weren't just talking through his hat. But how to find out for sure? Who could he find to infiltrate that seedy world for him?

Having declined an invitation to dine with William and his family, Edgar had his manservant bring him supper on a tray while he continued to mull over this problem.

And then it came to him. Goldie!

Just because he was a bachelor didn't mean that he had to be celibate. Much better to enjoy the delights of Goldie's girls than to even consider having a wife underfoot. Especially that old bag Belle Foster, who was still on the chase.

That night he had a quiet talk with Goldie in her private room. 'I need a little information,' he said eventually, over a bottle of her French champagne, which had cost him five times more than he'd paid for the same vintage already in his cellar.

'You know that's out of the question, Edgar. I never discuss my clients.'

'My dear, I wouldn't dream of asking you.' He chortled. 'I'm more interested in gentlemen who don't visit your worthy establishment.'

'Then I'd hardly know much about them.'

'Maybe you do. I mean gentlemen whose fancies don't include ladies.'

She laughed. 'Don't tell me you're that way inclined? I'm shocked at you.'

'That'll be the day,' he countered. 'No, I'm not interested in their games, only where they're held.'

'Not for the coppers?' she asked warily.

'Definitely not, I give you my word on that. It's a private matter, I'm trying to handle it delicately for a worried parent.'

She wasn't too keen but by this Edgar knew it was only a matter of price. He placed some notes on the table and Goldie picked them up. 'I'll see what I can do.'

On the following Saturday night Edgar instructed his trusted manservant, Brody, to bring round his small carriage.

'Do you wish me to drive, sir?'

'Yes. It's a private matter.'

Brody nodded. He presumed Mr Edgar would be visiting The Blue Heaven this evening. Private matters meant he didn't want his usual driver knowing his business, where he went and what he got up to. Drivers were an unreliable lot, they came and they went, but Brody had been with Mr Edgar for ten years now. And wasn't he just as capable of handling the horses as he did the household? Brody had been a jockey in his day and a damn good one at that, until weight got the better of him.

He never called the boss 'master' like some of his counterparts in toffy Brisbane houses, nor did Mr Edgar expect him to. Brody considered himself Mr Edgar's right-hand man, ready to turn his hand to anything, even cooking if necessary. They had a cook and a housemaid, both under Brody's jurisdiction, but sometimes when the cook didn't turn up, he took over without a fuss. Brody was the only one who lived in, so this big, cool house up on Wickham Terrace was a true bachelor establishment, and as a result, Brody prided himself, it ran more smoothly than most.

He was surprised when the boss told him to drive to a certain address down a gloomy back street in Fortitude Valley. When he brought the horse to a halt outside a drab workman's cottage, he lifted the flap and looked down at the boss. 'What now, sir?'

'We wait,' Edgar said, lighting a cigar and sitting back in the gloom.

As he watched, Edgar saw that there were lights on in the house but the drapes or blinds were drawn. Men came down the street, some alone, some in pairs, and slipped in through the gate, but he didn't recognize any of them – not that he needed to. He simply sat quietly, waiting. After a while the inmates of the house became curious about the dark vehicle parked outside the premises, and several men came out, ostensibly to walk up the street but in fact checking this possible problem.

One asked Brody casually if he needed advice. Perhaps directions?

'No,' Brody replied, and sat staring straight ahead, although this house, he'd noticed, didn't seem the right place for the boss to be seen. He hoped to God he wasn't going in. The whole thing made him very nervous.

'Just a minute!' Edgar called to the man who'd spoken to Brody. 'A word with you, sir.'

He was surprised when a fair-haired young fellow with a cheeky face stuck his head in the window. 'Good evenin', chum! Bit shy, are we? No need. You can come in with me.'

Edgar was tempted to strike the youth with his stick for his impertinence, but instead he opened the door. 'Get in.'

The youth leapt into the carriage, bouncing on the seat. 'Very comfy this. Your upholsterer's done a good job here. I know a bit about it I do, worked at it a year or so back. Now, what can I do for you?'

'I just wanted to have a talk with you.'

'That's what they all say,' the youth grinned. 'You'll find me very accommodating.'

'I'm sure I will.' Edgar brandished a pound note. 'There are nine more of these if you can give me some information.'

His visitor looked warily back at the house. 'I don't know about that. They don't like us to talk.'

'Even if I double the money?'

'Depends on what you want to know.'

'I just want to know if Fontana Sweepstone is a member of this . . . club.'

'Who? Oh, Fontana. Yes, he's a regular.' He put out his hand for the money but Edgar pocketed it again. 'Not so fast. If you will come with me and put that in writing, then the cash is yours.'

'The whole twenty?'

'Yes.'

The lad whistled, it was an enormous amount of money for a simple thing like that. 'You're not taking me to a police station?'

'No, just up to Wickham Terrace.'

'All right, but listen, mister, you won't want to pull a fast one on me. I've got a lot of friends.'

'I'm sure you have,' Edgar sniffed. He tapped on the window. 'Home, Brody.'

'Yes, sir!'

Edgar grinned in the darkness as he heard his manservant's snap of disapproval. He guessed that poor Brody was wondering what the world was coming to.

The youth's name was Ted Cameron, and he looked about him as Edgar ushered him into his study. 'Nice place you've got here,' he said, walking over to peer out of the open french doors. He seemed to be considering their suitability as a means of escape, if that were to become necessary.

'Will that be all, sir?' Brody asked stiffly.

'No. I want you to stay. I need a witness.' Edgar took pen and paper and sat at his desk. He placed the twenty pounds in front of him and allowed Cameron to sit.

He took down details of young Cameron, his full name, age, address and background. Then he began to question him about Fontana and his associates.

Cameron had no qualms about answering, but the more intimate the details elicited by his boss, the more Brody squirmed. He listened in shocked silence as Ted became more relaxed.

'Oh yes,' he boasted. 'Fontana was my boyfriend for a good while but he threw me over for another chap. Not that I cared. He was generous, was Fontana, but he could be mean, and he's a real flirt.'

'Let's get this clear,' Edgar said. 'As his boyfriend, does this mean you slept with him?'

'Slept with him? No, only sometimes when he was too drunk to go home.'

'By that I meant, did you have sexual relations with him?'

'Then why didn't you say so? Of course I did, and you gents needn't think you're going to make me feel bad about it.'

Brody couldn't stand it any longer. 'You mean you kissed him?' he blurted out. 'A man?'

Edgar kept writing, and Ted laughed. 'Come off it. He was my lover. Even though he's got another boyfriend, he likes to come to the house of a Saturday night for a bit of variety.'

'And is he there tonight?'

'Sure he is. A lot of blokes only come for a half-hour or so . . .'

'Do they pay?' Edgar asked.

'Some do, the new ones. It's sort of a gentlemen's club, if you see what I mean.'

This time it was Edgar who almost choked as his pen moved swiftly across the page.

Eventually he looked up. 'That's all we need, Mr Cameron. My man here will drive you back.'

His manservant bridled, but Edgar frowned at him. 'Mr Cameron is my guest. I promised him I wouldn't keep him long. Can you write, Mr Cameron?'

'Yes.'

'Then all you have to do now is sign this paper and add a few more words that I shall dictate to you.'

'And I get the twenty?'

'That's it. Now take up the pen and write: "I do declare . . ."' With some assistance in the spelling of the words, Ted Cameron managed to declare that his statement was true and correct.

'This won't get me into any trouble?' he asked, concerned now, but Edgar reassured him.

'None at all. You must be aware that your behaviour is illegal, but that's your business. I don't wish you any harm but I wouldn't mention this conversation to Fontana, he mightn't be so kind.'

Ted signed his statement and picked up his cap with the money. 'If they ask me where I got this, I can say I had a bit of a dally with an old bloke in his carriage.' He grinned happily at both Brody and Edgar. 'But hey! I don't even know your names.'

Edgar ignored that. He was delighted with the night's work and in a good mood now. As their guest made for the front door, he whispered to Brody: 'Now you see why I wanted you in the room all the time. I couldn't have that little snake claiming he had a "bit of a dally" with me. You don't have to take him all the way, drop him a few streets from that house. Then when you've put the carriage away I want you to witness this statement.'

'Be glad to, sir. Bloody disgustin' I call it.'

Edgar read the statement carefully then inserted the words: 'engaged in unnatural practices' in the space he'd left for that phrase. While it was true, he hadn't wanted to spook the young ruffian by having such a line staring at him.

With no time to waste now, Edgar arranged a private appointment with the Honourable Jed Sweepstone. The conversation went just as he had expected. Jed was appalled. His face went an ashen grey as he ran his hands through his thick white hair.

'You have proof of this?'

'I do. He must have offended one of his lovers, who came to me with the story.'

'Why you?'

'Why anyone? It was fortunate that it was me. I paid him to shut up.'

'Did you say "one of his lovers"?' Jed was distraught.

'Yes.'

'Oh my God! His mother must never know of this.'

'Certainly not. No one need know.'

The Minister poured himself a drink, and that seemed to calm him. He didn't offer one to Edgar. Recovering from the shock he turned on Edgar. 'And I presume I shall be expected to compensate you for your silence.'

'I wouldn't put it that way,' Edgar said, and went on to explain, in his best and most persuasive lobbying tones, that Jed had been procrastinating on signing the release of the much-needed land.

'You said you have proof. May I see it?'

Edgar placed Cameron's statement on the desk.

When Jed read it, he seemed to sway, and Edgar thought for a minute that he might faint, but he steadied himself, refolded the page and slipped it into a drawer.

'There are no copies?'

'I give you my word.' Edgar knew he could always rope Cameron in again, or another of his ilk, to provide him with more evidence if required. And he also knew that Jed was no fool. He would be well aware of the danger.

So the conversation continued in a courtly manner. While the Minister waited for a clerk to bring him the file on the proposed railway land, Edgar stroked Jed's conscience by reminding him that the people of the west, so long neglected, would be in the Minister's debt for generations to come.

It was only after Edgar Thurlwell had left that the Minister lit a match to burn that horrendous statement. Then he put his head in his hands and wept.

Chapter Six

Christmas, a time of cheer and goodwill towards all.

And so it should be! Edgar whistled happily as he trimmed his beard. Everything was coming up trumps, and to celebrate he was giving a dinner-dance this festive eve at the Great Northern Hotel.

It had been touch and go there for a while. The public response to his shares had been excellent, but he was still under-capitalized, with costs rising all the time, so he'd raised a three-thousand-pound loan from the Colonial Bank of New South Wales. The Sydney bankers were easier to deal with than the local fellows, more appreciative of the entrepreneurial spirit needed to push ahead with these great ventures.

And the co-operation of the Minister for Lands had clinched the deal. He hadn't mentioned to anyone up here, not even Lalla and William, that Sweepstone had finally come to the party. It wasn't necessary, they'd taken it for granted all along that the land would be made available to the railroad company.

He was so pleased with himself he did a little jig. For a big, bulky man, he was light on his feet, and tonight he would be able to trip the light fantastic with the best of them. 'Champagne and Roses' was the theme, and he wanted nothing but the best for his hundred guests, he'd told the manager.

'Roses, roses all the way!' he'd said, quoting a line he was fond of from a poem by Browning. 'That's how things will be for my company, and that's how it is to be on Christmas Eve for my guests. Do you understand?'

In the meantime, the managing director of Western Railroad could envisage all those little clerks and surveyors beavering away, block by block resuming that corridor of land all the way out to Longreach – land earmarked for the railroad. Everything was finally coming together, and once that line was under way he'd commence negotiations for the next, Brisbane to Bundaberg. He'd probably get a knighthood out of this.

The hotel manager, inspired by Mr Thurlwell's advice that money was no object, was delighted to be able to use his talents so freely in preparing for a truly elegant and memorable evening. He scoured the town for roses, and although they were in short supply at this time of the year he was able to make a good showing by adding scores of paper and silk flowers which he placed at higher levels so that they wouldn't be recognized as such.

Being something of a thespian who was often called upon to recite, he knew the Browning poem, and Mr Thurlwell's flamboyant repetition of that 'roses' line made him a little nervous. He was a superstitious man, and if he rightly recalled, that poem, 'The Patriot', had a sad ending. Still, taken out of context, it had a nice ring to it, as did the mounting costs for this function.

The Buchanans were invited, and as they waited with Belle Foster for their carriage, Clara took the opportunity to try to make Ben see reason about their property. 'We really must go home as soon as possible,' she said to him. 'I'd like to leave right after the New Year.'

'We can't do that, I'm too busy in town,' he said. 'And I don't know why you're in such a hurry. We can't do much out there.'

'There is something we can do,' she replied. 'I was thinking we should buy fodder here, as much as we can pack into box cars, and freight it out to Charleville. By train.'

He stared at her. 'Have you gone mad? That would cost a fortune.'

'It's better than doing nothing!'

'I've never heard of such a thing!' Belle said. 'You do get some queer ideas, Clara.'

'It's not a queer idea. The cattle need food. Imagine what a difference it would make it we could get a weekly supply of fodder and ration it out to the animals.'

'Nonsense,' Ben said. 'We can't afford such extravagance.'

'Why not?' Belle asked. 'Maybe it's not so silly after all. I've seen cattle dying in droughts and it's dreadful. I remember your father, Clara, having to shoot hundreds of the poor animals, and it nearly broke his heart.'

'We're already doing that, Mother. If we can't get water out there, at least we should be able to take feed.'

'The situation is hopeless,' Ben said. 'We'd just be sending good money after bad.' He didn't want to admit that he expected to do well on his shares very soon – he'd heard the whisper around the House that the Minister for Lands had granted the first corridor of land to Western Railroads.

'Then sell the place,' Belle said, 'and let's have an end to it.'

'I've tried,' Ben told her, 'but there are no takers. Who'd be mad enough to buy a station ruined by drought?'

Clara was alarmed. 'You've been trying to sell Fairmont Station without telling me? I don't want to sell. We have to hang on. It's our home.'

'With your ideas it'd be the ruin of us,' Ben snapped. 'I don't want to hear any more about it.'

'Very well, let it go for the time being,' Belle said. 'We're going out to enjoy ourselves, so I don't want arguments. I must say, that dress really suits you, Clara. Not your usual style. Where did you get it?'

'Phoebe helped me choose the style and the material. I wanted white but she said that this rose-pink crêpe would show off the beading much more.'

'It shows off more than the beading,' Ben muttered, glaring with disapproval at the plunging neckline.

Belle laughed. 'If she's got the bosoms to show, why not?'

As usual Phoebe was with her parents, but at their insistence was escorted by Robert Portnum, a nephew of the Governor, no less. He was tall, good-looking and delighted to partner her, so she made a determined effort to be cheerful, trying to throw off a vague sense of depression. It didn't help to see her mother take her seat beside Ben Buchanan and launch into an animated conversation with him, even taking the liberty of adjusting his bow tie. Phoebe was still suspicious of that pair.

But the dining room did look beautiful, decked with hundreds of roses, and the champagne flowed as the orchestra struck up a catchy tune. After a few glasses Phoebe didn't notice that she was really beginning to enjoy herself, that she was comfortable with all these elegant people whom she knew so well. And to top it off, Robert was an excellent dancer.

Sometimes Ben felt like Rip Van Winkle awakening from a long sleep, there were so many things he didn't know that were commonplace to his friends. He became an avid reader of newspapers to bring himself up to date with events, noting how prices had risen too. Cash had introduced him to the brothel, which he continued to visit occasionally, feeling rather guilty and knowing Oma would disapprove, but he had no social life.

Rod Callaghan had stayed on at the stables and had proved himself invaluable, so Ben had rewarded him with the title of manager and doubled his pay. His wife had been so thrilled she'd come to the stables to meet Ben and thank him personally.

'It's made a big difference to us,' she'd said. 'We can afford to send the kids to school again. We're very grateful to you, Mr Beckman.'

'Ben. Call me Ben.'

'Very well, Ben. And you can call me Alice. Rod and I are going to the band concert on Sunday afternoon. Why don't you bring a young lady and come with us?'

'I wouldn't know who to bring,' he said. 'I don't know any young ladies.'

Rod laughed. 'Listen to him! There are plenty of girls that'd be pleased to step out with the owner of this establishment, Ben.'

'News to me,' Ben muttered.

'He's too shy, that's his trouble,' Rod told his wife. 'By golly, you should see the way that Miss Thurlwell looks at him. All dewy-eyed she gets, when he's around.'

'Who? Phoebe?' Ben asked.

'Ha! You even know her name!' Rod crowed.

'Of course I do, she lives next door to me. You're not suggesting I ask her out?'

'No, that's aiming a bit high, she's gentry, but it proves my point, doesn't it? The girls are noticing you all right.'

'Don't tease him,' Alice said. 'If you don't want to ask a lass, Ben, you come on your own.'

'Can I bring my grandmother? She never goes anywhere and I'm sure she'd enjoy it.'

'She'd be welcome,' Alice smiled, 'and it's a good lad you are to be thinking of her.'

Before she left, Rod took her aside. 'You shouldn't be calling the boss a good lad. It's not proper.'

'No worse than you teasing him about girls,' she sniffed.

'You brought up the subject.'

'I know, I wasn't thinking. It'll be hard for him, what with his colour and people knowing he's been in jail.'

'Not with his money. He seems to have a bottomless well and he's turning in good profits now.'

Alice was thoughtful. 'That's the danger. I like him and I wouldn't want to see some gold-digging little hussy get her hands on him.'

Gussie Beckman, in her new hat, had a wonderful day with Ben and his friends, and she loved the band music. Sitting quietly though, Gussie never missed much, and she noticed that Alice Callaghan, who seemed to know a lot of people, went out of her way to introduce Ben to some very nice young girls.

'Good,' she said to herself. It was time Ben had some romance in his life. She was getting on, and she hoped to see her dear boy married and settled before she died. Gussie liked Alice; this was a very sensible woman who would know the temptations a young man like Ben would face if he wasn't steered in the right direction.

To Ben's surprise, she invited the Callaghans and their children to lunch at her home the following Sunday, already planning the menu, and they were happy to accept.

In such a small way, Ben's social life had begun.

Then there was Christmas Eve. Rod brought up the subject:

'It's usual to give the lads that work here a party on Christmas Eve, Ben. Have you made any plans?'

'Plans? No. I didn't know that was expected. What should I do?'

'Well, Cash was a bit mean. If there was any money about he'd spend it on himself, so he only put on a keg in the yard. But when old Mrs O'Neill was alive she'd have everyone, wives, girlfriends and kids too, over to the house. Gave quite a spread, she did. Everyone had a great time.'

'I suppose we could do that too, but it's a long way from here to our place. And if we have the party after work, the last ferry goes at seven o'clock.'

'Alice had an idea,' Rod said. 'You know Kathleen O'Neill has been doing some cooking for private parties?'

'No. Why would she do that?'

'To make money.'

'Who would pay her?'

'The people who have the parties and morning teas and things. Women are very particular about serving the best cakes an' all, to impress their pals. And Kathleen's as good a cook as her mother was. Alice says she's getting some real good customers too.'

'Good God!'

'So Alice says we should ask Kathleen to cater for our party.'

'And pay her?'

'She wouldn't do it for nothing.'

'Oh no, I'm happy to pay her, but it's all beyond me, Rod. Why don't we just ask Alice to see if Kathleen will do it for us, and see what happens. Miss O'Neill doesn't like me.'

'You'd have to tell Alice how much you want to spend.'

Ben shrugged. 'I haven't the faintest idea. Just see if Alice can organize it and give me the bill.'

Within days Rod reported that Kathleen had agreed to give them a staff party in her front garden at five o'clock on Christmas Eve.

'Wonders will never cease!' Ben exclaimed.

Only Gussie knew that this was the first party Ben had ever attended, and he almost backed out when she reminded him that he was the host. 'Don't let it bother you. I'll be there with you. You just have to make certain you talk to everyone and make a nice speech.'

'A speech?' He was petrified.

'For someone who can talk the leg off an iron pot, it'll be easy. You wish them a happy Christmas and thank them for their hard work.'

Kathleen had transformed her front garden into a fairyland of lanterns and balloons hung over long trestle tables covered in chequered cloths. There were paper party hats, and rattles and bungers, and baskets made of red crêpe paper along the tables, filled with sweets. On one side was the refreshment table, with ale, wine and cordials, and the two other tables were laden with cold chicken, savouries, pork pies, hard-boiled eggs and a fine assortment of scones and cakes. Everything cut neatly so that plates were not needed and the guests could help themselves as they pleased.

Ben was impressed. As plates were emptied Kathleen sailed out to replenish them. She even had a Christmas tree with presents for the children, and a fellow sitting on the veranda playing lively tunes on an accordion. But Alice was worried. How much would all this cost? Kathleen's parents had never put on a splurge like this. She went inside to find Kathleen writing up her account.

'This is what you're charging, eh?'

Kathleen nodded. 'Yes. I have to be careful not to leave anything out or I'll lose money.'

'I don't remember mentioning nothing about all them decorations and presents, nor half that food you've got out there. It wasn't supposed to be a banquet.'

'It's not a banquet, it's just the latest thing in party food.'

'And what if the boss jibs at the bill? I'll get the blame and where would that leave my Rod?'

'Mr Moneybags Beckman can afford it, I'm sure,' Kathleen said tartly.

'It's a mean thing to do, Kathleen. You're still carrying a grudge. Ben's done the best he could for you.'

'I don't need favours from him. I've catered well here and he can pay.'

She was nonplussed when at the end of his short speech Ben Beckman called for three cheers for Miss O'Neill for providing such splendid fare. However, on principle, she wouldn't reduce the bill, not even the loading for her time and use of her garden. She handed it to him just before he was due to leave and he took out his wallet and paid her without a qualm.

'Everyone had a great time,' he said, 'thanks to you, Miss O'Neill. And the food you served was marvellous. I think I ate too much myself. We've left a mess here, can I help you clean up?'

'No, thank you. It won't take a minute.'

But Mrs Beckman was there. 'Let him help, Miss O'Neill. You must be exhausted. All that cooking is hard work. If you don't mind, I'll just sit here under the trees awhile.' She smiled at Ben. 'This is the best Christmas I've had in years. So nice it was to meet all Ben's friends and see everyone so happy.'

He seemed to know his way about a kitchen. He took hot water from the stove and washed up in her big tin dish as Kathleen brought in the plates. He took down the trestle tables and then came in to ask her: 'What do I do with them now?'

'We'll just leave them. The men will come for them.'

'What men?'

'I hired them.'

'You did? That's clever. I wouldn't have thought of that.'

Forced to talk to him as she dried up the plates, platters and pots she had piled up in the kitchen, not being the tidiest of cooks, Kathleen realized he was much younger than she'd previously thought. She was twenty and she guessed he wasn't much older. Years in jail would harden a lad, she supposed, make him grow up fast. She'd heard his story from old Lennie, who'd been working at the stables when Ben had been arrested. At the time, still smarting from losing the business, Kathleen hadn't cared. Now she was touched by it, by the unfairness of nobs who had such power over ordinary people.

He collected all the rubbish and took it down to the bin in her yard to be burned.

'Nothing's fair in this life,' she said as she watched from the window. 'If Dad had lived we wouldn't have lost the business and I wouldn't be broke like this.' She looked about her. Not a scrap of food left, they'd gone through it like grasshoppers, so no leftovers for Kathleen. 'Oh well,' she said with a sigh. 'You've got money in your pocket this week, so stop complaining.'

When he returned she thanked him. 'That's all, you'll be pleased to hear. I've just put the kettle on. I'll see if your grandmother would like a cup of tea.'

Ben stretched, put his jacket on and sat at the kitchen table. This house was much the same as his own, he noticed. It could have been built by the same people, from the same plan, the only difference being position. The house up on Kangaroo Point was cooler. This one, on the flat, had no chance of a breeze, and it was hot now, stifling. Typical of Christmas weather, it had been a blazing hot day.

Miss O'Neill seemed to be taking her time, probably chatting with Oma. The kettle was boiling so he went over and shifted it to the side of the stove, then wandered out the front, glad of an excuse to vacate the heat of the kitchen.

She was standing at the bottom of the front steps, eyes wide in fright, hardly able to speak.

'What's the matter?' he asked her.

Kathleen ran her hands through her dark hair and shook her head, eyes downcast as if afraid to speak to him.

'What is it?' he insisted, stepping down. He thought she was about to faint, she looked so terrible, so he grabbed her arms to steady her.

At last she found her voice, and pointing, whispered: 'Ben! Your grandmother! I think she's . . . she's dead.'

He ran. She couldn't be! She was only dozing in the big chair. She looked so peaceful, she was only tired. Gently he tapped her cheek. 'Oma. Wake up. We'll go home. It's time to go home.' When there was no response, he panicked. 'Get a doctor. Get someone!' he shouted at Kathleen, but she was over the initial shock now and knew it was too late.

Kathleen blessed herself and stood helplessly by as he gathered the old lady in his arms, holding her to him, his face wet with tears.

It was Kathleen who found the doctor to issue the death certificate; who called in the women to lay out Augusta Beckman. It was Kathleen who stayed with him throughout the long, desolate hours of Christmas Day, knowing there was little she could do to alleviate his pain other than be some company in the stillness of the house.

After the funeral, while he stood out at the cliff, looking down at the river, she quietly removed Mrs Beckman's clothes from the house and sent them to the poor box at the church. Then she went out to join him.

'It's a fine view you have here, Ben.'

'Yes.'

'This river must be very old to have cut so deep into the land. How far is it to the coast?'

'A fair way,' he replied. 'I used to like to watch the ships coming and going from here.' He turned to her in despair. 'Why did she have to die now? Just when everything was turning out so grand.'

'I don't know these things. But she died so peaceful, Ben, never begrudge her that. I've given the clothes to the poor, they'll be grateful, but I haven't touched anything else. You can sort out everything when you're feeling better.'

'If ever,' he said dismally. 'I hate the thought of disturbing anything, she was so house-proud.'

Kathleen nodded. She didn't feel like trotting out all the rest of it – that these things pass, and so forth. He should be left to grieve.

'I had big plans to build a fine house here, but she wouldn't have it. She liked this house just as it is.'

'So what now?'

'Now? Nothing. It's queer, but I think I'll leave it be. I'm used to it again. They were happy here, my mother and my grandmother, and the house will remind me of them.'

From the balcony over the long room, Phoebe could see Ben out there on the clifftop, and she could see the woman with him, a young woman with dark hair.

She'd heard that Mrs Beckman had died and was waiting for a chance to go in and offer her condolences to Ben. But not too soon, for fear of intruding. And now he had that woman with him, whoever she was! She wouldn't go in with her there. She wanted to see him alone. After all, she was his oldest friend and it would be wrong of her not to pay a visit.

Phoebe realized she was jealous of the woman, and she didn't care. It was annoying to have that person hanging about him, marching in and out of his home as if she owned the place.

Several days later, when she was sure the woman had gone, Phoebe slipped away to knock on his door, but there was no answer. He was out. Probably back at the stables. She couldn't go riding this week, there were too many social events on her calendar, and anyway, she wanted to tell him how sorry she was about Mrs Beckman when he was on his own, not in front of his staff. This was very personal.

Finally, on the Sunday after the New Year, she found him at home. He was surprised to see her.

'Miss Thurlwell!' was all he could say as he hastily buttoned his shirt.

'Phoebe, remember?' she said softly. 'I've come to tell you how sorry I was to hear about Mrs Beckman. I would have come over sooner but I didn't like to.'

'Thank you. It's very nice of you.' He didn't seem to be sure what he was supposed to do next, and Phoebe made no move to leave.

'Are you feeling better? It must have been a terrible shock for you.'

'Yes, it was.'

'She was a very lovely lady.'

He nodded. 'I'll miss her.'

This wasn't working out the way Phoebe had planned. He was supposed to invite her in, not stand there in the doorway looking so dejected.

'Oh well,' she said, 'I'd better go. I didn't want to disturb you.'

'That's all right. Will you be riding again this year?'

'Of course. Perhaps you'll accompany me again one day?'

'I'd like that,' he said.

Phoebe went home disappointed. He had looked so miserable she'd wanted to put her arms around him, to kiss that sad face. Yes, to kiss him! Even depressed as he was, and caught off guard, with his brown hair no longer tied back but flopping loosely over his face, giving him more of a swarthy, sultry appearance. Making him look even more attractive than he did with it plastered neatly in place.

But he had said he'd ride with her again. 'I'd like that.' And she was sure he meant it. In which case, the sooner the better.

The trouble was, Lalla had become suspicious.

'Why this sudden interest in riding? Are you meeting someone?' she'd asked crankily one morning.

'Of course not! None of the dolts I know ever bother to ride. I wish I lived in the country. Clara Buchanan is going home and I won't even have her company.' She remembered how her mother had fawned all over Ben Buchanan at Edgar's party on Christmas Eve, so she added: 'Ben and Clara will be leaving any day now.'

'No they won't, Ben has too many commitments here,' Lalla said. 'None of the country people go home before the end of January.'

Phoebe shrugged. 'We'll see.' At least she'd deflected Lalla from the subject of the livery stables.

Clara was still arguing with Ben about returning home. 'If you won't come with me, I'm going back to the station without you.'

'You'll wait for me,' he growled.

'I can't. There's too much to do back home.'

Finally he agreed. 'Then damn well go! You're no help to me here. You make no attempt to talk to the right people or even to learn anything about politics. It's as if my career were of no interest to you at all.'

'If I didn't have so much to worry about at home I could stay here and do what I can, but you don't seem to have any interest in the property.' She began to weep. 'I hate all this politicking anyway, it's destroying our marriage.'

'Oh no! You're the one doing that. Don't go blaming me. I'm not responsible for the drought. The station's not making any money, I should sell the rest of the herds and shut it down.'

'You can't mean that! It's my home. And don't forget, Ben, my inheritance from my father went into that station too. I won't just walk away and let it go to ruin.'

'I wondered when you'd get around to that. Your share! Like hell it is! That's Fairmont Station, my station, for what it's worth, and don't you forget it.'

Clara couldn't believe how much he'd changed. And how much she'd come to dislike him. She'd always had her suspicions about her husband and Lalla Thurlwell, and their behaviour at Christmas Eve had almost confirmed them. Almost, because she didn't want to know. She wasn't as stupid as all these sophisticated people in the city thought she was.

Left at the table with Dr Thurlwell, who couldn't dance because he was suffering with gout, she'd pretended not to notice how often Ben had danced with Lalla. But there was still a little shine among the clouds. Lalla was married. He wouldn't leave her for a married woman. It would cause too much of a scandal. A single mistress would be more dangerous.

Not that she'd care if Lalla took him away from her. Not any more. But he was right, he did own the station, and a separation from him would cost her everything. Worrying, looking ahead, Clara could see herself landing back on her mother's doorstep, and that was almost as bad as having to put up with her husband.

But mothers like Belle did have their uses. She'd discovered that Clara had no money of her own, that even the station accounts were forwarded to Ben for payment.

'I know it's normal practice,' she told Clara, 'but it's demeaning for women to have to ask for cash for the slightest thing. I wouldn't have it when I was married to your late father, and I told him straight. Then when I married you dear departed stepfather, it didn't matter. I had plenty of my own.'

'It's no use, Mother. I've asked Ben to let me have my own bank account to run the station while he's away, but he won't hear of it.'

'That's to be expected. They don't like to lose control, they think women are silly with money. You compromise. Have a joint bank account, where either can sign.'

'He wouldn't do that!' Clara said.

'We'll see,' Belle retorted in a voice that Clara knew meant, consider it done.

And it was. A year ago, after a short, sharp confrontation with Ben, her mother had seen to it that the joint account was established. And to the woman trying to run a big cattle station it was a godsend. Ben was a notoriously slow payer, adding to the delay by quibbling, and now she could pay her staff on time and suppliers on delivery, removing the unpleasantness of having to operate on promises.

Now she was becoming so desperate to sustain her cattle, that joint account could be very useful if she could work out how to go about it.

She arranged to ride with Phoebe again, her last chance to see her friend before leaving for Fairmont.

'Is Ben going with you?' Phoebe asked.

'No. There are too many things to attend to here in Brisbane. He'll stay on for a few more weeks.'

'I think it's terrible you have to go home on your own,' Phoebe said.

'Not on my own, Phoebe,' she laughed. 'Trains are full of people, and I enjoy the ride on from Charleville out to Fairmont.'

'I meant without Ben. How can you run a station on your own?'

Clara glanced at her, wondering what she knew, but let it pass. 'It's not easy,' she replied. 'I have to muck in a lot, especially when the cows are calving. They often need help. But it's a most marvellous feeling to be able to rescue a newborn calf and put it on its feet. There are plenty of compensations.'

'Belle said you practically live on a horse out there, riding all day. It's a wonder you bother riding with me.'

Clara laughed. 'That's work. This is sheer pleasure, nodding along like this. Besides, I think I prefer horses to humans. Present company excepted, of course.'

When they returned to the livery stables, Clara stalled, chatting to the grooms about the horses. She wanted to talk to young Mr Beckman on his own, and for a while there she thought Phoebe would never leave. Finally she put her in her waiting gig, since the driver was becoming impatient, and after waving her off turned back through the gate to find the proprietor.

The new colt was a real brat, difficult to tame. He was strong enough but he'd never make a coach horse. He accepted riders now but wouldn't put up with the shafts, even when harnessed with other horses. So there'd be no sale to Cobb and Co.

'Very well, my friend. What am I to do with you?' Ben asked the horse. 'I can't take you back to the saleyards, I'd only get half the price. I'll have to find a private buyer.'

As he turned into the courtyard, leading the horse, he found Mrs Buchanan waiting for him. 'Want to buy a horse?' he asked her.

'This one?' she smiled. 'He's a beauty, but I can't feed my own right now. I wonder if I could have a word with you, Mr Beckman.'

'Of course. What can I do for you?'

'First, I heard you've had a death in the family and I want to extend my condolences.'

'Thank you,' he said. This woman bothered him. He'd met her before, somewhere, and still couldn't place her.

She came straight to the point. 'I wanted to ask you where I can buy hay, fodder for my cattle. Where do you get your supplies?'

'Various farms. The farmers bring me hay.'

'I need a lot. There's no feed out west. I want to buy as much as I can.'

'To send out to your station?'

'Yes.'

He whistled. 'That's a tall order. I never heard of anyone doing that.'

'But it's possible?'

'Yes, but it would cost you.'

'Either that or watch my cattle die.'

Ben handed the colt to a stableboy and walked with her to his office. 'I've been out your way. It's bad I know, but would a few drayloads of hay help?'

'I'm not talking about a few drayloads. I want to freight fodder to Charleville, by train.'

Just then there was a ruckus outside, men shouting, timbers banging.

He looked out of the window. 'It's the brat again, that colt! He won't pull so much as a donkey cart and he's got a set on one of the grooms.'

He laughed. 'The one who's trying to put him in his stall.'

'Perhaps you ought to see to it,' she said. 'I'm not in a hurry.'

Her words struck him like a bolt from the blue, bringing back a flash of memory as clear as it had ever been.

Ben strode over and soon shifted the horse with a jerk of the halter and a hard slap on the rump. 'You'll have to start bribing the devil with an apple or a lick of molasses, Harry,' he said to the groom, but his mind was on the woman in his office.

And on the boy who'd run screaming into the Thurlwell dining room, searching for Dr Thurlwell to come to his mother's bedside. On a room full of indignant voices raised against him. Except for one. He'd had a second of hope then. He'd looked to her when she'd cried out: 'Perhaps you ought to see what it's about, William?'

She'd been howled down and he'd been dragged away, never to forget the scene, nor the kind woman. And now she was in his office. Mrs Buchanan! Of course. She'd come here with Phoebe, she was a friend of the Thurlwells. It was her.

When he returned he'd made up his mind. 'I'll get the fodder for you. It'll take some rounding up but you can depend on me.'

Her eyes lit up. 'You could do that for me?'

'No trouble.'

'I'll be happy to pay you.'

'No, it will cost you enough for the loads. How many do you want?'

She took a deep breath. 'One a week. Could that be done?'

'We can try. I'll put the fodder bills on your husband's account here.'

Clara shifted uncomfortably in her chair. 'If you could refer those accounts to me at Fairmont Station, I'll attend to them. And I can pay the freight costs on delivery. I'd be obliged if you didn't mention this to my husband. He thinks it's a silly idea.'

'I suppose he does,' Ben shrugged, 'but it's worth a try.'

'Thank you. Now, Fairmont Station is via Charleville. That will find me.'

'Yes, I know. I rode across your land last year. Looking for brumbies. We met a couple of your boundary riders and they warned us there was no water out that way. But then we did find water at a rock formation called Winnaroo. Do you know that place?'

She nodded. 'That's Winnaroo Springs. It's a truly beautiful place and sort of a secret in our area. To preserve it. None of the locals would direct anyone there unless they were at death's door. The property is named after it. Winnaroo Station.'

'Who lives there?'

'No one. The owners ran into strife and left. We often took visitors there for an outing, with permission of course.' Clara smiled grimly. 'I must admit we've been trespassing a bit lately. Sneaking water out to fill the water-cart, a long, slow job even with a bucket brigade.'

'I suppose it would be, sloshing up that track.'

'Yes. It's frustrating to know the water's there. Brumbies can handle the slippery track but not cattle. They can't play at being mountain goats.'

'Fortunately,' Ben said.

'Unfortunately for the cattle. But yes, fortunately for the springs. If anyone were to force access by grading a proper track down to the water, I think it would ruin the place.'

'Surely no one would do that?'

She shrugged. 'Well . . . the station is up for sale. You never know what the new owners might do when they're desperate for water. I love that place but I'm glad it's not on our property. It would be a temptation.'

'There's no stock on that station now?'

'No. So the springs are not in any immediate danger. We just go on praying for rain and hope everything turns out all right in the end.'

The night was hot and very still. Clouds of mosquitoes had swarmed in at dusk and gone on their way, so Ben took a glass of whisky and a cigar out on to the back veranda, where he did his best thinking. Even the cigar reminded him, sadly, of Oma. It had taken him weeks to unwrap the Christmas gifts she had bought for him, some fine shirts and this box of excellent cigars.

He had completed the task set for him by Mrs Buchanan in consigning fodder out west, and had made arrangements for a steady supply, hoping it would be of some help. Occasionally her husband had come in for Talleyman and Ben had kept out of his way, feeling a little guilty about his part in her project, because he could see Buchanan's point of view too. It was a drastic measure.

Now that was done, and the saddlery was operating, he had other things to think about, and talking to Mrs Buchanan had reminded him. Diamond was dead. Oma was dead. And Dr Thurlwell was still sitting pretty next door, living like a lord. And, according to the newspapers which Ben studied each night, mixing with the high and mighty. Unassailable.

What had been his punishment? A few broken windows, for which Oma had paid. And Ben had paid too. Over and over, in a way that no man could forgive.

Angrily he marched inside and brought out the whisky bottle. He had no intentions of getting drunk. He still drank very little, but a couple more glasses might calm the fury that raged in him.

There was no way, legally, he could touch the worthy doctor. No way at all. While he was in prison, a hot-headed young fool, he'd thought it would be easy. Give him a hiding. Maybe even kill him. Burn his house down. Then the mad plan to build a bigger and better house. He was glad that Oma had talked him out of that. The Thurlwells would probably approve, he now realized. He would only be raising the value of all the houses in the street. A better idea would have been to pull the cottage down and build stables, with the smell and the flies they'd bring. But that would be cutting off his nose to spite his face. This was his home.

Ben had had enough of jail to even consider any rough-house retaliation. Any crime against Thurlwell would have him back there in double-quick time. And there was nothing he could do, financially, to upset the bastard. It would take years for him to catch up with their wealth. Landed gentry like them acquired their fortunes over generations.

So what could he do? Nothing. Diamond had not been worth a white man's attention, so Dr Thurlwell had gone happily on with his dinner party while she died, gasping for breath. And she had been too young to die. A few months short of her fortieth birthday.

But what about Phoebe? He wouldn't want to hurt her.

Rod Callaghan had nudged him again when Phoebe had arrived at the stables with Mrs Buchanan. 'There she goes,' he'd whispered. 'She's sweet on you, I can tell.'

Was she? It had been kind of her to visit after Oma's death. Only a kindness. But she had invited him to ride with her. Did that mean anything?

His thoughts seemed to stop in mid-stream. There was an ominous silence in the air. A cruel silence broken only by the strike of a match as Ben lit another cigar.

What if . . . He asked himself a question that seemed outrageous to him. What if he could romance Phoebe Thurlwell? What if she really were keen on him? A mad thought, but it could be true.

You'd have to take it very carefully, very gently, so as not to spook her, he told himself. She seemed to want to be friends with him, so was there a hope he could become more than a friend? She was bold enough already, riding with a coloured man. Few Brisbane ladies would even consider such a thing. It began to dawn on Ben that Callaghan was right.

And if he succeeded in winning the heart of fair lady, what would the great Dr Thurlwell think of that? His daughter and the despised neighbour! He'd probably have a heart attack. And good luck to him.

In the morning that idea dwindled to fantasy. Phoebe was just being friendly, she was well out of reach.

Nevertheless, the next time she came to the stables, he changed into correct riding gear, as well tailored as any in Brisbane, and, ignoring the stares of his staff, rode out with her.

'You're looking very smart,' she said.

'You force me to,' he said candidly. 'You always look so elegant, you can't be seen riding with someone who looks like a stableboy.'

'Believe me,' she laughed, 'you never look like a stableboy.'

The next time, she asked him who 'did' for him.

'Who what?'

'Who cooks for you and does the housework?'

'I do. I like to cook my own meals. I spent enough years watching my grandmother to be able to turn up a plain meal, which is all I need.'

'But the housework?'

'It doesn't take much to sweep a floor and make a bed.'

'You really ought to have a maid.'

'I don't want a maid. I don't want someone under my feet in the house.'

Phoebe seemed to consider this, and then she smiled. 'You're probably right. It must be marvellous to have a house all to yourself with no one pestering you about what you're doing and where you're going. I get hell if I'm late for meals, even if I'm not hungry.'

He still only rode with her on the odd occasion, as if, by chance, he could spare the time. And then the weather broke.

Phoebe returned from her ride drenched by a heavy shower, so he took her a towel as she stood under the dripping eaves.

'I nearly made it,' she laughed, unconcerned that her clothes were soaked, 'but the track turned into instant mud and it was a bit slippery, so I let Gracie take her time.'

'That was sensible of you.' He looked at the rising wall of blue-black cloud in the east. 'We're in for rain at last. I hope they get their share over the range.'

'So do I, I believe it's very bad out there. Mrs Buchanan said they haven't had any rain for years. It sounds impossible, doesn't it?'

'Yes, especially when it's so hot and humid here on the coast.'

She lingered. 'I suppose if it sets in, that's the end of my riding for a while.'

'Don't worry,' he replied, as if her concern was for the horse. 'We'll keep giving Gracie some exercise. She's been spoilt lately.'

'I'd better be off then,' she said. 'Thanks for everything. But since you're only next door, if you need any help at any time, let me know.'

'What sort of help?' he grinned.

She was too self-assured to be fazed. 'I don't know. You might get tired and need someone to cook your dinner.'

'Can you cook?'

She giggled. 'No.'

'Well then, when you've got nothing to do, you call out and I'll cook you a meal.'

'You'd better be careful. I might take you up on that.'

Phoebe left. Despite her apparent nonchalance, she was nervous. There was no doubt that he meant the invitation, that he liked her. But would she dare? It would be fun to have a man cook for her. Funny! A voice of caution reminded her of who and what he was, but she thought that rather unfair. He was a very sweet man, and, heavens above, she'd known him forever. What would be wrong with visiting him?

Everything, she told herself, from her parents' point of view. And, she had to admit, calling on a man in his own home, alone, wasn't the proper thing to do. Phoebe wondered where all these silly conventions came from. She wasn't a child, and she wasn't stupid. There were some men who might take advantage, and it was easy enough to pick the lechers, but Ben was different. He was a friend, like Barnaby. If this were Barnaby inviting her to visit, she'd have no qualms about it, so why not Ben Beckman? Just next door.

All she'd have to do was choose a time when her parents were out for dinner and the servants had gone off. No one need know. And to be able to really sit down and talk to him instead of making desultory conversation as they rode together would be very nice. He was such an interesting person.

And madly attractive. Her secret friend.

Rain pelted down. It beat a rhythm on tin roofs and thrust through to strategically placed pots and buckets, adding lilting plinks and plonks to its song, light-hearted percussion to balance the drum rolls of thunder from above. Houses with wide verandas were the envy of the occupants of other dwellings, who were forced to remain shut in, battling mould. Shopkeepers cringed as their awnings poured solid curtains of water and their customers remained in their homes, watching the swollen river nervously, afraid that it would once again flood their town.

After the first glad cries of 'Rain!' the steady downfall gave way to frustration as the wet season set in with a vengeance. It was no less frustrating in the west for people like Clara Buchanan, who still stared at hard blue skies dominated by a metallic sun that seemed to be nailed in place. But at least Clara had the first loads of hay which she was carefully rationing to her cattle, to the amazed delight of all her station people.

Phoebe was unhappy. Since her parents had curtailed their social activities, she couldn't escape, and worse, had to suffer Lalla's irritation, which was directed mainly at the servants but which put everyone on edge.

On a Sunday morning, with low banks of clouds moving moodily overhead, preparing for the next onslaught of rain, Phoebe spotted Ben working in his garden. She checked her printed cotton dress with its white pique collar, pleased that it looked suitably demure, brushed her hair out and tied it back with a large blue ribbon. The front of her hair had been cut shorter in the latest fashion to allow it to curl naturally, so Phoebe enhanced the blonde curls with a little spit and twist and then set off downstairs.

Wandering idly in the garden, or so it seemed, she was soon out of sight of the house and slipped through a gap in the hedge to stroll along the outside of the fence that overlooked the river.

Ben jumped up, wiping his hands on his already muddied trousers. 'Hello,' he said, making no apology for his rough clothes. 'This is a surprise.'

'I needed to get out of the house for a while,' she said. 'This weather is so boring I felt as if I'd turn into a mushroom if I stayed inside any longer.'

'I don't think there's any chance of that,' he replied appreciatively. 'You're looking as fresh as a daisy.'

'Thank you. What are you doing, for heaven's sake?'

'What's it look like?' he grinned. 'I'm gardening. Or trying to.'

'You're busy all week, why don't you get a gardener?'

'I ought to, I suppose. When I was a kid I hated having to do the garden, which in my case meant the weeding, but now I enjoy it. Probably because now I get to see things grow; I'm not just pulling up weeds.'

She moved away from him. 'These roses are in bud, they should be lovely in bloom.'

'If the grasshoppers don't get them!'

'Yes, we have the same problem.' Having made her visit, knowing she was holding him up, she turned back. 'Did you know that they are replacing horse trams with electric trams?'

'Good God! Are they?'

'Yes, they're unveiling the plans at the Town Hall next Saturday night. A gala function with the Governor and all. My parents wouldn't miss it come rain, hail or flood.'

'Are you going?'

'No. I wasn't invited.'

'Do you have any other plans for that night?'

'No.' Phoebe held her breath.

'Then would you like to join me here, for dinner? If you want to. I mean, it won't be anything special. Just something to do if you're home on your own.'

Phoebe almost said: 'Why not?' But recovered to accept more politely.

He walked her back to the fence. 'I know it's the done thing,' he said, with a glimmer of amusement, 'but maybe I shouldn't call for you.'

'No,' Phoebe laughed. 'I'm quite capable of walking a half a block.' To make light of it seemed the best way of avoiding mentioning that he would be far from welcome at his neighbours' house, and he took it well.

'Saturday, then.'

With the house quiet on that momentous evening, Phoebe wore a full cape over an Indian muslin dress, not too formal, but pretty enough for this occasion, and left her hair down for the same reason.

He had set the table in a small dining room, with a cream embroidered tablecloth and matching napkins, but had made no other fuss. No candles or special lamps. It was to be, as he had said, just a meal with him. And he was happy for her to come into the kitchen to help him serve chicken broth, chops cooked on the top of the stove, mashed potatoes and vegetables, followed by strawberries and cream.

She noticed his table manners were excellent, probably thanks to his grandmother, and he talked easily while they ate. When it came to the dessert Ben offered her champagne. A very expensive champagne it was too. She was thoroughly enjoying herself, after having worried all week that this could turn out to be a disaster. She'd been nervous that he might try to impress her and make her uncomfortable, and that she herself would have to guard against being patronizing since she had never before dined in a house without servants.

But there was no need for any of that. They both ate heartily, one course following fast on the next, and it was fun to be allowed to clear and serve with him, rather than have to sit at the table and be waited on.

Phoebe realized he was accustomed to the company of women, that this wasn't a bachelor establishment like Uncle Edgar's house. The female touch was everywhere, from the light curtains to the crocheted mats on the sideboard and the handmade silk flowers in the corner of the room.

Ben was interested in the electric trams. 'People say that soon horses won't be needed in towns at all,' he told her.

'I can't imagine that,' she replied.

'It could be right. I have to look ahead. I'm sorry, would you like coffee?'

'No thanks, I'm happy with the champagne.'

'Good.' He didn't invite her to leave the table and retire to the parlour. Instead he went to a drawer and produced pictures of motorcars. 'These vehicles will replace horses, I'm thinking. So I have to learn more about them.'

'What makes them go?'

'The newest ones that will soon be imported go on petrol, I'm told, and they'll travel at more than twenty miles an hour.'

Phoebe studied the pictures. 'I wonder if we'll have one.'

'They're all the rage overseas. But where'll they get the petrol? They can only carry so much before they conk out, so someone will have to have petrol shops.'

'I don't know what petrol is.'

'You're not alone. I'm not sure either, but I intend to find out.'

As Phoebe listened to him talking about motorcars she saw another side to Ben. He was ambitious, he wasn't content with the livery stables and the now-established saddlery. He wanted to move on, to move with the times, and she found it exciting. He was so close to her, but he might as well have been miles away, absorbed in the world of motorcars and mechanics and petrol sales.

When they'd finished the champagne he seemed to believe their evening was complete. 'I'll get your cloak and walk you to your gate,' he said.

And Phoebe was duly returned home, with his genuine thanks for her company. It was only nine o'clock when she let herself into the empty house, with the lamps all still lit.

She shrugged. 'Well, it was hardly romantic,' she said to herself. 'But what did you expect? You had a good time and he was the perfect gentleman.' She recalled passing a mirror in the hall and seeing them together: Ben with his dark, swarthy looks, and herself, so fair. 'Opposites attract,' she smiled. 'But is he attracted to me? Hard to tell.'

It came to her later that night that Ben would never have the cheek to romance her. She herself would have to find a way to initiate more interest in her as a woman, not just as a friend.

Barnaby was devastated. He felt that everyone was staring at him. Blaming him. And an awful sense of guilt shadowed him wherever he went.

The year had started off so well, for him anyway. Weeks of heavy rain had seen Brisbane awash but had made no difference to all the government clerks and pen-pushers busy in their own departments with their neat letters and files. As the rain eased Barnaby hardly noticed, except that the tennis club resumed games and summer tournaments, and he'd seen Phoebe there several times.

She'd been her old self again, pleased to see him and happily claiming that this year she'd take more lessons and beat everyone.

This caused laughter. 'You'd better start right now,' one of her girlfriends teased, since Phoebe usually ended up down the bottom of the lists.

'You'll see,' she grinned. 'I intend to take my tennis very seriously this year.' She turned to Barnaby. 'Guess what! We have a telephone in the house now. You'll have to telephone me, I believe there's a connection in Parliament House.'

'I don't like my chances,' he said. 'It's in the Premier's office.'

'Then maybe I could telephone him and discuss the weather,' she giggled. 'Do you think he'd mind?'

'Of course not,' Barnaby laughed. That's how it was with the new telephone exchange; people were making the connections but finding shouting into a mouthpiece a peculiar way to communicate. To most it was more of a status symbol.

He wished he could telephone Phoebe now, tell her he needed to talk to her, to talk to someone, but the Thurlwell household was the last place he could call. If it were possible, Lalla would pour boiling oil on him through that miracle of personal contact. At the very least he could expect a burst of vitriol from her or the Doctor.

He shook his head miserably. It had all started so innocently.

The itinerary for Theodore Prosser was almost complete, and Barnaby had drawn it up in fine style, having received approval from Prosser for the overall plan of progress. All he'd had to do was enlarge on it, giving details. Transport, mileage, accommodation and personages who could be expected to make them welcome.

Needing to make certain of the distances between these towns, he'd made his way to the Lands Department to take a look at the maps, beginning with the route from Rockhampton to Longreach. But the maps he needed were missing.

'The surveyors have them,' he was told. 'They can help you, their office is at the end of the passage.'

He found several surveyors hard at work but willing to assist. Looking over their shoulders he saw that they were immersed in hundreds of more detailed maps of the areas, carefully noting the size of blocks. From there they noted title deeds, with their attendant maze of parish, volume and description.

'I thought this work was all completed,' he said.

'Yes, but this is a new project,' he was told.

Barnaby saw that the route to Longreach was now pencilled off into blocks like dominoes.

'What's all this for?'

'The railroad.'

'Are they going ahead with it?'

'My word they are, this will keep us busy for weeks. We've had to put on extra surveyors to go out into the field to check every yard and make certain we've got it right. We can't afford mistakes.'

'What happens? Does the government resume the land? Those blocks you're marking off.'

'In a sort of a way,' a surveyor replied. 'But it won't be our headache, we hand on to the titles office. They'll be flat out organizing double transfers.'

'What's a double transfer?' Barnaby asked.

'The government resumes the blocks for essential services, so that the owners can't complain, and then the ownership has to be transferred to the Western Railroad Company.'

'The whole way? That'll cost them,' Barnaby observed.

The surveyor looked surprised. 'No it won't. They're building the railroad, they need the land.'

'You mean they're just being granted the land. For nothing?'

'Something like that.'

As luck would have it, Calvin Abercrombie had entered the room and was standing back, interested in this conversation. He was a Member of the Upper House, and unlike most of his colleagues, fiercely independent. He was a dedicated Labor man and a sworn enemy of Royce Davies, who, he claimed had sold his Labor principles to the money men.

'What were you saying, Mr Glasson?' he asked.

Barnaby pointed at the maps. 'I was just surprised,' he said, without malice, 'that land can be transferred in this way. I always thought that land for private enterprise would have to be purchased. But I suppose in this case . . .'

'Why in this case?' Abercrombie asked, his voice bland.

'A railroad is a costly venture, I guess they'd need government assistance.'

'To the extent that they own every inch of land along that route? That seems very generous. I would have thought the land belonged to the people.'

'It would be used for the benefit of the people,' Barnaby argued.

'And would the profits go to the people?'

'To the investors,' Barnaby said.

'Well now, you're a lawyer, Mr Glasson. Put it this way,' Abercrombie said, 'wouldn't you consider the people have also invested? When land is resumed the owners have to be compensated.' He turned to the surveyors. 'Isn't that right?'

'Yes,' the head surveyor replied. 'So much per acre.'

'And who pays for that?' he asked Barnaby.

'The government, I suppose,' Barnaby replied, the situation now becoming clearer to him.

Abercrombie persisted. 'So now we have the government, or let us say, the people, buying land and handing it over scot free to Western

Railroads. And let's take it a step further. What if the railroad plan fails? If it never goes through. Who would then own the land?'

'The company,' Barnaby said weakly.

'And you think this proposition is fair, or shall we say appropriate?'

Barnaby gave it some thought and then shook his head. 'No, sir, I don't.'

Abercrombie clapped him on the shoulder. 'Good lad. Now you see how these things slip through. No one gives them enough thought. Who ordered this wildly generous gift to the Western Railroad Company?'

'Our minister did,' the surveyor said. 'The Minister for Lands. But leave us out of it. We're just doing our jobs.'

'By all means,' Abercrombie said. 'Now come with me, Mr Glasson, I shall want a word with your boss, the Attorney-General.'

Reluctantly Barnaby had to take him along to Creighton's office, explaining to the secretary that the Member wished to see the Minister on a matter or urgency.'

Creighton was furious. 'Who asked you to interfere?' he shouted when Abercrombie departed.

'I didn't interfere, sir. I just happened to be there when Mr Abercrombie came in.'

'He claims it was your questions that alerted him to what he calls "shady dealings". What were you doing there?'

'I was just checking the distance between towns out to Longreach.'

'You did more than that. You quizzed the surveyors on work that had nothing to do with you.'

It was no use arguing with him. Barnaby retreated to his corner, trying to look busy, since he'd left his notes in the surveyor's office and didn't dare go back to the Lands Department.

Rumours were abuzz in the House. Abercrombie was threatening to bring the matter before the Legislative Council and was also demanding that the Chairman of Committees instigate an enquiry into how such a proposal could be approved. A meeting was arranged with the Premier, Barnaby heard, to try to hose down the trouble.

Several ministers, including Jed Sweepstone, attended, and Abercrombie, with three of his colleagues, arrived bearing copies of relevant maps, demanding the right to view the contract between the government and Western Railroad.

Gossip had it that the Premier was trying to tough it out, arguing that the Minister for Lands had every right to sign the contract, which was not in question, but which was a red herring to divert attention from the main issue. And it worked for a while. Until the frustrated Abercrombie went to the newspapers with his story of abuse of public monies. Then the whispers began.

It was said that Edgar Thurlwell had paid the Minister for Lands a prodigious bribe to release the land to him, but the Premier staunchly supported Jed Sweepstone as being a true and trusted friend and a man of great integrity, who would never stoop to a bribe of any sort. In the meantime, Parliamentarians who had accepted parcels of shares from Edgar began to distance themselves from the debate.

Lalla Thurlwell called on Ben Buchanan, at Edgar's request, to persuade him to put a stop to the harassment of the Minister. 'This trouble is coming from the Opposition,' she said. 'It's creating a scandal without any basis, but it could affect the company. Royce Davies is in Ipswich and can't be contacted, so Ben, as his deputy, you must act. Tell Abercrombie that he has to back off.'

'I can't. Abercrombie is up in arms. I can't stop him. After all, we're *supposed* to be the Opposition, Lalla, and it's a long time since we've had a big stick like this to beat the government with.'

'Whose side are you on? You know perfectly well that Jed Sweepstone wouldn't take bribes.'

'Of course I do. It's a mess but it'll blow over. In the meantime I have to go home. I'm leaving in the morning. Clara needs me at the station.'

'Since when?'

'Since we're afflicted by a very bad drought, or have you forgotten?'

'No, I haven't forgotten,' she said angrily. 'But it's convenient that you have to race to the rescue now, when you are needed here.'

'I'll be back when the House sits.'

'You mean you're running for cover. Are you afraid that an enquiry will show that you are holding shares in Western Railroad? Gifts from Edgar?'

'There was nothing illegal about accepting those shares,' he said coldly.

'And this is your gratitude for Edgar's support? For our support?'

He lit a cigar. 'Edgar knows about us, Lalla. That's why I stopped seeing you.'

She moved closer to him, with a small, seductive smile. 'Good Lord. Is that all? He would never hurt me, so what does it matter?' She reached up to stroke his face. 'Now that I'm here, darling, on legitimate business, why don't we make the most of it?'

But he turned away. 'Your brother-in-law threatened me. I don't like to be threatened. That's the message I want you to take back to him.' His voice hardened. 'Tell Edgar I said to go to hell.'

'And me too, I suppose?' she snapped.

Ben shrugged. 'I have a lot to do, Lalla. The maid will show you out.'

She grabbed her handbag and gloves. 'You'll be sorry for this, Ben Buchanan. You mark my words!'

'I doubt it,' he retorted, and rang for the maid.

Out of sight, out of mind, the Member for Padlow grinned to himself as he set about packing for the journey home. He agreed that Sweepstone would never succumb to a bribe. Why would he? He had money to burn. But with Abercrombie claiming corruption in high places, this was a good time to disappear. Just to be hauled up before an enquiry to have to admit he had accepted gifts of shares from Thurlwell could lead to claims of conflict of interest if push came to shove.

He took his rifle out to the shed to clean it, and spotted his yardman, a craggy old coot called Monty, who was cutting back a row of banksias. What with the rain and the heat, they'd grown like crazy in the last few weeks, and the heavily laden branches were flopping over the lawn.

'Leave that,' he called to him. 'I want you to go down to O'Neill's stables and tell them I'll be away for a while so they are to keep my horses exercised.'

Monty ambled over. 'You mean Beckman's stables, don't you, Mr Buchanan?'

'The bloody horses are at O'Neill's stables,' Ben snapped.

'Yeah. It was O'Neill's but Ben Beckman bought the place. You know, that young bloke, the half-caste.'

Jesus! The rifle nearly slipped from his grasp as the name came out of the blue. He'd almost managed to forget it from the time he'd first heard it. After that, discreet enquiries had reassured him that the bastard had bought himself longer jail terms, thanks to unruly behaviour, and was well out of the way. But that was years back. Was this the same person? He shuddered. He'd been to those stables several times and never spotted him. But would he know him now? Unlikely.

'Beckman?' he asked Monty. 'Wasn't he in jail?'

'So they say,' Monty replied. 'But it don't seem to bother him none. He's doin' well there. Owns the saddlery too.'

'Just a minute.' Ben went inside the house and made for his desk, where he shuffled papers until he came to the latest account from the livery stables. And there it was. Beckman's! Why hadn't he noticed it before? God Almighty! Clara had been there too, plenty of times. What if the bastard had talked to her?

Relief flooded over him. No, the wretch hadn't spoken to Clara, or to him, about his background, because he didn't know. Diamond was dead and only that witless old woman, Mrs Beckman, had guessed that he had fathered the bastard. Since he'd denied it, though, she couldn't be sure, so it was on the cards she'd said nothing to the kid. That was it! Beckman had come up in the world but he still had no idea that he was related to his customer, Mr Buchanan. Otherwise he'd have said something, come crawling to him with his tale.

But thank God he'd found out in time. Ben took the account and some pound notes out to Monty.

'I don't want a person like that in charge of my horses. Here's his bill, and some cash. Pay him out. Take my horses to another stable.'

'Which one?' Monty, by no means a willing worker, was put out by this extra effort.

'I don't know! The one in Essex Street, it's closer to here anyway.'

'But I'll have to make a couple of trips,' Monty complained.

'You can ride one and lead the others.'

'I'm not a bloody stockman! That Talleyman's hard enough to handle on his own.'

'Get him there and walk back for the others,' Ben grated, 'or you're fired!'

For that matter, Ben decided after he'd sent Monty on his way, he'd get rid of the bugger anyway. With the dry season coming on, nothing much would grow in the garden and the two women, the maid and the cook, could look to the odd jobs themselves in his absence.

The old villain took his time, but with his horses safely ensconced at the Essex Street stables, Ben gave Monty a few shillings and sacked him.

Cursing, the old man made for the nearest pub, where he spent all his money on rum, complaining bitterly about his tired legs and his pig of an ex-boss, but no one listened. Then he staggered back into town to his night job at The Blue Heaven. His work entailed emptying the pots and slops from the kitchen, keeping the dunny clean and stacking bottles ready for the bottle-oh in the morning, but he was so tired he sat in an old chair by the back gate and fell asleep.

It was Goldie herself who came across him after finding her kitchen staff in confusion on a busy night and rubbish piling up. She flung open the back door to usher a scullery maid out with bins, and spotted her yardman snoring in a corner.

She whacked him with her fan. 'Wake up, you lazy lump!' she shouted at him. 'Get out of here! I don't pay you to sleep on my time.'

Monty came up with a start. 'Cripes, I'm sorry, missus. I musta dozed off.'

'Go and do your dozing somewhere else. You're sacked!'

Monty only had two jobs. He wasn't about to lose both on the one day. 'Oh Jeez, I'm sorry,' he cried. 'Fair go! My boss, that bugger Buchanan, ran me off me bloody feet today. I've had to walk up and down the bloody town! He don't care about an old man's legs.'

'What for?' she asked, disbelieving.

'To get his horses. He took a sudden fit in his head that he didn't want them no more at Beckman's livery stables and I had to go and get them right then. Not tomorrow, nor the next day, but right then.'

Goldie was interested. 'Ben Beckman's stables?'

'Yeah. You know Mr Buchanan. He's so stuck up he decided he wouldna' have no jailbird looking after his nags.'

Jailbird? Goldie thought. Not likely. Those stables were well run. What difference would it make who was in charge? As for an ex-prisoner, that didn't make sense. A good percentage of the workers in Brisbane were convict stock.

'Get on with your work,' she said abruptly to Monty, and he was glad to oblige, leaping up to help the scullery maid.

Goldie returned to her parlour, thinking about this. More like it, Buchanan had just woken up, somehow, to the fact that young Ben was his son. Goldie was certain she was right. And she wondered if Diamond's son knew that his father was gentry. Pity the old lady had died, she'd have known. It occurred to Goldie then that she was probably the only person in the world now who knew the truth, and by God, one of these days, when she had time, she'd make sure the kid knew. It would be her pleasure to let young Ben know he came from high-stepping stock and pay back Buchanan for his treatment of her black girls.

One of these days.

The hardest thing for Jed Sweepstone to suffer was the well-meaning support of his wife and their friends, who could not conceive of him having done anything underhand.

Fontana came and went in his own way, hardly noticing the political storm gathering about his father.

Jed tried, but he couldn't bring himself to face his son with those dreadful accusations about his sexual activities. He was a gentle, kindly man who had led a sheltered life, he now realized, in the bosom of a very wealthy and loving family. His move into politics had been the result of his own quest to make a contribution to the country that had treated his family so well. A family that had progressed in classic style from rags to riches in three generations, beginning with the labours of a poor Yorkshire sheep farmer, who'd migrated to Sydney as a lad.

What could he say to Fontana? he'd asked himself. And what would his son reply? Would he answer truthfully? That in itself would be hard for a father to bear. How should he, himself, react to the truth? A more forceful parent might reach for the horsewhip.

On the other hand, to his regret, he'd always known that Fontana did not treasure the truth. Jed wondered where he'd gone wrong. Maybe he should have been a sterner father. He didn't know, and he worried about that aspect for weeks, more than all the political upsets. He believed he'd failed his son.

If he confronted the boy, Jed knew that Fontana would deny the charges, and might run to his mother for support. It was not beyond him. Annette Sweepstone had often had to stand between father and son over minor matters. But not this time. Jed was determined not to allow Annette to be dragged into it. He loved her dearly and would never permit her to have to face a scandal like this. Jed had no doubt that his wife had never even heard of the word homosexual.

So he made his decision. He informed his wife and his son that because of Fontana's dreadful behaviour at the Parliamentary tea party, in throwing cordial at a Member of Parliament, he had decided to send the boy to England. He tabled the passage tickets much as he would table papers in the House. A *fait accompli*. Fontana had three days to pack.

His son was delighted, absolutely thrilled. But Annette was taken aback. 'Why so soon, Jed? It hardly gives him time to arrange things or say goodbye to his friends. It's such a long way to go. We won't even have time to give him a send-off party.'

'Annette, I have enough problems at the minute. You saw the cartoon in the paper about Mrs Davies and her ruined dress. They are making a joke of the Parliament. If Fontana goes, that will reduce the pressure on me.'

'Don't argue, Mother,' Fontana cried gleefully. 'He might change his mind.'

'But Jed,' she persisted, 'you said this row about the railroad land was only a storm in a teacup. Just an excuse for the Opposition to get stuck into the government. What has it got to do with Fontana?'

'Nothing at all,' he lied. 'His presence just complicates things, that's all.'

Fontana sailed for England in the good ship *Australis*, and Jed shuddered at the calibre of the young men who'd come to the wharves to bid farewell to their friend, blaming himself once again.

But the storm over the grants of land did not go away. Daily the pressure increased, until Abercrombie discovered papers in the Lands Department showing that the Minister had at first disapproved of the release of the land, and then, believing that the railroad to Longreach would be in the best interests of the country people, had decided that the land should not be granted to the Company but leased. And then he'd changed his mind again, and approved outright titles.

The Opposition, through newspapers, with the House in recess, was baying for blood, claiming that a corrupt government had sold out the people. Since the Leader of the Opposition, Royce Davies, and his deputy were both out of town, it was Abercrombie who was making the running and emerging as an outspoken and strong leader. Labor and Independents were lining up as a formidable force under his leadership, which meant that Royce Davies' days as leader were numbered, and Ben Buchanan was forgotten.

The Premier was worried. He called the Minister for Lands, Jed Sweepstone, into his private office for a talk.

'We won't be able to hold out against this, Jed,' he said. 'When the House resumes they'll chew us up and spit us out. We're facing a vote of no confidence.'

'We have the numbers, we'll win,' Jed replied, embarrassed that he had to make such a statement.

'No we don't. Not any more. We're only a conglomerate of my supporters, the Ministerial Party, and some independents. We're not a party as such, while the Opposition is gaining strength now under a Labor banner. I can foresee a Labor government in this colony in the near future.'

'If you think it would help, I'm willing to resign, not only my ministry but from the Parliament,' Jed offered.

His friend was worried. 'If you do that, Jed, it's almost like an admission of guilt. What bothers me is why you switched from giving them leasehold to ownership so suddenly. Why didn't you come to me and talk it over? You must have had a reason, you're not a man to make snap decisions like that. Give me something to fight with.'

Jed went back to his office and wrote out his letter of resignation. He tidied his desk, collected his personal effects, called in his secretary to thank him for his loyal support, and in an emotional moment, handed him the letter to deliver to the Premier.

When he arrived at his palatial house in Toowong, Jed broke the news to his wife.

'Buy why, Jed?' she wept. 'You haven't done anything wrong. I know you. They don't understand.'

But Jed Sweepstone knew there was no other way out. Even the Premier, his old friend, was close to believing that he had been bribed by Thurlwell, and in a way, he had been. Not with money, but for the sake of family honour. But it was no less a bribe and he should have resisted. His own honour had been sadly lacking, so how could he blame his son?

He wrote a short letter to his wife, thanking her for her love which he had deeply valued all his life. He left no messages for anyone else. The political scene now seemed so trivial.

He walked down the garden to the river bank, well away from the house, watching the dear old river retreating with the tide and wondering how many of the ancient Aborigine tribes, now long gone, had trod these same shores.

'Everything passes,' he said to the ghosts of the past.

And then he shot himself.

The state funeral accorded the Honourable Jed Sweepstone was the biggest seen in Brisbane for many years.

To avoid more scandal, and to prevail on the Anglican bishop to take the service, the doctor had been persuaded to issue a death certificate stating that Jed had died by accident. Misadventure. Fallen in the swollen depths of the river and drowned.

But that didn't stop the whispers around Parliament House. Someone had it on good authority that the former Minister had shot himself, and it wasn't long before Barnaby heard about it and found himself the recipient of sullen, accusing glances. He was so upset he couldn't bring himself to go out and watch the funeral cortège pass by on its long, stately march from the church to the Toowong cemetery.

The following day, Mr Theodore Prosser arrived in Brisbane and Barnaby escorted him to his appointment with the Attorney-General. Creighton was still angry with his assistant and hardly acknowledged him as he took his visitor from the Australian Natives Association into his office. So Barnaby sat out in the corridor, a picture of gloom, certain that he would be replaced as Mr Prosser's guide and assistant on his tour.

Finally Prosser came out to inform Barnaby, in his booming, oratorial voice, that he would be lunching with the Premier, clearly delighted with his reception.

'I understand, young fellow,' he said, 'that we sail for Rockhampton on the first leg of our journey the day after tomorrow.'

'That's correct, sir.'

'Good. That will give me a chance to explore Brisbane before we leave. The ship sails at two in the afternoon. I expect you to collect me and my luggage at my hotel at ten a.m. and deliver me to the ship.'

Barnaby realized that this proud gentleman intended to treat him as his porter, but he didn't care. He was relieved to be able to escape Brisbane at this time. And to still have his job.

Chapter Seven

Chastened by that month-long blindfold of cloud, the sun emerged with less vehemence and cast a benign eye over the town, turning sodden greenery into sharp, springy relief. Colour crept out from the bushes to cheer with a new version of autumn. No sombre tones here. Blossoms and blooms rallied with dashing reds and golds and pinks and yellows and, not to be outdone, parrots flashed about flaunting their own brilliance while butcher birds blessed the clear air with glorious four-tone melodies. Fragile butterflies fluttered happily in their deep velvet shades as if to signal that all was well with the world.

'Best time of the year,' the Premier said to his Attorney-General, standing, hands behind his back, before the open window.

'Yes, indeed,' Creighton replied. 'Yes, indeed.' He had suggested to the Premier that his brother, Hal, be elevated to the ministerial vacancy brought about by the untimely death of Jed Sweepstone, and so would have agreed with his leader had there been a blizzard out there.

For his part the Premier was loath to fill that vacancy right now. Every one of his backbenchers wanted the job, and by making a choice he would put noses out of joint and face possible defections. As it was, the numbers were tight, and he was determined to hold on to government until he could push through the Enabling Act and send Queensland forth to federation. He turned to face Creighton:

'Your brother is very popular at Warwick,' he said. 'He's handling his electorate well, no doubt on your excellent advice. Nothing like having the strength of experience to call on.'

'Quite so. And he would also have my ministerial experience if he were to be honoured by the call to serve in your ministry.'

'Couldn't agree more. But is it fair to drop a new boy into the present hornets' nest? Abercrombie is on the warpath, and on the other side of the coin, Edgar Thurlwell is a tough customer with a lot of influence. The new Minister for Lands could find himself between the devil and the deep blue sea. If he stumbles, his career could be in tatters before he starts.'

'Sir,' Creighton said, 'I would be there to support him. To advise him.'

'Yes,' the canny Premier replied, 'that's true. And you know both of those gentlemen. I don't suppose you'd consider switching to the Lands portfolio?'

He kept a straight face as Thomas Creighton turned that suggestion down very smartly. 'With respect, sir, I think it would be a mistake for me to forsake my department at this critical time, what with all the work we're doing on the constitution.'

'True, true,' the Premier pondered. 'Really, Thomas, I think we'll leave the Lands portfolio for the time being. I'll take it over myself until all this blows over. It was a terrible shock to lose a good friend like Jed. I don't know why he didn't come to me. God knows what possessed a decent man like that to shoot himself.'

'The row over the railroad land must have been too much for him, I suppose.'

'But there was nothing illegal in what he did, was there?'

'No. Not illegal, but ill-advised. Especially since he changed the rules from leasehold to grants for Thurlwell.'

'Ah yes, for Thurlwell. I'm to see him this afternoon.'

'What will you do? Cancel Jed's orders to the surveyors?'

'I'll see. A lot of people want that railroad. I'm not happy about granting all that land to him, but if I renege on Jed's promise I'm placing myself onside with Abercrombie and admitting a serious mistake, if not worse, by the government.'

'What if we announce that railroads are to continue to be the responsibility of the state? That will shut Thurlwell out.'

'And also give the impression that the government will take over and build these railroads. Where will we find the money?'

'It's a ticklish situation,' Creighton agreed.

'Let me think on it a while,' the Premier said.

The talk with Creighton had gone well, the leader mused as his Attorney-General retreated. The man couldn't be relied on to keep his mouth shut, so he'd been given nothing, and no promises.

Late that afternoon he welcomed Edgar Thurlwell with a hearty handshake and a whisky.

He accepted Edgar's condolences on Sweepstone's death with a nod. 'It was very hard on his family,' he said, 'and on Jed's friends here in the House. I, for one, am inclined to take the death of my friends very hard.' He emphasized the last line while gazing at Thurlwell, because somewhere, somehow, the Premier believed that this fellow had been the cause.

'We will all miss him,' Thurlwell replied. 'A sad loss.'

They discussed the funeral, the eloquence of the bishop, the competence of the choir and the large number of wreaths that had spilled out on to the steps of the church, the Premier seemingly prepared to reminisce for ages, until Edgar, an impatient man, was forced to ask who would replace the late Minister.

'You'll forgive me for bringing up the subject, sir,' he said, 'but life must go on.' Edgar sighed. 'It will be up to me to do my utmost to co-operate with the new Minister. Plans are under way now to build the first of our railroads out to Longreach, and one can't even begin to assess the great benefits they will bring to our state.'

'The new Minister? Hmmm. I haven't had much of a chance to think about a replacement. But we'll see. All in good time. Was there anything in particular you wanted to discuss?'

'Since so much fuss is being made about the railroad, purely political, of course, I hope to meet the new Minister as soon as possible and reassure him that everything is going ahead as planned.'

'Such as?'

'My contract with the Lands Department.'

'I had no idea there was a contract,' the Premier said mildly.

'Well, let us say a gentleman's agreement. The late Minister was eager for my company to have the land, despite Abercrombie's objections. He did issue instructions for the Titles Office to proceed.'

'That's correct, but it's not exactly iron-clad. The new Minister would be able to use his own discretion on these decisions.'

'Surely there could be no reversal!' Edgar retorted. 'No company or corporation the size of Western Railroad can be subjected to chops and changes at the whims of new ministers who have had no part in the deliberations.'

'Of course not. Leave it with me, I'll look at it myself.'

'Thank you, sir. Your personal interest in this matter would be appreciated.' He picked up his hat and stick to depart. 'I understand that you are still in favour of federation, Mr Premier. Personally I can't see the value in it for our state, but then I've only been following the rather garbled debate in the newspapers so I wouldn't consider myself an expert on the subject. Perhaps you might care to join me for luncheon one day. I should be most interested in your views.'

With Thurlwell out of the way, the Premier relaxed behind his desk and lit a cigar. 'Free land for his vote on federation,' he laughed. 'That's an expensive price to pay for a few of your tame pollies, Edgar.'

He rang for his secretary. 'All that stuff I've been reading on the resumption of the corridor of land for the railway to Longreach is on the second shelf in the cupboard. Take it back to the department and file it. And here . . .' On his letterhead he scribbled the words: 'No action by order' and signed his name.

'Then go to the Titles Office and retrieve the maps. Give them the same instructions. And if anyone asks, just tell them this is a temporary measure.'

Left alone again, he leaned back in his chair. 'Temporary measure, nothing! It's buried. If you want that land, Thurlwell, you buy it yourself. And if this government decides to build railroads we shall not need your assistance.'

Edgar Thurlwell had an uncomfortable meeting with his bank manager.

'Your personal account is seriously overdrawn, Mr Thurlwell. When can we see some improvement?'

'My dear fellow, there's no problem. It's been necessary to divert some of my funds to the company, which is in good shape. You realize of course that the company will have far more collateral than is needed, as soon as all that land is granted to us.'

'It's going ahead, is it?'

'Of course. I spoke to the Premier himself yesterday, he's handling it personally.'

'Yes, but that's the company. Surely you could see your way clear to paying something on this substantial private loan.'

Edgar sighed. 'Very well, I'll transfer some monies into it later today. You might call it substantial but I call it trivial compared to our holdings. Good day to you, sir!'

He lunched with William and Lalla at their home, telling them that he'd had a private chat and a few drinks with the Premier, and that all was well. Although he really wasn't too sure; he'd been unable to prise a definite answer out of the Premier and it worried him.

They were delighted, and greatly relieved. Abercrombie, with his claims of corruption, had unnerved them. But when Edgar had a chance to talk to William alone, he produced some papers for his brother to sign.

'What are these?' William asked.

'Requisitions, authorizations for payments. As company chairman I need your signature.'

They had drunk several bottles of wine at lunch and now Dr Thurlwell was sleepy. He wished Edgar would take himself off and let him retire for a siesta. 'You're the company treasurer,' he complained. 'Why do I have to bother with all this?' He glared at the offending heap of papers and documents. 'Can't you attend to it, Edgar? I've been at the hospital all morning and I had a damnable time. Do you know that some of those snotty-nosed young doctors who call themselves surgeons are trying to push me off the board! They're claiming my methods are old-fashioned.'

Edgar had heard that talk in his club, and it was far more serious than William was admitting. Apparently he'd made some serious mistakes, refusing to give way to safer methods, and two patients had died. Edgar had no sympathy for his brother, who was usually half-sozzled, and indeed, had quietly made his own decision that if he were to go under the knife he wouldn't allow William near him. But that had no bearing on the matter in hand.

'Take no notice of them,' he advised. 'There's always a young buck ready to challenge men of experience. They always think they know better.'

'You're right, Edgar,' William mumbled as he signed page after page with hardly a glance.

'Tell you what,' Edgar suggested, to keep his brother's mind off the papers he was signing. 'Why don't you drop it to them that our company is thinking of donating a new wing to the hospital once we get under way? That will shut them up.'

'By God it would, wouldn't it? But could we afford it?'

'Those American millionaires with their railroads could buy all of Brisbane,' Edgar laughed. 'We mightn't fly so high but we won't notice a donation like that. Besides, it'll be tax-deductible. I'll make sure it is.'

William licked his finger to turn the pages, and his signatures flew.

'Make them legible,' Edgar cautioned. 'Did you know the Americans started railroads either side of the country and they met in the middle? Right on cue. That's what they call "know-how" but I call foresight. Have you finished?' He flipped through the pages to make certain that William hadn't missed any, and placed them in a leather case.

'Would you like a port?' William asked him, reaching for a bottle. 'This is an excellent year.'

'Good idea. But just one. I'm giving a small dinner party at the club tonight for Hal Creighton, of Warwick. He's breaking his neck to become a club member and I might be able to oblige, since I hear he's in line to be the next Minister for Lands.'

William's head was already nodding. 'Good show,' he mumbled.

His brother didn't open the leather case until he was safely at home. He smoothed out the most important document, the one that would satisfy the demands of his banker. A mortgage on William's mansion, Somerset House in Kangaroo Point, the monies to be directed to his brother Edgar's personal account.

There was no problem. Edgar told himself. He had already mortgaged his own house for 'the Cause', as he liked to call their great entrepreneurial venture, so why shouldn't William, who expected all this to be presented to him on a plate while his brother did all the planning and organizing? And if anything went wrong, he, Edgar, was also the company treasurer. He really didn't need his brother's signature on any withdrawals.

Phoebe walked through all the upheavals in a dream. She still had her secret life with Ben, seeing him as often as possible. Her family was upset by all the hoo-ha in the newspapers about the railway land, but it didn't seem important to her.

Barnaby went away but she didn't miss him. Then Ben told her that Mr Buchanan had shifted Gracie to another stable, but to Phoebe that was a relief. She felt she couldn't go the stables any more.

'Guilty conscience?' he'd asked, teasing her.

'I think so,' she said frankly. 'If I came there now I'd have to pretend I hardly know you, when it's not true.'

'Do you know me?' he asked.

'Of course I do. I know that you've grown into a very sane and sensible man, that you read a lot, judging by the number of books here.'

Ben laughed. 'No I don't, all the books in the house are in German.'

'Do you want me to bring you some books?'

'No. I haven't time to read them.'

'Of course, because you're too busy with all the catalogues on motorcars and petrol and stuff.'

'It interests me. When they're available, I'll buy a motorcar.'

'You'll what?'

'You heard me. Would you ride with me?'

Phoebe hesitated. 'I don't know. Can you imagine what a row that would cause?'

'Come here,' he said, walking out on to the vine-covered veranda that was lit only by a full moon sailing softly through wisps of cloud.

'What for?' she asked, stepping down from the kitchen door.

'I just wanted to look at you in the moonlight,' he said, taking her hands. 'You were such a gangly little girl, it's still hard for me to realize you're the same person.'

'I was too tall as a kid,' she said, 'and I hated it.'

'I was a bit of a squirt,' he smiled, 'but I grew bigger. I'm a lot taller than you now.'

'And some,' she said, but she wasn't smiling. They were so close, holding hands in the softness of the night, just looking at each other. And moving closer. There were no more words. His arms slipped about her waist and drew her to him, and her face had become nestled against his chest. That strong chest under his wide shoulders seemed like a haven to her, the protection she'd always craved. Phoebe lifted up her head and kissed the smooth skin under his chin. His lips came down to meet hers, and all the love she'd ever wanted in her life was in that kiss, that soft and loving kiss that lasted and lasted. He kissed her face, her eyes, her cheeks but always came back to her lips, with love, with love.

She attended the state funeral of Mr Sweepstone with her parents, wearing an outfit that her mother had chosen for her. From the crushed-velvet hat shaped like a luxurious mobcap, that allowed wispy strands of blonde hair to escape, to her gloves and shiny neat shoes, Phoebe was all in black. Her rustling silk dress with its taffeta petticoat and tightly corseted waist was a model of grace and propriety, the prim bodice buttoned through to the neckline, which was finished off with a collar band encrusted with jet beads. She was amazed at how well it suited her, and had to admit that Lalla's taste in clothes was impeccable. In fact, Phoebe realized, as the usher took them down the aisle of the church, with all eyes on her, she was outshining her mother. A new and exciting experience.

She wished Ben could see her. She doubted he'd be among the curious crowd milling outside. The sighting of celebrities wouldn't interest him.

Composing herself as the service began, Phoebe noticed that Fontana wasn't with his mother and all their relations in the front pews. Then she remembered that he'd gone to England. How awful, she thought, to have to hear such terrible news by telegraph and not to be able to get back for the funeral. Phoebe had known Mr Sweepstone as a kind and charming man, and as the eulogies began, she wiped a dampness from the corners of her eyes. She was feeling sentimental and her thoughts drifted to Ben, to their love.

For they were passionately in love now and it was all about them the minute she stepped into his house. Into his arms. It was in the welcome of the parlour, the simplicity of the small dining room and the gay rattle of the kitchen. It was in the trees and vines that shaded the river-front veranda, in the seclusion of the garden on the far side of the house where they walked, hand in hand, every little thing sharing their love which Phoebe believed was predestined.

They never spoke of their love. There was no need. The house and its surrounds was their enchanted garden. Safe from the world.

Lalla nudged her. Time to stand for a hymn. All of Phoebe's senses seemed to be sharpened now. The choir was superb, the service piteously impressive, the flag-draped casket in its carpet of wreaths was bravely mournful and the tears of the widow broke her heart. At the same time, common sense told her that it was in her own interests to refrain from antagonizing her mother now, so, quite deliberately, she'd become more pliable, more agreeable, consenting without argument to go along with Lalla on every point and occasion. She even sat in on Lalla's weekly card parties, all in the name of peace, to loosen the iron hand of parental control. And it was working, she told herself gleefully. Spared the daily confrontations, Lalla seemed to lose interest in her daughter, convinced she was now dressing and behaving as a young lady should.

'I saw your name in the paper,' Ben said, the next time she came to his house. 'Twice this week. Once at that funeral and another time at a dance for young people at Government House. One of the Vice-Regal younger set! Escorted by Robert someone. Who's he?'

'He's a nephew of the Governor. Are you jealous?'

'Of course I'm jealous.'

Phoebe giggled, delighted. 'Then you needn't be. Robert is madly in love with a country girl but her parents have taken her to Europe for the Grand Tour, so he'll have to suffer until she comes home.'

'How can he be in love with someone else with you around?'

'Very easily, my darling.'

To Ben's bewilderment, his dizzying liaison with this beautiful girl was out of hand. What had begun as a strident attack on enemy country by carrying off their pride and joy, their fair princess, was now his own problem. He loved her! He was madly in love with her! How could he not be? Even when he'd reminded her that they were worlds apart, she hadn't cared. She was fiercely independent and yet there was a softer side to her. With all her worldly blessings she was light-hearted, unassuming and a marvellous companion. And so loving he could hardly think of anything else. She was on his mind all the time.

Only two nights ago, she'd wandered into his bedroom, picking up the small reminders of his childhood. A carved ship that Diamond had bought for him at a fête, some readers, remnants of his lessons with Oma, two toy soldiers, a crab pot that he'd been meaning to repair . . .

When he'd come looking for her she'd turned to him. 'I love this room best. This is really you, not that other stuff you've been worrying me with, about that horrid jail. You shouldn't have been there and I won't have it mentioned ever again.'

He put his arms about her and then they were lying together on his bed, caught up in a passionate embrace. He could still feel her firm breasts against him and the wondrous curve of her body. God! She was so warm and loving and so naive! He'd had to put a stop to it. He'd had to get up and take her with him, smoothing her mussed hair and straightening her dress, take her outside into the air to walk for a while so that they could cool down. He was glad that no one else knew what had been in his mind when he first began to court Phoebe, cringing at the thought now.

Ben lay on the bed, the same bed, dreaming of her. He wanted her desperately and he didn't know what to do about it. She trusted him and he was afraid that if he went too far, even to satisfy his yearning to explore that lovely body, she might be offended. And yet she was so passionate, she confused him. Ben had only ever had sex with willing prostitutes, so what to do with a young lady who was driving him crazy? Perhaps a man should ask. Ask if he might unbutton her dress. Ask if he might . . .

No. That sounded ridiculous. He missed Diamond. Now that he was a grown man, he might have been able to talk to her about this problem.

The pretty lady who'd stood at his mother's graveside had also attended Oma's funeral and had turned out to be not so pretty and not so much of a lady. She was the notorious Goldie, the madam of The Blue Heaven, and the knowledge had surprised and amused him. If Diamond had known people like that, there was a lot he didn't know about his mother.

He'd wanted to ask Goldie more about his mother, but he'd never had the chance. And since Phoebe, he hadn't been back to The Blue Heaven.

The night seemed long. He couldn't sleep. He felt rather mean that he'd never invited Kathleen O'Neill back to the house, nor the Callaghans, but the place had a renewed feminine aura, even in the physical evidence. Phoebe left things about . . . a shawl, a brush and comb, hair ribbons, and even a long trailing muslin scarf that glittered with tiny beads. She'd hung that over the mirror in the hall in a playful mood to remind him of her. He couldn't bear to have to hide anything of hers.

And on that same night, walking with her out there, she'd put the question to him: 'What's to become of us, Ben?'

He'd put an arm about her and shaken his head. 'I don't know, Phoebe. I don't know.'

Travels with Theodore Prosser were proving to be irksome, irritating and at times downright infuriating. The man was pompous and demanding. Not only was Barnaby his porter, he was also his servant, never permitted to sit at table with him in public, and was at all times referred to as 'my man'. But Barnaby gritted his teeth and battled on.

They sailed directly to Cairns, and though Theodore was fêted by the captain on the ship, he was treated as a bit of a joke in the tropical north. People came to hear him speak, not because they were interested in what he had to say but because they had nothing else to do. Everyone agreed he was a great speaker and the audience cheered him with standing ovations.

Barnaby nearly split his sides laughing when one gruff town notable told him: 'Dunno what he's on about, but he's a bloody good talker. I'll give him that.'

By the time they sailed south to Townsville, the great orator was convinced he was winning audiences to federation, but Barnaby realized that it wasn't an issue in the north. They had too many pioneering problems to worry about. However, in quiet talks with various locals, he was able to establish that the concept of a new nation was worth their attention and managed to gain a few supporters.

Townsville was a disaster. The portly Prosser, unused to the tropical heat, was hoping for cooler weather, but within hours of leaving the ship he was overcome by exhaustion and refused to leave his hotel room. Fearing that his guest might have contracted a fever, not unusual in the north, the Mayor sent for a doctor, who pronounced that the patient was:

'Simply dead beat. Can't take the heat. Send him home!'

Rather than disappoint the patrons, Barnaby spoke at the meeting, in a more informal manner, preferring to field questions rather than talk for too long. Apart from the city fathers, the majority of the audience was composed of prospectors, from or on their way to the goldfields. These men, stargazers themselves, were amenable to change and were stirred by his words, charmed that they would be part of creating a nation. After the meeting they insisted on taking him to the nearest pub for a celebration. Any excuse, he discovered.

Then late monsoonal rains besieged the town, and Barnaby and his mentor were marooned in Townsville.

This was a huge disappointment to Barnaby, since he'd been looking forward to visiting the fabulous gold town of Charters Towers, which had already outstripped Brisbane when it came to wealth. In a vague way, he'd hoped some of that gold might rub off on him. Maybe some of his new friends might take him prospecting and he'd be able to find one of those six-pound nuggets they all talked about. The constant talk of gold during the next few days was insidious. During another drinking session he'd almost agreed with his new friends to chuck his job and come with them.

Prosser complained. Back on his feet, he paced the steamy hotel parlour, blaming Barnaby for this inactivity and demanding that another date be set for him to address the townspeople, but by this time itinerant players were performing at the School of Arts and Prosser had lost his chance. He became very angry when he heard that the meeting presided over by Barnaby had been a great success.

'How dare you push yourself forward like that?'

'I asked you, sir, and you told me to go ahead,' Barnaby replied.

'I was too indisposed to know what you were up to,' Prosser retorted. 'We leave here tomorrow for Charters Towers.'

'Sorry, sir, that's not possible. The rivers are flooded. Completely impassable.'

'I shall report you for this,' Prosser threatened, but Barnaby was becoming fed up with him.

'That's your prerogative. I have no control over the elements.'

Ten days later they sailed for Rockhampton, where Prosser refused to acknowledge Barnaby or introduce him to any of the town councillors. Or even allow him to join him on the stage at the meetings.

'The town clerk has been appointed to take me out to the country towns from here,' he told Barnaby, 'so your services will not be required.'

'Should I return to Brisbane?'

'Certainly not. You will wait here for my return.'

The laconic town clerk, one Hector Wordsworth, was not at all pleased at being seconded to these duties, and came to Barnaby for advice.

'Best of luck,' Barnaby laughed. 'Think like a servant and you'll get by.'

'Like hell I will!' Hector replied.

So Barnaby stayed to enjoy the river town of Rockhampton, careful to take all his meals at the hotel on Prosser's bill. Less than a week later, Hector was back in town.

'I left the old bugger to it,' he grinned. 'Had enough of him. Hardly anybody turned up at his meetings because he insisted that I change your advertisements, emphasizing that he was from the Australian Natives Association.'

'Oh no! I deliberately played that down in case it was misunderstood.'

'Too bloody right it was. Everyone thought it was a meeting for the blacks and they stayed away in droves.' He laughed. 'Even the Abos stayed clear, not knowing what was expected of them.'

It was Hector who took him about Rockhampton, introducing Barnaby to all and sundry, and it was then that Barnaby took courage and spoke not only of federation but of the fact that he would be standing for the new Senate when it came into being. His story created a great deal of excitement and he was even photographed for the local newspaper, which ran a front-page article entitling him, with blithe disregard for fact, as 'Our first national senator'.

Then came the news that Theodore Prosser had become very agitated at the poor attendance at a meeting in Longreach and had stormed from the stage, missing the steps. He was now in the Longreach Bush Hospital with a broken foot.

Barnaby drafted a telegram to the Attorney-General with great care. Freed from the muffling hand of Prosser, this was the opportunity of a lifetime.

He advised that Mr Prosser had met with an accident and would be laid up in Longreach for some time. He pointed out that while Mr Prosser had been ill in Townsville he had conducted the meetings with such an excellent response that he was sure the Premier would be delighted.

Aware of the Premier's determination to push through to federation, Barnaby knew those words would pressure his boss and lead him to agree to his next suggestion.

'Should I continue the good work or cancel all further engagements?' his telegram asked.

To his great joy the reply was a terse: 'Go ahead. Felicitations will be forwarded to Mr Prosser.'

Now it was his turn, and there'd be no going back. Pronouncing himself a Senate candidate had added the personal touch, which until now had been lacking.

He slipped quietly back to Brisbane and made for his rooms, where he found a note from Phoebe:

'I need to talk to you. Where have you been? Come and see me. Your friend, Phoebe.'

She'd cried wolf too often. She would have to wait. He had to sort out his clothes and set off on the Charleville route before Creighton realized he was in town and changed his mind. He scanned the newspapers. A Norwegian expedition with a Queensland surveyor were the first men to land on the Antarctic continent. Heavy rains in the north of the state . . . he knew about that. The Brisbane Art Gallery had been opened, at last, by the Premier on his return from a federation conference in Hobart. The row over grants of land to Western Railroad must have been resolved, since it didn't rate a mention.

Barnaby shivered. He still felt miserable about the death of the Lands Minister, but that too was no longer news. Suppression of gambling in Queensland, by legislation, was proposed, and had become the latest issue of contention, with both sides vicious in the condemnation of the other. He was glad to be out of the office, since Creighton seemed to favour the Bill.

'The bloody fool,' he muttered. 'It'll be impossible to police.'

He felt out of touch with Brisbane, almost anonymous, and was buoyed by a temporary sense of independence as he boarded the train for his first stop, the little town of Dalby.

No one seemed to care that he was only a stand-in for Prosser, since they'd never heard of the man anyway, and Barnaby was welcomed as the representative of the Attorney-General. And without Prosser to annoy him, he progressed from town to town in fine form, managing to draw audiences which, if not all that interested, were at least curious and prepared to 'give him a go'.

By the time he arrived in Charleville he was in high spirits. The monsoonal rains had swept south at last and the greening of the land had begun again. The local people were almost delirious with joy and relief as steady rain thudded down, turning the main street into a quagmire, but no one minded. The long drought was over!

To celebrate his final meeting, carried away by the excitement in the town, Barnaby decided to offer his audience a light supper. His cash advance was holding up well.

'Who could I get to provide supper?' he asked the aged caretaker of the hall.

'See Lottie Smith at the Shamrock Hotel. She does a good spread, and cheap too.'

So it was arranged that Mrs Smith and her ladies would provide a supper of sandwiches, cake and coffee for tenpence per head.

When he thought about it later, Barnaby knew his lone tour had been far too easy. By the law of averages something had to go wrong. And it did.

The hall was packed. With free refreshments on offer, the audience was in a genial mood. There were women present too, quite a lot of women for a change, since they'd heard that their sisters in South Australia had been given the vote. Talking with them before the meeting, Barnaby was surprised that they were so politically aware.

'We can read,' they laughed. 'Not much else to do of a night. We want the vote too. If there's to be a vote on this federation business, we ought to have a say. Don't you reckon?'

'Yes I do,' Barnaby replied. Although he hadn't thought about it before, he realized that the female vote could make a big difference to the result. 'I'll remind the Attorney-General,' he promised.

The Mayor led him on to the stage to introduce him, a stage that had a backdrop of an English rural scene, which, though faded, was a far cry from the surrounding countryside. They were accompanied by the usual pair of town councillors, who felt it their duty to be present and earn their share of the limelight.

Barnaby began by thanking the audience for attending and sincerely praised their fortitude in the face of that terrible drought. 'I'm so glad to be here with the rain,' he said. 'And I pray it keeps on coming down.'

'Hear, hear!' echoed through the hall.

He then launched into his, by now, polished speech, pointing out that he wasn't there to ram his opinions down their throats but to ask them to consider federation.

'Think of this huge continent as one nation. A country, if you give it a go, that can be a great nation called Australia. That will take its proper place among the nations of the world.'

There was a stir of interest in his audience.

'We can't go on forever,' he continued, 'as a motley collection of colonies, all going their own ways. We are Australians! You have it in your hands to be the makers of a new nation. Your children and their children deserve the right to stand proud as Australians . . .'

Barnaby looked at the sea of earnest faces, preparing to enter the minefield of independence where he would point out that federation did not mean cutting ties with Mother England, nor with their beloved Queen, who would remain Queen of the Commonwealth of Australia. And at the end of his speech he would tell them that he himself, a man who had studied the new constitution, would be a candidate to represent Queensland in the new Senate. But first a joke to lighten the mood:

'The convict days are over,' he said. 'We have to cast off the shackles that still weigh us down, and the only way we can do that is to stand up and be counted as Australians.

'I often think,' he confided, 'that the British must be kicking themselves. They should have left the convicts in their wintry land and come here themselves to our sunny clime.'

That brought a laugh, but one man commented drily: 'They're welcome to some of our sunshine, mate.'

'True enough,' Barnaby conceded, 'but their cold weather won't change and, God willing, we're seeing the end of the drought.'

As he carried on with his speech, Barnaby saw a man enter by a side door and take off his dusty hat and gunbelt, dumping them on a nearby table, to stand surveying the scene. He seemed familiar but Barnaby couldn't place him without turning to take a closer look.

Suddenly the man strode forward, addressing the Mayor in a loud, arrogant voice. 'Who is this fellow? What right has he got to be standing up there telling us what we should do? I say it's a damned impertinence!'

Barnaby was stunned. He recognized the intruder now. Ben Buchanan, MLA. The last person he needed to see. Where had he come from? With a sinking feeling of dismay, Barnaby remembered that Buchanan had a cattle station out this way. Damn!

As the Mayor stumbled to his feet to explain, Barnaby cut in, trying to make light of the interruption. 'Ah! Mr Buchanan. Welcome to the meeting. I'm sure you're well aware of my credentials. I represent our Attorney-General.'

Buchanan turned to the crowd. 'In other words he's a clerk. A man with no stake in the country, who has political ambitions. He's giving you all this hogwash about federation in the hopes that if he pulls it off, the Premier will reward him with a seat in the so-far non-existent Senate. Is that not true, Mr Glasson?'

'It is true that I would be a candidate, but . . .'

'There you are!' Buchanan jeered. 'What did I tell you?'

Barnaby heard an unpleasant muttering in the audience, and he knew he was losing them. He looked angrily down at Buchanan. 'I have as much right to be here as you do. You don't represent these people. You represent a Brisbane electorate. I'm surprised to see you here. You're always in town hobnobbing with the social set.'

He was surprised to hear a merry clapping from a small group of women, but the rest of the audience was now leaning forward with fervour, the meeting having taken a more interesting turn as far as they were concerned.

'Social set be damned!' Buchanan retorted. 'This fellow's talking revolution. We saw what happened when America cut loose from the mother country! War in their land, followed by an even bloodier war between their states! Do we want that?'

'No fear!' voices echoed.

'How can you listen to him?' Barnaby shouted. 'We don't want independence from England, just equality. There's no possibility of war. That man,' he pointed at Buchanan, 'is just a stooge for the Brisbane money-grabbers.' He recalled what Phoebe had told him about Buchanan, whom she disliked, about his arrangements with her Uncle Edgar. 'Who backed you, Buchanan? Western Railroad interests? They bought you the seat of Padlow, they gave you free shares in their company to be their mouthpiece.'

Buchanan laughed. 'How about that? I'm battling to bring more railroads to the bush and he's criticizing me!'

There was a thrust of chairs as people stood up to leave.

'Wait!' Barnaby yelled. 'Sooner or later there'll be more railroads. But not his way! You must have read that he and his mates are making a grab for the railroad land without paying a penny for it.'

'So what?' Buchanan said. 'It took twenty years to get this one track out to Charleville. To open up the country we want to move faster. We need that railway land, and we'll get it.'

'Don't bet on it!' Barnaby shouted.

A bulky man in a chequered shirt lumbered to his feet. 'Looks to me as if they're both a pair of go-getters. I'm for go-getting a drink, mates. Who's with me?'

The tables in the annex emptied as the members of the audience helped themselves to the food on the way out.

'I'll have your job for this,' Buchanan snarled at Barnaby before he strode away.

'Then I'll have yours!' Barnaby shouted after him.

The Mayor and his colleagues had made a swift exit out of the stage door, not needing to become involved in this argument, and Barnaby was left with the catering ladies, who commiserated with him.

Lottie Smith took him aside. 'I'm sorry about this, Mr Glasson. I think you're on to a good thing calling for us to be one nation, so don't give up, lad.'

She untied her long black apron. 'At least our nice food wasn't wasted. But you look out for Ben Buchanan. He's no good. You were right about him being in town all the time. His wife runs the property, she's a battler, one of the best. He doesn't do much, he's never changed.'

'From what?' Barnaby asked listlessly, more from a need to make conversation than interest, since everyone else had deserted him.

'From up north,' she said. 'I used to be their housekeeper at Caravale Station. His mother was a mean piece of work and he's no different. Next time he gives you a bad time, you ask him about Diamond.'

'Who?' he asked, startled.

'Diamond. A black girl. Smart as paint. She was his girl, if you get what I mean. But you know those housekeeping jobs – see nothin', know nothin', or you'll be out on your ear. Last I heard she was on the Palmer goldfields with him.'

'And he struck gold?'

'No, he came home broke. Had the fever up there. Then the old lady died, so he sold Caravale. Came down this way, married money and bought Fairmont Station. I feel sorry for Clara Buchanan, puttin' up with him. You look a bit tired. Can I make you some sandwiches to take back to your hotel?'

'I'd appreciate that,' he said.

He sat in his hotel room munching on the delicious roast beef sandwiches, disappointed at the collapse of the meeting, which would have to go into his report. As for the gossip about Buchanan, he didn't set much store by it. Even if the black woman, Diamond, was the same person he'd known, it was old gossip, and best left be. Diamond was dead, that was the end of it. Except that it did explain how she'd come by the gold she'd presented to her lawyer to sell for her. She must have struck it lucky at the Palmer goldfields.

'Interesting how things come out,' he murmured wearily as he climbed into bed. 'That Palmer River must have been a real treasure chest. I wish I could find a gold mine.'

He couldn't sleep. Wind shook and rattled the shutters and rain thundered on the iron roof with such force he half expected it to cave in. The noise was deafening. He pulled a blanket over his head and thought of Theodore Prosser.

He doubted if a man of Prosser's standing would have been subjected to such an attack by Buchanan. And if so, he wondered, how would he have handled it? Probably a lot better than he himself had, Barnaby had to admit, and that made him feel inadequate. Who was he, after all, the son of farmers, to be setting himself up against the establishment? To even be thinking that he'd have a chance for Parliament against the money men, the men of power who made the rules and looked after their own. And if he did lose his job, thanks to his abuse of a Member of Parliament, what then? Mantrell couldn't take him back; he was due to retire and his recently appointed partner would be taking over the firm.

In the morning a delegation of ladies came to him with a petition to take to the Attorney-General, begging for a vote for women, and he was happy to oblige. Even the Mayor dropped by to apologize for the débâcle of the previous night.

'Leave me a copy of your speech and I'll see the other councillors get to read it. I was impressed with what you were saying, Mr Glasson. By cripes! To have our own country, the way you said it, I tell you it made me proud. I'll back you any time.'

Chapter Eight

There'd been no word from the Premier, despite Edgar's requests for an appointment. Despite his insistence that Royce Davies keep up the pressure. But that fool was fast losing his grip, with Abercrombie making the running. Any day now he could roll Davies and take over as Leader of the Opposition.

Bribing Abercrombie was out of the question, and Edgar could find no mud to worry him with, so he began to turn his attention to the federation debate. Letting it be known that he was in favour and pressuring his tame pollies to switch to the Premier's side on this one, to curry favour.

Davies agreed, he went with the wind. Buchanan was a problem. Edgar wished he could shut him up, because he was writing that federation meant independence from the Old Country! The man had no political nous; this was the wrong time to wheel out that argument. He was a step behind the action. Couldn't he see that the Premier had the power to make or break the company at this point? The crucial issue now was the land.

He took up a pen and wrote to Buchanan, asking him to desist from criticism of the Premier for the time being, but then he tore it up. Awkward to ask that of a member of the Opposition. In writing.

But that was the least of his worries. Even with the public float, cash was a problem. Without the collateral of the land, the banks were leaning on him. Steelworks and manufacturers were demanding money, as were his Sydney coach-builders, claiming they'd be broke soon if he didn't resume the progress payments.

It was all one hell of a mess. Edgar had written to his friends, the American railroad tycoons, for advice and financial backing, which he knew they could well afford, but they hadn't even graced him with a reply.

Facing ruin, Edgar looked for a way out. He set up a private company called the New South Wales Steelworks, to hoodwink the public and nosy bankers, and began withdrawing money from Western Railroad, paying it into that facility. Then he raised his fees as managing director and treasurer to astronomical figures, knowing he wouldn't have to face his shareholders for another four months.

Recently he'd been introduced to Mrs Connie Downs, widow of a Charters Towers gold miner who'd owned the fabulously rich El Dorado mines. Although Connie liked to speak with a sob about her beloved late husband, friends had whispered to Edgar that her Charlie had been a womanizer of the first water. But he'd overstepped the mark in carrying off a young Chinese girl. Her father had come to her rescue and left Charlie with a knife in his gut. *Vale* Charlie. But that was beside the point. Connie's female friends were busy matchmaking, with Edgar the target.

For once, Edgar was happy to oblige. He began making arrangements to sell his house, claiming he would need a bigger home shortly, and that gave them heart. Connie was clearly thrilled, and anxious to please Mr Thurlwell, so anxious in fact that she took his advice and purchased shares worth ten thousand pounds in the NSW Steelworks, his non-existent company. Connie was content with the receipt he issued, trusting that Edgar would attend to all the rest of the paperwork for her. He was such a financial whiz, she was grateful for his attention to her little investments.

Then Edgar waited to see what eventuated. If the Premier gave him the nod for that land, which would carry excellent collateral, then everything could be put in order very swiftly. If not . . . well, life went on. It was a smart general who knew when to call retreat.

His sister-in-law watched developments between Connie Downs and Edgar with alarm. Edgar's money was family money. Why should that country frump be allowed to get her hands on it? That she was wealthy in her own right was immaterial. As his wife she'd have more. A lot more. And if Edgar died, then where would they be? Sharing assets with another Mrs Thurlwell, a scheming bitch if ever there was one.

Lalla was surprised at Edgar, the old fool, falling for her. She'd thought he had more sense. Connie was mutton dressed up as lamb. She had chocolate-box curls, a rouged face and a sweet little smile, which Lalla was certain hid a heart of concrete. She had made a beeline for Edgar right from the start, fawning over him, flattering him, wearing evening dresses practically cut to her navel to display those fat breasts under Edgar's nose. And he could hardly keep his hands off her. It was disgusting, at their age.

On this night, Edgar had invited her and William to a dinner party, but William had been called urgently to the hospital. Lalla tried to persuade him to ignore the message – they only called for Dr Thurlwell these days to assist when no one else was available – but he went anyway. The patient, he explained, was an important woman from Sydney, one of the Governor's set.

Rather than leave Edgar and Connie alone, Lalla decided to go on her own. She dressed with quiet good taste in an off-the-shoulder soft black velvet gown, her only jewels the pearl earrings Edgar had given her, and was pleased to find Connie in fluffy pink organza with a full skirt that made her look like the side of a house. She dripped with jewels, rubies and diamonds that clashed marvellously, Lalla thought, with the girlish dress, but Edgar didn't seem to mind.

'Doesn't she look an angel?' he said to Lalla, who felt like screaming while Connie purred.

'Yes indeed,' Lalla agreed, and when Edgar turned to speak to his manservant she said: 'What a lovely dress. Did you bring it with you from the goldfields?'

'No. I have my own dressmaker. She's wildly expensive but as long as she doesn't make for anyone else, I'm happy.' Connie gazed at Lalla with chilly green eyes. 'I know as a widow I should still be wearing black, but it's such a dreary colour, I couldn't bear it any longer.'

'You're quite right,' Lalla said. 'Very few people can wear black well.'

Playing the bachelor to the hilt, Edgar hadn't bothered with maids, and had his man Brody serve the meal, which gave Connie the opportunity to tease her host with little remarks about him needing a woman's hand in his household. Noting a glint of anger in Brody's reaction, Lalla made a point of agreeing with her while he was in the room. She knew she had an ally there. Brody served his master well and wouldn't take kindly to the introduction of a wife to the household.

In all she had a dreadful evening, until Connie choked on a fish bone. Lalla fluttered about, hoping Connie would asphyxiate herself as she coughed and spluttered and blubbered, while Edgar frantically stuffed dry bread down her throat. Since that didn't work, the two men hauled back her chair, pushed her head down between her knees, and thumped her on the back to try to dislodge the bone, which caused the hapless guest to pass wind in a noisy and most unladylike manner. And then vomit all over the pretty pink dress.

Serve her right, Lalla thought, she ate like a pig. She dashed through to the kitchen to call on the cook for assistance, since she had no intention of returning to the smelly dining room.

Apparently the bone had come up with the previous course, so the crisis was over, but Connie was in no state to remain.

'My poor angel,' Edgar commiserated as the cook brought Connie back from the bathroom with her dress sponged clean. 'What can I do for you?'

'Nothing, Edgar dear,' she whimpered. 'I'm so embarrassed.'

'Don't be, Connie. It could happen to anyone. I feel responsible for putting you through such an ordeal.'

'Would you like me to take you home, madam?' Brody offered, and Connie looked at him gratefully.

'If you would? I'm quite exhausted.'

'If you don't mind, Edgar, I think I'll go too,' Lalla said, and he nodded, seeming relieved to be rid of both of them. Lalla didn't want to stay anyway because she might have laughed, or criticized Connie, and she knew Edgar wouldn't tolerate that. He was savage in his criticism of others but reacted badly to any censure of his opinions. And he definitely had an opinion about this 'angel', Lalla thought, as he lovingly escorted the widow to his small carriage.

Arriving home early, Lalla went into the parlour, poured herself a glass of wine and sat waiting for William. She could hardly wait to tell him about this débâcle but more importantly, warn him that Connie, the angel, was becoming a problem. He was Edgar's brother, he would have to speak to him about this woman who was socially unacceptable. Not fit to be the wife of a man in Edgar's position, nor to bear the name of Thurlwell.

She was surprised when she heard the front door open. She hadn't heard William's gig come up the drive . . . and then she saw Phoebe walk quietly across the lobby. Lalla was out of her chair in a second to confront her daughter, who was not wearing a cloak or a hat, or even gloves, and who looked flushed.

Phoebe was definitely startled to see her.

'Where have you been?' Lalla demanded.

'Oh . . . just out for a walk,' Phoebe said lamely.

'At this hour? Who with?'

Phoebe shrugged. 'No one. I just felt like a walk.'

'In the street? You've come in from the street? Are you mad?'

'No, I'm not mad. Now if you'll excuse me, Mother, I'm tired. I'm going to bed.'

Lalla grabbed her by the arm. 'You'll do no such thing! You're lying! Where have you been?'

'I told you. Walking.'

'Rubbish. It's nine o'clock. You've been out with someone and they've dropped you out at the gate. Who is it that can't bring you to your door? And how dare you step out looking like that?'

'I'll go out as I please!' Phoebe sighed in a bored tone, and Lalla slapped her face.

'You won't leave this house looking like a streetwalker!'

Phoebe stared at her for a second and then slapped her back.

Lalla stumbled, shocked, nursing her cheek.

'That's the last time you'll ever hit me,' Phoebe declared. 'Consider yourself lucky I didn't take the cane to you like you used to do to me. Now get out of my way!'

As her daughter went defiantly up the stairs, Lalla screamed after her: 'You haven't heard the last of this!'

Phoebe knew that was true, and she was upset. Especially since she and Ben had had such a lovely night, and he'd kissed and kissed her before she left, so much so she'd been afraid her lips would tell on her. Now her mother had spoiled everything. She'd known that it would happen, that she'd be caught sooner or later, but she wished she hadn't let herself be provoked into returning her mother's slap. This wasn't the best time for battles, and there was sure to be another round in the morning when her father was informed. Phoebe decided to have a plain talk with Ben as soon as possible. She was tired of having to sneak out to see him, and although he was patient with her, he became tense whenever she mentioned her parents. And why wouldn't he? she worried. It must annoy him that he couldn't be seen in public with her, at her request, and that he always had to wait at home for her to find a chance to see him. It was demeaning too.

Maybe she should tell them about Ben and get it over with.

At breakfast, when he was never at his best, her father was confused by this latest row between mother and daughter, not certain who to believe.

'You must never walk alone at night, Phoebe,' he said. 'That's a foolish thing to do. Young girls don't understand the dangers.'

'I don't think she was alone,' Lalla said. 'I don't believe that tale for one minute.'

'Just don't let it happen again,' he told Phoebe, reaching for his newspaper.

'I'll see to that,' Lalla retorted. 'Whenever we're out in future, since she can't be trusted on her own, one of the maids will stay on duty. And if she wants to walk she can walk in her own garden.'

That does it, Phoebe thought. Now what? She could probably talk Biddy into turning a blind eye, but if she were caught, she would lose her job. And anyway, Biddy was no fool. She wouldn't let her wander off without an explanation so she would have to be told where Phoebe was going. Biddy would not approve. She wouldn't have a bar of it! The difference between Biddy and her mother was that the maid really cared about her. Dear Biddy. It wouldn't matter to her who Ben was, only that she should not be in a gentleman's home on her own at night. That was one of the 'occasions of sin' that Biddy had always warned her to beware of.

And where was Barnaby? He hadn't answered her note, the one she'd sent weeks ago. He should be home by this. In desperation Phoebe wrote him another letter, asking him to call. Telling him she needed his advice.

Phoebe knew better than to underestimate her mother. Even though she was practically under guard at night, Lalla made certain that whenever Phoebe went out during the day she was accompanied by approved friends or delivered in the gig by their driver and returned home in the same manner. Rather than write a futile note to Ben, Phoebe waited until the following Saturday and went to the tennis club as usual, telling the driver to collect her at five p.m. It was easy then for her to slip away in her long white tennis dress and boater hat and, taking back streets, to walk the five blocks to the livery stables.

She would never forget the look in his eyes when he saw her coming in the gate. The look of love. Not joy, not excitement, but a look that said that no one and nothing else existed in this world but her. He dropped the saddle he was carrying and walked over to her, this fine, handsome man.

'Phoebe,' he said softly, taking her hand and leading her to his office, closing the door behind them.

'I'm sorry,' she said. 'I haven't been able to see you. My mother . . .'

But he shushed her, taking her in his arms. 'It doesn't matter.'

Eventually he let her talk, listening quietly to her woes. 'They watch me now, Ben. What can I do? I know they won't let me see you, and I miss you so.'

'I've always known that we'd run into trouble, Phoebe,' he said, at length. 'So I'll do whatever you want me to do.'

'Like what? What can you do?'

'Stop seeing you? Stop causing you all these problems and let you get on with your life?'

'No!' she cried. 'You don't mean that! You are my life.'

'Then there's only one other alternative. Marry me.'

Phoebe stared at him. She couldn't pretend that marriage hadn't crossed her mind, but now that it was out in the open she was fearful. 'Could we?' she whispered. 'Could we get married?'

He stood before her and took both of her hands. 'That wasn't a very romantic proposal. I'll do better when you're not feeling so pressured. I love you, Phoebe, and I'm not poor. I can't say that I'll give you everything you want, because there are things that money can't buy. You know that as well as I do. You'll have to weigh up your losses.'

Confused, she muttered, 'You talk as if it's a business.'

'It's a very serious business,' he said. 'If I married you and made you miserable it would break my heart. I'd rather it happened now.'

She kissed him. 'I want to marry you. I love you too. I should be happy. Why are you frightening me?'

'You're already frightened,' he said. 'I saw it in your eyes. It's a huge step to marry a coloured man with a prison record. And it'd be hell on your social life.'

Phoebe pushed him away. 'I wish you wouldn't keep on about that coloured business. You're not a black man, you're no darker than a lot of white men who spend time in the sun, lighter, in fact. And your father was white. Who was he anyway?'

'I don't know. I always thought Oma was my real grandmother, that my mother had married her son. But she told me that wasn't true. She adopted my mother when she was a little girl.'

'Your mother,' Phoebe said vaguely. 'I liked her. I used to stutter . . .'

'We can talk about that another time,' Ben said gently. 'I want you for my wife, Phoebe, but you won't have the niceties girls like you expect. We couldn't announce our engagement, it would cause you too much trouble. The only thing we can do is just marry without a fuss. Could you handle that?'

'Yes!'

'You'd have to be very brave.'

'I don't want to hear any more of this,' she said angrily. 'You have proposed to me, Ben Beckman, and I've accepted. So now it's up to you.'

'Good,' he replied firmly. 'In three months' time, once you get used to the idea, I'll ask you again at my house, with roses and champagne and all the trimmings. If it's not to be, then we'll celebrate a friendship that can never be spoiled and call it a day.'

Phoebe was almost in tears. She realized that to insist the three months' delay wouldn't be necessary, was sheer bravado.

'How did you get so wise?' she asked him.

'From the love of three good women,' he smiled.

She waited for Barnaby on a park bench overlooking the river. This was the softer side of Brisbane, in direct contrast to the high red cliffs of Kangaroo Point. Parliament House, with its quiet dignity and green surrounds bordering the botanical gardens, seemed a strange place to Phoebe. On this lazy blue day it was hard to believe that it was the home of all the bitter debates and feuds that were constantly being discussed in her own house.

Biddy, her constant companion these days, had gone for a walk through the gardens which she loved, unconcerned that Phoebe had arranged to meet Mr Glasson during his lunch break. She liked Barnaby and had it in her head that romance could be blooming here, and Phoebe did nothing to disillusion her. She watched fish plopping in the river, wondering why they felt it necessary to jump out of the water like that. Maybe they were catching insects, or maybe they were just playing. Having a good time. She felt resentful that her life had become so complicated and wished a good fairy would come along and sort it all out for her.

Barnaby came hurrying down the grassy slope. He pecked her on the cheek. 'Sorry I've kept you waiting, I got held up. How are you? You're looking wonderful.'

'I don't feel it. But Barnaby, I'm so glad to see you. I missed you.'

'That's a good start,' he smiled. 'Do you want to walk?'

'No thanks. I'd rather sit here. And I wanted to warn you. Edgar had a letter from Ben Buchanan. He said you've been out west preaching revolution and he intends to lodge a complaint with the Premier. What on earth have you been up to?'

'Just going about my business, talking about federation, as I was instructed to do. And Buchanan did complain, not to the Premier but to my boss, the Attorney-General, the rat. I managed to talk my way out of it, so I've still got a job, but I had to promise not to ride my own hobbyhorse on his time.'

'What hobbyhorse?'

'To put myself forward as a candidate for the new Senate when it comes into being.'

Phoebe started to laugh. 'Really you can be quite mad at times. Talk about tilting at windmills. There won't be a Senate. Father says the federation stuff is a dead issue. And I didn't know you were interested in politics.'

'I've become interested. It's infectious. I often slip in to watch the politicians in action, and I meet a lot of them at the House. Some of them are such dills, it's not hard to think you could do just as good a job yourself.'

'You're a lawyer and a good one,' Phoebe said staunchly. 'You probably could. But has your political career come to a dead stop now?'

'No. The Senate can wait. I intend to ask the Premier's permission to stand for a state seat as a government candidate.'

'Well! Heavens! What seat will they give you?'

'They won't give me a seat. I'll have to work for it. I've decided to tackle Padlow.'

'Padlow?' She thought for a minute. 'Hang on. That's Buchanan's seat. You're going to oppose Ben Buchanan?'

'Yes.'

'Oh no. That's just marvellous! My parents will love that,' she said sarcastically. 'You'll be another one on the family ban list.'

'Why? Who's the other?'

She was quiet for a minute, staring unhappily at the fast-moving river. 'Barnaby, I need your advice.' She took a deep breath. 'I'm in love.'

His mood changed too. 'That's not the best news I've ever heard, but thank you for telling me. Anyone I know?'

She evaded that question, pretending she hadn't heard. 'It's not exactly the best news for me either. My parents won't approve. They hate him, and when I tell them we want to marry there'll be the most God-awful row.'

'Who is it?' he persisted.

'I can't tell you right now. I've been seeing him for months now and we're very much in love.'

'And he's been banned from your house?'

'No. He's never been to the house. They don't know anything about this.'

Barnaby was upset. 'Phoebe. This isn't like you to be so . . . well, underhand. Forgive me, I don't mean that to sound so bad. I know you don't get on very well with your parents, but to be seeing someone without their knowledge . . . Don't you think they'll have a right to be cross? And what sort of a man would propose marriage to you without even presenting himself to your father?'

'He's a very lovely man,' she argued.

'It doesn't sound like it. Honestly, Phoebe. What have you got yourself into?'

'Don't be angry, Barnaby. Tell me what I can do. We've got to the stage when this man says we should either separate for good or marry.'

'I'd take the first option,' he said firmly.

'I can't. I just can't.'

'Why? You're not . . .?'

'No, I'm not pregnant. I didn't say we were lovers, I said we were in love.'

He sighed. 'Your family will find out sooner or later. Who else knows about this?'

'No one.'

'Good God! Not even your girlfriends, Bunny and Leisha?'

'No.'

'And can this dark horse afford to support you?'

Phoebe grinned. 'Was that a pun? Yes, he's quite well off.'

Barnaby clasped his hands in front of him. 'You asked my advice, Phoebe dear, and I've given it to you. What more can I say?'

'You might tell me what would happen if we eloped.'

'I'd tell you not to do that, for God's sake. At least give your family the chance to accept him. If you love him, he can't be that bad. Face them.'

'It's not possible.'

'For God's sake, it has to be possible. Who is this fellow? Do you want me to have a talk with him?'

'I don't know. Maybe. But you might talk him out of it and then I'd hate you.'

'So you're going to hide with him all your life? Someone has to meet him! The more you tell me about this clandestine love, the more I'm disliking him. If you want me to understand you'll have to introduce me to him, otherwise, in your best interests, I'll repeat, break it off now.'

She wavered. It hadn't occurred to her that Barnaby might want to meet him. But it could be for the best. It would be a relief to have someone, a friend like Barnaby, talk to him. To know about them.

'It's Ben Beckman,' she said with a defiant lift of her head.

'Who?' he cried, astonished. 'Diamond's son?'

'Yes, and don't tell me about the jail business. I know all about it. I've known Ben since I was a kid, Barnaby, they're next door, remember? All I want to do is marry the boy next door,' she added, parodying a popular song.

He shook his head. 'Oh Lord! There'll be hell to pay!'

'That's what I was trying to tell you. In fact, Ben reminds me of you. He told me that I have to go away and think about such a serious step—'

'Only this time you really are serious,' Barnaby said ruefully.

'Yes. Here comes Biddy. I have to go. Promise me you'll see Ben, talk to him, then you'll know why I love him so much.'

'I'll make an appointment,' Barnaby replied, sounding officious he knew, but how else was he supposed to react? Ben Beckman! Good God! The Thurlwells would go after him with shotguns. Or have him arrested again. Did Ben have any idea what he was up against?

The scandal didn't come with a bang. It sort of seeped in like that worrisome summer mould. Starting with a dusting of sickly green powder on boots and suits left in dark closets, mould spread slyly, secretly, a malicious fungus, feeling its way, dreading the light. But open the door to a room that has been closed, blinds drawn for a month or so in the season of heat and humidity, and the ogre has run rampant. Blackened walls tell the sorry tale and the evil thing is exposed.

And so the scandal began with a grumbling butcher, though no one took much notice because he wasn't the cheeriest of souls at the best of times. The wife of the owner of the general store just down the road commiserated with him eventually, because they were having the same problems with unpaid bills.

'Go up to his house and bang on his damned door and demand your money,' she railed at her husband, waving a sheaf of accounts at him.

'You can't do that to gentry. I could lose his business altogether. He's a good customer.'

'Good customer be buggered! This isn't England. Those folk are no better than us. If they don't pay they don't get no more supplies.'

He didn't go banging on the door though, he thought he'd wait a bit longer. But it still rankled with Iris, his wife, who told everyone brazenly that they could do without Mr Thurlwell's business. She even threatened to go round there herself and give him a piece of her mind.

'Won't do you any good,' a woman said. 'My sister's his cook and she's been laid off for a month. Mr Thurlwell's gone to Sydney on business. You'll have to wait till he gets back.'

So the tradespeople let it rest. Not so Connie Downs. She planned to give Edgar a welcome-home party when he returned from Sydney, to make up for that last horrible night and to show him that she could entertain just as well as that snooty sister-in-law of his. And not knowing which ship he'd be returning on, she waited a few weeks and then began to instruct her driver to pass by his house every time she was out, even if it did mean several detours.

At last her vigil paid off. The drapes were drawn back and the windows were open. Connie bounded down from the gig, opened the gate and strode up to the front door to give the brass knocker a short sharp rap.

She was expecting the manservant, Brody, to open the door but instead she was greeted by a young girl.

'I'm Mrs Downs,' she said. 'I should like to see your master.'

The girl grinned. 'You mean my father?'

Connie blushed, believing Edgar must have visitors. 'I beg your pardon, my dear. I wished to see Mr Thurlwell, but if he's busy . . .'

'That's all right,' she replied. 'But you've got the wrong house. Mr Thurlwell doesn't live here any more. He's moved. We bought the house and we just moved in this morning.'

'Oh dear. What a mistake I've made! Could you tell me Mr Thurlwell's new address?'

'I'll ask my father,' she said, and ran to enquire.

'He's moved to the suburb of Hamilton,' she informed Connie, 'but we don't know exactly where. When you see him would you tell him we're holding mail for him.'

'Yes, of course.' Connie went home, not displeased. Hadn't Edgar talked about buying a new house, a bigger house? A hint in itself that a change in lifestyle might include a wife. And Hamilton! Trust Edgar! There were some beautiful properties up there. What a rascal, she smiled to herself. Here she was preparing to surprise him and he's stolen a march on her. What had he called her? 'My angel', and slipped her a kiss while Lalla wasn't looking. Well, she wouldn't spoil his surprise. She'd wait for his summons. But the silly man! He should have called on her to help him shift his belongings. Packing and unpacking was such a business.

In several corners of the banking fraternity three men were feeling very much in the dark. The manager of the new South Pacific Banking Company, who had approved a loan on Dr Thurlwell's mansion at

Kangaroo Point arranged by his brother, was perturbed that the first monthly repayment on that mortgage had not been made. He wondered if a reminder might offend.

At the Bank of New South Wales an accountant was perturbed that the Western Railroad Company, even with the support of public investment, was sinking deeper into the red, and not a sleeper had been laid. The last time he'd mentioned this to the manager he'd received a curt rebuff and been told the company was secure, it had plenty of collateral. But now he was unable to locate the actual premises of the New South Wales Steelworks, a firm that had been receiving a steady stream of funds from the Railroad Company. He wondered if he should risk further reproof by making more enquiries.

Dudley Luxton, manager of the Bank of Queensland, sat behind closed doors and pondered the Thurlwell joint account. True, after their last talk, Edgar had strolled in to deposit two thousand pounds, by no means enough but a gesture of goodwill that had calmed Luxton's fears. Temporarily. Then the manager had taken two weeks' holiday with his family at the seaside, returning refreshed only to find the account in even worse shape, well over the overdraft limit. Edgar had been making substantial withdrawals and his brother William, whom Dudley rarely saw, had carried on scattering cheques about the town like confetti.

That made Dudley very angry. They might have put it over his assistant manager but not him. Trouble was, though, Edgar was still in Sydney. But then a glimmer of light brightened the manager's day. What better time to lower the boom than when Edgar was out of town? He was a formidable character, given to shouting and desk-banging at the slightest note of criticism, and it took all of a man's stamina to stand up to him. An unnerving experience.

Why, he wondered, were wealthy people such poor payers? Did they regard their creditors as beneath contempt? Or were they of the view, which Dudley thoroughly abhorred, that it was smarter to use other people's money? He decided it was time to bring the Thurlwells to heel.

Lalla was the first to meet the ogre but she didn't recognize it.

'What is this?' she asked William as she opened her mail. 'The hat shop has returned your payform. Obviously you haven't signed it properly or something. For heaven's sake be more careful, William. You're always making mistakes like this.'

He sighed. 'They're called cheques, Lalla. Cheques. Let me see it.'

He studied the cheque and handed it back. 'It's quite in order. Send it back to the shop.'

'Why is there a bank stamp on the back?'

'Because it has been to the bank and someone there has made a mistake. It's not my fault.'

In the next week more and more cheques found their way back to Somerset House, and so William dashed off a letter to the manager of the Bank of Queensland, complaining about the incompetence of his staff. To which Dudley Luxton replied that he was sorry this difficulty had arisen, inviting the Doctor to come to his office to discuss the matter.

'More like it!' William grunted. 'I'll call on him when I'm good and ready.'

But it was Connie who inadvertently opened the floodgates. Connie didn't believe in accountants, she could add and subtract without their help, and she had no truck with bank managers, believing that if they were so wise with money they'd be wealthy themselves. No, she kept her money in three different banks in case, as has happened in Victoria only recently, one of them went bust. But she did have a sharebroker and she enjoyed her discussions with him.

Scanning her portfolio of shares, she told him to include the ten thousand shares in New South Wales Steelworks which she had recently purchased.

'Never heard of them,' he said.

'Ah. That's because I have inside information,' she replied.

'Do you have the share certificates,' he asked, 'so that I can record them?'

'No, not yet.'

That night, he took the unprecedented step of calling at her home. 'Mrs Downs, I have some unsettling news. I have made extensive enquiries and there is no such company as NSW Steelworks. Nor can we locate Mr Thurlwell.'

'He's moved to Hamilton,' she replied, but her stomach gave a lurch. She still hadn't heard from Edgar.

'Where in Hamilton?'

'I don't know,' she admitted. As he worried at the subject, her upset stomach sent bile to her throat, which she held down by anger which soon turned to rage.

'It appears,' the broker continued, 'that Mr Thurlwell has not returned from Sydney. I sent a telegram to the firm that is building railroad coaches for his company, and received a reply. If Mr Thurlwell has been to Sydney, they haven't seen him and they wish to contact him urgently.'

When he left, Connie poured herself a double whisky, and then another, and paced the house most of the night. She knew what she had to do next. Call on Dr Thurlwell and his stuck-up wife and demand to know Edgar's whereabouts.

Barnaby found Ben Beckman at the stables. They seemed only to have met previously on abnormal occasions, prison problems and funerals, so

Ben was delighted that he'd made the time for a social call, for, at first, that was what it seemed. He took Barnaby on a tour of the stables, then the saddlery, where four men were hard at work.

'You're doing well,' Barnaby commented.

'I'll do better,' Ben told him. 'I've ordered a motorcar.'

'A motorcar? What will you do with that?'

'Learn how it works. It might be ages before I can have one shipped here but I've got a chap lined up to come with it.'

'You're not going to try to build them?'

'No. That's too hard. But people will be buying them so I'm thinking of a depot with fuel for them and a place where they can be fixed when they break down.'

Barnaby laughed. 'I hear they break down a lot.'

'Good. I'll have a mechanic to sort them out. And I could even hire mine out instead of horse cabs. Plenty of possibilities, don't you reckon?'

'Eventually,' Barnaby said. 'But I wouldn't rush things. People here are very conservative.'

They walked back through the stables to the paddock, where one of the grooms was exercising a horse, and sat on the fence to watch, talking like old friends now that Ben's miseries were behind them. Sitting on a fence like this in the cool of the evening, just smoking and yarning, reminded Barnaby of his own home. His father liked nothing better than to prop on the rail fence beside the dairy for a quiet smoke at the end of the day. It was what he regarded as 'men's time' before they washed up and went into the house for dinner. Not that his father talked much, mainly about the farm, and sometimes words of advice for his son. Even though he was not that much older than Ben, Barnaby felt he had assumed the paternal role here. Or rather he'd had it thrust upon him by Phoebe. No! Further back than this, he realized with a start. Diamond had pushed Ben into his care when he was only a kid, up on that stealing charge.

He still felt guilty about pocketing that extra cash she'd given him, and he'd never taken a bribe since, but he consoled himself that he'd earned his keep as her son's minder. Or had he? Was there worse to come?

A young woman waved to them from the house next door and Ben waved back.

'Who's that?' Barnaby asked.

'Kathleen O'Neill. She's a grand girl. Her father used to own this business. Have you got a girl?'

Barnaby was startled. This was supposed to be his question to lead on to the main subject. 'Er . . . no,' he said.

'I'll have to introduce you then,' Ben replied. 'You'd like her. And she's a great cook. Do you want to come over and meet her?'

'Not just now. There's something else I wanted to talk to you about.'

Ben ground out his cigarette with his boot. 'Phoebe?' he asked. 'Did she tell you about us? She said you were her friend.'

'Yes, she did.'

'And?'

'Ben, do you really think they'd let you marry her?'

'No.'

'Then what are you thinking of?'

Ben slipped down to lean against the fence, facing Barnaby: 'It's hard for me to think of anything else. I want to marry her because I love her, and I think she really loves me. And I'd look after her, Barnaby.'

'Would that be enough?'

'I don't know. What did you say to Phoebe?'

'I told her it couldn't work.'

Ben shrugged. 'At least you're honest.'

'Has it ever occurred to you that Phoebe is a girl who has to have her own way and this might just be part of it. She loves to shock people. To make her own rules. She's always been like that.'

'A rebel? Yes, I've noticed.'

'Ben, you've been rebelling since you were a kid, with good reason I admit, but have you considered this might be the attraction? If you'll forgive me for saying, a flame that could die out fast, given the setbacks.'

'Are you in love with Phoebe?'

'Yes and no. I was. I was mad about her, but I've accepted that I'm not in the running.'

'I thought so,' Ben said without rancour. 'Then you, of all people, must know how I feel about her. I won't give her up. I could never do that. Unless she says it's over. Then, I hope I can take it on the chin like you have.'

'Oh Christ!' Barnaby said. 'Why don't we go to a pub and have a drink?'

'I don't drink in bars,' Ben told him. 'I never look for trouble.'

Barnaby had forgotten that Ben, with his olive skin and the darkness around his eyes, could still be barred from pubs as an 'Abo' if anyone cared to take offence, but that seemed secondary now. 'For someone who never looks for trouble you haven't done a bad job. And now, when you've got it made, when everything is going smoothly, you're lining yourself up for real trouble.'

'I don't have any choice,' Ben said. 'But this time, if Phoebe decides to marry me, I won't lose.' His voice carried the threat reminiscent of his belligerent prison days. 'They won't beat me this time,' he said harshly.

Barnaby shuddered. This wasn't the genial young businessman now, this was Diamond's son. He'd seen that same look in his mother's eyes when she'd demanded the release of her kid, no matter what it took. A look born of bitterness and a startling clarity. She'd understood what was required. He wondered if Ben did.

Nevertheless, Barnaby decided, he would like a drink and a bite to eat rather than retreating to his rooms with a bun and a pork pie. He liked Ben. He seemed more of a friend than the self-seeking civil servants who were his present associates. More real.

If he'd only give up on this suicidal plan to win Phoebe.

'A friend of mine owns the Regency pub down the road,' he said. 'We can go there. You won't have any bother. If you start in this motorcar business, you bring the contracts to me. I'll check them out for you. All new fields have a lot of fly-by-nights.'

They sat in an alcove off the saloon bar of the hotel, like old pals. Their ages seemed to have melded. They ate substantial platefuls of pork sausage and mash and washed them down with glasses of claret.

'I don't drink much,' Ben said.

'Neither do I,' Barnaby told him solemnly. He called the waitress: 'Another bottle here.'

They talked and talked, Barnaby about his tour and his political ambitions, Ben about his saddlery and his horses. About everything except the subject of Phoebe. They dug into a platter of bread and cheese and ordered more claret.

Barnaby told him about the last meeting he'd held in Charleville, which had nearly cost him his job thanks to Buchanan.

'That reminds me,' he mumbled, in his cups now. 'I met a woman who knew your mother. Or at least I think she did.'

'Who was that?'

Barnaby tried to think. His brain was fuzzy. 'Forget her name. It will come back to me. She didn't like Ben Buchanan either. I told you about him ruining my meeting. Does his name ring a bell?'

'Yes, they had horses at my stables. Mrs Buchanan's a charming woman. Had me organize freight of fodder out to their station. Thank God that drought is over, they must be relieved. One of those days I ought to go back and have a look at that country now that things are better.'

'What you ought to do,' Barnaby said, 'is introduce me to your friend Kathleen O'Neill. Why not now?'

'No. It's too late. She'd think we were drunk and bite our heads off. My grandmother died at her house, you know. Quietly and peacefully under the trees in her garden.'

'God rest her soul,' Barnaby intoned. 'But she wasn't really your grandmother.'

'No.'

'Your mother, Diamond. She found gold. Was it on the Palmer goldfields?' Temporarily, Barnaby's head had cleared. He ate another slice of cheese.

'Yes. She found her tribe there. Irukandji. They showed her the gold. It was no use to them. Oma said she went back years later to see them. Her family. But they were gone. Dead or scattered by the whites.'

'Did she ever work out west?' Ben hadn't reacted to the Buchanan name except to refer to Mrs Buchanan, but that wasn't the point.

'Yes, I think so. Oma said she was a lady's maid. Went out to a big station.'

'Where?'

'I don't know. The place where they had the big gold strikes.'

'Charters Towers?'

'Yes.'

'Have you ever heard of a cattle station called Caravale?'

'No. Why?'

Barnaby was tired now. The drink or the hour, he wasn't sure. 'Because a woman in Charleville told me that's where she worked.'

'Could be,' Ben said. He fished some notes from his pocket. 'Let me pay. I've had a good night but I have to go home while I can still stand. I'll get a hansom cab. Can I drop you off? Where do you live?'

'I've got rooms in Albert Street. They're not much but they do me.'

Ben was astonished. He thought lawyers, being professional people, would live in grand houses. Especially lawyers like Barnaby Glasson who worked for the all-important Attorney-General. By the time they reached Albert Street, Barnaby was staggering so Ben carted him up the stairs, took his key, lit the lamp and dumped his friend on his bed. Out cold!

There was no kitchen, no bathroom, no balcony to get the air, only two rooms, the bedroom and a sitting room which was dominated by a large desk and a table covered with books and papers. The windows stared at a blank brick wall next door. The carpet was threadbare. The walls needed painting.

'Is this how they live?' he asked the lonely, depressing room. 'It doesn't seem right.'

When Barnaby Glasson came home from the office the following evening he found Ben sitting on the front steps. 'I've got an idea, Barnaby,' he said.

'If you want me to buy a motorcar, forget it,' Barnaby laughed.

'No. I wanted to remind you that I live alone up on the Point. And there are two empty rooms in the house. If you are interested you could have Oma's room. That's the one across from the parlour. I'll have it done up for you.' He hesitated, suddenly shy. 'I mean, you don't have to accept, it's just an idea.'

Barnaby was nonplussed. 'It's good of you to offer, but I don't know. I've never thought about shifting. I've been living here since I first came to town.'

'You'd have the run of the house. A kitchen at least, and a garden. Room to move about. And I wouldn't bother you. You could come and go as you please.'

Barnaby thought about it. Ben did have a lovely position up there, fresh and airy, a change from his own rooms, which were unbearably hot in summer and never saw a glint of sun in winter. But they were cheap. 'What rent would you be asking?'

'Rent? I never thought about rent. You don't have to pay. I told you the room isn't being used. You can buy your own food though. Please yourself.'

'I'd feel better paying rent.'

'Don't be so stuffy. I'm not doing you any favours. The room is there if you want it.'

Barnaby was tempted. He could get the ferry to work from there and that would be very pleasant. 'What would Phoebe say?' he asked.

'It won't bother Phoebe. And if we do marry, could you see us living next door to my in-laws?'

Barnaby laughed. 'Good God, no!'

'Give it a try then. If it doesn't suit you, I wouldn't mind if you moved back into town. If I'm lucky in love I'll be moving out myself, eventually, but I won't sell the house.'

'Could I move in at the weekend?'

'Any time you like,' Ben said.

There wasn't much to pack, only his clothes and books and a few odds and ends. As he loaded them into the hired cab, Barnaby realized he hadn't accumulated much in years of work, except some better suits that he needed to keep up appearances at Parliament House. And a large collection of shirts. Every time he forgot to take the bundles of dirty linen to the Chinese laundry he had to dash out and buy a new one.

The girl, Kathleen O'Neill, was there to meet him when he arrived at the house on the Saturday afternoon. 'You must be Mr Glasson. Come on in. Ben's still at work. Saturday's a busy day for them.' She ushered him into the front bedroom. 'Doesn't it look nice? When he told Alice he had a friend moving into the house she said we ought to get it ready for you.'

'Who is Alice?' he asked.

'Alice Callaghan. The wife of Ben's manager. Ben said we could do what we liked. So we came out here to tidy up. The room had hardly been touched since his grandmother died. Then he got a better idea. Told us to get rid of everything and put in new furniture for you.'

'That's very kind of you,' Barnaby stammered.

'Not at all,' she grinned. 'We had the fun of Cork, Alice and me, buying all new furniture. Even the desk. Ben said you would need a desk. Do you like it?'

'It's wonderful!' Barnaby looked about the stylish room, obviously the largest in the house, that smelled so fresh and new, even down to the bed linen and the curtains. The women had put a bowl of flowers on the mahogany dressing table.

Kathleen insisted on helping him unpack, chatting away as if she'd known him forever. 'I believe you're a lawyer,' she said. 'Where's your office?'

'At Parliament House. For the time being, anyway.'

'Oh my!' Kathleen was startled. 'You must be very important.'

'Not really. I just have to study legal matters and make reports on them.'

'Well, you must be good at it. Can I make you a cup of tea?'

'Thank you. I'll just finish up here.' He picked up a box of books and put them on the desk. Why was he surprised that Ben had other friends? He must meet a lot of people in his line of work. With a sense of discomfort Barnaby realized that though he himself had a few friends, mostly at the tennis club, there were none he could call on to help like this.

'Do you know his girlfriend?' Kathleen asked him.

'Who would that be?'

'Oh, go on with you. If you're to be staying in his house I'll bet you do. Miss Thurlwell.'

'How do you know about her?'

'She comes to the stables and he goes all starry-eyed when she's about. He thinks no one notices, but everyone does. She's so gorgeous a person couldn't be missin' that one.'

Barnaby didn't comment.

'Don't worry. We won't say anything. I believe she lives next door in that grand house.'

Too soon, she had to go, this perky Irish girl. Barnaby offered to run down the road to get her a cab. 'Lord no,' she cried. 'I can't afford a cab.'

'Kathleen, I'll pay for it. It's the least I can do.'

'Don't be wasting your money now! I'll take the ferry.'

'Then let me accompany you to the landing.'

He took her arm as they walked down the steep path, wondering if Ben had paid these ladies for their work. If not, he would like to show his gratitude by buying Kathleen, and Mrs Callaghan too, of course, a really nice present. It was a windfall not to have to pay rent, a lift to his savings. His father had told him when he started receiving wages that he should 'tithe' himself. 'No matter how hard, lad, put away ten per cent of your wages every month. Put it in the bank and leave it there. One day you'll be looking for a wife and you'll need your nesting egg.'

It had been a struggle but Barnaby had followed his father's advice with stolid determination, not only to save money but because, every time he saw his dad, he was asked how much he had in the bank. The response, a nod of satisfaction, made it worth the trouble.

He handed Kathleen on to the ferry and then, on impulse, jumped aboard too, and paid the ferryman. Then when they reached the town side of the river, he decided he might as well walk her home from there, since the afternoon shadows were drawing in.

On the return journey across the river Barnaby realized he'd walked right past Phoebe's house without giving her a thought.

Lalla Thurlwell was irritated when Biddy gave her the name of her visitor. 'Good God! What have I done to deserve this? I hope she doesn't count herself as one of my friends. Where did you put her?'

'In the front parlour, madam.'

'Very well. Let her wait.'

Connie wasn't surprised that she was kept waiting. It would be typical of Lalla. She'd hardly be in the kitchen baking or having to tidy herself up from scrubbing floors. No, the delay was deliberate, to put her in her place.

As a matter of fact Connie, too, had delayed. She'd given her stockbroker two more days to make further enquiries so that she was sure she was on solid ground. There was no doubt now that Edgar was a cheat. She wondered why she was always attracted to cheats, or whether that was just the nature of men. She'd come from a poor family in Ipswich. Her dad had been a coal miner and her mum was always poorly, so Connie had worked at home for a pittance doing piecework for a shirt factory. Just as night followed day it had been inevitable that Connie too would marry a coal miner.

When she and Tommy became engaged, Connie's dad had been pleased as punch, throwing a party for them in the little worker's cottage, so small it would fit in the front garden of the house Connie now owned. But her mum wasn't so pleased. 'He's a drinker, Connie,' she'd warned. 'I don't trust him.'

And she'd been right. Tommy spent all his money on booze and owed everyone money. When Connie refused to lend him any more he became angry and marched out. Then she found that the jam jar where she kept her shillings was gone. They never saw Tommy again.

Charlie Downs was different, a teetotaller and a smart dresser. His father owned the flourishing Commercial Hotel. 'Seeing all those drunks is enough to put a man off the booze for life,' he told Connie, and that was enough to endear him to her.

Charlie boasted he'd make a fortune one of these days, and as soon as they were married he announced that they were off to the goldfields.

His father laughed. 'You'll be back. Findin' gold ain't as easy as it sounds.' But he gave them a stake and everyone turned out to bid them farewell as Connie and Charlie set off in a wagon piled with camping equipment and the picks, shovels and sluices needed to search for gold.

They headed north-west for the Cape diggings, full of hope, but the goldfields turned out to be hell. Pure hell, Connie recalled, like living in an open madhouse. She had never met so many terrible people. They worked hard all day coping with the heat and dust and flies, and at night they listened to the drunken fights, screaming women, gunshots, and the occasional riots. Often Charlie would leave her alone in the tent at night, going off to find out where they might have better luck, since they'd worked claim after claim without sighting colour of any sort.

As Connie became acclimatized to this rough life, she bought herself a rifle and defended her patch with a fury that matched any ugly intruder. Then came the big day when Charlie struck a gold-bearing reef. They worked that out for months and bought a fine house in Charters Towers.

Everyone said Charlie had the Midas touch, and he surely did. Every time he staked a new claim you could bet he was on to something, and the money was rolling in. But it was then that Connie began to find out what else her husband had been up to. Women told her that even when they were working their first claim, Charlie had been out chasing everything in skirts. Including harlots. While she'd been stuck in that tent fending off rats, animal and human.

Connie began to pay attention, and she soon discovered that he was cheating on her in the township too, so she confronted him but he wasn't concerned.

'A man has more needs than a woman, Connie,' he said. 'I give you your share, don't I?'

After that he began bringing women home. Brazen hussies who cavorted with him in the other bedroom, treating her with contempt.

She considered leaving Charlie, but why should she? Her husband was one of the richest men in town, a town where riches were aplenty. She had servants now, a full larder and a cellar full of the best wines money could buy. Being a publican's son, Charlie had no objection to others drinking; in fact he was a generous host. Connie developed a taste for French champagne, which she drank with her women friends, at breakfast. And at lunch. And at dinner. And she had no trouble surrounding herself with merry company.

Sometimes women asked her why she put up with Charlie and his philandering, but Connie just smiled. It wasn't as if she was enduring scandal. The west was wild, the town was wilder still, Charlie's behaviour bothered no one compared with the open whoring and lawlessness all about her. Charters Towers and its surrounding goldfields were beyond scandal.

It was only a few weeks after Charlie's fiftieth birthday, when he was still claiming to be the lustiest man in town, that he came across the pretty little Chinese girl. Connie was out that night, playing cards with her friends. Somehow he had enticed the girl into the house. He was good at that, golden-tongued with the ladies, people said. And he'd raped her in that other bedroom.

When Connie came home she found him dead, his torso knifed from throat to groin. A ripped satin cheongsam lay dismally on the floor. And the bed was disgusting, awash with blood, Charlie's blood.

She wrapped him in a blanket, carried his skinny body down the back steps and out into the darkness, stepping carefully and purposefully through the deserted unlit back lanes to dump him well away from her home. Then she returned to change her clothes, put her hat on and step out again. This time by the front door.

Connie called on a woman she knew, an elderly matriarch of the Chinese community, well respected and a damn good mah-jong player. Connie had never beaten her yet, but the fun was to keep trying even though she lost a lot of money. Madame Ling Lee always played for money.

Madame Ling permitted her a private audience in a smoky, incense-filled room, and the women had a quiet conversation.

Within the hour three silent black-clad Chinamen slipped into Connie's house and removed every skerrick of blood from the room, including the horribly stained linen and mattress and the pathetic little cheongsam. A few minutes later, without a word, a slippered coolie bore a new mattress into that room, settled it on the bed frame, bowed to Connie and retreated. Calmly Connie remade the bed with fresh linen and her best lace bedspread. Enough was enough. To find Charlie in bed with his guts spilled would be a scandal, even in Charters Towers. Now it was over. And when the body was found she'd be the grieving widow. A rich grieving widow.

All of these things crossed her mind while she waited for Lalla, anger churning away. Neither Tommy nor Charlie had been as bad as Edgar Thurlwell seemed to be, unless someone had an explanation to excuse him. Tommy had just been bad in the drink, and Charlie, well, he'd been a cheat too, but an ordinary man, never pretending to be high-falutin' society like this one, leading a woman on. And by Jesus, if he had, they'd all better look out, all of the bloody Thurlwell clan!

'Why, Connie!' Lalla said as she came forward in a softly draped cream crêpe de Chine dress. 'How nice of you to call.'

'I was just passing,' she smiled, knowing this was a dead-end street, 'and I thought I'd pop in.'

'Just passing?' Lalla murmured with raised eyebrows. 'I see.' She didn't offer her visitor tea or coffee and Connie noted the deliberate snub, but not to worry, just another nail in the coffin.

'I was wondering how I could get in touch with Edgar,' she said.

'My dear, he's in Sydney. Didn't you know?'

'Where is he staying in Sydney?'

'I really have no idea. One of the best hotels, I presume.'

'And when is he due back?'

'Connie, I'm not his keeper. Edgar has business to attend to in Sydney. When he has completed that business he will return. I'm sorry if he hasn't been in touch with you, but that's Edgar. A bachelor, you know, he's much sought after in company.'

'I'm sure he is. I was hoping to give him a little welcome-home party when he returns. But how can I leave him an invitation if I don't know where he lives.'

Lalla peered at her. 'I realize you were rather upset when you last dined at Edgar's house, but surely you can't have forgotten the address.'

'Of course not, but Edgar has moved. He doesn't live there any more.'

Lalla seemed pleased. She sat at the edge of a winged chair near Connie. 'My dear, may I speak in your best interests? Sometimes men say things like this to ladies, to well . . . lessen the blow. I mean, you're a very nice person, but Edgar is a bachelor, and you're not the first lady to set her cap at him—'

'The house is sold,' Connie said, interrupting the patronizing sermon.

'There you are,' Lalla continued. 'I do wish men would come out with what they have to say rather than resort to subterfuge. I hate to have to tell you this but his house has not been sold.'

'Yes it has. Another family is living there. They say he has moved to Hamilton.'

'I think you must be confused.'

'No I'm not. And if he has moved to Hamilton he must be back in Brisbane. I'd appreciate his address.'

Lalla fluttered a handkerchief. 'Are you sure you're feeling well? I really don't have time for this.'

'No, you wouldn't. And if you can't, or won't, give me Edgar's address, then kindly let me have the address of the NSW Steelworks.'

'I don't know anything about such a firm, but one would expect it to be in New South Wales.'

'Then could you ask your husband, since I'm told it is a substantial company and a supplier to Western Railroads.'

'My husband is not at home.' Lalla stood. 'Now, if you will excuse me, I'll have a servant show you out.'

'Well you might,' Connie said, picking up her handbag. 'In my opinion your husband's brother has done a bunk and you people, for your own purposes, are covering for him. It's no use turning your back on me, Mrs Thurlwell,' she called, as Lalla walked over to ring the bell for Biddy. 'Inform your husband I require the address of those steelworks. And of your brother-in-law, of course.'

'Show her out,' Lalla said as she swept past Biddy. 'Damn cheek of her! The woman is demented.'

Edgar relied on his man Brody in many ways. Apart from being an excellent servant, he was a fellow who heard things. Who made it his business to hear things. He was a great talker, but a better listener, and in his time off he frequented several taverns where persons of his class gathered, including servants who worked for the high and mighty of the town.

He knew the housekeeper who worked for Creighton, the Attorney-General, and over a few drinks was able to discover from her that the Creighton family were hoping to be able to boast another Minister in their ranks. Hal Creighton, the Member for Warwick, looked like being elevated to the role of Minister for Lands.

'They're all excited,' she said, 'just waiting for the nod. A real feather in their caps that'll be, and there'll be a big party to celebrate, you can bet on that.'

'Hal Creighton,' Edgar mused, on hearing that information from Brody. 'He's as weak as piss. Keep after her, Brody. I need to know the minute it's announced so that I'll be on his doorstep first up.'

A couple of weeks later Brody returned with depressing news. 'Seems the Premier has decided to hang on to that portfolio himself, for the time being anyway. No party in sight for the Creightons.'

'Can't you find out anything about the land deal?'

'Not from house servants, they wouldn't know what I was talking about. But I did meet a little clerk from the Lands Department, he hangs about the River Inn too. Sweet on one of the barmaids that works there.'

'He might be a good source. Try him. And here, Brody,' Edgar gave him a fiver, 'test him out and if needs be see if this helps.'

The clerk was pleased to have met a pal like Brody, who was a regular at the River Inn and who didn't mind shouting a few drinks. And he liked to talk about his job, especially within earshot of his beloved Gertie, explaining to Brody the intricacies of his work and the splendid opportunities for promotion.

'There's not much you wouldn't know about what goes on there then?' Brody said, impressed.

'I don't miss a thing, mate.'

After several evenings in the clerk's company Brody asked him what was happening with that railroad to Longreach. The whole town was wondering when that land would be released and the railroad get under way. 'Jobs, mate,' he said. 'There'll be a rush for them jobs.'

'Don't know much about that,' the clerk had to admit.

'And I thought you was the gent on the spot,' Brody laughed.

'I could find out if I wanted to.'

'A fiver says you can't,' Brody grinned, 'but I reckon my money's safe. You're all talk.'

For a week Brody waited and Edgar brooded, and then the clerk accosted Brody at the inn. 'You owe me a fiver.'

'What for?' Brody asked, as if he'd forgotten.

'That railway land. I told you I could find out. The whole show is dead. Buried.'

Brody wanted to make certain. 'What's that supposed to mean?'

'The file's marked "No action" and blokes in the office say Western Railroad Company hasn't got a hope in hell of getting that corridor of land for free. And what's more, they reckon it's blackballed. They wouldn't get it even if they paid for it. Now hand over my fiver.'

'That does it,' Edgar told Brody, 'start packing.'

'Are we broke, sir?' Brody asked, but Edgar laughed.

'By no means. It's just time to move on. Those people who want to buy this house will be pleased, I'll sign the contract today. Cash up. As soon as the shipping office opens, go down and buy two first-class tickets on the first ship leaving Brisbane.'

'Two first-class, sir?'

'If you want to come with me, you'll be travelling as a gentleman's gentleman, Brody. It's fitting.'

'Sounds all right to me. Where are we going?'

'America, eventually, but just get us out of Brisbane first.'

'Righto,' Brody grinned. Life was looking up.

When he'd left, Edgar opened his safe and surveyed all the cash he'd been hoarding for a rainy day, pleased that the sale of the house would add another thousand or so. It didn't bother him that he was holding money given to him in good faith by Connie. She had plenty more. Or that the mortgage on William's house had released to him a considerable bonus. William had been leaning on him for too long; it was time he stood on his own feet. All those cheques to the nonexistent steelworks had bled as much as he could from the railroad company, on top of his director's fees. He rubbed his hands with pleasure. 'Serve them all right,' he said to the open safe. 'If the government had backed me, this wouldn't be necessary. People get the government they deserve. Let's see how long the Premier lasts when the shareholders find that Western Railroad has collapsed!'

He didn't care about Lalla. She'd besmirched the Thurlwell name herself with her affairs, especially with Buchanan. He'd had Brody keep an eye on the pair of them when Buchanan had first leased that apartment in town, which Lalla had decorated for him.

'I'll bet she did,' he said grimly. 'The bloody whore.' What a fool William was.

Edgar picked up a little leather bag with a drawstring. It was heavy. And so it ought to be. This delightful little cache of gold had been intended for Phoebe, the only person in the world he cared about. A girl after his own heart. He'd enjoyed the way she stood up to Lalla and had William bluffed. Pretty as a picture too, and stout of heart. He really should leave the gold for her, but then who knew which way the wind would blow from now on? He might need it himself. He put it back and locked the safe, then went off to find the good strong pigskin suitcase with the locks that would be his bank from now on.

This was Thursday. Two ships were leaving on Saturday. The *Locheil* for Sydney and the *Eastern Star* for Singapore.

'I thought the *Locheil* would be best,' Brody explained. 'She goes to Sydney, then on to New Zealand and Hawaii.'

'Excellent. And you were able to get berths?'

'No trouble, sir.'

'You're right. It will look much better if we head for Sydney. Business, you know.'

He left Brody to give the cook temporary leave, informing her that he'd be back with the master within the month. And he called on William and Lalla to tell them he was sailing on the *Locheil* for Sydney in the morning to check on the progress of the coach-builders. Before he took his leave, he pressed a gold nugget into Phoebe's hand, only one. It was only worth a couple of hundred but the thought was there, he told himself sagely as he winked at his niece.

The *Locheil* sailed on schedule in the early-morning light, with Edgar resting in his cabin, keeping an eye on that pigskin suitcase, and Brody up on deck watching the sailors at work as they headed downriver for the coast. He was excited; this was a great day indeed.

'By Jove,' William said to them as he turned the pages of his newspaper.

'Our Edgar's a lucky chap. Always was.'

Phoebe agreed. She hadn't told them about the present Edgar had slipped into her hand as he was leaving, it was their secret. She'd had to rush away on her own, clutching the mysterious lumpy gift to see what it was. Gold! It was a jagged, uneven nugget of gold, she was sure. She'd seen those glittering treasures in jewellers' windows often enough. As soon as she could, she'd take it into town to be valued.

'Why now?' Lalla asked William.

'Hang on.' The Doctor adjusted his spectacles. 'I'll read it to you.'

Lalla sighed and put down her coffee cup. She hated him to read at the breakfast table and worse, to read bits out to them. To be fair, that irritated Phoebe too; she liked to read the paper herself, not find out the news second-hand.

'There's been another shipwreck off the coast of New Zealand,' William read. 'Off the North Island. It went down in heavy seas, having been cast upon rocks, and was therefore too badly holed to remain afloat. The shipwreck took place during the night and by early morn some survivors made it to shore to raise the alarm. No further information is available as yet but it is feared that more than sixty lives might be lost.'

'Oh dear,' Lalla said. 'They say that the Tasman Sea between Australia and New Zealand is always rough.'

'Yes, but the ship, Lalla! The ship! It was the iron clipper *Locheil*, travelling between Sydney and Auckland! Edgar was aboard. He would have disembarked in Sydney where it took on new passengers. Poor souls, how awful to think they would have been stepping aboard on a voyage to death.'

'That's terrible!' Phoebe said. 'Edgar probably knew some of them.'

'I think it's dreadful,' Lalla said. 'Our coastline is littered with wrecks. It's a wonder the governments don't do something about it.'

'Nothing they can do about the elements, my dear. No doubt we'll hear more of it when Edgar comes home. It could be the captain was incompetent.'

'When *is* Edgar coming home?' Lalla asked.

'Any day now, I should imagine. It would take time to examine all the aspects of the building of those coaches. He's a hard master, he'd want everything to be exactly as specifications demand. Then he'd have to wait for a ship returning to Brisbane.' William chuckled. 'Not that he'd mind, he does enjoy Sydney.'

'Where is he staying?'

'I don't know. The Australian Hotel as usual, I suppose.'

Lalla nodded. That stupid woman had managed to unnerve her, just a little, with her outrageous suggestions. 'Do you know of a firm called New South Wales Steelworks?'

'Yes. They'll be supplying the rails for the trains to run on. Edgar was fortunate to find them. It's much cheaper to have them made here than to have to import them from England. No doubt he'll have to check on them too, it's imperative that the rails are of the highest quality.'

'May I have the paper now?' Phoebe asked him, and he handed it over. 'Certainly. I must be off. I'll call on Mrs Carroll. She's still in hospital, refusing to leave until she's fully recovered. She only had her appendix out and should have gone home days ago; there's nothing wrong with her now.'

'That woman has always been a hypochondriac,' Lalla sniffed.

Somehow, Lalla found, she couldn't settle down that morning. She did the flowers herself, since the servants could never arrange them properly or remember that the white roses always went in the long room with no other colour but a background of greenery. The tale of someone living in Edgar's house still nagged her. It was probably Brody and some servants. But maybe it wouldn't hurt to take a look.

She instructed the driver of her gig to pull up outside the house. 'Will you be going in, madam?' he asked, ready to assist her down.

'No. Just wait here a minute.'

There were two children playing in the front garden, and Lalla was affronted. How dare servants allow their children into Edgar's garden! He'd hear about this.

The postman came along the street, blowing his whistle. When he came to Edgar's house he turned, recognizing Lalla.

'Why, Mrs Thurlwell! I've got letters here for Mr Edgar and I haven't got his new address. I reckon he wouldn't like me to send them back to the post office, they might get lost.' He handed her a small bundle held together by a rubber band.

To add to Lalla's confusion, a woman came from the house to meet the postman. 'This here's Mrs Doctor Thurlwell,' he told the woman cheerily. 'She'll take them letters off your hands.'

'How do you do, Mrs Thurlwell,' the woman responded, impressed. 'It's so nice to meet you. I've seen your pictures in the paper often enough. I won't be a second, I'll get the letters for you.'

She dashed inside and returned with a small basket containing more letters. 'You can keep the basket,' the woman said. 'I made it myself.'

'Thank you,' Lalla conceded, although she felt flushed and nervy.

'Where will I send Mr Edgar's mail? Now that he's moved?' the postman asked her.

'To us, Somerset House, Kangaroo Point,' she managed to reply. 'Mr Thurlwell is in Sydney on business at present.'

'Ah well, that explains it,' he replied. 'Leave it to me. I'll see none get lost.'

She sat stiffly in the gig as it spun away down the sandy road, not daring to even look down at the basket beside her.

'Oh my God,' she breathed to herself. 'Oh my God. He *has* sold the house without a word to us. Why would he do that? Why?'

The journey into town and over the bridge, down through South Brisbane and on to Kangaroo Point, seemed endless, and even though it was a pleasant sunny day, to Lalla the sun seemed to be beating down on her with grim determination. She felt her face burning and perspiration dampening the silk bow at her throat, but she remained erect, head up, every yard of the way, every monotonous beat of the horse's hooves.

Phoebe was sitting on the veranda by the open front door. 'Mother, while the gig's here, may I go into town? I have some shopping to do and it's not fair to Biddy to take her away from her work and then have her running late for the rest of the day. And besides, I'm getting fed up with being under surveillance all the time, I'm going to—'

Lalla cut her short, 'Do what you like!' and swept past her.

Her daughter stared, shrugged, and made for the gig. She was already dressed for town, because she'd been determined to make a stand this time and go. If not in the gig, then by the ferry. But obviously her term of punishment was over. Typical of Lalla to push her to the limit before giving in.

'Queen Street,' she told the driver.

Having shown the nugget to a jeweller, she then decided to visit Ben at the stables.

'Look what I've got,' she told him. 'My Uncle Edgar gave it to me. Isn't he sweet?'

He weighed it in his hand. 'Worth a bit, I'd say.'

'Three hundred and twenty-three pounds to be exact,' she said. 'The jeweller suggested I might want to have it melted down and made into a piece of jewellery, but I thought I'd just have it mounted and keep it like that. What do you think?'

'I like it as it is too,' he replied. 'It's a piece of history. You must ask him which goldfields it came from.'

She touched his bare arm. 'I've missed you.'

He wrapped his arms about her. 'Not as much as I've missed you.'

'I have so,' she smiled, 'and I think the ban has been lifted, I'll be able to visit you again, at the house.'

'Barnaby Glasson called on me,' he told her.

'Yes, I asked him to. Now tell me the bad news. Did he say we ought to say our farewells and go our separate ways?'

'He did.'

'Oh God,' she groaned. 'I hoped you'd talk him round.'

'Well . . . I think having said his piece he's given up on us. He's not for us or against us. But we did have a long talk, in fact we had a night out together.'

'Without me? You wretches!'

Ben released her and sat on the edge of his desk. 'He's been very good to me, Phoebe, for years. Ever since I was a kid. In his capacity as a lawyer. Too complicated to explain now, but I found a way to repay him. He has moved into my house.'

'Barnaby has? Why?'

'Have you seen his rooms? Where he lived? Just a couple of dreary rooms in a rabbit warren of a place.'

'No, I haven't. But that's not unusual, Ben. Most young men like him whose families live out of town take digs or rented rooms.'

'I didn't realize that. Anyway, I offered him one of the spare rooms at my place, and after some persuasion, he accepted.'

'For heaven's sake! But what a good idea! As long as you don't mind, it'll be much nicer accommodation for him.' She laughed. 'A real bachelor establishment now! I'll have to watch you two. And Barnaby can be our chaperon. Is that why you invited him?'

'To be honest I didn't think about that. I only hoped you wouldn't mind.'

'Of course not. It's your house.'

He looked at her thoughtfully. 'I also told Barnaby that if you accepted my proposal we wouldn't be living there. So eventually if he finds the house convenient I'll rent it to him.'

'I have accepted your proposal, Ben Beckman, and I have no intention of changing my mind.' She kissed him. 'And I'm ahead of you, my darling. I've always known that we couldn't possibly live next door to my parents, but you love the house so much I have been dodging bringing up that subject.'

'You've still got plenty of time to think about marriage,' he reminded her.

'I've done that. But you've posed an interesting question. Where will we live?'

'Anywhere you like. I'll buy another house. That'll be your decision. But there's one more thing, Phoebe. Barnaby thinks I ought to do the right thing. I ought to call on your father when or if we decide to marry.'

'No!' she said vehemently. 'No! Definitely not! Good God, Ben, you know my parents better than he does!' Phoebe suddenly had a picture of the boy forcing his way into their house, screaming for help for his mother. And another of the smashed windows. And another . . . more blurred. Of Ben's grandmother coming to their front door to plead for the boy, who'd been taken away by the police. And being coldly dismissed by her mother. But she hadn't gone. She'd been on the front veranda talking to someone. Pleading for help. That memory sidled into her consciousness but only to the edge, it wouldn't take form. It had been an exciting time, with all that smashed glass. Probably old Mrs Beckman had tried to appeal to her father as well, and received the same rebuff. It had been so sad.

Phoebe burst into tears. 'Don't do it, Ben. Please, I beg you, keep away from them. I'm frightened. Promise me you won't do it.'

He held her close. 'Phoebe, love. Don't cry. If you'd rather I didn't then I won't. I just want to do what's best for you.'

'Then stop making it so difficult for me!' she sobbed. 'Are we getting married or not?'

'Yes,' he said gently. 'Yes. I love you dearly, Phoebe Thurlwell, and I want you to be my wife.'

She wept. She kept on crying. 'What's wrong now?' he asked her, alarmed.

'Nothing. Nothing at all,' she smiled through her tears. 'It's just such a relief. At last I know what I'm doing, I know where my life is going. Tell me you love me again. And again. I wish we weren't in this office, it's so . . . so public. Anyone could come to the door . . .'

'The way I feel now it's just as well we're in the office,' he said. 'Come on now, I have to get back to work.'

The world was a special place for Ben that morning. The polished blue skies gleamed and beamed, the men smiled as they worked, and horses were led by in amiable procession. Everything was in order. As usual he joined the men at the lunch break in the shady lean-to behind the shed. It was a sort of meeting place where most sat on the ground, leaning against the wall, while the more enterprising had commandeered old benches and chairs. Ben wasn't particular, he sat wherever there was a space, on this occasion at the end of a bench.

Lunchboxes were out, and tobacco pouches and newspapers, and the men about him were talking, joking, when suddenly his hearing seemed to go haywire. It was instantaneous, as if his ears had switched to another range, altering his perception of what he heard. The voices about him were normal, in tone at least, neither louder nor softer, but their accents sounded foreign. He could understand them, no problem about that, they were discussing their favourite topic, horse-racing, and which nags had the best chance on Saturday. But this was all wrong. Confounded, he continued to listen intently, not saying a word, listening to these men whom he knew so well, speaking in hard, sharp sounds that were alien to him.

And yet everything was normal, or appeared normal, to them anyway.

He tried to diagnose what was happening to him. It felt as if he were a Frenchman, understanding English but aware of their accents. But he wasn't a Frenchman and they were speaking his language. His native tongue. English.

Or were they? Maybe it wasn't his ears. Maybe his brain had reverted to the lost language of his ancestors, his mother's ancestors.

Before he could consider this further, everything snapped back to normal. No one had noticed anything strange happening, and it was too peculiar a sensation for him to try to explain. He took out his tobacco to roll a smoke and looked across at Rod Callaghan, who was seated on the ground leaning against a post, his long legs stretched out in front of him. Rod was half dozing, using the break to rest mind and limbs.

'Rod,' Ben said quietly, from a good ten feet away, 'don't move.'

Rod's eyes blinked into focus. 'What?'

'You heard me,' Ben said, his voice still quiet but firm. 'Don't move.'

They stopped instantly and everyone was very still. No one moved a muscle. They all knew what that warning meant. A snake or a dangerous spider. Snake probably: spiders hid in dark corners, snakes came out to sun themselves.

Rod was tense. He allowed his eyes to move down to see the snake sliding along beside his arm, and he looked to Ben in despair to do something. There were no firearms to hand. The men who could see the snake now passed the message along to the others by eye contact only. Ben had seen plenty of snakes at the quarry and he recognized the coppery tones and streamlined head of a brown snake, a particularly venomous character, known to be very nervous.

So was Ben. As he stood up carefully and began to advance towards it, he remembered that all animals feel threatened by size; many of them will roll over or drop down to avoid further aggression. He could hardly reduce his size, but he did lower himself to a crouch, moving forward, maybe to distract the snake, he wasn't sure. It was watching him now, tongue flicking. He moved slowly on, watching as the snake nestled its thick body further down beside Rod's leg.

Its tail was visible now and Ben moved sideways, wondering if he'd be fast enough to grab that tail before the snake grabbed him. He began talking to it softly, muttering to it as if it were a wild horse, trying to calm it, trying to tell the snake he wouldn't hurt it, all the time wondering if he could get hold of that tail.

But the snake was too fast. It might have read his mind. It reared up as if to strike at him and then shot past him into the undergrowth, disappearing so swiftly everyone was taken by surprise.

They all ran out of the lean-to, shouting: 'Catch him! Kill him!' But Ben wouldn't allow it. 'Leave him to me.'

He took a forked stick and a hessian sack and searched out the snake, hooking him into the bag. 'Get me a canvas bag!' he shouted to Rod.

'What for?' Rod cried.

'Because he can bite me through this one,' Ben yelled.

With the snake safe inside the two bags Ben set off to release it into bushland, ignoring the complaints of his staff, who'd rather have seen it demolished.

When he returned Rod shook his hand. 'Thanks, Ben. I owe you. That was too close for comfort. I could almost feel those fangs in me. But I didn't know you spoke Abo.'

'Not very well. Only a mixture of dialects. I learned them in jail.'

Rod laughed. 'Well, I'm mighty relieved that bloody snake got the message. He understood and took off like lightning. You must have got his dialect right.'

'What do you mean?'

'You were right beside me. You were talking Abo to the thing.'

'Oh.' Ben was as surprised as Rod. He had thought he was speaking in English.

'Strange things happen, I suppose,' he said to himself as they all went back to work, the crisis over.

Without a qualm, Lalla ripped open Edgar's mail, to find bills and more bills. But that wasn't unusual; everyone received bills. She had often observed that without this irritating mass of paper, the postmen would have little to do and would probably only have to make one delivery per day.

William's mail was on his desk, so she opened that as well. But all she could find were several invitations and more of those damn bills. Nothing to give them a hint that Edgar had sold the house, or even a letter from him.

She had promised to attend a card party for ladies this afternoon at Belle Foster's house, a regular monthly occasion, but decided against it. Connie Downs might be there, since she'd tacked herself on to Belle. For that matter she seemed to have ingratiated herself with everyone who knew Edgar, part of a strategy, of course, to snare the man. But after yesterday's episode, Lalla would not be seen in the same room as her. From today Mrs Downs could consider herself blackballed. All doors would be closed to her. Lalla would see to that.

By the time William arrived home, his wife was in a very bad mood, and noting this, the Doctor announced that he would take a nap before dinner.

'No you won't,' she snapped. 'I wish to talk to you.'

'Can't it wait? I'm rather tired.'

'I'm sure you are! It must be exhausting drinking with your friends at the Club all the afternoon.'

'No more than usual,' he said sagely, 'especially since I have some good news. That federation business is all over. None of the chaps are interested any more. Even the supporters have to admit that the bubble has burst. It's just not the time for such high-falutin' ideas. Told them all along, I did,' he crowed.

'Oh, shut up!' she said. 'That's nothing new. The Premier has been losing ground on it for months. He can't get it through Parliament and he never will. There's something else I need to discuss with you. Why didn't you tell me Edgar has sold his house?'

He sank into an armchair. 'Where did you get that notion?'

'From Connie Downs. She came to visit me yesterday and her attitude was nothing short of insulting.'

'Yesterday? This is the first I've heard of it.'

'Never mind that. What about Edgar's house?'

'You're talking in riddles, woman. My brother's house is intact as far as I know, and there has been no sale.'

'That's where you're wrong. I went over there today. It has been sold and the purchasers have moved in.'

William blinked. He was feeling rather tipsy and this nonsense was confusing him. 'If Edgar had sold his house he would have told me.'

'Since he didn't tell you, and the new owners are under the impression he has bought a house in Hamilton, I want to know what is going on.'

'How would I know? He never said a word to me. Maybe he is getting serious with that Downs woman and has planned to move into a bigger house. He knows you don't like her. Probably dodging having to tell us beforehand. Present us with a *fait accompli* so to speak, so that we can't talk him out of it.'

Lalla contemplated this, tapping a finger on the edge of her chair. 'If that's true then she's just cut her own throat. But I have a nasty feeling there's more to this. You've got a lot of the books in your study pertaining to Western Railroad. I want you to look up the address of NSW Steelworks.'

'Now?'

'Right now. I'll help you.'

'Is this really necessary?'

'Yes.'

They searched through the two large drawers where William kept the railroad papers and contracts, letters and statements, in no sort of order.

'This is a terrible muddle,' she complained. 'I don't know how you can ever find anything.'

'I've been busy,' he muttered. 'I've been meaning to sort them out but Edgar keeps dumping more and more on me and I simply don't have the time. I'll attend to it at the weekend.'

'You do that,' Lalla snapped. 'But I can't find anything to do with that steelworks.'

'That's not surprising. Edgar has most of the papers in his office.'

'In what office and where?'

'I don't know. In that Hamilton house, I suppose. What is this all about?'

'Mrs Downs claims that Edgar, to put it in her words, has done a bunk.'

William was shocked. 'By God, you were right about her, Lalla. I never heard such tommyrot. We could sue her for that.'

'She also gave me the distinct impression that there is no such firm as NSW Steelworks.'

'She what? The woman's mad! They're our suppliers.'

'But you, you damn fool, don't even know where they are located. First thing in the morning you will go and find out, if only for my peace of mind.'

'How do I find out?' he wailed.

'How would I know? Ask the bank. Ask some of your precious friends at the club, but find out. Until Edgar gets back, or I have the answer to throw in Connie Downs' face, I'm not inclined to go out in case she makes a scene again.'

'My dear, you've really let that wretch get to you. Now don't be worrying.' He hauled himself from his chair to put a reassuring hand on her shoulder. 'Leave it to me. I'll sort it all out in the morning. Now I really must take a nap. You should too.'

As he trod heavily up the stairs, William wished Edgar would cease his cavortings in Sydney and come home. Stuffed in his pocket were two mystifying letters that had been hand-delivered to the rooms he shared on The Terrace with another physician. They were both from banks demanding money. One was from a house he'd never heard of, the Pacific something, obviously one of those newcomers to the banking world, trying to cash in on the Queensland gold boom. And, naturally, with no idea what they were doing. That letter had claimed payment on some mortgage, so William had shoved it aside, refusing to read on. It had nothing to do with him. He sighed. Banks were not what they used to be. In his day they never made mistakes.

And then there was the other letter, from Dudley Luxton at the Bank of Queensland. That was sheer impertinence.

William sat on the edge of the bed and picked nervously at his nails. He needed another drink but Lalla was down there like the Keeper at the Gate. Luxton's letter had informed him that no more credit would be extended to W. & E. Thurlwell until substantial payments were made on the overdraft.

What credit? He didn't need credit. And there wasn't any overdraft. The Thurlwells never required credit. Had all of these bank managers lost their grip? While still signing themselves one's most obedient servants!

Damn fools! William felt extremely anxious. He realized now why his cheques had been returned. 'Bounced' was the latest horrible term. He'd used it himself, he had to admit, in dealing with some of his patients' dishonoured cheques, and had been shocked at their cheek. And he recalled now that those accounts had remained unpaid.

It was beginning to dawn on him that until Edgar came home, if Luxton persisted in this attitude, he had no money. Only a few hundred in cash at the surgery. How could he tell Lalla that?

The nap was forgotten. William took a bath and went downstairs, looking forward to the blessed relief of a few good belts of sherry before dinner, having made up his mind. He would send a telegram to Edgar at the Australian Hotel in Sydney, his home away from home, asking him to return immediately and also asking him to telegraph to him the address of the NSW Steelworks, to set Lalla's mind at rest.

Edgar would sort it all out. Edgar would run rings around the likes of Dudley Luxton. And when the matter had been resolved, he, William, would insist that they remove their business from the Bank of Queensland. Luxton's insulting attitude towards the Thurlwells would cost him dearly. As for calling on him to enquire the whereabouts of one of their own suppliers, not on your life! He would never step inside the doors of the Bank of Queensland again.

Federation was a dead duck, and no one seemed to care. No one except Barnaby Glasson, who was now seeing all his work on the constitution going down the drain. So he hung about his temporary office in Parliament House, waiting for his next assignment.

Politicians had begun to meander back into town, preparatory to the opening of Parliament in March, and he was disgusted to hear the Speaker, Harold Sutcliffe, boasting that he had never been in favour of union, and that it was a great load off his mind to be able to get back to the real issues that concerned this state.

Word had it, his colleagues told him, that the Attorney-General might send him over to work on the new Bill banning gambling. To Barnaby that constituted a fall from the heights of glory to the shallows of silliness, and he began to consider resigning from the Attorney-General's department and going it alone. Hanging out his shingle as a lawyer. Maybe not here in Brisbane – there was too much competition – but in a country town. Like Charleville, for instance. But then that would be the end of his political ambitions. Even if he could survive, financially, it took years to be accepted in country towns, and he had his heart set on the seat of Padlow. On going after that bastard Buchanan, right here in Brisbane. Maybe he shouldn't have boasted of such a wild ambition to Phoebe, then he wouldn't feel so bad at having to back off.

At last, though, he got the call from Creighton. 'His Holiness', the staff called him behind his back.

'Looks like you're the bunny,' the assistant secretary whispered to Barnaby as he brushed his hair and straightened his tie before entering the holy of holies, the great man's inner office. 'You're for the gambling Bill. Just remember not to make any bets on the Melbourne Cup or you'll get burned at your own stake.'

'Very funny,' Barnaby said to all the grinning faces.

'Ah, Glasson,' Creighton said as Barnaby stood before him. 'Mr Prosser is back in town.'

'Is he, sir? I didn't know. I hope he has recovered.'

'His foot's still in plaster but apparently his voice isn't affected. He wishes to see you.'

Barnaby's expression must have given him away because the Attorney-General continued: 'I don't blame you for looking glum. I'd say you are in for a well-deserved bawling-out, Glasson. But a word of advice. Take it like a man and don't involve this office. You get me? If a word of criticism floats down to me, you're fired. I don't think I can make that any clearer. Can I?'

'No, sir. Where should I go to meet Mr Prosser?'

'You are to present yourself at the Premier's home this evening at nine p.m.'

Barnaby shook in his boots. 'At the Premier's home?'

'Yes, I presume you know where Sir Samuel lives?'

'Yes, sir.' Who didn't know that leafy estate on the hill?

'Mr Prosser has many important friends in the Australian Natives Association all over the country. The Premier felt it was the least he could do, in the face of Prosser's unfortunate accident, to have his people meet the gentleman when the ship berthed to take him to his own residence, rather than the poor chap having to deal with an hotel.'

'Ah yes. Of course,' Barnaby echoed, petrified. Being bawled out by Prosser would be bad enough, but in the company of the Premier of Queensland! He felt sick. Surely it would be kinder of them to sack him now and get it over with.

Creighton spoke to him as if he were a ten-year-old.

'Now wear your best suit. Shine up your boots and see that your nails are clean. And you could do with a haircut, your hair's as thick as a mop!'

Annoyed by this lecture, Barnaby looked at him coolly. 'Should I go to the front or the back door, sir?' But the sarcasm was lost on his superior. 'I think the front would be best. After all, you do represent my office.'

He didn't have his hair cut. But he did plaster it down with pomade, making certain that the parting was as sharp as a blade.

Duly, at nine o'clock on the dot, Barnaby Glasson presented himself at the door of the residence of the Premier, and was ushered into the presence of Theodore Prosser, who was reclining in a large chair, his plastered foot, with the toes sticking out, resting on a stool.

'There you are, Glasson! Punctual. Good!' Prosser said. 'Sit yourself down, we've got work to do.'

'I'm glad to see you looking so well, sir,' Barnaby said. 'I hope your injury isn't bothering you too much.' What work? he wondered.

'Not at all. At least not now. At first the pain was excruciating. Damned excruciating! But I'll say this for country folk, they looked after me right well. And the matron at the hospital is a fine woman. Mrs Woodside. Do you know her?'

'No, sir.' Barnaby was bewildered. How could he possibly know the woman? And Prosser! He was positively genial. Maybe they'd put him on laughing gas out there.

'Nursed me herself,' Prosser continued. 'Best of treatment. I told her she was wasted in the bush. She ought to come down to Sydney, and by Jove, she might just do that. A widow, you know . . . Pass me my pipe and that tobacco. Samuel keeps only the best.'

Barnaby solemnly did as he was bidden, providing matches and an ashtray as well, and grinning to himself. Had Theodore the widower found love in the outback? Sounded like it. No wonder he was cheery.

'I hear you had a spot of trouble at Charleville?'

'Yes, sir.'

Prosser laughed. 'That'll teach you! Experience counts. Who was the fellow again? The one who accused you of inciting revolution?'

'Mr Ben Buchanan. Member for Padlow. He lives out that way.'

'That's right, yes. And he succeeded in breaking up your meeting. I heard all about it, and I've seen his written complaints about you.' He wagged his pipe at Barnaby. 'Wouldn't have happened with me up there. I'm accustomed to dealing with interjectors, no matter who. He wouldn't hard dared pull a trick like that on me.'

Barnaby nodded. It was a moot point but he wasn't prepared to argue.

'But we won't worry about Buchanan or his ilk now. There's been a change of plan, a change to the constitution, and this time we'll win.'

Not again, Barnaby thought dismally. How many more amendments did he have to look at?

'Have you heard of the meeting at Corowa?' Theodore asked.

'No, sir.'

'Then you will. Everyone will. It's a town on the border between Victoria and New South Wales, and a meeting was held there by a large body of delegates from the Australian Natives Association and stalwarts of the Federation League. Are you following me?'

Barnaby nodded again.

'Oh, what a great day it must have been. I wish I'd been there,' Theodore enthused. 'They came to the conclusion, as we all have, that it is a hopeless endeavour to try to get lethargic and downright opposing politicians all over the country to agree on federation. One might as well say, too, it would be impossible to get all those gents to agree on anything.'

'I'm afraid so,' Barnaby said.

'Exactly! Now to cut a long story short, that convention voted to add a preamble to the proposed constitution rather than amend it. They intend to override those stonewalling politicians and go straight to the people. Have the people elect delegates to draft the final constitution for their own new nation. What do you think of that?'

Barnaby was stunned. 'Can it be done?'

'My bloody word it can. It's a simpler exercise to ask persons to put themselves forward as delegates and let the electors decide who goes. It leaves the anti movement with not a leg to stand on. No opportunity to vote no! Brilliant, in fact.'

Barnaby thought about this for a while. 'I'm not against the proposition, sir, but isn't it more of a republican stance than in the British tradition?'

'I suppose it is, but that can't be helped. Your Premier is a wily chap. He knows that Joe Blow out there will pay a damn sight more attention to union if he gets his say right up. Give 'em a chance to thumb their noses at politicians, Glasson my lad, and they'll be at the polls with bells on.' He puffed on his pipe and leaned back in a glow of satisfaction. 'Other countries have united the hard way, by wars. We'll show them Australians have more sense.'

'Or less interest in brawling over the idea,' Barnaby grinned.

'Maybe so. But I predict there'll be no revolution. This is a matter that must be decided by the people, the electorate at large, not by the bumbling self-interest of the states.'

'I hope it works,' Barnaby said. 'Once we have a constitution it will still have to go to referendum.'

'But we're halfway home,' Theodore said firmly. 'There's a folder on the table, it will provide you with more information and notes on the Corowa convention. Once the constitution is decided on by the new delegates the yes/no campaign will begin in earnest. I shall probably return to Brisbane as a campaign consultant.'

The door opened and the Premier came hurrying in.

Barnaby jumped to his feet. 'Good evening, sir.'

'Evening, Glasson. I'm sorry, Theodore, my other guests are slow in departing. Has our young lawyer here got the gist of things?'

'I believe so,' Theodore replied. 'I've done my best.'

Thanks for nothing, Barnaby thought, still standing. It wasn't all that hard to understand, I'm not completely stupid.

'Good.' The Premier turned to Barnaby. 'Now, Mr Glasson, I have a suggestion for you. We'd like you to resign from the Attorney-General's office. To resign from government employ altogether.' He walked over to the sideboard to study a glass bowl of silver-wrapped chocolates, testing them with his fingers. 'All hard centres,' he said, disgusted. 'No good to me, they give me the toothache. Remind me to have them replaced, Theodore.'

I might have known I'd get fired, Barnaby thought. And I hope they do give him toothache. Bloody old Prosser has only been stringing me along, waiting for the old boy to come in and give me the boot.

'Is that all right with you?' the Premier asked him.

'As you wish, sir,' Barnaby shrugged. He wasn't about to beg.

'It would be best if you went into private practice,' Sir Samuel continued. 'You're young, and sharp, and you know your law. You should do well.'

'Thank you for your confidence, sir, but I couldn't afford to go out on my own. I should have to find a firm that would employ me.'

'No, no. You don't want any interference from other partners. What you have to do is open your own office and employ a legal clerk who can hold the fort in your absence.'

In the face of this futile plan, Barnaby shook his head. 'I'm sorry, sir. I can't afford my own legal office. It's out of the question.'

'Oh no it's not. These things can be arranged. We want you to be a delegate to the next convention. We want you to stand as a representative of the people, and being the first to throw your hat in the ring, you'll have a damn good chance. But you have to disassociate yourself from politics and politicians, hence the need to set up in private practice.'

At once Barnaby understood what all this was about, and he was thrilled. But he also realized that it was essential to make certain these men didn't send him out into the world on sixpence and a promise.

'Exactly what would these arrangements be, Sir Samuel?'

'We could put business your way. One year's rent on your offices would be helpful too, don't you agree?'

'Yes, sir, but I'd need campaign funds.'

'Don't you have any money of your own?' Theodore asked.

Barnaby glanced at the Premier with a smile. 'It's not possible to save on the salary of a government clerk.' Only a small, necessary fib.

'I suppose not,' the Premier said. 'But that's not a problem. Open a trust account for donations from supporters and we'll see some of it goes your way. I have to get back now. Find yourself legal rooms and let my secretary know. He'll handle all the details, you have my word on it.'

He shook Barnaby's hand. 'This matter is to be kept private. You are an ideal candidate, Mr Glasson, because you have applied yourself to the constitution with such diligence. We need people down there who know what they're talking about, and there aren't too many around. I can only wish you good luck.'

Barnaby walked for half an hour before he found a cab to take him over to Kangaroo Point, but it gave him time to think about this marvellous opportunity and the responsibility that had now been placed on his shoulders. Even if he lost the race to be elected a delegate, he'd won, having achieved his own firm, but somehow that seemed a rather mean assessment. The Premier had faith in his ability, and had placed his party support behind him, so he had to work at it. Get it right.

'Anyway,' he cheered as he walked into the house and threw his hat in the air, 'who cares! I didn't get sacked, I got bumped upstairs! And boy, what a bump!'

Ben was in the dining room, surrounded by more catalogues on the intricacies of motorcars and their engines, and Barnaby thought how great it was to come home and have someone to talk to.

'You're in a good mood,' Ben said. 'What happened to your hair? It looks as if it's pasted on.'

'It is,' Barnaby laughed, heading for the bathroom to wash out the thick pomade.

As he towelled his hair dry he told Ben his news:

'I'm not working for the government any more.'

'Why? Did you get the sack? You expected it.'

'Not exactly. I'm going into private practice, and the Premier has asked me to be a delegate to the constitutional conventions. Not as easy as it sounds, of course. A delegate has to be elected by the people. New rules.'

'And this is what you want to do?' Ben asked.

'Can't wait, on both counts!' Barnaby said gleefully. 'Especially since they're backing me financially.'

'That's great,' Ben said. 'I've some good news too. I talked to Phoebe today and she turned the tables on me. She won't abide by my rule of three months' grace. She insisted *I* make up my mind now. So we've agreed to marry.'

'Oh God! And you want me to celebrate the fact that you're walking into a hurricane!'

'Just do the best you can,' Ben said amiably. 'Tomorrow night, Rod and Alice Callaghan are taking me to see a friend of theirs, a priest. Oma was a Catholic, Phoebe's an Anglican, and I'm nothing in particular, as far as religion goes.'

'A Catholic priest won't marry you.'

'I know. But Alice says he's sensible and very nice, and it wouldn't hurt for me to just have a talk to him. They're as worried as you are. You're all making me nervous.'

'Is Phoebe going with you?'

'No. I just said I'd talk to the chap because he's not involved. So I won't be home tomorrow night; you'll have to do your own cooking.'

'Ah well. Best of luck,' Barnaby said. 'I'm going to be a real legal eagle, and you're on your way to married bliss!'

The Tasman Sea was rough. But both Edgar and his gentleman's gentleman were good sailors, and they withstood the heavy seas with hearty humour. They fought the winds in their daily march about the sturdy decks and derived pleasure from the massive lift and fall of foam-slicked waves and the sheer devilment of defying the great turmoil that surrounded them.

Less hardy voyagers had the opposite reaction to the incessant imbalance, and ran for the rails, or for the tender care of stewards in their cabins. This was a bonus for Edgar and Brody, who took full advantage of the sparse attendance in the first-class saloon and dining room to enjoy the excellent service provided by the good ship *Locheil*, and many a card game with other fortunate shipmates.

They had stepped ashore in Sydney for the few days that the *Locheil* was in port, but held their cabins. Edgar did not visit any of his usual haunts, nor did he approach any of Western Railroads' suppliers, and with Brody as his only company, he made the best of it. They had a riotous time visiting the taverns in the Rocks district, which Brody knew well, but they were careful. Edgar carried his pigskin suitcase with him at all times and Brody, acting the bodyguard, was armed. He had a pistol strapped to his waist under his overcoat, and a knife in his boot. And they returned to the ship at night.

As they neared the coast of New Zealand, Edgar was in high spirits. A couple of days in the Land of the Long White Cloud, and then they'd be on their way to Hawaii. And thence to America.

'We might even stay over a few weeks in Honolulu,' he informed Brody. 'A gentleman can have a high old time in those islands.'

At no time did they mention what they'd left behind. The slate was wiped clean. Brody was a man who never looked back, and Edgar had come to appreciate his attitude. For a servant he made an excellent companion. Better than most, he was inclined to admit, and a damned good card player when needed to make up a four.

As they neared the coast, heading for Auckland, storms raged and the seas retaliated with a power that sent the ironclad ship staggering and plunging, caught in a battle of the elements. Even the best of sailors fought for handholds as they tried to keep their ship on course, battening down against the furies.

Brody was still on his feet but Edgar had succumbed. Violently ill in his cabin, he cursed the ship and its captain, declaring they'd sail on from Hawaii in a decent vessel. Brody did his best. He fed his master brandy to settle his stomach and put him to sleep until the worst was over, and then he went up top to get some air because he was feeling a bit queasy himself.

All hands were at work to keep the ship steady, so he took himself down that night to the deserted saloon. It was near to two o'clock when he helped himself to a bottle of Spanish liqueur. 'Made by monks,' he mused as he swallowed the sweet and fiery liquid. 'And by all that's holy,' he grinned appreciatively, 'they do a fine job. Just the thing for a stormy night, especially since there's nary a soul about to be asking me to pay for this expensive stuff!'

Halfway through the bottle he was in a nostalgic mood, and inclined to sing a bit. He was having trouble remembering the words; nevertheless, it was a grand old night, with the furies out there fighting themselves, and him in here safe and sound with a bar all to himself.

When the crash came the bottle nearly snapped his front teeth. He was just about to take another pull at the sweetest drink ever made when the bloody saloon dropped on its side.

'Jesus!' he said, as he tried to pick himself up. 'The monks pack a bigger wallop than potheen!'

But then the room itself, the saloon, reared up at a very nasty angle, and he knew it wasn't the drink as he slid across the room, still clutching the bottle.

'I think we've hit New Zealand,' he announced, sitting on the floor. Then, as he heard the wrenching, ripping sounds, and the shouts from above, Brody was suddenly sober.

'Jesus bloody Christ!' he shouted.

He was the first to race down the corridor to pull Edgar from his bunk. 'Get up, boss! Quick! The bloody ship's hit somethin'. There's water rushin' in already.'

Edgar was groggy. He allowed Brody to shove him into his dressing gown and push him out of the cabin, and up steps and more steps with the world at a crazy angle, but the more air that entered his lungs the clearer Edgar became. People were screaming and shoving all about him.

'What's happening?' he asked Brody as they climbed from shelter into blinding rain and the onslaught of attacking waves.

'The ship's run aground,' Brody said.

In the teeming blackness he supported Edgar down the dangerously sloping deck. 'Everyone's runnin' berserk,' Brody told him. 'There are only a couple of lifeboats, and they're down this way. Hang on to me and we'll get there.'

'Did you bring my suitcase?' Edgar shouted over the scream of the wind and the terrifying sound of groaning timbers.

'No time for that,' Brody said. 'Here's a longboat. Every man for himself.'

'You bloody fool!' Edgar shouted at him. 'Go back and get it! The pigskin case, with the money and the gold.'

'There's no time. The ship's sinkin' fast.'

'I'm ordering you.' Edgar punched Brody in the back. 'Go and get it, you stupid bastard.'

'Get it yourself,' Brody retorted. He let go of Edgar to fight through the dark figures surrounding him for a place in the longboat, that was already being lowered into the sea only a few churning yards away.

Edgar shouldered back the other way. By the time he reached the gangway leading to the saloon, he was congratulating himself on not panicking, once he'd grasped the situation, by not risking that dark sea that was probably full of sharks.

Admittedly the ship had a dangerous list, but this side was dry. He lurched on to his cabin, thankfully in first class and not down in the bowels of the ship, and felt about under the bunk for the precious suitcase. Grasping it firmly, he headed out again, just as a surge of water came hurtling down from the hatches.

'Help!' he screamed, as he clung to his suitcase, fighting to wade then swim towards the freedom above him, that he knew was just up there above him. Then he realized that he wasn't the only one screaming; he was trapped in a chorus of screams, terrible sounds that he vowed, not recognizing his own dying moments, he would never forget.

'Ah well,' Shaun Brody, one of the survivors of the *Locheil* shipwreck, said to the New Zealand reporters. 'That's life.'

For weeks he searched the shores near where the *Locheil* had gone down ostensibly assisting in the search for survivors, or bodies; in reality looking for a pigskin suitcase. But he searched in vain.

The newspapers reported that Mr Brody, though technically a servant, had been travelling first class as a gentleman's gentleman, a category unknown in these parts. But as Brody was happy to explain to reporters, it meant that he was a cut above a butler. Offers of employment flooded in from the status-seekers among rich New Zealand sheep farmers and the owners of superb horse studs.

Because he'd always loved horses, Brody studied the latter offers with care, and found that one of his would-be employers was a Mrs Carmel O'Shea. A widow. She managed to persuade him to take over the management of her lavish household.

Within six months he and Carmel were married, and three years later their four-year-old prize filly crossed the Tasman Sea with them to win the famed Melbourne Cup. It bolted in.

When a stranger asked Brody if he'd known Edgar Thurlwell, Brody couldn't recall the name. Being a gentleman of property, he had no wish to be reminded that he was once in service.

Chapter Nine

The shocking news of Edgar's tragic death had not yet reached his family, since the New Zealand authorities were very thorough in their investigations. Finally, when the search was abandoned and enquiries completed, the list of sixty-two souls lost at sea was published and forwarded to the authorities in Sydney, home port of the ill-fated *Locheil*.

Edgar's family at Somerset House were busily engaged in their own affairs. Lalla had been appointed Chairman of the Ladies' Committee for the preservation of parks and gardens, with the Governor's lady as patron. Money had to be raised, so she had no choice but to attend several functions, the first being a high tea at Government House. This prestigious appointment called for an entirely new wardrobe in the latest fashions, so her first priority was to send for her dressmaker. To Lalla's horror, the woman refused to come.

Phoebe, too, was taking stock of her wardrobe. Since she and Ben had at last come to a decision, Phoebe was calmer, not so concerned about the actual date as about quietly adding to her glory box, a matter of major importance for a bride-to-be.

Her father was worried. Dreadfully worried, and bewildered by mounting debts and the absence of his brother, who could easily make sense of all this botheration.

While he was doing his rounds at the hospital he found that Mrs Carroll was still ensconced in a private room, and that annoyed him. He had too many troubles of his own to be putting up with her today.

'I believe you're leaving us this morning,' he said to her, endeavouring to summon up his bedside manner.

'Certainly not,' she replied. 'My side is still sore. Pass me that hand mirror. If I put a foot to the ground I'm certain this gash will open up.'

'You need have no worry about that, the stitches have been removed and you're healing up nicely. I'll have a carriage brought round for you and you can go home to celebrate a successful operation.'

'Peculiar ideas you have about celebrating,' she snapped, 'after the agonies I have suffered. You doctors are all the same, you simply don't understand pain!' She looked at him meanly. 'And what's this I hear about your Phoebe? Just because I'm stuck in here doesn't mean I'm out of touch. I believe she has a steady beau and an engagement is imminent.'

'And that means you *are* out of touch,' he retorted. 'My daughter has many social engagements but she's not stepping out with anyone in particular.'

'Much you know! My friends tell me she is regularly seen at the Beckman livery stables in the company of the proprietor. That young fellow, Ben Beckman.'

'Never heard of him.'

'Aha! Don't pretend with me, Doctor. Of course you know him. The fellow lives next door to you. The coloured chap.'

William was stunned. He dropped his aloof stance. 'Mrs Carroll, I beg of you not to repeat such a statement, it's just not true.'

'Oh dear,' she smiled. 'It happens so often, fathers are the last to know what's going on in their families. But believe me, Dr Thurlwell, it is true. My brother, the magistrate, has seen her there with him many a time. It's common knowledge among the people at the livery stables. He was rather surprised that you didn't put a stop to it. After all, a fellow like that, he's hardly suitable . . .'

'It is not true,' William insisted.

'My dear, it is just as well for you to hear it from me, since you seem to have been left in the dark. People are even saying that they're lovers and that she visits him in his house, unchaperoned.'

Dr Thurlwell charged out of the room, and Mrs Carroll settled back in her bed with a smile. She intended to remain in this hospital for another two days, by which time her aggravating old mother-in-law would have returned to the family station out west, and good riddance for another year.

William stumbled out of the hospital, forgetting his other patients, praying that what that awful woman had said was not true. Surely Phoebe wouldn't associate with the likes of that fellow? Then he remembered Lalla making a fuss about Phoebe taking a walk at night on her own. It was an odd thing to do, but Phoebe was inclined to do mad things at times.

What if she hadn't been walking alone at night? What if she had been in there, visiting that scoundrel? He wiped his forehead with his handkerchief as he walked towards his driver, who was sheltering with the gig in the shade of a tree. That was it! Lalla had caught her coming in, hatless, hardly dressed for the street. And the girl had lied. The lies could only mean one thing: there was something going on.

As he was about to step into the gig, he turned to ask the driver, 'You take my daughter to O'Neill's stables, don't you?'

'You mean Beckman's stables, sir? Yes. Took her there yesterday, as a matter of fact.'

It pained William to have to stoop to eliciting information from servants, but at this point he had little choice. 'Do you know any of the workmen at that place?'

'Yes, Doctor, most of them.'

'I see.' William pondered this, knowing he was making the driver nervous. 'Now listen to me and listen well. I have some questions to ask of you, and if I hear you have lied to me, you'll be out of a job in a blink.'

His driver clutched his cap from his head and bit his lip.

'Have you heard any gossip at those stables about my daughter and that fellow Beckman?'

'What sort of gossip, sir?'

'Don't play the fool with me, man. Answer the question!'

'I did hear that they are sort of friends, Miss Phoebe and Ben.'

'Ben, you say. I presume he is the proprietor. Obviously it *is* common knowledge. What I want to know is how far this friendship has gone.'

'Oh, it's not for me to say, Doctor.'

'It is for you to say. Take my warning to heart. If *you* can't say, what are the workers there saying?'

'They're bettin' that they'll get married, but gosh, sir, that ain't gospel. I wouldn't want to be puttin' you wrong on this.'

'Thank you, that will do.' He climbed into the gig. 'Take me up to the Terrace.'

He sat in his room with the door firmly shut and took a bottle of port from the base of his medicine cabinet. There was no doubt in his mind now that the half-breed had somehow inveigled himself into his daughter's company, and that the silly girl had fallen for him. How could she be so stupid? She'd make a laughing stock of the family. If she hadn't already done so. He could just imagine Lalla's reaction. There'd be hell to pay!

Maybe the scoundrel had already seduced Phoebe, which would account for this marriage talk. He shivered. He'd have to put a stop to this affair right away. But what if Phoebe were pregnant? He gulped down a second glass of port. The bastard should be horsewhipped for daring to force his attentions on his daughter! He should be run out of town or shoved back in jail where he belonged.

Jail! God in heaven, he'd almost forgotten the man's record. He was a thoroughly bad lot.

William almost choked in rage and disgust. He would put a stop to it, of course, but that fellow had to be punished. And smartly. Let him know that he couldn't play fast and loose with the Thurlwell family and get away with it. What would Edgar do in this situation? He wouldn't sit about like this, he'd act, and act swiftly. As William's anger increased he saw the gardener slouch past his window, wheeling a barrow. The man was a ruffian and not very bright. He'd been battered about the head in too many tent fights at fairs, and William had given him the job here to please a friend. The ex-pugilist had been so grateful, since he was also allowed to live in the shed at the back, that to him, Dr Thurlwell was a god.

Sometimes he could be embarrassing, following William about like an overgrown puppy, always asking if there was anything he could do for him. William watched him now, wondering if it might be time for 'Punchy' Duncan to earn his keep. He was still very strong and had a grip of iron. William winced, recalling how he always tried to avoid Punchy's enthusiastic handshakes.

He wandered outside and to Punchy's great delight, found time to sit down on a garden seat and have a chat to the gardener.

Punchy listened with growing concern to the Doctor's much simplified tale of woe.

'He put his hands on your little daughter?' Punchy was shocked when he managed to get the tale squarely in his head. 'By cripes, if I knew where to find him I'd give the bastard the hiding of his life. He wouldn't be touchin' her again when I finished with him.'

'It would seem the right thing to do, to protect my daughter's good name,' William muttered, as if the idea were only hypothetical. 'To warn him off once and for all. I'm at my wits' end to know what to do about him. The police won't do anything.'

'Coppers never do nothin',' Punchy growled. 'Why don't you let me have a bit of a talk with him? I owe you, sir, you bin bloody good to me.'

'Maybe you should. But it would have to be our secret. I couldn't have my wife hearing about it. This is men's business.'

'Too right it is,' Punchy echoed. 'It's men's business.'

He was working under the lamp at the dining room table when he heard the knock at the front door. It was about nine o'clock so he smiled to himself, thinking it might be Phoebe, glancing at her shimmery scarf hanging on the wall mirror as he passed to open the door.

A huge man stood silhouetted in the doorway against the moonlit night.

'Yes?' he asked the stranger, but instead of a reply a fist like concrete smashed into his face and Barnaby was thrown back into the passageway. Unhindered, the attacker lumbered after him, pulled him to his feet and Barnaby felt bones crush as that fist smashed into his face again. Other blows followed, as he was punched in swift succession in the chest, the stomach, around the head again. He could taste the blood streaming down his face. In a daze he saw the dark figure leave as suddenly as he had entered, slamming the door behind him, and then there was darkness.

When Ben came home he found Barnaby barely conscious on the floor, in a pool of blood. 'Jesus! What happened to you?'

He picked him up and carried him to his bed, aware now that Barnaby had been the victim of a bashing, right here in Ben's own home. He used wet towels to swab his face and try to bring him round, but quickly realized that Barnaby's injuries were too much for him to cope with, so he propped him up on pillows and ran all the way down the road to busy Vulture Street to find a horse cab. They were all busy so he paid a couple five pounds to get out and let him have their cab in this emergency.

At the hospital he informed the matron that this patient was a personal friend of the Premier's and demanded a private room, the only other one being occupied by a Mrs Carroll.

By this time Barnaby's face was barely recognizable, having ballooned into a mass of purple bruises. Ben waited outside while a young doctor saw to the patient.

'He's in a bad way,' he told Ben. 'Broken jaw, cheek-bones damaged, collar bone broken and I'd say a few broken ribs. Just pray he hasn't got internal injuries. What happened? Did he get run over by a wagon or something?'

'No,' Ben growled, 'he took a very thorough bashing.' He didn't add that he'd seen this sort of thing before, in the jails.

'Where did it happen?'

'At home. Probably robbers. He must have disturbed them.'

'Anything stolen?'

'I didn't have time to check. I wanted to get him here as soon as possible.'

'Good man. Will you report this to the police?'

'Bloody oath I will. But if I can find who did this they'll be your next customers. Is there anything I can do for Barnaby now? I want him to have the best treatment.'

'Nothing you can do really. We'll look after him.'

Ben considered this. 'I think I'll go home and try to figure out what happened, but I'll be back as soon as I can. Are you sure he'll be all right?'

'We'll have a better idea tomorrow. We may have to set the broken bones. I can do that or you can request the senior surgeon, Dr Thurlwell.'

'That butcher!' Ben exploded. 'Don't you let him near Mr Glasson.'

The doctor grinned. 'I'm Nathan Stein. I'll take care of him.'

On the way home in a cab through the dark streets, Ben grew certain that his house had been robbed, but he wasn't too concerned about his own private 'bank'. No one in the world knew about that, and thieves would have to be very lucky to find it. He had removed the floorboards under his bed and placed down there a small safe which contained most of Captain Jack's haul, replacing the boards and covering them with lino.

But the house was intact, except for the bloodied carpet runner in the hall and the overturned coat rack which Barnaby must have grabbed at for support. Nothing was missing. Barnaby's papers, in neat piles, were still on the table.

Ben walked about surveying the scene. The only lamp that had been lit in the house was well inside in the dining room. The thieves must have thought that no one was home, since, from outside, the house seemed to be in darkness. And they could have gained entry easily. The back door and all the windows were open. Since nothing had been stolen, poor old Barnaby must have put up a fight and they'd decided to quit. It must have taken a couple of the bastards to make such a mess of him.

Ben wandered into his mother's room. It was still the same, with the iron bed and the pristine white lace bedspread and the pretty white pillows. Oma had kept all the spare bed linen in the big dresser, and Ben's winter clothes were hanging in the wardrobe. Diamond's box, he noticed, was still under the bed, untouched. Several times he'd thought he ought to go through that box and do something about the contents, but like Oma, he'd felt that was all he had left of his mother, so he'd left it untouched. As a kid he'd peeked in, turning over bits and pieces, but had found nothing interesting except a sharp sheathed knife, which he'd considered pinching but had thought better of it.

Ben smiled. Had he taken that, he might really have met the hard end of the leather strap.

He sat on the bed, thinking of his dear mother who had loved him so much. He wondered again what she would think of his plan to marry Phoebe, and there in her room, he had the uncomfortable feeling that she was disapproving.

'Why not?' he asked her. 'It's not payback any more. I love Phoebe. You would love her too. You knew her, Diamond.'

The stony silence in her room chilled him. Had there been someone to argue with he'd have felt better. He thought about Barnaby again. Why had he been beaten up at the front door? Was it usual for thieves to calmly walk in through the front door? He remembered Diamond's routine when he'd asked her questions. Think about it, she'd say, and come back and tell me. It was the tribal way of teaching, she'd explained. Go and look and learn.

He took another tour of the house. Barnaby had been battered to the floor. The thieves needn't have run. Bottles of liquor were on the sideboard in the dining room. A saucer on the ledge held a pile of small change that Ben often emptied from his pockets. Several ornaments on the shelves were silver, real silver, worth quite a bit, Oma's possessions.

Ben had never taken stock of his household before. The ornate carriage clock on the mantelpiece, the silver picture frames, and Diamond's favourite treasure, a gold nugget, shaped like a jagged star, still sitting on its velvet base under its glass case. They'd been there for so long, Ben had taken them for granted. The damn house was full of dear little treasures the two women had accumulated that were probably worth a packet. What crook would pass them by? Christ! In jail they'd steal a flea-ridden blanket if you weren't watching.

What sort of thieves were these?

He went back into Diamond's room and stared at a sketch done of his mother by a street artist, working in crayon, that they'd lovingly placed in a silver frame.

'Thieves?' he asked Diamond. 'Robbers?'

He'd lived with thieves for four years. The coldness of the room had become an atmosphere of suspicion, of danger, and Ben recognized it. Barnaby wasn't the intended victim at all. Ben was! Barnaby had taken a beating intended for him. And who would want to do that?

Ben Beckman went outside to stand and stare at the mansion next door. It was in darkness now, gloomy and forbidding, an impregnable monolith, safe from childish thoughts of sticks and stones. He remembered Diamond's death and those harsh years he'd spent in prison, and was glad now that she hadn't known about that. It had been bad enough for Oma. Diamond would have suffered even more than he had.

'By Jesus!' he said softly. 'There'll be payback for this.'

The only person who would have sent a thug to do him over had to be Phoebe's father. A man who lacked the courage to face him and who had sent someone else to do his dirty work. At that moment Ben hated that family, and uneasily felt a shift in his emotions towards Phoebe. Did he really love her, or was it just a fantasy?

That was the question the kind old priest had put to him, recognizing the social differences between the couple. And Ben had vehemently declared his love in the presence of Alice and Rod Callaghan.

Ben had liked the priest, as Rod had said he would, because he was so easy to talk to. He hadn't approved or disapproved, just encouraged Ben to talk it out and warned him that he would be taking the girl down a hard road. But none of them knew that Ben's first interest in Phoebe had welled from a savage instinct to exact revenge on her family.

'Think it over very carefully,' the priest had said to him.

'That I will,' Ben said now, but his voice was hard and uncompromising. 'This time they won't beat me, I'll marry her as soon as possible.'

Needing something to do, he returned to the house, rolled up the bloodied carpet and threw it out into the yard, intending to buy another. Then he took a bucket of soapy water and a scrubbing brush and cleaned the blood from the floor and walls of the hallway. Standing by the open front door to allow the night breeze to flow inside, he remembered the first time Phoebe had climbed the fence to save him from the snake, and his heart softened. She'd been so sweet. She still was.

And thinking of her father, his enemy, he said to himself, 'I've got a serpent at the gate now, not out there on the cliffs. But by God, so have they! I'm not a helpless kid any more, Dr Thurlwell, and you'll get more than your windows broken this time.'

He took a bath, found clean clothes and pocketed a wallet of cash to pay for Barnaby's treatment, not knowing what hospitals charged. He woke the driver who was still waiting outside in his cab. 'This'll cost you, mate,' the driver complained.

'You'll get paid,' Ben snapped.

William was early to his rooms the next morning to slip a few quid to Punchy, who told him gravely: 'That bloke won't be botherin' your little girl again, sir, I gave 'im a message he won't forget in a hurry.'

'You're a good friend,' William replied solemnly, 'but don't forget, this is our secret. I wouldn't want to get you into trouble.'

'Ain't no trouble,' Punchy said happily. 'He was a pushover. None of them Abos know how to fight, he went down like a sack.'

The 'Abo' he was referring to, Ben Beckman, was sitting anxiously by Barnaby's bed.

Barnaby was awake and looking even worse than he had last night, his face heavily bandaged and his eyes only slits in the purple bruising. He couldn't recall what had happened from the time he'd heard a knock and gone to answer the door, and was desperately trying to talk to Ben through a mouth heavily plugged to stop the bleeding.

'Don't try to talk,' Ben told him. 'You got beaten up by robbers but you must have fought them off, because they didn't get a chance to rob the house. You're a hero.'

It was easier for Barnaby to write his requests with paper and pencil, and Ben carried them out to the letter. He went to the Premier's residence, introduced himself to Mr Prosser and explained that Mr Glasson had been attacked by thieves.

'Bless me,' Prosser said, his foot still in plaster. 'We seem to be having a run of bad luck. Poor Mr Glasson! How frightful! Are you sure he'll be all right?'

'Yes. His only worry is that he wants to assure you he will be able to carry out the duties assigned to him. A few broken bones won't stop his mind working.'

'Stout fellow! Of course he's young. They heal quicker.'

'And he's very well thought of in Brisbane.' Ben added his own opinions. 'He told me he hopes to be a delegate to the next convention and he'll get plenty of support.'

'Is that so? I knew we were on the right track.'

'You chose well,' Ben said. 'All of my friends,' he lied, 'are in favour of federation, and we will be supporting his candidature financially.'

'That's excellent news.'

'I want to report this attack on Mr Glasson to the police,' Ben said, 'but I think a letter from you would carry more weight.'

Prosser looked at him keenly. 'I gather you are of Aborigine descent. Is that why you need my written complaint?'

'Yes, sir. I am of Aborigine descent and I make no apology for that. I have substantial business interests in Brisbane. Mr Glasson has always handled my business affairs and this is my chance to repay his confidence. But times haven't changed that much. A complaint from a man who is part Aborigine would not carry the weight of a letter from a gentleman like you.'

Theodore Prosser grinned. 'Smart fellow, I'll say that for you. What did you say your name was?'

'Ben Beckman.'

'German stock, eh? Father a German?'

'Yes, sir,' Ben lied again. 'A sea captain.' From now on he would give the white men what they wanted to hear. 'Went down with his ship on the Barrier Reef, but he saw to it that I was well educated.'

'Did he by God? I hope you appreciate it.'

Ben smiled as he pocketed the letter. Prosser had dashed off his outrage on expensive notepaper which bore the Queensland crest and the heading: 'Premier's residence'.

He took the letter to police headquarters at Roma Street. It was important to him to establish his own credentials, his own connections with people in high places now, to ward off any further trouble that the Thurlwells might instigate.

Impressed, the Superintendent of Police took charge of the matter. 'A guest in your house, Mr Beckman? I'm very sorry to hear about this. You can assure Mr Prosser and the Premier we will investigate this attack thoroughly.'

Although he was still worried about Barnaby, it was a great day for Ben to be treated with such respect by the police hierarchy. He had not offered any reason for the attack, apart from agreeing with the police that Barnaby could have disturbed thieves, because he wasn't ready yet to implicate Phoebe's family. They'd hear about it soon enough; let them worry then.

William certainly did worry. He was aghast at Punchy's mistake!

Having set the plan in place to give Beckman the punishment he deserved, he didn't say a word at home about Phoebe's involvement with the fellow. In fact that night he'd been feeling quite smug, considering he'd made a rather clever move. No one could point the finger at him.

Two days later, his evening was ruined by the newspaper account of a dastardly attack on the well-known young lawyer, Mr Barnaby Glasson. He took the paper and repaired to his study without mentioning that item to Lalla or Phoebe. He could always claim he hadn't noticed it.

He'd had no idea that Barnaby Glasson had taken up residence next door. He blamed Punchy for assaulting the wrong man and decided not to say anything to the gardener; it would only confuse the idiot and Lord knew what he'd do next.

But when he saw a policeman walking up the drive he nearly had a heart attack. How could they have tracked the assault back to him so quickly? Had Glasson recognized Punchy? Had Punchy talked? 'Oh my Lord!' he wailed. What could he do? Deny it, of course. Deny everything. Whatever had happened had nothing to do with him.

His knees were so wobbly that he was unable to lift himself from his chair when Lalla, looking very worried, brought the policeman into the study.

'This policeman,' she said to William, 'has some bad news that he says he must deliver to you personally.' She stood firmly, arms folded, making it clear that she intended to remain to hear this news.

'Perhaps you should sit down, Mrs Thurlwell,' the policeman suggested kindly, and waited as she did so.

He cleared his throat. 'It is my sad duty to inform you, sir, that your brother Mr Edgar Thurlwell did not survive the wreck of the *Locheil* which went down off the coast of New Zealand.'

'Oh good God!' Lalla cried. 'You almost frightened the life out of me. Of course he survived. He had to survive because he was not on board the ship. These sort of mistakes are unforgivable.'

William was so relieved he felt light-headed. 'My wife is right, Constable. Edgar Thurlwell disembarked in Sydney. We were very sorry to read about the loss of the *Locheil* but grateful that my brother had a lucky escape.'

'I'm afraid I have to disagree, sir. Mr Thurlwell did not disembark in Sydney, he continued on towards Auckland. The passenger list has been checked and rechecked.'

'And was his body recovered?' Lalla asked acidly.

'No, ma'am.'

'Well, there you are!'

'Very few bodies were recovered, ma'am. The ship went down too fast, and in the dead of night. I wish I could say this is wrong, but survivors have attested that Mr Thurlwell was aboard, and they include his manservant, a Mr Brody, and two officers who knew him quite well, having voyaged with him from Brisbane and on that fateful crossing of the Tasman.'

William was still trembling and shaking his head when the constable departed.

'It can't be right!' he wept. 'Edgar can't have drowned, my own dear brother!'

But Lalla was made of sterner stuff: 'Pull yourself together, William. I want to know what your *dear* brother was doing on that ship.'

'How can you be so cruel, Lalla?'

'Very easily, when I think of what has been happening lately, and what that woman said to me. I'm terribly afraid she could be right. What has Edgar been up to? That's what I want to know.'

'Maybe he is still in Sydney,' William said hopefully.

'And maybe he's not!' she snapped. 'And if he's not, then it's better for all of us that he's at the bottom of the sea. We can at least go into mourning while we try to discover what he's been up to, and the extent of his estate. As his next of kin you would naturally inherit. Has he left a will?'

'I don't know,' William sobbed. 'I have no idea.'

'Then send a messenger to his lawyer, advising him of Edgar's demise and asking him to call on you urgently. In the meantime we will naturally cancel all engagements, and I shall have to arrange a memorial service.'

She went to find Phoebe. 'We've had some dreadful news. Your Uncle Edgar was on board that ship *Locheil* that went down, and the police have just advised he was lost at sea.'

Phoebe burst into tears. 'Oh no! Poor Edgar, that's terrible!'

'Go and see to your father, he's most upset. And don't leave the house. We're in mourning and I shall have to find you some more suitable clothes. You only have that one black dress.'

Phoebe was surprised that her mother didn't seem to be too broken-hearted, but then she supposed someone had to take charge at times like this. Poor Edgar. The last time she'd seen him he'd given her that little gold nugget, not knowing it was his farewell gift.

Edgar had left no will, and diligent as he was, the lawyer could not unravel his former client's affairs, since they were too closely involved with the Western Railroad Company. In desperation he called in an accountant recommended by the stock exchange. Within weeks it was evident that Edgar had absconded knowing that the Western Railroad Company could not survive an overwhelming accumulation of debts.

The two men were shocked to discover that Thurlwell had been siphoning off money under the guise of the New South Wales Steelworks. Other cheques had been signed by Dr Thurlwell, which meant that he was also implicated in this deceit.

Hurried meetings were held at the stock exchange to try to stave off the collapse of the company because of the adverse effect it would have on other shares, but the situation was hopeless.

'In my opinion,' the accountant said, 'Dr Thurlwell was just a pawn in this. Apparently his brother took out a mortgage on the Doctor's house as well, possibly in an attempt to balance the books somewhat, but on finding that money wouldn't help, he simply pocketed the cash along with other monies and left the country.'

'Legally, though,' the lawyer pointed out, 'the Doctor is still accountable.'

It was Buck Henry, President of the Turf Club and a leading stockbroker, who spoke up. 'William is an old friend of mine. He might be a ditherer, but he's not dishonest. He has suffered losses even greater than most shareholders, including the death of his brother. William, sadly, had great faith in Edgar. We have to keep this scandal down to a minimum. It will serve no purpose to hound William except to give the newspapers an excuse to drag the story on and on. In which case we'll all face loss of confidence in investments.'

'What do we do then,' someone asked.

'We simply issue a statement that due to a proliferation of debts that company has had to be wound up.'

'The papers will call it a crash,' a voice growled.

'Yes, they will,' Buck agreed. 'That can't be helped. Bankruptcy proceedings must follow and that will take time, time for the scandal to become old news. But I doubt the company has enough assets to pay investors a penny.'

'I bought a thousand shares in the company myself,' Edgar's lawyer complained.

'So did I,' Buck told him calmly. 'It was a grand plan but it just did not succeed, so let's make an end to it.'

Finally it was left to Buck Henry to break the news to William and Lalla that not only was the company bankrupt, but as far as he could make out, they were too.

'I would suggest that you sell the house to dispose of that unfortunate mortgage,' he told them.

Lalla was furious. She didn't care that Buck Henry was witness to her rage. 'You fool,' she shouted at William. 'You bloody fool! You signed for a mortgage on this house and we didn't see a penny of it. Your scoundrel of a brother took the lot! How could you be so stupid?'

'We'll just have to sell,' William said. He was so shocked he could hardly comprehend any of this. 'Would you like a drink, Buck?'

'No thanks, William. I have to be on my way. But if there's anything I can do, you know you only have to ask.'

It had been an embarrassing scene and he was glad to escape.

As soon as he left, Lalla turned on William again. 'We will not sell Somerset! Never!'

'What else can we do?' he said, sunk in gloom.

'We'll repay the mortgage, and the bank. You'll have to start taking more patients, you've been doing precious little the last few years. Time you got back to work. And I'll sell my jewellery. That's a start. We've got plenty of wealthy friends, we'll simply have to borrow from them to stay on our feet.'

'I wish you hadn't spoken to me like that in front of Buck,' he said miserably. 'It was very bad form.'

'Bad form!' she shouted. 'It is your duty to look after your family, and look what you've done! You've ruined us!'

William had had enough of her. 'I'm not the only one to fail in my duty. I expect a mother to look after her daughter, to see that she is guided into society, to see that she makes a suitable marriage. But not you, you're too busy with your own social accomplishments.'

'What rot are you talking now?'

'I'm talking about Phoebe. I had to hear the gossip at the hospital! That she's planning to marry that wretch next door. The son of that black woman. Don't talk to me about duty, you obviously haven't been able to instil it in our daughter.'

Lalla tore out of the room to stand at the bottom of the stairs, screaming for Phoebe to come down.

Biddy rushed into the safety of the kitchen.

'What now?' the cook asked.

'God knows,' Biddy replied nervously. 'There's terrible things going on in this house.'

Phoebe was in a very nervous state. Her mother had harangued her for hours, it had seemed, about her 'filthy' association with Ben, and at the same time had informed her in no uncertain terms that her uncle was a thief and a rogue and the family was bankrupt. Ruined!

She'd approached her father gently, hoping not to upset him any further by trying to explain, but it was a terrifying experience to find him in tears. He was drinking heavily and seemed not to care about anything any more.

In desperation she'd sent Biddy next door with a note for Barnaby, asking him to call on her as soon as possible.

Biddy, instead, had spoken to Ben and returned to tell Phoebe that

Barnaby was in hospital, having been attacked by an intruder right there in the house. 'Mr Beckman's very angry about it,' she'd said.

'You are not going anywhere,' Lalla told her. 'We're in mourning and that is the best possible excuse to keep the scandal at a distance. You've seen the newspapers relishing the crash of the Railroad Company. Do you want to be run down by reporters? For once in your life, try to do something right.'

Phoebe was so overcome by all this disaster that she obeyed her mother and stayed in the house. Not knowing what to expect, she was too frightened to go out, even to try and see Barnaby. Or Ben. They would have read in the papers about Edgar's death and the failure of the company, the insinuations of fraud! She was so shamed she wasn't even ready to face her two best friends.

Her parents were constantly arguing. Even over the memorial service for Edgar. Lalla flatly refused to make the arrangements and warned William that even if one were held she would refuse to attend, and so would Phoebe. Not that she had any say, Phoebe thought. It was all too awful. And then when a gentleman came to the door to assess the value of her mother's jewellery, Phoebe felt so sorry for Lalla, knowing how much she loved her beautiful gems, that she brought down the gold nugget and added it to the collection on the table.

'Where did you get that?' Lalla asked.

'Uncle Edgar gave it to me.'

'Good! We'll sell that too.'

In the face of all this confusion Phoebe seemed to be losing touch with reality. Nothing was as it should be. Nothing at all. Confined to the house, she walked about in a daze. Edgar dead! This was the closest she had ever come to death, and the suddenness shocked her, as did his terrible fate. She tried to push the picture of the drowning man from her mind, but in her dreams she thought she heard him screaming. And no one seemed to care now. There was hatred of the dead man in this house instead of mourning. No one sent condolences.

She hadn't heard from Ben, not even a note of sympathy, and the fact that Barnaby was in hospital seemed to her just another unreal affliction to add to the plagues presently besetting her family.

The newspapers were vicious in their condemnation of the Thurlwells. Angry creditors came to the gate, hammering and shouting, but were refused entry. Letters requesting Lalla's resignation from committees replaced invitations, and whenever the new telephone rang it was left to Biddy to ward off the inevitable abuse.

Overwhelmed by the disgrace heaped on them, Phoebe became silent and withdrawn, wandering aimlessly about, not wishing to be the cause of any more concern to her parents, who had enough to deal with. When she heard that her father's services were no longer required at the hospital and he had been asked to vacate his rooms on the Terrace, she hardly registered that information. Even when Lalla complained bitterly that their last source of income was gone.

'We'll have to get rid of the servants,' William said.

'Certainly not,' Lalla retorted. 'I can't run a house this size without servants. You find the money! Borrow it! I refuse to be humiliated any further.'

It was Biddy who told the Doctor that Phoebe wasn't well. 'She's not with us, sir. And she's cryin' in a funny way. Tears runnin' down her face and her doin' nothin' about it. She just sits starin' for hours.'

So the Doctor gave his daughter sedatives which Biddy thought made her dopier, though it wasn't for her to say.

And then one day Belle Foster came to call.

'Times like this you find your friends,' Phoebe heard her say to Lalla, in her booming voice. 'I've heard all about it and I'm glad to see you're not hanging your head. Chin up, I say. Boom and crash, that's what money's all about.'

The two women were closeted in the parlour for a long time, and then they sent for Phoebe.

'Mrs Foster has been very kind,' Lalla said. 'She has decided to go out to visit Clara at the station, and we think it would be best at this time if you accompanied her.'

Phoebe looked at her mother suspiciously, trying to focus on Lalla's sudden change of tone, but she was so nervy she had no fight left in her. In fact she welcomed the opportunity to escape.

'It's a long journey. I would appreciate your company,' Mrs Foster said. 'And a holiday in the country will do you good.'

'Thank you,' she replied, her voice hollow. The way she felt these days, she wished she could stay out there with Clara forever. The house had become a lonely place, and Brisbane, she already knew, was no longer her happy home town, what with all the horrible things people were writing in the paper about her family. They had become social outcasts.

Ben could at least have sent her a note of comfort by this, but there wasn't a word from him either. Maybe he, too, was one of those fair-weather friends Mrs Foster spoke about. In her shattered state it occurred to Phoebe that Ben had thought he was marrying money, and now that they were bankrupt he would start looking elsewhere for a wife. These things were not unheard of. That night she cried herself to sleep, not even sure what, specifically, she was crying about. She felt more in tune with her father than anyone else. She simply couldn't handle all this, she didn't want to have to care about anything.

* * *

Young Mr Glasson was quite a celebrity in the hospital. The police came to interview him, accepting his written replies with great respect. The wife of the Attorney-General came to visit, and even the Premier's secretary, a dour gent, arrived bearing best wishes from the great man himself.

Several of the apprentice nurses managed to find opportunities to call in on him to make sure he was comfortable, and a Miss Kathleen O'Neill and her friends made the best of visiting hours to try to cheer him up. And then there was the tall and handsome Mr Beckman, who came at all hours, ignoring the rules, without a whit of complaint from Matron who was usually very strict.

Although Ben's appearances at the hospital created interest among the staff, he was, in fact, busy carrying out Barnaby's instructions, searching for a suitable legal office so that his friend could begin in private practice as soon as he recovered. Ben suggested that Barnaby might not want to return to his house, but Barnaby was adamant that he would not be frightened off.

He was a little hurt that he hadn't heard from Phoebe, but Ben explained that the family had their own troubles, and brought in a few back copies of newspapers for Barnaby to read.

Barnaby was shocked at the tragedy and trouble that had struck the Thurlwells, and asked Ben if he'd seen Phoebe.

'No,' Ben replied, and left it at that.

He had considered slipping a note to her through Biddy, whom he often saw walking up the street, but decided against it. How could he write and commiserate with her when he wasn't sorry at all? It was the best spot of reading he'd done in years. How the mighty doth fall! He was only sorry he'd had no part in it. The story was the talk of the town. He'd even heard that they'd be selling the house and moving out. Jubilation upon jubilation! What a relief to be rid of them. And poetic justice for Dr Thurlwell for sending an attacker into his home.

The police had visited the house, and had talked again to Barnaby, who could recall only that a man, a big fellow, had shoved inside and attacked him.

'Definitely a knuckle job,' the police sergeant told Ben. 'No weapons used on your mate there. Just bare fists, going by the injuries, but there are plenty of bruisers like that about Brisbane. He'll be hard to find, but we'll keep on it.'

At last Barnaby received a letter from Phoebe, who was upset to hear he'd been hurt but was unable to visit because of problems at home. She also asked him to tell Ben that she was going out to Clara Buchanan's station with Mrs Foster for a little while.

That was the best they could make of the long, rambling pages, so unlike Phoebe's usual clipped notes that neither of them could take much comfort.

'Poor Phoebe,' Barnaby managed to mumble. 'It must be terrible for her. A break will do her good.'

'I suppose so,' Ben said, but he was hurt. Why had she chosen to write to Barnaby? Surely she could have slipped in to see him by this? Or sent him a note.

Then his conscience began to bother him. Had he gone too far? So pleased to see her parents getting their comeuppance that he hadn't considered her feelings? On the other hand, he wasn't exactly on the other side of town. She was obviously too self-absorbed to give him a thought.

For the rest of the day he worried, wondering what to do for the best, hoping that when he returned home he'd find some message from her. But there was nothing.

'That does it!' he said to himself. 'It's stupid to hang about like this. I'll have to go in there and talk to her. Even if it does cause ructions.'

Somerset House was well lit but quiet, and he couldn't help admiring the mansion as he walked up the drive. He mounted the steps to the front porch, feeling confident, wishing he'd made this move months ago. It had been foolish to keep their meetings secret for so long. He should have come to her door before this, like any gentleman caller.

Biddy opened the door, understandably surprised to see him.

'Good evening, Biddy,' he said quietly. Firmly. 'I'd like to see Miss Phoebe.'

'She's gone, Mr Beckman. Gone to the country.'

'Already?'

'Yes, sir, they left this morning.'

Ben's confidence slid away. Once again he felt intimidated by the splendour of that entrance hall behind the maid, and the glittering chandelier he remembered so well.

'Fairmont Station, via Charleville,' Biddy whispered to him.

'Thank you,' he said, retreating.

He retraced his steps to the gate, walking stiffly, feeling that eyes were on him from those windows, laughing at him. She'd gone, without a word. And here he was, making it obvious to them that she hadn't bothered to inform him!

Ben was so angry he resolved to write to Phoebe demanding an explanation, but by the time he put pen to paper he had relented.

'Give the girl a chance,' he told himself. 'She's been through a lot.' And of course, he had to admit, he loved her too much to address her like that.

His letter was gentle, wishing her well, telling her not to forget to write to him, and simply signed: 'Always, Ben.' He smiled as he sealed the letter. If he wrote how he really felt it would take pages. He was already missing her.

If not exactly heaven, Fairmont Station, to Phoebe, was close enough. All the space in the world to move about, with her cares left firmly behind her. She needed this chance to feel free again, released from the sombre walls of her own home, and the opportunity not to think. Not to have to face problems of any sort. Before they left Brisbane she had become so listless and out of focus, unable to concentrate on anything that was said to her, that she knew her presence was upsetting her father even more.

She'd heard him remonstrating with Lalla, demanding that she leave 'the girl' alone and stop taking out her frustrations on her daughter.

'Can't you see,' Phoebe had heard him say, 'that the girl is close to a nervous breakdown?'

'If anyone is to have a breakdown around here it's me!' Lalla had retaliated. 'You take the cure in your whisky! I have to attend to everything. She's always been a pig-headed little wretch, and taking up with that blackfellow is typical of her atrocious behaviour. She didn't even have the grace to deny it! The sooner she's out of here the better.'

Phoebe wondered what a nervous breakdown was. She'd heard the words often enough but had never actually seen anyone suffering from that ailment, so she asked Biddy.

'I'm not sure, me darlin',' Biddy replied. 'I think it's when people are just plain tired out.'

Is that all? Phoebe had pondered. In which case Father's right. I'm just plain tired of everything, even of worrying about Ben.

When they arrived at the cattle station, Ben Buchanan was civil, taking charge of their luggage, and Clara was so excited she couldn't stop talking.

'Mother, I'm so pleased you've come to visit at last. Isn't it marvellous the drought's over? The rainy season is still with us, but I'm sure you won't mind a bit of wet weather. Everything's springing up green again! And Phoebe!' She threw her arms about her friend. 'How wonderful that you could come too. We'll have such fun. We won't have to ride on busy town roads out here. But you're looking so thin and pale!'

Phoebe saw Belle turn a warning frown on Clara, who didn't seem to notice. 'Never mind. We'll fatten you up. And I've got a horse for you, you'll love her. The smartest little filly. Her name's Cleo.'

'Clara! It's damp out here,' Belle interrupted. 'Could we please go in?'

'Yes, yes, of course!'

Two Aborigine girls in cotton shifts stood shyly at the end of the veranda, watching as the visitors were ushered into the house.

Phoebe remembered someone saying that Ben Buchanan had chosen this property because the homestead was so spacious, and she had to agree. It was a very large house and most attractive, painted white with a red roof. The country-style verandas softened it, creating such a restful atmosphere that Phoebe wondered why she suddenly felt so emotional, almost close to tears. Relief, she supposed, at finding refuge out here, miles from anywhere.

Belle insisted on making straight for a parlour where she could put her feet up. Her ankles had swelled from sitting in the train for almost twenty-four hours, so without a qualm she removed her shoes and stockings and called for her slippers.

While the Aborigine maids were attending to her mother, Clara took Phoebe on a tour of the house, showing her the reception rooms, formal and informal dining rooms, her sitting room and Ben's study, and the wings that housed the bedrooms. The house had been built around a central courtyard which looked rather strange. Tables and chairs were arranged out there under an ugly roofing of chicken wire.

'That was covered in wisteria,' Clara said, 'and it was just beautiful, but we couldn't spare the water during the drought, so it died off. We had to cut it all back. But it's beginning to grow again.'

Phoebe's room was very pleasant, with a large double bed covered in a light patchwork quilt, but after traipsing about after Clara, nodding and nodding, she felt confused again. Open french doors looked out on to the veranda, and beyond that a line of trees, and from there a great silence of country, a vast expanse of nothingness, it seemed to her. Much as she liked Clara, she wished she would go away and leave her alone.

'Are you feeling all right?' Clara asked her anxiously.

'Yes, thank you. I'm fine,' Phoebe replied, and to her shame, found she was crying.

'I'm sorry,' she said, fishing for her handkerchief. 'I'm sorry, Clara. I'll be all right in a minute.'

But Clara put her arms about her 'Oh Phoebe,' she said. 'What have they done to you? Don't apologize. Cry! Cry it all out. Don't bottle things up. I know, I'm good at it.'

Phoebe was put to bed. She barely touched the chicken broth Clara brought up to her, or the apple pie and cream that she'd hoped might tempt her, so Clara gave her a very small dose of the sleeping draught Dr Thurlwell had prescribed and sat with her until she was sleeping soundly.

Her mother and Ben had finished their dinner when Clara came in to join them for coffee.

'What's wrong with Phoebe?' she asked Belle. 'She's in a terrible state. She's not the same person any more.'

'I know,' Belle said. 'It's been like transporting a deaf-mute bringing her along with me, but I explained to people that she's simply not well. I told them it's a great pity – we met several very eligible young gentlemen *en route* – they're not seeing her at her best. Phoebe really has a quite exhilarating personality.'

'I've never noticed,' Ben said. 'She always seemed to me to be a fractious person. It's a relief to see her tamed a bit. She drives her mother mad, you know.'

'And vice versa, I wouldn't be surprised,' Clara snapped.

'You never understood Lalla,' Belle said to Clara. 'You never tried. She's a very strong woman and that's no sin. I'm impressed at the way she is holding up against all her present travails. Not many women would have the guts to sell off their jewellery within days of having the roof fall in. She did that, you know.'

'With what choice?' Ben said bitterly. 'That family has cost me a fortune. I've lost a heap on that bloody railroad. Word has it we'll be lucky to get two and six in the pound on our investment.'

'Word is wrong,' Belle said. 'You'll get nothing. It's pretty clear that Edgar took off with all available funds when he saw the writing on the wall. The government refused to grant the railroad land. The company was already deep in debt and that was the final blow. No collateral.'

'In other words, the Premier caused this crash,' Ben said.

'Not necessarily,' his mother-in-law replied calmly. 'Edgar was a carpetbagger. He came to town with a grand plan and used the anti-federalists, like us, to bolster support. Give him his due, he was a great talker.'

'He was a bastard, Belle, and you know it.'

'None of us knew that at the time,' she retaliated.

'Drowning was too bloody good for him!'

'A lot of people would agree with you,' she said. 'Including Lalla. He's ruined them too.'

'I didn't know that,' Clara said. 'I thought selling the jewellery was to pay off Edgar's debts.'

'Oh no,' Belle told her. 'Edgar busted them right well too.'

'When Parliament reopens I'll give that bloody Premier hell,' Ben said, 'and I'll have all those investors at the back of me. He won't get away with this.'

'That's as may be,' Belle said. 'How much did you lose in the crash?'

'Plenty, thanks to the insidious operations of the Thurlwells. I don't believe William and Lalla are broke at all. They were as thick as thieves with Edgar. Lalla's an actress of the first water. I'll bet selling off the jewellery was a front. I read in the papers that there's a huge amount of money missing. Don't tell me they're not well covered. If you believe they're broke, Belle, you're a lot more naive than I thought you were.'

Belle picked up her glass and swallowed a gulp of port. It was not often that Ben saw his mother-in-law thrown off balance.

'It's possible,' she admitted.

'For God's sake, Belle! Edgar and William were directors of the company, and Lalla knew every move. Directors of companies like that know when to jump. They don't give a damn about their investors, they take the money and run.'

'I did meet a Mrs Downs who claimed they prised ten thousand out of her and she never even saw a share certificate,' Belle conceded. 'She claims Lalla knew about it all along.'

'The poor woman,' Ben said. 'And I suppose you didn't believe her?'

'Why would I? It seemed too outlandish. The Thurlwells have always been wealthy. The house alone – and its position, of course – are fair comment, not to mention the contents. Lalla never skimped. Why would they want to do this Downs woman out of a few thousand?'

'For a damn good reason,' Ben said bitterly. 'They knew they were going down the drain and didn't even have the decency to warn their friends.'

'That's a bit harsh, Ben,' Clara said. 'Maybe they didn't realize until it was too late.'

'Then tell me why there is so much money missing? And why the directors, our dear friends, started paying themselves outrageous fees?'

'Oh well, what's done is done,' Belle said.

Ben dumped his napkin on the table and stood up. 'Oh no it's not. They've left me in a financial mess. Now that the drought has broken I'm selling this property, it's saleable now. I've been carrying it too long.'

'There's no need to sell now,' Clara said. 'This is our home. I don't want to sell. We're restocking the herds. Everything will be all right now.'

'Until next time! Did you tell your mother how you actually bought fodder and had it delivered out here? More expense for me!'

'It saved some breeders,' she fired back. 'You'd have let them die.'

Belle intervened. 'I didn't come out here to listen to arguments. We've time enough to sort that out. I'm going to bed. Clara, ask the girl to bring me some hot milk with a dash of rum. It makes me sleep better.'

In the quiet of her bedroom, sipping her drink, Belle wondered just how much Ben had lost in the Railroad Company crash. By the sound of things, she guessed, a lot more than he was prepared to admit. In which case, if he needed money, this would be a good time to sell. They still had the house in town. And besides, she was getting too old to be traipsing all the way out here. In a few more years it would be beyond her. She grinned. 'You've become too reliant on home comforts, you old fool.'

It would be good to have them living in town. A person needed family about when one was getting on.

Clara didn't rush Phoebe. She let her rest and wander about the homestead as she wished. Phoebe didn't even remember the horse, so Clara made no mention of riding, waiting for her to ask.

'I'm glad you're here,' she said to her mother. 'I'm busy about the station and won't be in much during the day. It's a relief to have you here to keep her company. She doesn't seem to be interested in anything. I don't know what to do for the best.'

'In the first place,' Belle said, 'throw out that medicine her father prescribed. I don't believe in that muck. It makes people so numb they don't know what they're doing. Tell her it's all gone. She's a perfectly healthy girl, she'll pull herself together soon enough. It's not just Edgar's death and all that financial scandal, you know, there's another problem. Her mother told me she's got herself entangled with a very unsavoury character, even to talking marriage.'

'Oh no! Who?'

'A half-breed called Beckman. Apparently he's a thoroughly bad lot.'

'Ben Beckman?' Clara was amazed. 'From the livery stables?'

'I don't know where he comes from.'

'But . . .' Clara stuttered. 'I know him. We both know him! Phoebe never said anything to me.'

'Obviously! She has good reason to keep him quiet.'

'He's really quite a nice chap, Mother, but I find it difficult to believe there's anything between them.'

'You'd better believe it because it's true. Phoebe hasn't denied it. And if she mentions him to you, discourage her, for God's sake.'

Clara was nonplussed. 'I had no idea!'

'Now you do, and that's the reason why her mother wanted her out of town. She has to stay here until she comes to her senses. We have to watch the mail. She is not to receive any letters from him, nor is she permitted to write to him. Out of sight, out of mind.'

'How can we do that? It doesn't seem right.'

'It's for the best. I promised Lalla, so don't go making a fuss, Clara. We have a duty here.'

Barnaby might have known it was all too good to be true. He had set up his office and found a law clerk, Timothy Bedlow, to assist him, but there was still no word from the Premier.

The lease on his two-room office had been drawn up and Barnaby had paid the first two months' rent, but the promised assistance hadn't materialized.

'Words are cheap,' he said to Tim, wondering how long he could survive in this shaky venture.

'Write to him,' Tim advised.

'I don't like to do that. It sounds like begging.'

'Just make it a gentle reminder, nothing specific.'

'I suppose I could do that. I don't want his staff knowing my business, which would mean that all the rest of the people I used to work with would know too.'

So he did write, simply mentioning that he had enjoyed their discussions and was looking forward to hearing from the Premier.

While they waited for a reply and watched the door for clients, Timothy resumed his studies, not displeased that Barnaby had plenty of time to assist him. Eventually, one fine afternoon, Barnaby went out for a walk. But once away from the office he decided to take a cab and visit Kathleen O'Neill, on the off-chance that she might be home.

She was. And she was delighted to see him, a cheerful note at this depressing stage of his career.

Kathleen invited him in and insisted he stay for tea. She was impressed that he had opened his own legal practice and even had a clerk working for him.

'I'm so proud of you,' she said. 'There'll be no stopping you now.'

He wasn't so sure about that, but he returned to the office in a much better mood, having arranged to meet Kathleen for lunch in the park the following Sunday.

'I think you're in love,' Timothy grinned. He had heard how the afternoon had turned out.

Barnaby sighed. 'I wonder if it is possible to refrain from falling in love until one knows if the feelings are reciprocated?'

'In a perfect world,' Timothy said.

'We'll see,' Barnaby reflected. His love for Phoebe had caused him too much heartache. He couldn't go through that again. Kathleen, with her dark good looks, was a very desirable woman, but by no means flirtatious, accepting him as a friend. He'd had enough of being the best friend. He really was quite fond of her, but if she ever started to tell him about a boyfriend or any of her beaux, he'd disappear from the scene!

A few days later a solemn young man with a drooping moustache called on Barnaby at the request of the Premier.

'My name is Jeremy Hobson,' he informed Barnaby, looking down his nose at Barnaby's still bruised face as if the young lawyer had been involved in a street brawl. 'Sir Samuel has authorized me to see to a year's rent on these premises.'

Barnaby was so relieved he could have shouted with joy. Instead he nodded sedately. 'That was our agreement.'

'Very well. The name of your landlord? I shall attend to it.'

That suggestion didn't sit too well with Barnaby, who regarded it as somewhat of a slight, as if he might abscond with the precious rent money, but he deemed it wiser to agree.

His duty done, Hobson turned to leave.

'Just a minute,' Barnaby said. 'There's the matter of my campaign expenses. I was to open a trust account.'

'Ah yes.' Hobson flicked out his card. 'This is a party matter. I shall operate the trust account. If you do have any such expenses, Glasson, send me a detailed and witnessed account. And keep in mind that extravagances will not be tolerated.'

When he left, Barnaby laughed. 'Pompous little ass! Half a slice is better than none. At least the rent's paid Timothy, my good fellow. What say we shut up shop and retire to yon tavern?'

Legal work began to trickle in. Some wills, property settlements and disagreements. Some minor criminal cases. Disputed fines. They even took on some rather foolish libel cases, back-fence arguments, so keen were they to build up the practice. And even though Barnaby was still losing money, he had Timothy to bolster his ego. He was a good lawyer, and given luck and chance, he could succeed.

'We'll get there. Give it time,' Timothy told him. 'One day I hope you'll let me put my name out there with yours.'

Barnaby was still living at Kangaroo Point, and there hadn't been any more problems with intruders. The police hadn't been able to locate his assailant, and as far as Barnaby could make out, it had just been a failed robbery. But Ben was still touchy about it.

'I wish you'd stop brooding,' Barnaby said. 'I got beaten up, that's all. It isn't uncommon in Brisbane and it's not your fault. And you shouldn't have paid my hospital bills, they were my responsibility.'

'Forget it,' Ben replied. 'Is business picking up?'

'Slowly. But we're coming along.'

'That's good. My bank manager asked to see me today.'

'Oh God!' Barnaby shuddered. He had an innate fear of that breed of man.

'Nothing to worry about. It's the other extreme. The stables are doing fine and the saddlery's making money. I've got orders lined up for months. I knew if I got O'Neill's good tradesmen back I couldn't miss.'

'Half your luck.'

'Yes, well he says I've got money accumulating in the bank and it's time I began to invest.'

'He's right. Why don't you?'

'After what happened next door? I'm not keen on investments, letting other people lose my money.'

'Your mother did. She bought gold shares.'

'Yes. But she'd been there. She knew the goldfields and she had friends out there. To people like us it'd be hit and miss.'

'What about your motorcar?'

'Still a long way down the track. They seem to be inventing better ones all the time. I don't want to import one that will be superseded before it leaves the factory.'

Barnaby watched as he wandered restlessly about the house. 'For a man who has just been beamed on by a lordly banker,' he said, 'you're none too cheerful. What's the matter?'

'I'm bored. Rod Callaghan is doing such a good job as manager they'd hardly notice whether I'm there or not. And I'm worried about Phoebe.'

'She can't come to any harm out there, she's probably having a great time.'

'That's the trouble. I've written to her twice and she hasn't bothered to reply. It's been weeks. And it's my own fault! When I heard the Thurlwells had gone broke, I didn't care. You know the background. I hoped they'd end up in the poorhouse. I should have tried to contact Phoebe but I didn't. I couldn't face her and say I was sorry about all that.'

'It's understandable, but you shouldn't take it out on Phoebe.'

'I know. I did go in to see her eventually but she'd left for Fairmont Station without a word to me.'

'Not much you can do then, except wait for her to come home.'

'I'm thinking of going out there.'

'Uninvited?'

'What else can I do?'

Barnaby stared, suddenly remembering the woman in Charleville who'd told him the story about Buchanan and Diamond. 'But that's Buchanan's station,' he cried, startled.

'So what? I know you don't like him, but I'm not calling on him. I just want to see Phoebe. I won't want to stay.'

'I don't think it's a very good idea,' Barnaby said cautiously.

'Anything is better than staying here and worrying. I have to see her.'

'By the sound of things you've already made up your mind.'

Ben leaned against the mantelpiece, considering this. 'Yes, I suppose I have. I've sort of had it in mind for the last week or so. Been exercising one of the horses, a big chestnut called Rapper, to get him fit for a long ride.'

'Why don't you take the train?'

'I'd rather ride. It'll be more interesting and give me more freedom of movement. I might as well enjoy myself on the way in case she doesn't want to see me when I get there.'

Barnaby climbed out of bed at dawn to see Ben off. He certainly did have a fine horse, and the best of equipment, thanks to his expert saddlers.

'You ought to come with me,' he said to Barnaby. 'I can wait another day.'

'Don't tempt me,' Barnaby said, experiencing a twinge of envy at missing out on this adventure. 'I've got work to do. Or rather, I've got to find more work. And by the way, here's a name for you at Charleville.' He passed a slip of paper to Ben: 'This woman, Lottie Smith, is married to the proprietor of the Shamrock Hotel. You ought to talk to her.'

'Why?'

'Because she knows the Buchanans. She could be very helpful.'

'I'm only going to see Phoebe,' he said, 'not the whole territory.'

'Don't count on it,' Barnaby warned. 'I wouldn't be surprised, now that I've had time to think about it, if Phoebe hasn't been hustled away to drop you out of the picture. She could have told her parents about you.'

Ben strapped on a rifle. 'You're getting close, Mr Lawyer. Why do you think you got beaten up? Hasn't it occurred to you yet that it was a mistake? I'll see you in a couple of weeks.'

He swung on to his horse and cantered out through the open gate, past the Thurlwell house and down the road.

Barnaby stood stunned. Was that what had happened?

He wished Ben hadn't left so quickly. There was more he'd meant to say to him. He had been to Charleville, admittedly with not a lot of luck, but with credentials as a minor personage. Ben, with his swarthy looks, would be noticed as a coloured man in country towns where they were more aware, and more biased, than people in Brisbane. From generations of hit-and-run wars with blacks in the west the antipathy remained. On both sides. Barnaby prayed that Ben wouldn't take his white upbringing for granted out there in the bush where no treaty had ever been drawn up.

Chapter Ten

Was this the same place? Even though Ben had heard that the long-awaited rains had finally broken the drought, he was unprepared for the transformation that confronted him after he crossed the range. The dustbowl had been replaced by a greening of the vast landscape.

Where once dread had reigned, optimism now gleamed throughout the bush. Dormant seeds had struck and tangled grasses burst into life along the muddy road, carpeting the endless wild scrub. Gum trees, hardy survivors of the bad years, that had drooped in despair now lifted up shiny red-tipped leaves in delight. Even whitened dead trees, still standing, and the untidy beaten logs littered about, no longer invited pity. They seemed to be a necessary part of this miracle, as if the picture would be incomplete without them.

On this long and solitary ride Ben avoided the towns that he and Cash had visited. He had enough supplies not to have to bother with them; he wanted to make his own way without reminders of that last terrible journey. Travelling the same route, he tried not to think of Cash, blaming himself for being such a simpleton, eager for a friend, impressed that Cash had befriended him. He could still see Cash's cold eyes when he'd turned on him, ready to kill him. The shock remained, more than Cash's death. And it depressed him.

On past Dalby he stopped to assist a family whose heavily laden wagon was hopelessly bogged. Even the combined strength of two horses and two men hadn't been able to drag it out. Ben helped them unload, with a woman and several children waiting nearby, and then they dug the vehicle out of the mud, corrugating the road with saplings to assist it to firm ground. When the crisis was over, he stayed yarning with them for a while over a lunch of tea and damper, then rode on, feeling no need for company.

That afternoon he camped by a river, enjoying the riches of the formerly desolate land. Thousands of birds wheeled and settled in the scrub along the now swiftly flowing river. He watched flocks of budgerigars and lorikeets and corellas, all keeping with their own kind, and wondered about humans. Wondering if the birds ever cross-bred. Wondering about himself.

Gentle pink and grey galahs scratched in the bounty of grass seeds, mumbling contentedly, and he was cheered by them. Then a row started between two cockatoos and two crows, all of whom had decided to claim the one branch. The fight made him laugh. There were plenty of other spaces but no, this lot were determined. The white cockatoos, no longer prepared to be bullied by fat black crows who'd survived the drought easily by picking the eyes from dying stock, screeched like fishwives, flapping and pecking at the cunning crows who dived for footholds under their opponents' wings rather than match their strong beaks against this onslaught. In the end the crows gave up and flew away and the cockatoo pair settled, snuffling and preening in indignation.

Ben wished he knew more about the bush and its inhabitants. The eventual silence was seductive and to him overwhelming. This was his mother's land, her earth, and part of him, he realized. He belonged out here. Last time, he'd ridden out west simply bent on making money, on finding those wild horses, noticing nothing much but the desolation. 'Come to think of it,' he remarked to himself, 'Mandjala and Djumbati never complained about the drought, they seemed to take it for granted.'

The peaceful surrounds gave him room for contemplation. 'It's too simple to say I came out here as a white man,' he told himself, 'not able to appreciate the country. Whites love the land too. I came out as a townie, a man brought up in a town, with little knowledge of the bush. Now I'm just discovering there's more to life than making money.'

Diamond had done her best. Money, and keeping her head down, had been her rule, but unfortunately her son had been too young to learn the second part of that lesson. Running madly to that house and smashing windows was exactly the sort of behaviour Diamond would have forbidden, no matter what the provocation.

Night brought doubts that Diamond might not be too keen on his marriage plans either. In his first thoughts he'd imagined her as happy as he was, but now he wasn't too sure. Marrying a white girl, and a 'socialite' at that! In no way could such an idea be construed as keeping a low profile in Brisbane. But then . . . for all he knew, Phoebe could have changed her mind. He was tempted to turn back, to avoid the hurt of rejection.

In the morning, though, he was in a much better mood, the dawn chorus of birds lifting his spirits. He tramped into the bush to find his horse, which was quietly grazing in a patch of open country, and brought it back to the river, scaring off a couple of kangaroos that had also come down to drink.

When he set off again he decided to head for the blacks' camp near the Sailor's Drift goldfields, in the hope of finding his two Aborigine friends. It was, he knew, a delaying tactic, born of nervousness. He was afraid to hear from Phoebe that she had decided not to marry him. But he did want to see Mandjala and Djumbati, he kept telling himself.

Four days later he stocked up with rations at a general store cum grog shop on the busy track to the Drift, interested to hear that the gold was still holding out in various spots adjacent to the original diggings.

'Lookin' for gold?' the storekeeper asked him.

'No. I tried prospecting once, hardly found any colour at all.'

'Where you headed?'

'Just travelling. Fairmont Station eventually.'

The storekeeper watched as Ben strapped on the refilled saddle bags. 'That's a fine horse,' he said. 'And that saddle wouldn't come cheap. You watch out for outlaws, they're busy out this way.'

'So I've heard.'

Ben rode off with a grin. 'That'd be poetic justice!' he said to himself. But he adjusted the rifle at his knee, and moved his leg to feel the knife, Diamond's knife, strapped against his shin.

He had meant to by-pass the goldfields, but the countryside had changed yet again. The blacks' camp that he had known had disappeared, and in its place was a moonscape of mounds and hillocks right along the river bank, with not a tree or bush left standing. Tents and humpies were scattered among the familiar trappings of miners' claims, primitive racks and ladders and rushing sluices, while the inhabitants toiled for that elusive gold. Watching from a hilltop, he even had an urge to go down there and try again, to stake a claim one more time. The lure of gold was hard to resist. What if he got lucky and struck a reef?

'And what if you don't?' he muttered to himself. Prospecting could be exciting to start with, but it was hard work to be on the losing side. He decided not to ride down to the diggings, and instead travelled the extra miles round the perimeter until he came to a creek, obviously a tributary of the main river. Following that west, he eventually came across a family of blacks who were building fish traps in from the shallows.

This time the tribal people only gave him a glance and went on with their work.

Ben addressed them politely and asked if they knew Mandjala or Djumbati. 'They are friends of mine,' he said in English, and again in a dialect, but two of the men shook their heads, shrugged and then ignored him. He hung about for a while, smoked his pipe as their work proceeded, constructing a network of low fences like a miniature farm. But in the end, he gave up and left. They didn't need intruders.

As he rode a little further, seeking a campsite for the night, he saw a mob of brumbies, about twenty strong, galloping away in the distance and was pleased that they too had survived the drought. 'They're smart,' he said to his own horse. 'And the country is too big. There'll always be brumbies now, they've become part of the land.'

He remembered his mother telling him that when the Aborigines first saw men on horseback, having no knowledge of such an animal as a horse, they'd been petrified, thinking they'd seen a man with four legs. And he wondered if the fables that Oma had read to him from picture books had come from the same ancient folklore. He recalled a sketch of a man with the body of a horse but couldn't place the fable. His childhood seemed an eternity ago.

'Righto,' he told his partner, the horse, as he dismounted. 'We'll sleep here tonight and tomorrow we head west and I'll see if I can find the road to Fairmont Station. Someone will know. I'm a bit lost now, everything looks so different.'

And what then? he asked himself.

'Then I just ride up to the station. Mrs Buchanan knows me, she won't mind. And I'll ask to see Phoebe, and have a talk to her.'

He knew that the big stations always had accommodation for travellers in their outbuildings, and he'd be happy to doss down with their stockmen. It wasn't as if he were asking to be put up at the homestead. There was no worry about that. The reception he received from Phoebe, though, might be more awkward. But he wouldn't embarrass her, he just needed to talk to her. And to see her! God! How was it possible to love someone so much that even a glimpse of her would be sheer joy?

That night Ben Beckman slept soundly under the stars. He knew in his heart that she did love him and wondered if she would be waiting for him. Realizing that a letter might not get there in time, he'd sent her a telegram via Charleville, which would then be delivered by mail, to tell her that he was on his way. He hoped that plan had worked, although out here everything was so slow and off-hand, his telegram might still be sitting in Charleville. Not that it mattered. Within two days he'd be at the station.

What a joy this station was! Phoebe doubted if she could ever thank Clara enough for 'taking her in'. For giving her the chance to pull herself together.

It was difficult for Phoebe, even now, to remember the first week or so at the Fairmont homestead, she'd been in such a daze and upset at being parted from Ben. She knew she'd spent a lot of time on the veranda, which was covered in shady green creepers like a leafy grotto, trying to read but absorbing nothing. And she'd gone for walks with Belle, down to the lake and round all the outbuildings to be introduced to the stockmen, and the blacksmith and his wife, and several of the Aborigine workers, only to be embarrassed because she had promptly forgotten all their names. A social crime as far as Lalla was concerned.

Beyond all common sense, Phoebe had been so dismayed at her lack of manners that she'd dodged and hidden whenever any one of them came into sight. They must have thought she was mad.

And she probably was, Phoebe mused as she waited for Clara. Ridiculous to let a thing like that throw her, but there it was. She had been so concerned with making a good impression and not presenting herself to these people as the vague girl from Brisbane, that she'd made a right mess of it. And here she was still thinking of such a trivial matter when it was over. She knew all their names now.

And she loved her horse, Cleo. They'd become fast friends too. Riding out with Clara early in the morning, checking waterholes, mustering cattle, was all very tiring, but Phoebe was actually helping and was proud of herself. Even if it had taken two weeks for her to gain the courage to ride out of the home paddocks.

This afternoon they rode back along the shores of a wide lake that was gradually refilling, flocks of birds returning to settle again.

'I can't imagine the lake empty,' Phoebe said. 'It must have been terrible.'

'Yes, it depressed me every time I came by, just a big useless gap where water should have been, but it's looking good now.'

'And it's all so peaceful. I love it out here, Clara. It's so good of you to have me.'

She was grateful to Clara for taking her as she was. Belle had nearly driven her mad, or madder, she thought, by asking her, several times a day, how she was feeling.

Every day Phoebe had given the same answer: 'Very well, thank you,' but with a nervous mistrust of her own reply. It had been difficult for her to explain her confusion.

Clara hadn't asked. Hadn't enquired at all. Hadn't insisted, like Belle and Ben, that she ate her meals. That she played the piano for them when she couldn't find a familiar note with the music staring her in the face. That she played dominoes when she couldn't match a five with a five. A terrifying time when Phoebe, appalled at her lack of co-ordination, had felt as if she were somewhere above, watching herself being so stupid, watching as she made an idiot out of herself. Completely unable to tell this imposter who was impersonating her to sharpen up. To tell them that this was *not* her at all. A humiliating experience.

Not once had Clara asked how she was. Not once had she taken her arm to guide her to the bathroom as Belle did. Not once had she spoken to her in the patronizing way that her husband did.

Only Clara and the two maids, the black gins, old Ruby and little Sissy, had treated her with respect despite her stupidity. Phoebe liked Ruby; she was a grey-haired woman who'd been with Ben's family forever. Clara said she'd inherited her. Ruby had come south as Ben's housemaid when he'd sold the property in the far north and moved down here.

'A treasure,' Clara had told Phoebe. 'She speaks good English and a number of Aborigine dialects, as well as being a ferocious housekeeper. I used to be scared stiff of her. She was trained by Ben's mum, who apparently was one of those dogmatic old birds, even worse than Belle. Strict as anything around the homestead, you know, dress for dinner and all that. Thank God we're past that ridiculous formality now.' She turned to face Phoebe. 'Do you think I'm foolish to love this place so much?'

'The station? No. I think it's just marvellous. I'd love to live in the country.'

'Ben wants to sell. It's not just the drought, he prefers town. But I want to stay here.'

'I don't blame you. But what if there's another drought?'

'Droughts, floods. That's country life anywhere. We'll just have to save money so that we can handle these setbacks. It's unfortunate—' Clara cut short what she had intended to say, and finished lamely with: 'we were so unprepared.'

She couldn't say that if Ben hadn't invested so heavily in that Railroad Company they wouldn't be so short of cash. Nor could she mention having bought fodder for their stock with the assistance of the owner of the livery stables, Ben Beckman.

Then there was the matter of the letters. And a telegram which had arrived a few days ago, from that gentleman, advising Phoebe that he was coming to visit her. Clara felt guilty about that too. She had complained, again, to her husband and her mother, that it was terrible to intercept a guest's mail.

But Belle was firm. 'We're only carrying out Lalla's instructions, and, don't forget, the wishes of Phoebe's father. He is appalled! Blaming Lalla for allowing this to happen.'

'I still think it's wrong,' Clara said. 'Maybe he's not suitable as a husband in their eyes, but Phoebe should be allowed to make up her own mind.'

'Suitable!' Ben had been furious. 'That's the understatement of the year. The man's a half-caste and a jailbird! Isn't that enough? I won't have such a person on our property. I won't have her introducing a fellow like that into my home. He can get the hell out of it! He's not coming here.'

'There's no need to get so angry,' Clara said to him. 'I don't know why you're making such a fuss. If you hadn't interfered, he'd have received her letters and remained in Brisbane. Phoebe wouldn't invite anyone out here without telling us.'

'I think the whole affair is disgraceful,' Belle sniffed. 'The girl ought to be ashamed of herself. I agree with Ben, a lout like that is simply not welcome here.'

'There isn't much we can do about it now,' Clara said. 'If he does turn up we'll have to tell Phoebe. Anyway, she'll probably see him.'

As they stabled the horses Clara was apprehensive. She had a feeling that all this subterfuge could blow up in their faces. She desperately wanted to speak to Phoebe about this boyfriend of hers, but she didn't dare. Lalla and Belle had handled the whole thing so badly she wouldn't know where to start. How to explain that she'd been a party to withholding Phoebe's mail?

Fortunately, Phoebe was still thinking about Fairmont.

'Can't you insist on staying here?' she asked.

'I could, but it would mean a fight.'

'Then fight!' Phoebe said, with a sudden display of her old self. 'Don't let them push you around. I'm on your side.'

Clara was thoughtful as they made their way up to the house. Finally, she took Phoebe's arm. 'I will!' she said. 'I can fight them. I'm staying.'

'Good on you!' Phoebe laughed. It was about time Clara stood up to her husband. Phoebe wished he'd go back to town. She'd never liked him and now it had become evident that it was mutual. He had been positively rude to her the last few days. Parliament would be sitting again soon, so he'd have to go, thank heavens. And she couldn't help but notice how he treated Clara, snapping at her all the time, and that annoyed Phoebe even more.

It would serve him right if I paid him back, she thought meanly. Wouldn't I just love to drop it to Belle that he'd been having an affair with my mother? That'd make old Mrs Foster switch sides very swiftly. She was the real power round here, and it irritated Phoebe that she never seemed to notice the harsh way Ben spoke to Clara. Possibly she thought that if Clara was prepared to put up with it, then it wasn't of any importance.

She supposed the situation wasn't much different from the way Lalla yelled at her husband. People are strange, she said to herself. But how much more pleasant it will be here when Clara's husband departs. Worth waiting for.

Buchanan wasn't just furious, he was shocked. Not at that stupid Thurlwell girl's choice of husband – he didn't care if she married Chink the Chinaman – but at discovering that the boyfriend was threatening to visit his home. Seeing that address at the top of the disgusting letters – Kangaroo Point, next door to the Thurlwells – left him in no doubt that this was Diamond's son. He was convinced the fellow was deliberately dogging him, even ingratiating himself with Phoebe Thurlwell for the same reason. He wanted no part of the Thurlwells any more and wished the girl would get the hell out of his house.

But what did the half-caste really want? To come here and claim to be his son? He'd get short shrift with that tale. Diamond was dead and he'd read in the paper that the old woman was too, so there was no one left to back his claim. Not a soul.

But he still worried. In the north, where his former station Caravale was located, there were a lot more blacks, and no one cared about white men taking their sex with gins, but down here, closer to civilization, that practice was kept to a whisper. In fact he'd even heard stuffy men referring to it as polluting the white race, so he'd been careful to keep well clear of the few gins who worked on this station. There were more interesting specimens at Goldie's house in town.

He'd already acted to keep this bloke Beckman off his property, ordering the boundary riders to watch out for him and chase him off, not needing to make excuses to them, although he had a valid reason in protecting Miss Phoebe. And he himself had taken to patrolling the main road leading to the sign which announced Fairmont Station. Where he went and what he did on his own land was his own business, so it wasn't necessary for anyone to know why he was keeping watch on that road with a loaded rifle.

The sun was high and the flies were bad, so he rode away from the turn-off to his homestead and down the track to have a smoke in the shade of a big pepper tree. This was the site of one of the first old huts in the district; now only the chimney remained, and the pepper tree, planted by some wise old coot. For some reason the flies weren't too keen on these trees so they created a refuge from all but the most persistent of the sticky, irritating insects.

He dismounted and sat on the rotting log that had also been there for years, since this was a favourite smoko spot for stockmen with the same idea. The flies were bad this year. Everywhere you rode, your back would be covered in the bloody things, waiting their chance to annoy. The women had taken to wearing nets on their hats. As he lit a cheroot he wondered about flies; there seemed to be no rhyme or reason to the plagues that lasted for months. Wet season or dry, it didn't make any difference, a plague could descend on them at any time. He remembered one year, when he was a kid, they'd been so bad up north that the family had taken their meals sitting under a huge net that his mother had hung from the ceiling.

They'd had fly-wire doors, but they were only for the kitchen, to protect the food, not for humans trying to eat it. This homestead was much the same, so he'd had removable fly-wire doors made to fit the french doors that led from the dining room to the veranda.

He finished the cheroot, stubbed it out in the dirt, and continued his contemplation of war against flies. He had argued that these Queensland houses should be completely protected from flies and mosquitoes by fly-wire, even if it meant getting rid of the beloved french doors, but he'd been shouted down. Defence claimed that fly-wire stopped the much-needed breezes. Ben dozed, his horse dreaming quietly beside him, appreciating the respite under the pepper tree.

A traveller woke him, and he was on his feet instantly.

'Sorry to disturb you, sir,' the rider asked, 'but is this the way to Fairmont Station?'

Ben cursed his stupidity at being caught out like that, his authority diminished. He affected the slow bush attitude, making for his horse and swinging into the saddle before he replied: 'Who wants to know?'

He didn't have to be told. This was Beckman! He *had* seen him at those damn stables but the penny hadn't dropped. And Jesus! Here he was, right at his gate.

'The name's Beckman,' the fellow replied amiably.

Ben Buchanan took stock of him now, out of mixed emotions of anger and curiosity. He was a hefty bloke, muscles hard. The sign of hard yakka, probably from the prison years, he thought maliciously. Clean-shaven and even-featured, he lacked the wide nose of the average Aborigine, and his steady eyes, though brown, were not as deep and dark as Diamond's had been. But the skin gave him away, that creamy-olive shade, sign of the tar-brush.

'What's your business?' he demanded.

Something about this rider's stance and the set of his jaw reminded him of Diamond's steely arrogance. She could be a dangerous bitch, so he'd have to watch the son. The last time he'd seen Diamond, up there in Cooktown, he'd given her a hiding. Which she'd richly deserved for being so high-handed. And she'd pulled a knife on him, forcing him to back off. And her just a bloody gin! He still smarted at that shock.

'Just visiting,' Beckman said. 'I've come to see someone on the station.'

'One of the blacks?' Ben asked, putting him in his place.

'I don't know any of the blacks out here,' Beckman said quietly. 'I've come to see Miss Thurlwell who, I believe, is staying at Fairmont.'

'Have you?' Ben retorted. 'Well, I'm afraid you're wasting your time. I am Buchanan and this is my station.'

'I know,' Beckman said. 'You had horses at my livery stables in Brisbane. I would like to see Miss Thurlwell.'

Ben resisted a shudder. So he did know who he was! The bastard, in every sense of the word, was playing with him. 'Miss Thurlwell has made it very clear to me that she doesn't wish to see you, so the best thing you can do is turn about and make tracks.'

'Not until I've had a chance to talk with her.'

'Are you defying me? Who do you think you are?'

'I am simply a friend. I won't be staying—'

'You can be bloody sure of that!'

'Then can I see her?'

'No.' In a swift, well-practised move, the station-owner's rifle was out and trained on Beckman. 'I told you to make tracks. Now get going!'

Taken aback, Beckman stared at him. The two horses, aware of tension, shuffled uncomfortably sideways but the loaded rifle remained steady.

'Mr Buchanan,' the visitor said softly, 'I don't like having guns pointed at me.'

'I don't imagine you would after years in jail,' Ben grinned, now in full control. 'But you should be used to it. Now take that rifle from its pouch and throw it over there into the scrub.'

'Why?'

'You know Abos aren't allowed to carry arms. Do as you're told!'

He saw the angry tilt of Beckman's head at that studied insult and was pleased with himself as he watched the half-caste obey him, slowly and carefully, one hand raised in fear.

But he misinterpreted the emotion. Ben Beckman was not frightened, only amazed. What was going on here? All he wanted to do was to talk with Phoebe. He hadn't expected an armed guard in the person of Buchanan himself.

'There's no need for this,' he said as he threw his rifle away. 'I won't make any trouble.'

'I'm damn sure you won't,' Buchanan snapped.

All at once, Ben was nervous. As he closed the flap on his rifle holster he loosened the knife in his boot. This man was mad. The hatred in his face was unmistakable. But why? It occurred to him then that nothing changed: he was faced with the old feud, whites against blacks, and he'd committed the worst crime of touching one of their women. That seemed to be the only reasonable explanation, and out here he knew only too well that these station owners were a law unto themselves.

'Now turn around and get going!' Buchanan said.

Slowly, very slowly, Ben urged his horse about, acutely aware that Buchanan hadn't added the expected: 'And don't come back!' Out of the corner of his eye he saw the muzzle of the rifle slowly lifting and knew that if he did turn and ride away he was about to get a bullet in his back.

He slipped the knife out by its blade, because that was the way it rested in its straps, upright, ready for action, and wheeled his horse as if moving out. Then he twisted suddenly in the saddle and hurled the knife.

Buchanan had left it too late. With his finger on the trigger, waiting for the retreating target, his shot went wide as the knife plunged into his shoulder.

Unarmed now, Ben didn't wait to check. A knife thrust at that distance, unless very lucky, couldn't do a lot of damage. He spurred his horse and galloped wildly down the road.

With the thud of his horse's hooves, and of his heart too in that lucky escape, he didn't hear Buchanan coming after him, only the report of the rifle shot and the almost instantaneous hesitation as his horse pulled up with a shock and then crashed to the ground.

'Oh God, no!' Ben shouted as he realized that the horse had been hit. He leapt free and dived into the thick scrub, then, keeping low, ran on and on through the high sharp grass, stumbling over heavy logs and dodging behind trees until he knew that he was well hidden. A man on horseback would have to negotiate this obstacle course with care.

He worried about the horse. There'd been no time to find out if it had only suffered a flesh wound or if it had been seriously injured in the fall. Rapper was a fine horse, a beauty. Ben had chosen him for himself when he'd first bought the stables. He'd got his name from his habit of rapping on the gates of his stall with his hooves when he decided he wanted attention. An imperious four-year-old, strong as an ox and with a brain to match, he didn't deserve to be lying out there hurt. Ben hoped he had managed to get to his feet and taken off; he'd find him again eventually.

And if Rapper were hurt, too badly to survive, Ben worried, what could he do? He had no means of putting him out of his misery. He groaned, wishing he, rather than the poor horse, had collected the bullet.

Ben waited nearly an hour, but then he couldn't stand it any longer. He had begun edging back towards the road when he heard the shot. Buchanan had some heart in him after all. He wouldn't have been firing at nothing, since his prey was well out of sight. It had to be the horse. He sank down on the ground, shattered. Why did Rapper have to be the victim?

For a long time, he waited, hidden in the scrub, afraid to move or make a sound in the stillness of the afternoon, when all creatures in the bush were silent. The fact that Buchanan had tried to kill him seemed to have taken second place to the death of his horse. He was so furious at the attack by this madman that he was determined to come back. Buchanan could count on that.

Eventually, when the coast was clear, he stole out to find that Rapper was dead, with a bullet through his head. There was another in his rump which had caused him to stumble and break a foreleg. But he was bare. The saddle and bridle rig, as well as Ben's packs containing food and money, were all gone. Everything. He might as well have been ambushed by outlaws, so complete was the theft. But Buchanan was no outlaw, he'd simply made a point to Ben, leaving him out in the scrub, miles from anywhere without transport, sustenance, or the means to provide for himself. Not even a waterbag.

'That's all right, Mr Buchanan,' Ben said as he covered the horse with brush for some protection from the hordes of flies that had already settled on the carcass. 'For now. But we've got a score to settle.'

He decided to make for Charleville, more than forty miles away, keeping off the roads for fear of pursuit, but not being a bushman he had to use the roads as a guide. It was heavy going tramping through the bush with the occasional detour to check that he wasn't lost, and by sunset he was very tired and thirsty. He then had a change of plan, figuring that the road would be safe enough at night, and gritting his teeth began to lope along the white strip between the dark bush, hoping he was going in the right direction since there were no signs to help a weary traveller.

Nocturnal animals startled him occasionally with a flurry of leaves or a sudden dash across his path, and a dingo howled somewhere nearby, the mournful tone fitting his mood. Soon he had to slow to a walk, trudging along, but determined to keep moving all through the night.

By the time the pre-dawn glow lit the sky Ben was exhausted, so he headed into the bush again and collapsed. Sleep came easily and when he awoke the sun was well up. 'About seven o'clock,' he said, groggily pulling himself to his feet. 'And no breakfast, chum! On your way!'

But the position of the sun worried him. Charleville he knew was to the east. The sun rises in the east. Then why was it lifting over there, almost behind him? For a minute, as he recommenced his trek, he thought he might have turned about and was retracing his steps, but he knew that couldn't be. He had pulled off the road to the right and he was sure he was still on that side. To make certain, Ben went back, cursing, to see that he had trampled grasses and flattened ferns when he'd stopped on this side.

'It isn't important,' he told himself, 'these roads twist and turn. Bullock teams and wagoners made them in the first place, detouring to avoid big trees and rocks and any other sort of obstacle. Just keep going.'

He had no idea how far he'd travelled since the horse had been killed, and only annoyed himself trying to work it out. But he must be a good distance away from Fairmont Station, and now he needed help. If he stuck to the road he'd have to find someone or sight a house. Or cross a creek. Water would fix him up, he could do without food for a while. He picked up a pebble and stuck it in his mouth to restore some saliva, a trick he'd learned working in the quarries where water for the prisoners was only doled out at mealtimes. He couldn't think of Phoebe, or anyone else, it was hatred of Buchanan that kept him going down the long, dusty road that tantalized him with mirages. Far in the distance, though, and it was no mirage this time, he could see a turn in the road and that gave him heart. As he came closer he felt better still because he could see a gate, a clumsy gate made from saplings and the usual three rungs of wire.

The road hadn't turned, it had come to a dead end. Some time during the night, half asleep, tramping on, he must have forked off along this bloody useless stretch. But up ahead he could see two chimneys lodged behind a clump of trees. At least he'd found a homestead where he could get some help.

He made his way up the mile-long track, nervously noting that it seemed overgrown, even allowing for the recent rains. There were no wheel marks of the odd wagon or buggy . . .

He passed under the shade of the sturdy trees to a completely overgrown circular drive and the remains of a homestead that had been burned to the ground a long time ago. Only the two brick chimneys were left standing at either end of what must once have been a fairly big house, where young trees and even wild flowers were now blossoming from the ash.

'Oh Christ!' he said, stalking the area. He banged on a rusted iron water tank, then dropped stones down a well but heard only a thud instead of the promise of water.

Quite a bit of the land had been cleared around this house on a hill but the trees were fast fighting back, springing up all round to meet the encroaching bush.

In spite of his disappointment Ben studied the area, appreciating that this must have been a fine homestead and property in its day. The circular drive in front was witness to the fact that the people who lived there must have been house-proud. Broken stone jardinières lay at the base of crumpled steps, signs of better days, and a stunted red geranium still blinked a welcome.

But no one, he pondered – certainly not the owners who had taken such care in siting their house – would overlook the necessity of permanent water. They wouldn't have relied on that old well and the rainwater tank.

He marched around the house, scanning the area, and sure enough, down there, only about a half-mile away, was a steady line of towering gums, far stronger than the rest of the straggling bush. As he watched he saw birds gliding down into their foliage.

Ben began to run, praying that for once, in this maddening country, he'd got something right. He crashed in among the tall gums, shoving aside the undergrowth, slipping down into a gully to fall, fully clothed, into a gently flowing creek. It was no river, the bed was full of snags and reeds, but the waters, like the trees out there, were now reclaiming their territory and Ben was grateful for it. He drank and splashed and drank again. He threw his boots back to the shore and sat wallowing in the middle of the creek. He didn't know where he was. He had no idea. But today was today.

The master of Fairmont Station was in no mood for Ruby's fussing when she saw he was hurt. He sat on a box in the tool shed and tore off his shirt. 'Shut up your chatter! Get some water and eucalyptus and clean this up.'

As far as he could see, twisting his head to examine his shoulder through the dried blood, the wound wasn't too deep. The knife had glanced off the bone, but it had hit him with such force that at first he'd thought it had cracked a bone. And it still hurt like mad every time he moved his arm. If it hadn't been for the knife he'd have got Beckman, and that would have been the end of it. But now, if there were any complaints, he could say he was attacked first and he had the knife wound to prove it.

He'd dumped the nigger's gear, all of it, down an old mine shaft. No one would ever find that lot. But for the time being, it was best to say nothing. He didn't feel like answering to the women, especially with Phoebe Thurlwell in the house. And he doubted her boyfriend would be back, he'd been given the message, loud and clear.

Ruby rushed back to wash the wound and pour the eucalyptus oil over it, swabbing gently with a dry cloth.

'What happen, boss?' she asked, concerned for him.

'A branch,' he said. 'I rode headlong into a spiky branch and it stuck me. Nearly knocked me off the bloody horse.'

She wagged her head at him. 'You be more careful, boss. Not be ridin' mad out there.'

'Is it deep?' he asked, to make sure.

'No, not too bad. The bones there? Bones hurt?'

He winced as her deft fingers dug into his shoulder.

'No, bone not broke. Him bleedin' again, but I tie him up for you.'

With Ruby's treatment he wasn't surprised it was bleeding again, but he'd back her experienced old hands against those of some fidgety doctor, and her reply reassured him. He sat silently while she bandaged his shoulder with some clean strips of sheeting that she kept in her 'medicine' box.

'Now get me a clean shirt.'

The wound was just an ache now and he was feeling quite pleased with himself. He'd had a lucky escape and the injury was easily explained. There were always accidents in the bush, and compared with the really bad falls, this was a trivial matter. And he'd got rid of the menace. Beckman would know he couldn't go to the police; the knife attack would be held against him. No one would take the word of a half-caste against that of a pastoralist who was also a politician and who would claim that he was simply defending himself from the assailant by shooting his horse from under him.

Ruby had lived on Caravale Station up north. She'd come down to this station with the boss and the rest of his property. She watched him put on his shirt and stride away, shaking her head. 'Mr Ben,' she whispered to herself, 'what you bin up to this time? You always bin a bad boy right from when you was a kid. That ain't no branch stuck you, that a knife!' She sighed and packed up her medicine box.

Ben Beckman had come to the same conclusion as his attacker as he prepared to set off again. If the tables were turned and he was accused of throwing the knife first, he'd be in real trouble. Not that he intended to go to the police; this was a private matter. He didn't want Phoebe drawn into it. She was the only explanation he could give the police for wanting to enter Fairmont Station.

He wondered what tale Buchanan would take back to the homestead. The man was a lunatic, that was for certain. Guarding Phoebe with a gun! Had she really been so adamant that she didn't want to see him? As he pulled on his boots he knew he ought to give it away, go back to town and wait for her to come home. And let Buchanan get away with trying to kill him? Buchanan, who could be in league with his old friend William Thurlwell! That might be the real source of this trouble, the great doctor again.

The rage in him surfaced again. If he had a horse, and a weapon, he'd turn right back and make for that station again.

'But you haven't,' he said, 'And you're going to walk until you find that bloody town, if it takes a month.'

'You talk to your own sel'p,' a voice said, and Ben whirled about to find Mandjala grinning down at him.

'Good God!' he shouted. 'Where did you come from?'

'Bin trackin' you. Back longways.'

'But how did you know I was out this way?'

'People say you come askin' about.'

'They said they didn't know you.'

Mandjala shrugged and pointed with his thumb over his shoulder. 'Your horse dead. Some feller shoot him?'

'Yes. He would have got me if I hadn't hidden in the bush.'

The bushman shook his head. 'No one follow you. Where you goin'?'

'To Charleville.'

Mandjala burst into shouts of laughter, thumping his sides with merriment and pointing a bony finger at Ben: 'You bloody fool lost!' He pointed north-east. 'Big town go that way.'

'Don't rub it in,' Ben growled. 'I'm hungry. You got any tucker?'

This seemed to amuse Mandjala even more. Obviously, since he was still only wearing a plaited belt and lap-lap and a new innovation, a sleeveless shirt made of flannel, he wasn't carrying supplies. He took a short sharp boomerang out of his belt, still cackling with laughter, and dropped it beside him as he squatted in the sand by the water's edge. 'Plenty tucker here,' he said.

'Glad to hear it,' Ben retorted. 'Where's your spear?'

'White men get cranky seein' spear. White men think war spear.' Mandjala spat irritably. 'More better no carry spear now.' He drew an arc in the sand. 'You bin travel thisaway since the horse. Goin' round like the moon.'

'Then why didn't you catch up with me sooner?'

Mandjala explained that Ben had been easy to track and not in any immediate danger. He'd thought it 'more better' to pick up the trail of his enemy from the place of the dead horse to make sure this unknown man would not return.

Ben listened fascinated. He wished he'd known that he'd had a foot-soldier guarding his rear. Mandjala had tracked Buchanan right into his property, although he hadn't seen him. He was able to tell Ben that the horse had been carrying extra weight on his return journey . . .

'Yes, my saddle and all my gear,' Ben said.

All of which, he heard, had been dumped down a shaft several miles 'this side' – Mandjala tapped his left arm – of the track to the homestead.

'Any chance of pulling it out?' Ben asked, but Mandjala shook his head. 'Too much far down.'

Not that it mattered, Ben thought. A saddle wasn't much help without a horse, but the money would have saved him bother in Charleville. And the arrogance of Buchanan not to care that he could be throwing money down that shaft along with a bloody expensive saddle!

'That fella, him live in that station,' Mandjala warned.

'I know. He's the boss.'

His friend's eyes widened. 'Then better you run. You in big trouble fightin' a boss.' He slipped his hand into his shirt and pulled out the knife. 'This belonga you?'

'Yes!' Ben was pleased to have retrieved something, especially Diamond's knife. 'Where did you find it?'

'On the road. You cut him, this boss?'

'Yes.'

Mandjala stood up. 'You make a fire.' And marched off into the scrub.

'What with?' Ben asked helplessly, left alone again. He wasn't even carrying matches, they were in his pack with his pipe and tobacco at the bottom of some damn shaft. And he knew that he'd be on the receiving end of Mandjala's hilarity when he returned to find his half-Aborigine friend sitting there as useless as a knot on a log. So all he could do was wait as the skies darkened and his stomach rattled, and think about these events.

Mandjala had tracked Buchanan for miles right into his property, without being seen by anyone. Ben wondered if he could get as far as the homestead without problems. He didn't want to put his friend in any danger. But he was one hell of a tracker.

'Not that I'm any judge,' he admitted. 'I could have been followed by a herd of elephants and probably wouldn't have known.'

But there were blacks on all the stations: stockmen, housemaids, rouseabouts, paid nothing but their keep to serve the squatters and their families. Could Mandjala take a message for him and have it passed on to Phoebe, without any of the station white folk finding out? He had nothing to write with, and word of mouth could be too difficult and possibly too dangerous for any of the black staff. What if Phoebe objected to being approached by one of the blacks and reported it to the Buchanans? Interrogations and upsets could follow.

They ate well. Mandjala cooked yams and a fat bush turkey over the fire, which he'd had to light by rubbing two sticks together in his palms as Ben, under instruction, dropped crumbled dry bark about the sticks to catch the sparks. Apparently they weren't just any sticks either, they had to come from a stringy-bark tree, Mandjala informed him. For future reference, Ben presumed, but he'd still rather have matches.

Mandjala asked him if he had any 'baccy' and was broken-hearted to hear it had gone down the mine shaft too. Far more precious to him than the money or the saddle.

Ben enquired of Djumbati and heard that the young man had taken a wife and gone back north to work with her on a station.

'Horse-ridin'!' Mandjala said contemptuously.

'Don't blame him,' Ben said. 'Young men have to find a way to live somehow.'

But to Mandjala this was a sell-out.

The idea of sending a message to Phoebe by way of the blacks still lodged in Ben's mind, but his first priority was to buy a horse and new equipment.

'Will you take me to Charleville tomorrow?' he asked Mandjala, who seemed relieved.

'More better you go home, eh?'

'No. Not yet.'

Mandjala looked at him knowingly. 'That boss fella, he got your woman, eh?'

Ben was startled. 'No, she's just visiting his house.'

The old man nodded and smiled, staring down at the fire, as if he'd guessed all along that the battle had been over a woman.

They began the run at first light, a chilly morning, the land wet with dew. Ben travelled well to start with but then began to trail behind his guide who was taking him cross-country in a direct line for the town. Obstacles were no bother to Mandjala. They climbed through fences and cut through herds of staring cattle in cleared areas, and at one stage were even followed by a trio of curious emus, striding out, thinking maybe this was a race of sorts. When Ben turned to stare at them they fled.

They traversed rough country, pushing into timbered gullies and out again to march uphill until they came to a wide valley.

Ben slumped, exhausted, on the hillside.

'How much further?' he asked for the third time.

'Ten miles,' Mandjala announced wisely for the third time, so Ben climbed to his feet and battled on, trying to match the black man's pace.

At sunset Mandjala led him to a deserted bough humpy, probably used by stockmen. It was unfurnished except for a slab table but Ben was glad of the shelter, missing his canvas tent. He was almost too tired to eat, especially when Mandjala cooked a possum for them, but he managed to get some of the meat down.

The black man preferred to sleep in the open and Ben was touched that Mandjala had provided shelter for him. They could easily have bypassed this leafy refuge, he'd never have noticed it.

In the morning the efficient guide took him up a hill and pointed to a road below them, half hidden by bush. 'Him fella go on to big town.'

'Ten miles?' Ben asked with a grin, and Mandjala nodded, pleased.

As it turned out, it was less than five miles to small farms on the outskirts of the town, and Ben was soon trudging up the main street of this drab outpost.

At the saleyards, Ben discovered that IOUs were all very well if you were known, but weren't extended to dusty tramps, so he marched past a dozen ramshackle pubs until he came to the Shamrock Hotel, a similar wooden building with a small veranda right on the street, and found Mrs Lottie Smith.

She was a tall, spare woman with a weathered face and greying hair bunched in a knot at the back of her head, and she was wearing a plain black dress with a black apron. A no-nonsense type this one, he thought, as she eyed him suspiciously, and so he hurried to introduce himself.

'You're a friend of Mr Glasson's?' she asked. 'And how is he?'

'Very well,' Ben said, deciding to skip details.' He has his own practice now, in Brisbane.'

'And what can I do for you?' she asked, not giving him a chance to exchange more pleasantries before he broached the important subject of money.

'I'm in a bit of a fix,' he said. 'I own a livery stables in Brisbane and I was out here on business and . . .'

'You mean you're broke?'

'Not exactly. I only need a loan. I'm good for it.'

'Where's your horse?' she asked. 'I saw you comin' down the road and you haven't even got a horse. Or a swag.'

'That's right. My horse died. I had to leave my gear and leg it the rest of the way.'

'Where from? Where did it die?'

The interrogation was irritating him but he remained polite. 'About ten miles out on the road,' he lied, for brevity.

'And you left your money with the dead horse?' she asked incredulously. 'That's a good one.'

'Mrs Smith,' he said patiently, 'I've run out of cash. Barnaby told me to look you up when I was out here. I thought you might be able to give me a loan. I'll pay you back with interest. I'm good for it, I can assure you.'

She glanced over her shoulder at the burly man standing at the bar behind her, obviously Mr Smith, and shook her head. 'We're not a lending society, mister, but I'll tell you what. You go to the bank. If you're good for cash they'll lend it to you.'

'Why would they?' he asked. 'If you won't help what hope have I got at a bank?'

She sighed and cast her eyes heavenwards at his dullness. 'We're not so out of touch here as you might think. Go to the bank over the road there, ask for Seth Collins, he's the manager and the teller all rolled into one. If you're who you say you are, he can telegraph to Brisbane and get you sorted out.'

Ben brightened up. 'Mrs Smith, you're a treasure. Why didn't I think of that?"

She relented. 'I'm sorry, but you have to understand our position. We get a lot of con men coming through here. Cleaned out from the goldfields. Have you been out to Sailor's Drift fields?'

'Yes,' he said and strode across the road to the bank. He had been intending to ask them to telegraph to Barnaby, but the fading print on a board outside informed him that this overgrown shed was the First National Bank. This Mr Collins could telegraph directly to Ben's own bank in Brisbane.

But Mr Collins took a while to convince. 'Who's going to pay for the telegram?'

'I'll pay when they reply.'

'What if they've never heard of you? Who'll pay then?'

Ben persisted, begged, and finally lost his temper. 'Send the bloody telegram, damn you! Tell them I need you to advance me a hundred pounds, make it two! My account is at the head office of your bank and I'm a good customer. If you don't do this for me, by Christ I'll see to it that you're out of a job the minute I get back to Brisbane!'

'Two hundred pounds is an awful lot of money,' Collins wailed. 'They'd never advance that to someone like you.'

With a shock Ben realized he wasn't just up against the con man problem but the colour bar as well.

'You're supposed to be a bank manager,' he grated, 'now behave like one. The amount of money I require is none of your business.'

He marched Collins over to the telegraph office and stood over him while his message was written out and sent.

'Won't get a reply until tomorrow,' the telegraphist announced. 'I close at one o'clock, got my other job to do.'

'What's his other job?' Ben asked.

'He's the postmaster,' he was told. 'He opens the post office after he's had his lunch.'

It was all to do with the arrival of the train, Ben heard, and as he walked back to the Shamrock he told himself he ought to go home. Collect his cash, hire a horse, go back to Mandjala who was waiting out there by the humpy, have a yarn with him for a while, then head back to Charleville and board the next train for Brisbane. He'd never travelled in a train, it would be very pleasant.

And very unpleasant to have to admit that they'd beaten him again. Even tried to kill him.

'Not a chance,' he muttered. 'You'll stay right here and find out what's going on.'

Lottie's husband, Bellamy Smith, gave her the nod when he heard that the bank was arranging to advance Ben some cash, so she agreed to stand him for accommodation and meals until he was 'flush' again.

'You can have the bungalow out the back,' she told him. 'We're not as flash as the Royal Hotel, that being new, but the Shamrock's clean.'

'And that's a true fact,' her husband added proudly. 'I got a wife and the best housekeeper in town in one hit. You want a beer, Mr Beckman?'

'I certainly would, and have one yourself.'

'Right you are. I'll put it on your slate.'

He had to hand it to her, Lottie could cook. She served dinner for her husband and four men, including Ben, on a long table in a kitchen that shone from the results of her scrubbing and scouring; from the pots that hung over the wide stove to the pine benches and cabinet stacked with sturdy china.

The men made short work of large bowls of thick pea soup, roast pork and platters of steaming vegetables, and rhubarb sponge, finished off with hunks of fresh bread, butter and jam. The talking was mainly of horses, since they'd heard the newcomer owned livery stables.

After a stroll round the town Ben sat in a corner of the saloon reading old newspapers from a pile in the corner. At closing time, while Lottie swabbed down the bar and washed the glasses, Bellamy brought two pints over and sat down with Ben.

'Just because you're on the slate don't mean you have to join the temperance club,' he said. 'This one's on me. Bad luck about your horse, eh?'

'Yes.' Ben wasn't inclined to enlarge on that subject.

But Bellamy, his day's work over, was in a talkative mood. 'How come a bloke your age gets to own a livery stable? Belonged to your daddy, did it?'

'No. My grandmother left me some cash. I was lucky.'

'You sure were, by gum. Doing well, is it?'

'Yes, I've got a saddlery there as well.'

'Smart lad, we could do with one out here too. Blokes have to send to Roma for good saddles. Beckman? Your daddy a German? They're good farmers. Met a lot of them out Toowoomba way.'

'No, the Beckmans adopted my mother.' No one had ever asked Ben these questions point-blank like this. He looked at Bellamy's rosy face and kindly blue eyes and knew the man was only making conversation, so he couldn't be bothered lying. He'd had enough of lies for one day. 'I don't know who my father was,' he shrugged, 'and I don't much care. My mother was a full-blood Aborigine. She's dead now but she did well by me.'

'That's easily seen. You've been well brung up,' Bellamy said, lighting his pipe and settling back for a yarn. He noticed Ben looking at him and suddenly had a thought. 'Sorry, mate. Would you like a smoke?'

'If it can go on the slate,' Ben laughed, 'I'd give an arm for a smoke.'

'Ah cripes, you shoulda said so before. We've got some good pipes there on the rack. Hey, Lottie,' he called. 'Will you bring young Ben here a pipe. And two more pints.'

'My shout,' Ben reciprocated and Bellamy nodded in agreement.

Ben smiled to himself. Bellamy Smith was no fool, a yarn was fine, but business was business.

'So what was your mum? A Brisbane black?' Bellamy asked. 'I like to know about people, where they come from and how they get about. Do you know we had some blokes here last week from Finland. Can you beat that? I was real sorry when they left.'

'No. My mother was Irukandji, from the far north. Up near Cooktown.'

'Irukandji, eh? I heard about them from diggers down from the Palmer River goldfields.'

'You know of that tribe?' Ben was startled. This was the first time he'd come across anyone who even knew the word.

'Sure I do. You ask any of the old diggers. They were a tough mob, gave no quarter. The Palmer was their territory and if you ran into any of them, say your prayers! God knows how many diggers, whites and Chinks, they bumped off. That's what made the Palmer River so treacherous. Gold was there all right, by the ton, but you had to get past the Irukandjis and it was hard enough trekking through jungle from the coast in that heat without having to dodge spears.'

Bellamy had a score of diggers' yarns to relate about the murder and mayhem on the Palmer trail and about the huge fortunes made by lucky prospectors. Ben was enthralled.

'Your ma, she didn't tell you about the Palmer?'

'Not a lot,' Ben replied. 'But then I was only a kid. I was more interested in seafarers. I wanted to be a sea captain.'

'Ah well. That's kids for you. I wanted to be a policeman. Joined up for a while but quit. A mug's game chasing bushrangers through this country. Like looking for a needle in a haystack. Or, pardon me for saying so, driving poor bloody blacks off their own land. Them Irukandjis, they're gone now too, scattered I hear say. The numbers and the guns beat them in the end.'

'Yes. I know that much,' Ben admitted.

'And how did your ma get down to Brisbane? To safety?' Bellamy asked.

'I'm not sure, I'm a bit hazy about that,' Ben replied. Bellamy Smith had raised his interest in these old tales now. He decided that when he got home he'd take a proper look in Diamond's box, where the only item among the papers that had caught his eye was the knife, the knife that Mandjala had retrieved for him. There was another old trunk in her room containing the Captain's logbooks, but they were written in German. He'd have to find someone to translate them for him.

'You should know about these things,' Bellamy told him. 'Your kids and their kids will want to know. My granddaddy was a convict!' He laughed. 'Lottie don't like me to tell people that, she come out here from England free, as a servant girl, and did well for herself, got good posts because she was educated.'

Ben was feeling mildly defensive, so he was glad to be able to say that his mother had been educated too. By her German foster parents. 'I do know she worked in Charters Towers for a while,' he added.

'So did Lottie,' Bellamy said. 'She was the housekeeper on a big station out there. Hey, Lottie,' he called, 'you ever know a black girl in

Charters Towers back then by the name of Mrs Beckman? Or, I suppose,' he added with a wry smile, 'Miss Beckman.'

'Let me think,' Lottie said, coming over to join them with her glass of brown sherry.

'Lottie knew everyone up there,' Bellamy said, 'and she never forgets a face. That's why she was nervous of you, Ben, she thought your face was familiar. You gotta understand that the con men who hit these towns are not your average rouseabout, they could talk the leg off an iron pot. You're a good talker too, so we was right on our guard. Been caught too many times.'

'Can't say that I remember any black girl called Beckman,' Lottie admitted finally. She was about to add that gins never had surnames but thought better of it in case she offended their guest. Bellamy was a good judge of character and he'd taken a shine to Mr Beckman. Lottie had been listening to their conversation on and off.

'Tell me this,' Ben he said. 'Do you know Buchanan? He's a Member of Parliament and owns a cattle station west of here.'

'Sure we do,' Bellamy said.

Lottie's small green eyes narrowed. She took off her apron and folded it on to her lap. 'Did Mr Glasson mention him to you?'

'He said something about him. Apparently Buchanan has differing political opinions,' Ben replied casually.

'He spoiled Mr Glasson's meeting, that's what!' she said indignantly. 'Why do you ask? Are you political too?'

'No. That's Barnaby's field. We share a house, Barnaby and me. He talks politics and I talk horses and motorcars, so we get on well.'

Bellamy picked up on a new subject of conversation. 'You know about motorcars, Ben?' he asked with enthusiasm. 'You ever seen one?'

'Just a minute,' Lottie interrupted. 'We were talking about Mr Buchanan. Is he a friend of yours, Ben?'

'I wouldn't say that,' Ben said evenly. 'In fact I don't think Mr Buchanan likes me one scrap.'

'Why not?' she persisted.

'He's not the sort needs a reason,' Bellamy said. 'You be careful, Ben. He's God round here.'

'There's always a reason,' she snapped, and turned to Ben. 'I noticed your clothes when you walked in. You're wearing good clothes and smart riding boots. They weren't meant for marching. You've walked a lot further than ten miles, your boots are worn to a frazzle. How far have you really come?'

Bellamy was worried. 'Now Lottie, this isn't our business.'

She looked at Ben. 'How far have you walked and what *did* happen to your horse?'

'A long way,' Ben admitted. 'And Buchanan shot my horse.'

'Oh Jesus!' Bellamy spluttered. 'Whatever you do, don't go to the police. They're hard against colour out here.' He headed for the bar and lifted a whisky bottle from under the counter. 'I'm for a decent drink.' He poured himself a small shot of whisky, wanting no part in this conversation.

'Was he shooting at you or the horse?' Lottie persisted.

'Me,' Ben shrugged.

'Why?'

'I'm not sure but I'll find out. There's no need for you people to worry. I'm not about to report him to the police. I know the system. I have a friend staying on his station and I decided to visit her, and he hunted me off. That's all. I'm not going back looking for trouble, I just need to find out more about him.'

'I can tell you,' Bellamy called from the bar at the end of the room, 'if he don't want you on his property, then you don't go there. Right?'

'Agreed,' Ben said. 'Put a whisky on my slate, will you? I've had a long day.'

As she and her husband climbed into their high iron bed, Lottie's mind was racing. She hated Ben Buchanan. When his mother died, he'd sold Caravale Station, leaving Lottie to find her own way back from the north, after years of service to his family. Not a word of thanks to their housekeeper, nor even a reference, although she had asked him several times. And to make matters worse, when she'd checked her wages, which accrued over months on the station books when one wasn't in need of spending money, she'd found she was twenty pounds short.

'The amount is correct,' he'd said, 'there's no mistake.'

Lottie, from her own careful book-keeping, had written up her wages and drawings for a full year, and shown it to him, pointing out that he was, indeed, mistaken, but she never got that twenty pounds. And it still rankled.

'There were no educated black gins living in Charters Towers in my time,' she said to Bellamy.

'Ah well, maybe the lad was exaggerating a bit,' he replied.

'Except one,' Lottie added. 'I mentioned her to Mr Glasson. Maybe that's why he told Ben to look me up. She came out to Caravale with a woman visitor, as a lady's maid. She was neither fish nor fowl. The missus wouldn't have her in the house because she was black, but she was too well dressed and well spoken to cope with the blacks' camp. I didn't know what to do with her so I made up a bunk for her in the old creamery and she was all right there. I never heard her surname, never thought to ask. She was simply called Diamond.'

'Why didn't you tell Ben? She could have been his mum.'

'Because Diamond had an affair with Buchanan. He never could keep his hands of the black gins and she was a very beautiful girl. The affair lasted just as long as it suited him and then he ordered her off the station.'

'Go on!' Bellamy said, enjoying this extra bit of gossip.

'But he underestimated Diamond. She was very proud, and a fiery girl, so there was a real row. In the end the blacks smuggled her off the station for her own safety. But she was in love with him, poor girl.

'Not long after that the station wasn't doing too well so he joined the rush to the Palmer, where all he got was the fever.'

'Ah yes,' Bellamy said. 'That took out a lot of the diggers.'

Lottie sighed. 'Some girls never learn though. He was so ill he was brought into Cooktown and the word filtered back that Diamond was looking after him. People had seen her with him. She nursed him back to health.'

'But what would she be doing up there?'

'Listening to you two it's becoming quite clear she was trying to find her tribe, her family. Always asking questions of the local blacks. The Palmer was Irukandji country, her tribal home. That's why she was there. She found them. I'm sorry to hear she died but at least she did find her own people'

Bellamy whistled. 'And she'd have been just as safe with the blacks as she was with the whites up there. She could have gone in and out of the Palmer as she pleased. I wonder if she found gold?'

'If she did, she never gave it to Buchanan.' Lottie smiled with satisfaction. 'But the other side is more interesting. The timing is right. I wouldn't be surprised if that young man out there in the bungalow is his son.'

'Whose son?'

'Buchanan's. After all, she called him Ben!'

'And you think that's why Buchanan chased him off his property?'

'It's a possibility. I know that wretched man, and he wouldn't have been shooting at the horse.'

'Well, we have to keep out of this, Lottie. I reckon it's best if you don't say no more about it.'

'Of course, you're quite right,' she said, slipping down under the covers, smiling to herself.

In the morning she took Ben a cup of tea. 'I was thinking,' she said to him, 'I never met a woman of your mother's description in Charters Towers, nor anyone by the name of Beckman. But there was one girl who was at Caravale Station when I was housekeeper there. Her name was Diamond.'

Ben almost knocked over the steaming mug of tea. 'Diamond? Yes! That was my mother's name. You knew her? That's wonderful!'

'She was only there a little while,' Lottie said. 'She was a very nice girl, but a mite too trusting for that company.'
'Why?'
Lottie closed the door. 'Promise me you'll never mention this to my husband. We've got a lot of competition here, there are twenty hotels in this town and he can't afford trouble.'
'I promise,' Ben replied eagerly.
'Ben Buchanan was Diamond's lover.'
He flushed, startled. 'Are you sure about this?'
'Oh yes. It was quite a scandal. She never told you?'
'No.'
'Then I didn't either,' Lottie replied. 'Drink your tea. It's all past history now and Buchanan's not worth bothering about. Bellamy's right, you should pack up and go home.'
When she left, Ben sat stunned. Embarrassed. There were so many questions he wanted to ask Lottie but he dared not. In his heart he knew there was more to this than she was prepared to tell him, and it began to dawn on him who Buchanan could be. And the realization was not pleasant.
He remembered the policeman in Mitchell who'd said he never forgot a face and that Ben seemed familiar. Had he seen in him the face of Buchanan, who was well known on that route? Ben jumped up and stared into the small mirror over the washstand.
'No!' he said angrily. 'No!' He refused to admit that there was any resemblance between him and the man who'd tried to kill him.

Phoebe, in her own mind, only called *him* 'Buchanan'. She refused to think of him as Ben because he was so different from her own dear Ben, who was kind and thoughtful and had a wonderful sense of humour. Not so Buchanan.
This last week, since his accident, he'd been impossible. Imperious. It was like living with a god. A god who'd hurt his shoulder in a joust with a tree and acted as if the members of his household were to blame. Phoebe supposed that since she had been on the station for a while now, she'd become part of the furniture, so he no longer hid his cranky moods. She wondered if she were imagining that he seemed to be particularly annoyed with her for some reason. She couldn't help noticing that he rarely addressed her and on many occasions when she'd passed him in the house or the yard he'd ignored her, cut her dead.
Maybe he was just deep in his own thoughts, distracted, not noticing her. That could be the explanation, but whatever, it was uncomfortable, and she began to wish she could go home. Her father had written to her, waffling on, telling her that he hoped she was having a wonderful holiday

and that everything was fine at home and to stay as long as she liked. With a note at the bottom that her mother sent her love. But she hadn't heard from anyone else. It seemed that the world had forgotten her now that she was acting the part of an apprentice station hand, getting about like Clara in shirts, men's moleskins and riding boots.

Not that she could keep up with Clara, who could ride as well as any of the men. Phoebe spent a lot of time watching fearfully as Clara hurtled into the scrub after cattle, riding at a furious pace, her horse twisting and turning after the lumbering beasts, dodging trees at the same time. And back in the yards, she roped cattle with the same expertise.

No wonder she loves it out here, Phoebe mused. It must be marvellous to be that good at something. How I envy her!

Riding back to the homestead for lunch, on this particular day, Phoebe congratulated Clara. 'I never knew you could ride like that. It must have been boring for you just trotting along with me in Brisbane.'

'A change but still enjoyable,' Clara laughed.

'But how on earth did you learn to ride so well?'

'You learn young in the bush, and I fell off a lot! But the horses have to know what they're doing too or there'd be more calamities. And I never tire them, so they don't make mistakes.'

'Is that why you change horses at lunchtime?'

'Sometimes more often, depending on what work has to be done. There are always plenty of fresh horses for the stockmen in the home paddock, and I make sure they use them. So does Ben. He gets very angry if they work the horses too hard.'

Phoebe sighed. If he could be bad-tempered about the slightest thing at the homestead, his anger must be something to see when he did have something to complain about.

'I wish I could ride as well as you,' she said to Clara.

'It takes years,' Clara replied simply. 'And a knowledge of the cattle, which ones are smarties and which ones are just dumb. You can't expect to be a rough-rider in a matter of weeks.'

'No. What I really meant was that you're good at what you do. I'm no good at anything. Not a thing. I can't even cook or sew.'

'You could learn.'

'But I don't particularly want to.'

'So thank God for servants,' Clara grinned.

'I've come to the conclusion I must be a very boring person,' Phoebe said dismally.

'You're far from that. And you're a competitive person, Phoebe, you like to win.'

'You've never seen me playing tennis!'

'Then you just haven't found anything to interest you enough to make the effort. If you want to be good at something you have to care.'

'Good at what?'

'That's up to you. Most women are happy to be good wives.' She looked at Phoebe. 'Anyone on the horizon?'

Phoebe pretended not to hear that. She leaned over to lift the wire catch on the gatepost and push the gate open, stopping to close it again as Clara led on down to the stables.

After lunch Ben disappeared and Clara was off again, so Phoebe stayed at the cleared dining room table to play dominoes with Belle for a while. She never went out in the afternoons. Even though she wasn't as saddle-sore as she'd been earlier, by midday she'd had enough. Too tired to ride all day.

Keeping to her own schedule, Belle went to her room at three o'clock for her afternoon nap, so Phoebe studied the large bookcase, eventually selecting *Northanger Abbey*, which she had read at school and found boring, but maybe her taste had improved. She took it out to the front veranda to settle in one of the deckchairs, and was well out there, too far to retreat, before she saw *him*, sitting there reading a newspaper. She'd thought he was out somewhere about the station.

'Oh!' she said, choosing a chair on past him. 'I hope I'm not disturbing you. I often come here to read of an afternoon. Clara keeps so busy I can't keep up with her.' Thinking that startled comment could be construed as a criticism of the boss who was resting up while his wife worked, Phoebe tried to retract, fumbling for the right words. 'I mean, she's so interested in everything on the station, isn't she?'

'Yes. And I'd appreciate it if you took less interest.'

Phoebe blushed. 'I beg your pardon. I didn't realize I was getting in the way. If you'd prefer I didn't ride near the cattle in the mornings then I won't.'

'I'm talking about the sale of this property,' he snapped. 'I'm well aware that you are siding with Clara on that matter.'

Phoebe could hardly deny that accusation. 'I'm sorry if I've offended you. I was just hoping you'd come to some compromise. She really does love this place, every stick of it. Surely you could work something out.'

'Of course!' he sneered, rustling his paper. 'It's very easy to work something out with you here encouraging my wife to defy me. Let me tell you, I've had just about enough of it!'

Her blush had disappeared and she felt her face draining of colour in the chill of his attack. There had been times when, despite her dislike of him, she'd thought him handsome, with good strong features and rakish hair that flopped down on his forehead, but the jutting, belligerent jaw and those flint-like eyes now dispelled that image. Raving at her like this he was ugly. And a bully.

'Enough, do you hear?' he was saying. 'Your family has caused me enough trouble as it is. I'm faced with a serious lack of funds thanks to that outrageous fraud instigated by your people. And you have the gall to sit here trying to tell me my business.'

Phoebe was appalled. 'Mr Buchanan, I very much regret what has happened. I don't know what to say about that except that I really am very sorry that you lost money.'

'A heap of money,' he corrected her.

'I suppose so.' Phoebe refused to stoop to the pitiful stance of reminding him that she was a guest in his house and therefore should not be subjected to this abuse. She knew that the financial losses through the community and among their friends were substantial, but this was the first time it had been slammed home to her. And she guessed it wouldn't be the last, so she'd better make ready for it. 'I can only say,' she added, 'that my family has suffered too. My father is a trusting man, he could never have imagined that his brother would have the capacity to ruin him. My parents have been left in a dreadful situation, through no fault of their own. I can't allow you to speak of them like this.'

'Oh you can't? And how are you helping them? By running about town with a half-caste who is also a jailbird? By making them a laughing stock on top of all their troubles? Oh, you're a great help!'

He stuck his face back in his newspaper, as if to dismiss her now that he'd said his piece.

Phoebe struggled out of the ungainly deckchair and stood up. 'What did you say?' she asked, very deliberately, her anger matching his now.

'You heard me.' He had decided to ignore her. He didn't even bother to look up.

'Mr Buchanan,' she blazed at him, 'I am seeing a young man. But he is a gentleman, which is more than I can say for you.' She clasped her book and marched past him making for the front door to go inside, to get away from him, wondering how he knew about Ben and smarting from the insults. Then she suddenly turned back to retaliate: 'As I said,' she glared at him, 'my friend is a gentleman. He wouldn't dream of having affairs with other men's wives!'

She wished she could slam that front door as she rushed past, but it was never closed and was held in place by a heavy brick doorstop neatly encased in a piece of carpet.

But in the refuge of her room, with the door firmly closed, she sat on the bed and shook in a nervous reaction. What had she done now? Nothing less than trading insults with her host. She could hardly recall how it had all begun and she preferred not to try to reassemble her jumbled recollections. The last bit was bad enough. She half expected him to thump on her door and order her out of his house. Rather, she hoped he would. To provide her with an opportunity to escape this embarrassing situation.

'He won't do that though,' she told herself. Phoebe had grown up in the company of politicians, and she knew he'd weigh up the repercussions first. It was a bit late for him to complain about losing money to the Thurlwell family company, and there was also the chance that his guest might enlarge on her crack about other men's wives.

P'raps I could tell Clara I'm homesick and would like to go home, she considered. But Clara would find that very strange, since only this morning she'd been enthusing about being on the station.

'Damn!' she said out loud. She was in a hole and she'd have to find a way out. And anyway, how had Buchanan known about Ben? she wondered. Lalla must have told him. Or told Belle. In which case they all knew about him. Clara too.

Phoebe felt let down by everyone, but there were no tears this time. She was past all that. She would have to look to her own future, beginning with Ben. And if he didn't want to marry her she would have to find a job. Other women did, she'd think of something.

In the next room, closer to the front veranda, Belle Foster was sitting thoughtfully, far from sleep.

That girl Phoebe, she mused, certainly has recovered from her nervous collapse. And she's full steam ahead now. A chip off the old block. Not William, but Lalla. She'd often noticed that mother and daughter had been constantly at loggerheads. Because they're so much alike, she decided. Very determined women.

Belle had taken off her dress and her corsets, in preparation for her nap, and was slipping on a silk kimono and tying a net on her hair as she heard them outside. The raised voices had her out of the french doors in an instant and running to the corner of the veranda to find out what this was about. Standing there in her stockinged feet, pressed against the wall of the house, hidden from them, Belle heard it all.

Scowling, she hurried back to her room as the exchanges between them ended with Phoebe storming inside.

'Other men's wives, eh?' she said to herself. The girl might not have meant Lalla but for a long time Belle had been suspicious of her son-in-law and Lalla Thurlwell. And whoever it was, Phoebe had slammed back at him with certainty. And Belle believed her.

She grinned. Phoebe had defended her boyfriend with a vengeance! Serve Buchanan right, he'd hit below the belt insulting her over her family's financial woes, and the girl had been right to try to defend them.

One of the reasons Belle had tried to encourage her daughter to spend more time in Brisbane was to keep an eye on her husband. But Clara wasn't the type to manage a wayward husband. Who was? If men were inclined to play up there wasn't much the wife could do about it.

And why should she? Clara was a good wife, why should she have to stoop to undignified complaints? Or put up with a man who was making a fool of her? And of her mother!

Belle tapped her fingers on the bedside table. She had some thinking to do.

After a while she padded across the room to the washstand, poured water from the jug into the china basin, took a fresh facecloth from the cabinet and sluiced her face and neck to refresh herself, since she'd missed her nap. Then she towelled herself briskly as she weighed up the pros and cons of a switch to Clara's side in this argument about the station.

Much as I should have enjoyed having them living closer to me, she thought, Clara would be as miserable as hell and no damn company. And her husband would be free in his beloved Brisbane to resume his womanizing! There were so many single women and widows about Brisbane, what if one of them really got her fangs into him? Where would Clara be placed then?

Belle was sitting at the dressing table brushing her hair by the time that thought lodged, and she banged the brush down. Had Clara thought of that? By God, she might have! What was wrong with the girl that she couldn't confide in her own mother? She was such a mouse where he was concerned, she never criticized him to her mother, just accepted his unfortunate attitude, which wasn't rare. Girls didn't seem to have any gumption these days!

Except, Belle grinned, picking the brush up again, for the Thurlwell girl. She really let him have it.

It seemed to Belle then that Clara might be aware of the danger. If the property were sold the payment would go straight into his pocket. Fair enough if one were dealing with an honest and decent husband. But if not, he would have control of Clara's inheritance. He would be free to do what he bloody well liked. Maybe even leave her.

'The hell you will!' she said, pinning up her hair. 'Not with her dear father's money you won't!'

Maybe Phoebe had been giving Clara moral support to defy her husband, as he had said, because Clara was certainly digging her heels in, refusing to sell.

'And,' Belle admitted, talking to the mirror, 'selling did seem to me to be a good move. But I can't be expected to know what's going on behind the scenes, what with his smooth-tongue talk and her stubborn silence.'

Now she dressed with extra care. She stood in front of the wardrobe mirror in her good brown dress and pinned a diamond brooch at the collar. On her right hand she wore the big emerald ring encircled with diamonds.

'Whatever you do,' she told her image as she smoothed the rolls of grey hair from her face, 'you mustn't let him know that you overheard that conversation. If he's forewarned, he's forearmed. You don't need him to know that you're on to him and that you'll be checking up on him in Brisbane.'

Since the night was cool Belle wrapped a shawl about her shoulders, making for the door. 'He might be a leading politician and a social swell,' she muttered to herself, 'but to me he's just another self-serving wretch.' And no gentleman, she remembered with a smile.

And, she thought, it went to prove her long-held opinion that this country didn't need any more politicians. None of them were worth their salt. We've already got local mayors and councillors and state members of Parliament, we don't need another mob based somewhere down south running roughshod over the whole country.

With a pleasant smile on her face Belle Foster swept down to the parlour, looking forward to a few sherries before dinner.

At the same time, in Brisbane, Barnaby Glasson was discovering that this attitude prevailed among the ordinary people he'd hoped to win over to his cause.

After a succession of poorly attended meetings, his clerk, Tim, seemed amused.

'As far as I can see, you have, so far, identified two trains of thought, one lot who don't want any more politicians and another who couldn't care less.'

'I know,' Barnaby groaned. 'The only people who turn up at the meetings are the protesters against federalism. At least in the country people came to listen.'

'Because it was an outing,' Tim said. 'Nothing better to do. It's harder in Brisbane. Why don't you just give it away and concentrate on the law practice?'

'I can't do that. I want to be elected as one of the Queensland delegates. And besides, Sir Samuel's federalist people have set me up here. I owe it to them to continue the fight.'

Tim laughed. 'Seems to me that whenever a politician walks into the State House a little man with a hammer gives him a bump on the head and suddenly he has a bright idea. Then when the swelling goes down the idea is forgotten.'

Barnaby laughed. 'And the next time the little man with the hammer taps him on the head he dashes off with a new bright idea?'

'Something like that.'

'You think they've forgotten me?'

'Where are all the clients they promised you?'

'It takes time,' Barnaby replied defensively, knowing Tim was right. Somehow he'd have to rustle up more customers.

'I think I'll take a stroll down to the Roma Street police station,' he said. 'I know a few members of our constabulary. They ought to be able to put a few of their customers our way. Before I got involved with constitutional matters I used to see myself as becoming a leading light in criminal law.'

'Aha!' Tim said. 'You've had a tap on the head!'

'A couple,' Barnaby replied without enlarging. He was recalling the solutions to Ben Beckman's problems, and becoming more streetwise. He'd have another talk with Sergeant Dolan. There was no point in sitting in his office twiddling his thumbs when the watch-house was full of prospective customers. Dolan might be persuaded, for a small remuneration in each case, to refer some of them to him. Especially the ones who could afford to pay for a defence lawyer. Worth a try, he decided as he picked up his hat.

He returned with a smile on his face. He'd had an amiable conversation with Dolan in the pub next door to the police station. The Sergeant had been pleased to see him again. 'Out on your own now, lad,' he'd boomed with a hearty grin. 'I always said you'd go far.'

In a quiet corner of the pub, Barnaby put his proposition to Dolan, this time with more confidence.

'The Lord helps those who help themselves,' Dolan replied, sinking a pot of beer. 'And I'm sure to find plenty of lads and a few lassies who'll need your services. Leave it to me.'

And just like that, the deal was done, with no mention made of their previous association.

As he walked back through the door Tim winked at him and nodded towards Barnaby's office. 'A gentleman to see you, Mr Glasson.'

Another client, Ben thought. This must be my lucky day. He hurried into his office to find Dr Thurlwell waiting for him.

The Doctor raised himself from the chair with the aid of a stick. He looked very tired and worn. 'Good afternoon, Mr Glasson.'

'It's still Barnaby, sir. Do be seated. It's nice to see you.' He replaced his hat on the stand and took his seat behind the desk. 'How is Phoebe?'

'She's very well. Still out at Fairmont Station, having the time of her life by all accounts.' The Doctor looked about him. 'Good premises you have here. Doing well, I hope?'

'Just getting started really.'

'Ah, but you had an excellent mentor in Joseph Mantrell. A fine lawyer. I hear he has retired.'

'That's right, sir.'

The Doctor was silent then, so Barnaby filled the void by enquiring after Mrs Thurlwell, to hear that she too was very well.

Since William Thurlwell seemed very nervous Barnaby was forced finally to ask him if there was anything he could do for him.

'Yes, there is,' the Doctor mumbled, taking some papers from his bag and placing them before Barnaby. 'I want you to attend to this.'

Barnaby turned over some legal documents and looked up in surprise. 'This is a mortgage document. A mortgage on your house. But it has been drawn up by the South Pacific Banking Company. Shouldn't you see them?'

'No. I want nothing to do with them. I didn't even know my home was mortgaged.'

Bewildered, Barnaby rechecked. 'But you've signed the mortgage agreement.'

'My brother drew that up and had me sign it. I didn't know, didn't notice what I was signing.' He pulled out a handkerchief and wheezed into it. 'There were so many documents relating to the Railroad Company . . . I didn't know . . .' His voice trailed off. Then he looked up at Barnaby. 'Is it legal?'

'I'm afraid so, sir. Forgive me for saying this, but if Mr Edgar were alive you might get away with claiming that he forged your signature. Under the circumstances, though . . .' He shook his head. 'May I say I was very sorry to hear of Mr Edgar's death. It must be a very confusing time for you.'

Even though he had at times been in the Thurlwell bad books, Barnaby now felt sorry for Phoebe's father, who seemed to have aged years since he last saw him. And it dawned on him that it must have taken quite an effort for the Doctor to consult him, since the Thurlwells were well acquainted with Brisbane's top legal men. Why me? he asked himself.

'They're demanding money from me to pay that mortgage,' the Doctor said suddenly. 'And I don't have the money. We lost everything when the Railroad Company failed.' He produced another sheaf of papers and shoved them over to Barnaby. 'Look at this! Bills. Bank demands. Threats to sue! It's all beyond me. I want you to do something about it.'

With growing alarm, Barnaby studied the pages, stalling for time as he tried to shuffle them into some order.

In the end he said quietly, 'I think you'd be better to have an accountant go through all this with you, sir.'

'Don't talk to me about accountants!' William cried. 'I've had enough of the upstarts at the bank. Our personal bills will be paid. I can't do anything about the Railroad Company, but these will be paid and I want you to see to it.'

'Do you have other assets?' Barnaby asked.

'Yes. The house. Somerset House.'

'But it's under mortgage.'

'I know that,' the Doctor said testily. 'I want you to sell it for me.'

'There are house and property agents—' Barnaby attempted to explain, but William interrupted.

'Yes. That's what to do. Engage an agent and sell the house. Pay off the mortgage and these bills with what's left. I don't want anything to do with it.'

'But surely there's some other way?' Barnaby said.

'Not according to the bank. And I won't give them the satisfaction of selling me up. I'd prefer that you handle the matter in a more dignified way.'

Barnaby escorted the Doctor to the door. He wanted to ask how Phoebe felt about the sale of the house but didn't dare. And he supposed the question would be pointless. She'd be just as upset as her parents obviously were.

Tim whistled as they tried to sort through Dr Thurlwell's papers, listing the amounts owed. 'They'll have to get a damn high price to cover this,' he said. 'So you make certain you put your account on the top of the list, or you won't get paid either.'

'That's what worries me,' Barnaby said. 'Their daughter Phoebe is a dear friend of mine. I'd feel like a leech draining them, adding my bill to the list.'

'Don't be a fool,' Tim argued. 'I'll bet the Doctor wouldn't have waived his bill for you.'

Chapter Eleven

Accustomed to his role of boss – the big boss, in station terminology, since the foreman was also called boss by all the staff – Ben Buchanan was still in a state of shock.

The cheek of that girl! How dare she talk back at him! Didn't she realize *who* he was? A Member of Parliament, holder or one of the highest offices in the state. And a highly respected pastoralist. It was appalling that he should have to put up with her and her snide remarks when she was nothing but a charity case, a refugee from a disgraced family, staying under his roof, reliant on his goodwill. Which had run out. She had to go. But in the meantime he was anxious to hear from the two men he'd sent to town.

The Rawlins brothers, Moss and Mungo, had worked on the station for years. Neither of them was very bright, except when it came to cattle, but they were loyal to the big boss and carried out his orders without question. He'd sent them into town on the pretext of giving them a few days off in return for their hard work with new herds the drovers had brought in, but had told them to look out for a half-caste called Beckman and keep an eye on him. Report on his every move.

That was why he'd been sitting on the veranda, watching the track, waiting for them to return and report to him.

By nightfall a cold south wind was blowing so he pulled on a leather jacket and strode out of the back door, away from the homestead, to the outbuildings.

The blacksmith was shutting down his shed.

'Have you seen the Rawlins boys?' Ben asked.

'They just come in now, I heard. Be still down at the stables I'd say, boss.'

Both of them, Ben thought. Good. That means he's gone.

He found them emerging from the stables, their saddles hooked on their shoulders. Moss and Mungo treasured their saddles, they never left them about for anyone else to use.

'How did you go?' he asked them.

'Found him all right, boss,' Mungo said. 'He came tramping into town on shanks's pony. Didn't even have a mount so we couldna' missed him. Gawd knows where he came from.'

That pleased the boss. A forty-mile hike would do the bastard a world of good. 'Then what?' he asked.

'He put up at the Shamrock and hung about for a few days. Then he goes on a buyin' spree. Got everyone talkin'.'

Ben was startled. That was Lottie Smith's pub. What was he doing there? Had that old bitch been talking to him? Were they in cahoots? With growing fear he began to worry that he was right: there was a lot more to Beckman's appearance at his gate than his excuse of wanting to see the girl.

'Of course they'd be talking,' he snapped at Mungo. 'Since when do Abos stay in pubs? They're not even allowed drink in bloody bars without a licence and papers signed by the local police. I told you this bloke is bad news. He's done time. How did he get away with it?'

Mungo scratched his right ear. 'I dunno. I never saw him go near the coppers. Folks in town were talking about him and his cash. They say he stood over Seth Collins at the bank and made him telegraph Brisbane for money for him. I dunno how they do that. Beats me. But it worked. Yesterday was when he done all the spending.'

His brother interrupted. 'He's got colour all right, boss, but he don't act like no Abo I ever seen. Talks and dresses like a white man. Acted like he owned the bloody place yesterday, bought a good mount, saddle and gear. Spent a fair whack at the store on clothes and supplies.'

'And no one took any notice of him?'

'I wouldn't say that,' Moss grinned. 'A stranger in town, you couldn't miss him.'

Mungo glared at him. 'That's not what the boss was talkin' about. Since when do Abos get the run of the town?'

'Since idiots like you let it happen,' his boss retorted.

'You only said to watch him,' Moss complained. 'And we done that. He rode out this morning.'

'Where to? Towards Mitchell? Heading back to the coast?'

This time the brothers looked at each other, hesitating, until Mungo replied, 'Well . . . not exactly. But he's left town.'

'Which way did he go?' the boss's voice was menacing.

'Thisaway,' Mungo admitted, 'but then he took off into the scrub. Might be he was heading for the diggings, cross-country.'

'And you didn't follow him?'

'We didn't know as we were supposed to,' Moss said apologetically.

'You mean you lost him!'

'The bugger was armed,' Mungo said. 'We didn't want to get too close.'

'He was what?' Ben felt as if the whole district was conspiring against him. 'An Abo comes into town, marches into the pubs without a licence and then calmly buys what? A rifle and ammo?'

They nodded in unison.

'Abos are strictly forbidden to carry arms. Or didn't you remember that? Have you all gone mad?'

'You shoulda thought of that!' Moss accused his brother.

'Why me?' Mungo snapped. 'I was doin' most of the watchin' while you was hangin' about that floozie.'

Ben was furious. This was his land, his territory. He wasn't about to allow that bastard to ride roughshod over him, making a fool of him. And he bet, somewhere along the line, that Lottie Smith was at the back of this, the money-grabbing old cow. He should have fired her from Caravale Station as soon as his mother died instead of letting her hang on, poking her long nose into his business. He'd get her for this.

'Is McAlister still sergeant of police?' he asked them.

'Yeah. But he was outa town,' Mungo said, pleased to find an excuse. 'He wouldna' put up with no cheek from an Abo.'

Exactly, Ben thought.

'I'll give you a letter in the morning, Mungo,' he said. 'I want you to take it to town and hand it personally to McAlister. And no one else. Do you think you can get that right?'

'Sure, boss. I'll be ready when you are.'

Clara called out to him as he stormed past the parlour, heading for his study: 'Dinner's ready. We're waiting for you, Ben.'

'In a minute,' he replied sharply. If her mother hadn't been with them he'd have told her, and her brat of a friend, to eat dinner on their bloody own. He was fed up with the both of them. But he wanted to write the letter now, while its main points were in his head. He'd been composing it all the way back from the stables.

McAlister was just the man he needed right now. As a boy, Alan McAlister had lived on a remote cattle station west of Rockhampton, until they'd been attacked by blacks. His mother and father had been killed and his uncle savagely wounded by spears. The lad, hidden in a cupboard, had escaped notice, and as soon as the marauders had left he'd ridden sixty miles, right through the night, to find help. By the time a posse of volunteers had thundered up to the McAlister homestead it was too late. His uncle had also died. Alan had grown up a bitter man with a fierce hatred of blacks. Where they were concerned he went well past the letter of the law – everyone knew that, and understood – but he'd proved to be an excellent lawman and now nearing sixty he would soon be retiring.

Ben took a sheet of his parliamentary stationery, which he would use for added impact, and began to scribble notes before actually penning the letter. First would come his greetings and disappointment that Alan would be retiring, since he doubted anyone could replace a man of his capabilities.

Next – he hated to bother him but he had received several complaints which he felt should be brought to the sergeant's notice – business people in the town were blatantly breaking the law. Probably, he added, through greed, but that was no excuse.

He outlined the offences: a half-caste Aborigine who went under the name of Beckman had been in the town for several days flaunting the law by drinking and being accommodated at the Shamrock Hotel without a licence. Keeping in mind that the said Beckman also had a record, having spent years in jail.

'That,' he said to himself with smug satisfaction, 'will bring McAlister down on old Lottie and her husband like a ton of bricks.'

Next, he noted, he should inform Alan that the half-caste – he crossed out half-caste and wrote 'blackfellow' – had also purchased a rifle and ammunition in Charleville, which had shocked several residents.

And so on.

He was penning the letter with great care when Clara came to the door. 'Ben, dinner will be getting cold.'

'Then start without me,' he said crankily. 'Can't you see I'm busy? I won't be long.'

The envelope also carried the state seal so Ben addressed it with care in his best handwriting. He then folded his letter in the correct manner: one half-fold of the page and two folds inwards so that it would fit the small envelope and the recipient would find it opened out without further ado.

Then he placed it inside a much larger envelope, sealed it with the all-important wax stamp available only to a gentleman of his parliamentary status, and addressed it to Sgt Alan McAlister.

He called one of the black maids and told her to run down and give it to Mungo and no one else, and instruct him to head for town at sunup.

In Charleville, Ben had noticed that, as a stranger in this one-street town, he was something of a curiosity, but it hadn't bothered him. Re-equipped, he rode out, this time sure of his directions, having walked the route. Learned it the hard way, he smiled to himself as his new mount cantered down the road. This was a sturdy grey horse which the dealer had tried to tell him was a pure-bred even though he had the hefty gait of a brumby strain, and powerful shoulders to match. But Ben hadn't argued. It was called Pepper, which he'd thought at the time the Irish horse-trader had just invented, since he didn't seem to be too familiar with the animal, keeping well back and pointing him out in the paddock. And he'd asked almost double what the horse was worth, but Ben had paid up without argument, not caring that he was being taken for a ride.

But once off the road into the bush he soon found that Pepper could be the animal's true name. He doubted it could have been long broken in. Smelling the freedom of the scrub, Pepper took off like lightning, determined to dislodge his rider and find his way back to his mob.

'Oh! You're a bossman, are you?' Ben said to the horse, glad that he remembered to buy hobbles, otherwise he'd lose this mount. Ducking to avoid branches and hauling the horse aside to prevent him from slamming him against trees, Bed had a wild ride until he was able to take control again. He was angry, not with this horse but with Buchanan, thinking of that other poor animal now lying dead on a lonely road. 'You'll pay for that,' he said through gritted teeth, but he had to acknowledge the depressing fact that he had no idea how this could be accomplished. Despite his high-ranking status the man was a criminal and a coward, but there was no way Ben could retaliate without landing himself in jail again. White laws were too powerful.

After mulling over this problem for far too long, he tried to think of Phoebe but that didn't help. He felt he was losing her. So it was with a sense of relief that he sighted Mandjala waiting patiently by the old humpy. The quiet Aborigine seemed to Ben to represent normality in this confusing place.

As he unpacked some supplies the horse began playing up again, neighing, pawing at the ground, pulling away into the glow of the setting sun, always to the west. Ben needed Mandjala's help to hobble the animal. When at last he was quieter, moodily snorting in disgust, Ben laughed. 'He's a real villain. We'll have to watch him or I'll be tramping back to Charleville again.'

Mandjala nodded. 'That fella Winnaroo mob wild horses. Him wanna go home.'

'Oh yes! Winnaroo!' Ben looked about him. 'Everything is so different now since the rains, like a new country. Where is it from here?'

'Horse knows.' Mandjala grinned. 'That way. Into the sun. Going on past that burnt-up whitefeller house.' With a sigh of satisfaction he sucked on the clay pipe that Ben had bought for him. 'White men call that land Winnaroo too, but people all gone now.'

Ben was interested. 'That's Winnaroo Station? Of course! It adjoins Fairmont Station.'

His friend, having no aversion to whitefellow food, was more interested in the corned beef and strange tins that he was unpacking, but Ben's mind was racing. 'The Buchanans. They know about the Winnaroo Springs, so Phoebe would know too. Or it shouldn't be hard for her to find out. She could ride over there and meet me. It can't be too far.' Mandjala, he knew, could judge the distance exactly from the homestead to the springs but he couldn't translate it.

'Mandjala,' he said, taking out a pencil and some writing paper, 'if I put a message on a page like this could you get into Fairmont Station with it?'

The Aborigine nodded agreement without hesitation.

'Could you ask someone there to give it to Miss Phoebe, in secret.'

'Miz Fee-bee,' Mandjala repeated slowly, pleased that the pronunciation caused him no trouble. 'Black girls work in big houses. They givemup to Fee-bee.' Then he laughed. 'Good joke, eh? Keep secret?'

'Yes. I want to ask her to meet me at the Winnaroo Springs.'

'Good place,' Mandjala agreed. 'Him fella horse be happy.'

'Yeah, too happy. I'll have to rope him down.'

In the morning Ben emerged to see a white ibis fluttering around near the humpy. Since it was unusual to see a bird like that so close to the ground with a human nearby, he walked over to investigate and was immediately saddened to see another bird lying dead nearby. Its mate still flapped about, frantic in its distress, hoping, maybe, that it would revive, refusing to leave the poor still body.

'Look here,' Ben called to Mandjala.

'Ah!' the old man cried, throwing up his hands. He looked up to the sky for the hawk that had probably felled the ibis but there was no sign of it, only the bloody stain on the bird's feathers.

He lowered himself to the ground to sit cross-legged a few yards from its broken-hearted mate, watching as it fluttered over the body, landing on its black stilt legs and lifting off again as soon as it touched ground. Ben squatted further back out of the way.

Gently Mandjala picked up a stick and snapped it in half, startling the bird but not enough to frighten it away. Then he leaned forward and placed the broken sticks apart, near to the dead bird.

He began to sing in a low, monotonous chant until at last, tiring, the bird came to rest, standing awkwardly, head drooping as if listening to his song.

When the chant stopped, the ibis turned away to step daintily through the grass, head dipping as if feeding, from habit. Then, confused, it came back again, not knowing what to do. For a long time it wandered about and Ben's thoughts drifted to his mother, remembering the time Diamond had sung to the snake. He was always upset when he thought of her and wondered when he'd ever get over it. He'd been able to accept Oma's death, even though that had been a shock; why couldn't he do the same with Diamond? When he looked again the bird had disappeared.

'Where did it go?' he asked.

'She had to go back to her nest for the babies,' Mandjala replied.

He took the dead bird, wrapped it in bark and placed it on a high branch. 'This bird totem my people,' he said. 'I put him away to help her stop crying.' Then he looked at Ben. 'What totem your fambly?'

'I don't know. Snake I think, but I don't know which one.'

Mandjala shook his head in disgust.

Later Ben lit the fire, with matches, and sizzled some beefsteak in the ashes with potatoes. He'd kept that meat aside as a surprise for Mandjala, who ate with relish.

'Why did you break the sticks back there?' he asked.

Mandjala tapped his head. 'So she know. Broken. Gone. Wild things they doan unnerstand dead. Sometimes they love so much they nebber leave, they die too. I tell her that fella a spirit now so she mus' stop crying.' He folded his arms and sat back. 'You my frien', Ben. You tell me why you still cryin'.'

'What?' Ben was startled and not a little embarrassed. 'I'm not crying.'

'Last time you come walkabout here you was allasame cryin' inside, just like her. Back of me I feel you cryin' still.'

'No I'm not,' Ben denied. 'I'm worried about the girl, Phoebe.'

Mandjala moved his shaggy grey head from side to side. 'Worry not allasame cryin'. Come one day she tell you to put down your cryin'.'

'Who, Phoebe?'

'No, the snake woman.'

Ben was so astonished, sitting there by the embers of their fire with only the burping of frogs and the occasional cries of settling birds to break the massive stillness about them, that he could feel the hairs standing up on the back of his neck. He didn't want to ask but he had to.

'What about the snake woman?'

Mandjala poked in the ashes with the stubby remains of a sapling as he considered the question. 'She is a spirit now,' he said, 'but she can't go yet.' His voice sounded more confident, and Ben didn't know if he were imagining it, but Mandjala's English seemed better and his eyes were glazed as if he were in a trance. 'She can't go until you are safe.'

'I'm safe now,' he retorted.

'Too many no-good fights in you. When you put them down, she can go and the crying will be over.'

Ben didn't know what to say to that, and Mandjala seemed to have lost interest. He dropped several handfuls of nuts on to the embers, watching them heat and crack open, then whipped them out and dropped them beside him to cool.

What fights? Ben asked himself, feeling defensive, but he knew he hadn't forgiven Dr Thurlwell, nor his new enemy Buchanan. And he would never do that.

But there was something else. Coming out to see Phoebe had given him the excuse he needed to absent himself from the stables. He reflected that his life had become boring, going to work every morning at the same time and returning home every night at the same time, with Sundays off. It was too regimented, and he'd had his share of regimentation. Added to that, Ben found that he had to make work for himself during the day because everything was running so smoothly at both the stables and the saddlery. He would surprise the stableboys by grooming the horses himself and spent quite a bit of time in the small factory learning how to make saddles, even though such detailed work didn't appeal to him.

There was always the eventual interest in motorcars of course, but that was a long way off.

Maybe he wouldn't feel so restless when he was married. The joy of having Phoebe at home, waiting for him, would have a settling influence, he was sure. Then he smiled. Or it could make it harder for him to leave her and take himself off to boring work!

He supposed it would all work out in the end, but there was still a hollow feeling inside him, a strange sense of failure.

They waited dinner for him at Clara's insistence and when he did arrive to take his seat at the head of the table Belle was surprised to find him in a cheerful mood, talking of the latest news of Brisbane where plans were afoot to build another much-needed bridge across the river.

Phoebe was very quiet, hardly saying a word, intimidated by him since their altercation this afternoon, but Belle wasn't worried about her now. She'd survive.

'I was thinking,' Belle said, as they began the main course of roast beef and Yorkshire pudding, 'that Clara could be on the right track after all.'

'What about?' Ben asked.

'About retaining this property,' Belle said calmly. 'My word, this pudding is excellent. Just right.'

'And why would you say that?' he asked evenly, almost patronizingly, although she saw the cold glint in his eyes.

That's right, my lad, Belle thought. You take care how you address me. I'm not your wife. And I've got a fat bankroll to back me up.

'The station is restocked, it's faring well and with natural increase you'll be able to cover your losses.'

'And if we have another drought next year?'

'You've been a cattleman long enough, Ben. You know these things come in cycles. It could be a decade before the rains fail again.'

Clara, at first dumbfounded at her mother's sudden change of heart, was now delighted. 'That's what I've been saying. We've got time now to steel ourselves against droughts. We can sink more wells, and save money, not be spending so much . . .' She faltered on that line, wishing she hadn't said that. It was Ben who did all the spending, living it up in Brisbane and investing in failed ventures.

Her mother sighed. Trust Clara to put her foot in it. But no matter. 'You could still remain on those boards in Brisbane, Ben,' she said quietly. 'Those remunerations are not to be sneezed at.'

'I'm glad you appreciate that,' he retorted, 'but you don't seem to understand Belle, that restocking costs money. Despite what Clara thinks, I have had a great deal more experience than her and this property is not fully restocked. We could easily carry another two thousand head.'

'It will take time,' Clara said.

He turned on her fiercely. 'How often do I have to tell you we don't have the time! We don't have the money to carry on!'

Belle smiled. 'You worry too much, Ben. That's your trouble. For a start you could sell that house in Brisbane. It's an imposing residence and since you have had it redecorated and refurnished it's looking very grand. I'd say you could get top price for it.'

'I see,' he replied very slowly. 'And in my capacity as a Member of Parliament where do you suggest I should reside? In some cheap hotel room?'

'Quite a few of them do when they come down from country centres,' she said, 'since that occupation carries no salary. But one could not expect that of you. My residence is hardly a cottage, in fact it's twice as big as your Brisbane house, with only me rattling about in it. It's meant for entertaining,' she added in a wistful voice, 'with its lovely gardens. You'd be most welcome to stay with me when you come to town. Both of you.'

'I wouldn't want to impose on your generosity,' he countered.

'You wouldn't be doing that, for heaven's sake! You'd be making an old woman very happy.' Belle was about to add that after all, she was presently enjoying his hospitality, but remembered that Phoebe was too, and wisely decided not to include her in this very important conversation.

'I'll think about it,' he said, pushing away his plate with its half-eaten meal.

A glance at the disappointment on Clara's face told Belle that she hadn't succeeded in convincing him yet, so a little more pressure was required. This wretch of a man had to be pinned down.

She finished the glass of claret before her, and adjusting her glasses, peered down the table. 'I'd do more than think about it, my dear. It's all very well to be on these boards, but as everyone knows they're apt to switch and change, depending on who's popular this week and who isn't. And if you happen to lose your seat in Parliament then, to the people behind the scenes who hold the reins, you could have outlived your usefulness.'

Belle watched as he poured himself another glass of claret from the decanter. It was a threat, a double threat, and he knew it. She had enough pull in Brisbane to have him yanked off any board, and as an outsider, not residing in his electorate, he'd need plenty of support to retain that seat.

Then, as if to cheer him up, she turned to Clara. 'You'll be forty next month. The bonds that your father put aside for you will come due. Quite a tidy sum, running into thousands I believe. That should help to pick up the financial slack on the station.'

'Bonds!' Clara was so excited she knocked over her glass, which, fortunately, was empty. She was gaping as she righted it. 'I didn't know about any bonds.'

'That's because you never listen,' Belle said serenely. There were no bonds, but if Clara could hold on to the station and her investment in it, then she would need more capital. And cash from a source like this was a more tactful way of placing money at Clara's disposal than an outright contribution to the station by her mother.

Overjoyed, Clara looked to her husband. She'd missed the cold message her mother had just delivered to him. 'Ben, you must listen to Mother. She's right. It's more important to own land than to rely on salaries. You chose this station yourself and you made a good choice. We can't give up on it now. And with this extra money . . .'

He shoved back his chair and stalked out of the room.

'And how was your day?' Belle asked Phoebe.

'Very nice, thank you,' the girl mumbled. 'Very nice.'

She hated this man who could sit so confidently at his table ignoring her discomfort, knowing she'd be mortified trying to stuff down a meal that was nearly choking her. If she had remained in her room, or even failed to eat her dinner, Clara would be concerned, and Belle would be asking questions and Phoebe wasn't up to it.

Not looking forward to this next encounter with Buchanan, she'd determined to sit quietly in her most ladylike manner and just get through it. But as the conversation progressed she was fascinated. There was no need for her to speak at all, indeed had she done so it would have been intrusive. Belle Foster had at last come round to her daughter's point of view, and about time! And she was letting *him* know, without sounding offensive, that he'd better change his tune too. Or else. Phoebe was thrilled, he was taking a real pasting, losing the argument. She wouldn't have missed this for the world! Clara had won the right to stay on the property.

When Belle had insisted that he should use her house as his Brisbane residence, Phoebe had dropped her head to hide the glee in her eyes. What a laugh! Moving in with his formidable mother-in-law would be like placing him under guard. Apart from the relationship between Buchanan and Lalla, which she hadn't been able to help noticing, Phoebe had heard plenty of gossip about him in Brisbane. He was known as quite the ladies' man but naturally, no one would be so cruel as to mention it to Clara.

Phoebe wondered if Belle had heard the gossip, and then dismissed that thought. No one would be game to criticize anyone in Mrs Foster's family, right or wrong, she'd be likely to tell them to mind their own business. No. She'd seen the station for herself now. Seen that it was recovering from the drought, Phoebe decided, and realized it would be foolish to sell. Thank God!

After dinner Clara, still excited and enthusiastic, brought out the station books and ledgers, which she kept diligently, to prove to her mother that there was no need to worry any more. Especially with the assistance of the windfall of bond money, the property would be showing a profit again in no time.

Leaving them to it, Phoebe took her book and retired to her room. Now that she was feeling so much better and her friend Clara was in high spirits, it was a good chance for her to tell them that she had decided to return home. She had to get away from him, it was intolerable to be staying in his house now. She would say that she was concerned about her parents and really ought to be home in case she was needed. Someone could take her into Charleville in the buggy, and she was quite capable of taking the train from there. She'd seen several women travelling alone on the journey out, even down in the rougher second-class carriages. It would be fun to do the journey on her own.

Preparing for bed she pulled back the covers and plumped the pillows in a heap so that she could sit up and read, and it was then that she noticed a note under a pillow.

A note? Smiling, she thought it might be some cheery little message from Clara. Maybe Clara was so thrilled about the latest developments that she wanted to share her joy with Phoebe later. On the quiet.

But it was a note within two envelopes. For protection. As she looked at the pencilled words she stared in shock.

The letter was signed by Ben Beckman! Her Ben!

She looked about the room, bewildered. He must he here. On the station! But why the secrecy? Her first thought was to rush outside on to the veranda to look for him but she steadied herself and sat down to read the letter.

Her face was grim when she'd finished it. She'd thought they were her friends, Belle and Clara at least, but they'd all conspired against her. Ben hadn't received her letters and although he'd written to her, where were they? It dawned on Phoebe then that they'd intercepted her letters, ingoing and outgoing. That she'd been kept from contact with Ben by their deliberate actions. She was so angry she felt like barging out and confronting them there and then, but she read on. He had attempted to visit her but had been turned back at the gate. He didn't say by whom.

How dare they! Was she a prisoner here?

'We'll see about that,' she snapped.

But Ben was here. Waiting for her. At Winnaroo Springs. And she did know where that was, Clara had shown it to her.

She'd heard them talking about the springs often enough and one day when they were checking boundary fences, which were in a constant state of disrepair thanks to roaming gold prospectors who simply smashed through them in casual disregard of other people's property, Clara had taken her to the crest of a hill and pointed them out.

Phoebe had expected to see an oasis of tall greenery across the flats, but instead there was only a vast spread of grassy plains with young trees sprouting everywhere, just the same as on the Buchanan property.

'Where?' she'd asked.

'See that big outcrop of rocks,' Clara said, 'with a cliff face to the west. In there. The springs are inside. It looks such a solid core of rock that we didn't know it held springs until a few years back.'

'Would the owner have known about it?' Phoebe asked.

'I'm sure he would have but he never let on. Old Tom McCracken was a crafty fellow.'

'Then why did he quit the property if he had water there.'

'The springs wouldn't be enough to water a station and the creeks dried up. He had started putting in wells, probably following the underground course of the springs, but he came to grief routing cattle from the scrub. He used to ride like a maniac and his horse fell. He was gored by a bull and died a few days later. His wife tried to hang on, with the drought getting worse, but the cook she had at the time was a drunk. He ended up setting fire to the kitchen and before she, or any of the men, could get back to the homestead, the whole place was on fire.'

'What happened to the cook?'

'He got out and then he bolted, which was just as well. If she'd caught him she'd have shot him. Anyway, that was too much for her. She sold all the cattle, paid off the men and quit the land for good. The property is up for sale but I haven't heard of any takers yet.'

Winnaroo Springs. Phoebe was almost sure she could find her way alone to that boundary, but she'd have to be careful. She'd never ventured that far, more than twenty miles, without Clara, and the bush had a terrible sameness about it so it would be easy to get lost.

There was no way she could reply to Ben, since she had no idea which one of the black housegirls had smuggled the letter into her room. It had to have been one of them but she didn't dare ask. Phoebe was thrilled with Ben's resourcefulness. He was a very determined man, one of the many things she admired about him. And she would show him that she could be equally resourceful. Instead of riding cross-country and taking the risk of becoming lost, she'd ride straight out and follow the boundaries. But which way?

Phoebe was tired, she couldn't remember in which direction they'd been travelling when Clara had shown her the site of the springs. This station was massive. Where on earth had they been that day? She wished she'd taken more notice, but even that would have been hard. Clara made constant detours to water the horses and for dozens of other reasons.

She had to force herself to climb into bed to try to get some sleep, but as she lay there she made her plans for the next day.

It seemed only minutes later when Clara woke her. 'Come on, sleepyhead. Do you want to come out with me this morning?'

Phoebe squinted from under the eiderdown at the pale morning. 'Oh, it's cold,' she said, snuggling down. 'I don't feel up to it this morning.'

Clara laughed. 'Yes, it is cold. Very well, you have a good rest. I'll see you later. Would you like breakfast in bed?'

'Thank you. I would.' She knew that the cook preferred guests to have breakfast in their rooms rather than spoil her kitchen routine, since Clara and Ben were served at six o'clock or earlier, and that suited Phoebe very well.

Even though she was anxious to be on her way, she stayed in bed until Sissie, one of the black girls, brought in her tray. Sissie was all smiles as usual, telling her to eat up while the sausages and eggs were still hot. Nothing amiss. No glances at the pillow. Phoebe still had no way of telling who had brought the note.

But as soon as Sissie left, Phoebe was out of bed, snatching at the food as she dressed. This was to be a busy day so she ate every scrap, mopping up with toast, and drank the hot tea. Then, with angry resolve, she packed all of her clothes into her suitcase, leaving aside only the necessities for the day. Later they would discover she had gone. They didn't deserve an explanation. None of them. She would meet Ben and ask him to take her straight to Charleville, from where she could go by train to Brisbane.

She shoved the suitcase under the bed and finished dressing in her riding clothes and heavy suede jacket. Before she left she looked about the room. When Sissie came in to make the bed she wouldn't notice anything different. The room was as neat as Phoebe always left it, with the wardrobe and drawers closed and Clara's crystal dressing table set in place on the lace runner. As an afterthought, she rummaged in her suitcase and pulled out her nightgown, throwing it on the bed. She didn't want Dorrie searching for it to put it in its rightful place under the pillow.

When she arrived home, Phoebe decided, she would write to Clara explaining why she had left and her disappointment at the treatment she had received at their hands, even though it had obviously been instigated by her mother. She would ask Clara to send her luggage on.

She stuffed handkerchiefs in her pocket, and a small roll of pound notes into an inside pocket, wrapped a scarf around her neck, picked up her riding cap and left the house via the veranda.

A black stockman saddled Cleo for her. 'Goin' down to the stockyards, missee?' he asked, excitement in his voice.

'No,' she said. 'Why?'

'Big musterin' for brandin' goin' on down there,' he said, as if disappointed that he had to stay and work at the stables.

'I think I'll just ride down to the gate,' she said. 'It's quieter. By the way,' she asked him as she mounted the horse, 'where are the Winnaroo Springs?'

'Them out there,' he said, pointing over past the homestead, 'long ways.'

'Thank you,' Phoebe replied as she rode off.

Moss heard the last of the conversation as he came out of the stables. His horse had thrown a shoe and was being re-shod. It should be ready by this. As he marched down to the blacksmith's he wondered why the city girl would be going to the springs. He'd taken visitors over there himself, it was the talk of the district, but ladies didn't go out there alone.

Being a single-minded fellow, Moss discussed this with the blacksmith, who also thought it was a matter for concern. 'Bloody fool women,' he said. 'Gotta peek into everything! She'll get lost out there sure as hell and we'll be up half the night lookin' for her. You better tell the missus.'

'She's out roundin' up strays,' Moss said. 'I gotta get down to the yards. We're shorthanded with Mungo away.'

'Then tell the big boss. He's thereabouts. He'll have your hide if that girl don't come in by dark with you knowin' about it.'

He was right. Moss didn't want this responsibility. He collected his horse and rode down to the mud and mayhem of hundreds of cranky cattle as they were being herded through the maze of fences and gates to be seared by the Fairmont branding irons.

The boss was there, standing astride rails in the centre of the action, shouting at the men to keep the cattle moving, and shoving them through the tight runs with the whip and the boot. Moss didn't have a chance to speak to him then, he had his own work to do, but when the first mob were through and they stopped for smoko he ambled over to Buchanan.

'I was wonderin',' he said, 'if that Miss Phoebe's gonna be all right? Ridin' off on her own, like, to them Winnaroo Springs.'

'What are you talking about?' the boss said impatiently.

'Miss Phoebe. She rode off to the springs.'

'Don't be bloody stupid! The springs are over on McCracken's station.'

'Ah well . . . yeah.' Moss didn't like being called stupid in front of the other blokes. He should have minded his own business, he thought, as he hunched his shoulders and moved away. If Buchanan was such a know-all, let him handle it.

The boss drank his black tea from an enamel mug and stared moodily into the campfire. That bloody fool got everything mixed up. But then he began to think about it. What if she *had* headed for the springs, alone? Why would she do that? She never went far on her own, and that was a fair way. And why there?

The answer jolted him. Had Beckman contacted her? Had he arranged, somehow, for her to meet him there? Mungo had said they'd lost him, and they thought, the pair of idiots, that he could have been headed this way. Jesus! He suddenly realized that Phoebe Thurlwell would believe Beckman, that he'd been fired on first. It wasn't a matter of the courts any more, it was her big mouth. She already hated him. She'd shout it to the rooftops, and even though he could deny it, in the hotbed of Brisbane politics, mud stuck.

He whistled to Moss, who put down the branding iron he was reheating in the small stone fireplace and came lumbering back.

'How do you know she went to the springs?'

'I heard her asking the way,' Moss replied sullenly.

'Bloody hell!' the boss said with feigned irritation at having his work interrupted. 'Get your horse. We'll head her off.'

Moss swung on to his horse, feeling vindicated. And he was a bit proud to be riding off with the boss himself even though he knew the rest of the blokes would be too involved in their work to take much notice. They'd think they were just going after another mob of cattle, not on an easy ride to catch up with the young lady,

But it wasn't an easy ride. The boss rode hard, heading straight for the springs.

As they forded a creek Moss was confused. 'She'd never have got this far, boss. She wouldn't know the short cuts.'

'Exactly. I'm not riding around the scrub all day looking for a bloody female. We'll go to the springs and wait. And if she doesn't turn up then we'll find her on the way back.'

Moss had his reservations about that idea. If he had his way they'd split up and criss-cross this patch of country right now. Before she got any further. But he supposed the boss knew what he was doing, and besides, it was getting him out of a day's hard work. The blokes would be cursing by this, being short three hands. And he bet the missus wouldn't be too pleased. She'd be real crook on that girl for messing up the day's schedule.

Mandjala had been welcomed in the blacks' camp on Fairmont Station with great joy. They hugged him and smiled and wept to see him again, for he was an elder of the scattered clan, held in great respect as a wise man who was gravitating, they all knew, towards the great honour of being a magic man, a keeper of the secrets.

He sat in the shade by the waterhole and talked to them of old times and new times, with laughter and with sadness, and his message letter was taken with due care, its destination assured. It passed from hand to hand on to a runner who took it as far as the dairy where some of their girls worked, and it was then slipped to one of the housegirls. Neither Mandjala nor any of his friends knew exactly how the white girl would receive the message, they just knew it would be done.

In the morning, some of the young ones went off to watch the big marking parade of the cattle, but Mandjala stayed with his friends, listening to their stories and answering, to the best of his ability, their questions of tribal protocol, much undermined these days. He had carried out Ben's instructions, the girl would know he was there at the springs. It was up to her now. Mandjala still felt an uneasiness about Ben's relationship with this white girl but accepted that he didn't understand their ways, even though it seemed to him that Ben was trying to steal a girl from another clan. A clan that did not approve the match. Such a situation was always trouble. But then, the young man had never had proper guidance, he mused sadly.

Winnaroo Springs was still a wondrous place, so full of the secrets of an ancient past. The rough fences that they'd built were long gone, trampled by horses, the remains of sturdy saplings engulfed by stringy grass. The track was wider now, the undergrowth shouldered aside by horses and men, but regrowth had already begun, determined ferns surging forward like a small army, battling for space.

With an ache of regret, Ben remembered Cash and his wild ways. His treachery had cut deep because at that time he'd been Ben's only friend, and like Willy his childhood friend, he'd proved to be false. But it had been his own fault, he'd been too eager for company, too eager to be accepted. Was he still? he wondered. Being a boss had made a difference, the question never seemed to arise any more.

If Phoebe had received his message – and had decided to make the effort to meet him at the springs – she couldn't possibly be here before noon today, so he led his horse down the steep winding track to make camp at the sandy edge of the deep waterhole. Then, with Pepper well roped and time on his hands, he set off to explore the area.

He scrambled over rocks and boulders as he circumnavigated the hidden lake, finding shallow caves with Aborigine signs and hand paintings on the walls. Ben studied them, interested, because he knew they spoke of the legends of the Dreamtime, but he couldn't interpret them. Continuing on, a difficult climb at times, he kept searching for a route to the top of the cliffs because from there he'd have a great view of the surrounding countryside, a lookout from where he could watch for Phoebe.

But no matter how hard he tried, he couldn't make it to the top. Gazing about him, accepting defeat, he realized that this was a crater, the cone of an ancient volcano, so heavily wooded on the inside it had been hard to distinguish.

'Oh well, that's that,' he said, and moved on, fascinated by the proliferation of ancient cycads and bush orchids that he came across, listening to the songs and twitterings of so many birds, busy in their own domain, and watching the swift little rock wallabies that dodged past him, taking the heights with ease.

'It's a greenhouse, an aviary and a private zoo, all in one,' he said to himself, looking down at the dazzling water below him.

Ben began to feel that he owned this lonely pool of tranquillity and looked forward to showing it to Phoebe, certain she'd be as enthralled as he was by the beauty surrounding them. He hadn't specifically asked her to come alone but he hoped she would. By now she'd be aware that he wasn't welcome at Fairmont.

Once again doubts arose. What if she ignored his request? What if she didn't want to see him?

'Oh well,' he shrugged, answering his own questions. 'Camping here for a few days won't be a hardship. After that . . . we'll see.'

They had reached Boundary Creek and started to head across McCracken's property towards the landmark of rock, but they still hadn't set eyes on the girl. The ride had taken the two experienced horsemen only two hours, so Moss figured if she was on the right track she'd be at least an hour behind them. That was if she hadn't fallen off and broken her neck, or stopped to pick flowers, which ladies seemed to like to do.

'Do you reckon she'll make it?' he asked the boss, still believing it would be smarter to turn back and find her now, but Buchanan ignored him and cantered on at a slower pace with his destination in sight.

At the base of the huge rock, which always seemed so much smaller from the other property, the boss reined in.

'You wait here,' he told Moss. 'She has to come from this direction, so watch out. I'll take a look around.'

'Suits me,' Moss said, dismounting and reaching into his pocket for his tobacco pouch. 'I'll give you a coo-ee if I sight her, but I reckon she'll be a while yet.'

Buchanan didn't like this place. He'd grown up on Caravale Station, so deep into Aborigine territory that the Charleville district seemed almost like a suburb to him. From the first time a stockman had brought him over here and shown him the hidden entrance to the springs, he'd been wary. Aborigine superstitions were ingrained in him because he'd seen so much of their culture. He'd seen men die after the bone-pointing ceremonies and he'd learned to keep away from their sacred places, they brought bad luck.

He looked up at the towering rock, like a monolith in the middle of the plain, and shuddered, riding quietly, hugging the base. While he had no respect for the breed, he had plenty of healthy respect for the Abos' mysterious and secret 'business', and this was a sacred place if ever he'd seen one. Bad joss, the Chinamen used to call Aborigine secrets, and they were always careful never to cross an Abo magic man or intrude on bora grounds.

He'd only been in here once before, and while Clara and her friends had been cooling off in the waterhole he'd explored the interior of this walled jungle and found the caves with the ochre paintings.

When he came back to the group he'd heard them saying that this place was probably once used by the blacks, but that they were all long gone.

Like hell they are, he'd thought. The paintings were as fresh as they'd been when they were put there, maybe centuries ago, which meant that chosen ones, magic men from each generation, had come, and were still coming, to renew the paint. Not that they'd be about now, no one ever saw them, that was another secret. But the bloody place still bothered him.

And more so now because he was certain that Beckman was hanging about here somewhere.

'Bad joss for him too,' he said softly as he tethered his horse, took his rifle and loaded it before moving towards the entrance between the scattered boulders. Beckman wasn't outside, he'd made sure of that, so he had to be in there. Trapped. There was no other way out. If he was careful he could get a snipe shot at the bastard, finish him off and drop the body into the dense undergrowth where the dingoes would make short work of it. The plan was so perfect he could feel himself becoming irritated at the thought that maybe Beckman wasn't here after all. Doubting his explanation for her sudden and sly journey out this way.

But he was here now, and he had to make sure. He didn't care whether the girl made it or not. If she got lost, he almost laughed, it would be her bad luck. Bad joss again. As for Moss, if he happened to hear a shot, he'd be so slow off the mark it would be all over before he came to investigate. And it could be easily explained. Wild duck. A pot shot. Missed.

At each bend down the track he waited and then stepped out to move stealthily on again.

And then, suddenly, there he was! Beckman! Coming towards him up the slope. He hadn't heard him coming. Clara had said he was going deaf but that was rubbish, he could hear as well as anyone. Besides, the half-caste, who'd stopped short, looking up at him in shock, was barefoot.

'Hands up!' he shouted, in full control this time, pleased to see that Beckman was unarmed. Or was he?

'What do *you* want?' Beckman said angrily, his hands high.

'I want the knife first.'

'What knife?'

'Raise that trouser leg and if you make a wrong move I'll blow a hole in you.' It would be easier to take him deeper into the crater to shoot him, rather than having to lug him down and leave blood on the track.

Jubilant, he saw the leather strap. 'Undo it and throw it, pouch and all.' He was only yards away, rifle trained, so Beckman had no choice. Using one hand, the other still raised, he released the pouch with the knife and tossed it aside.

Buchanan couldn't resist boasting. 'You beat me last time. I forgot about the knife. Did she teach you to carry a knife like that? You, a town nigger?'

'Who are we talking about?' Beckman replied coldly.

'A woman called Diamond.'

Beckman looked up at the older man standing over him, and nodded. 'I thought so. She didn't teach me, but it is her knife.'

'No use to you now, is it?'

'That's obvious. What do you want with me? I've never bothered you. I never realized I had any connection with you until you attacked me when I came to your gate.'

'The hell you didn't!'

His prisoner looked at him calmly; he didn't seem to grasp that he could count his life in minutes now. 'That's interesting,' he said. 'So there is a connection? For what it's worth, I have got a live father after all.'

'You've got nothing! Your mother was a whore. You could take your pick of fathers but I don't want you about pointing the finger at me.'

'And that's why we're here?'

'Yes.'

Ben stood very still. There was no denying that this maniac needed to kill him to defend his reputation, and no point in begging for his life. He couldn't bring himself to do that anyway. But even at this late hour he wanted to know more about his mother. He felt she was close to him now, in death. Waiting for him. As if this meeting of the trio were preordained. 'My mother is dead now,' he said.

'I know that.'

'And I know she was with you in the north.' Ben meant on Caravale Station, and he was surprised when Buchanan nodded.

'Yes, that's true enough. I got the fever on the Palmer goldfields and she hauled me out. I have to admit I admired her. She had plenty of grit.'

'Did she go with you to the Palmer?'

'No. She just turned up, probably a camp follower with the rest of the whores.'

'My mother wasn't a whore. Stop saying that!'

'Jesus, you're wet behind the ears!' He was in no hurry and seemed to have a need to talk. 'When she was on my station, working as a lady's maid, I was mad about her. I can tell you that now. She was gorgeous, I'd never met an Abo like her in my life.'

Ben winced but let him talk, watching for an opportunity to act.

'She was intelligent too, and literate. But I wouldn't marry a black gin and as soon as she heard that, she was trouble. She had to go.' He shrugged. 'She headed for Charters Towers, and don't try denying me on this. I knew Diamond's every move. She worked in a Chinese brothel, and with a name like hers she was famous. Her mate Goldie is the madam at The Blue Heaven in Brisbane. But I suppose *you* never went there.'

Ben ignored that. 'But she still helped you when you got the fever on the Palmer goldfields?'

'So what? Turn around and start walking down. Keep your hands up. And walk wide on that bend so I can see you.'

The track was still damp and slippery, Ben, in bare feet, could tread easily but he knew Buchanan, wearing boots, would have to take care. As he rounded the corner he turned back. 'Can I ask you something else?'

'Like what?'

'Did you find gold on the Palmer?'

'No. I was too ill. It was all a big bloody waste of time.'

'Diamond wasn't there as a whore. She was up there to find her tribe. Her own family.'

'Oh yes. I remember something about that.'

'Irukandji, they were called.'

'Yeah, bloody cannibals the lot of them! How does that make you feel?'

'It doesn't bother me. She should have let you die.'

'Bad luck for you she didn't.'

Ben stopped. He had to have the last word. It was important. 'And you didn't know about her gold?'

'What gold? We had the same row all over again in Cooktown. Just because of the months we spent there she thought I'd marry her, or at least take her back with me to Caravale. A nigger whore! Jesus! That turned into a real fight, and the bitch pulled a knife on me. Your dear sweet mother was swift with a bloody knife. She always carried it.'

'She would have needed it, a black woman among white men,' Ben retaliated.

'Sure enough, but she made the biggest mistake of her life pulling it on me. I threw her out. Back on the dunghill where you all belong.'

Ben laughed. 'You're the one who made the mistake! Diamond had found gold. Her tribal people showed her, they always knew, but it didn't mean much to them. You threw out a very rich woman.'

'You're lying!' Buchanan cried angrily.

'Why would I? She lugged home a fortune in gold. She bought the house on Kangaroo Point.'

'That belonged to the German woman.'

'Oh no! Diamond owned it all. Her gold kept us all those years in considerable comfort.'

Ben realized now that the news had thrown Buchanan off guard, and at once he saw his chance. A broken loya vine, shoved aside by a passing animal, or even a human, was coiled, twisted and black, just by Buchanan's neck.

'Don't move!' he shouted, pointing. The familiar warning of snake.

As Buchanan's eyes flicked to his left Ben sprang forward to grab the rifle, but Buchanan was too quick. He jammed the rifle butt into Ben's throat, sending him staggering downhill. Then he was over him again, kicking him as he tumbled down, a heavy boot connecting with his head and his back as he tried to regain his balance, to clamber back to his feet.

'You don't think I'd fall for that old trick, do you?' Buchanan was shouting, as he rammed his boot in. 'Get on down there!'

Even with his head ringing from the blows, Ben could hear them coming. He wondered why Buchanan didn't seem to care. Why he was so intent on lashing out at Ben that he was prepared to ignore the danger?

Despite the blows, despite the fact that Buchanan was reversing the rifle and lining up to shoot him, Ben scrambled to his feet and hurled himself, rolling and tumbling, away from the track.

They came hurtling round the bend, a mob of wild horses led by a brutal stallion, charging downhill, heading for their waterhole, trampling anything in their path. Buchanan had his back to them. He went down under their hooves, screaming, trying to escape the onslaught. As soon as he saw a chance, Ben dived forward to grab Buchanan's outflung arm and dragged him to safety just as more brumbies slammed past them.

As suddenly as they had charged through, they were gone, down the slope. And all was quiet. Ben lay beside Buchanan, puffing from the effort and aching from the battering this man had given him.

Wearily he turned his attention to Buchanan, who was still alive but lying crumpled in the damp grass. His face was bloodied, a leg badly twisted and an arm looked to be broken. For all Ben knew he could have other injuries, but right now he had to get him to the station, to a doctor.

Until the brumbies left he didn't dare go down for Pepper; that mad horse would be uncontrollable with all his mates about.

With an effort that tested every painful muscle, he lifted the heavy limp body from the ground and began staggering up the slope, treading carefully, praying that the brumbies would dawdle at the waterhole, knowing that when they decided to leave they'd exit at the same breakneck speed.

'What's going on here?' Moss had become bored with standing about staring into space, so, forgetting his instructions, he climbed back on his horse and trotted down the western aspect of the rock, only to see a stranger stumble from the springs, carrying the boss. And Jesus, what a mess he was in! Out cold by the looks of it, and covered in blood. Instantly he had his rifle out and cocked, pointing at the stranger's head.

'Put him down!' he shouted.

'I can't! Not yet!' the man yelled at him. 'Help me, I have to get him clear of the track!'

'You're Beckman!' Moss said, stunned.

'Shut up and give me a hand. He's a dead weight.'

Quickly Moss adjusted his rifle, shoved it back in its pouch and slid down to assist Beckman.

They placed the boss gently on the ground in the shelter of some boulders, and Moss stared. 'Jesus Christ! He's in a bad way. What the hell happened?'

'Brumbies,' Ben said. 'He was on the track . . .' he began. This was no time to dredge up the fight. 'And brumbies came galloping in.' He looked confused. 'I don't think he heard them coming.'

'His hearing's shot,' Moss said. 'You just about have to shout in his ear or stand in front of him. The blokes all bet he does more lip-readin' than listenin'. I reckon he'll be a bloody sight worse now.'

Ben nodded as he examined Buchanan. 'He's taken some clouts to the head, this arm's broken and that right ankle's smashed. His breathing's harsh. I'd say he's got chest injuries too.'

'Then we'd better get him back to the house.'

Ben had seen plenty of injuries like this from brutal bashings by prison guards, and he knew it would be dangerous to put a man in this state over a horse. They needed a stretcher. 'I don't think he'd make it,' he said. 'We can't tie him on a horse, he's too badly hurt.'

'What do we do then?'

Just then the brumbies thundered out into the clearing and took off for the scrub, heads tossing, their leader plunging ahead. Moss grabbed the reins of his mount as it reared in fright.

'You'll have to get going,' Ben told him, 'and make it fast. Go back to the homestead, tell them to send for a doctor and in the meantime get a wagon out here as soon as you can.'

'Yeah. I think that'd be the best thing to do,' Moss said slowly.

'Then go!' Ben shouted. 'I'll do what I can for him here.'

Moss was well on his way before he wondered what Beckman had been doing at the springs. He looked as if he'd taken some bumps too, carrying a few bruises of his own. Buchanan had been looking for that bloke. It seemed to Moss that it was just as well he'd found him. And Mungo was wasting his time in town.

In the distance he saw the girl riding towards him. 'That bloody girl!' he growled. 'She found her way after all, and made damn good time.' But he was in a hurry, he didn't have time to chitchat with her. He was inclined to by-pass her in his haste but thought better of it and galloped over to meet her. 'You goin' to the springs?' he said nastily, without bothering to greet her.

'Yes,' she said. 'You're Moss, aren't you?'

'That I am. You keep goin', you might come in useful. If it hadn't been for you we wouldn't be in this bloody mess.'

'What mess?'

'The boss is lyin' back there, half dead, thanks to you. He was lookin' for you!' he snorted, then wheeled his horse and cantered away, gathering speed. Disgusted with her.

Phoebe was frightened. She urged Cleo towards the landmark, petrified of what she might find ahead of her. Until now she'd been very pleased with her progress. She'd met a group of station Aborigines within the first hour of her ride, and even though they were headed in the opposite direction, they took the time to help her. Two lads ran gleefully ahead for at least a mile, to lead her on to the right course.

* * *

Moss was right. Buchanan had been badly injured, and there was Ben fixing a rough splint to his arm. He looked up with a grim smile. 'Thank God you're here. Will you hold these pieces of wood for me while I bind his arm.'

'Is it broken?' she asked, dismounting but standing back in horror. Buchanan's face and clothes were covered in blood.

'Yes. I've set it but it's hard to keep the splints in place. Give me a hand.'

'I can't,' she shuddered. 'Will he die?'

Ben ignored the question. 'You can and you must, Phoebe.'

His voice was so curt she dropped to her knees as ordered and tried holding the two short sticks, but they slipped away.

'For God's sake, you've got hands, not just fingertips. Use them!' he snapped. 'Hold them firmly.'

'I'm frightened I'll hurt him,' she wailed.

'You can't hurt him, he's unconscious.'

There was blood on her hands and that made her nauseous. As he began to tie the rough splints in place with thin, supple vines, she let one of them slip again and he swore: 'Jesus! Hold them steady.'

'I'm trying,' she retorted.

'Try harder!'

When that was done he turned his attention to Buchanan's right leg, which was askew. Phoebe thought she'd faint.

'Get his boot off,' Ben said. 'I have to go down to my camp for some blankets to keep him warm, he'll be in shock.'

'You're not going to leave me here?' she cried. 'What will I do if he wakes up?'

He stared at her as if she were suddenly a stranger. 'Help him,' he said caustically, and then he was gone.

Petrified, and angry that Ben should treat her like this, she bent over to undo the laces on a blood-soaked boot. She wanted to help but this was sickening. Why couldn't he understand that she'd never had to face anything like this before? Never in her life!

Afraid that he'd be even more cross with her, she worked feverishly to remove the boot, which wasn't easy, and then she knew she'd have to take off the sock, already stiff with drying blood.

Blowflies hampered her efforts, and she kept brushing them away, trying to keep them from Buchanan's battered face at the same time, almost retching when she saw his foot. A bone was sticking out from the skin at his ankle.

He coughed and a small trickle of blood came from his mouth.

'Are you all right?' she asked him, grabbing handkerchiefs from her pocket to dab at his face, feeling it was a futile question but that a voice might comfort him.

He coughed, grimacing in pain.

'I'm here,' she said. 'It's Phoebe. You're going to be all right.'

His eyes fluttered open to search her face, as if looking for answers.

'Moss has gone for help,' she told him. 'You mustn't try to move.' Settling down now after the shock of this encounter, Phoebe lifted hair back from his badly grazed face. 'You've had an accident, but you'll be fine.'

What sort of an accident? she wondered. What had happened here?

'I think he's conscious,' she whispered to Ben when he returned. 'His eyes were open a minute ago.'

He nodded as he wrapped the blankets about their patient, then he split Buchanan's trouser leg from the ankle. 'Not much I can do here,' he muttered, 'except bandage it up and hope for the best.'

Phoebe watched as he tore two shirts into strips, binding the ankle and then using the rest of the makeshift bandages to firm the splints on Buchanan's arm. He had brought a waterbag with him, from inside those rocks, wherever the springs were, and began to swab Buchanan's face with a damp cloth.

'Would you like me to do that?' she asked timidly.

'Yes. Thanks, Phoebe. Try to clean the cuts as best you can, they've collected a lot of grit. I'll go back and get my horse and the rest of my gear.'

'What happened?' she asked him.

'He got trampled by brumbies.'

'Where?'

'There's a track just by those rocks that goes right down to a waterhole. He was on the track when the brumbies came galloping in.'

'But what about you? You've been hurt too. Your face is bruised and you're limping.'

'I fell trying to dodge them,' he lied, too weary to explain. Some other time, he thought. If ever.

'Moss said this was all my fault,' she said dismally.

'Did you tell Buchanan you were coming to meet me?'

'No.'

'He must have found out somehow and beaten you here. He probably guessed you were coming to meet me. It's not your fault at all.'

'Who turned you away from Fairmont?'

'He did.'

She nodded. 'I might have known it!' She looked up at Ben. 'You haven't even said hello to me.'

Ben leaned over and kissed her. 'Forgive me. I'll make it up to you. I was never so pleased to see you in all my life as I was today.'

'You didn't sound like it,' she complained.

'Well . . . I had to attend to your friend here.'

'I'm sorry for him, I really am, and I hope he'll be all right. But he's no friend of mine.'

'We'll talk about that later,' he replied. 'Moss is bringing back a wagon. We'll have to stay out here until they come from the homestead, so we won't have much shelter. It will be getting chilly soon. I'll have to light a fire to keep him warm.'

As he walked back down the track he was tired and depressed, resenting being saddled with this responsibility. His instinctive concern for Buchanan irritated him too but he shrugged it off: 'I couldn't just leave him there.'

His chores completed, he tried to make Buchanan more comfortable by the fire, placing a pillow of clothing under his head and erecting a small canvas humpy over him to protect him from the dew that was beginning to settle as the light faded.

Phoebe made tea in the billy and they sat huddled across from Buchanan, watching helplessly as he moaned and then drifted into ominous silence.

Worried, they had little to say. Phoebe told Ben she had enjoyed the station although Buchanan had been difficult. And then she explained that she'd been very upset when she'd realized that her hosts had withheld her mail, deliberately keeping them apart. She could hardly add that this man had spoken of Ben in the most awful way, referring to him as a half-caste, claiming that she was making a laughing stock of her family by associating with him. She could never repeat such cruel remarks to Ben. How would he feel if he knew that he'd saved the life of a man who despised him?

Ben wasn't feeling much at all. He was staggered to think that a man could be so paranoid as to want to kill him simply because he might lay claim to be his son. That was the last thing he was likely to do! Diamond might have loved Buchanan but she'd seen him through the eyes of passion. All Ben saw was an arrogant white man who'd grown up on an outback station, one of the infamous fraternity of whites who believed they had the right to kill blacks if it suited them, and the power to carry out their monstrous crimes.

He'd heard enough about them from the blacks in the prison, but this was the first time he'd seen the brutal arrogance first-hand. And it had nearly cost him his life. Ben didn't care that the man was a so-called respectable pastoralist and a Member of Parliament, he would be ashamed to admit any relationship with scum like this.

So he, too, kept back the truth. He told Phoebe that he'd met

Buchanan at the gate to the property and been ordered to leave. And that, guessing Phoebe was coming out here to meet him, Buchanan had ridden ahead with Moss to send him on his way.

'You talked to him?' she asked.

'Yes. I got the message I wasn't wanted around these parts.'

'And that's when the horses came through?'

'Yes.'

'If you hadn't been there he would have died.'

'Moss was outside,' Ben shrugged.

After a while Phoebe said: 'I'm still upset with Clara and Belle Foster for deceiving me, but my mother was at the back of it. She doesn't want me to marry you.'

'And what about Phoebe Thurlwell? Does she still want to marry me?'

Phoebe wished they were anywhere but in this horrifying situation. She'd thought this meeting would be so romantic, that here alone with him, after all this time, they'd be able to throw off all restraints and reaffirm their love, but the presence of this badly injured man, of Buchanan himself, intimidated both of them.

'Yes,' she whispered. 'You know I do, Ben. Will you wait for me and take me back to Brisbane?'

He put an arm about her. 'Of course I will.'

Moss arrived first. 'Is he still alive?'

'Yes,' Ben said. 'He's awake every now and then.'

'The wagon is on its way.'

The wait seemed interminable. Phoebe lay down on Ben's bedroll, pretending to sleep. Ben squatted by the patient, poking at the fire, and Moss paced about restlessly as cold stars lit the sky and the massive sweep of the Milky Way rose majestically above this silent outpost.

Fairmont homestead, usually so quiet at night, now seemed like a busy village. Dogs barked, lamps blazed as the wagon rolled up the track and the accompanying riders milled about, shouting at the crowd of anxious station hands to stand back.

The journey home, riding behind the wagon, had been long and slow, taking a winding route to accommodate the vehicle and keep the patient as comfortable as possible. Even though someone had thought to line the tray of the wagon with a straw mattress, and Buchanan, under blankets, was strapped on to it, Phoebe gritted her teeth, feeling for the injured man as it bumped and jarred through trackless country and, of necessity, over rocky creek beds.

'It'll be a blessing if he has passed out again,' she said to Ben, who was riding beside her, and he nodded in agreement.

Four more men had ridden out with the wagon in case of accident – a bog, or a broken wheel perhaps – but the driver had taken great care and they were not needed except as an escort.

There was no moon to light their way, so two of the riders trotted ahead with lanterns, guiding them. Phoebe shuddered. It was an eerie convoy with the red glint of the lamps up ahead and a blackness behind them.

The swish and rumble of the wagon wheels and the jingle of harnesses seemed overly loud to her, as if they were trespassing on this mysterious land, and Phoebe was comforted by Ben's presence. Above her, tall trees rustled, and yet there seemed to be no breeze. Dark leafy branches brushed against her as she rode by, startling her every time. From the deep darkness of the surrounding bush, bright eyes glinted, disembodied, spooky, and even though Phoebe knew they were only small harmless animals, they unnerved her. The ride itself, like a funeral cortège through a gloomy forest, was an ordeal. She was saddle-sore, cold and hungry and she was being returned to the house she'd quit that morning. She wouldn't be surprised if they'd discovered that packed suitcase by this, in an effort to make sense of why she'd taken off so suddenly that morning.

Moss was riding ahead. He would have given them the news that she and Ben were out there with Clara's husband. Phoebe tried to measure Clara's confusion against her own embarrassment at having to return and explain herself. And introduce Ben.

Would Clara be angry? Would she blame her for causing all this trouble? None of the drama now unfolding in this chilly darkness would have happened if she'd stayed home. She looked at the silent men accompanying the wagon. What were they thinking? Phoebe rode head down, numb, shamed by her part in this tragedy.

She hadn't noticed that they were passing by the other side of the lake near the homestead, and as they approached, hundreds of birds, only black shapes now, shot from their roosts, wings flapping and battering just over the heads of the riders.

Phoebe's nerves were already on edge. She screamed and her horse reared, but Ben was nearby. He grabbed Cleo's reins and calmed her.

'Are you all right?' he asked Phoebe.

'Yes, I'm sorry. The birds came up so suddenly they startled me. We're nearly at the homestead, thank God! It's been a horrible day.'

Clara came running down to meet the wagon, but it was the doctor who took charge as the men carried Buchanan into the house, past Belle Foster and the group of housegirls who were huddled behind her on the veranda. She gave Phoebe a quick kiss on the cheek. 'I'm glad you're back,' and picked up her skirts to hurry up the steps and see to her husband.

A breathless hush settled on the homestead then, in contrast to the clatter of their arrival. The men took the horses and the wagon and drifted away, the women disappeared into the house and a lone dog sniffed silently about, trying to detect the cause of the commotion.

Phoebe was stiff and sore as she made for the steps. Ben had helped her down from the horse and she'd taken it for granted that he was following her, having handed both animals over to Moss, but when she looked back he was moving away with the other men.

'Come inside,' she called to him.

He came back. 'No. You go. I'll doss down in the men's quarters.'

'But Clara will want to see you.'

'In the morning. She's got enough to think about now.'

'What about me?'

He kissed her on the cheek. 'Phoebe, you need your rest. You've had a long day.'

'But I want you to come in.'

'No,' he said firmly. 'Now be a good girl and do as you're told.'

Moss was waiting for him at the gate leading down to the outbuildings. 'I been tellin' the boys if it wasn't for you the boss'd be a corpse by now. They said for you to come on over and have some supper. And there's room in the bunkhouse for you.'

'Thanks. Where can I wash up?'

'In the tin shed over there.' Moss had noticed when he returned to the springs that Beckman had changed his clothes, getting rid of the other shirt and trousers that had some blood on them. A real dandy, he thought, as he waited. But dandy or not, being a half-caste, Beckman couldn't stay in the house, which suited Moss. There was something he had to tell this bloke, if he could without letting Mungo know. To Moss, the man was a hero, he'd saved the boss's life. Well, so far, anyway. And he'd earned a quiet word of caution.

Mungo was back. And Mungo had told him to shut his trap about them keeping a watch on Beckman in Charleville. The boss had known what he was doing. It was for them to keep out of it.

'I'll bet the boss knew he was out there,' Moss grinned to himself. 'They think I'm dumb but I got eyes.' He had no doubt now what it had all been about. He figured that the boss, known to be a ladies' man, had laid a claim on pretty Miss Phoebe only to find Beckman, her boyfriend, was in town. He bet the boss had made for the springs to warn off Beckman before she got there. But he'd had the bad luck to be run down by the brumbies. 'Bein' deaf,' he mused, 'can't be no joke. I hope it don't happen to me.'

When Beckman emerged he took him over to the cookhouse. At the door he said: 'You stayin' long?'

'Just the night. I'll be heading back to town tomorrow.'

'Ah, right,' Moss said. Then he added: 'I'd give Charleville a miss if I was you,' and ducked into the smoky shed without giving Beckman a chance to respond. He'd done his best.

'How is he?' Phoebe and Belle both looked up anxiously as the doctor came in.

'He should survive but he's taken a pounding. With these cases,' he said wearily, 'it's best not to move them for a few days. His face looks worse than it is but his chest's the worry, a few broken bones there. I've strapped him up because I don't want to operate if I can help it. I'll know better tomorrow. Ribs are best left to heal themselves if they aren't poking into the lungs.'

'You can't operate on him here,' Belle said.

'No. He'll have to go into hospital anyway. That leg looks bad. The ankle's smashed. We'll do our best.'

'What does that mean?' Belle asked warily.

'Just what I said, Mrs Foster. Time will tell. His arm's broken too but it's been set just fine. I've strapped that up again so he can't move it, and when we get to the Charleville hospital we'll put a plaster on it. All we can do now is keep him quiet, I've given him a sedative.'

He went back to the sickroom and Belle turned to Phoebe. 'I don't like the sound of that at all.'

'I suppose they try not to worry people,' Phoebe replied, although it seemed to her that the doctor wasn't sure what to do. One minute he was saying the patient shouldn't be moved and the next minute he was talking about taking him to hospital.

Belle glanced at her as if to make a comment, possibly about her presence at the springs, but she changed her mind and went in to relieve Clara.

Rather than disturb anyone, Phoebe made for the kitchen, where the cook, Mrs Dimble, was waiting for news of the boss.

'The doctor said he's as well as can be expected,' Phoebe said in answer to Mrs Dimble's question, realizing she was quoting her father's stock reply.

'Ah, the poor man. There's always accidents in a place like this. You never know what's going to happen next. Would you like something to eat?'

'No thank you,' Phoebe sighed.

'What about some hot soup then?'

Phoebe stayed in the warm kitchen, taking her time over the rich, thick soup and picking at some bread and cheese, rather than face her hostess.

But it was Clara who came to her, sitting down at the kitchen table with her. 'Ben is feverish. Mother and the doctor are attending to him. Surely to God he can't get any worse than he is now.'

'Oh Clara, I'm so sorry,' Phoebe said.

'Don't blame yourself. Where's Mr Beckman?'

'He's sleeping in the men's quarters.'

Clara was surprised. 'I wanted to talk to him.'

'I know, but he didn't want to bother you. He said he'd see you in the morning.'

Clara nodded. 'You went out there to meet him?'

'Yes.'

'We found your suitcase. You weren't planning on coming back?'

'Clara, I'd just as soon not talk about that now. I've caused enough trouble.'

'Why didn't you at least tell me?'

'Because I knew you'd disapprove. And because I found out you were withholding my mail.'

Clara's face reddened. 'Yes. I'm sorry about that. Everyone seemed to think it was for the best.'

'Well it wasn't. I was really upset, but it doesn't matter now. If it hadn't been for me this terrible thing wouldn't have happened.'

'Not entirely. Ben could easily have caught up with you before you got to the springs. Why did he have to go all the way out there?'

'I don't know,' Phoebe said. 'He probably thought he was doing the right thing.'

'How? By finding out who you were meeting and sending him away?'

'I imagine so. He shouldn't have interfered. Even if he had caught up with me, Clara, I wouldn't have turned back. I had to see Ben. I hadn't heard from him until yesterday. God, that seems years ago! I didn't know what was going on.'

'You heard from him yesterday? Telling you to meet him at the springs? How did you come to hear from him?'

'I'd rather not say.'

Clara shrugged. 'Fair enough. Do you really care that much about Mr Beckman?'

'Yes, I do.'

'Even though you know that it's not a suitable match for a girl in your position?'

Phoebe bridled. 'Why can't people understand? Ben's a lovely man . . .'

'I know he is. He helped me to get fodder out to the station, and now he has saved my husband by rescuing and caring for him. I am very grateful and I'll tell him so. But that doesn't alter the fact that you'll have a hard road ahead if you marry him.'

'I fail to see that. He's a good and caring man and he can afford to support me quite comfortably.'

'That's not the point. You don't know anything about Aborigines.'

'Really, Clara, that's a ridiculous argument. Ben's father was white and he wouldn't know how to live like a black any more than I would.'

'I simply meant,' Clara said quietly, 'that life can get complicated, even for men like Mr Beckman.'

Phoebe refused to continue this argument, so Clara walked over to shift the kettle on to the centre of the stove. 'Would you like a cup of tea?'

'Yes please,' Phoebe replied. 'Are you angry with me?'

'Only about as angry as you were with me over your letters.'

'Could I have them now?'

'Mother burned them,' Clara said. 'I'm sorry.'

Regardless of their anxiety about the boss, the station work had to go on, so the men turned out at dawn to line up for breakfast of mutton stew and potatoes and scalding hot tea, before tramping away into the mist.

Ben was up too but he ate his breakfast more leisurely before wandering outside to take a look at Buchanan's station. The homestead up there on the hill was quite grand, and down here in the work area he had the impression of being in a small township as he passed stables and blacksmith, harness and tool sheds, then a dairy and various storerooms. There were at least twenty horses in the home paddock, spare mounts, he guessed, and further out he could see the mustering yards and the mobs of cattle being herded in. Turning towards the house he came across the remnants of a large orchard with only a few trees left standing – survivors of the drought, he supposed – and beyond that he saw two black girls working in a long vegetable garden.

He'd heard about these stations, that they were mostly self-supporting except for the basics of flour, tea and sugar, and now he was seeing one first hand, finding it very interesting.

He retraced his steps to enquire of the blacksmith the whereabouts of the blacks' camp.

'Go across that paddock,' the burly man pointed, 'pick up the foot-tracks and follow them down through the scrub. They shift about a bit but you're bound to come across someone.'

'Thanks,' Ben said, ready to leave.

'You got family here, mate?' the blacksmith asked, and Ben jerked back in surprise, thinking of Buchanan. Then he realized that the blacksmith was referring to the Aborigine community. He was so accustomed to being accepted as white these days, that that too was a shock.

'No,' he said. 'I don't have any relations here.'

'Ah well. You're welcome to take a look about. You done a good job lookin' out for the boss. I hear he's a bit better this morning.'

'Good,' Ben said, although he didn't care one way or another.

As he strode across the paddock, intending to look for Mandjala before he left the station, he saw the old man coming towards him with a grin on his face. 'You fix that big boss good, eh?'

'I didn't hurt him. It was the brumbies.'

'People say that. Me, I don't reckon so.'

'It's true.'

They squatted on their haunches at the edge of the bush to talk, and Ben told Mandjala what had happened. The old man sat quietly, listening without interrupting.

When Ben came to the end, relating how he'd pulled Buchanan from under the hooves of the brumbies, Mandjala spat. 'Bloody mad! That feller kill you!'

'Forget him! I'm not worried about him any more.'

Mandjala nodded. 'Your mumma. Her medicine too strong for that feller. She bin watchin'.'

'You think she sent the brumbies?' Ben laughed.

Mandjala eyed him crossly. 'Plenty thing you doan know,' he growled.

'Righto. But I came to say goodbye. I'm going home.'

'The girl? She go too?'

'I hope so.'

Obviously Mandjala disapproved, but he made no comment and Ben stood up. 'You've been a good friend. I won't forget you. Maybe we'll meet again some day.'

The old man looked up, squinting into the early-morning glare. 'No goodbye. Not time yet.'

A flock of white ibis filed across the blue sky in steady formation, and Mandjala pointed to them. 'They go home now. Winnaroo.'

Ben accepted this little piece of information solemnly since it seemed to be important to Mandjala, and then shook his hand and left.

Mrs Buchanan was waiting for him as he walked up to the front of the house, a deliberate move on his part for his own self-respect. He would not go to the back door of Buchanan's house.

'Come and sit here with me,' she said, indicating chairs on the veranda, and Ben was relieved about that too, since he had also decided that he would not go into the house.

'Would you like a cup of tea?' she asked when they were settled.

'No thank you. I've had breakfast.'

'So have I. So we won't bother. I have to thank you once again, Mr Beckman, but this time I don't know how to thank you enough.'

'How is he?' Ben asked, to be polite.

'A bit better, I think. The doctor is still here, which is a relief to me. But it looks like we'll have to take my husband into Charleville hospital so they can operate on his ankle.'

'I thought so. It looked bad to me.'

'Can you forgive us for interfering between you and Phoebe? I'm embarrassed that your correspondence was never delivered.'

He was tempted to remind her of the boy who'd crashed into the dinner party at the Thurlwells' so long ago, when she'd been the only one who'd attempted to speak up in his defence, but he chose not to. He was tired of the past, finished with it. As Mandjala would say, he'd put it down.

'Don't worry about it,' he said. 'The station looks in good nick now. I can't get over the change. Last time I was out this way it was dying from the drought.'

'The blessed rain,' she smiled. 'When the first rain came we all ran out and stood in it, getting soaked. It was wonderful! Phoebe should be up by this. Would you like me to call her.'

'Yes. If it's convenient.'

Clara took his hand. 'I hope we can be friends again.'

'Of course.'

Phoebe came out. Her long hair tumbled loosely about her face and she was wearing a shapely check dress in a shade of blue.

'You look gorgeous,' he said, kissing her since Mrs Buchanan, tactfully, had not returned.

'I feel fine now. I was so tired last night. What are you doing today?'

'Going home.'

'Already?'

'No point in staying on now. Do you still want to come with me?'

'Yes. I think so. Clara can cope. She doesn't need me around and her mother, Mrs Foster, is none too pleased with me. I'm already feeling I'm in the way. It will be a little awkward leaving like this, but it can't be helped. When do you want to go?'

'Whenever you're ready.'

It was more than awkward. Clara accepted Phoebe's decision but Belle was angry. 'Young ladies don't travel alone with a man, especially that person. What will your mother say?'

'We're only riding into Charleville,' Phoebe retorted. 'We'll catch the train from there. Excuse me, I have to change.'

When she was packing again, Clara came into her room. 'You will need your luggage, Phoebe. You can't take it on your horse. I'll lend Mr

Buchanan a packhorse. He can leave it in Charleville. Someone will collect it later.'

'I'll have to leave Cleo there too,' Phoebe reminded her.

'Oh yes. I'm sorry, I forgot Cleo. She wouldn't want to leave the station, she was born here.'

The two women hugged each other. 'You take care now,' Clara said.

'You too. I hope Ben will be all right.'

'It will take a while, but we'll look after him. I'll see you in town one of these days.'

Chapter Twelve

'Good luck!' Clara had called as they rode away from the homestead, leading the packhorse, but it wasn't until they left the property far behind that Ben could relax.

Phoebe was subdued. Only Clara had come out to see them off, the other woman hadn't appeared at all, so it had been a rather dismal departure for her, he guessed. He noticed, too, that she grimaced as he legged her up into the saddle, still creaking from the long ride yesterday. For that matter so was he. His back ached, legacy of the savage kicks Buchanan had served on him before being run down by the brumbies.

But he was lucky. The luckiest man alive today. Phoebe was with him, looking brisk and beautiful in a tailored riding suit, and they were going home together.

Deliberately he rode on past the spot where his other horse had been shot, noticing that the carcass had been removed, probably on Buchanan's orders. But he was still determined to put all that behind him and when they came to a clearing by the roadside he reined in the horses.

'Why are we stopping?' she asked.

'Because it's just you and me now.' He helped her down and took her in his arms. 'Do you still love me?'

'Yes,' she said fiercely. 'But you've been so cool to me I feel as if I'm just a nuisance! Everyone else back there thinks so.'

'You're not a nuisance! Good God, I'm just so happy you're coming with me.'

'I would have left with you yesterday if everything hadn't gone wrong.'

'Yesterday? Why?'

'Because I'd had a row with Buchanan.'

'What about?' he asked uneasily.

'Because he accused my family of being frauds and cheats.'

Ben had almost forgotten that the Thurlwells had been involved in the crash of the railroad company, but he couldn't pretend to be upset about that.

'A fine host,' he said lamely.

'Oh, he can be very cruel. He treats Clara like dirt. And I know it's an awful thing to say, but now that he's hurt, he'll need her. I heard the doctor telling Clara's mother that he could lose his foot. And there's still a chance he could die, but they haven't told Clara. Do you think he'll die?'

'Not him. He's a tough bastard.'

She was startled. 'You know him?'

'I met him at the stables. Where I also met Clara, and you. Remember?'

'Oh yes. Of course. And you met him again at the springs. I suppose you talked about me? He disapproved of you too.'

How could he tell her that neither he nor Buchanan had mentioned her? That she had nothing to do with their conversation. It startled him to recall that in the intensity of the confrontation with Buchanan he hadn't given Phoebe a thought.

In his mind's eye he defended himself: I was too busy trying to stay alive.

'And thinking of Diamond,' a voice seemed to answer. 'Of the past, not of the present.'

'Your mumma. Her medicine too strong,' Mandjala had said.

Suddenly Ben realized that he'd been stalling, encouraging Buchanan to talk, wasting time, in a hopeless situation against a man with a gun, because somehow, from the mists of time, he'd know that Buchanan would lose.

'Never mind,' he said to Phoebe. 'That's over now, he's got his own battles to fight.' He kissed her. 'Stay here with me awhile and tell me how much you've missed me.'

Phoebe felt safe, reassured, to be once again in his loving arms, to know that he cared so much for her, but Belle Foster's stinging rebuke, in front of the doctor, just before she left the house, still rankled: 'You silly girl. You don't know what you're letting yourself in for.'

They made good time on the long open stretches of road and arrived in Charleville mid-afternoon, making straight for the railway station.

Ben found the station master and came back to tell Phoebe that there would be a train leaving for Brisbane the next day.

'Ten o'clock,' he said. 'That will give me time to make arrangements for the horses. I'll send Pepper back to Clara with my compliments, he deserves a good home.'

'Where will we stay in the meantime?' she asked.

'There's one fairly decent hotel in the main street, the Royal. We'll take a couple of rooms there and tomorrow we can have a look about the town.'

'Not much to see,' she said as they rode into the sleepy town. Flies buzzed, horses dozed at rails outside the hotels, a few people, making their way along the tree-lined street, stopped to stare at the strangers. Phoebe peered into dim shops without enthusiasm, thinking there'd be time enough in the morning to do a little shopping. But for now she was tired, looking forward to a cold drink, a hot bath, and a pot of tea, in that order.

'The Royal!' Ben said with a flourish, stopping in front of a two-storeyed timber hotel, a new building, she was pleased to see, painted a drab bone colour with a brown trim. Phoebe smiled and walked ahead of Ben, who was tethering the horses, to step in through the front door.

The publican, a heavy-set man with a red face, leaned over the lower half of a stable-type door that led to the bar and called to her, 'What can I do for you, miss?'

'I'd like two rooms, please. Two good rooms.'

'I can manage that,' he replied. 'And our rooms are the best in town. I'm Will Turner, my wife is out at the minute.'

By the time Ben joined them the publican had produced his lodgers' book and written in Phoebe's name. He looked up expectantly for the other name.

'Mr Beckman,' Phoebe said.

Turner raised his head slowly to get a better look at Ben and then closed the book. 'I'm sorry, I can put you up, miss, but you'll have to find someplace else, mister.'

Phoebe stared at him. 'You just said you have two rooms.'

'Only one,' he persisted.

Ben came forward with a sigh. 'If you're worried about the cash I'll pay in advance.'

'Not here you won't.'

'Why not?' Phoebe demanded angrily.

'Because I don't want to lose my licence, that's why.'

'Phoebe, just a minute,' Ben said, moving her aside. He confronted the publican. 'Why would you lose your licence by putting up a traveller?'

'Because the likes of you are not allowed on licensed premises without a permit.'

'What do you mean,' Ben asked, 'by the likes of me?' Although it was beginning to dawn on him.

'Abos,' Turner shrugged. 'You must know the law. Aren't you the one been staying at the Shamrock?'

'Yes.'

'Well, they nearly lost their licence for breaking the law. They let you stay there and Sergeant McAlister got wind of it. He's a real stickler, keeps this town in order, I can tell you. He lowered the boom on the Smiths and would have shut them down only you'd left.'

'That's ridiculous,' Phoebe cried. 'Mr Beckman is a very respectable gentleman.'

'So he might be, miss,' Turner replied. 'In which case there's no problem. You trot off down to the police station, Mr Beckman, get yourself a card. After that, as far as I'm concerned, your money's as good as anyone else's.'

'Is that really necessary?' Phoebe asked him.

'Essential,' Turner said.

He came out of the bar. 'I'll take your suitcase up, miss,' he said, collecting her luggage. 'It's room three, right on the front. Bathroom down the passage.'

Phoebe turned to Ben, her face crimson. 'It's outrageous! How dare they humiliate us like this!' She glared through the open door at the dozen or so men propped up at the bar. They were listening intently, their faces impassive. 'Does this mean that you couldn't even go in there? Take a drink with that lot of drones? They're only stockmen and labourers!'

He shrugged. 'That's right. I'm sorry, Phoebe. I forgot.' As indeed he had since he and Barnaby always drank at the same pub where the owner hadn't bothered him. But he hadn't known about this card system. The subject hadn't come up.

'But you're really white!' she persisted.

Ben took her arm and walked her quietly to the door of the hotel, away from those staring faces. Her claim that he was 'really white' worried him. 'The law might say I'm really black,' he countered, forcing a smile to ease the situation for her.

'Oh! You are not!' she retorted. 'It's a damned impertinence, but I suppose you'll have to get one of those cards.'

'I couldn't do that.'

'Why not? I'll come with you.'

'No. I will not go to a police station and ask for a card, a pass to move about as freely as anyone else. Anyone white.'

'But you wouldn't have any trouble. You heard Mr Turner. As long as you have the silly card you can stay here and everything will be all right.'

Ben shook his head. 'No, Phoebe. It's the principle of the thing. I'll never go cap in hand for something like that.'

She tried to soothe him. 'Come on now, don't be so stubborn. Who cares about their stupid rules? Just do it to shut them up and then we can relax until it's time to catch the train.'

'I've never been on a train,' he murmured. 'I might have to produce a card for that too. Especially since we'd be travelling first class. I could be relegated to second class. Or the box car.'

Phoebe was becoming irritable. 'Ben, stop inventing problems. If you have to get a card, then get it! What do we care?'

'I care. Why don't you just go on upstairs and make yourself comfortable?' He saw the publican come down and disappear into the bar, his eyes averted.

'And what will you do?'

'I'll camp out again. I've been camping all the way out here, what's the difference?'

'There's a lot of difference,' she said angrily. 'You're with me. I don't want you dossing down by the river like a . . . What I mean is, there's no need for it.'

'Like a blackfeller?' he said. 'You meant like a blackfeller.'

'What if I did? You're just being stubborn.'

'I suppose you're right. But I have no intention of applying for a card.'

'You're being as stupid as they are. I can't believe you're doing this to me!'

'And what about next time it happens? In another town, at another place, another hotel? Will I have to keep on getting permits? I have to fight this.' As he spoke he saw the shock on her face. Phoebe had seen this incident as a one-off. Now that he was making her think it through, what he saw depressed him beyond words. She wasn't interested in his need to oppose this rule, or at least not give it credence by submitting to it. Poor Phoebe, she was suddenly forced to look ahead and was thoroughly shaken by what she saw.

'Very well,' she said stiffly. 'If that's your last word, I'll go in. Where will I meet you later? Here in the street?'

'There's a café down the road a bit. We could have tea there.'

'Are you sure you'll be allowed in without a card?' she asked tartly.

'It's not a licensed premises.'

Phoebe shrugged as she turned away. 'I'll meet you there at five thirty. But I think you're making this very difficult for both of us.'

Ben decided that his next priority was to test the railway system, but here at least there was no problem. The station master unlocked his ticket office and sole Ben two first-class tickets.

'You live in Brisbane?' he asked Ben.

'Yes.'

'Me, I'd rather the bush. I was offered a town station but I says to them. "No fear!" Too much rush and bustle. Give me the country any time.'

'I'm inclined to agree with you,' Ben said thoughtfully. Despite the trouble Buchanan had caused him and the stupid rule he'd just run into, he loved the country. They were only incidental matters. Out here a man could feel part of the land, there was so much to do and learn, so much about the bush and the wild life that was lost to town folk. Already he was rebelling at the thought of having to return to the daily round of work at the livery stables, of spending most of his day sitting in his office checking accounts and pay sheets for both of the businesses. A boring life, he told himself, not for the first time. So why don't you make a change?

As he strode back to the main street a woman called to him, and he turned to find Lottie Smith hurrying after him.

'I'm so pleased to see you,' she said. 'I heard you had trouble over at the Royal.'

'Not really,' he grinned. 'I ought to apologize to you for causing you trouble.'

She shook her head angrily. 'Not at all. We had a row with the police sergeant, who's a mean piece of work at the best of times. We couldn't convince him that the ban didn't apply to people like you. It's only meant to keep the peace. We couldn't serve tribal blacks anyway, all the other customers would leave.'

'I had the impression the publican at the Royal was on the lookout for me.'

'Exactly. We've all been warned off. But you take Jacky Dunne. His mother was black but he comes and goes as he pleases because his dad, a white man, died and left him Ballymore Station, just south of here. He's a property-owner, he can put "Esquire" after his name, so he doesn't need to carry a permit.'

'But I own property too,' Ben said.

'We told the Sergeant that but he said he was acting on a complaint. A written complaint.'

Ben nodded. 'Don't tell me . . . Buchanan?'

'Himself,' she replied. 'A word from the Member of Parliament and we all have to jump.'

'Not me,' Ben said.

'Good for you. But we still can't put you up without a permit, it's too risky.'

'Don't worry abut it, Lottie. Let me work it out.'

'I heard you have a lady friend with you. Where's she?'

'At the Royal, she's quite comfortable.'

'That's good. But I wanted to ask you. They say Buchanan had an accident. Is that true?'

'Yes. He got in the way of some brumbies, he's badly hurt. I think they'll have to bring him into hospital.'

'Oh, well. I can't say I feel sorry for him.'

'Lottie,' Ben said, 'thanks for everything, but I have to go. We're leaving for Brisbane in the morning and I have a few things to do.'

'You take care then. Maybe we'll see you again some time.'

'Count on it,' he grinned as he walked away, heading for the offices of a stock and station agent.

The manager greeted him. 'Monaghan's the name. What can I do for you?'

He was a wiry little fellow with sharp eyes but he had a ready smile for this prospective customer. You're a stranger in these parts?' he added.

'More or less,' Ben said absently. 'I wanted to enquire about a property out here.'

'Buy or lease?'

'Buy.'

'Excellent. I've got several grand properties on my books. Now that the drought's over it's the right time to buy. Now let me see.' He walked over to his desk. 'How long are you staying? I could take you out on inspections—'

'Winnaroo Station,' Ben said. 'I'm interested in that one. Is it still for sale?'

'Surely is, sir. The best around. But it don't come cheap, let me warn you.'

'I heard it's unoccupied.'

'For a very short time. This one won't last.'

'And there's no homestead.'

'That's true, but it wouldn't cost much to put up a house. Bachelor are you sir?'

'Yes.'

'Then you won't need anything flash. Not for a while I suppose?' he smiled at Ben.

'I don't have a lot of time,' Ben said. 'I'm leaving for Brisbane in the morning. I know Winnaroo, Mr Monaghan. It will take a lot of money and muscle to get it operating again. I need more details about the property, but I won't pay a fancy price. Can you have the information for me by eight in the morning?'

'Certainly. And your name, sir?'

'Ben Beckman. If the price is right I'll wire you a definite offer when I get to Brisbane. My solicitor,' he said, thinking of Barnaby, 'will handle the sale for me.'

Monaghan was delighted with this arrangement. 'The station will need restocking,' he said. 'And I'm your man in that department.'

He was a great talker, Ben found, and it was with difficulty that he finally managed to escape to meet Phoebe at the café.

'I have just been informed,' she told him tersely as he dashed in the door, 'that this charming establishment closes at six o'clock, so I have ordered for you.'

He kissed her on the cheek, taking in the 'charming' establishment, a rough shop-front café buzzing with flies that were attracted by the smell and presence of grease. Ben grimaced, realizing he'd made another mistake bringing her to this grimy place. 'I'm sorry, Phoebe. You don't have to eat here. I'll take you back to the hotel.'

'No you won't,' she said, cleaning the cutlery with the grubby tablecloth. 'I've already ordered, so don't make a fuss.'

To his immense relief she laughed: 'The menu is a classic. You can have steak and eggs, chops and eggs, sausages and eggs or "the lot", so I ordered "the lot".'

'Perfect,' he grinned. 'Just what I wanted.'

'And what have you been doing?'

'Bought the train tickets, met Lottie Smith from the other hotel where I stayed last time I was in town. Found out that as a gentleman of property I don't need to carry a permit anyway.'

'Then you can stay at the hotel.'

'Not in the eyes of the local police sergeant, and it's not worth an argument.' Because he was determined to distance his name from Buchanan's, he did not tell her that Buchanan was at the back of it. That would only lead to more questions.

'You're so stubborn,' she said.

Ben took her hand across the table. 'So are you, my love. If you had your way I'd be pounding on doors, demanding to be let in.'

'Demanding your rights,' she corrected.

'With a permit in my hand. No fear. I'll never do that. Here's our dinner.'

Despite the unsavoury appearance of the café, the meal, served by a stout, sweaty woman, was passable. She also brought them a plate of buttered bread and a jug of gravy. Ben had forgotten how hungry he was and he polished his meal off with gusto, but Phoebe picked at hers, claiming she was too tired to eat.

After the meal they strolled up the street, looking in windows, feeling a little more relaxed, until they reached the front door of the hotel where men stood about watching them with curiosity.

Ben saw her embarrassment again under those stares, and gloom settled on him as she turned quickly away from him and hurried inside. He was almost tempted to run and beg for that permit to spare her this unwanted attention: he should be able to stand by her at all times. Instead he walked down the lane beside the hotel to collect the horses and take them over to the livery stables and arrange for them to be delivered back to Fairmont Station.

Since he had nothing better to do, he joined in a card game with the stablehands and later that night his new-found friends insisted he take one of the spare bunks in their shed.

As he stretched out on the hard bunk, all he could think of was Phoebe, and how to make her happy. He was crazy about her, madly in love with her. It had been hard enough to sit with her in that dingy café when all he wanted to do was to take her in his arms, and it had been a wrench to have to leave her at the hotel like that, deprived of any privacy. And tomorrow there would be that long train journey, sitting together and yet apart, under scrutiny by other passengers at a time when he desperately needed to be alone with her. To have a long talk with her as they'd been able to do, so long ago it seemed, at his home in Kangaroo Point, just the two of them, talking about everything and anything, comfortable in each other's company.

Had all that sweetness between them dissolved now? he wondered. Spoiled by outside pressures? No, he couldn't allow that. He was already making plans for their future. He would keep the house in Kangaroo Point, that would be their town house, and he would sell the stables and the saddlery and buy Winnaroo Station. There he would build her a lovely home, a beautiful station homestead that she would be proud of. He would run cattle, and, more importantly, a horse stud; he'd make Winnaroo Stud a show place. He still hadn't touched the bushranger's cash, now he had good use for it.

Phoebe would be living next door to her friend Clara, and as for Buchanan, if he survived, Ben decided he'd have a good talk with that gentleman. And this time he'd be laying down the rules: 'You stay off my patch and I'll stay off yours.' He would not brook any more trouble or interference from that quarter. Buchanan had a lot more to lose in a battle of wills than he did.

His mind was so busy ploughing over all these plans that Ben was convinced he wouldn't sleep a wink; but sleep he did, in quiet content.

Phoebe slammed the bedroom door behind her and tore off her hat and gloves. She tried to tell herself that all was well, that she couldn't care less about the people in the hotel who had nudged and whispered as she'd passed by, or those stupid men who'd grinned as she'd pushed through them at the door. She loved Ben and she didn't care who knew it.

But doubt seemed to be crouched in the room with her, nagging, wearing down her resolve.

Being forced to eat in that dreadful café with him had been yet another humiliation, especially since the hotel dining room had looked so inviting, with its starched linen, shining silver and floral displays. Feeling sorry for him, she'd tried to make a joke of it, even pretending that she wasn't hungry rather than eat that revolting food served on cold, greasy plates.

'Tea!' she said, disgusted. She'd been expecting tea and cake at that hour, not a shearer's meal. But she'd had to stay for his sake, pleased to see that at least he'd been fed. She felt as if she were responsible for his welfare and that annoyed her too. If he weren't so pig-headed they could be sitting downstairs now, like normal people. But here she was, locked in her room so early in the night with nothing to do but stare at the wall, while Ben was out there somewhere, God knows where. Sleeping under a tree probably. It was all too much.

Angrily she stuck her head out of the door and called to a housemaid to bring her some coffee and cake. Then she sat on the bed, tapping her foot, until the girl returned.

'No cake, miss, but Cook sent up pudden. It's real nice, treacle pudden with cream,'

'Thank you,' Phoebe said, taking the tray. 'That will be all.'

The hot pudding was delicious, and the coffee too, so Phoebe felt a little better. She did love Ben, she really did.

'Well I think I do,' she said to the room. 'Or maybe I'm just losing my nerve. Everyone's wearing me down. Why can't people leave us alone?'

Miserably she undressed, telling herself that she was Phoebe Thurlwell, she'd always done exactly as she'd wanted to do and she saw no reason to change. 'In all my life,' she said defensively, 'Ben's the only person I've ever really cared about. I won't let people or these trifling incidents rattle me. He needs me. He does. I won't let him down.'

The bed was comfortable, the sheets satin-soft and the eiderdown warm and fluffy. It had been a long and tiring day and Phoebe luxuriated in this respite from all the confusion. She was soon asleep, dreaming of Ben, lovely erotic dreams that he was here with her, making love to her, holding her safe, so handsome, so loving. She awoke in a mood of content, the dreams, as they were apt to do, having coloured her morning with a rosy shade of happiness. The last she would experience for quite a while.

Having retired so early, she was up and packed before the breakfast bell. Several men were already in the dining room when she came down, and they glanced at her in appreciation, which should have displeased her but didn't. Phoebe knew she was looking her best. The holiday at the station had done her the world of good. She had left her cloak and hat on the hallstand and was wearing her straw-coloured hair down, softly waved about her face and held up at the crown with a blue ribbon and a few clips, allowing the strands to curl down on her shoulders. Her tailor-made blue travelling suit was by no means country-style and she knew it, but today Phoebe Thurlwell was making a statement to this town of Charleville.

She was who she was, and she wanted them to know it! On her lapel she wore the lovely pearl brooch that Clara had given her when she'd heard that Phoebe and Lalla had sold their jewellery. It matched the pearl buttons on her heavy silk jacket. A jacket that was nipped in, emphasizing her small waist and giving way to a rustling, beautifully cut skirt.

She ordered her breakfast and was sitting alone at her table when the waitress ushered in two women.

'You can sit here with this lady,' she said to them.

The elder of the two women stared frostily at Phoebe. 'We'd rather not,' she replied imperiously, and they stalked away to choose their own table.

Phoebe felt her face flame. She watched as they were served before her and wished she could go over to swat them or tip their porridge into their laps.

No attempt was made to seat any other guests at her table, which was set for six, and the waitress was in no hurry to serve her, so she sat alone, the centre of attention. Phoebe considered storming out, but couldn't bring herself to do that, to back down. Instead she beckoned to the waitress and whispered to her that if she wasn't served immediately she could expect trouble.

'I'm sorry, miss,' the girl said, simpering.

'You will be!' Phoebe threatened, and her three-course breakfast magically began to appear.

Not that Phoebe ate much. She lingered long enough to prove her point, taking her mind off the company by studying the décor, deciding that Lalla would hate this room with its red velvet drapes and red-embossed wallpaper, quite out of place for a country hotel, which should have an airy rural ambience rather than this phoney, stuffy attempt at grandeur. Then she went outside to pay her bill.

The publican's wife was in the office. 'It's been paid,' she said curtly, 'by that gent out there. We brung down your luggage. He's got it. Outside.'

'How very kind of you,' Phoebe retorted. 'I look forward to meeting you again one day.'

It was only bravado of course, Phoebe knew, but it was enough to startle the woman, and that would have to suffice. Ben was waiting for her. Outside. And that hurt. She wanted him to put an arm about her, the dream lingering, or at least give her a kiss of greeting, but he was intimidated by the interested stares and simply picked up her luggage to walk with her to the station.

When they boarded the train they found that the two women who had snubbed Phoebe in the dining room were also travelling in their carriage – or dog-box as it was known, consisting of just two rows of seats facing each other – so Phoebe had to endure their stares until the women alighted at the next station, leaving only three men sitting with her and Ben.

Phoebe was glad they'd gone, until the next stop when they all stepped out to stretch their legs and she saw that the women had not left the train but had merely removed themselves to another carriage.

The studied insult depressed her. She hoped Ben hadn't noticed. Their conversation was stilted under the watchful eyes of the other travellers, and as the hours passed Phoebe saw their disapproval when Ben insisted she stretch out on their seat with her cloak over her and her head on his lap. Telling herself they didn't matter, Phoebe eventually slept into the night, holding his hand, feeling him beside her, protecting her from the real world.

The train arrived in Brisbane at eleven a.m., an hour late, and they were arguing even before the hansom cab clattered out over the bridge.

'Just drop me at the house,' Phoebe said. 'I'm exhausted. I need a bath and a rest before I can face anyone.'

'I can't just leave you at the front door and run away, Phoebe. You're not a foundling.'

'It's for the best,' she replied wearily.

'No it's not. You've come home with me. No more deception. I'll deliver you to your home, to your parents, introduce myself, and then leave as any gentleman should.'

'It's a mistake, I tell you! You don't know them.'

'And they don't know me. It's time they did. Unless you've had a change of heart. Don't look away.'

'I'm not. It's just nice to be home.'

'Then you still care for me?'

She was irritable. 'Of course I do.' She pulled away from him. 'Don't maul me. People can see us.'

'I'm sorry,' he said, offended. 'I didn't mean to upset you.'

'Oh, I'm sorry too. I'm not upset. I'm just tired.'

'Of course you are. Twenty-four hours in a train is no joke. You must be exhausted. But wait until you hear all my good news. I've got some marvellous plans.'

'With motorcars?' she replied listlessly.

'No. We'll have a motorcar, but this is much better.'

'That's nice.' Phoebe said as the cab neared her front gate. 'Just let me off here and go on home, Ben.'

'No. We're both home. We've come home together, Phoebe. My darling, don't take fright now, everything will be all right, you'll see.'

'What are you doing home?' Lalla was startled to see Phoebe come in the front door. She'd thought she was still out at Fairmont.

Phoebe's response was swift. 'This is still my home, I believe,' she said acidly, and Ben, carrying in the luggage, was disturbed by the coldness between mother and daughter. He'd expected difficulty over his presence but not this outright antagonism, which, he felt, went far deeper than his involvement.

Mrs Thurlwell was a beautiful woman, fine-featured, her fair hair softly groomed into the fashionable wide rolls that framed her face, and the likeness between the two women was remarkable. But that was all they seemed to have in common. She remained standing at the foot of the stairwell, making no move to come forward and welcome her daughter.

Phoebe seemed to take this for granted, and anyhow, she was too busy staring about her. 'What's happened here? The house looks empty!'

'We sold most of the furniture at auction,' her mother replied coldly, across the gulf.

'But why?' Phoebe was shocked. 'All the beautiful things!'

'Because we had no intentions of letting them go with the house.'

'Oh my God! Are you selling the house too?'

'It's sold. We're moving to Sydney.'

'You've sold Somerset!' Phoebe's voice was a cry of pain. 'Mother, you never said. You never told me! Why do you shut me out like this?'

They seemed to have forgotten him so Ben stood patiently, waiting for this crisis to pass, as Phoebe burst into tears.

'Are things this bad?' she cried.

'It was necessary to sell,' her mother replied, unmoved.

'But Somerset! It's always been our home!' Phoebe wept. 'Isn't there anything we can do?'

'Stop your whimpering!' Mrs Thurlwell said, and Ben could almost have liked her for her stoic attitude, knowing that the loss of this gracious house would be a wrench for her too. Until she inclined her head in his direction: 'And who is this person?' As if she didn't know!

Phoebe came back to earth with a jolt. Trying to match her mother's reserve, she coolly placed her cloak and hat on a chair before replying. 'Mother, this is Mr Beckman. My fiancé.'

Mrs Thurlwell peered at him, her green eyes ice-cold, and without acknowledging him, turned to Phoebe. 'Is this what we've come to?' Without another word she swept across the white-tiled lobby, opened a door and called to her husband: 'William! You're needed out here! Your daughter's home.' Then she glided away, head erect, to disappear into the rear of the house.

'I told you so!' Phoebe snapped at Ben, as if he had encouraged her mother's bad manners.

'So?' he said calmly. 'I'm still in one piece.'

But was he? When the Doctor came rushing out, delighted to see Phoebe, embracing her, Ben's heart thumped. Here was the enemy, face to face. His throat constricted and he was afraid his voice would fail him when Phoebe introduced him. 'Be polite,' he kept telling himself. 'The past is the past. For Phoebe's sake, leave it there.'

'How do you do?' Dr Thurlwell said distantly when Phoebe introduced them, making no attempt to offer his hand.

'Ben and I are engaged, Daddy,' Phoebe announced.

'Don't talk nonsense,' he said. 'But I'm glad Mr Beckman has finally shown himself. You must know, Mr Beckman, I do not approve of your association with my daughter.'

'I'm sorry about that, sir, but I want to marry Phoebe. I love her and I will take good care of her.' He hated having to enlarge but he did so for her sake. 'I can afford to support Phoebe quite well,' he added.

'Possibly you can, though not in the manner to which she is accustomed.'

Ben could feel his anger rising. The man was already snubbing him by not inviting him in; this wasn't a matter they should be discussing standing in the lobby. 'Was accustomed,' he said quietly, deliberately, looking about the stripped room.

Thurlwell's pink whiskery face reddened. He ignored that remark and continued: 'I don't need to explain my reasons for rejecting your suit, Mr Beckman. The whole idea is preposterous and you know it.'

Phoebe intervened. 'Daddy, don't be so stuffy. You don't know Ben. It's time you talked to him.' She saw Biddy coming down the stairs and called to her: 'Biddy! I'm home! We've been on a train forever. Could we have coffee in the parlour?'

'Yes, miss,' Biddy smiled. 'It's nice to have you home again.'

But the Doctor wouldn't budge. 'Mr Beckman. Your presence in my home offends me. Would you kindly leave?'

Ben shrugged. 'I suppose I couldn't expect any more from a man like you. You haven't got the guts to talk this out as Phoebe wants you to do. You prefer a more underhand approach.'

Thurlwell flinched and looked away. 'Leave my house, I said!'

Ben knew he'd hit a nerve, that he'd been right all along about the attack on Barnaby. 'Where's your footman now, to throw me out?' he asked. 'You never do any of your dirty work yourself, do you?'

'Ben, stop!' Phoebe cried. 'My father's not well. Leave him alone!'

'Like he left Barnaby alone?' Ben grated. He turned on her father. 'Who did you pay to beat me up? In my house, right next door!'

'I don't know what you're talking about!' Thurlwell stuttered, backing away.

'Of course you do,' Ben retorted. 'But he made a mistake, didn't he?

He beat up the wrong man. Barnaby took the beating meant for me.'

Phoebe clutched his arm. 'Ben, stop! Please.'

'Why should I?' he snapped. 'I've kept quiet, trying to do the right thing by you, trying not to upset your family. They object to me!' he said harshly. 'I wouldn't refuse aid to a dying woman! I wouldn't send a kid to jail for breaking a few windows. And I would never send a thug to settle my arguments as he did. Look at him. He knows what I'm talking about.'

'Get out!' Thurlwell shuddered.

'I'm going, sir, and you can consider yourself lucky I didn't point the police in your direction, or you'd have been up before the courts quick and lively.'

'That's enough!' Phoebe was distraught.

'Yes it is,' Ben said. 'Phoebe, I love you, despite your family and their cowardly attitudes.'

'Shush!' she said, taking him to the door. 'Just go home and calm down. Abusing my father! How could you! You've ruined everything!'

'There wasn't anything to ruin, Phoebe. I've just cleared the air.'

Before he left Ben looked up and saw Lalla standing above them, looking down from the top of the staircase as if she were merely an interested spectator, unaffected by the scene.

'I'm sorry, Daddy,' Phoebe said, pouring coffee for him. He was badly shaken. 'Ben didn't mean all that, he was just upset. He cares for me very deeply. You have to understand that.'

'He's a frightful person!' her father insisted. 'Promise me you won't see him again.'

Lalla came in, took her coffee and sat apart from them, picking up a magazine.

'I can't do that,' Phoebe cried. 'What did Ben mean? That you had something to do with that attack on Barnaby?'

'Lot of nonsense! The man's mad.'

Lalla looked up. 'For goodness' sake, William, stop lying! It's obviously a Thurlwell trait. Any fool could have guessed what happened next door. Who did you send? That brute who works at your rooms?'

'Who?' Phoebe demanded.

'That creeping Jesus of a gardener, I forget his name. Glasson's a lawyer. He could have sued your father for a fortune, but I suppose he realized there's nothing left to go after.'

'Is this true?' Phoebe turned on her father.

'I was only trying to scare him off,' he replied feebly. 'I simply wanted that fellow to know we were serious about having him stay away from you.'

'That's terrible! And poor Barnaby! You didn't care what happened to him?'

'It was a mistake. And I won't have you criticizing me, Phoebe. Don't you realize how upset we are about all this? I was only trying to protect you. I made enquiries. Apart from the fact that he's a coloured man, that fellow's name isn't really Beckman. Mantrell arranged that by deed poll. He was no relation to that old woman. So on top of everything else, he's illegitimate. God knows who his father was. Some tramp who'd taken up with the gin. Is that the heritage you want for your children?'

'Oh, forget about it,' Lalla shrugged. 'I've given up on her. If she's fool enough to marry him she'll get what she deserves. Every door in Brisbane will be closed to her.'

'She won't marry him. This is just a passing fancy, she'll get over it. If you'd been more interested in your daughter than your own affectations it wouldn't have come to this.'

'That's right,' Lalla said airily. 'Blame me.'

'You've never cared for her. She simply fell for the first person who appeared to love her, to take an interest in her. It was probably our family fortune that attracted him in the first place.'

She laughed. 'Then he's made a bad mistake too, hasn't he?'

Phoebe wasn't listening to their arguments; she'd learned to switch off from them years ago. But the mention of the old woman, Mrs Beckman, had shifted something in her memory. Ben's father? What was it? She recalled being here in the front parlour, by the broken windows, a long time ago. The old woman had been sitting on the veranda talking to someone. Her father? And she'd been pleading with him not to send the boy to jail.

But it wasn't her father, it was Buchanan. A guest in their house. And the little girl had been eavesdropping. As usual, Phoebe recalled. What the hell had she heard? Something interesting. Buchanan had been angry and Mrs Beckman almost in tears. She needed his help. Why him? Gradually it came back to her: because she was claiming that young Ben was his son, and he was denying it. And Phoebe had thought what a strange thing that was!

She looked at her parents, wondering if she ought to say something. She could be wrong. And anyway, what difference would it make to them? Diamond was still his mother.

As if somehow her thoughts were transferred, Lalla said to her: 'You've had a lot of excitement at Fairmont. How is Ben Buchanan? The papers are full of the story.'

'He was very badly hurt,' Phoebe said, not wanting to be side-tracked from these more interesting memories.

'Trampled by brumbies! Horrible!'

'And that's another thing you haven't explained, Phoebe,' the Doctor said. 'I'm very disappointed in the Buchanans. The papers claim that the fellow next door saved his life. I want to know what he was doing out there.'

'Surely you don't expect her to tell you the truth?' Lalla said scornfully. 'That's the last thing I'd expect around here. Phoebe, we're moving to Sydney in a fortnight. Staying with my sister Blanche, for the time being. She has a lovely home on the harbour. It's just as well you've come home, you can get your things packed and help me finalize arrangements.'

'I asked you a question,' William reminded Phoebe.

She ignored him. 'You expect me to go with you, Mother?'

'We can hardly leave you stranded here. You'd be the first to complain.'

'And that's why you're not worried about Ben. Well, I'm not coming with you. I won't leave him.'

'Yes you will,' her mother said calmly. 'You're not entirely stupid. You've got a fortnight to change your mind. After that, you're on your own.'

This time Phoebe marched out of the front door, not caring who saw her, to confront Ben Beckman.

He was so relieved to see her, his face lit up with delight, and she almost weakened. When he smiled he was so handsome, but she'd now seen another side of him. Hard, uncompromising. When he bent to kiss her she pushed him away. 'You were so awful to my father! I had no idea you hated him so much.'

He stood back, allowing her to enter, and followed her down to the dining room. 'What do you want me to say?'

'You could apologize to him. I told you he's not well.'

'Would you like a cup of coffee?' he asked as she pulled out a chair and sat down with a bump.

'No. I'll have a glass of that wine you and Barnaby drink.'

'The white wine is better. A good year.'

'Very well.'

Ben took down two of Oma's crystal glasses and poured the wine. Even though Phoebe was angrier than he'd ever seen her, he was feeling a lot better. More in control than he could ever recall. A little light-headed in fact, having downed a couple of whiskies when he first walked into the empty house. Barnaby wasn't much of a housekeeper. He'd only found some mouldy cheese, unappetizing leftovers and stale bread in the cupboard.

'Well?' Phoebe demanded.

'You know I can't apologize.'

'It makes you feel good, does it? To bully an old man?'

'Yes,' he said sharply. 'It did! He's had that coming for a long, long time. And he's not so bloody old either, so put away your violin. What is he? Forty-eight? Fifty? The same age as my manager, Rod Callaghan, who's in the prime of his life. Grow up, Phoebe!'

'You're the one who needs to grow up,' she retaliated. 'Nursing grudges all your life. Can't you see their point of view? We're asking a lot of them.'

'Because my mother was black?'

'Yes! And for people in their circumstances their reaction is normal. You knew that. You've known it all along. Why did you have to antagonize them?'

'You're overreacting. If I'd clutched my cap and said "yes sir, no sir" I'd still have been thrown out, so don't resort to fairy stories, Phoebe. They've met me now, they know who I am and it is immaterial to me whether they accept me or not. The decision rests with you, not with them.'

Sullenly she studied her glass. 'Why didn't you tell me your father was Ben Buchanan?'

That hit home. The surprise on his face, the dismay, she thought angrily, was some recompense for the misery they were putting her through. She resented all three of them. Ben, Lalla and her father. They were all so pig-headed, they deserved each other. Lalla's threat hung over her head. She'd have to choose. And soon. She could see her mother's cold, pitying gaze if she chose to stay.

And with what? She couldn't expect a penny from them, so she'd have to rely on Ben for financial support, even before they were married. The very idea of having to ask him for money, to admit that her parents, the people she was trying to defend, had dumped her, was a humiliation she doubted she could face.

He was just sitting there, staring at the table, toying with his glass.

'Who told you that?' he said eventually.

'Never mind who told me. It's true, isn't it? Why does everyone keep things from me?'

'That's what you said to your mother. She'd have told you in good time about the sale of the house. Everything doesn't revolve around you, Phoebe. People have their own problems. For your information, it is possible that Buchanan is my father, and that gives me nothing to cheer about. I despise the man.'

'You saved his life!' she said.

'I'd have saved *your* father's life too, given no choice, but I don't have to like him. And what difference does it make who my father is?'

'I don't know,' she replied. 'I don't even seem to know *you* very well.'

'Yes you do. You've been dodging this issue all along, Phoebe, hoping it will go away. But it won't. I love you. I'll always love you, I'd give you the world if I had it. I'm here for you,' he smiled, 'for better or worse. Have faith in me, not in what other people think or what might have been for you. If you can't do that, then—'

Phoebe interrupted him. 'I won't have another ultimatum, Ben! Don't do this. What was the surprise you wanted to tell me about?'

'It's not important now.'

'Never mind then. I'd better go.'

'Don't go yet. Barnaby will be home soon.'

Phoebe gathered her skirts and jumped up. 'Barnaby! Good God! I'd forgotten he lives here! I don't want to see him. Is he all right now?'

'Yes, he's fine. Wait for him, he'll want to see you.'

'Not yet. I can't.'

She was practically running as he followed her out to the gate, determined to avoid Barnaby. Ben was afraid she was slipping away from him, and he made an effort to cheer her up. 'Listen, Phoebe,' he said. 'It's the Brisbane Cup on Saturday. Why don't we go out and enjoy ourselves for a change. We'll take a picnic.'

'Yes, all right,' she said anxiously. 'I must go, Ben.'

'So! The hero returns!' Barnaby laughed. 'Welcome home.'

'What hero?'

'It's in all the papers that you saved his life. Our beloved MP. What did you do that for?'

'Sheer accident, believe me.' He looked keenly at his friend. 'I met Lottie Smith too. That was no accident, was it?'

'I thought you two might have something in common.'

'Or someone?'

'Possibly. Was I right?'

'I don't know for sure, and I don't care. But Buchanan was a jump ahead of me. He's bad news. You could have warned me! But forget about all that, I brought Phoebe home with me.'

'Great! How is she?'

'She's very well. Looking marvellous, of course, but she's worried and confused about everything. Her parents have sold the house—'

'Yes, I know. I found Thurlwell a buyer very smartly through an agent friend of mine, got a good price for him, sorted out the mess that he called his accounts, leaving him with a few quid from the wreck, sent him a bill, and he came in to my office and abused me!

'"After all, you've been a guest in my house often enough, Glasson,"' he mimicked the doctor. '"I expected some gratitude!"'

'Did he pay you?'

'Of course not.'

Ben laughed. 'Nothing changes. Phoebe is upset, though, about you. Her father *was* at the back of that thumping you got. It was supposed to be me. You must go and see her.'

'Ah, poor Phoebe. I will. But what's for dinner? I've had a long day.'

'Dinner! There's hardly a crust in the house and I haven't had a decent meal for days. Let's go down to the pub and eat up big.'

Over the meal Barnaby explained that the business was picking up but his campaign to win election as a state representative had fizzled out. 'No one takes me seriously. I'm a nobody. I'm just not well enough known. And that's what I wanted to talk to you about. I don't want to sound like a vulture, but how is Ben Buchanan? The papers give conflicting reports.'

'Why do you want to know about him?'

'Because if he's not well enough to continue, the seat of Padlow becomes vacant, and I want to go for it. If I can win that seat I'll have enough clout to be elected to the convention. I could handle both easily.'

'Then you'd better throw your hat in the ring,' Ben said. 'He'll have to resign. He's in a bad way and I'm sure he'll lose his foot. He won't be back in town for a long time.'

'I'm trying not to look pleased. Parliament, here I come!'

'Good. Now I have some news. I'm selling the stables and the saddlery and buying a cattle station called Winnaroo, on past Charleville. It's the most marvellous place.'

'What!'

'In your capacity as my lawyer you can settle up all the details for me. And I promise I'll pay the bill.'

'And how does Phoebe feel about this?'

'She doesn't know yet, but I think she'd enjoy a cattle station. We'd live a freer life and as an established pastoralist my colour won't be such a problem.'

'I thought they were down on colour out west.'

Ben laughed. 'I talked about that with a station agent, Monaghan, yesterday morning. There are other station owners with the well-known touch of the tar-brush, but no one bothers them. Cattlemen employ staff and keep those little towns going. Money talks, Barnaby. Besides, I'm bored here in town.'

'What about the house?'

'I won't throw you out. Do you want to lease it?'

That night Ben decided not to tell Phoebe that he was arranging to buy Winnaroo. At this stage it might sound like a bribe. As if he were giving her some place to hide from the world, when in fact he saw the station as an opportunity to be an integral part of a community. To bring up their kids in the wide open spaces with plenty to do. Winnaroo would be a wedding present for Phoebe.

'I refuse to sit at home like a prisoner,' Lalla said. 'We have nothing to be ashamed of. We always go to the Brisbane Cup, so we shall go again tomorrow, William.'

'I'm going too,' Phoebe said.

'Good.'

'With Ben.'

Her mother sighed and sat back in her chair: 'Very well, do what you like. He won't be permitted in the members' enclosure, so I hope you enjoy yourself out there with all the harpies and hooligans.'

To Phoebe, her mother's disdain was the last straw, because she knew she was right. For the rest of the day she wandered the garden, worrying. She did love Ben, desperately, but could she go through with this? The pressure was too much. Sydney was sounding better by the hour, away from all these upheavals. Ben would just have to give her more time, surely that wasn't too much to ask? If he really loved her he would. There were so many things to think about.

She sat on a garden bench looking out over the river, feeling terribly sad. About everything.

Her parents had gone on ahead, thank God. Today, especially, Phoebe needed to avoid any unpleasantness.

It was a beautiful day, perfect winter weather, sunny and warm with golden wattle blooming everywhere; and the marvellous tang of glistening eucalypts gentle in the air. A magpie sang, clear notes soaring into the blue like a carillon, and Phoebe stood on the front porch looking out over the lovely garden, appreciating it more now, since it would soon belong to someone else.

She watched as Ben drove the spanking new gig up to the front steps. How normal it seemed, she thought sadly, that a young man should be calling for her at her home in this manner, jumping down to hand her up beside him, a large picnic basket and tartan wool rugs nestling behind the seats. But it wasn't normal, nothing was real today. Not the house, nor her escort, it was all a façade, ready to crumble.

'You should have let Biddy make up the lunch hamper,' she said to him.

He grinned. 'Don't worry, it's all done beautifully, compliments of Kathleen O'Neill. She caters well. As far as I can see we've got chicken and savoury things and scones and cake, and champagne of course. Even tablecloths and napkins,' he added enthusiastically.

Phoebe felt a pang of jealousy at the mention of Kathleen's name – he often spoke of her – but pushed it aside, determined now. 'I'm sure we'll have a lovely picnic. But Ben, do you mind if we don't go to the races?'

He looked at her, surprised, as he turned the gig out of the gate, urging the horse on to the road. 'No, of course not. What shall we do then?'

'I'd rather have our own picnic down by the river. There are some beautiful spots on past the bridge.'

'Your will is my command, lady,' he smiled. 'It's a glorious day to sit by the river, I'd like that. Just the two of us. Who needs all the noise and dust of race meetings?'

He found a lovely grassy spot on the tree-lined bank by the wide yellowy-brown river, so quiet and tranquil that Ben was delighted. He walked down to stare at the fast-flowing waters as she unpacked their lunch. 'It's really a magnificent river, isn't it?' he called to her. 'From up on the Point it looks so much smaller.'

Phoebe agreed, and they settled down to enjoy the spread that Kathleen had prepared, which, she was happy to allow, was delicious. As was the champagne.

'To us,' Ben said softly. 'To us, Phoebe.'

They talked about this and that. He told her a little about Buchanan, not much. About Barnaby, and their expectations that he had a great career ahead of him. About the stables and the saddlery that Ben had decided to sell to his manager, Rod Callaghan, on easy terms. Phoebe listened politely, immersed in her own thoughts, not thinking to ask him what he planned to do instead. He looked so handsome, so relaxed, stretched out there on the grass beside her, that she wished they could be together like this forever. But it was not possible: the hard mean world was out there, waiting to spoil everything, to destroy them.

'What a perfect day,' he said, reaching into a corner of the hamper. 'Now look here, missy. I've got a present for you.'

Phoebe's heart sank as he handed her a small velour box. She opened it slowly, reluctantly, and found a beautiful sapphire ring set in gold.

'Oh Ben,' she said. 'I can't accept this.'

'Why not? If you don't like it you can change it. This is my way of asking you to set a date for our wedding. Your engagement ring.'

She looked glumly at the ring. 'Ben, I'm sorry. I'm going to Sydney with my parents.'

'I see,' he said tersely. 'I thought something was bothering you. For how long?'

'I don't know.'

He looked so shocked, so stricken, she wanted to put her arms about him and tell him it was for the best, but she couldn't afford such closeness. On this day, when she was battling to be decisive, she'd never been so sexually attracted to him. Wildly, contrarily, she wanted him to make love to her, for the first and last time, here in this lovely lonely place, so that she could say goodbye to him once and for all. And not be pining after him.

'Is that why we didn't go to the races?' he asked her.

'Sort of.'

'You didn't want to be seen with me?'

'It's not that. I can't bear to see you hurt all the time. Like you were in Charleville.'

'I wasn't hurt, Phoebe. You were. And you were afraid I'd be snubbed at the races too, weren't you?'

'Yes, I was,' she said defiantly.

'People get snubbed for all sorts of reasons,' he said. 'You told me your mother insisted on going to the races today. I'll bet she knew she would be in for her share of snubbing, but she had the guts to go.'

Phoebe stared at him. 'I can't believe you're throwing her at me. She hates you.'

He took her hand. 'How many times do I have to tell you? I love you. All of these things can be overcome. I've got plans for us—'

'I don't want to hear your plans, Ben. I can't listen any more. It just won't work. I know I'm being selfish, a coward if you like, but I can't marry you. I just can't face all the trouble and all the talk. I'm not used to it. I won't.'

He shook his head, disbelieving. 'Tell me you don't love me.'

Phoebe reached out and touched his face as gently as she dared. 'Don't ask me to say that. I'll always care for you.' But she was reminded of her mother's cynical comment, only last night:

'Oh, for God's sake, William, if she insists on marrying him, let her! Tell her you'll approve if he accepts our terms.'

Appalled by Lalla's intention to humiliate her even further, Phoebe turned the tables on her mother. 'You needn't bother,' she'd said caustically. 'I've decided to go to Sydney too. Barnaby said it's a marvellous city. I'm quite looking forward to it!'

William was delighted. 'Oh my dear! That's wonderful.'

Lalla shrugged. 'Typical! Whatever I suggest you can guarantee she'll do just the opposite!'

Touching his face had been a mistake. Ben recognized the tenderness and drew her to him, kissing her, murmuring to her: 'You can't leave me. I won't let you.'

Phoebe responded desperately, the bittersweetness of this moment to be remembered always, and as he lowered her on to the softness of the rug she clung to him. All the passion she had felt for him welled up in a rush of emotion, and there was joy all about her as this dear man made love to her in the dappled stillness of the afternoon.

Shadows began to steal away the sunlight just as surely, Phoebe thought, as time was running out for them. She knelt, busying herself by packing up the hamper and folding the rugs.

Ben lay flat on the grass, watching her, his chin resting on the cup of his hand.

Eventually he spoke. 'Was that goodbye?'

Phoebe avoided his eyes, refusing to reply.

'I thought so. Is there anything I can say, or do, to make you change your mind?'

She shook her head.

It was time to go. There was a chill in the air.

Phoebe handed him the small jewel case containing the ring. 'I'm sorry,' she said lamely.

'No. You keep it. I want you to have it. Call it a farewell gift. And God speed.'

Goldie was at the races that Saturday. The critical stares of snobby women didn't bother her. In the company of Caleb Moreton, who was an old rascal and rich enough not to give a damn about anyone, she was just as entitled as they were to be in the members' enclosure. It was a men's club, they only got in because of their men too, so who were they to be looking down on her? She was wearing her best green taffeta with a jaunty bustle and a large chapeau decorated with green and silver imitation roses, to please Caleb. His jockey's colours. And she looked very fetching. The attention she was getting from the men proved that. She and Caleb were having the time of their lives, betting up big and drinking champagne at their table out on the lawns.

The talk was all about Buchanan. It was definite they said. The doctors had decided his foot would have to come off, and a couple of surgeons were preparing to leave for the Charleville hospital to perform the operation, since he was still too ill from other injuries to be brought to town. Everyone was sorry for poor old Buchanan, and Goldie listened sourly. She wasn't. Buchanan had left town again without paying his bill. And this wasn't the first time. He was as mean as hell. She could hardly send him a bill, so she'd just have to wear it until he turned up again. If he ever did.

It had intrigued her to read that young Ben, Diamond's son, had rescued him, and she wondered how that had come about. No one, however, had mentioned any connection between them, so apparently Buchanan was still keeping that quiet. There'd been a comment from Buchanan's wife about the debt they owed to 'the young man', so it didn't seem that she knew either.

The more they speculated about poor Buchanan's chances, the more

Goldie became irritated. He was sounding like a saint now, but she knew better. And so did some of her girls.

She noticed that the Thurlwells, another source of gossip, were sitting at the next table. The Thurlwell name was mud in town now since Edgar shot through with the company cash and got himself drowned, the villain, but his brother the doctor and his wife were still playing the socialites – he in his shiny topper and she in a grey silk hat to match her outfit. Goldie wondered how women like her could dress so plain and look so smart and expensive.

They didn't seem to be having much fun though. He looked as glum as a landed fish since few people even stopped to acknowledge them, but she held her head high with a haughty gaze. Goldie liked that. She was always one for the underdog. She turned towards Mrs Thurlwell and gave her a wide smile, only to be thoroughly and deliberately ignored.

'Huh!' Goldie said to herself. 'Up you too!'

She saw that awful Mrs Crawford bearing down on Caleb's noisy table, pumping on her white parasol as if to hasten her progress, and Goldie watched her nervously. This was one woman who could spoil her day. President of the Anglican Women's Committee, Mrs Crawford was always taking up petitions to have The Blue Heaven closed down, and at times it had been touch and go, necessitating bribes on Goldie's part and extra pressure on her important customers. Goldie had always vowed to herself that if these women managed to run her out of town she'd see to it that their husbands were make a laughing stock. There were pamphleteers who'd pay well for her list of clients, to hold toffs up to ridicule.

But with a snort in Goldie's direction, Mrs Crawford passed on by, to stop and address the Thurlwells. Goldie, afraid that she might complain to them about the woman at the next table, leaned back to hear what she had to say.

'Good afternoon, Doctor. And Lalla,' Mrs Crawford said, in a sugar-sweet voice. 'Don't get up,' she added as the Doctor attempted to scramble to his feet from a wobbly chair.

'How are you Lalla?' she asked.

'Very well thank you, Agnes. And you?'

'Not the best since my operation, but I'm not one to complain, as your husband would know.'

'You're looking well enough,' Thurlwell retorted.

'Oh I always do. That's my trouble. People don't realize how much I suffer.'

'Poor you!' Lalla Thurlwell said sarcastically, and Goldie quaffed some more champagne with a giggle. What a put-down!

Mrs Crawford bridled. Although there were empty chairs at their table, they hadn't invited her to join them, and Mrs Thurlwell's studied snub made it worse.

'That reminds me, Doctor,' she said. 'I was right, wasn't I?'

'Right about what?'

'What I told you in the hospital, my dear! That your daughter is having an affair with that Beckman fellow.'

'My daughter isn't having an affair with anyone,' Mrs Thurlwell replied in a voice like ice.

'Oh well. Choice of words perhaps, but I was the first to enlighten you, wasn't I, Doctor? That she was seeing that coloured boy. I hear they're going to be married.'

This time Dr Thurlwell made it to his feet. 'My daughter has nothing to do with that sort of riffraff! And if you continue with these allegations, madam, you shall have a libel case on your hands!'

In a flurry it was over. Mrs Crawford sailed away. The Thurlwells were silent. Mrs Thurlwell ordered more wine and sat studying her racebook while her husband gazed into the afternoon sun.

Riffraff, was he? Goldie thought. Diamond's son. Hadn't he done well at the livery stables? Pulling them back into shape after the death of Cash, who'd been a ne'er-do-well anyway. Young Ben Beckman was a respectable person, a bloody good kid and a credit to his mum. How dare these crooks call him riffraff after they'd diddled half the town out of their savings.

And if young Ben was riffraff, what was Buchanan? He, of course, was socially acceptable. A pillar of the community! She recalled a rumour that Buchanan had been getting into Mrs Thurlwell's bloomers, and looking at her now, a very attractive woman with a dumpy, sexless husband, it didn't surprise her.

Old Crawford's story about their daughter and young Ben had a ring of truth. They'd have to know one another, she realized, they lived next door, up on the Point.

That night, with The Blue Heaven in full swing after the big race meeting, Goldie kept all this in mind.

She took her lunch in bed the next day and emerged to find that the maids had done their work well. Everything was in tiptop order again. But she was still angry at the way those people had spoken of Diamond's son, and her anger shifted to Ben Buchanan, the Member of Parliament, Mr High-and-Mighty, who had ill-treated her girls and never paid his bills. Who'd broken Diamond's heart. Her friend.

Goldie was still a little drunk and very hungover. And feeling very emotional. All along she'd known that the skinflint Buchanan would never have supported Diamond and her son, so with natural curiosity as to how Diamond had come to be so affluent, she'd worked it out for herself. Cooktown. The Palmer River. Gold! It was the only answer. Buchanan had dumped her and she'd suddenly turned up in Brisbane, rich. Anyone who could give away fifty pounds was bloody rich! Diamond had found gold and disappeared out of that place in a hurry. She'd even beaten the customs officers. No one would think to ask a black gin boarding a sailing ship for the south to declare gold and pay duty.

A maid brought her a black coffee laced with brandy and Goldie drank it gratefully. She felt she ought to look out for Diamond's son. Someone should raise the ante on his behalf. The world should know that he was Buchanan's son as well. But then he mightn't like that, she decided tipsily. Branding him as illegitimate when the late Mrs Beckman was his very respectable grandmother.

No. There was another way of swiping at Buchanan, of laying down the rules once and for all, without embarrassing young Ben in any way. When she had time she would attend to it. But right now, Goldie decided, she'd better go back to bed.

Clara had been at his bedside in Charleville for weeks. Ben was not a good patient. Up until the last minute he'd flatly refused to allow them to cut off his foot, and for days after that he'd been delirious, shouting and screaming abuse at the doctors and nurses. Especially the nurses. Sometimes he'd been reduced to tears, demanding that someone else should nurse him, someone who really knew how to look after him. Someone who cared about him, because, he'd cried in his demented state, no one else did.

'Diamonds,' a nurse whispered to Clara. 'He wants to know where his diamonds are. He thinks we've stolen them.'

'Never mind,' Clara said. 'Just bear with him. There aren't any diamonds.'

Gradually the ordeal was over and he began to recuperate, but his right lung had been damaged and bed-rest was essential. At least his broken right arm was healing well, as were the injuries to his face, although there the scars would remain. Every time Clara looked at his broken nose and the red weal that shot from the end of an eyebrow to his chin, she could have wept for her handsome husband. But the loss of his foot was another matter. The doctors were promising that they could construct a peg-leg for him but he called the very idea monstrous, claiming he'd rather be dead than be seen wearing such a thing.

So that was where she was placed when it came time to put him into a good solid wagon and take him home to Fairmont. At first reporters from various newspapers had converged on the Charleville hospital, upsetting everyone, and then letters of encouragement had come from friends everywhere, wishing Ben well, and Clara had spent her evenings at the Royal Hotel answering them. Even the Premier had written, which was kind of him since Ben sat on the opposition front bench. Or had done. To avoid another confrontation, Clara had asked the doctor to suggest to Ben that he might consider retiring from Parliament but she needn't have worried.

The doctor reported that it was her husband's idea to resign.

'Surely,' he'd said, when the subject was broached, 'they don't expect me to carry on with my duties in my state of health. They can go to hell! Had they elected me Leader of the Opposition when I had earned the right, I should have considered it my duty to hang on, to get back to Brisbane as soon as possible. But not now. I shall resign and leave them to face a by-election for my seat. And I hope they lose it.'

'That was easy,' the doctor told Clara. 'He doesn't seem to realize that returning to Brisbane is out of the question for a very long time.'

On the day they were due to return to Fairmont, Clara collected their mail at the post office and flipped through it in the hospital waiting room as the nurses prepared Ben for the journey. There were still more letters to Ben from well-wishers, quite a few business letters, several for Belle and one for her in a handwriting she didn't recognize.

When she opened this letter, written on coloured paper, she was surprised to find it was unsigned, and a little nervous. Anonymous letters were horrid things. But maybe the writer had forgotten to sign it, she thought hopefully. It started off pleasantly enough, even though the writer wasn't much of a speller.

Dear Mrs Buchanan,

The papers told it good about your husband's accedent and about a young man called Ben Beckman who did a brave thing to resscew him from under the hoofs of wilde horses. Mr Beckman is true blue, you aught to know this. He should not be looked down on by peeple who aught not to throw stones.

Oh dear, Clara smiled. If this person had signed his or her name I should be able to write back and assure them that no one looks down on Ben. But that gave her a spasm of guilt. Hadn't she told Phoebe it wouldn't be a suitable match? A different matter entirely, she told herself, and read on.

Mr Beckman was well brort up by his mother who was called Diamond. A black woman but edjicated. No backwoods gin her. Yore husband is his father, Ben Buchanan. She called the boy Ben after him see. This is no lie. I don't want nothing eccept that boy deserves more respect.

Clara stared at the stumbling writing, reading it again and again. It was not true! A vicious, cowardly lie!

But what had Ben called out in his delirium? Diamonds. Or was it Diamond? A woman. Was he calling for her? Surely not?

She glanced about at the other people in the waiting room. They all seemed to be staring stolidly at her, like a row of reproachful jurors, as she stuffed the letter deep into her handbag. Clara was so shocked she couldn't think what to do. What to say. How could she dare to mention this to her husband?

All the way home she clutched her handbag, afraid that the letter would fall out and somehow be read by others. And what if her mother read it? Found out about this? She'd demand to know the truth of it. Belle seemed to thrive on confrontations but Clara hated them.

As soon as she dared, with Ben settled in their bedroom, Clara drifted into the kitchen, and when no one was looking, pushed that dreadful letter into the stove fire, poking at it to make sure it burned to an ash.

But the devastating accusation nagged at her. She hated the person who had sent it. Who had been demanding respect for Ben Beckman? Such nonsense! Had Beckman himself instigated the letter, to unsettle them? Somehow she didn't think so. But had Phoebe known about this? She doubted that too. Facing their criticism of her association with Beckman, Phoebe wouldn't have overlooked that weapon, she'd have thrown it at their feet and left them standing!

So. It wasn't true. She shouldn't let a crank letter worry her.

Several days later she caught up with old Ruby, the black housekeeper, in the laundry. Ruby had practically retired now since Clara had learned to run her own household with the help of the cook and two maids.

'Mr Ben,' Ruby said sadly. 'How he gonna get about wit no foot?'

'He'll learn,' Clara said. 'People do. And when he gets better he can still ride.'

She watched while the old woman hauled steaming sheets from the copper with a stick and dumped them in a cold tub. They were heavy.

'Can I help you?' Clara asked.

Ruby grinned. 'I still got two good hands, missus.'

'That you have,' Clara smiled. 'Strong hands too. You've been with my husband a long time,' she added.

'Since he was a bubby,' Ruby said proudly. She loved to tell people that. It made her feel superior to all the other blacks on the station.

'When he was sick he was asking for someone called Diamond,' Clara said. 'Do you know who that would be?'

Instantly Ruby's shoulders tensed and she turned away. 'Don't know nothin' about Diamond.'

'Do you know where she is now?' The question was a trick, unfair, Clara knew, to put to a woman struggling with an alien language, but it served its purpose.

'Diamond long gone,' Ruby said irritably. 'Long time ago.'

'But you knew her?'

Ruby was silent, plunging the stick into the remaining linen in the copper to force the soapy water to do its work.

But Clara had learned to get through to this tough old woman by observing the giggling black girls. She tickled Ruby on the neck and under her arms until she doubled up, chortling. 'You naughty lady, jus like dem silly girls.'

'Oh go on! You love it,' Clara laughed. 'You knew everyone at Caravale Station. Did Diamond work there? Come on, tell me or I'll tickle you more.'

'No! No!' Ruby giggled. She stood up and took a deep breath. 'That Diamond! She doan work for no one! She high-class gin. Look black. Talk white.' With the innate love of stories passed on through generations, Ruby warmed to her subject. 'Magic men say Diamond daughter of big-fellow tribal chief way north. You savvy? In the hot country.'

'Palmer River?' Clara asked, her heart sinking. Ben had often talked of the awful time he'd had in his failed search for gold. He'd said if he hadn't gone down with the fever he'd have come back a millionaire like so many others.

'Dunno,' Ruby shrugged.

Clara had to choose her words carefully now. Ruby could clam up fast. The Palmer connection, possible connection, was a dead end. She returned to Ruby's territory, Caravale Station.

'The old missus, my husband's mother. She wouldn't have liked having a gin about who didn't work.'

Ruby rolled her eyes, agreeing. 'She plenty mad. She done hate that Diamond girl.'

Clara noticed that Ruby was carefully, too carefully, avoiding any mention of involvement between her beloved Ben and this woman Diamond. What was a non-working gin doing on the station? A gin from a distant tribe? She wouldn't have any skin relatives there.

Something about this story was frightening Clara. She'd heard enough. 'So Diamond left, never to be seen again,' she said in a light-hearted attempt to extricate herself from this conversation, but Ruby turned to her, whispering, 'Bad joss there. Missus send bad blokes to kill Diamond. But Diamond come back and put a spell on the missus. Send her crazy. Then she burn the house down.'

'Diamond burnt the house down?'

'No. Old missus crazy as a dingo in the trap. He eat off his own foot. She burn her own house down. The missus done that. We never see Diamond no more.'

'Oh my God! What did Ben do?'

Ruby shrugged. 'He go too. Lookin' for gold.'

Clara hid in the spare room, the one Phoebe had occupied. Ben was right not to tell her these things. These horrible things with confused images of mysticism and truth. Like him she knew a fair bit about Aborigine lore, some of which they affected to take with a grain of salt but knowing, deep down, it was territory best not to explore. And Ruby, true to their superstitions, was probably inventing the story of spells to account for a normal fire. They weren't unusual, house fires. Take the Winnaroo fire. No one claimed that there was any other reason but the stupidity of a drunken chef. No spells. No bone pointing. Normal.

But Ben had always hated Winnaroo Springs. Often in his cups, never when he was sober, he would claim the springs were an eerie place, a bad place, too many ghosts, but no one took any notice of him. Sober, he forgot, but come to think of it he rarely joined parties of their visitors heading out to enjoy the most beautiful swimming hole in the district. If at all, after the first visit. She couldn't recall. And in the end, look what had happened to him there.

Clara shuddered. She made her way along the passage through to the parlour and the dining room, turning up lamps as she went. She wouldn't allow all this superstition to bother her and a blaze of lights made her feel better. It was silly to be worrying about things that had happened long ago, and especially to take an anonymous letter to heart. She was glad she'd burned it and she certainly wouldn't mention it to Ben. What had happened before they met was his business.

Her mother called to her from the parlour: 'Here's a bit of news, Clara! Come in here.'

'What is it?'

'Front page in your local paper. Winnaroo Station has been sold.'

'Has it? That's good. Does it say who bought it?'

'It certainly does. Mr Ben Beckman.'

'From Brisbane? From the livery stables?'

'That's what it says here. Phoebe's friend. What do you think of that?'

Clara flopped into a chair. 'I don't know what to think.'

'Do you suppose Phoebe's coming with him?'

'I've no idea.'

'Of course you'll have nothing to do with him.'

Clara sighed. 'Mother, if he's to be our neighbour we'll treat him as any other neighbour.' She stumbled on her words. She'd almost said 'with due respect'.

'You know yourself that goodwill between neighbours on these big properties is important,' she added.

'Your husband won't be too pleased about it.'

'He won't have any say,' Clara snapped. 'He's already under obligation to Mr Beckman so he'll just have to learn to shut up.'

Something tells me he will too, she smiled to herself as she walked over to check on him. I don't have any quarrel with Mr Beckman, I think he'll make a very good neighbour.

The new Winnaroo Station homestead was a show place and Sergeant Paddy Reilly, who'd taken over the district when McAlister retired, now had an excuse to get a look at it. Word had it that the owner, Beckman, was a tough character. A bloke who worked like a madman getting that place operational and kept his men working at the same pace, brooking no cheek from anyone. Of course, they said, being a half-caste he'd have to be a firm boss or the likes of the stockmen out here would soon have his measure and would run all over him.

But Reilly had met several of the Winnaroo men in Charleville, and they had no complaints. 'The quarters are new, the grub's good and he pays well,' they said. 'Turning out to be a pretty good bloke all in all,' they admitted.

Reilly consulted a scratch map as he rode along. There were crossroads up ahead and he'd been warned not to take the wrong fork which would lead him well out of his way to Fairmont Station, but now he couldn't remember which was which.

Fortunately someone had had the sense to put up a sign, and he was relieved to see a board nailed to a tree, indicating that Winnaroo was off to the right.

At the boundary gate he spotted a fencing gang hard at work. 'G'day lads,' he called. 'Where can I find the boss?'

'That's me,' a tall fellow replied, striding over to greet him. Beckman looked no different from the rest, in a sleeveless flannel shirt and coarse trousers.

Reilly dismounted and introduced himself. 'Got some messages for you, Mr Beckman,' he said.

'Since when do police deliver messages?' Ben grinned.

'When they're new to the district and getting to know people. How is everything with you?'

'Going well. Takes time to get things organized, but I've got a good man buying stock for me and the herd is growing. It's a great property and I've got a lot to learn, but I ought to be able to make a go of it. Would you like to stay for lunch?'

'I wouldn't say no. Here's a telegram for you.'

The telegram was from Barnaby, informing Ben that he would be in Charleville shortly, campaigning as a constitutional representative for Queensland, and was looking forward to seeing him. Also that Biddy Donovan, who used to work for the Thurlwells, was out of work and could he place her?

The two men rode up the long track to the house, and as they rounded a bend and began to climb the hill, Reilly whistled. 'Ah now. There's a fine place.'

'The old homestead was burned down but I chose a different site for this one, closer to the river.'

The solid hewn-stone building had broad verandas and a tower room on top that intrigued the policeman.

'I had to build very high up because the river floods,' Ben explained, 'but I still didn't get the view I wanted, hence the tower. From up there I can look across to Winnaroo Springs. I'll show you later.'

'Well, you must have a grand view,' Reilly said as they stepped up into the house. 'I love the smell of fresh timber, cedar is it not?' he asked, admiring the polished floors.

'Yes. The place is only half-furnished yet, but I'll get around to that in time. I've been too busy to bother so far.'

They sat in the sunny kitchen, enjoying a bottle of beer before lunch.

'Nothing's private in this country,' Reilly said with a laugh. 'Your telegram is from Mr Glasson.'

'Yes. He's found me a housekeeper; that will be a big help. And he's coming to visit.'

'That's what I wanted to talk to you about. As a Member of Parliament, for the Brisbane seat of Padlow, I believe, some of his supporters want to give him an official welcome.'

'That's good.'

'Yes. They're arranging a function to be held at the Royal Hotel. Since you're a friend of his they'd like you to come.'

Ben nodded. 'And you're here to issue me a permit to walk into licensed premises?'

'Times change, Mr Beckman. My predecessor had his ways, I have me own. 'Tis true there are blacks who have to show they know how to behave before they can be served, even in pub grounds. Nothing I can do about that. One step at a time. But I'm for a bit of common sense.'

'You mean I'm acceptable?'

'No. I mean I don't see anything to be acceptable about. You're another citizen of the district and I'm pleased to make your acquaintance.

Can I tell them that you'll be attendin'?'

'I'll be glad to.'

Sitting at a long table in a stiff shirt that cut into his neck, in company with twenty mainly bearded gentlemen, Ben enjoyed the dinner but felt he had earned it, as he was then forced to endure addresses of welcome to the honoured guest, Mr Barnaby Glasson, followed by Barnaby's speech and then more long and rambling speeches. Everyone, it seemed to Ben, except himself, had to have a go.

From there they tramped across the road to the hall, where a public meeting was to be held to hear Mr Glasson, MLA, speak on the subject of 'Australians Unite'. But it wasn't just Barnaby, Ben groaned to himself, shifting on the rock-hard chair, four of the other gents were on the stage with him and they all had to have their say too, reruns of their previous speeches. By the time Barnaby was on his feet, Ben was struggling to stay awake, thinking that the people in this crowded hall must be hard up for entertainment, but he listened attentively, or appeared to do so, and was the first to lead the hearty clapping when Barnaby finished speaking.

'It was a great night, wasn't it?' Barnaby said to him when they were back at the hotel, on their own at last.

'If you say so.'

'Oh go on! You enjoyed yourself.'

'If this is politics, you can have it. I'd rather watch grass grow.'

'My dear fellow, you're looking at one of the first senators in the Australian parliament, if I can keep up the momentum. So stop complaining.'

Biddy Donovan walked about this sparkling new house, hugging herself with sheer joy. This was to be her home, a real home, with a proper bedroom of her own, not just a share of the cold bunkroom next to the wine cellar back at the Thurlwell house.

She'd had a bad time of it the last six months. The Doctor had promised her that the new people would keep her on, so even after all the other staff had left Somerset House she'd stayed to see the family on its way. She and Miss Phoebe had both cried. It had been hard to say goodbye after all these years, for Phoebe had been like her own little girl. Later she'd found a pretty handkerchief sachet on the kitchen table, a parting gift from Phoebe. It had contained a lace handkerchief, and inside that, a five-pound note.

And Biddy had needed that cash. The new people arrived and immediately dismissed her, telling her that Dr Thurlwell had made no such arrangement. They'd brought their own maids with them.

She had a little money put aside, and found a cheap room while she looked for a job, but then came another blow. Her father had died in prison.

Broken-hearted, Biddy insisted on paying for a proper funeral for him, with a Mass said, and stood alone by the graveside thinking the world had come to an end. She hung on, taking odd jobs where she could find them for a few shillings here and there, until she was cleaned out and behind in her rent.

Then she saw Mr Glasson's photograph in the paper and remembered Miss Phoebe's two friends up there on the point. A bachelor establishment! They knew her, they might need someone to clean for them.

And that was how she came to be out here. Mr Glasson had said that he couldn't afford a maid, which surprised her – she'd always thought politicians were made of money – but he knew just the place for her. At Winnaroo, as Mr Ben's cook and housekeeper.

Biddy was careful not to mention Miss Phoebe. She'd heard all the rows in the house about them, and for a while there she'd thought Phoebe would defy them and marry him, but it had all got too much for the poor girl. And then there was her mother's cruel suggestion. She was a mean piece of work, that one. She'd sell her soul for a bankroll, let alone her daughter. What a fight that had been. The daddy of them all! Phoebe had picked up the magnificent crystal water set that her mother treasured and had decided to pack in her own luggage so that it wouldn't be broken, and hurled it across the room, tray and all, smashing the lot.

'Don't you dare!' she screamed at her mother, and Biddy, shocked, had stayed out of sight.

So. Mr Glasson had brought her out by train to Charleville, and there was Mr Ben to meet them.

Telling her not to worry about the cost, they'd put her up at the Royal Hotel, in a splendid room, like a real guest, and gone about their business. A dinner party and a public meeting of some sort. Biddy would have liked to go over for a listen – she'd seen the hall all decorated outside with a big banner – but she'd never dare. She wanted them to know she knew her place.

At dinner time, she'd gone down to the kitchen to ask if she could have a plate of soup or something, but the women there were very kind. Her gentlemen, they told her, were at a function in the commercial dining room, but she was to sit in the main dining room.

Biddy cringed. 'Oh no. I never done that.'

'You're a guest in the house, paid for, and as good as any of them,' the cook said. 'You go on out there and we'll look after you. Who are you anyway?'

Biddy explained that she was on her way to take up a new position as housekeeper at Winnaroo Station, and as she spoke a sense of pride crept into her voice. At forty-seven, accustomed to service, this was a new experience for her.

Four women worked in that kitchen, and they were interested in the newcomers, so Biddy was introduced around, noticing that the capable cook, while carrying on a conversation with her, kept up her dexterous carving of three different roasts and the serving of vegetables and gravy.

'Next time you're in town, Biddy,' she said, 'drop in and see us. You don't have to be a loner out here. Now go on inside and have your dinner.'

Nervously Biddy sat at a small table in the dining room. Her table manners, after years of serving the rich and powerful, were impeccable, and when she had the courage to lift her eyes, she frowned. A lot of them were eating like pigs, pointing with cutlery, even ladies, and gradually she settled back with a smile. Biddy enjoyed her first meal in a posh place.

It was a long way out to the station in the buggy, with Mr Ben driving and his horse tied on the back, but Biddy enjoyed every minute of it. The two young men joshed and teased all the time, and asked her opinions, which she was fain to give, not wishing for her new boss to think she was even a mite forward. But she'd never been out of Brisbane before and she took delight in the grand countryside, with hardly a soul to be seen if you didn't count the kangaroos that stopped to stare at them as if they belonged in a zoo with the roos looking in. Ah, it was a blessed day!

This morning they'd gone riding off. Mr Ben had to show Mr Glasson some springs. All the men, who had their own cook, she'd been told, were out somewhere. Chasing cattle, she presumed, not sure why they'd be doing that. She had the tower house all to herself. She had her black apron on and she walked from room to room with a firm and busy step, taking note. The essentials of furnishings were there, beds, tables and the likes, but nothing in the parlour or dining room, and no drapes or curtains.

'We'll attend to that,' she said to herself. 'What a shame Miss Phoebe isn't here to see what a darlin' place you've built. It's a dream of a house, with a lazy lovin' feel about it. All wide open, no fuss, no bother, no need for footmen in fancy clothes.' She climbed up to the tower room, also unfurnished as yet with glass all about, and looked over the great river.

'Oh dear God,' she prayed, 'I never asked for much in me life. Let me do good here. 'Tis a job and a home in one. Don't let him send me away. I've no place else to go.'

It was time, Ben knew, and with an excuse to visit Fairmont Station, he rode over with his head stockman, Jules Mannering, who at one time, had worked at Fairmont.

Mrs Buchanan welcomed them politely, a little nervously, Ben thought, and they retired to the station office to discuss fencing problems on their miles of boundary. Both Jules and Mrs Buchanan knew more about it than he did, so Ben made a suggestion:

'Can I leave you to this? I'd like to visit Mr Buchanan.'

'He's not very well,' she said sharply.

'I'll be very quiet.'

Clara looked at him, and then turned to Jules. 'Excuse me a minute.' She took Ben outside. 'Now listen to me, Mr Beckman—'

'Ben.'

'Very well. Ben. It's no use beating about the bush any more. It's just not my way of doing things. I have to get this over with. Was your mother's name Diamond?'

'Yes.'

She drew in her breath, as if from a blow, but persisted. 'So now what? What are you up to? I want the truth from you.'

He put an arm about her and led her away from the house. 'You and I seem to have the tail end of a story. Your husband knew my mother. That's all I know, and it's all either of us needs to know. Before the accident at the springs we talked. He knew who I was and he had a bee in his bonnet that I might lay some claim on him. I would never do that,' he said. 'I make my own way. So you have to let me talk to him. My buying Winnaroo has nothing to do with you or him. I like the place, I love it. I was bored in town, I had nothing to look forward to. The sameness was getting me down. Surely you can understand that?'

'Yes, of course. I'm sorry. This is all very embarrassing. Perhaps you could see him some other time.'

'No. I have to get it over with.'

She hesitated, and then gave in. 'Oh well. I'll just see if the room is tidy.'

The station office was in the rear wing of the house, and as Ben waited on the veranda he hoped he was doing the right thing. This was the house he'd vowed never to enter, but circumstances had changed and if he were to run the neighbouring property well he needed the co-operation of the Buchanans. Clara Buchanan at least.

An elderly black woman was walking across the yard carrying a basket. Suddenly she stopped dead and stared at Ben. She came closer, peering at him, and then her face broke into a wide smile, as if she knew him.

Ben nodded politely to her, and without a word she turned to continue on her way, still smiling broadly.

Clara came back. 'He's ready. I didn't tell him you were here, though. Are you sure you want to see him?'

Buchanan was lying on the bed in his dressing gown, propped up on pillows, with a plump eiderdown over him.

'Get out of my house!' he grated, the minute Ben walked in the door.

'Is that the way you treat your rescuer?' Ben asked him.

'Pack of lies! You were too busy trying to save your own skin. Come to gloat, have you?'

'Yes. Why not?'

'Get out!'

'I'm going. I suppose you know I've bought Winnaroo.'

'Where'd you get the money from? Steal it?'

'None of your business. And that's what I came to tell you. I want nothing to do with you bar the normal neighbourly activities, which I should prefer to conduct through Mrs Buchanan.'

'Got you scared, have I?'

'Don't kid yourself, you bloody fool! And if you're considering a shot in the back sometime, forget it. I've placed my birth certificate, with your name on it, with other papers in my Brisbane bank. The other papers include complete details of your attacks on me, duly notified and witnessed, plus instructions that if any accident should befall me, the police are to be informed and your movements and activities are to be investigated. So you'd better pray, Buchanan, that I keep fit and well.'

'Blackmail is it now?'

'You're still stupid, aren't you? Buns for brains. You've got nothing I want. Nothing. And you keep well away from my station or you might have another accident.'

He marched out of the room to find Mrs Buchanan again. While he'd been speaking to Buchanan he'd noticed the flat patch under the cover where the foot should have been, but had seen no point in mentioning it.

'How was he?' Clara asked as he joined her and Jules in the office.

'Bit cranky,' Ben grinned, 'but no worries. He'll get over it. He looks better than I thought he would.'

'Yes. The doctor said he'll soon get sick of crutches and then he'll see the sense of strapping on the peg-leg. It will be hard for him but the men are all willing to help him.'

As he and Jules were leaving, Ben turned back to her. 'You must come and visit. Any time.'

'I'd like that, Ben. Have you heard from Phoebe?'

His face clouded. 'No,' he said shortly. 'Have you?'

'No. I've written to her in Sydney but I haven't had a reply. I hope she's all right.'

Ben made no comment. He thanked God for Winnaroo, for the busy life he now led that helped to keep thoughts of Phoebe from his mind. It had been hard at first, to fight off the depression that had assailed him when he'd lost her, but he'd kept telling himself that he'd suffered a lot more, physically, when he was younger, so he could overcome this too.

'Have you got everything you need?' he asked Jules.

'Yes, Mrs Buchanan has been very helpful.' Jules had wanted to talk to her about the cattle and animal husbandry since she was quite an expert on the subject, and she'd said they could have copies of stock sheets, on loan, to set up their own station journals.

Clara shook hands with them. 'I know you'll do well,' she said, 'and if I can help at any time, don't be afraid to ask.'

On the way home Ben grinned to himself. His talk with Buchanan had been necessary, to keep him in line. There were no papers in the bank nor was there a birth certificate. While he was packing up the house at Kangaroo Point he'd found a clipping from a newspaper in Diamond's box. It was a photograph of Ben Buchanan, and Oma had written on it: 'Father of Ben Beckman.'

He'd burnt it.

It was Clara's idea for him to have a housewarming.

'This is a much better position,' she said to Ben when she came to visit. 'More chance of a breeze in summer. And the house is lovely. Did you design it?'

'No, the builder drew up the plans. I just told him where to put it and that I wanted big rooms with high ceilings. I'm not exactly a small person, and with no shortage of space I thought he might as well spread out. They're not too big, are they?'

She strolled across the two front rooms with their big open fireplaces, and twirled about. 'No, of course not. They're splendid.'

'I don't know what I'm doing with two parlours either side of the front door,' he said, almost apologetically, because he wanted her to approve of his house. It wasn't as large or as formal as the Buchanan homestead, which he'd taken the opportunity to glimpse as he'd walked through, but more rustic somehow. 'The builder said it gave balance to the house.'

'It does,' she said. 'It will be a great place for entertaining. People can really spread out with both sets of double doors opened up.'

He shrugged. 'I can't see myself entertaining.'

'Why not? You town people seem to think we do nothing out here but herd cattle and chase about on horses. We have a lot of fun, Ben. Everyone entertains. I'd put a piano in this room if I were you.'

'A piano?' He was astonished. 'Who would play it?'

'There's always someone who can play the piano. You ought to have a housewarming! Such a beaut house, it deserves to be christened.'

He was embarrassed. 'I don't think so. I mean, it's nice of you to suggest it, but I wouldn't know who to invite.'

'Haven't you got friends in Brisbane?'

'Yes. Some.'

'Good. Invite them. You've plenty of room to put them up. People adore being invited to the country for the weekend. And you made a good impression in town, I heard from Sergeant Reilly. But apart from them it's time you met the other station people out here. They'd travel a hundred miles for a good party. I could put some of them up.'

'Whoa!' he said. 'You're going too fast for me. I don't think this is a very good idea. Face facts, Clara. They mightn't want to meet me.'

'You won't find out sitting on your hands. If you shut yourself off from people they'll think you're some mad hermit. Parties don't cost much, Ben, and people appreciate hospitality.'

'It's not the money,' he said.

'Then what?' she persisted.

'I don't know,' he said again. 'I'll ask Biddy. She runs the place.'

Biddy? Clara thought as he disappeared into the back of the house. Who's this? Interesting for a single man to have a woman in the house. She'd heard no mention of a woman. Clara hoped she hadn't put her foot in it, talking about a party.

It had been weeks since Ben had made that visit to her husband, but she'd sent Moss over several times to liaise with Jules and to make sure the new cattle coming on to this property were free of disease. Co-operation with neighbouring stations was essential. Surprisingly, her husband hadn't said much about his visitor except that he didn't want that half-caste pushing his way into his company.

'Not much chance of that,' she'd said drily, and taking Ben Beckman's advice, had left it at that. He was right. Forget it.

Clara was sure now that he was her husband's son. Her stepson. The resemblance was there in the facial structure and in young Ben's straight brown hair, unusual in an Aborigine and of the same texture as Buchanan's. She'd never noticed it before she received that letter. And why should she?

But if neither the father nor the son would admit to it, then there was no problem. Except that Clara had always wanted children of her own but had never been able to conceive. She found it rather sad that there had been a child out there all the time. Coloured or not, she'd have mothered him. And look how he'd turned out. The nicest man! She wished he was her son. Maybe the woman, Diamond, wouldn't mind if she took a little interest in her stepson. Could be she'd approve. 'I'm on your side, Diamond,' she said, as if to ward off bad joss.

Since Ben hadn't come back to Fairmont, on this day Clara had decided to ride over with Moss and Mungo, and he'd been delighted to see her, although a little shy now.

Eventually he came back. 'I'm sorry to keep you waiting, but she was working in the vegetable garden and insists on cleaning up for you.'

When Biddy arrived hastily tucking a white blouse into her long black skirt, Clara was overcome. She ran forward and threw her arms around Biddy. 'Oh my dear! How lovely to see you! I didn't know you were here, Biddy. How did this come about?'

While the women talked, Ben stood looking into the wide flagged fireplace that had not yet seen a fire, leaning on the polished mantelpiece, fighting off his distress. Would he ever be free of Phoebe? Of her damn family! As they spoke of old times at Somerset House he despaired. What was this talk of a party? Just an excuse to paste over who he was. Or rather who he was not. He was his own boss now, in a position to ward off humiliations, not invite them. He just wanted to be left alone.

But it was not to be. The two women had the reins. Biddy thought it would be a wonderful idea to have a housewarming.

'Mr Ben,' she said, 'I'd love to do it. I know how, you can be trustin' in me not to let you down. I'll do you proud, I promise you.'

Finally they convinced him. To agree, that was all. In his mind's eye Ben could envisage only a miserable turnout and steeled himself for the first and last party at his Winnaroo homestead.

That night Biddy was excited. Too excited, in her efforts to please him, talking too much, she realized afterwards. But he was interested. 'What a shock it was to them,' she said, 'when old Edgar was drowned.'

'Was it true,' he asked, 'that he took off with the company funds? How would he do that?'

'I'm sure I don't know. But he skinned a lot of people, and his own family too. Forged Phoebe's dad's signature and mortgaged the house. Grabbed that money too. That's why they sold the house.'

'I never understood what that was all about,' he said.

'Oh, the rows in the house that caused,' Biddy told him. 'She gave the Doctor hell!'

'Who? Mrs Thurlwell?'

'Who else?'

'So her husband was a crook. Serves him right.'

'No. He weren't no crook. He was just a dope. Half the time he never knew what was goin' on. And Miss Phoebe, she was always stuck in the middle of their fights.'

Biddy stopped. 'I'm sorry, Mr Ben. You don't like for me to speak of Miss Phoebe, I know.'

'That's all right,' he said wearily, sitting back in his chair. He always had breakfast and lunch with the men, and dinner here in the kitchen with

Biddy, so that she wouldn't be lonely. Sometimes he wondered what those other fine rooms were for. 'Would you like a glass of this red wine?'

'If you don't mind.'

'Not at all.'

Biddy tasted the wine and shuddered. 'It's a bit rough. We'll have to do better for the party. But as I was saying, poor Miss Phoebe was always in the middle. Her mum was always playing her off against her dad. Making points, you know.'

Ben half listened as Biddy reminisced. Seeing Phoebe on their last day together. Dreaming of her, luxuriating in this closeness with her, through Biddy. Just this once, allowing her back into his thoughts.

'I have to say I heard that row about you,' Biddy continued. 'She fought them, never you believe she didn't, but her mother, that woman, she always knew where to hit the hardest. Cook used to say she'd be a star turn on a dartboard.'

'Ah well, that's over now,' he said.

'And so it is, more's the pity. But when Mrs Thurlwell told her husband he ought to approve your marriage, you could have knocked me down with a feather. I knew there had to be a catch in it.'

Ben shook himself to attention. 'Phoebe's mother suggested it?'

'Indeed she did. She wasn't too complimentary about you, if you'll forgive me for saying. But she told the Doctor he ought to give you the go-ahead. For a consideration.'

'A what? What sort of a consideration?'

'Payment. Sort of a dowry in reverse. She said they were entitled and you could afford it. "Make him pay her worth," she told the Doctor. That's when Miss Phoebe really hit the roof. Yelling at her mother. Smashing things!'

'Phoebe did?'

'Oh, she's got a temper, that girl.'

'I noticed. But Biddy, tell me all that again. Are you sure you've got it right?'

'As sure as God's me judge!'

Ben went for a long walk outside that evening, and finally decided that the housewarming would have to be postponed. He had more important matters to consider.

As far as they knew on Winnaroo Station, the boss had gone to Brisbane on business. But in truth he'd travelled much further than that. The city of Sydney loomed tall. Traffic clattered. Pedestrians clung to their hats in the windy streets. Street vendors shouted. Crowds interlocked seeking entry and exit at the doorway of a huge emporium. He saw a motorcar trundling past and ran alongside it for several blocks to admire the marvellous black and red machine, envying the gentleman in a white coat and soft cap who sat grandly atop, grasping the steering wheel.

Reluctantly he turned back. No time now to be side-tracked, even by a motorcar.

He dodged across the road and approached the entrance to the park, stopping a couple to enquire if this was Hyde Park.

'Indeed it is,' the gentleman replied, and Ben tipped his hat, moving on along the shady paths, watching for Captain Cook's statue, which the porter at his hotel had told him, with a wink, was a good spot for a rendezvous.

'Why not here in our garden lounge?' he'd said. 'All the society people come here.'

'I suggested that in my letter,' Ben replied, grateful for the man's interest. 'But the lady didn't agree. She chose Hyde Park.'

'You can't miss it. Couple of blocks down that way.' He pointed.

Ben found the statue and having walked around it a few times, in deference to the great sailor, and stared up appraising the handsome face, he took refuge on the sunny side, out of the wind, and waited. She was late.

On this Friday morning there weren't too many people about. Some strollers. Elderly gents seated on park benches. A nanny with two small children wrapped up like roly-poly dolls. To his eye, the famous park was rather plain, lacking the exuberance of Queensland greenery, but then everyone to his own.

Though he'd been nervous, sick to his stomach even, about the outcome of this meeting, he'd enjoyed every minute of the short steamer voyage that had taken him interstate. And he'd relied on the advice of a gentleman on the ship to direct him to a good hotel. Everyone he'd met had been so helpful, Ben was already very fond of this city.

Within hours of arriving in Sydney his letter had gone to Phoebe at the address Biddy had given him, hand-delivered by a messenger from the hotel.

It had been a long and lonely day. Ben smiled grimly, remembering how he'd hung about the hotel, waiting for a reply. Waiting for her to come to see him in the gracious garden lounge of the Australian Hotel. Hoping she'd come.

The reply directed him to Hyde Park the following morning and Ben sent the messenger back with his affirmation. At least it was a start. There was communication. If she'd said the Blue Mountains, he'd have gone there. Anywhere.

At that moment he saw her walking towards him, so elegant in a fashionable hat with ostrich feathers brushing the breeze, and sleek fur tails linked lazily over a warm grey tailored suit. People stared. Ben stared. Did he have the nerve to match this woman?

'Good morning, Mrs Thurlwell,' he said. She seemed taller than he remembered, but then he guessed that she was wearing high heels hidden by the long skirt.

She nodded coldly, not extending a gloved hand.

'Would you like to sit down?' he asked, indicating a nearby park bench.

'I suppose one must,' she said, making certain there was plenty of space between them on the bench. 'It's chilly here.'

'It was your idea,' Ben said. 'Are you always in the habit of opening your daughter's mail?'

'When it suits me. Besides, Phoebe doesn't live with us. I thought it could be important.'

'Where does she live?'

'That's a matter we could discuss.'

'You don't intend to tell me?'

'It's possible.'

He wished he could stand. Everything about this woman seemed to place him at a disadvantage. 'How is Phoebe?' he asked her.

'Extremely well. How did you know where to find us?'

'Biddy works for me now.'

She shrugged. 'Of course. Servants know everything.'

'Biddy also told me that you would approve my marriage to Phoebe for a consideration.'

She didn't bat an eye. 'If she'll have you.'

Her self-possession, the sheer cheek of her, almost unnerved him, and he struggled to keep his temper. He had a plan and he was determined to work through it.

'We'll see about that. So. A consideration would be in order?'

'I don't see why not. You've caused us a great deal of unhappiness.'

'And that's why you're here? Righto, what's Phoebe's address?'

She fingered a small silver earring and gazed over the gardens, watching a dog chasing a ball down the rise.

He laughed. 'I suppose you think I might dash off with Phoebe and you won't see the money.'

'I don't trust you and I don't trust her.'

'I'm feeling better all the time. By the sounds of things Phoebe hasn't forgotten me.' He took a sealed envelope from an inner pocket. 'There's a cheque here for five thousand pounds. It's the best I can do. I've had a great deal of expense lately. The address, please?'

She produced a small notebook with a pencil attached, and with a sigh of resignation, as if he'd forced her hand, wrote down an address in

Manly. Then she took the envelope and buried it deep in her handbag. 'Can I have your word that this cheque will not bounce?'

'It won't bounce, I promise you.'

'And if she doesn't marry you?'

'Then the cheque will be returned to me. Naturally.'

'Yes,' she said tersely, 'of course. You may tell her she has her father's permission to marry you if she must.'

'And yours?'

'Phoebe never takes notice of me.' She stood, straight-backed, serene. 'I must go. I have a luncheon appointment.'

'Just a minute. Where is Manly?'

'It's a common little beach place on the other side of the harbour. She's staying with friends. Peculiar people, but that's always been Phoebe's taste!'

He took the ferry across the harbour, sitting on deck, studying the scenery to take his mind off the challenge ahead. Phoebe might not want to see him. She was so attractive there could be another man in her life by this time. Bound to be! But he had to see her and ask her one more time to marry him. 'To be honest,' he said to himself, 'just to be able to see her again would be some recompense for all this effort.'

Phoebe's mother had faded from his mind. Meeting her hadn't been so bad after all. In a way Ben felt sorry for her. All the airs and graces couldn't disguise the greed of a woman who'd stoop to such a shabby deal. Not once had she given any indication of how Phoebe would react, of how she already had reacted. No wonder Phoebe was so touchy, so confused. She would flare up at slights to him, and then just as angrily demand he compromise. He guessed she'd spent so many years confronting her mother, and losing, that it had become a pattern. She'd wanted to marry him but at the last minute the pressure had been too much and she'd lost her bold resolve.

'This time,' he said to himself as the ferry neared the wharf and the other passengers were preparing to disembark, 'her mother has lost the battle. Let's see how that affects her daughter.'

He was sitting on the sandy steps of the weatherboard cottage when he saw her coming up from the beach, barefoot, hat in hand. Ben braced himself. The first sight of him would tell all. Any hesitation, a forced smile – even, God forbid, dismay – would give him the answer he sought and send him home.

Phoebe crossed the road, saw someone there, blinked in the glare of the sun, and then her face lit up with delight.

'Ben! It's you! Ben! Where did you spring from?'

She ran. She was in his arms and the first hurdle was over.

Phoebe made tea and found some currant buns, and he carried the tray out to a rickety table in the scruffy garden while she talked and talked about her young friends, a married couple who had a draper's shop just down the road. 'I used to go to school with Dolly,' she explained. 'And I met her on the ferry one day. She invited me to stay and I love it out here. You must come over and walk in the surf with me. It's wonderful. And at night you can lie in bed and listen to the waves pounding and pounding . . .'

'I'd like that,' he said. 'With you.'

She smiled, a little embarrassed

'Come back with me.'

'Oh Ben. I don't know. We've made the break. Leave it at that.' Then it hit her. She looked at him. 'How did you find me?'

'Biddy works for me now. She gave me your address at Bellevue Hill and your mother gave me this address.'

'Good God! What possessed her to be so amenable?'

'Five thousand pounds,' he said calmly.

'What?' White-faced, Phoebe pushed away from the table. 'How dare you? Do you think I can be bought? Or sold, for that matter?'

'Calm down, Phoebe,' he said easily. 'We keep going off at tangents. Forget that for a minute.'

'I will not!'

'A minute, I said! I was stupid. I had a surprise for you and I never told you, what it was. As for your parents suggesting I pay them, Biddy told me about that.'

'Biddy shouldn't have!'

'Sit down! When last I saw you, I was in the process of buying Winnaroo Springs cattle station but I didn't tell you about it because I was afraid you'd think—'

'That you were trying to cajole me into marrying you? Bribing me?'

'Something like that. But maybe a bit worse. That we were withdrawing to Winnaroo, that I was suggesting a way to avoid public scrutiny.'

She chopped savagely into a crumbling bun. 'Thanks a lot.'

'You should have told me about your mother's brilliant idea, and I should have told you about Winnaroo. We've been too busy analysing things instead of getting on with our lives. I'm sorry about that.'

'Oh, don't blame yourself,' she said. The familiar defeated voice was back again. 'I ran for cover, Ben. I didn't believe I could cope with a mixed marriage, as it is referred to in the kindest circles.'

'What about now? When you've had time to think about it?'

'Now,' she said coldly, 'I can tell you. I've missed you so much it has been difficult but I've adjusted. I hated living at my aunt's place so I managed to prise an allowance out of my father to move out here. Dolly and her husband are so normal compared with all that unrealistic snobbery I grew up with that I feel stronger now.' She laughed. 'Let's say I've undergone a course in ego-stripping and it's been good for me.'

'I liked your ego. Don't throw it all away. Why don't we go inside to your bedroom and find out if you still love me?'

'No, it's too late. I really am pleased to see you. But I'm angry with you for paying my mother that money. Why didn't you talk to me first?'

'I didn't know where to find you. And besides, you were so upset about it, according to Biddy, I wanted to put myself in your place. To go through with it and get your father's permission. If they really meant it.'

'And so you paid her. Did you end up buying Winnaroo Station?'

'Yes. Clara comes over quite often. Buchanan stays home. The station is restocked, I have an overseer called Jules, and Biddy is housekeeper. And ten stockmen on the payroll. In time I'll have a horse stud too. But you have to see the house. It's a tower house on a hill, brand new. It's a wonderful place, Phoebe. You'll love it. Come back with me.'

'You paid my mother! I can't forgive you for that. You played right into her hands. I thought I was free of her but I'm not at all. She'll be laughing now.'

'I don't think she'll be laughing.'

'Of course she will. How could you lower yourself to do that?'

Ben sat back with a grin. 'Look out! Your ego's showing. It wasn't so hard after all. I got your father's permission for us to marry. I got your address. I found you.'

'And you paid for me.'

'I gave her a cheque.'

'Good. It will take time to be cleared in Queensland. Cancel it.'

'I couldn't do that.'

'Why not?'

'Because your mother didn't look at the cheque. I rather think that would have been beneath her. She simply took the envelope and placed it in her handbag. Maybe she is accustomed to dealing with gentlemen, but I'm no gentleman. The cheque was made out to you. Loud and clear. I double-checked that with my Brisbane bank before I left. No one else can cash it.'

'You did what?'

'You heard me.'

'So she's got a useless cheque?'

'No, she's holding your wedding present, and I expect you to cash it.'

Phoebe started to laugh. She grabbed the remains of the currant buns and threw them up into the air. Still laughing, she ran round the small table and flung her arms about Ben, causing him to topple with her into the grass.

Dolly appeared at the back door. 'Is someone being attacked here?'

'Yes, he is,' Phoebe called, sprawling beside him. 'This is my very devious friend and fiancé, Ben Beckman.'

Coda

Winnaroo homestead was ablaze with lights and the strains of a Strauss waltz drifted over the gardens. Inside, ignoring the heat of high summer, couples swayed to the romantic music, while others preferred to gather on the veranda where even a slight breeze was welcome.

Over the years, Phoebe Beckman had entertained many of their friends at Winnaroo, but this night was special. All over the country people were celebrating the first New Year's Eve of the new century. But adding to the excitement was the dawning of an important day, 1 January 1901.

Huge bonfires were at the ready in cities, country towns and far out into the bush; in back yards and parks and along the seashore; in valleys and on mountain slopes, everywhere in the great open spaces where people could assemble. Many claimed that when all these bonfires were lit they would be seen from the stars and no one disagreed. No one wanted to disagree because this was a night for dreamers, for a people full of hope for their future, as the stately Southern Cross hung low overhead, a symbol, it seemed, of their impending nationhood.

Just before midnight, Ben and Phoebe brought in their two children as the countdown to twelve o'clock began, to join in the cheers and the singing of 'Auld Lang Syne' in the crowded parlour.

When the singing had died down, the MC for the evening, Sergeant Reilly, stepped forward. 'Ladies and gentlemen! I ask you to charge your glasses again. On this day, at Centennial Park in Sydney, a great event will take place. Today, federation will be proclaimed. A new nation takes its place on the world stage as all of our states unite. I give you the grandest toast I've ever had the honour to propose: Australia!'

A second round of champagne corks popped as cheers and more toasts followed, and Reilly, who took his duties seriously, checked his list.

'One more,' he called. 'Our host and hostess have asked that we wish our good friend, Barnaby Glasson, all the best in the coming elections. And ask him to say a few words.'

Barnaby put down his glass, stalling for time. He was suddenly nervous. For months he'd been travelling throughout the state, making so many speeches that he was just about talked out. But the moment of truth was drawing close, and he worried that the confidence of his friends could be misplaced. What a fool he'd look if he failed, only managing to scrape up a few votes. And even if he did make it to the Senate, was he up to the task? What madness was this that he should be aspiring to the Federal Government?

He spoke quietly. Humbly. Thanking them for their support. 'But,' he continued, 'compared with what's happening in Sydney today, the inauguration of the Commonwealth of Australia, I'm only small fry. This is Australia's day. Not mine . . .'

Barnaby was interrupted by a small voice from the crowd. It was Ben's six-year-old son who called out: 'When are we going to light the bonfire?'

'Now there's your proof,' Barnaby laughed. 'He's got his priorities right. We shouldn't be standing about here, we have to join with our fellow Australians and light up. Let's go!'

Out in the home paddock, the twenty-foot-high bonfire was set ablaze and standing back, everyone linked arms as the twigs and brush took hold of the inner logs and the fire crackled into life, flames soaring into the sky.

Children raced madly about and the grown-ups swooped after them to keep them safe as the burning heap began to crash down, showering sparks about the perimeter. When it was reduced to smouldering embers it was time to make for the homestead again, for supper.

Phoebe kissed Ben. 'It's a beautiful party, isn't it?'

'So are you, Mrs Beckman,' he said, taking her in his arms, oblivious of the smiles of guests who passed them in the lamplit garden.

'Still the lovers,' Barnaby commented, following them up the path. 'I should be jealous, but I'm so happy for you.'

Phoebe turned back to him. 'It's time *you* were married, Barnaby.'

'One thing at a time, my dear. I've been kept moving so much lately I never seem to be in the same town long enough to get to know people, let alone court a young lady.'

'Marry the girl next door is my advice,' Ben grinned. 'I found it a very good move.'

'Spare me!' Barnaby cried. 'The people who live in your old house on the Point, Phoebe, have a daughter. She's thirty and as wide as she's tall. A widow and a religious fanatic. She keeps coming over with new texts for me to read and offering to pray with me. I'm thinking of putting a chain on the gate.'

'That won't work,' Ben said. 'She'll come over the wall like Phoebe did!'

'Get away with you!' Phoebe laughed. 'I only fell out of the tree.'

Later, Barnaby and Ben had time for a quiet talk.

'So what happens now?' Ben asked him.

'Well . . . in a couple of weeks Mr Barton will open the campaign for the first federal elections. All that has happened so far is that he heads an executive council. It's up to the people to elect a Parliament.'

'They say Labor is very strong in Queensland.'

'True, but I'm sticking with Barton's party. He's middle of the road, he should be able to form a government. And I don't want to start off in opposition. That's if I get to start at all.'

'Win or lose, it's worth a go, Barnaby. When are the elections?'

'About the thirtieth of March. So I won't be seeing you before then. I've got to work even harder now.'

You'll get there. It's going to be very exciting waiting for the results. I think I'll build another bonfire especially for you on election day. Have it ready for our own little celebration out here.'

'And if I lose?'

'We'll think about that when the time comes. Where will you be?'

'In Brisbane, in my office. I'll probably sleep there for a week, too nervous to leave.'

For Barnaby's friends, the weeks dragged, and when the two election days finally arrived there was a long wait for the results to filter in from remote areas. Ben and Phoebe never did manage to arrange a party, but resolutely, to the delight of his children, Ben built another bonfire.

Eventually, late one afternoon, Reilly rode out, mystified, to deliver an unsigned telegram.

'Who's it from?' he had to ask them.

Ben smiled proudly. 'It's from Senator Glasson.'

'He got in!' Phoebe screamed. 'How do you know? What does he say?'

'Only three words: "Light the bonfire." '